DISSONANT VOICES

OLEG GRIGORIEVICH CHUKHONTSEV, poetry editor at *Novy Mir* since 1986, was born in Moscow in 1938. He graduated in humanities from the teachers' college for the Moscow region in 1962, but had already begun publishing his poetry in magazines and journals by 1958. In 1968 one of his poems, suggesting, à propos of Ivan the Terrible's reign, that treason was a just repayment for tyranny, touched off the fury of the General Staff, thus precipitating several years of official ostracism. It was only in 1976, at the age of thirty-eight, that his first slender volume, *From Three Notebooks*, was published. The book was well received, and was followed in 1983 by a more substantial collection, *Rooftop Window*, in 1989 by *Like Wind and Ashes*, and in 1990 by a selected edition of his work. Today Chukhontsev is acknowledged as one of the leading poets of his generation. He also works as a translator and literary critic. He is married to the writer Irina Povolotskaya and lives in Moscow.

Dissonant Voices is the first Harvill "Leopard", an occasional series presenting the best of contemporary Literature in translation and in English, published by Harvill and reflecting Harvill's own list though not exclusively drawn from it.

LEOPARD 1

DISSONANT VOICES

The New Russian Fiction

Edited by Oleg Chukhontsev

HARVILL
An Imprint of HarperCollins *Publishers*

First published in Great Britain in 1991 by Harvill
an imprint of HarperCollins Publishers
77/85, Fulham Palace Road,
Hammersmith, London W6 8JB

9 8 7 6 5 4 3 2 1

BRITISH LIBRARY CATALOGUING IN PUBLICATION DATA

Dissonant voices.
I. Chukhontsev, Oleg, *1938*–
891.730108 [F]

ISBN 0-00-271199-0
ISBN 0-00-271182-6-pbk

Photoset in Linotron Galliard by
Rowland Phototypesetting Limited,
Bury St Edmunds, Suffolk
Printed and bound by
HarperCollins Book Manufacturing, Glasgow

CONTENTS

EDITOR'S PREFACE

I have never in my life managed to read a single preface right to the end and I have no idea of why or how they come to be written; if they are that essential, let mine err on the short side and stick to the main point.

So, what is the main point? The short story (or novella) is a favourite form of Russian literature. It is the one most subject to the whims of the passing moment and yet the most durable. Herein, evidently, lies the secret of its attraction.

If you leaf through old literary journals or thumb through bound sets of newspapers and their literary supplements you will find that many authors with substantial novels to their credit, or at least the better of them, started with short stories, and that is itself eminently indicative. For a start – so as to avoid misunderstanding – one should immediately reject any doubt on the score of the short story's inadequacy or lack of substance. On the contrary, of all the prose forms, the short story (or novella) is the most rigorous and virtually the most demanding: a conservatory for tradition and a launchpad for experiment, a form offering the artist inexhaustible scope for his inventive talents.

This is not the place for literary theorizing, or lengthy historical excursions, that seek merely to confirm received truths. I will simply say that in times of spiritual crisis and social cataclysms, during which the major forms simply serve as storehouses of subject material, it is the short story, as the most sensitive form, which is best able to respond to events and retain its topicality.

Such, for example, was the case at the beginning of the century, before the first Russian Revolution of 1905, when the short story carried more weight than the novel (when the highest praise was to be compared to Chekhov): such was also the case later, at more than one time (e.g. the dynamic short stories of the 1920s or the lyrical-confessional ones of the 1960s).

That being so, one could safely predict an upsurge in this form in the watershed years of the 1980s, were it not for two circumstances which distorted the overall picture: the backlog of novels accumulated over previous decades which had been impounded by the KGB or rejected by the literary journals at one time or another had unexpectedly re-emerged on the surface of the literary maelstrom of that time in conjunction with the tidal wave of socio-political writing which engulfed all the printed media. At the start the short story had to take second place, but its break-through as a new conception became thus all the more inevitable.

This volume is an attempt to present the short story of the 1980s in terms of its own dynamics and introspection. It stands to reason that any anthology is incomplete and the editor is no less than others aware of the yawning gaps which could well, at his direction, be covered by the inclusion of other names – and there are many such, both in Russia and abroad in the Russian diaspora. But then one cannot, as Kozma Prutkov* remarked, encompass the unencompassable, and there is nothing more tiring for a reader than repetitiousness, a degree of which would be inevitable, if one were to attempt academic comprehensiveness. And besides, the actual size of the collection imposed its own conditions.

I nevertheless venture to hope that this assembly of names and texts, for all their incompleteness and subjectivity of selection, is reasonably representative. They are, in my view, very substantive names and representative texts, varying in style, in moral and spiritual stance and with, perhaps, only one trait in common: independence of approach, individuality of style. They are all, even those of them who have yet to make themselves heard, not choirboys but soloists.

First of all there are well-known Russian prose writers, from Astafiev to Bitov, who emerged in earlier, difficult years and have confirmed in these no less difficult years their high artistic reputation, even though it needs to be pointed out that in terms of social stance these authors occupy distinct, frequently diametrically opposed positions.

There are also a good dozen new names in this collection, writers who have attracted attention comparatively recently, among them a number of distinctly young authors, such as Bakin and Ermakov, and also slightly older ones, such as Pietsukh and Lavrin, but both the former as well as the latter are talented short story writers of whom much may be expected.

* Kozma Prutkov: a fictitious writer of the mid-nineteenth century (the creation of two talented poets) whose comically pompous sayings became part of the Russian language, and whose satirical verses and plays attacked the bureaucratic and mundane aspects of Russian life.

Finally there are masters of the craft who are no longer with us, such as Tendryakov and Dombrovsky, whose hitherto unpublished works have recently been appearing and are very much of present-day relevance.

One should also, of course, refrain from classifying the unclassifiable: writing, as everyone knows, is a one-off affair, each bit of it is interesting in its own right. The fact that the overall picture these writers paint is both vivid and gloomy, both expressive and unbearable to look at, is something else. Their picture, after making all due allowance for creative invention and idiosyncrasy is, I would say, very much an objective one. True, there is a lot that is sad in it, many losses, many deaths, but does our history suggest anything different? And the deaths in question are of very different kinds: the death of the boy in Makanin's "Those Who Did not Get into the Choir", so banal as to be terrifying, the majestic death of the buffalo in Iskander's "Broadbrow", and the pseudo-heroic death of the bookcase and its occupant, the retired colonel, in Lavrin's "The Death of Egor Ilich" – is this all not part of our life? . . .

When returning from Siberia in the summer of 1989, I discovered for myself, in a strange, mystical way, the fact that literary invention can be horribly real, can be documentarily substantiated. Settling back in my seat on board the plane, I started reading for the first time, in the literary journal *Enisey*, Zazubrin's "The Chip", a story about revolutionary terror in those same regions over which I was flying. Reading it I was chilled with horror and revulsion and remember putting it aside so as to calm down. Enough, I decided, and laid it to one side, and, by way of temporary distraction, took up a newspaper. Glancing through *Izvestia*'s contents I came upon the following announcement ". . . On the premises of former NKVD outhouses trenches filled in with soil have been discovered, from which already more than three hundred human skulls have been extracted. To judge from the position of the bones, the victims were simply tossed into the pits. Some of the skulls were shattered and had bullets in them." The item was from Irkutsk.

I was struck by the coincidence. "The Chip" was not fiction, but the terrible truth set down by the writer. Bones and boulders. And whoever it is – D503*, the builder of the "Integral" or S-854† from "Socialist City" – the distinction is immaterial.

* D-503: the narrator of Evgeny Zamyatin's dystopian futurist novel *We*.

† S-854: the prison number of the protagonist of Alexander Solzhenitsyn's *One Day in the Life of Ivan Denisovich*.

In his poem "Thirteen Ways of Looking at a Blackbird", Wallace Stevens has the lines:

> I do not know which to prefer,
> The beauty of inflections
> Or the beauty of innuendoes,
> The blackbird whistling
> Or just after.

I recall them with some reason, for neither do I know the answer.

It does seem to me that the artist is actively haunted not by this mad world's reality so much as by his own inner conclusion or sense of perception – depending on the individual – and inside the world's cacophony he hears above everything the call of his own blackbird.

So, to close this preface, may I invite you to take a look at life, such as it is disclosed here, through the eyes of the authors concerned and to listen with redoubled attention to its call in the hope of picking something up and coming to some understanding of it. And if it comprises twenty-six different points of view, rather than one or thirteen, then it is the more probable that each person will find something in it that calls just to them.

This life is, after all, whatever one may say of it, the only one we have, and it has its charms as any life does. And there is always the hope that old Mother Palanya's miserable door in Petrov's "A Bit of Winter" – history's chip – will, when spring comes, start floating down the river and, cast adrift on the swollen waters of the Iskona, eventually fetch up on some blissful, far-off shore accompanied by, maybe, a single surviving boot, and that you also will, together with old Nikitich, unwrap the simple message inside the cellophane and sigh disconsolately: "Yes, you're right, it'll be over there too . . . We've got geese and herons and flamingoes down here, but up there, you know . . . there's still a bit of winter left. Bullfinches and jackstraws in the trees . . ."

God permitting!

OLEG CHUKHONTSEV
Moscow, January 1991

VLADIMIR ZAZUBRIN

The Chip: A Story about a Chip and about Her

I

OUTSIDE THE WAGONS began to move their huge steel feet, shaking the stone building to its very foundations.

In Srubov's office, up on the second floor, the copper ink well lids began to jangle. Srubov went pale. The investigating officer and the members of the Cheka Central Committee hurriedly lit themselves a cigarette. Each one sat behind a thin wall of smoke, eyes fixed firmly on the ground.

Down in the cellar, Father Vasily raised the crucifix above his head, and intoned: "Brothers and sisters, let us pray together in this, our last hour."

The priest wore a dark-green cassock, and had a round, bald head and a heavy, drooping belly. He stood in the corner of the room, a mouldy Communion bread in his hand. Black, shadowy forms crept softly down from their bunks, falling to the ground with a low moan.

From another corner, where Lieutenant Snezhnitsky sat with a blue face, came a wheezing sound. Skachkov, once an ensign in the tsar's army, was trying to choke him to death with a small noose made from a pair of braces. He was in a hurry to get it over with, afraid that the others might notice what he was up to. With his broad back facing the door, he had Snezhnitsky's head firmly between his knees and was pulling. He intended to finish himself off too – that was what the sharp piece of glass was for.

And still the wagons rumbled to and fro outside. No one in the three-storey stone building had any doubt what those wagons were for – they had come to take away the corpses.

Like a fat, hairy snake, the arm holding the crucifix slithered out from inside the cassock's wide sleeve. Pale, ashen faces raised themselves up slowly from the floor. Eyes, colourless, lifeless, bulged out of their sockets, swollen with tears. Few were able to make out the crucifix in any detail. Some saw merely a narrow silver plate-like object, others a shining star. For the rest of them, however, there was nothing but a black void. The priest's tongue stuck to the roof of his mouth, and to his cold, purple lips.

"In the name of the Father, and of the Son . . ."

Grey sweat clung to the grey walls. Beads of perspiration hung down from the corners of the room, like fine, frozen white lace.

The priest's words crept across the floor, rustling like dead leaves. The people in the cellar squirmed restlessly. Like the walls, they were covered in a cold sweat. But they were shaking with fear, whereas the walls remained rock-steady in their indestructibility.

The commandant wore a red peak-cap, red riding breeches, a dark-blue soldier's shirt, a brown English shoulder belt and shiny boots. He had a crooked Mauser which he carried without a holster. With his rosy, clean-shaven face he might have been a hairdresser's model. He entered Srubov's office without a sound, and then froze just inside the doorway, where he straightened himself up to his full height.

"Everything ready?" asked Srubov, scarcely looking up.

The commandant answered tersely, in a voice so loud he was practically shouting.

"Ready."

He remained absolutely still, the only movement coming from his dagger-like eyes, which sparkled as brightly as glass.

Srubov and the others in the office all had the same eyes, the same limpid sparkle, the same expression of intense anxiety.

"Bring out the first five," ordered Srubov. "I'm coming now."

Without hurrying he filled his pipe and took leave of the others in the room, shaking their hands and looking around him all the while.

Morgunov did not offer his hand. "I'll come with you," he said. "Just to have a look."

It was Morgunov's first time in the Cheka. Srubov said nothing, but frowned slightly. He put on his black sheepskin coat and red, long-eared fur hat. Once out of his office he lit up his pipe. The tall, bulky Morgunov, dressed in sheepskin coat and papakha fur hat, had to stoop slightly as he followed Srubov out into the corridor. From the ceiling hung a row of light bulbs, like incandescent blisters. Pulling his hat over his ears, Srubov closed his mouth and half shut his eyes. He looked at the grey, square, wooden floorboards under his feet. It was as though they had been threaded together and then drawn out the length of the corridor. They crawled under Srubov's feet, and

Srubov, without knowing why, began to count them quickly:
". . . three . . . seven . . . fifteen . . . twenty-one . . ."

There were grey squares on the floor, and white ones on the walls
– these were the signs announcing the various Cheka departments.
Although he did not look at them, Srubov saw them. They too seemed
to be drawn out on a long thread.

. . . Secret Oper . . . Counter-Rev . . . No ent . . . Gangster . . .
Crimin . . .

Srubov reached sixty-seven, and then lost count. He stopped, turned
round and looked exasperatedly at Morgunov's ginger moustache.
And when he understood why he had stopped, he frowned and waved
his hand dismissively. He moved off again with a click of the heels,
mentally reproaching himself: ". . . senti-ments . . . senti-ments . . .
senti . . ."

He was in a bad mood, and quite unable to snap out of it.

". . . Senti-ments . . . ments-senti . . ."

On the first landing he came to there was a sentry. And to make
matters worse, he was still being observed by this unwelcome witness,
walking behind him. Srubov hated the idea that he was being watched,
that everywhere was so bright. Up more steps, and Srubov was on his
way again.

". . . two . . . four . . . five . . ."

An empty landing. He started counting again.

". . . one . . . two . . . eight . . ."

They reached the first floor, and another sentry. They walked past
him, side by side.

Up more steps.

And more.

They came to the last sentry. Faster now, through the door, out
into the yard, out on to the snow. It was much brighter here than in
the corridor.

Here there were soldiers armed with bayonets, enough to make a
whole railing. Morgunov, meanwhile, was thoughtlessly walking right
next to Srubov on his left side and making a nuisance of himself with
his incessant conversation.

Father Vasily was still standing with the crucifix raised above his
head. Condemned men and women were kneeling all around him.
They were trying to sing in unison, but each one sang something
different.

"And with the saints eternal re-e-e-e . . ."

There were only five women. As for the men, they couldn't be heard. Fear had wound strong steel hoops around their ribcages, and had a tight grip on their throats. They croaked in thin, broken voices: "Wi-ith the sai-ain-aints . . . the sai-ain-aints . . ."

The commandant also put on his sheepskin coat, which in his case was yellow. He went down to the basement with a white piece of paper. On the paper was a list of names.

The bolt on the cellar door rumbled heavily as it was drawn aside.

Those who a few seconds earlier had been singing now had no voice left. Their mouths were full of burning sand. Not all of them were able to get up. They crawled into the corners of the room, on to their bunks, or under their bunks. Just like a herd of sheep – except for their cat-like whine. The priest, propping himself up against the wall, stammered quietly: ". . . re-e-e-e . . ."

And with that he loudly polluted the air.

The commandant waved his piece of paper in front of him. His voice had an earth-like quality about it, raw and oppressive. He called out five surnames. Five people suddenly felt crushed, choked. None of them could find the strength to move. The air in the cellar began to smell like a stirred-up cesspit. The commandant held his nose in disgust.

A Cossack captain with a long moustache stepped forward and asked: "Where are you taking us?"

They all knew where they were being taken – to the firing squad. But none of them had heard their sentence officially pronounced. They all wanted to know exactly, conclusively. Anything was better than uncertainty.

The commandant spoke in a solemn, stern voice. Looking them straight in the eye, without any trace of emotion or embarrassment, he declared: "To Omsk."

The captain sniggered. Sitting down again, he ventured: "In a wooden box?"

Colonel Nikitin also found the situation amusing. He arched his broad guard's back and chuckled to himself.

What he didn't see was that out from underneath him, and from underneath his neighbour, General Treukhov, tiny streams trickled down their bunks. The streams formed a little swamp-like pool on the floor, from which steam began to rise.

Five of them were led away. The tightly closed cellar door prevented any of the others from leaving with them.

The spy-hole in the door also clanged shut. The wagons outside could now be heard more clearly. To those locked inside the cellar they sounded like huge clumps of frozen earth smashing against the cellar's iron door. As though they were being buried alive."

"Chu-chu-chu-chu-chu. Fr-chu-chu-chu. Fr-chu-chu-chu."

Standing up by the wall, Captain Bochenko placed his hands firmly on his hips and raised his head. With a wink at the dimly lit lamp hanging from the ceiling above him he declared: "They won't find me, mate."

So saying, he got down on all fours and slipped under a bunk.

In the corner of the room, Lieutenant Snezhnitsky's blue tongue hung lifelessly from his mouth for all to see. Skachkov made sure the commandant didn't notice it. As for Skachkov, he had not yet slit his own throat. He had a broken piece of glass ready, but just kept turning it over in his hand, unable to make up his mind whether to go through with the deed.

Suddenly, the tiny incandescent blister on the ceiling burst open, spraying a filthy, black, tar-like substance into everyone's eyes. Darkness filled the room. With the gloom came not panic, but despair. They couldn't just sit down and wait. But the only way out was through those walls – or through the brick floor. They began to crawl along the floor, squealing like animals, attacking the damp stones with their nails and teeth.

The narrow, snow-covered yard looked to Srubov and the five prisoners with him like a long room made out of white-hot metal. Revolving slowly as if at the bottom of a three-tier stone well, this room seized those who had entered it and hurled them through a narrow hatchway leading to another cellar at the opposite end of the yard. In the narrow gullet of the spiral staircase two of the prisoners lost their breath and collapsed, their heads spinning. The other three all stumbled, forming a pile of human bodies on the soil-covered floor.

The second cellar had no bunks, and was shaped like an upside-down "L". The shorter of the two sections of this stone letter, further away from the door, was shrouded in pitch-black darkness. The other section of the room – the long stem of the "L" – was filled with light. There were lamps on the ceiling which were placed at five paces from each other, and which became progressively brighter the further one went into the room. The floor was covered with little protuberances and tiny holes. No one could ever hide in here. The walls, the bricks of which formed rocky crags, fitted each other perfectly, as if their sheer, perfectly formed edges had been welded together. Above the walls, the ceiling hung down heavily like an empty, sagging belly. There was nowhere for the five prisoners to run. Besides, there were guards everywhere – behind them, in front of them, alongside them. Everywhere they looked there were rifles, swords, revolvers, and red, red stars. There was more iron, and there were more weapons, than there were men.

A white "wall" stood at the junction of the main, brightly lit section of the room and the shorter, dark part. Here, five doors, pulled off their hinges, had been placed against the craggy brick wall. Next to these doors stood five Chekists, each one with a large revolver in his hand. The cocking piece of each gun was drawn back, raised in the air like a black question mark.

The commandant told the prisoners to stop and then barked the order: "Undressed!"

The word hit them with all the force of a body blow. All five of them went weak at the knees with fear. Srubov felt that the order was addressed to him, too. Without thinking, he unbuttoned his coat. At the same time, however, his mind tried to reason with him, to make him see that his action was absurd, that he was an officer of the Cheka and that he was there to oversee the execution. Srubov needed a great deal of effort to regain control of himself. He glanced at the commandant, at the other Chekists – no one was looking at him.

The prisoners' hands trembled as they undressed. Their fingers, numb with cold, would not obey, refusing even to bend. Buttons and hooks would not come undone. Cords and laces became entangled. The commandant chewed on his cigarette, and shouted at them: "Come on! Come on!"

One prisoner had got his head stuck in his shirt, and was in no hurry to extricate himself. No one wanted to be the first to be completely undressed. They cast sideways glances at each other and deliberately took as long as they could. Kashin, a junior commissioned officer in the Cossack army, had not even begun to take his clothes off. He was sitting on the ground, his face distorted by fear, arms clasped tightly around his knees. He stared emptily at the toe of his torn boot, now a faded red colour. Efim Solomin went up to him, holding his revolver in his right hand, behind his back. With his left hand he patted Kashin on the head. Kashin winced, and opened his mouth in a gesture of surprise, his eyes now fixed firmly on the Chekist.

"Gone all thoughtful, have we, pal? Or jus' scared?"

Efim spoke quietly, in a drawling voice, still stroking Kashin's hair.

"Don't be afraid, pal, don't be afraid. You're not gonna snuff it for ages yet. Nowt to worry 'bout. Let me jus' take yer jacket fo' yer."

And affectionately, although at the same time firmly and assuredly, Efim's left hand unbuttoned the officer's trench coat.

"Don't be afraid, pal. Now, let's have yer sleeve."

Obediently, submissively, Kashin stretched out one arm, and then the other. Tears ran down his face. But he didn't notice them. Solomin was now in total control.

"Now yer trousers. It's OK, it's OK, pal."

Solomin had honest, blue eyes, and a wide face, with high cheekbones. His chin was covered in grubby basts, while a thin fringe sat on his upper lip. He undressed Kashin like a solicitous hospital orderly. "Now yer pants."

Srubov was painfully aware of the hopelessness of the prisoners' situation. It seemed to him that the violence committed against these people was at its most intense not in the act of execution, but rather at the moment of undressing. To be made to take off one's clothes and stand on the bare ground, naked amongst fully clothed men – this was humiliation in the extreme. At the same time, the anticipation of death was made even harder to bear by the apparent banality of the situation. And then there was the filthy floor, the dusty walls, the cellar itself. Maybe they *had* all dreamed of becoming President of the Constituent Assembly, or prime minister under a restored monarchy, or even Emperor. Hadn't he, Srubov, also dreamed of becoming People's Commissar, not just of the Russian Soviet Socialist Federation, but even of the World Soviet Socialist Federation? Srubov felt that he, too, was about to be shot. Beads of cold sweat pricked his back like tiny needles. He tugged nervously at his shoulder strap and his wiry beard.

A naked, bony man was standing up, his pince-nez gleaming in the light. He was the first to be fully undressed. The commandant pointed at his face.

"Take that off."

The naked man bowed slightly towards the commandant and smiled. Srubov saw the man's slender, intelligent-looking face, and his small light-brown beard. It was the face of an intellectual.

"But how will I manage without it? I won't be able to see the 'wall'."

There was something naive and child-like in the man's question, and in his smile. A thought suddenly occurred to Srubov: no one was going to shoot anyone. The Chekists, for their part, burst out laughing. The commandant dropped his cigarette.

"By devil, you're a fine fellow. Don't worry, we'll show you the way. Now remove your pince-nez."

Another prisoner, a fat man with a thick mat of black hair on his chest, spoke out in a deep bass voice.

"I wish to make one last statement."

The commandant turned to Srubov, who came closer and took out his notebook. He began to take notes, not stopping to think, to question whether, given the circumstances, there was in fact any sense in this man's making a statement at all. He was merely glad that the final, decisive moment could thus be delayed a little longer. The fat man, for his part, lied, contradicted himself and deliberately spoke as slowly as possible.

"Down by the little wood, between the river and the marshes, in the bushes . . .'

He told them that the White detachment in which he had served had buried a large quantity of gold somewhere. None of the Chekists believed him. They all knew that he was merely playing for time. At the end of his statement, the condemned man suggested they postpone his execution, and that they let him show them where the gold was buried.

Srubov put his notebook back in his pocket. The commandant chuckled and, slapping the naked man on the shoulder, said: "Stop winding us up, old man."

By now all five prisoners were totally naked. They were rubbing their hands together in an effort to keep warm, and shifting from one bare foot to the other. Their outer garments and underwear were all piled together in a multicoloured heap. The commandant made a sign with his hand which meant "Stand still".

The fat man with the black hairy chest let out a wail and burst into tears. Another man, a convicted gangster, with a vacant, indifferent look on his face, went and stood by one of the windows. He stood firmly on his huge flat feet, his crooked, hairy legs placed wide apart. A third prisoner, a former cavalry captain from one of the tsar's punitive detachments, whose legs were now totally lifeless, cried out: "Long live the Soviet regime!"

Vanka Mudynya, with his large, flat nose and big, clean-shaven face, went up to the prisoner and pressed his revolver against the man's body. He shook his sailor's fist, with its bulging sinews and prominent tattoos, at the man. With a sleepy grin on his face, he slobbered: "Don't shout – you'll get no mercy from us."

Another prisoner, a Communist found guilty of accepting bribes, lowered his round shaven head and muttered quietly to the ground: "Forgive me, comrades."

At this the jovial man with the little brown beard, who was now without his pince-nez, made them all laugh. He stood up, and made an idiot of himself by smashing his face against a door. "So that's how those doors are made," he said to himself. "Now I've got the light on them I can see they've got no hinges. Well, I'll know next time."

Again Srubov thought that these prisoners were not going to be shot.

But then the commandant, still laughing, gave the order: "Turn round."

At first the prisoners didn't understand.

"Turn round to face the wall, with your backs to us."

Srubov knew that as soon as they started to turn round the five Chekists would as one raise their revolvers and shoot each of them at point-blank range in the back of the head.

By the time those who were naked had understood what was required of them by those who were not naked, Srubov had had time to refill his pipe and light it again. Now the prisoners would turn round, he thought, and that would be it. The guards, the commandant, the Chekists with their revolvers, Srubov – all had white faces, and all looked particularly tense. All except Solomin, who was perfectly calm. He looked no more preoccupied by all of this than if he had been doing a mundane, run-of-the-mill kind of job. Srubov fixed his eyes on his pipe, and on the burning tobacco inside it. But he still saw the pale Morgunov open his mouth to gasp for air and turn his face away from the prisoners. Some force or other drew Srubov towards the five naked men, and he turned his face, and then his gaze, in their direction. The fire in his pipe suddenly came to life. He felt a painful ringing in his ears. Damp, white lumps of dead meat hit the ground with a thud. Each Chekist swiftly withdrew a few paces, a trail of smoke issuing from his revolver, before uncocking his weapon. Spasms ripped through the dead men's legs. The fat man gave a piercing scream and breathed his last. "Is there such a thing as a human soul or not?" thought Srubov. "Maybe that scream is the soul leaving the body?"

Two men in grey overcoats carefully tied ropes around the corpses' feet, and then dragged them off into the dark recesses of the cellar, round the corner. Two similarly dressed men threw shovelfuls of earth over the steaming rivers of blood. Solomin, his revolver tucked inside his belt, began to sort out the clothes left by the dead men, diligently placing underpants with underpants, vests with vests, and putting all outer clothes in a separate pile.

The next group of five prisoners to be selected for execution contained the priest. By now he had lost all self-control. Barely able to drag his large frame along on his stumpy legs, he kept repeating in a faint, high-pitched squeak: "Holy God, Almighty God."

His eyes were bulging out of their sockets. Srubov recalled how his mother used to make gingerbread larks out of dough, and give each one raisins for eyes. The priest's head looked just like the head of one of those larks, fresh from the oven, with its raisin eyes swollen from the heat. Father Vasily fell to his knees.

"My dear brothers, do not kill me . . ."

But for Srubov, this priest was no longer a human being; he was merely a lump of dough, a lark made out of dough. He couldn't feel sorry for someone like that. His heart filled with malice, and he ordered curtly, through clenched teeth: "Stop whining, you holy windbag. Moscow does not believe in tears."

Srubov's harsh, vulgar outburst acted as a spur to the other Chekists. Mudynya, rolling his cigar between his fingers, shouted: "Give him a kick up the backside – that'll shut him up."

Semyon Khudonogov, a tall man, unsteady on his feet, and the short, squat, bow-legged Alexey Bozhe got hold of the priest, threw him to the ground, and began to remove his clothes. The priest, whose movements were sluggish, trembled all the while like a rickety pane of glass in a rotten windowframe.

"Holy Father, Almighty God . . ."

Efim Solomin intervened.

"Lay off the old man. 'e can undress 'imself."

The priest went silent, gazing at Solomin with dull, lifeless eyes. Khudonogov and Bozhe stepped back.

"Don't make me take my clothes off, lads. Members of the clergy should be buried in their vestments."

Solomin offered a few kind words.

"Yer'll be too 'eavy in all tha' gear, pal. I' weighs yer down, all tha' gear does."

The priest was lying on the floor. Hitching up the bottom of his long grey overcoat, Solomin squatted over the priest and began to unbutton his heavy quilted cassock.

"It don't matter if we take yer clothes off. Then you can go in the bathhouse and work up a good sweat. If yer clean – I mean real clean – then dyin's not so tough. Now you just get rid of all that skin off yer back. Yer jus' like my little birdy – an' it's time I let yer spread yer wings."

The priest was wearing fine white linen. Solomin carefully unwound the tapes from his ankles.

"If yer keep all tha' gear on, then we're murderers. And we ain't no' murderers, but executioners. An execution, pal, is sumit grand.'

One of the officers asked for a cigarette. The commandant gave him one. As the officer lit up, the smoke made him screw up his eyes.

"Shooting us won't solve your transport problems. And you've still got to find food."

These words sent Srubov into an even worse mood.

Two other prisoners were undressing, cracking jokes and chatting away about nothing in particular as if getting ready for a sauna. They seemed not to notice or see anything, and not to want to see. When Srubov looked at them more closely, however, he saw that this was all just a game – their eyes were lifeless, and swollen with fear. The fifth prisoner, a peasant woman, was by now completely undressed. She stood in front of one of the revolvers and calmly crossed herself.

Meanwhile, the man with the cigarette, the one whose remarks had so annoyed Srubov, was refusing to turn round.

"I want you to shoot me in the mouth."

Srubov cut in sharply: "The rules cannot be broken. We only shoot prisoners in the back of the head. I order you to turn round."

The naked officer's will was weaker than Srubov's. He turned round. In the surface of the wooden door he saw a myriad of little holes. All he wanted was to become a tiny, tiny fly, to crawl into one of those holes, to hide for a while, and then to look for a chink in the cellar through which to fly to freedom. (In Kolchak's army he had dreamed of completing his military service at the head of a corps, as a full general.) And suddenly the tiny hole which he had picked out for himself in the door became a gaping cavity. The officer plunged effortlessly into it and died. The pupil in his right eye, which was still open, was now as wide and as veiny as the new hole in the door, made by the bullet as it passed through the officer's head.

Father Vasily's stomach looked just like a lump of dough which had fallen from a pastry board on to the floor. (Father Vasily had never wanted to become a member of the very highest orders of the clergy, just an archdeacon.)

Once again, a rope was tied around the dead prisoners' feet, and they were dragged off into the unlit section of the cellar, round the corner. All of these people – each in his own way – had dreamed of living a good life and being someone important. But what's the point of bringing this up, now that there was nothing left of each of them but a hundred or so pounds of fresh meat?

The next five prisoners were not brought in until the bodies had been removed and the blood covered up. The Chekists rolled their cigars between their fingers.

"Efim, yer toad, are yer always tha' pally with 'em?" asked the stocky Bozhe.

Solomin scratched under his nose.

"Why should yer tease 'em an' be nasty to 'em? They're only enemies 'til they're caught. Here they're just dumb cattle, see. If yer wanna kill a cow on the farm, yer gotta be nice to it. Yer gotta go up to her, like, an' stroke her, an' say, 'hold on there, moocow, steady now, girl'. An' then she'll stand still for yer. An' it's the same here, only the blow's gotta be even more accurate, see."

There were five executioners in all – Efim Solomin, Vanka Mudynya, Semyon Khudonogov, Alexey Bozhe and Naum Nepomnyashchikh. None of them had noticed that the last group of prisoners had contained a woman. All they saw was five fresh, bloody hunks of meat.

Three of them worked just like machines. Their eyes were empty, glazed over with a lifeless sheen. Everything they did down in the cellar they did almost without thinking. They would wait for the prisoners to get undressed and stand up, then they would mechanically raise their revolvers, fire, step back quickly, and replace their spent cartridge clip with a fresh one. Then they would wait for the bodies to be taken away and for five more prisoners to be brought in. Only when those who were condemned began to shout and protest would their blood boil with a burning rage. At this point they would start swearing, and shake their fists, or the butts of their revolvers, at the prisoners. And then, as they raised their weapons to the heads of those who were now naked, they would suddenly feel a cold shiver run through their hands and chests. This was the fear of missing – or of merely wounding. It was essential that they kill their victims instantaneously. If not, and if the half-alive prisoner began to scream and spit blood, then the cellar would suddenly become unbearably stuffy, and they would be gripped by the urge to run out of there and go and get themselves blind drunk. But they were too weak to do that. Someone huge and powerful would always force them to raise their hand quickly and finish off the wounded prisoner.

This was how Vanka Mudynya, Semyon Khudonogov and Naum Nepomnyashchikh carried out their executions.

Only Efim Solomin felt himself completely relaxed. He was con-

vinced that shooting White Guards was just as necessary as slaughtering beasts. And just as he couldn't feel any malice towards a cow who
obediently stuck out its neck for him to slit, so he bore no resentment
towards these condemned prisoners who offered their shaven heads
for him to aim at. That's not to say that he felt sorry for them. Solomin
knew that they were enemies of the Revolution. And he served the
Revolution willingly, conscientiously, as he might serve a good master.
He wasn't shooting anyone – he was merely doing a job that had to
be done.

(Whom he shot, and how he shot them, was ultimately of no
importance to Her. All She wanted was to destroy Her enemies.)

After the fourth group of five prisoners. Srubov could no longer
distinguish between their faces or their bodies, nor could he hear their
shouts or their groans. The smoke from the tobacco and the revolvers
together with the steam from the blood and the vapour from their
breath combined to form a ghastly pall. Through the haze, white
bodies were just visible, limbs hideously contorted by spasms tearing through them in the last few moments before death. Those
prisoners who were not quite dead would crawl on their hands and
knees, praying. Srubov watched, silently puffing on his pipe. More
bodies were dragged aside, more blood covered over with soil.
After each group of dead, naked prisoners another group of live, naked
prisoners would be brought in. Group of five after group of five, on
and on.

At the dark end of the cellar, a Chekist would take hold of ropes,
lowered through an opening in the ceiling. He would wind them
around the necks of the dead prisoners, and shout to those waiting
above: "Pull!"

The corpses, limbs dangling, would be hauled up through the
ceiling, and disappear. Meanwhile, more live prisoners would be
brought into the cellar, each one soiling his underwear from fear,
sweating with fear, sobbing with fear. The rumble of the wagons' steel
feet went on and on. One muffled last breath and then up from under
the ground on to the yard outside.

And still they hauled up more bodies, and more bodies.

The commandant came up to Srubov.

"The whole thing runs like a machine, comrade Srubov," he said.
"Like a factory."

Srubov nodded his head and remembered the white-hot "room" in
the yard. The room was revolving, hurling people from one cellar to
another. And all over the building, fires were blazing and machines

were pounding. Hundreds of people were employed around the clock. And there, in the cellar, he could hear "rrr-akh-rr-rrr-akh", as with a resounding clang and a sharp crackle automatic drills bored holes into skulls. Red-hot splinters of metal were shooting off in all directions. Bloody, clotted brain matter came spurting out like lubricating oil. (When people bore or drill, in order to build an artesian well or to find oil, they don't just cut through the earth. Sometimes they have to go through thick layers of rock, and veins of ore, in order to reach the earth below. In the same way, steel drills are often needed to cut through all the layers of bone in the skull, and bore through the porridge-like quagmire of brain tissue, and pipes have to be used to direct all the spurting jets of blood into sewers and drains.) The cellar was now awash with fresh blood, and the air reeked with the stench of human sweat and faeces. The room was filled with a thick, smoky haze. The light from the blinding, incandescent eyes on the ceiling had to force its way through the mist. The walls were soaked with cold perspiration, while the soil-covered floor writhed in frenzied convulsions. A red and yellow jelly-like substance, putrid and sticky, clung to the feet. The air was now heavier for all the lead. Breathing was difficult. This was indeed a factory.

"Rrr-akh-rrr-rrr-akh!"

"Pull!"

"A-a-a-a-gh!"

"I have conclusive evidence. Stop the execution."

"Rrakh-akh-rrr."

"OK, get undressed. Get undressed! Stand still. Turn round."

"A-a-a-a. O-o-o-o."

"P-a-akhakh."

"Pull!"

"Long live the Emperor! Go ahead and shoot, you Red swine. Lord, have mercy. Down with the Communists! Have mercy. I've shot some of you, too, you Red bastards."

"Rrr-rrr."

"Pull!"

"I die an innocent man. A-a-a-gh."

"Shut up!"

"Rrr."

"Pull!"

"I beg yo-o-o-ou."

"Rrr-u-u-khkhkh."

"Pull!"

Vanka Mudynya, Semyon Khudonogov and Naum Nepomnyashchikh all had deathly pale faces. They wearily unbuttoned their coats,
the sleeves of which were red with blood. As for Alexey Bozhe, the
whites of his eyes were swollen by excitement at the sight of blood.
His face was splashed with blood, his yellow teeth showed through a
bloody grin, and his moustache was covered in black soot. In an
unruffled, straight-faced, matter-of-fact manner, Efim Solomin wiped
thick clots of blood from under his nose, and from his moustache and
beard. He straightened the dirty peak of his green, red-starred cap,
which was half hanging off. (But does She really find any of this
interesting? All She has to do is make some people kill, and order
others to die. That's all. The Chekists, and Srubov, and the condemned
prisoners are merely insignificant pawns, tiny screws in the huge
mechanism, already hurtling out of control. In this factory coal and
steam feed Her anger. She is the only boss here, at once cruel and
beautiful.) Srubov, wrapped up in his black fur coat, and his ginger-
coloured fur hat, felt Her breath in the smoke from his smouldering
pipe. Sensing the proximity of that new, intense energy, he tensed his
muscles and his veins, in order to send the blood quicker round his
body. For Her and for Her sake he was prepared to do anything. Even
murder, if it was in Her interest, filled him with joy. And if necessary,
he would not hesitate to fire the bullets into the prisoners' heads
himself. Let just one Chekist try and chicken out, or back down from
his responsibilities, and he would lay him out on the spot. Srubov was
filled with a joyous sense of determination.

For Her and for Her sake, he thought.

But it wasn't always so straightforward. A young, handsome White
Guard, for example, refused to get undressed. Pursing his thin, aristocratic lips he announced in an ironic voice: "I am used to being
undressed by a lackey. I refuse to do it myself."

Naum Nepomnyashchikh angrily thrust the barrel of his revolver
into the man's chest.

"Get undressed, you bastard."

"Fetch me a lackey."

Nepomnyashchikh and Khudonogov grabbed the stubborn prisoner
by the feet and threw him to the ground, next to General Treukhov,
who was lying there almost unconscious. He gasped desperately for
breath, and began to pray in a weak, hoarse voice. His throat hissed,
like water being poured on to burning hot sand. In the end, they had
to undress him themselves. As they pulled his red-striped trousers off,
Solomin spat, and turned away in disgust.

"Phoo! 'Old yer noses, everyone. 'E's gone an' shat 'imself."

The guard, now totally undressed, stood defiantly, arms folded, refusing to budge. He proclaimed arrogantly: "I refuse to turn round in front of scum. As a Russian officer I command you to shoot me in the chest."

With that he spat in Khudonogov's eye. In a fit of rage, Khudonogov thrust the long barrel of his Mauser in the officer's mouth. Smashing through the man's clenched white teeth, he pulled the trigger. The officer fell backwards, his head jerking and his arms flailing helplessly. Convulsions ripped through his body, causing the muscles of what was obviously once quite an athlete to ripple like marble. For a moment, Srubov felt sorry for this handsome young man. He had once felt the same sense of pity at the sight of a strong thoroughbred stallion, writhing on the ground in agony from a broken leg. Khudonogov wiped the spit from his face with his sleeve. Srubov snapped at him sternly: "Calm down, will you?"

Then he added, in a voice which betrayed both his authority and his irritation: "Bring in the next five. And quick about it. Stop dithering."

The next group of prisoners contained two women and Ensign Skachkov. He still hadn't cut his throat. Even now, fully naked, he held the small piece of glass in his hand.

A big-bosomed, fat-bottomed woman with her hair brushed up high was trembling, reluctant to go to the "wall". Solomin took her by the arm.

"Don't be afraid, luv. Don't be afraid, my beauty. We're no' gonna hurt yer. See, there's another bird 'ere with yer."

The undressed woman gave in to the dressed man. Her smooth legs and slender ankles shaking, she stepped across the warm, sticky slime on the floor. Solomin led her carefully across the room, a look of intense concern on his face.

The other woman was a tall blonde. Her hair had come loose and was hanging down around her knees. Her eyes were blue, her eyebrows thick and dark. She spoke with a slight stutter, and with a voice like a child's.

"If you only kn-knew, comrades . . . how much I want to live, to live . . ."

They were all entranced by her deep-blue eyes. The Chekists did not raise their revolvers. Each one of them had eyes as black as coal. From their hearts down to their feet they felt the sweet, weary ache of desire. The commandant said nothing. The five of them stood still, each one holding a smoking revolver in his hand. But they all had their eyes fixed on this woman. Everything went quiet. Beads of perspiration dripped down from the ceiling on to the floor, where they broke up with a soft thump.

The smell of blood and fresh meat awoke in Srubov an instinct which he shared with all animals, if not with the earth itself. He wanted to grab hold of this blue-eyed woman, to hold her close to him, to sink his claws and his teeth into her, to be transported by a hot, red wave of ecstasy ... But She whom Srubov loved, to whom he had promised everything, She was here too (although any kind of comparison between Her and this blue-eyed woman was obviously absurd). And because of this, Srubov took two decisive steps forward and drew his black Browning from his pocket. Placing the weapon right between the dark arches formed by the woman's eyebrows, he pumped a nickel-plated bullet into her white forehead. The woman's whole body collapsed on to the floor, where it lay sprawled out. A sliver of blood snaked across her forehead and on to her light-brown hair, twisting and spiralling like red sea coral. Srubov did not lower his arm. Instead he turned and shot Skachkov through the temple. Next to him the big-bosomed woman lay unconscious. Solomin bent over her and with a big bullet ripped off the roof of her skull with its magnificent coiffure.

Srubov put the Browning back in his pocket and retreated. At the dark end of the cellar the corpses, which by now were piled on top of each other, reached up to the ceiling. Little streams of blood flowed from them right down to the bright end of the cellar. Srubov, in his sleepy state, saw a whole river of red. In the intoxicating haze everything looked red – everything, that is, except the corpses. They were white. There were red lamps on the ceiling. The Chekists were dressed all in red. In their hands they held not revolvers, but axes. It wasn't corpses that were lying on the floor – they were white-trunked birch trees. Birch trees have resilient bodies. The life in them is very stubborn and never gives up without a fight. If you try and chop them down they bend, and creak, and when, after a long time, they eventually fall, they come crashing down with a loud thud. They lie on the ground, their dying boughs trembling. The Chekists were throwing the white logs into the red river. On the river they were tying them together to make rafts. And they kept on chopping, and chopping, sparks of fire shooting off from the wood with every blow.

The foam from the red river was gnawing at the banks of brick like blood-covered teeth. A line of rafts made from white tree trunks was floating down the river. Each raft contained five trunks, and on each one were five Chekists. Srubov was jumping from raft to raft, giving orders, showing them he was in charge.

And then, just before dawn, as the night, exhausted by red insomnia, with red, swollen eyes, began to shake, the river's bloody waves caught fire in a blinding flash of light. The red blood burst into flame like bright molten lava. And it wasn't the ground which was shaken with fear – it was the whole earth that trembled. The volcano erupted with a thunderous roar.

"Trr-akh-rrr-ukh-rrr."

The cellar walls came crashing down and were washed away. The yard outside, and the streets and the whole town were submerged. More and more molten lava came pouring out of the volcano. Srubov was tossed immeasurably high by the waves of fire. The bright, radiant expanse blinded him. But in his heart he felt neither fear nor doubt. Srubov stood resolutely, with head held high, while the earthquake raged around him. As he gazed intensely into the distance, one thought alone occupied his mind – Her.

2

The moon was pale with fever. Its fever, and the freezing cold air, made the moon shiver slightly. Its breath formed a shimmering, glistening gossamer-like haze. Above the earth, this haze became clouds of dirty cotton wool, while down below it swirled along the ground like fresh milk.

Frozen blue snowdrifts covered the earth like rows of hunchbacked figures in the milky mist. Enveloped in blue snow, slivers of which lay on the windowsills and hung down from the roofs, the frozen, many-eyed walls of the white, three-storey building with a bluish tinge.

With a look of feverish haste written on their pale faces, two men, standing on a wagon, and dressed in different yellow sheepskin coats (although at night they wore black ones), would send nooses down into the cellar's black throat, and then wait with backs arched and arms stretched out in front of them.

The cellar would call out with a sigh, or a cough: "Pu-u-u-ull."

And then up would come the corpses, hauled up on the ropes, as if exhaled or spat out of the smoke-filled throat like phlegm or thick, warm saliva, blue, yellow and blood red in colour. Once loaded on to the wagon, they were trampled on like phlegm or saliva, and spread all over the floor. When the pile of blue, frozen corpses, bent double like bulging snowdrifts, reached higher than the sides of the wagon, they were covered with a grey tarpaulin, which spread over them like a thick mist. Then the wagon would move its steel feet, extricating them from the deep blue snow, breaking the drifts' hunched backs and crunching through their white bones. Finally, it would set off through the prison gates with its iron frame clanging and its engine snorting in quick, short breaths, its whole bulk dripping with the dark, ruddy sweat of oil and blood. Shrouded in its grey mist, each grey wagon would make its way to the cemetery, rocking the streets and the houses as it rumbled past. Those who lived along its path knew only too well what it was and where it was going. Dragged from their beds by the commotion, they would press their sleepy noses against ice-cold windows, their faces freezing to the glass. And their trembling knees and their shaking bed and the rattle of the crockery and the window-frames would make these people cover their heavy, festering eyes in fear, as from their stinking, sleep-filled mouths came the helpless, spiteful, horrified whisper "The Cheka . . . It's from the Cheka . . . It's the Cheka transporting its cargo."

Back in the yard, Srubov, Solomin, Mudynya, Bozhe, Nepomnyash-chikh, Khudonogov, the commandant, two men with shovels and the guards (guards who now had no one else to guard) – all of them, like the wagons, crunched through the hunched backs of the snowdrifts (although *their* feet were not made of steel but were animate, human feet, and by now extremely weary). Solomin walked next to Srubov and ahead of the others. He had blood on the right sleeve of his overcoat, on the right side of his chest and on his right cheek. In the moonlight it looked like soot. He spoke in a weak but cheerful voice – the voice of one who has undertaken an enormous task which, although difficult, nevertheless serves an important purpose.

"Yer know that tall, 'andsome one – the one that got shot in the mouth? It would 'ave bin good to pair 'im off with that blue-eyed bit. Would 'ave given good stock, tha' would."

Srubov looked at him. Solomin spoke quietly, his arms outstretched like an earnest businessman. "What's he talking about?" Srubov wondered to himself, before it struck him – Solomin was talking about people. With his tired eyes, all Srubov could make out was the bunch of crucifixes, miniature icons and amulets in Solomin's left hand.

"What have you got those for, Efim?"

Solomin smiled brightly.

"Toys for the kids, Comrade Srubov. Can't get toys anywhere these days. Just ain't any."

Srubov remembered his own son, Yury, little Yurasik, dear little Yukhasik.

The men behind him were laughing and swearing. They were talking about the prisoners they had just shot.

"The priest signed the confession – and the general did too . . ."

Srubov gave a sleepy yawn. He turned round to look at them with his pale, white face.

"The cheerful sort, like that geezer in the pince-nez, are always easier to kill. But them what whine . . ."

It was Naum Nepomnyashchikh. Bozhe only half agreed with him.

"They're always so club-footed, though . . ."

They spoke brashly, their heads raised in cheerful self-confidence. Srubov's tired brain had to make a considerable effort to grasp what they said. He realized that it was all just empty talk, mere bravado. They were all exhausted. They were straining their necks in an effort to hold up their leaden heads. And they were only using vulgar language in order to cheer themselves up. A foreign word suddenly appeared in Srubov's memory – they were all *doped*.

It took Srubov a long time to reach his office. He closed the door and locked it behind him. He turned the key in the lock and examined the door handle. It was clean; there were no marks on it. He held his hands under the light – there was no blood on them, either. He sat in the armchair and then jumped up again, bending over to look at the seat – that was clean too. There was no blood on his coat, or on his fur hat. Opening the safe, he reached behind a pile of papers and pulled out a quarter-litre bottle of spirits. He poured himself exactly half a tea glass of the liquid, which he then diluted with some boiled water from a carafe. Standing in front of the fire he shook the muddy liquid and peered closely through the glass – there was no red in it. The liquid gradually became clear. Srubov raised the glass to his lips, before the same word once again triggered itself off in his memory – *doped*.

It was only when Srubov had finished his drink and taken a few paces up and down the room that he noticed he had left behind him a red dotted line which formed a neat, sharp-pointed triangle from the door to the table, from the table to the safe, and from there back again to the door.

Just at that moment the bronze knick-knacks on his writing table began to stare at him impertinently, and the metal couch raised its thin bent legs off the floor in a gesture of distaste. The figure of Marx, hanging on the wall, stuck out his white, shirt-clad chest. Catching sight of him, Srubov flew into a rage.

"To hell with you and your white shirts, Comrade Marx."

Angrily, painfully, Srubov picked up the bottle and the glass and walked heavily over to the couch. "Just look at you, you tight-fisted aristocrat. Just what you deserve." He deliberately kept his boots on. He stretched himself out and knocked the pen holder on his desk with the heel of his boot. The ash-blue upholstery was covered with mud, blood and something wet that looked like snow. Srubov put the quarter-litre bottle and his glass down on the floor beside him. He longed to plunge into a river, or the sea, and wash himself spotlessly clean. As he lay on the couch he finished off his drink. The liquid burnt his mouth, like pure, neat alcohol. And his brain, intoxicated from the spirits, from the charcoal fumes in the cellar, from the fatigue, and from insomnia, produced drunken thoughts that were almost completely nonsensical, almost totally in-coherent.

"Just why does Marx have a white shirt, anyway?"

Some of Srubov's thoughts – the more moderate and liberal ones – wanted him to deliver her baby by Caesarean section, others – those more reactionary and resolute – to abort it. His most persistent and black thoughts, on the other hand, urged him to kill both Her and the baby. Hadn't they done the same thing in France, where they'd rendered this once great, healthy, fertile woman barren, where they'd dressed Her in velvet, diamonds and gold, where they'd made Her worthless and weak-willed, and turned Her into nothing more than a kept woman?

In the meantime, just what was the Kolchak counter-revolution? It was a small room in which there was very little air and which was filled with tobacco smoke and the stench of vodka and of human sweat. In this room was a writing table covered with pieces of paper, some blank and others used up, and with bottles, some empty and others full to the brim with vodka or spirits. There were whips lying on this table, whips made of leather, or rubber, or wire, or whips made of rubber and wire and lead, and revolvers and explosives, stone blocks and grenades. Whips, revolvers, grenades, rifles and explosives were every-where – on the walls and on the floor and on the people, both those sitting at the table and those sleeping under or next to the table. During the interrogation the entire room, either drunk or hungover, would hurl all it had at the prisoner – leather, rubber, wire, lead, iron or empty bottles – ripping its victim's body to shreds, flaying him alive, howling with the force of dozens of mouths, pointing dozens of threatening fingers at rifle barrels.

The Kolchak counter-revolution was another room too. In this room, the writing rable was covered with papers and heavy green cloth. At the table a captain or a colonel with scented moustache, always polite and well spoken, would stub out his cigarettes on prisoners' faces while he signed their death warrants.

And there he was, surrounded by Marx's white shirt, the squeamish couch and the immaculately clean baubles on his desk.

Well yes, yes, yes, yes, yes . . . Yes . . . Yes . . . Yes . . . But . . . But . . . but . . .

"How sweet it is to fire a bullet into a wild animal's mouth," thought Srubov. "But is it really possible to crush worms, when there are hundreds, if not thousands, of them crawling under your feet, and as you crunch them pus-like blood splashes your boots, your hands, your face?

"As for Her, She is not an idea. She is a living organism. She is a pregnant peasant woman, a woman who wants to bear Her child, to bring it into the world.

"Yes . . . Yes . . . Yes . . .

"But to those raised in Roman togas or Orthodox cassocks She is, of course, an incorporeal, infertile divinity with classical or biblical features dressed in a classical or biblical robe. She is even sometimes depicted like this on revolutionary banners and posters.

"For me, though, She is a pregnant peasant woman, a fat-bottomed Russian peasant woman dressed in a torn, lice-ridden, dirty sackcloth blouse. And I love Her as She is – a real, living thing, not a figment of anyone's imagination. I love Her because in Her huge river-like veins there flows bloody lava; because in her bowels there is a healthy rumbling so loud it sounds like peals of thunder; because Her stomach bubbles as it digests its food, just like the kitchen stove bubbles as it cooks; because Her heartbeats sound like the subterranean stirrings of a volcano; because She thinks great, maternal thoughts about the child which She has conceived but to which She has not yet given birth. And in cellars, in innumerable cellars, She shakes out Her blouse, brushing it and Herself clean of all the lice, worms and other parasites, many of which try to cling to her with their suckers. And what we have to do, and what I have to do again and again, is crush those parasites, crush them harder, and harder still. And when I crush them they exude pus, and more pus, and even more pus. And we're back again with Marx's white shirt. And outside the frost sticks its icy face to the window and breaks the glass. And under the window the thermometer which the merchant Innokenty Pshenitsyn once used to read shows minus forty-seven degrees."

The pale dawn filtered into the office, which had once been Innokenty Pshenitsyn's but was now Srubov's. But the building, which had once belonged to Innokenty Pshenitsyn but now belonged to the local Cheka, never noticed the dawns or the dusks, the nights or the days. It did not even know what they were. For with all the hammering on typewriters, the rustling of papers, the clicking of dozens of heels and the slamming of doors, it never went to bed, never got any sleep from one day to the next.

And cellars Nos. 3, 2 and 1, where Innokenty Pshenitsyn had once kept his cheeses, his sugar loaves, his sausages, his wine, and his preserves, now housed something else. In the semi-obscurity of No. 3 cellar the shelves had been replaced by bunks, the rows of cheeses by rows of prisoners, the sausages by sausage-shaped arms and legs. But the fat red rats with their long, bare tails still scurried cautiously, furtively about as they had when the cheeses and the sausages had been there. Once the prisoners, shaking wearily but uncontrollably, had dozed off, the rats would sniff the air, with a twitch of their hypersensitive whiskers and nostrils, and a sparkle in their sharp-sighted eyes. With their infallible sense they would identify those prisoners most soundly asleep, and begin to gnaw at their boots. Nevedomskaya, whose case was currently being investigated, had had all the fur on her high, warm galoshes eaten by the rats.

As for the rats in cellar No. 1, once the corpses had been removed, they would fight with each other, squealing and screeching, each one trying to be the first to burrow under the soil lying on the floor and lick up all the human blood beneath. Their little tongues, sharp, red and hungry, were like tongues of fire. And their tiny, sharp, white teeth were stronger than stone, stronger even than concrete.

The only cellar where there weren't any rats was cellar No. 2. They didn't shoot anyone in No. 2, or send any prisoners there for long periods of time. It was here that prisoners were kept for the last few hours before their execution.

A sign, covered in splashes of red paint, and fastened to the front of the white, three-storey building, peered out through the grey frosty haze into the murky dawn light. The black letters on the red background formed the words "Local Extraordinary Commission". Underneath this, in brackets, was a title at once more laconic and more clearly recognizable: "(Gubcheka)". The same sign had once declared, in gold letters on a black background: "Wine. Provisions. Groceries. Innokenty Pshenitsyn".

The heavy, red velvet flag flying high above the building was swollen with blood. Flapping in the wind, it sprayed forth blood from its tattered fringe and threadbare tassels.

Meanwhile, the last grey wagon, dripping with the dark, ruddy sweat of blood and oil, was bringing a detachment of Chekists, each with his iron shovel, back to base. It rocked the cemetery, the streets and the houses along its path. As it came through the gateway, rumbling along on its heavy steel feet, it rocked the white, three-storey stone building too.

3

At night the white, three-storey stone building with the red flag on its roof, with the red sign on the wall, and with the red stars on the caps of its sentries, would peer out at the town from behind the gleaming, hungry, square eyes of its windows. Opening its wrought-iron gates as if baring frozen teeth, it would devour prisoners by the armful, chewing them, swallowing them in its gullet-like stone cellars, digesting them in its stone belly and then purging itself of them as spittle, sweat or excrement, throwing them up like vomit out on to the street again. And towards dawn, it would yawn wearily with a creak of its iron teeth and jaws, and poke red tongues of blood out from under its gate.

Every morning, the lights would be switched off and the square, eye-like windows would be dark again. The blood red of the flag, and of the sign on the wall, and of the stars on the sentries' caps, would flare up brighter than ever. Brighter, too, the bloody tongues creeping under the gate, licking the pavement, the road and the feet of passers-by. Every morning, telephone wires would reach out from the white building to other buildings containing Soviet institutions, with all their different-coloured signs, making their way through the town like metal tentacles.

"It's the local Cheka on the line. Inform them immediately . . . From the local Cheka. We must produce within twenty-four hours . . . The local Cheka want this done as a matter of urgency . . . make it your personal responsibility . . . Have an explanation ready for the local Cheka by tonight . . . The local Cheka want . . ."

It was the same for all of them, for all the buildings with their different-coloured signs indicating the different Soviet institutions.

Large buildings and small buildings, stone buildings and wooden buildings, they all pressed themselves close to the black earpieces of their telephones, and all listened attentively, excitedly. And they all did what the Cheka demanded – immediately, without delay, within twenty-four hours, before closing.

In the local Cheka building, on the other hand, men armed with rifles stood on each landing, in each corridor, in each doorway, while other men dressed in leather jackets, soldiers' shirts and trench coats, and armed with revolvers, sat at tables full of papers, or rushed, briefcase in hand, from room to room, and girls, unarmed, pretty girls and ugly girls, girls well dressed and girls not so well dressed, chattered away over their typewriters. Men with special powers, agents and Red Guards from the Cheka battalion lit their cigarettes and conversed in the smoke-filled commandant's office, while waiters from the cafeteria went around the different departments, their trays laden with red clay cups full of weak tea and sweets made from rye flour and treacle. Visitors arrived in torn fur coats (in the Cheka you always went around in a torn coat – if you didn't have one you borrowed one from a friend), sheepishly presenting their passes, while witnesses waited impatiently for their interview, and visitors and witnesses alike lived in fear of being accused and arrested themselves.

Every morning Srubov's desk was piled high with grey bundles of letters. They came in all sorts of envelopes – white ones, yellow ones, envelopes made from newspaper or from old archive material. The addresses came in all kinds of writing: the jaunty, elaborate hand of an office clerk, the jittery, ligatured script of an intellectual, the illegible scrawl of an illiterate. The letters, too, went from painstakingly traced ringlets to regular, square-shaped, typewritten characters. Srubov never lost any time in tearing the envelopes open.

"I think the local Cheka should know . . . Makes no secret of his two wives. This is a threat to the Party's authority . . . Yours, a well-wisher."

"As a committed Communist I simply cannot . . . It's an outrage . . . Some visitors call the maid 'my girl', or 'darling', whereas the Soviet authorities have clearly stated that the word should be 'comrade', and you . . . This should be brought to the attention of whomever it concerns . . ."

Srubov lit his pipe. Making himself more comfortable in his armchair he picked up the file marked "Top Secret" and "Personal". He tore off its newspaper covering.

"I found vodka in the therd company of wite comander Gat . . ."

Further down the white sheet of writing paper were details of what Kolchak's army had done in Siberia and what the Soviet forces were now doing. Then came the conclusion: ". . . and so he (I mean the company comander) has got to be distroyd, becos he's stoping the workers and the pesants from uniting and preventing the red forces from joining together. Signed, acting political instructor Pattykin."

Srubov frowned and puffed on his pipe.

On a sheet of ivory paper someone had painted a watercolour of a black sepulchral mound with a stake driven into it. Underneath the painting was the inscription: "Death to the Bloodthirsty Chekists".

Srubov pursed his lips nervously and threw the sheet into the bin.

"Dear comrade chairman, I would like to get to know you, becos I think you chekists are realy fasinating, with your lether trench coats and your velvet collars, and your revolvers round your waists. Your very brave with your red stars on your chests . . . Lets meet . . . I'll wait for you at . . ."

Srubov chuckled and tapped his pipe on the baize-covered table. He threw the paper away and brushed the smouldering tobacco from his desk. There was a knock at the door. Without waiting for a reply, Alexey Bozhe walked into the room. He placed his large red hands on the table and fixed his red eyes firmly on Srubov's face. He spoke his question firmly, slowly.

"Are we gonna do it today?"

Srubov knew what he was talking about, but for some reason asked: "Do what?"

"Change shifts."

"What do you mean?"

Bozhe's square, flat face with its high cheekbones twitched in displeasure, and his black, overgrown eyebrows came together in a frown. The whites of his eyes went red.

"You know very well what I mean."

Of course Srubov knew. He knew that since spring now the old peasant had been desperate to get back to his ploughed field, that the old worker was missing his factory, that the old bureaucrat was soon exhausted now he was officially retired, and that some of the old Chekists began to pine miserably for the opportunity to take part in executions or at least to attend them if they had not done so for any length of time. He knew, too, that the profession left its indelible mark on each of them, that it instilled into them professional traits of character (in other words, traits particular to that profession alone), that to a certain degree, at least, it conditioned their spiritual aspirations and inclinations, and even their physical needs. As for Bozhe, he too was an old Chekist, and in the Cheka he had only ever worked as an executioner.

"I got no more strength left, Comrade Srubov. I've done nowt these last two weeks. I jus' get drunk all the time – what else yer wan' me to do?"

The square, angular figure of Bozhe, with his thick neck and narrow forehead, helplessly paced up and down the room, his red, swollen eyes fixed on Srubov.

Srubov thought about Her. She destroyed Her enemies, he said to himself, but Her enemies could inflict wounds on Her. And that was what Bozhe was – Her blood, the blood from one of Her wounds. But when blood flowed from a wound, Srubov thought, it inevitably went black, festered and rotted. Anyone who sought to turn the means into an end in itself would be swept from Her path and would be destroyed, would simply rot away. All ends were great only if She was striving towards them, only if they were Her ends. Otherwise, they were meaningless. Without Her, outside Her, all ends were meaningless. Srubov did not feel at all sorry for Bozhe, did not pity him in any way.

"If you get drunk I'll send you down to the cellar."

Next, able seaman Vanka Mudynya entered the room, swinging his arms as he walked. He came in without knocking, and without being invited, and stood by the desk next to Bozhe.

"You called me, so I've come," he declared.

He held a grudge against Srubov, and spoke without looking at him.

"Do you drink, Vanka?"

"Yeah."

"I'm going to send you down to the cellar."

Mudynya's cheeks flared up, as if he had been slapped in the face. He tugged nervously at his black seaman's jacket. Srubov's words stung him like a sharp insult.

"That's jus' no' fair, Comrade Srubov. Right from the first day o' the Revolution I've supported the Soviet regime, an' now yer puttin' me in the same hole as them Whites."

"Then don't drink."

Srubov's voice was cold, indifferent. Mudynya kept blinking and pursing his thick lips.

"It's no use sendin' me down to work at the 'wall' – I can't go on. I shot a thousand of 'em wi' no problem, an' no drinkin'. But when I 'ad to shoot me own brother, see, then I started on the bottle.

'S image 'aunts me, like. When I see 'im, I says to 'im, 'Andryusha, stand still,' an' 'e turns round, like, an' gets on 'is knees, and says to me, 'Vansha, me own brother' . . . Agh . . . Ev'ry night I see 'im . . ."

Srubov suddenly felt uneasy. Thoughts came to him in bunches, in shreds, in knots, in tiny fragments. They were all muddled up, and he couldn't make head nor tail of them. Vanka drank, and Bozhe drank. But didn't he drink too? So why couldn't they? Of course, there was the Cheka's prestige to think about. They hardly made much secret of their drinking. Yes, that was it. But then, he wondered, did She have total rights? And what did She know? Well, what *did* She know? Wasn't it in the nature of rights to apply to both sides, and in the same way? He could see nothing but chaos. Chaos and more chaos. He waved his hands dismissively.

"All right. Now get out. And try not to be so open about it in future."

The two men left, closing the door behind them. Srubov immediately buried himself in another letter, so as not to have to think. Anything, so as not to have to think.

"I don't usually take sides, but . . . particularly as he's a worker with responsibilities . . . The Republic needs kerosene . . . and to use this kerosene for his own ends by bartering it for twenty pounds of potatoes . . ."

One after the other Srubov read letters about two pounds of salt, a pound of bread, half a pound of sugar, ten pounds of flour, three nails, a pair of shoe soles and a dozen needles which someone or other had used to pay for something from someone else (and this despite the fact that the Soviet authorities allowed the private acquisition of goods only with a warrant containing the appropriate signatures, and stamped by the relevant government office). And if all this lot had been authorized by a warrant then that only proved that the warrant had been illegally drafted and wrongly issued.

Srubov took in three or four other pieces of information: a counter-espionage agent had assumed a false name; the furs in the local Council of National Economy stores were continually being stolen; a former member of a tsarist punitive expedition had wormed his way into the Party. And more "well-wishers", observant people who saw a great deal, but remained neutral, outsiders, independent of the Party. The sheets of paper rustled in an obsequious whisper. Those who had sent them all wanted to bring what they had to say "to the attention of the relevant authorities". With a servile gesture they took Srubov by the arm and dragged him to their bedroom, where they showed him the contents of their chamber pots (perhaps they were drunk; perhaps doctors could examine them and find out whether they were or not). They shook out in front of him all their dirty washing, or someone else's, perhaps belonging to someone from their family, or a relative, or someone they knew. They would claw their way like mice into someone else's cellar, or basement, or larder, and go through all their rubbish. As they did so, they would smile ingratiatingly or grimace cringingly at the noble guardians of society's morals, nodding their heads and asking: "What do you think, eh? What do you make of that? Eh? Nothing? Doesn't that smell of counter-revolution? And just look at this. And isn't this suspicious? No? Eh?"

They would always finish by taking Srubov quietly to one side and declaring quite indifferently that, of course, this was no concern of theirs, that it was merely their moral duty to inform "whomever it may concern" of the facts.

Srubov drew a red pencil line across the resolutions. At the bottom of the page he signed his name with two bold letters: "A.S.". He ripped open some more bundles of letters. He went through them impatiently, hastily, missing out every other line. Of all the mail sent to him most were anonymous letters, petty, trivial tip-offs from well-wishing informers. Any important information came from secret agents, and was sent directly to Comrade Yan Pepel at the Secret Service department.

Srubov couldn't read any more. He'd had enough. He got up and began to walk around the room, taking big strides from one corner to the other. His pipe went out and he sucked on it, chewing the end. He was irritated by the impression that a layer of dirt clung to his body. Srubov shrugged his shoulders. He unbuttoned his shirt collar. His vest was completely clean – he'd put on a fresh one the previous evening after his bath. All his clothes were clean and so was he. And yet the feeling that he was dirty just wouldn't go away.

His office contained an expensive writing table with luxurious marble ink wells. The plush armchairs were very comfortable and the walls were covered in brand-new wallpaper. Everything in Srubov's office was clean, yet this was a cold, harsh cleanliness that sparkled arrogantly. And it made Srubov feel very uncomfortable.

He walked over to the window. Down on the street below, people were riding in cars and trams, or walking along the pavement. Pedestrians were hurrying about their business, office staff with briefcases or housewives with shopping baskets, a multicoloured assortment of people, some with bags, others without bags. Those not on foot were all either people with briefcases or people with red stars on their caps and on their sleeves. Soviet citizens pulled heavily laden toboggans, dragging them along the road like horses.

Hundreds of tiny nerve-like wires reached out from Srubov's office right across to the other side of this busy street and beyond. Srubov had at his disposal hundreds of volunteer informers, a whole staff of permanent secret agents. He felt that he too was watching, listening and dissembling along with each and every one of them. He was kept constantly informed of other people's thoughts, intentions and actions. His job took him down into the world of the black marketeer, the gangster and the counter-revolutionary. He had to stretch out his hand into this world, with all its dirty tricks and its mud-slinging, and clean it up. A foreign word, one which recently had become particularly appropriate to him, formed itself in Srubov's brain and stretched out of it letter by letter, like a crooked staircase: s-a-n-i-t-i-z-o-r. It even made him laugh. The sanitizor of the Revolution. Of course, Srubov had no dealings with proper people, only with the dregs of society. And they really did make one rethink one's values. What had once been prized was now considered worthless totally superfluous. If people were honest then he had nothing to do. His task was to pour into the muddy, blood-red river of the Revolution all the dross, the rubbish and the dregs, to keep Her pure underground springs free of any filth or poison. And still that long foreign word stuck in his head.

". . . Mudynya and Bozhe are two hardened frontline soldiers, true, genuine comrades," he thought to himself. "Both have been awarded the Order of the Red Star. Ivan Nikitich Smirnov knew them on the Eastern Front, and it was to them that he was referring when he said, 'If I die, I hope to die alongside lads like them . . .' But what about the vodka? And what about me? And what significance do any of us have – I, Mudynya, Bozhe, any of us – what significance do any of us have for Her?".

Then there was the letter from his father. Two days had gone by since since he had received it, yet he couldn't get it out of his head. It wasn't his own thoughts, of course, that bothered him, but his father's . . . "Imagine that you had the task of constructing the fate of humanity, of ensuring happiness, peace and tranquillity for all, but that to achieve this you had to make just one tiny creature suffer, to build everything on this one creature's tears. Would you consent to be the architect of this new edifice? Your father would not accept such a task. But as for you . . . You think that you're going to erect the building of human happiness on top of all those who have suffered, who have been shot, annihilated . . . Well, you're wrong . . . Future generations won't want this 'happiness' founded on so much human blood . . ."

Yan Pepel coughed impatiently, which made Srubov start. He walked over to his desk, sat down in his armchair and without thinking motioned to Pepel to take a seat. Srubov listened without listening, gazing at Pepel with vacant, expressionless eyes.

Pepel finished his piece and stood up to go. But before he could leave, Srubov asked him: "Do you ever, Comrade Pepel, think about the problem of Terror? Have you ever felt sorry for those who have been shot, or rather, are being shot?"

Pepel was wearing a black leather jacket, black leather trousers, a large black belt around his waist, and tall, black, polished boots. His face was clean-shaven and his hair was neatly groomed. He raised his head with its long, thin aquiline nose and closely cropped angular beard, and fixed his cold, stubborn blue eyes on Srubov. With his left fist the size of a cobblestone clenched tight in his pocket, he spread the broad palm of his other hand across the holster of his revolver.

"I be worker, you be intellect'l. I got hatred, you got philos'phy."

That was all he said. He didn't like long, drawn-out conversations. He'd grown up in a factory. He'd had nothing above his head or under his feet for ten years but drive belts that hissed like snakes, cutting tools with screeching teeth and wheels that whirred round so fast it made one dizzy just looking at them. There was no time to talk to anyone. One couldn't even turn round. Consequently, Pepel wasn't very generous with his words. But during those years he had picked up a keen eyesight, something which served him well now. And his spirit had acquired the steel inflexibility of the machine. From the factory he went straight to the war, and from the war straight into the Revolution, in order to serve Her. But he remained a worker at heart. And at his desk in his office he could still hear the hissing of drive belts slithering along the floor, and the clicking of the cogs on the gear wheels of life. He felt as if he was in a workshop rather than an office, at a workbench rather than a desk. He always wrote illiterately, but quickly. The pieces of paper would fly like wood shavings from his desk to the secretary's typewriter. Whenever the phone jangled to life, he would pick up the receiver and listen with one ear, while with the other checking the tap-tap of the typewriter. If the sound was interrupted, or stopped altogether, he would bark: "Come on, get that machine moving. Quickly!"

Then he would shout into the telephone: "All right. Go on."

Now and again he would give a few instructions to his agents, and exchange the odd word or two with visitors. Only a quick word, mind. No time to sit down: he had to go and check the machine. Make sure the factory was working at full capacity.

And now, after he had been to see Srubov, he himself had a visitor, whom he held in his pincer-like gaze, and who sat in the armchair as if gripped in a vice. Pepel began firing questions at the man.

"What? Can we trust you? All right. An' d'yer support the Soviet regime? Total support? Right. Now let's be totally logical 'bout this . . ."

Then Pepel wrote down on a piece of paper something which he didn't want the typist to hear.

"Whoever suports the Soviet regim shud be preperd to help it. Are you preperd to be an informer?"

The visitor, stunned by the unexpectedness of the question, muttered an answer which expressed something halfway between refusal and consent. But Pepel had already written the man's name down on his list. He thrust a typewritten sheet of paper – instructions for informers – into the man's face.

"Agreed? A'right. Have a read through this. You have our complete trust now."

Of course, Pepel didn't trust him, just as he didn't trust dozens of other colleagues. He never failed to double-check the work of any one of them. After more than two years in the Cheka he had stopped trusting anyone.

Meanwhile, Srubov had another visitor, the flabby, bald Colonel Krutaev with his grey moustache and his shabby officer's overcoat. He crept quickly into the room in tiny, shuffling steps, bowed politely and sat down with a smile.

Krutaev sat on one side of the table, Srubov on the other.

"Even while I was in prison, Comrade Srubov, I wrote to you expressing my long-held sympathy with the Soviet regime."

The colonel uninhibitedly crossed his legs.

"I was convinced and I remain convinced," he continued, "that I would make an extremely valuable colleague and a devoted, committed Communist."

Srubov wanted to spit at Krutaev, to slap him in the face and to stamp all over him. But he restrained himself, chewing on his moustache and catching his beard with his teeth. He said nothing, content merely to listen.

Krutaev drew out his thick, flabby lips into a sickly-sweet grin and pulled a silver cigarette case from his pocket.

"Do you mind? Want one yourself?"

Leaning across the table, the colonel offered Srubov a cigarette. Srubov declined.

"I intend to prove it to you today, Comrade Srubov, committed Communist and shrewd officer of the local Cheka."

Srubov still said nothing. Krutaev popped his hand into the side pocket of his coat.

"Just look at him. What a rogue, eh?"

He handed Srubov a visiting card with a photograph on it. The man in the photograph, who was called Vladimir, had an interesting, slightly swollen face. He wore a captain's shoulder strap, and swords, and was dressed in full ceremonial uniform.

"Well?" he asked.

"It's my wife's brother."

Srubov shrugged his shoulders.

"What's all this about?"

"His surname, dear Comrade Srubov?"

"Who is he?"

"Klimenko. Captain Klimenko, commander of the counter-revolutionary army."

Srubov didn't let him finish his sentence.

"Klimenko?"

Krutaev was pleased with himself. With a sparkle in his old, faded eyes, he grinned fiendishly.

"You see, I'm not even sparing my own brother."

Srubov wrote down the details of Klimenko's address, as well as the false name which he had assumed.

On his way out, Krutaev carelessly remarked: "Oh and Comrade Srubov, I'd like two hundred roubles."

"Why?"

"Expenses occurred in obtaining the card."

"You just picked it up at home."

"No, I got it from friends."

"You bought it from friends?"

Krutaev coughed, and went on coughing. The blue veins on his brow swelled up suddenly, and his forehead turned a crimson colour. His eyes went red and tears welled up in them. Srubov placed his hand on a marble paperweight. All he had to do was pick it up, raise his arm and fling the thing at the colonel's temple – that would put an end to his coughing.

"I beg your pardon, Comrade Srubov, I bought it from a servant. It cost me exactly two hundred roubles."

Srubov threw two hundred-rouble notes on the table. Krutaev took them and went to shake Srubov's hand. Srubov, however, directed Krutaev's gaze to the sign on the wall that read: HAND SHAKING IS NOW ABOLISHED.

Krutaev once again drew his lips into a sugary grin. Bowing and scraping in his threadbare galoshes that seemed to stick to the floor, he scurried over to the door. Srubov felt the urge to fling the paperweight at his hunched back.

Through the open door came the sound of conversation and the tramping of boots. It was Chekists going to the cafeteria for lunch.

That evening there was a meeting of the local Party cell. Mudynya and Bozhe sat half drunk, with inane smirks on their faces. Solomin, just back from a search, was deep in concentration, rubbing his nose and listening attentively. Yan Pepel was also there, his face presenting its usual mask of grey indifference. Spending every day scheming, deceiving others and making sure others didn't deceive him, he had learnt how to rid his expression of the slightest sign of any feelings or thoughts. Srubov sat smoking his pipe. He was bored. The person reading the report was a political worker from a Cheka batallion, a clean-shaven youth, who was talking about the RKP's housing programme.

In the reading room next door non-Party Red Guards from the Cheka battalion sat playing draughts, rustling through newspapers and smoking. Vanda Klembrovskaya, an interpreter with the Cheka, was playing a tune on the piano. The Red Guards sat listening to her, shaking their heads.

"I'll never know what tune that janglin's supposed to be."

They could hear a sound like raindrops falling on the wall outside and on the floor above them, raindrops dripping softly down staircases. Srubov thought it must be raining, that the rain was breaking through the roof, through the ceiling, and that thousands of raindrops were splashing loudly on to the floor below. He remembered Levitin, Chekhov, Dostoevsky. Why them, he thought, in surprise. As he was leaving the meeting it suddenly came to him – Vanda Klembrovskaya had been playing Scriabin.

4

She could bury her trembling hands in the narrow pleats of her skirt, and her half-closed eyelids could hide the glimmer of trepidation in her eyes. But Valentina could not conceal her heavy breathing, nor the look of fear on her cold, powdered face.

Open suitcases lay on the floor. Piles of freshly ironed linen lay in neat squares on the bed. Each drawer in the chest had been opened and emptied of its contents, each lock with its flat tooth raised in a gesture of impotent defiance.

"Andrey, you've been coming home every night recently looking as white as a sheet and stinking of spirits, and your clothes have been covered in blood . . . No, this is awful. I can't stand it." Valentina was overcome with emotion. Her voice broke as she tried to speak.

Srubov gestured towards their child, who was asleep.

"Not so loud."

He was sitting on the windowsill, his back to the light. His head, dishevelled hair and square shoulders formed one black shadow which spread across the window, blocking out the scarlet and gold reflections.

"Andryusha . . . You were once so close to me. I used to understand you so well . . . Now you've shut yourself off from the outside world, you live behind a mask . . . You've turned into someone else . . . Andryusha," she said, moving closer to him. She sank sideways and rather awkwardly on to the bed and threw the white pile of linen on to the floor. She caught hold of the iron bedstead, and sat up against it, holding her head in her hands. "No, I can't stand it. Ever since you started working in that awful place, I've become afraid of you . . ."

Andrey said nothing.

"You have enormous, absolutely limitless power, and you . . . I'm ashamed to be your wife . . ."

She hadn't finished everything she wanted to say. Andrey quickly took out his silver cigarette case. In a gesture of annoyance, he tapped the end of his cigarette firmly against the lid. Then he lit up.

"Go on, then. Finish saying your piece."

After every swing of the pendulum on the clock on the wall, one of its springs hissed. It was rather like someone limping along a wooden pavement, striking the ground firmly with the heel of his good leg but dragging his other, bad leg along behind it. From the high cot, where little Yurka was sleeping, came the sound of heavy nasal breathing. Valentina said nothing. The glass in the windows had gone grey and was covered with a thin yellow deposit. The chest of drawers, the beds, the suitcases and the baskets looked to Srubov like dark, swollen tumours. The corners of the room were merely soft, shadowy drapes, and the room itself lost all its straight lines, turning into nothing more than a dimly lit sphere. All Andrey could see was the bright point of his lit cigarette. As another bright point burnt into his chest, he felt a searing pain in his heart.

"You don't want to talk? Well then I'll talk. What you're ashamed of is that all sorts of narrow-minded scum think your husband's an executioner. Isn't that it?"

Valentina gave a start. Raising her head, she saw the sharp red eye of a cigarette staring at her. She looked away.

Andrey threw the still burning cigarette end away. From the floor where it lay, the tiny fire, no bigger than a pinhead, pierced his eye. His eye hurt just like his heart.

"Not just narrow-minded people . . . There are Communists who think that too . . ."

There was one other thing she wanted to say. She spoke with a voice full of desperation, a voice that she had to try very hard to make even barely audible.

"And I'm sick of having to share my rations with Yurka. Others can manage it, but you can't, even though you're a Cheka officer."

Andrey stamped heavily on his cigarette. He was angry now. He wanted to shout a torrent of abuse at her, to humiliate her, to spit at her, at this woman whose very proximity made him feel spat at, humiliated. He was painfully ashamed to be married to someone as small-minded, so spiritually remote from himself. He flicked the light switch on. He saw suitcases, piles of things jumbled together in a heap. He saw the two of them, strangers now. He said nothing, despite his urge to speak. He recalled the first time he had met Valentina. What was it that had drawn him to this weak-willed, ugly, petty-minded woman? Yes, yes, she had humiliated him, insulted him by her closeness, precisely because she had made herself out to be someone totally different from the person she was in reality. She had craftily guessed his thoughts and desires, and had hypocritically echoed them, pretending them to be her own. But all one had to do was become intimate with a woman for her convictions, her very thoughts, to become identical with one's own convictions, one's own thoughts. Five years they had been together. How absurd it all was. Was there still anything which attracted him to her? Yes, there was, even now that she had made up her mind to leave him. But what that something was, Srubov couldn't say.

"So you're going away for good then?"

"For good, Andrey."

In her voice, in the expression on her face, there was a resolve which he had never noticed before.

"Well, you're perfectly free to do so. It's a big world out there. You'll meet someone and I'll meet . . ."

He felt sick. Why did he feel sick? Was it because of that little which remained intact from his relationship with Valentina? What about his son? He belonged to both of them. He was the flesh and blood of both of them. And then there was that insult. She'd called him an executioner. It wasn't so much a word as a scourge. It burned into him with its unbearable, searing heat. It made deep scars in his soul. The Revolution obliged him to act the way he did. Yes, that was it. The Revolution should feel proud that he had fulfilled his every duty. But there was still that word, that terrible word. He wanted to hide under the bed, in the wardrobe. He wanted no one to see him – and to see no one.

5

Srubov saw Her every day dressed in rags of two colours, red and grey. He was deep in thought.

For those raised on the hollow zeal of bourgeois promises She was red and was dressed in red. That wasn't true though. One couldn't describe Her merely as red. The fire of insurrection, the blood of Her victims, the call to arms – all this was red. But the salty sweat of days filled with toil, the destitution, the call for men and women to work in Her factories – that was grey. She was a mixture of red and grey. And their red banner was a mistake, an error of judgement, a half-truth, mere self-deception. A grey stripe should be sewn on to it. Or perhaps it should all be grey. Or perhaps a red star on a grey background. No one should deceive themselves, or be under any illusion. The fewer illusions, the fewer mistakes and disappointments – the clearer and more sober the perspective.

Srubov continued his thoughts. Hadn't this red banner become tarnished, hackneyed, just as the words "social democrat", too, were now tarnished and hackneyed? Wasn't this fact understood by the executioners who worked for the proletariat and their revolution, and weren't they trying to hide behind it? Hadn't the same banner once flown above the Tavrichesky, and Winter Palaces, just as it had above the Communist training school at Samara? And wasn't it under the same banner that the Kolchak division had once fought? And Gaide-man, Vandervelde, Kerensky . . . ?

Srubov was a fighting man, a comrade and the most ordinary human being, with big, dark, human eyes. But human eyes need red and grey, they need colours and they need light, otherwise they become melancholy and lose their lustre.

Every day, Srubov was surrounded by red, grey, grey, red, red-grey. There was grey and red in the house searches he conducted, in the naphthalene softness of the trunks he rummaged through, in the terrified stillness of other people's apartments, in the requisitions and the confiscations, in the arrests and in the faces twisted with fear, in the dirty rows of prisoners, in the tears, in the requests for clemency, in the executions, in the smashed skulls, in the heaps of steaming brains, in the blood. That was why he went to the cinema so often, and why he liked the ballet. That was why, one day after his wife had left him, he was sitting in the theatre waiting for the start of a show by a new ballerina.

The theatre contained more than just the orchestra, the footlights and the stage. There was the audience too. And for the time being, as the orchestra were late and the curtain still down in front of the stage, the audience had nothing to do. With their hundreds of eyes, and their dozens of binoculars and lorgnettes, they were watching Srubov. Wherever Srubov looked he saw tiny circles of shining glass and eyes, more eyes and even more eyes. From the chandeliers, the binoculars, the lorgnettes and the eyes came beams of light, all focused on Srubov. A barely audible whisper reached him from the stalls, the boxes and the gallery, as if wafted on a breeze.

". . . Chairman of the local Cheka . . . Supervises what goes on in the cellars . . . Local executioner . . . Red gendarme . . . Soviet Secret Police . . . Chief robber and pillager . . ."

Srubov felt nervous. His face was white and he kept turning from side to side in his chair, rubbing his beard up into his mouth and biting on his moustache. His eyes, simple, human eyes which needed colours and light, grew dark and filled with hatred. And although his weary brain craved for peace, it was further strained by the thoughts which whizzed around it like arrows.

"I know you," Srubov addressed them silently. "You are Soviet employees, sitting in free seats at a Soviet theatre. Half of you are wearing shabby English trench coats with the shoulder straps pulled off. Half of you are the wives of former landowners and are wearing patched-up dresses and dirty, crumpled fur stoles. You sit there goggle-eyed, whispering to each other, keeping your distance from me as if I had the plague. You stinking, rotten swine. Do you write denunciations against each other? With the most patriotic expression of the deepest patriotism, you write out whole pages of them! You're nothing but vermin. I know – oh, I know! – that there are even those among you who have wormed their way into the Communist Party. There are even so-called "socialists" here. Many of you have clamoured, and still clamour, howling ecstatically, for the foe to be crushed without mercy . . . Vengeance and death . . . Smash them, destroy them, you rotten scoundrels. We shall cover our enemies in crimson blood. But, you'd better beware the Chekists, you swine. The Chekists are second-rate people. You scum, you hypocrites, you work-shy bastards – in your books and your newspapers you say you have nothing in theory against the Terror, you accept that there is no alternative. And yet you despise the Chekist, the very person conducting the Terror which you accept. You claim the enemy has been disarmed. But as long as he remains alive, he won't have been disarmed. His main weapon is his brain. General Krasnov, and many tsarist military cadets, have all escaped from our grasp. You are bestowing upon the terrorists and the socialist revolutionaries the halo of heroism. Do you really think that Sozonov, Kalyaev and Balmashev weren't executioners just like we are? Of course, with them it was done on a beautifully prepared stage, in a fit of zeal. With us, on the other hand, it's a much more mundane affair, just another job to be done at work. And work is what you're frightened of more than anything else. The work we do is monumental, arduous, black, dirty work. You don't like unskilled labourers or unskilled labour, do you? You like everything to be spotlessly clean, even your toilets. And yet you despise the sanitizor, the one who cleans everything, and you turn your back on him. You like your steak rare, with plenty of blood, and yet you think 'butcher' is a dirty word. You all, from the 'Black Hundred' member to the socialist, approve of the death penalty. And yet you shun the executioner, and always depict him as some snake-like Malyuta Skuratov. Whenever you talk about the executioner, it's always with revulsion. But let me tell you, you swine, that we executioners deserve respect . . ."

Srubov could not stay and wait for the start of the show. He got up quickly and made his way to the exit. He felt eyes, binoculars and lorgnettes directed towards him from all sides, from behind him and from in front of him. He hadn't realized that he had pronounced the word "swine" out loud. As he left he spat at the floor.

When he arrived home his face, pale with emotion, was twitching nervously. An old woman in a black dress and black shawl opened the door for him. Looking him in the eye inquisitively, but affectionately, she asked him: "Are you ill, Andryusha?"

Srubov gave a feeble shrug of the shoulders. He gazed at his mother with his heavy, weary eyes, eyes from which all the colour and all the light had gone, and which now expressed nothing but a dull sadness.

"I'm tired, mother."

He was now lying on the bed. He could hear the rattle of plates in the dining room. His mother was getting the dinner ready. But all Srubov wanted to do was sleep.

He dreamed about a huge steam engine, with lots of people on it. The chief engineers, up on top, were sitting at their command posts, working levers and turning wheels, and all the time looking far ahead into the distance. Sometimes they would lean over the catwalk railings to gesture or shout something to those working below them, or to point to something ahead of them. Down below, workers were feeding fuel into the engine, pumping water and running around with oil cans. These people, who were all thin, were black from the soot. And below them, alongside the engine's wheels, shiny disc-shaped knives span round. Near the wheels were Chekists, Srubov's colleagues. The discs were revolving in a bloody mass which, when he looked closer, Srubov could see was in fact worms. Columns of soft red worms were climbing up the engine, threatening to clog the mechanism and wreck it. The rotating knives cut them down again and again. Red, unbaked dough fell under the engine wheels and was squashed into the ground. The Chekists stood all the while near the knives. All around them was the smell of meat. But Srubov couldn't understand why the smell was of cooked, rather than raw, meat.

Suddenly the worms turned into cows. Cows with human heads. The cows began to crawl up the engine as the worms had done. The metal disc-shaped knives couldn't cut them down fast enough. Red dough kept falling, again and again, under the engine's wheels. One of the cows had deep-, deep-blue eyes. Its tail was a length of maiden's golden hair, tied into a plait. It crawled over Srubov, who looked it right between the eyes and stuck his knife into it. Blood flowed out from the wound, the smell of which hit Srubov in the face, and reminded him of cooked meat. Srubov felt the air become stuffy, and started to choke.

Two meat cutlets were lying on a plate next to his bed. Next to that lay a fork, a piece of bread and some milk. Unable to stir her son from his sleep, his mother had left the food for him. Srubov woke up and cried out: "Mother, why have you left this meat for me?"

His mother didn't hear him. She was asleep.

"Mother!"

Opposite the bed there was a cheval glass. Peering into it, Srubov glimpsed his pale face with its pointed nose and huge frightened eyes. His hair and beard were dishevelled. Srubov began to mutter to himself in horrified whispers. His double in the mirror mimicked him, repeating his every movement. He called out like a child: "Mummy! Mummy!"

But she couldn't hear him. She was asleep. Everything was quiet. The pendulum clicked from side to side, dragging its bad leg along with it. The clock hissed. Srubov felt very cold, as if he were frozen solid to the bed. He saw his double in the glass, a crazed expression on his face, keeping guard over him. Srubov wanted to call his mother again, but he couldn't even move his tongue. He had no voice left. All he could do was stare at the mirror, at the figure jabbering silently in front of him.

6

Izaak Kats, a friend of Srubov's from school, who had also been with him at university and in the same underground Party unit, was now a member of the local Cheka Central Committee. It was Kats who had signed the death warrant for Srubov's father, Pavel Petrovich Srubov, a doctor in medicine. This was the very same Pavel Petrovich, a Moscow doctor who had a black beard and wore gold glasses, who had often playfully rubbed Kats's curly ginger hair while the latter was still a preparatory school student, and referred to him affectionately as "Ika", and whom Kats used to call respectfully "Pavel Petrovich".

Before his execution, as he was undressing in the damp, stuffy cellar, Pavel Petrovich had said to Kats: "Ika, tell Andrey that I died without any ill feeling towards him or towards you. I know that people can sometimes be blinded by an idea to such an extent that they lose their ability to reason correctly, to separate black from white. Bolshevism is a temporary, unhealthy phenomenon, a fit of madness which has affected the majority of the Russian people."

The naked, black-bearded doctor bent his silvery-blue head to one side and took off his gold-framed glasses, passing them to the commandant. Wiping his hands, he stepped forward towards Kats.

"And now, Ika, allow me to shake your hand."

Kats couldn't stop himself stretching out his hand to Doctor Srubov, whose eyes, as always, expressed nothing but kindness, and whose voice was as soft as velvet.

"May you recover from your disease as soon as possible. Believe me as an old doctor, believe me as once, when you were a schoolboy, you believed me, when I cured you of scarlet fever, believe me when I tell you that your disease, a disease shared by the whole Russian people, is without doubt curable, and, given time, will disappear without trace and for ever. I say for ever, for once an organism has been struck down by a disease it develops a sufficient amount of antibodies to resist it. Farewell."

At this, Doctor Srubov, afraid he might lose his self-control, turned round quickly and walked with his back arched over to the "wall".

Izaak Kats, a member of the local Cheka Central Committee, whose duty it was that day to attend the executions, had to fight very hard not to succumb to the urge to run away.

On the night that Doctor Pavel Petrovich Srubov was executed the local Cheka Central Committee member Izaak Kats received a telegram notifying him of his transfer to the same post in the town where Andrey Srubov was working. On the first day after his arrival, Izaak Kats was sitting in Andrey Srubov's flat and drinking coffee with him. Srubov's mother, an old woman with a white face and dark hair, wearing a black dress and a black shawl, was in the kitchen making the coffee. She called her son out from the dining room and whispered to him in the dark hallway: "Andryusha, Ika Kats shot your father and now you're sitting at the same table with him."

Gently stroking his mother's face with the palm of his hand, Andrey Srubov whispered back: "Mama dear, there's no need to mention that, or even to think about it. Let's have another cup of coffee, eh?"

He didn't want to talk about it or think about it. But Ika Kats felt awkward not talking about it, and so he did. As he spoke, he stirred his coffee with the spoon, which jingle-jangled in his cup, and looked closely at his red hand with its ginger hairs and blue veins. He hung his curly ginger head over his steaming coffee, inhaling its strong, heady aroma mixed with the sweet smell of boiled milk.

"He had to be shot. The old man had organized the 'Association for Ideological Struggle against Bolshevism', or AIS. He had dreamed of creating AIS groups all over Siberia, and of eventually uniting the scattered forces of the anti-Soviet intelligentsia. During his interrogation he referred to the members of the intelligentsia as 'AISists' . . ."

As he spoke, he kept his face lowered over his coffee cup. Srubov listened, slowly filling his pipe, without looking at Kats. He had the impression that Kats didn't want to talk, and was only doing so out of politeness. He tried to convince himself that his father's execution was necessary, that as a Communist and a revolutionary he ought to accept this wholeheartedly and unconditionally. And yet something drew his eyes to Kats's hand, its short red fingers gripping the cup filled with brown liquid. This was the hand which had signed his father's death warrant. With a tense, false smile and considerable effort he parted his lips and said: "You know, Ika, when one ingenuous Chekist asked Kolchak during his interrogation how many people he had shot and why, Kolchak replied: 'You and I, sir, are adults, wouldn't you agree? And as adults, let's talk about something more serious, shall we?' Get it?"

"OK, I won't mention it again."

Srubov was taken aback by the fact that Kats agreed with him so readily, and that his red, clean-shaven, fleshy face, with its hooked nose and its green, swollen eyes, displayed a stony indifference to the whole question. When Kats stopped talking and began drinking his coffee, swallowing it loudly, thoughts began to race through Srubov's head. These thoughts were an attempt at self-justification. But justification before whom? Perhaps before Her, or before himself. Srubov's eyes were filled with an expression of pain, of shame and of the desire, the passionate, irresistible desire, to justify himself. And if he daren't do so out loud, then he longed to be able to justify himself in his own head, in his own thoughts, to justify himself again, and again, and again.

"I have absolutely no doubt," he said to himself, "that each person, and therefore, my father, is nothing more than flesh, bones and blood. I also know that when someone is shot their corpse is nothing but flesh, bones and blood. So why am I afraid? Why am I now scared to walk in the cellar? Why do I keep goggling at Kats's hand? Because freedom implies the absence of fear. Because being free means above all not being afraid. Because I am not yet totally free. Yet I am not guilty of anything. Freedom and power after centuries of slavery are not things to be taken lightly. If you remove the bandages from the disfigured feet of a Chinese girl she will fall over and begin to crawl around on her hands and knees, until she has learnt to walk normally, until her feet have grown again. Even with enough determination and willpower to fill an ocean, she'll still be unable to walk because of those crippled feet of hers. Such feet, no doubt, are what prevented Napoleon and Smerdyakov from achieving their aims. But don't we all have crippled feet? It's useless trying to exercise them, to learn how to use them properly – what we need is to acquire a different skin, to be born again."

Kats finished drinking. Without putting his cup down, he uttered something which may or may not have been meant for Srubov.

"Of course, one can talk or cry or philosophize about it all. We can each of us have a good weep. But bring people together as a class and they become cruel, implacable, merciless. A whole class will never stop before a corpse – they'll step over it. And if you and I go soft, they'll step over us too."

As these words were being spoken, one hundred and twelve people in cellar No. 3 could feel their knees shaking, their hands trembling and their teeth chattering. The commandant, who wore red riding breeches under his big sheepskin coat, and who had a rosy, clean-shaven face, held a white sheet of paper in his hand. On the piece of paper was an order for one hundred and twelve prisoners to collect their things together and move to another cellar. It was this order that was the cause of all the shaking knees and the trembling hands and the dry mouths and the tears and the sighs and the moaning. One hundred and twelve people had taken part in an uprising against the Soviet regime. They had all been arrested with weapons in their hands and all knew that they were going to be executed, and that if they were being ordered to collect their things together and follow the commandant, then they were following him to their execution. And so it was that one hundred and twelve people walked out of the cellar, dressed in black and chestnut-coloured sheepskin coats, smelly fur coats, full-length and half-length coats, in coats and jackets of various colours made from the pelts of dogs, deer, goats or calves, in shabby papakha caps and long-eared fur hats, in high fur boots with their stitching undone, and in simple felt boots. Each one carried with him the pile of things which he had already folded together in the spacious commandant's office, and left behind him the dampness, the gloom, the rats, his damp and rickety bunk, the fear, the torpor in which he had waited for death, the days of semi-consciousness and the nights of sleeplessness. They all made their way along wide, brightly lit marble staircases, along landings where sentries stood like statues and the air, filled with electric light, was warmed by the dry breath of radiators, finding themselves eventually in what was the concert hall for the local Cheka and Cheka battalion social club. The long, multicoloured, hundred-headed, stinking animal crept forward, accompanied by the soft rustle of fur jackets and boots, obediently following the commandant up to the third floor, where it covered all the chairs of the concert hall with its motley fur.

On the piece of red towelling which served as the stage curtain was the inscription: NO PEASANT WHO HAS BEEN BETRAYED WILL BE PUNISHED BY THE SOVIET REGIME.

They made out the words with difficulty, reading syllable by syllable. As they did so they began to sigh with barely suppressed joy and hope, fidgeting excitedly and whispering to each other. But there were other inscriptions on the walls, printed on green Christmas tree trimming, inscriptions whose messages were frightening, horrifying, and whose meaning contradicted the earlier message: DEATH TO THE ENEMIES OF THE OCTOBER REVOLUTION, DEATH TO THE ALLIED ALLIANCE AND ITS SERVANTS.

The motley fur began to tremble, and then to wrinkle. The whispering too became louder, more nervous.

"Dea-a-ath . . . D . . . Dea-dea-th . . . Dea-dea-death . . ."

The hall was filled with the stench of sweat, soiled underwear, foot bindings, rancid sheepskin and cheap, strong tobacco. The commandant ordered a small window to be opened, and the motley, shaggy-haired beast breathed heavily through its nostrils, eagerly filling its lungs with the fresh dampness of melting snow, intoxicating its body with the earth's first cold sweat. Anxiously, uneasily, the beast began to fidget, jabbering and making the chairs creak. The healthy, strong beast was drawn to the earth, filled with the urge to sink its teeth into the earth's black breast, to cling to it with its huge body drenched with sweat after all its labours.

Srubov and Kats came into the room and saw on the faces and in the eyes of the arrested peasants the grey, desperate colour of longing. They understood that this longing was caused by inactivity, by the stuffy atmosphere in the cellar, by the intolerable burden of waiting for death. What they all longed for was the land, and the chance to work the land once again. Srubov walked quickly, with straight, broad steps, out to the front of the stage. A tall figure, dressed in black leather jacket and trousers, with black beard and black hair, and his revolver at his side, he stood against the red curtain like a cast-iron statue. He stared boldly into the eyes of the powerful, motley beast which had by now calmed down again. His first word was in the form of an address which he pronounced with the triumphant joy of the victorious lion tamer.

"Comrades . . ."

He spoke softly, slowly, almost singing the word, in the same way that he might stroke an animal's tough, wiry hair. His words sent a tingle along the motley fur. Like a lion tamer, calmly opening the cage of a tamed beast, Srubov announced slowly: "In an hour's time you will all be freed."

One hundred and twelve pairs of eyes were suddenly ablaze, gleaming with joy. The motley beast began to growl in joyful excitement. Meanwhile an unceasing, inebriating smell of melting snow streamed through the window. The beast breathed harder now, opening its nostrils wider, its head spinning with the ecstasy of spring. Srubov too felt light-headed from the intoxicating breath of the approaching spring, from the intoxicating, animal-like joy of one hundred and twelve people. Large, fiery clusters of words broke through the beast's chest, which was swollen with joy. Sparks of sun-drenched, blinding rain flew all over the beast's motley fur, stinging and scorching it, and setting it alight with tiny red, blue and green fires which burnt holes in it.

"Comrades, the Revolution is not about apportioning blame, or executions, or the Cheka."

In the sea of fire in front of him the black, charred figure of his executed father flashed momentarily before his eyes, then burned itself out and disappeared as suddenly as it had appeared.

"The Revolution is the brotherhood of the workers."

After the show in the concert hall the now liberated motley beast ran through the open gates of the prison and out onto the street. As it ran, it growled with delight, its hundreds of feet resounding noisily on the pavement beneath it.

The Chekists were drunk with a joyful, unaccountable, intoxicating, animal-like lust for life. That night the white, three-storey stone building, with its red flag and red sign and the sentries by its gates and in its doorways, witnessed something which it had never seen before.

Laughing and shouting loudly, colleagues from the local Cheka walked out through the gates. The chairman of the local Cheka ran ahead of the rest of them like a little boy, grabbed hold of a handful of snow and shoved it into Vanka Mudynya's face. Rocking with laughter, Vanka cried out: "I'm going to rub snow all over that little chairman's face of yours, Comrade Srubov."

A sombre-faced Bozhe held on to Mudynya. Two cold white balls suddenly hit Srubov on the back and neck. Srubov threw a snowball back into the group of Chekists, who, just like schoolboys, jumped out into the middle of the street, at the junction with the main road, and with loud screams began to bombard each other with snow. With every pellet of snow came a peal of laughter – first a pellet, then a peal. They were all filled with a genuine, unaccountable, intoxicating, animal-like lust for life.

Srubov was white from head to toe, plastered all over with snow. Snow had even landed on untouchable faces – sentries' faces.

The tired men, all of them wet behind the collar, with dripping, red-hot hands and cheeks, said goodbye to each other and went their different ways.

On the corner of the street Srubov shook Kats's hand, looking at him with dark, but clear, sparkling eyes.

"Goodbye, Ika. Everything's OK, Ika. The Revolution is life itself. Long live the Revolution, Ika."

At home Srubov ate his dinner with a hearty appetite. When he had finished he got up from the table and took hold of the sad, darkly dressed woman who was his mother. He danced with her around the room. His mother tore herself away, not knowing whether to be angry with him or to laugh. Trying to get her breath back after the furious whirls of the unexpected waltz, she shouted: "Andrei, you've gone mad. Stop it, Andrei . . ."

Srubov laughed, and replied: "Everything's OK, Mama. Long live the Revolution, Mama!"

7

The prisoner under interrogation sat in the middle of the room, a bright light shining in his eyes. Behind him and to the side of him there was nothing but darkness. In front of him sat Srubov, face to face with him. All the prisoner could make out was Srubov and two guards standing at the edge of the illuminated part of the room.

Srubov was busy reading the papers on his desk, and paid no attention to the prisoner. He didn't even look at him. As for the prisoner, he tugged nervously on the wretched-looking stubble that was his moustache, and tried to prepare himself for Srubov's questions. He kept his eyes glued on Srubov, waiting for him to begin the interrogation. In vain. Five minutes passed by in silence. Then ten. Then fifteen. The prisoner began to doubt whether there would even be any interrogation. Perhaps, he thought, they had called him to tell him they were setting him free. Thinking about freedom made the prisoner feel happy and relaxed.

Suddenly, unexpectedly, came the question.

"Your name, patronymic and surname?"

Srubov spoke without even raising his head, as if the prisoner weren't there. He rearranged the papers on his desk. The prisoner gave a start and answered the question. Srubov didn't bother to write down what the man said. All the same, a question had been asked. This meant that the interrogation had begun. He would have to answer their questions now.

Another five minutes of silence. Once more the question "Your name, patronymic and surname?"

The prisoner was confused. He had been expecting a different question. He answered falteringly, but then began to reassure himself. After all, he thought, there was nothing unusual in their asking the same question twice. There was another pause.

"Your name, patronymic and surname?"

This time, the question smashed through his hopes like a hammer. Srubov, for his part, pretended not to notice anything was amiss.

There was another pause. And still the same question.

"Your name, patronymic and surname?"

By now, the prisoner's strength was drained, and his body hung limp. He sat on the stool, with no support for his back, unable to collect his thoughts. He was far from the wall – he couldn't even see it. He was surrounded by a hollow darkness. There was nothing to lean against. All he could see was the light shining in his eyes and the guards' rifles. Finally, Srubov raised his head and looked at him sternly. Instead of asking another question he began to reel off details from the man's life, including the unit in which the prisoner had served, where it was stationed, what its functions were and who had commanded it. Srubov spoke with great confidence, as if reading straight from the man's service record. The prisoner shook his head and said nothing. Srubov had him firmly in his grasp.

The prisoner had to sign a statement. Without reading and with his hands trembling, he wrote his surname at the bottom of the page. Only as he was handing the long sheet of paper back to Srubov did he realize the horrifying meaning of what he had just done – with his own hand he had signed his death warrant. The last sentence of the statement gave the local Cheka Committee the right to make him pay the ultimate penalty.

". . . took part in executions, floggings, and the torture of Red Army soldiers, participated in arson attacks against whole villages."

Srubov put the piece of paper away in his briefcase. Then he ordered casually: "Next one."

He didn't say anything else about the man. Not even who he was, or who he wasn't. Srubov hated those prisoners who were weak, and who gave themselves up without a struggle. He liked adversaries who were cunning, bold. He liked to have to fight to the bitter end.

The prisoner joined his hands suppliantly.

"Have mercy, I beg you. I'll be your agent, I'll betray them all to you . . ."

Srubov didn't even look at him. He addressed the guards once more, with a sense of urgency in his voice.

"Next one, next one."

Since the interrogation of the man with the straggly moustache, Srubov's soul had begun to shiver squeamishly. He felt as if he was crushing woodlice.

The next prisoner to be interrogated was an artillery captain. His sincere face and his honest, self-confident air won Srubov over to him. The Chekist immediately began talking.

"Were you a long time with the Whites?"

"Right from the start."

"In the artillery?"

"In the artillery."

"Did you fight at Akhlabinny?"

"You bet I did!"

"Then it was your battery that was in the wood by the village?"

"Yes."

"Ha-ha-ha-ha-ha!"

Srubov unbuttoned his trench coat and his undershirt. The captain was taken aback, but Srubov laughed and uncovered his right shoulder.

"Look how you left me."

On his shoulder were three pink and blue scars. The shoulder itself was withered.

"I was wounded by shrapnel at Akhlabinny. I was a regiment commissar then."

The captain nervously twisted the ends of his long moustache and stared at the floor. Srubov, though, spoke to him just like an old friend.

"It doesn't matter. Just something that happened in the heat of battle."

They talked a long time, but this was no interrogation. The captain did not figure on the list of those wanted by the police. Srubov was able to sign a warrant for his release. As the two men said goodbye, they stared at each other hard and long, with a look that expressed the simple respect of one human being for another.

When the captain had gone, Srubov lit up his pipe, and smiled to himself. He wrote down the man's name in his notebook so as not to forget it.

He suddenly heard a commotion coming from the next room. There was a muffled cry. Srubov listened closely. Once more he heard the cry, which seemed to be coming from within a hollow barrel. It sounded as though steel hoops were being pressed tightly around the barrel, and water was being poured into it through its cracks. The shouts had come from a mouth which had a hand placed over it.

He went out into the corridor.

Up to the door marked: ACTING INVESTIGATOR.

It was locked.

He knocked on the door, which hurt his hand.

Then with his revolver.

"Comrade Ivanov, if you don't open the door I'll break it down!"

But neither did he break it down, nor did Ivanov open it.

Behind the door was a black Turkish sofa. On the sofa sat a woman under investigation, whose name was Novodomskaya. Her legs were white, and bare, and she was dressed in white shreds of lace. Her underwear was white. So was her face.

Ivanov, on the other hand, was red, and drenched in sweat.

Half an hour later, Ivanov, who was now under arrest, and Novodomskaya found themselves in Srubov's office. They sat side by side in armchairs by the left-hand wall. Both were pale, and both had large, dark eyes. Over by the right-hand wall, on a sofa, sat Cheka officers. They all wore trench coats, patched-up soldiers' shirts, leather jackets and trousers of various colours, black, red and green.

Everyone was smoking. Dull grey faces looked out from behind palls of smoke.

Srubov sat at his desk in the middle of the room. He had a large pencil in his hand and as he spoke he crossed things out on the sheet of paper in front of him.

"Why don't we rape her if we're going to shoot her anyway? What temptation for a working man's soul."

Novodomskaya was terrified. She gripped the chair's cold little leather arms with her cold hands.

"We're allowed to shoot her, so we must be allowed to rape her. Everything's allowed . . . And what if every Ivanov . . ."

He glanced to his right and to his left. No one said a word. They all just sat there, sucking on their cheap grey cigarettes.

"No, not everything is allowed. Only what is allowed is allowed."

He snapped his pencil in two and threw it violently down on to the table. He stood up sharply, his shaggy black beard jutting out in front of him.

"Otherwise, the Revolution will be replaced by the reign of religious superstition and the Terror will give way to nothing more than wanton depravity.

He picked up another pencil.

"The Revolution is not about what my left foot wants. The Revolution is . . ."

He scribbled something with his pencil.

"First . . ."

He pronounced the word slowly, pausing between each syllable.

"Or-ga-ni-za-tion."

He stopped.

"Second . . ."

He scribbled something else, and then spoke as before.

"Pla-nn-ing. And third . . ."

He ripped up the piece of paper.

"Cal-cu-la-tion."

Srubov got up from the table and started walking around the room, turning his bearded head to the right, then to the left. As he walked he pressed himself close to the wall and picked up bricks off the floor. He put one brick next to another until he had a whole row of them. These bricks were the foundations which he cemented together, and on which he placed walls, a roof and pipes. The whole thing represented one block of a huge factory.

"The Revolution," he declared, "is a factory."

Each machine, each screw had its own place.

And what was the energy source for all of this? It was steam, compressed in a boiler, and electricity, whizzing round the earth like a thunderstorm.

The Revolution could take its initial steps forward only when the energy source had been contained within the iron-hard boundaries of order and expediency. Electricity was electricity only as long as it remained within the steel network of wires. Steam was steam only as long as it stayed in the boiler.

The factory started to work. Srubov stepped inside his brick construction, walking between the machines, prodding them with his fingers.

"This is our machine. What makes it work? It is driven by the fury of the masses, channelled by them as a means of self-defence . . ."

Srubov's thoughts entered the heads of all those listening to him and piled up high inside them like strong iron tiles.

Srubov finished talking and stopped in front of the commandant. With a frown on his face he stood still for a moment and then said in a completely steady voice, the voice of a man who would tolerate no objections: "Now shoot them both. Him first – that should convince her."

The Chekists rose immediately, noisily, to their feet. They left the room without looking back, without saying a word. Only Pepel turned round in the doorway and remarked sternly: "Thas' right. No time for philos'phy in t'Revolution."

Ivanov sat with his head sunk on his chest and his mouth wide open. He always walked straight, but now all he could manage was an awkward hobble. Novodomskaya gave a little squeak. She sat with an alabaster face, staring at the floor with unseeing eyes. Srubov noticed that her high warm galoshes were torn (the rats in the cellar had eaten them).

Glancing at his watch, he stretched a little, walked over to the telephone and dialled.

"Mother, is that you? I'm on my way home."

Recently Srubov had begun to fear the dark. By the time he got home, his mother had lit a fire in every room.

8

Srubov saw a wondrous sight. The Whites and the Reds were spinning a grey web – a web made from the tedium of everyday life.

Srubov's everyday life.

The Whites drew the web from institution to institution, from headquarters to headquarters, tying it with minute but strong knots around the three-storey stone building, pulling all the loose ends of the web together in the same place, beyond the town, in the crumbling little hovel occupied by the local allotment attendant. The Whites spun their web at night, in dark backyards and lonely alleyways, hiding from the Reds, believing that the Reds could not see them, convinced that the Reds were unaware of their presence.

The Reds wove a web-like net parallel to the Whites' net, thread for thread, knot for knot, loop for loop. But they drew the ends of their threads to another place, to the white three-storey stone building. The Reds went on spinning night and day, not stopping for a break, even for a single minute. They hid from the Whites, certain that the Whites could not see them, convinced that the Whites were unaware of their presence.

The Whites and the Reds both worked hastily, with a sense of urgency. Both pinned their hopes on the strength of their web, counting on it to foul up the other web and cause it to tear.

But it was in this very haste, this urgency and this vigilance, and in the imminent entanglement of one web with the other, that the stuff of Srubov's everyday life was to be found. To go for whole weeks on end without sleep, or to sleep, fully clothed, at a desk, on a desk, on a sledge, in a saddle, in a car, in a train compartment, or at the end of a carriage, to eat nothing but cold snacks, to eat standing up, to receive people, to meet people, to interrogate people, to give instructions to dozens of agents, to read through, write or sign hundreds of sheets of paper, barely able to hold one's head up, barely able to drag one's feet along with fatigue – this was everyday life for him now. Srubov had been working eight days now like this, round the clock, without ever being able to undress, falling asleep in his armchair at his desk or lying down for an hour or two on the sofa, facing a constant filthy avalanche of people, stuck in white mountains of paper behind bluey-grey clouds of tobacco smoke. (Working in the Cheka, one tended to see nothing but red-grey, grey-red, the Reds and the Whites, the Whites and the Reds. Their webs had been interminably entangled for more than two years now.)

And now, now that all the preparations had been made; now that all the instructions had been given; now that colleagues armed with warrants had been dispatched to the right places and were doing the right thing at the right time; now that the white, three-storey building was empty and quiet (there was just one company from the Cheka battalion stationed on the ground floor); now that, on the night from the eighth to the ninth of the month they had to wait for the results of last week's work; now that there were exactly two hours remaining before the swoop, the searches and the arrests began, all Srubov wanted to do was close his red eyes and go to sleep. Instead, he had to open the black morocco leather file on his desk. As he rummaged with one finger in the piles of shreds and scraps of paper the file contained, he went over in his mind the shreds and scraps of his thoughts. Propping his heavy head up with his hand, he yawned and began to smoke.

In front of him lay a large piece of ruled paper. He read it.

"In France they had the guillotine and public executions. We have the cellar. That way we carry out our executions in secret. Public executions place a halo of martyrdom, of heroism, around the head of the criminal, even the most terrible kind. Public executions serve as propaganda points for the enemy, for they give him a moral advantage. Public executions leave the relatives and friends of those executed with a corpse, a tomb, a few last words, a last request and the knowledge of the exact date of death. In that way, public execution does not mean total destruction.

"An execution carried out in secret, in a cellar, unannounced by any formal sentence, and leaving no traces visible to the outside world, overwhelms the enemy by its suddenness. Its effect is that of a huge, merciless, omniscient machine, seizing its victims and mashing them like a meat grinder. After the execution there is no exact date of death, there are no last words, no corpse, not even a tomb. Absolute emptiness. The enemy is completely destroyed."

There was a form, at the top of which were the words "Chairman of the local Extraordinary Commission for Combating Counter-R . . .". The bottom of the page had been torn off unevenly. On the strip of paper that remained was a list.

1. 9 o'clock – meeting with Arutevy.
2. Ask the steward why rotten fat has been served this month.
3. Tomorrow – town meeting.
4. Give Yurasik the money to buy himself some shorts and some sweets.

Srubov came across the signed report of a search. Something had been added in blue pencil at the bottom of the page. "Terror should be organized so that the work of those carrying out the executions should be virtually identical to the work of the chief theorist. One says, 'Terror is necessary'; the other presses the firing button on his machine gun. The main thing is that no blood should be seen.

"Future 'enlightened' human societies will rid themselves of their superfluous or criminal members by means of gas chambers, various acids, electricity or deadly bacteria. Then there will be no cellars and no 'bloodthirsty' Chekists. Learned scholars with learned expressions on their faces will quite calmly put live people into huge retorts and test tubes, and with all kinds of chemical compounds and reactions and distillations imaginable will turn them into shoe polish, vaseline and lubricating oil.

"And when these wise scientists start to work for the good of mankind in their laboratories, then we won't need executioners, or murderers, or wars. Even the word 'cruelty' will disappear from use. All that will be left will be chemical reactions and experiments . . ."

There was also something from a notebook.

1. Place a decree in the newspaper concerning the registration of all types of rifle and similar weapons.
2. Get some advice from NACHOSO.
3. Make a systematic list of thoughts about Terror.
4. Chat with Professor Bespaly about electrons.

The next thing Srubov saw was a scrap of glossy drawing paper. The design of a machine gun had been drawn on it. There was a postscript – "Project for the mechanization of . . ."

On the inside of a used parcel cover was something written in fine red ink.

"Our work is *especially* difficult. It is not for nothing that our institution is called the *Extraordinary* Commission. It goes without saying, of course, that not all Chekists are extraordinary people. One of my well-placed friends once told me that when a Chekist has shot fifty prisoners, he deserves to be shot as the fifty-first. Nicely put, that. Apparently, then, we are first-rate people who happen to find Terror theoretically necessary. Fine. As a rough analogy let's suppose that there are insects which are destroying cereal crops. These insects have enemies, which are also insects. The agronomists set the second lot of insects on the first lot, and the second lot eat the first lot. The agronomists get their loaves of bread, but as for the unfortunate ravaging insects, they are no longer needed and so never get a chance to munch on the white bread."

Srubov's head was heavy, his eyes were red and leaden sleep pressed down on his shoulders and on his back. He folded the black file on the desk, covered it with his chest, his face and his beard and fell into a deep, deep sleep.

From beyond the windows, out in the blue, murky darkness, came the sound of feet scurrying along the pavement, the crunch of boots on frozen puddles, the murmur of voices, and the soft rustle of the crowd, as waves of people made their way droningly to early morning service. Up in the cathedral tower, the bell, the biggest and the oldest in the world, grey-green with age, lazily licked its grey-green copper teeth with its black iron tongue and boomed: "O-o-o-mim-o-o-omim -o-o-omim . . ."

Srubov's office was filled with tobacco smoke, a stuffy heat, bright light from an electric chandelier and the constant, frenzied jangle of the telephone receiver. It was as if metallic flies had crawled into both of Srubov's ears and were buzzing around inside them. "Z-z-z-dr-r-r-dr-r-r-r-z-z-z . . ."

They had achieved their aim – Srubov was awake again. His head was even heavier than before, however, and his eyelids stuck together. He had a dry, bitter taste in his mouth. But his thoughts were immediately sharp and clear. The day had begun.

It certainly had. With his left hand he kept the telephone receiver pressed against his ear. From down the telephone line came reports and instructions of various kinds. Srubov held his gaze on the town map on the desk in front of him. With his right hand he drew little crosses on parts of the town seized by the revolutionaries, on areas where conspirators were still holding out, and in those places where arms were being stored. He tore through the Whites' slender, entangled web, cutting it to pieces, with short, slanting pencil lines. A bitter, ironic grin spread across Srubov's lips.

Damp, blue night still hung over the town. It was pierced by the fiery lights from the illuminated churches, and the sound of bells ringing out with Easter joy, of the throng as they shuffled along, of people exchanging kisses, three kisses for Easter. Christ is risen! But She also stood above the town, with a bitter grin on Her face and a wicked gleam in Her eye. With Her bare foot She stamped heavily, imperiously, on the sickly-sentimental joy of the worshippers, and on the sweet white pyramids of cottage cheese and Easter cakes. The lights in the churches, in pots and lampions on ledges, went out, the bells became silent, and the rustle of feet faded to nothing, to be replaced by the scurry of people running away and hiding in their homes. A stillness now hung above the town, a strained, terrified stillness. The inky blueness of the spring night reflected the blue of Her vigilant, hate-filled eyes.

Srubov did not stay in his office. He called Kats back from a raid and left him sitting in his office armchair while he went for a drive around town.

With a triumphant roar and a snort, and a flash of its headlamp eyes, the powerful steel beast sped off. But there were no Whites to be seen anywhere. The Whites were hiding in backyards, and basements, and in the gloom of street corners.

Srubov recalled the arrest of the White ringleader, the local allotment attendant Ivan Nikiforovich Chirkalov, formerly Colonel Chadaev in

Kolchak's army. The colonel had conducted himself with a composure bordering on arrogance. Srubov had been unable to resist a sarcastic comment.

"Christ is risen, my dear Colonel."

Getting into his car, Srubov added to himself: "Well, life's certainly not going to be any sweeter for you on this side of the garden fence, my friend."

Chadaev had said nothing, merely pulling his peak-cap down over his eyes. There had been frightened ladies in elegant dresses with him, and men in frock coats and dress shirts. Solomin, imperturbable, unruffled, sniffed as he went through their trunks, disturbing them in their naphthalene-shrouded slumbers.

"Tell uz 'ow many ov you bourgeois there are. We'll leave each ov yer a fur coat and take all wot's left."

As Srubov had surveyed the pile of confiscated weapons his heart had beaten proudly, joyfully, and a powerful red force had flowed through his muscles.

Everything else merged together in a confused mass inside Srubov's head – night, day, streets, more streets, one patrol after another, the wind rushing through his ears, the vibrating car seat, the car door being slammed, the weak feeling in his legs, the noise, the heaviness in his head, the shooting pain in his eyes, the apartments, the rooms, the alcoves, the beds, the people, people forced to stay awake, traces of sleeplessness imprinted on their faces, sleepy people, people taken by surprise, people asleep, frightened people, Chekists, Red Army soldiers, rifles, grenades, revolvers, ordinary tobacco, cheap tobacco, and grey-red, red-grey and White and Red, Red and White. And then, after a night, a day and another night, there were visitors to receive and prisoners' relatives to see.

The thing these relatives all asked about the most was the prospects for release. Srubov listened attentively, but indifferently. Although he was sitting in his armchair he was as if perched at a great height, from where he could not see the visitors' faces, or even their bodies. As they moved about below him, they were reduced to the size of tiny black dots, nothing more.

An old woman would ask about her son, sobbing.

"Have pity on him, he's my only one . . ."

She would fall on to her knees, wiping her cheeks, wet with tears, with the corner of her head scarf. Her face would seem to Srubov to be no larger than a pinhead. Bowing and scraping before his feet, she would lower her head and then raise it, a pin illuminated by a flashing electric light. Then she would plead, in a voice barely audible: "My only one."

But what could he tell people like her? The enemy would always be the enemy, and it made no difference whether one treated them as members of a family or as individuals. And anyway, what did it matter whether there was one more of them or one less?

Srubov had no time for people today. He had even forgotten they existed. Their requests did not disturb him or touch him in the slightest. He found it easy to say "no".

"We don't care whether he's your only one or not. He is guilty and must be shot."

As one pinhead disappeared another would crawl out in front of him.

"He's the only breadwinner in the family, my husband . . . five others, all children."

The old story. The same old story.

Family circumstances could not be taken into account.

The pin would go red, and then white. One look at Srubov's face, with its stony, impassive, deathly-pale expression, would strike terror into it.

Eventually, all the little pinheads would leave. He was the same with all of them – cold, implacable, brutal.

One dot moved forward, coming right up to the table. It stepped back to reveal a small dark pile on the table. Srubov slowly realized what had happened – a bribe. Without coming down from the unattainable heights where he sat, he spoke a few ice-cold words into his telephone. The dot in front of him went black with fright, and babbled incoherently: "You don't take it. Others of you will. It has happened . . ."

"We will find those who have taken bribes. Then we'll shoot them along with you."

There were other visitors, but they were also dots, pinheads. All the time he was receiving people, Srubov felt relaxed, perched up in the immeasurable heights. It was just a little chilly up there. That was probably why his face was stony white.

Families, relatives and friends could always, of course, supplicate, tremble, weep, stand in a queue with tiny bundles tied with string, or bring the prisoners sweet Easter cakes or shortbreads or painted eggs – the white, three-storey stone building remained firm, implacable. Its brutality, its impartiality were as regular, and as predictable, as clockwork.

Family members might bring buns and sweets even after prisoners had been photographed with their numbers chalked on their chests, and after they had made the journey from cellar No. 3 to prison, and from prison, bound, to cellar No. 2, and thence to No. 1, and thereafter to the cemetery; when outside in the yard the draft reports of their cases, the final versions of which already lay in the official archives, were smouldering on the rubbish tip (every day, drafts and scraps of paper swept up in the various departments of the local Cheka building were burnt); when fat, yellow, bare-tailed rats had gnawed through their bodies with their strong teeth, and with their sharp red tongues had licked their corpses clean of blood.

The white, three-storey stone building, with its red flag, its red sign and its sentries, impassively bared the cast-iron teeth of its gates, and stuck out its blood-red tongues covered in the white spittle of slaked lime (in warm weather the blood which collected from the wagons used to remove the corpses was always sprinkled with slaked lime). The building knew nothing of the grief of those who worked within it, or of those who were brought to it, or of those who visited it.

9

At a Cheka Central Committee meeting, it was established that the White forces had been organized in the following way. Group A – fifteen units of five, comprising some of the best frontline officers in Kolchak's army, taken for the most part from employees of Soviet institutions. Their collective task was to occupy the Party training school and artillery store. Group B – ten units of five, including former officers, former merchants, small-time entrepreneurs, shopkeepers, soldiers and a few Red Army commanders. Their job was to take the main telegraph office, the telephone exchange and the headquarters of the local Party executive committee. Group C – seven units of five, drawn from the local riff-raff. Their objective was the railway station.

After taking their appointed targets and stationing a sufficient number of men for their defence, the plan was to unite all three groups, and then, provided that a certain number of Red Army units switched sides, to attack the local Cheka headquarters, engaging those troops still loyal to the Soviet regime.

Apart from these thirty-two units of five, the Whites could also count on the support of sympathizers and others who could be called upon to play subsidiary roles.

Sitting in the Central Committee meeting, Srubov felt very comfortable. He felt as if he were perched incredibly high up and that the others were somewhere way, way below him. And from where he was he could see all of the Whites' craftily constructed, entangled web as if it were in the palm of his hand. Srubov ripped through the web, proudly rejoicing in the realization of his own strength.

The investigator read out his report.

". . . active member of the organization, whose task . . ."

Srubov listened to everything with great interest. It was dead quiet in the office. Kats had a cold and could be heard trying not to breathe too noisily through his nose. An electric light flickered on and off at irregular intervals.

The investigator ended his report and looked silently at Srubov. Srubov responded with a question.

"Your conclusion?"

The investigator shivered, then rubbed his hands and shrugged his shoulders before pronouncing: "I propose that this man be made to pay the ultimate penalty."

Srubov nodded, and then turned to the others.

"The suggestion is to send this man to the firing squad. Any objections? Any questions?"

Morgunov went red and buried his face in his teacup.

"Well, of course."

"You mean he's already been shot?"

Srubov felt happy. Kats, blowing his nose, confirmed things.

"Yes, he's already been shot."

"Let's have the next one."

The investigator ran his hand over his bristle-length hair and began another report.

"The organization's arms supplier was . . ."

"What shall we do with this one, comrades?"

Kats bent down and dug his hand into his pocket for his handkerchief. Pepel concentrated on lighting up his cigarette. Morgunov stirred his spoon pensively in his tea. Nobody seemed to have heard the question. Srubov said nothing. Then one voice spoke out resolutely for all of them.

"Carried."

Surnames, more surnames, and even more surnames. Ranks, duties and titles. On one occasion Morgunov objected to the sentence, and began to argue, saying: "In my opinion, this man is not guilty . . ."

Srubov cut him short with a voice full of resolve and malice.

"Shut up, you sentimental fool. The Cheka is a tool in the class war.

Understand? If it's war, then there can be no courtroom hearings. We do not dispute the principle of personal accountability, we just operate it differently from an ordinary court or a revolutionary tribunal. What matters most for us is the position an individual occupies in society, the class he belongs to. This, and only this, is what counts."

Yan Pepel raised his clenched fists in an emphatic gesture of support for Srubov.

"No room for philos'phy in t'Revolution. Shoot 'im."

Kats also spoke out in favour of shooting the man, and then began to blow his nose violently.

Srubov was still perched up on high. He did not feel fear, nor did he think that what he was doing was cruel, or morally inadmissible. As for wondering about what was ethical and what was unethical, moral and immoral, that was just a lot of preconceived drivel. Of course, those little pinhead people thought that all that rubbish was necessary. But why did he, Srubov, need it? All he had to do was make sure all those pins didn't rise up in insurrection. As for the means with which to achieve this end, well, they were neither here nor there.

And yet at the same time, Srubov somehow felt that that wasn't quite true. Not everything was allowed. Everything had its limits. But how could one prevent oneself from crossing those limits? How could one refrain from going beyond them?

Srubov saw the investigator's white face, and the wrinkles between his eyebrows. But he wasn't listening to his report. He was wondering how one could stop at the line which marked the limit of what was allowed. And where was this line? He was standing with one leg on a very tiny point, while with his other leg and his two arms he tried to keep his balance. It wasn't easy. It was only towards the end of the meeting that Srubov felt able to stand firmly on both feet. He was very happy to have found a way of staying on the boundary line. He had discovered that everything depended on a sharp-pointed, three-sided pyramid. He had also discovered, of course, that this pyramid was to be found in his own brain. Its constituents were iron determination and absolute purity. It was made exclusively from electrons which analysed and checked his every action. Srubov smiled and ran his hand over his head. His hair pressed in one tightly packed mass against his skull – there was no way the precious pyramid could escape. He calmed down.

Srubov was the first to sign the minutes of the meeting. Pressing his pen hard against the paper, he wrote in large clear swirls: "Srubov".

From the letter "u" he traced a fine thread and attached it to the end of a long fat stick which stood for the letter "b". The whole signature resembled a tightly curled wood shaving stuck on the end of a stake. The other committee members hesitated for a second. All of them hoped that somebody else would pick up the pen.

Yan Pepel resolutely took hold of Srubov's pen. Opposite the word "members" he hastily scratched his name: "Yan Pepel".

Srubov frowned sombrely. He felt a blast of cold air hit him in the face, as if the minutes sheet were really a snow-covered pit. The living feel uncomfortable standing by a grave. It's something alien to them. Yet it's right under their feet. Srubov's signature was separated from the name of the last prisoner to be sentenced by a single centimetre. A centimetre higher and Srubov would have found himself amongst those condemned to death. The thought even occurred to him that a secretary could easily make an error when retyping the list, and put his name with those above it.

As everyone was getting ready to leave the meeting, Srubov's attention was suddenly drawn to the back of Kats's close-cropped neck. Without thinking, Srubov cracked a joke.

"What an elegant officer's neck you have, Kats. A nice flat, wide neck. No bullet could miss it."

Kats frowned, and went pale. Srubov suddenly felt awkward. Without stopping to glance at each other or say goodbye, they both left the room.

10

The last piece of paper (containing the last flashes of rapidly fading reason) which Srubov slipped into the black file was a crumpled sheet, torn unevenly and covered in crooked, twisted lines that looked like blue veins.

"If we had wanted," it read, "to shoot all the members of the Chirkalov–Chadaev organization five at a time in the cellar, we'd have needed a lot of time. To speed things up a bit, we took more than half of them to a place just out of town. We immediately removed all their clothes and stood them on the edge of a grave dug in the form of a ditch. Bozhe asked for permission to 'quarter' them (to hack them up into squares), but this was refused. Then we shot ten of them with a bullet in the back of the head. Some of the prisoners were so terrified, they sat on the edge of the ditch with their feet dangling over the side. Some wept, or prayed, or begged for mercy, or tried to run away. The usual scene. But they were surrounded by a line of cavalry. The cavalrymen didn't let a single one of them through. If anyone tried to escape they cut him down. Krutaev howled at me, pleading: 'Call Comrade Srubov! I have valuable evidence. Stop the execution. I can still be of use to you. I am a committed Communist.' When I went up to him, he didn't recognize me. He just kept rolling his eyes senselessly and howling: 'Call Comrade Srubov!' We had to shoot him all the same. We had discovered that he had too bloody a past, and we were getting tired of all the complaints against him. And anyway, he'd already outlived his usefulness.

"But I was struck, and pleasantly so, by the majority of these people. It was obvious that the Revolution had even taught them how to die with dignity. I remember reading when I was still a lad how in the war with Japan the Cossacks had forced the Japanese soldiers to dig their own graves, and had then placed them on the edge and cut the heads off them, one by one. I admired the tranquillity of these Orientals, the imperturbability with which they each waited for the mortal blow. And now I am lost in admiration when I think of that long row of naked people, illuminated by the moon, frozen in total silence and passivity, like a lifeless column of plaster and alabaster statues. The women seemed particularly unruffled. I must say that women, as a rule, are better at dying than men.

"A voice cried out from the pit: 'Finish me off, comrades!' Solomin jumped into the pit and on to the corpses, and began walking on them, turning them over, finishing off any he found still alive. Conditions weren't very good for shooting people. Although the moon was shining, there was still plenty of cloud around.

"As the moon illuminated the blood-covered faces of the dead prisoners, the faces of corpses, I somehow began to think about my own death. Just as these people are dead, I said to myself, so one day you'll be dead too. The law of life is a harsh but a simple one: be born, reproduce, and die. And I started to think about man: can we really have any doubt that man, boring into the ethereal expanse of the universe with the eyes of his telescopes, tearing through the earth's natural borders, digging in the dust of centuries gone by, deciphering hieroglyphics, rapaciously grasping the present, rushing boldly into the future – man who has conquered the earth, the water and the air – can we really have any doubt that man will one day be immortal? One lives, one works, one loves, one hates, one suffers, one learns, one accumulates a wealth of experience and knowledge, and then one ends up a stinking piece of dead meat . . . How absurd . . .

"We returned to base just as dawn was breaking. Walking up to my car, I trod on an ant hill. Dozens of ants poured into my boot. As I got into my car and drove off I reflected that even a tiny insect like the ant is prepared to wage a deadly war for the right to live, eat and reproduce. An insect like that will eat another insect's throat out. Yet all we do is philosophize, pile up various abstract theories and sit there racked with anguish about it all. Pepel maintains: 'No room for philos'phy in t'Revolution.' And yet I can't do anything without ' 'philos'phy' . . .

"Is that really all there is to life . . . be born, reproduce, and die?"

11

Then came the nights spent in the psychiatric clinics. And the two months' leave. And his removal from his duties as chairman of the local Cheka. And the longing to see his son. And the lengthy period of alcoholism. It was all rather a lot for just a few months.

And now there was this interrogation. Srubov sat emaciated, his face yellow, with deep-blue bags under his eyes. He was just a pile of bones in a leather suit. He had no body as such, no muscles. His breathing was a series of gasps and wheezes.

Kats was conducting the interrogation. His face was a round teapot, his nose a sharp-pointed spout aimed at the floor. Srubov wanted to block up the end of that spout. The Head of the local Cheka was actually sitting at his very table and playing with him like a toy. With his red paw Kats grabbed his white ivory pen and dipped it into the well in front of him, smearing it with ink. This interrogation was so painful for Srubov that he felt he was being physically tortured. If only they would ask him some questions. Instead, he was getting a lecture from Kats all about the authority of the Party and the prestige of the Cheka. All the while he had this spout in front of him, now pointing up and up, digging into him and tearing at his very heart.

Srubov tore at his beard. He clenched his teeth. He held Kats in his fiery, hate-filled gaze. A sense of insult ran through his veins like sulphuric acid. It burnt him as it raced round his body. He could restrain himself no longer. He jumped up and thrust his bearded face at Kats with the words "Listen, you shit, I served the Revolution with my own blood, I gave it everything I had, and now I'm just a has-been, a lemon from which all the juice has been squeezed. And juice is what I need. If I've got no blood left then I need alcoholic juice, get it?"

For a split second Kats, the investigator and chairman of the local

Cheka, became Ika again. He looked at Srubov with large, friendly eyes.

"Andrey, why are you so angry? I know you have served Her well, but why did you have to lose your self-control?"

Because Kats was fighting with Ika, and because this internal conflict hurt him so much, he frowned painfully and said: "Look, put yourself in my position. Just tell me what I was supposed to do when you began denigrating Her, dishonouring Her virtue?"

Srubov waved his hand dismissively and started pacing round the room. The bones in his knees crunched as he walked. His leather trousers creaked noisily. He didn't look at Kats. Why take any notice of that nonentity? She was standing in front of him, a mighty, voracious mistress. He had given Her the best years of his life – more than that, he had given Her *all* his life. She had taken everything – his soul, his blood, his strength. And now that he was a worthless piece of junk She had discarded him. Her insatiable appetite could only be satisfied by young, healthy, full-blooded men. She had no time for has-beens like him. He was being thrown away, like leftovers down a rubbish chute. How many others, the life sucked from them, their strength drained, no longer needed by anyone, lay strewn in Her wake? Srubov could see Her clearly, in all Her brutal splendour. He wanted to collect all the invectives he could muster, mix them together with the bitter taste of blighted hope, roll them into a ball of fire and fling them in Her face. But he hadn't the strength. His tongue wouldn't move. Srubov could also see that She was a beggar dressed in blood-stained rags. It was this destitution which produced Her brutality.

He, the invalid, the scrap of leftover food, was still alive and wanted to stay alive. But the cleaner had come to sweep him up with his broom. There he was, sitting opposite, his nose still stuck up in the air like a teapot spout. He didn't want to be thrown down the rubbish chute. They had decided to destroy him, but he wouldn't let them. He'd hide – they'd never find him. Life, life . . . Let his cap stay on the table. With a sly, malicious grin he turned to Kats:

"Mister Chairman of the local Cheka, I am not yet under arrest, am I? Then may I be allowed to go to the toilet?"

He slipped through the door. He almost ran along the corridor. Kats, now Kats, the chairman of the local Cheka once again, blushed with shame at his momentary weakness. Turning the telephone receiver violently in his hand, he asked the prison warden whether he hadn't seen anybody wandering about on their own. He lit up a cigarette and began to wait for Srubov. As he did so, he calmly, resolutely, signed a warrant for Srubov's arrest.

But Srubov was already outside. The pavement was packed tight with people. He stretched out his long bony legs as he ran down the middle of the road, waving his arms in the air. The wind blew his hair up on end and tossed it about. Curious passers-by stopped and pointed at him. He saw nothing. All he could remember was that he had to keep running. Several times he changed direction by turning into another street. The names of the streets, and the numbers on the houses, were of no importance to him. All he wanted to do was hide. He lost his breath more than once, and fell over, but each time he picked himself up and continued running. Somewhere doors slammed, and others opened. He began to think that he would escape after all, that they wouldn't catch him . . .

And then all of a sudden his luck ran out and he came up against a black, impenetrable wall blocking his path. Behind him stood his double. He must have been running after him all this time. Srubov hadn't once turned round, so he hadn't seen him. Now his double was happy – he'd caught up with him. Srubov opened his mouth wide like a fish to gasp for air, twisting his face contortedly.

He hadn't noticed that he was in his own flat, standing in front of the cheval glass.

This time he was not afraid of his double. In an instant he made up his mind to destroy him. His axe virtually jumped into his hands from on top of the stove where it lay. With all his might he struck his double full in the face, all the way from his right eye to his left ear lobe. His double, like an idiot, even broke into a loud laugh in the split second before the axe struck. He was still laughing as he was strewn all over the floor in tiny glittering pieces.

One foe had been destroyed. Now it was the wall's turn. They were wrong if they thought they were going to make him stand against that wall. Nobody was going to shoot him. He would fool them all. Let them think that he was getting undressed – he would smash that wall down and break through it to freedom.

Behind him in the doorway was the white, horrified face of his mother.

"Andryusha, Andryusha."

Plaster came crashing down. Then a yellow beam fell to the floor, landing on its side. Wood chips flew in all directions. Srubov swung the axe harder and harder. The blade flew off its handle, but Srubov didn't give a damn. He would use his teeth. He would gnaw at the wall, claw through it with his fingernails and run away to freedom.

"Andrey Pavlovich, Andrey Pavlovich, what are you doing?"

Someone was tugging at his shoulder. He had to see who it was. Perhaps his double had picked himself up off the floor. So he hadn't killed him outright, then. Srubov found himself staring at a short, stocky man with a black moustache. Ah! It was Sorokin, the lodger. Sorokin was a pathetic little philistine of a man who worked for the local Social Security. He was going to have to conduct himself in a dignified manner if he wanted to get rid of this little shit. Srubov proudly raised his head.

"First of all, I'll thank you not to get familiar with me and to keep your grubby hands off me. Second, I'll have you know that I am a Communist and I do not recognize my 'Christian' names, names that come from all those Saints Andrey or blessed Vasilys or whatever . . . If you want to speak to me, then kindly address me by my proper name, which is Has-Been . . ."

For some reason Srubov suddenly felt tired. His head was spinning. He had no strength left. Had he been poisoned by those charcoal fumes? He wanted to go for a car ride, out of town. Maybe he should ask this pathetic little philistine; he would probably be willing, even delighted, to take him. He could see his mother smiling and nodding her head.

"Go for a drive, Andryusha, go for a drive, son."

When he got to the hallway they let him put on his coat. On his head he put his lightest kepi. The lighter the better, he thought. As he reached the doorway he turned round. He was shaking, trembling.

"Mother dear, don't forget to give little Yury his cutlet for breakfast today . . ."

His mother didn't answer him. She was crying. Srubov had the impression that the car did not run on petrol at all, but was in fact drawn by horses – or not so much horses as an underfed nag. Never mind. The main thing was to get into the car. He didn't mind Sorokin either, really. At least he was someone to talk to.

"You know, Sorokin, I've just come from a huge factory. It's in operation twenty-four hours a day."

That seat wasn't very comfortable, though. Perhaps he could lie down? He would have to ask.

"Sorokin, is there a bed near here? I'm horribly tired."

He was a funny bloke, this Sorokin. Like a block of wood with eyes. Never said a word. He wasn't a very good dancing partner either – grabbed you round the waist like a bear.

Out of the corner of his eye Srubov caught sight of an orchestra parading a red banner. The orchestra weren't playing. He could hear the tramp-tramp of feet marching in time.

A red banner unfurled itself before Srubov's eyes, enshrouding him in a red mist. The stamping of feet sounded like the banging of axes on rafts (he could never forget that sound). Srubov felt that he was once again floating down a blood-red river. Only this time he wasn't on a raft. He had broken away from his raft and like a solitary chip was now bobbing up and down on the waves. Rafts went past him. He could see multidecked passenger ships sailing close to the bank. Srubov found a little absurd the thought that hundreds of people travelling and working on those ships, with their compact, red faces and their tensed, swollen veins, were pointing long, long pipes up to the sky and drawing with them like pencils, tracing astrakhan sheep in smoke on the light-blue paper sky. Just like children. That sort always drew astrakhan sheep in their exercise books.

A stinking haze hung over the river. Steep, stone banks rose high above it. A blue-eyed mermaid bobbed along towards him. In her golden hair she wore a red coral diadem. Alongside her swam a shaggy-haired, big-breasted, fat-bottomed witch. A fat goblin covered in thick black hair walked on the water as if it were dry land. Out from beneath the water came arms, legs, and blackened, half-decomposed heads that looked more like tree stumps, covered in women's hair which was matted together like seaweed. Srubov went pale, unable to close his eyes from terror. He tried to shout out, but his tongue was frozen to his teeth.

More and more rafts floated past him . . . And multidecked passenger ships sailed by in an unbroken line.

The orchestra came level with Srubov's horse-drawn cart. It thundered into life. Srubov held his head in his hands. What he heard was not the stamping of feet, nor the beating of drums, nor the blare of trumpets – it was the earth shaking, rumbling, crashing down around him, a volcano erupting, blinding him with its red-hot, bloody lava, its black, burning ash raining down on to his head and on to his brain. Srubov was forced to bend under the weight of the burning black substance as it poured down on to his back, his shoulders, and his head. He had to cover his scalp with his hands to protect his brain from the black, scalding liquid. Yet he could still see what was flowing out of the fire-breathing crater: a river, which was narrow, and a dull, blood-red colour at its source, but which became wider, brighter and cleaner as one followed it towards its middle, and which, at its mouth, spilled over into the vast gleaming emptiness, flowing out into a boundless, radiant sea.

More rafts floated past, and more ships sailed by. Srubov gathered his last ounces of strength, shook off the heavy black gunge from his shoulders and flung himself at the nearest multidecked volcano. Its sides, however, were slippery smooth. There was nothing to cling on to. Srubov jumped down from his horse-drawn cart on to the road, waving his arms about. He tried to swim, tried to shout out something. But all he could do was splutter: "I . . . I . . . I . . ."

The black searing mass of black ash weighed down on his back, his shoulders, his head and his brain, burning deeper and deeper, and pressing down harder and harder.

Meanwhile, that very same day, the Red Army soldiers from the Cheka batallion were in their club playing draughts and cracking nuts as they listened to Vanda Klembrovskaya playing something "incomprehensible" on the upright piano.

Efim Solomin, perched high up on a box, was speaking at a meeting.

"Comrades, our party is the RKP, our teachers are Marx and Lenin – we are like choice grains of wheat. We are Communists – we're what yer might call the real wheat. But those outside the Party are useless husks – they're the chaff. Do people outside the Party really understand where we're goin'? They'll never understand. We had an example of this with one of our own men. But wot's clear is tha' people reckon the Cheka are just interested in killing people. OK, so Vanka kills people, and Mitka kills people. But don' they see that it's not jus' Vanka who's doin' it, or Mitka, but the whole world; that it's not killin' but execution, and that's sumit wot goes on all over the world . . ."

With the broken glass of their conspiracies, with the strychnine of sabotage, they drew Her blood. Her belly, or, as they say in the Bible, "womb", was swollen from the child She carried, and from the hunger She endured (they were already starving in Povolzh, in Moscow, and in Peter's city). Covered in wounds and blood – Her own as well as that of Her enemies; for weren't Srubov, Kats, Bozhe and Mudynya really Her own blood? – She stood, a broken figure, in rags of grey and red, in a dirty, lice-ridden blouse. But She stood tall, Her naked feet planted firmly on the great plain, watching the world with vigilant, hate-filled eyes.

24 April 1923

Translated by Graham Roberts

Frostbitten Hands

AS A CHILD shortly after the Revolution, I went to the Robespierre Music School. When I was told that it was forbidden to attend school barefoot, my musical education came to a halt at the allegro of a sonata. But my musical education was as nothing compared to my humiliation on hearing the headmaster's opinion of boys who insulted his establishment by attending barefoot, like street urchins.

"We have no money for shoes," I told him.

"Well buy a second-hand pair at the market then," he said. "They're cheaper."

"Mama won't let me wear old shoes, she's afraid of infection," I said.

"I fully sympathize with your predicament," said the head, "but I have to consider the reputation of the school."

I went out of his office, my ears burning. On the way home I decided to say nothing to Mama about the shoes. I knew she would buy me some if she knew about my disgrace, but to do so she would have to sell her own felt boots or warm scarf, or else cut down on food – and I knew it would be she and my father who went hungry, and that despite all difficulties, I would always get the best.

Endless dreams about money!

I would find a purse with ten, no fifty million roubles in it, or a ration card for boots, or I would receive a present . . . Then I would buy some new lace-up boots, as shiny as the glass side of a photo negative, and a new pair of trousers, and a jacket and an overcoat, and I would go to school looking like little Lord Fauntleroy, and the headmaster would sidle up to me, and I would look at his boots and sneer – or rather laugh quietly to myself – because they were old and merely polished. Then at the school concert I would play a sonato better than he himself could play it, and he would rush over and say: "Please forgive me for being so foolish and rude as to tell you not to come to school without shoes on . . . !"

I realized I would have to make some money to buy a pair of boots. This was not easy for a boy of twelve at a time when many adults were unable to find work; but I was lucky. One of my friends took me round to the office of the *Craftsmen's Gazette*, where I learnt that all craftsmen were obliged by law to subscribe to this paper, whether they wanted to or not. I was given a receipt book, to enable me to bring enlightenment to the town's tailors, hatters and watchmakers, and a pointed Red Cavalry helmet, which I was to wear during working hours to make me look important, and I was told I could keep ten thousand of every million roubles that my subscription drive brought to the paper.

Little did I realize what a crown of thorns this job would be.

At that time Mama worked in one of our innumerable Government departments, whose offices moved almost daily. She had an acute social conscience, and she and her workmates enthusiastically carried the department's notional wealth from street to street. Since I was virtually unsupervised, I had little trouble slipping out of the house. Wearing short trousers and my cavalry helmet, I ran barefoot to Gorlits the binder. He stood behind his bench making up boxes. (He wasn't binding books at the time.)

I said: "Citizen Gorlits, please read this Government Decree!"

I felt myself blushing from head to foot, and the words stuck in my throat.

Gorlits read the decree, pushed his spectacles back on his forehead, sighed and stared at me.

"I know your papa,' he said. "He bound books in my workshop when Bloody Tsar Nicholas was on the throne. Everyone in this town respects him. Everyone says he is a decent man. And you come to me dressed up in that outfit, and try to take the bread out of the mouths of my children! Do you know what bread costs these days? I shall go to your papa at once and tell him what his beloved son is up to! I don't expect he knows anything about it!"

"It's the only job I could get!" I stammered, wishing I could fall through the floor.

"All right, I shall subscribe to your newspaper, because people will only keep on coming if I don't," he said. "There, take your ill-gotten gains!"

After him I went to Perets the clock-mender, and Sypunov the bootmaker, and they all berated me for taking a job no decent person would touch.

Sypunov was the most uncompromising of them all. He refused even to read the Decree, commented even more contemptuously than the others on my choice of employment, and showered me with curses;

but in the end he too was forced to subscribe to the *Craftsmen's Gazette*.

On his shelf, still on the last, was a pair of new boots – the answer to all my dreams. "How much are those boots?" I asked, handing him his receipt.

"You won't be able to afford them," said Sypunov. "I'll charge you so much you'll have to eat cattle cake . . ."

I spent the whole of that summer and early autumn in a state of constant humiliation, amassing enough capital to buy boots. Finally the day came when I brought back from the market a brand-new pair of lace-ups, as highly polished as mirrors. Beaming with happiness, I showed them to Mama.

"Where did you get them from?" she asked.

"I bought them at the market," I said.

"But how did you get the money?" she demanded, and I could see from her face that she imagined I must have fallen into bad company on the street.

"My God!" she said, when I had told her the whole story. "I never thought I'd live to see the day! Have you no shame? I've given birth to a monster! You've dragged our good name through the mud just to buy yourself a pair of boots. Are you sure you're not hiding anything else from me?"

From then on I was strictly forbidden to leave the house without special permission, and I barely managed to persuade Mama to let me out for the half-hour I needed to hand in my notice and return my helmet and receipt book.

Autumn passed, and winter came. I had a new suit made out of a green plush door curtain, with dark fading patterns of lilies and winding stalks on the back. I also had a new overcoat, cut from Mama's old cloak, and I was bought a new fur hat. The only thing I didn't have was a pair of gloves. I had worn my old pair after the first snow fell, and had lost them after less than an hour, playing snowballs. I concealed this from Mama, and whenever I went out I pretended I had them, so that she assumed I was properly dressed.

One day Mama came home from work and said to me: "Tomorrow morning you must go to the warehouse to get our rations. This month, I'm getting twelve pounds of flour sweets instead of the usual food and salary. Here's a sack. Don't forget your gloves."

It was a bitterly cold morning. The streets were empty. A freezing wind blew in from the steppe. The thermometer outside the chemist stood at minus twenty-six degrees.

I arrived at the warehouse and joined the queue on the street. My hands were red with cold, like a goose's claws. Mama had made my coat herself, and since she considered it impolite to put one's hands in one's pockets, there were no pockets, and the sleeves were too narrow for me to push my hands up them. I put my left hand behind the coat's lapel, but then my right hand froze. I was terrified of losing my place in the queue in case I wasn't let in again. I was probably too late anyway, for the queue was terribly long. The time dragged. My legs ached, my teeth chattered, and my hands . . . I blew on them; I unbuttoned my coat and put them under my armpits – it was a desperately cold day.

At last I crossed the threshold of the warehouse and shuffled down the steps towards the counter.

The most improbable things happen.

I took one glance at the man weighing the goods, and gasped. It was Sypunov the bootmaker, one of my subscribers to the *Craftsmen's Gazette*. He had recognized me too. He peered over the counter at my feet to see if I had shoes on, then said: "Got yourself enough money, did you? Stealing it from honest people?"

The whole queue stared at me.

"He went round collecting subscriptions to a newspaper," Sypunov explained, as though demanding justice. "He threatened to fine us – he got a kopeck for every one he sold. Knee high to a grasshopper, but he's already a thief. He'll be a nasty one when he grows up."

I forgot all about my hands. I wanted to freeze to death. Anything rather than have to hear him and see the crowd staring.

When I reached the counter, Sypunov said: "Two thirty. Lunchtime! You'll have to go out, comrades! We shall be closed for an hour."

"Give me my rations, I have to go home," I begged. And added, much to my own surprise: "My mother is ill, there's no one at home."

It was a pointless lie. "We're not giving out anything before lunch," Sypunov replied. "Eat your subscriptions if you're hungry!"

"Give him his rations!" people called out from the queue. "He hasn't stolen anything! What's he done wrong? Look at him, he's blue with cold. He's freezing!"

"It freezes my blood just to look at him! He got his way then. Now he's not getting a thing. Let him wait. Out you go now please, citizens!"

We went out into the street. Dust, scraps of paper and needle-sharp hailstones were driven along in the wind, and yellow leaves hit the paving stones like iron. I stuffed my hands inside the bag. A little girl with dimples on her cheeks went past in a blue hood. "What a funny muff you have, little boy!" she said.

For a moment I was warm. I turned away, unwound the bag, unbuttoned my coat and plunged my hands into the pockets of my trousers.

The little girl turned back and shouted: "Velvet trousers, velvet trousers!"

I pulled my hands out of my pockets, heroically did up all the buttons, and resigned myself to the next insult. The girl turned round once more, but she had run out of taunts. The people in the queue pushed their noses into their collars, shifted silently from foot to foot, jumped up and down and clapped their hands, like cab drivers waiting for customers. The time dragged as though it too had been nipped with frost. Eventually Sypunov came back, undid the padlock, flung open the metal-bound doors, and we all descended once again into the warehouse. He fussed around with some accounts, scribbled something, spat on his pencil, then said to me: "Give us your card, scum!"

With stiff fingers I pulled the card out of my pocket, and Sypunov threw twelve pounds of congealed sweets into my sack. I hoisted it on to my shoulder and set off.

A large orange sun loomed out of the frosty haze like a hemisphere of Mars. The wind hurled handfuls of sand into my eyes, and froze my lips. I could barely carry the sack, and had to hold it on my shoulder with both hands. I felt a lump in my chest, as though my hands were transferring the pain there so I could endure it, and wouldn't die. I pulled the sack down from my shoulders, put it on the pavement and stood over it, smearing the tears across my cheeks with my left hand, and thrusting the right hand behind the lapel of my coat.

A woman stopped, and said: "Are your hands frostbitten, little boy? Do they hurt? Go home at once and put them in cold water! It's a pity there's no snow to rub them with. You must tell your mother to get you some gloves. Have you got a mother, little boy?"

Without replying, I hoisted my sack on to my shoulder again, gripped the knot with both hands and stumbled off down the street.

Mama had come home for lunch and she opened the door to me.

"What's the matter with you?" she shrieked, staring into my face. "Where are your gloves?"

I stretched out my hands, and she seized them and squeezed them painfully in hers. She brought a saucepan of water, and I thrust into it my lifeless hands, which seemed not to belong to me any more. Mama bent over me. Oh, how old she had grown in the last few years . . .

Translated by Catherine Porter

VLADIMIR TENDRYAKOV

On the Blessed Island of Communism

BLIND THEMIS PLAYED a subtle joke in arranging for Khrushchev to bring Stalin to book. The butcher's judge was a man whom Stalin considered a clown.

I saw Stalin only once in my life – on 7 May 1945, when parading with endless thousands of my fellows across Red Square past the Mausoleum. I remember being struck by his small stature – his forage cap with its stiffened band barely projected above the parapet – and by the limply senile gesture of his avuncular hand, evoking a volcanic roar from the frenzied, ecstatic masses in the square. I, of course, was as much a part of that stentorian hysteria as the next man . . .

Khrushchev I saw and heard on many occasions, from afar and from quite close at hand, although I had not, alas, spoken with him or been permitted a handshake.

There was one meeting which I do think worth recording. I had the honour conferred on me of spending a whole day in Communism. Just so, exactly that, in the assiduously promised, intensively publicized Communism, inside which any sensible citizen of our country has long ago given up any thought of finding himself.

1

15 July 1960. I received a telephone call from the Board of the Union of Writers.

"Please call in tomorrow during working hours. Something very important."

Since, to do it justice, the Union of Writers had not overburdened me with its attentions, particularly on important matters, I dutifully called in at Vorovsky Street. There I was handed an envelope containing a glossy ticket looking like a holiday pass and made to sign for it.

The pass specified that Comrade Tenkov, VF, and spouse were invited to attend a meeting of Party and Government leaders with personalities in the field of science and the arts; please arrive at 9 am. On the reverse was a route map: along the Kashira Highway, turn off at Kilometre No. 120, in the direction of the Semyonovsky State Farm.

"Shall we provide you with transport?" I was asked.

I wished to remain independent.

"I have my own car."

What I had was my much-travelled Moskvich, which I washed maybe twice a year – when the inspiration came to me, or in very special circumstances, such as its annual technical inspection. The meeting with the Government was just such a transcendental occasion and I made a mental note that I would give it a wash.

But I failed to keep my promise: that day I returned home late at night and by the time I got up the next morning, the hands of the clock pointed past eight o'clock, so there could be no question of a car wash – I really had to get a move on to ensure that, if I were late, I should not be hopelessly so.

I scrambled into my one and only light suit, rushed out together with wife towards my unwashed Moskvich, and charged through Moscow in the direction of the Kashira Highway.

"More haste, less speed . . ." I am always at odds with such old saws, so that on the outskirts of Moscow I craftily arranged for a tyre to puncture. Whereupon, shedding my light-coloured but suffocatingly thick jacket, as hot as a peasant's jerkin, cursing our cantankerous car, the Government's initiative, myself and my totally guiltless wife, I set about changing the mud-caked wheel, as the sun burned down on me. Meanwhile, past us along the highway sped effortlessly the black Zils and the monumental Chaikas – a novelty still at that time – with their carriagework glittering immaculately, bound, inevitably, for the destination towards which I too was making all speed.

Finally the wheel was on, the boot slammed shut, hands were hastily rubbed with a rag – and it was full speed ahead. I squeezed from my unwashed steed all she was able to give, not bothering overmuch with the road signs, driving on the left when need be, with our glossy invitation ready to hand. If the militia were to stop us, I'd shove the omnipotent document under their noses: it's not as if I'm off to visit my Uncle George; you should not be condemning me but giving me top marks for zeal. The highway was thick with militia patrols – they had posts almost every kilometre – but I suppose they must have guessed from the sheer effrontery with which I violated all traffic regulations that I had a glossy pass ready for them and they limited themselves to staring after me with severe expressions on their faces. It was only when I committed the really heinous offence of overtaking the black limousines on the left at the approach to a level-crossing barrier, and unceremoniously planting myself alongside a Chaika, that a militia representative with the shoulder boards of a lieutenant colonel and a look of deep injury came up to me. He did not even ask to see my driving licence, nor enquire where I was going in such a hurry, and, alas, the glossy pass did not have to be produced. The lieutenant colonel confined himself to saying reproachfully: "That's not on, you know. You could cause an accident driving like that. That's bad."

And he so touched my heartstrings, and caused me to feel such genuine shame, that when I set off again I continued to get what I could out of my poor unwashed one, but without crossing the bounds of decency.

All of a sudden, I sensed that the highway around me was empty: there was just one ramshackle old lorry jolting around in front of me – no sign of any black limousines or any proud Chaikas with their gold-plated bustles . . . And I realized that I had erred from overzealousness – having sped past the cherished turn-off indicated on the reverse side of the pass. There was nothing for it but to do a U-turn . . .

There it was: the familiar rectangular "brick"; the no-entry sign, at the side of the road, excluding any casual caller, and then a ribbon of asphalt across the fields leading to a pine grove.

Our Moskvich found itself in a queue of cars winding past a solid, four-kilometre fence painted a regulation military khaki-green.

The young soldiers with their blue cap bands and blue flashes broke into a smile when I steered up alongside the gleaming Zils and Chaikas. Through our lowered window, I could hear one of them saying pointedly to his colleague: "Take a look – Mr Private Enterprise has turned up!"

I showed him my pass, which I was keeping handy. They saluted with immense deference and I drove in under the shade of the pine trees, looking around me in bewilderment – where was I supposed to put the car? The somewhat narrow drive, not more than one car's width, led to a small asphalt turning circle. A young man came up to us.

He was tall, broad in the shoulder, willowy. He did not so much walk as glide. The dark suit he wore, which set off his broad chest and slender waist, produced discreet, almost musical folds at the elbows. His head was curlier than Pushkin's and his face, with its regular, manly features, was capable of registering nothing but open goodwill. Without a trace of a shudder, he placed his powerful hand, in its stiff sleeve with the brilliant white expanse of cuff, on the handle of our long-unwashed car door, flung it open and cooed to my wife: "Good day. Welcome. If you please . . ."

And my wife, confused by his magnificence, his courtly deference, climbed out of the Moskvich on to the hallowed asphalt. The greeter slammed the door shut and motioned casually to me.

"You drive on! On you go."

How about that!

There is something about me which, for some reason, always evokes mistrust among doormen and waiters. Doormen keep me at arm's length; waiters warn me unceremoniously that the beer in their establishment is dearer than that on sale in the kiosk across the road.

Once the misunderstanding was cleared up, our greeter was profuse in his apologies, but still he insisted that I move on. My wife, who had just set foot on the promised land, clambered back into the car and we rolled on along the narrow track – onwards into the depths of the woods.

Suddenly the trees came to an abrupt halt. We emerged through gates, past other servicemen with blue flashes, into the open fields under a dazzling blue sky, and into the full heat of the burning sun. Cars were parked tightly behind each other on both sides of the road, and I realized I had crossed the border of the area where hospitality and benevolence were the order of the day and had landed back in the zone with free-for-all rules, where it's everyone for himself and the devil take the hindmost.

Here were the Zils and the Chaikas, the Chaikas and the Zils, their bodywork shimmering with polish, their windows bright and clean, their nickel glittering hotly. Alongside each car, its driver was relaxing in the sun. They, like their cars, were all of a kind, standard issue, tubby, sauna-red, disinclined to effort. Even at a distance I could sense their contempt for me – a rum sort of chap who had wormed his way into such a brilliant social gathering in a clapped-out and disgustingly dirty little Moskvich.

Nonplussed at their august disapproval, I kept on going, peering from side to side in increasing confusion and despair – surely a gap would appear in their imposing ranks into which I could squeeze? No; no such luck. I must have driven a good kilometre before the relentless lines came to a halt and the open fields began again. At that point I turned about and parked my unwashed one in the spot it commanded – on the uttermost fringe of the glorious vehicular gathering.

I locked the car and exchanged a glance with my wife.

"Let's go!"

"Let's go."

And off we went, at the mercy of the sun, once more along those daunting ranks, raked by the contemptuous glances of the guild of VIP chauffeurs. The sun had acquired barbaric strength and that, plus their glances, and the light costume in which, in fact, I could parade in winter without benefit of an overcoat, were, with each step I took, making me hotter, and hotter. I started to boil, at first quietly, then loudly and more loudly still, cursing everything I could think of – the bright, sunny day, the cloudless sky, the well-fed asses on the verges, the idea of a meeting in the back of beyond. And the sweat poured down my back, under my light jacket, and I desperately wanted something to drink . . .

The road ahead of us was bisected by a small ravine. On the other side of the little bridge with its handrails one could now glimpse the gates in the green fence and a soldier standing beside them. Only a wee bit more . . . But how one needs a drink!

Quite unexpectedly, from directly below the bridge, the figure of a man in a straw hat popped up – for all the world like a plastic toy out of a bath – and planting itself like a startled statue in our path, enquired in a light tenor voice: "Where are you making for?"

"What d'you mean 'where'?" I replied in astonishment. "Here!" – and I nodded at the gates.

My explanation was not all that clear, but I was beyond improving on it. However . . .

"Please carry on!" Straw Hat promptly hopped back under the bridge.

There were only some fifteen paces left to the bridge when I suddenly went cold under my jacket.

"Wait a mo', what about the pass?"

The pass was back in the car, beneath the windscreen.

The military personnel saluted us, heard me out sympathetically, and shrugged their officer's shoulder boards.

"We can't."

"You realize that only an idiot would venture here without a pass. I do have one, believe me. We'll die if we have to get ourselves there and back in this heat."

"We believe you. We sympathize. But we can't."

I could see that they did believe me, and I understood them perfectly well – to allow me in before I was able to flourish my scrap of glossy cardboard at them was to commit the gravest crime imaginable to them, was to admit to the uselessness and senselessness of their own

existence. There I was, standing before them, pitiable, sweating, dead
to the world, and wondering whether to say to hell with the whole
idea, and just scamper back through the heat, turn my unwashed one's
nose homewards . . . True, the military were decent kids – they'd been
sympathetic.

Suddenly one of the "decent kids" glanced to one side, waved his
hand and said imperiously: "Over here!"

A most peculiar car came towards us, even odder, as it so happened,
than my Moskvich – a run-down Pobeda, likewise long unwashed and
covered in dust. Behind its wheel sat a large-nosed chap of evident
Jewish origin.

"This is what you do: take these comrades back to their car and
then bring them back here. Is that clear?"

"I've got trouble with my big end . . ."

"Your orders are: take these comrades there and bring them back!
Is that clear? Please, get in."

And we, brimming over with gratitude, clambered inside the musty,
dusty, smelling-of-something-sour Pobeda. No sooner had we moved
off than our driver began complaining disdainfully: "My big end is
falling apart. I'm just making out on the one shock absorber. I'll not
get as far as the garage."

We listened, in guilty silence, but we were driving past the lines of
cars on parade, past the recumbent chauffeurs.

The pass had dropped down below the windscreen and while I
groped around for it, the Pobeda, together with its driver, disappeared
without trace.

And yet again, at the mercy of the sun, we toil onwards and ever
onwards . . . How one longs for a drink! I use my pass to protect my
overheated crown. I have stopped cursing anyone, stopped swearing;
I boil inwardly, afraid of exploding.

Finally our faltering steps take us up to the little bridge with its
handrails. Our goal is now within reach.

From underneath the bridge the figure of Straw Hat, a grey-brown
leprechaun, pops assertively into view.

"Where are you making for?"

I was beside myself.

"You must need glasses, damn it! It's the second time we've come
past. What in the hell do they pay you for!"

The leprechaun's shoulders drooped, his hands fell to his sides, his
wrinkled face creased forlornly under his hat.

"What are you so upset about?" And, in his high tenor voice, now plaintively defenceless, he added: "After all, I'm only doing my job."

And popped back below the bridge.

For the second time that day I experienced remorse: in fact, is it really his fault if he is reduced to earning a living by such a strange form of employment – under a bridge? What's more, I'm here as the guest of the high and mighty – in other words, someone to be reckoned with – and it's so easy for me to deal with him in a high-and-mighty way . . .

But no time was left for going into all the nuances: we were already approaching the wide-open gates. I flourished my magical pass – "Open Sesame!" – and received a deferential salute as we crossed the magic threshold.

We are immediately plunged into blessed shade. And the rustle of the pine branches above our heads. And the cool, aromatic, deliciously enveloping breeze. Another world.

I want a drink, I'm dying of thirst . . .

Hardly had I pronounced these words to myself than, on the instant, as if by the wave of a magic wand, I saw in front of me amid the trees a little stream; and in its ripples was a table, under which the necks of bottles protruded directly from the water – Borzhomi, Essentuki and other mineral waters, lemonade – to choice. Behind the table a plump, smiling, young girl in a starched headdress presided over an array of crystal goblets, which she filled with mineral water, the bubbles popping inside the chilled glass.

I rushed towards the table, took my place behind another thirsty customer, all ready with my customary belligerence to repel anyone who might jump the queue. But the girl from the fairy tale was already handing me a goblet filled to the brim, and smiling at me.

The water was cold, impregnated with a natural spring freshness.

"Aah, thanks! Is it possible to have another."

"My pleasure."

Another goblet perspiring with condensation, and another smile.

"Thank you."

"Another one?"

"No, that's just fine."

I rummage in my pocket for small change and I get ironic but not malicious looks from all around – what a simpleton!

I then realize where I am. How could money come into it? Here everything is free – the scent of pine, the cool moist atmosphere, the kindness of the fresh-cheeked young girl in the headdress and the burbling of the stream.

2

In my early childhood, even before I went to school, we used to hear the phrase "Communism is on the horizon!"

The horizon, as everyone knows, is an apparent but nonexistent line which unfailingly recedes as one draws nearer to it. We were proceeding towards Communism and Communism was receding from us.

And what actually is Communism? What should it look like?

We always lived frugally: we fed poorly, dressed badly; queues at shop counters and communal, frowsty, overcrowded flats were our lot in life. Thus the nirvana of Communism was seen as a horn of plenty, which would guarantee everyone a more than bountiful supply – to the the point of surfeit.

Karl Marx ridiculed this housewifely perception and called it Spoon Communism. He gave the world the formula "From each according to his abilities, to each according to his needs." It is a suspiciously philanthropic and vague formula. And there is no one who has provided any better explanation of Communism. His successors confined themselves to mere assurances of its coming: "It's on the horizon!"

Is there any reason for surprise at the tendency of the unenlightened majority to define Communism for themselves in terms of a superficial, but highly tangible, criterion; if there is money in circulation, that means there's no Communism; if all that thrice-accursed money is dead and buried, its advent has been achieved.

They accepted no money from me for my mineral water, nor will they likewise for the ceremonial dinner which undoubtedly awaits us in due course. The purse I have in my pocket is today the one thing I don't need.

3

"If you'd like to have a dip, go ahead . . ."

Some veteran "islander" who had arrived here half an hour or so ahead of me, and had had time to look around and get his bearings, uttered the words.

Hell! Here the offer is made before you've had time to formulate the wish. I suddenly felt how clammy I was, how my flesh was all encrusted with salt, and what a relief it would be to get into the water, but . . .

"Who was to know that for a meeting with the Government you needed to come equipped with your swimming trunks?"

"That's no problem, they'll provide you with trunks . . . and thank you for the privilege. Take this path which comes out on to the shore of the lake; you'll see to one side two bathing cubicles, a men's and a women's . . . And if you want to go for a row, they'll find you a boat . . ."

The degree of courtesy evidenced was such that it remained only to comply – if for no more than my very own good and wellbeing.

A number of unsophisticated young body builders, Russian-style, homebred Apollos and Mercurys, were wringing out and distributing swimming trunks. But there was one regrettable hitch: there weren't enough trunks to go round, so I got a pair of shorts, already used by someone else, but then conscientiously wrung out.

The sizeable pond was in a clearing in the pine forest. It had natural banks of grass and reed, not government-embellished ones. Of course, all around its extremity there were asphalt paths, benches and wooden booths politely offering bamboo fishing rods. And somehow on this occasion there were no anglers to be seen . . .

At the last such meeting of cultural personalities and members of the Government the reservoir banks had been studded with anglers and their rods – one every ten to fifteen paces, standing there motionless. Konstantin Paustovsky, himself a keen angler, told me of how he, in his simplicity of soul, sat down beside them and, without any ulterior thought, indulged his curiosity.

"How're they biting?"

The angler stayed silent, his impassive glance riveted on the motionless float.

"What are you using for bait? Grubs or worms?"

Answer came there none. Only then did it dawn on Paustovsky that it was not the river fish the angler was interested in, and that he must accordingly have been given strict instructions not to enter into conversation.

This time the banks were unpopulated; there were no anglers on official secondment, and the guests were not interested in fishing rods.

There was much animation at the men's cubicle and the faces around me were all familiar, as if I had happened upon some branch meeting of the Moscow section of the Union of Writers. Alexey Surkov was shaking ants out of his trousers and complaining with a frown: "They're eating me alive, just like a vicious critic."

"Better be patient," I ventured to advise him. "They're on Government orders."

Surkov laughed. When he was not discharging his senior functionary's duties, one could have a joke with him, even on serious matters. Slightly to one side of him there was Leonid Leonov, wheezing loudly as he slowly dressed. And in the water under the bank an encounter was afoot: Valentin Kataev was battling his way towards the spherical figure – resembling the moon adrift on the water – of a broadly smiling Dorizo, and complaining loudly: "Did I have to travel a hundred and twenty kilometres to come face to face with the same ugly mug I keep bumping into on Vorovsky Street!"

From the water's safe haven Nikolay Dorizo rewarded him with a smile of gentle, disarming imperturbability.

A short distance away was a figure stuffed with strawberries and cream, sporting a tie, a snow-white blouson, beautifully pressed trousers, with his hair quite dry, so he had obviously not been in for a swim and, evidently, was not proposing to, but was simply resting. Until just recently he had been a modest employee of *Komsomol Pravda* ... Alexey Adzhubey, Khrushchev's son-in-law! We had had one chance encounter sometime in the past, had even clinked glasses to each other's health; now we were studiously avoiding each other's gaze. I had the impression that he was waiting for me to seek inevitably – for was I not bound to try! – to intercept his gaze and offer a deferential greeting. But here he was a host and I was a guest and it was his duty to meet and greet. Togged up in my damp governmental drawers, I scrambled into the water, without any recognition from Adzhubey and making out that I, for my part, failed to recognize him.

Afterwards, refreshed, at peace with the world, I went for a stroll in the shade of the pines and bumped into friends and acquaintances, with whom I either exchanged greetings or paused for a gossip.

Everyone was studiously polite to each other; their faces glowed with the spirit of human kindness; each was overcome by gentleness, ready to forgive injury, to love his enemies – the spirit of Christmas and goodwill towards mankind, and all that. Here we had Ehrenburg fussing over Gribachev, while I, with tears in my eyes, embraced Kochetov.

However, you cannot long remain in a state of transcendental illumination at the sight of "wondrous things to behold"; you involuntarily take a further breath and find yourself right back in this sinful world of ours. I suddenly realized that I had the entire day ahead of me to spend strolling along the asphalt paths in the shade of the conifers, right up until the evening, with its promised dinner and ceremonial speeches. And the ignoble thought intruded: "In fact, it's a bit on the boring side . . . is this Communism of theirs."

But the Government had not yet put in an appearance. Surely it was due to introduce an element of variety.

4

This was the second such meeting with the Government. I had not had the honour of being invited to the first one – more's the pity; it had shaken the participants rigid.

On that occasion Khrushchev had, as they say, really put it away, and had launched into a full-blooded rendering of "Down the Road to Petersburg . . ." over the dinner table.

At the start he confined himself to constant interruption of speakers, irrespective of rank or status, throwing in juicy impromptus, like "The Ukraine is not one of your trussed chickens!" And the jokes he cracked were such as to cause even the sempiternally white-as-a-sheet, seen-it-all-before Molotov to blush.

After that Khrushchev had a go at Marietta Shaginyan. No one could recall what actually provoked it. In response to some casual remark by the elderly lady writer, he shouted in her face: "You tuck into our Russian bread and bacon, don't you!" And she took instant offence: "I'm not accustomed to having crumbs of bread thrown in my face!" And ostentatiously left the festal table, went off and sat down in an empty bus, where she set about abusing the Government to the Government drivers. All of which, however, had not the least impact on the proceedings.

Khrushchev, by now well over the top, got stuck into the subject of ideology and its place in literature – "The 'embellishers' are not such bad lads . . . We shan't stand on ceremony with those who foul our nest on the sly!" – to the rapturous yells of the loyalist littérateurs, who began there and then to point the finger at their colleagues: "Let them have it, Nikita Sergeevich! They've now got their own organ, *Literary Moscow*!"

The *Literary Moscow* almanac had been launched on the initiative of a group of writers. Officially, it was responsible to no one; in practice it was entirely subject, as were all publications, to the whims of the censor. Yet its independent status evoked apprehension none the less. Kazakevich, generally recognized as its main initiator, for some reason this time escaped individual attention, and Khrushchev unexpectedly vented all his royal wrath on Margarita Aliger, whose only fault was to have been one of the contributors to the inaugural issue."You're an ideological wrecker! An eructation of the capitalist West!"

"Nikita Sergeevich, what are you saying . . . ? I'm a Communist, a Party member . . ."

Small, fragile, skin-and-bones Aliger – a woman of moderate views, the author of orthodox verse, never harbouring a single hostile thought towards the Government – stood confronted by the maddened, purple-faced head of one of the mightiest states in the world and in a diffident, thin girlish voice tried to answer Khrushchev back. But Khrushchev broke in on her: "You're lying. I don't trust Communists like you. But I do trust Sobolev, and he's non-Party."

The stately Sobolev, a former aristocrat, a former alumnus of the Petersburg Corps de Pages and author of the well-known novel *Capital Refit*, bobbed up and down in assent and shouted obsequiously: "That's right, Nikita Sergeevich! That's right! They can't be trusted!"

Khrushchev grew increasingly violent, everyone present cowered and stayed put, afraid to move. During that time the clouds had thickened, it started to thunder and there was a torrential downpour. So that was it: the Lord Almighty had decided to take a hand in the tragedy being played out before His eyes, and had resorted to some old-fashioned dramatic effects.

The awning stretched above the festive tables bulged under the weight of water and some of it dripped on to the members of the Government. As if from beneath the earth brave lads in well-pressed suits sprang up, armed with mops and stakes, and started to prop up the sagging canvas, and to pour the water off – on to themselves. The torrents flowed over their heads and on to their immaculate suits, but the lads carried on fighting the good fight – noble sons of Atlas supporting the governmental canopy. However, the thunder never stopped, the downpour persisted and Khrushchev carried on ranting.

"You pretend to be friends. You're fouling our nest on the sly! You dream of bourgeois democracy! I don't trust you . . ."

Margarita Aliger, downcast, stood to attention and no longer tried to get in a word edgeways.

The guests clung fast to their tables, shrinking with fear under the wrath of the mighty, as well as from the streams of water which were pouring through the awning – the young Atlases were concerned only with shielding the members of the Government. An embarrassed Mikoyan politely regaled those nearest to him with select wild strawberries from the governmental table. And Sobolev never stopped chanting: "You can't trust them, Nikita Sergeevich! You're right to be cautious, Nikita Sergeevich."

His wife, a sour-faced lady in a broad-brimmed hat, twitched at her husband's sleeve and whispered something to him. Her husband heeded the call, and said in a tetchy sort of way: "I have the right to your respect, Nikita Sergeevich, but there's no way . . . there's no way in which I can get a garage for my car."

His wife wagged her broad-brimmed hat in energetic assent.

But the thunder continued to split the sky, and the well-soaked Atlases continued holding aloft their outstretched mops. From somewhere among the guests, a pale Samuel Marshak, his face tense, muttered from time to time: "Talk about Shakespeare! It's quite beyond the master's wildest dreams . . ."

To cap it all, Sobolev, as a result of his efforts and overexcitement, had . . . a stroke. He was removed from the ceremonial meeting on a stretcher, with his wife in black gloves up to the elbow running alongside and fanning her stricken husband with the broad-brimmed hat.

Margarita made her way to the exit on her own; people were scared of going up to her now she had been branded as an outcast. Only Valentin Ovechkin caught up with her, took her by the elbow and made a great show of escorting her away. Some of the sodden Atlases moved after them . . . No, it was not his championing of the disgraced poetess that bothered them, but the mushroom . . . Under one of the governmental trees Ovechkin had happened upon a large specimen of a *boletus edulis* and had given way to temptation and picked it. With one hand he was propping up Aliger and in the other he held his mushroom . . . Why a mushroom? Might it not be a camouflaged bomb? The Atlases stayed with them all the way to the exit.

The rain stopped. The sun re-emerged.

A few days later the rumour ran around Moscow that Nikita Sergeevich's conduct at the reception was being condemned . . . even by those close to him.

Certainly, the last such meeting was still fresh in everyone's minds. Today everyone was awaiting Khrushchev's appearance with keen interest: how would he behave? Would he have another rush of blood to the head? Or would contrition suddenly drive him in the opposite direction – towards sweetness and light? The ways of the Lord are unfathomable. With Khrushchev anything was possible.

5

It seems that Winston Churchill, on learning shortly before his own death of Khrushchev's fall, rewarded the world with what was to be virtually his last witticism: "This man was always inclined to jump the abyss in two strides."

Marx employed the idea of revolutionary leaps as the basis of his own theory; we applied them in practice. Khrushchev wanted with all his soul to take a mighty leap across the abyss between existing socialism and fabulous Communism. Item No. 1! – and to overtake prosperous America in terms of meat and milk production! Item No. 2! – and leave her languishing inside the unprepossessing confines of reality, with Russia safe inside the land of the fairy tale! Orders were given: slaughter cattle stocks to provide more meat! The only fact they overlooked was that the cattle had first of all to be raised to maturity. A great country soared upwards but failed to clear the abyss – instead we collapsed. An oversight? Of course not, heaven preserve us! We again jump into the realm of hyperabundance – this time with maize as our launching pad . . .

One account I heard was that in the Murmansk region – only slightly smaller than England and a lot larger than Bulgaria – on the sunny slopes of the few existing valleys sheltered from the wind, an area of some twenty square miles had been given over to cold-resistant potatoes and cabbages. And this was where Khrushchev had given orders for two square miles to be replanted with maize!

"But it simply won't grow there, Nikita Sergeevich," people bravely ventured to tell him.

"But supposing it does? What a political resonance that would have!"

But what if . . . ? The argument of a jumper who honestly believes that he'll find a launching pad in the middle of the abyss.

Government leaders are often distinguished by the banality of their thinking. Great thoughts, far-reaching discoveries, never occur overnight in millions of heads, and there is no such thing in nature as mass-scale enlightenment. Great thoughts and discoveries are the perquisite of those able to think that much deeper than others, the perquisite of those who are champions in the field of intellectual ability and power of thought. And time, a great deal of it, is needed for the prosaic masses to understand and accept what the champions of human thought have mastered. It took more than two decades for Copernicus's discovery to gain general acceptance.

But your Government politician is concerned with questions of everyday life, with problems generally requiring an immediate answer. He cannot wait for centuries or even decades in order to be understood. Hence the political leader is compelled to take refuge in generalized stereotypes, in trite notions, thus taking his intellectual cue from some sort of general projection of society's own level of banality. However hurtful it may be, in the case of prominent political figures who are leaders of men and direct people's lives, wisdom and brilliance are qualities distinguished more by their absence than by their presence.

Napoleon, for example, cannot be called a fool but how fruitless his thinking proved to be. He contributed nothing that was to the benefit of mankind. And what is the good of a stultified, futile intelligence? It has no greater merit than does folly.

Abraham Lincoln and John Kennedy, before revealing themselves to be the intellectual superiors of the man in the street, pretended at first to make common cause with pedestrian, standardized ways of thought and sought to appease them; only after they had risen above them, were they removed.

The same Churchill, renowned for his slyness, resourcefulness and wit, acquired the reputation of a profound politican, but how often did he act with astounding obtuseness, without suspecting it. Let's open his Memoirs at random. This, for example, is his version of events, put forward in all seriousness . . . "May 1942. Almost all of Europe had been swallowed by the Hitlerites, and German forces were deep into Russia." This was when Churchill, on the one hand, and Molotov on behalf of Stalin on the other, met in London for talks. Did they discuss the question of how to defeat a terrifying, dangerous opponent? . . . No, they bargained with one another over who should have the Baltic States and Eastern Poland. They set about dividing up, with intense mistrust of one another, a fragment of the skin of an as yet unkilled, indeed powerful and dangerous bear. And did so with such fervour that the question of how one was to kill the bear seemed to them not of the essence. "Apart from the question of the Treaty," Churchill says en passant, "Molotov came to London to ascertain our views on the opening of a Second Front. Accordingly I had an official talk with him on the morning of 22nd May." Full stop! Casually, en passant – this matter is not worth attention. A course of action of risible stupidity, especially in the light of subsequent tragic events: the Germans, whose skin was being so avidly divided up, launched a new, intensified offensive against Russia, took a 600,000-strong army formation prisoner on the outskirts of Kharkov, and advanced up to the Caucasus and the Volga. And then, many years later, well-informed Churchill recounts authoritatively, without a trace of irony, in his Memoirs that that was how it was: they divided it up, and got through their business; that is, he remains a victim of his own previous stupidity.

Stupidity can easily grow into amorality. When Churchill learnt from Stalin that collectivization in the USSR had been achieved at the price of the murder and exile of ten million "small men" – for want of a better expression! – his reaction was not one of horror and condemnation but of magnanimous justification: "A generation would no doubt come to whom their miseries were unknown, but it would be sure of having more to eat and bless Stalin's name." Yea verily, blessed are the poor in spirit for they know not what they do. In this context Khrushchev proved infinitely more perspicacious: no such words as those ever passed his lips.

Yet, in himself Khrushchev was incalculably, sublimely stupid, stupid as only Russians can be, though, in fact, there was nothing to distinguish him from other prominent politicians and he suffered from their common failing. Of course, his high-and-mighty self-assurance morally deformed society, and tended to produce liars, toadies and cruel, unforgivable scoundrels – such as the "Ryazan miracle worker" Larionov – who made careers for themselves from official extortion.

But the strange thing is – and such paradoxes do occur in history! – that it was precisely Khrushchev's braggadocio that enabled him to accomplish a progressive transformation in our country. Artful Sir Winston never brought as much benefit to England as did Nikita Khrushchev to the Land of the Soviets by his one speech to the Twentieth Party Congress! . . .

However, we have become sidetracked from our subject and meanwhile the hospitable hosts have honoured us with their presence.

6

Without any particular ceremony, without forewarning, the members of the Government suddenly appeared on the asphalt path among the pine trees. A smiling genial Khrushchev, in a light jacket, an embroidered Ukrainian shirt done up by a coloured string at the neck, a garment popularly nicknamed a "Jew-baiter"; Voroshilov, quaking with decrepitude, in a civilian hat; Mikoyan with his two-way nose over his funerary moustache, still untouched by grey. But not the two faces which used to stare at us from the public hoardings – of Molotov and Kaganovich, both senior participants in the last meeting. They had failed to give satisfaction and Khrushchev had kicked them out. No, he hadn't hidden them away behind barbed wire, hadn't had them shot in the cellars as was Stalin's wont with his suite of Molotov and Kaganovich clones, but had simply pushed them out of Olympus: to hell with you, make do on your pension! Another to share their fate was Shepilov, who had "adhered to them". The contemptuous epithet hinted at the lack of political clout of the person in question. A lightweight? May well be, though not for such as me. This particular lightweight was in command of the country's culture – gave orders and directed people, promoted and demoted, dished out favours and meted out punishment. For some unknown reason, he always put me in mind of Lensky's lament: "Where, oh where art thou gone? . . ."

The Government had appeared and immediately an intense, syco-phantic hullaballoo developed around it. The arts-and-literature figures – not all of them, obviously, but those who considered themselves of sufficient note to pretend to a degree of intimacy, elbowing each other out of the way, with the happiest of smiles on their perspiring faces – started a general free-for-all to see who could get nearest. The corpulent figure of Sofronov was there in the fray, puffing, giving no quarter, and holding firm against assaults; Gribachev's bald head glittered in the sun; Leonid Sobolev, bent almost double in his desire to show respect, was mincing forward, little step by little step, having now become the recipient not only of a garage – how unutterably modest their family dreams had been – but also of the Union of Writers of the Russian Federation, newly created for him. Sergey Mikhalkov, the incomparable "Uncle Styopa", never one to pass up an opportunity for self-advertisement, kept bobbing up, here, there and everywhere.

The Ukrainian composer Maiboroda managed to burst through on Khrushchev's right side, thrust aloft his flat, wide-boned, glistening countenance, closed his eyes and melodiously intoned:

> "I gaze at the sky
> And wonder awhile . . ."

Khrushchev, a broad smile on his face, took up the refrain in an uncertain baritone:

> "Why am I not an eagle,
> Why have I not wings . . ."

People kept surging forward to get at him, looking him in the eye, pushing and shoving, getting hemmed in, and smiling, always smiling ... They were all solid, portly, superbly dignified figures. Were you to meet any one of them in the street or in one of the corridors of power, you would find it impossible to imagine that such a lordly personage were capable of stooping to such petty manoeuvres.

Here was the verdant island of Communism; within its narrow bounds, to be favoured with the monarch's notice was of merely moral significance – HE had noticed, remembered, named your name, shaken your hand. How pleasant! But tomorrow everyone present would find themselves outside the bounds of this delightful island, adrift on an ocean, subject to its pitching and its tossing, where someone was always drowning, someone being hurled aloft, where one had to be strong and skilful in order to stay on the crest of the wave. And each one who had continued to edge closer, to touch the omnipotent hand, was counting on taking away with him a particle of that autocratic authority. Hence the crush, the carousel, the to-ing and fro-ing, the cheeks puffed out in a broad smile – the tournament of the knights in favour!

I stood to one side, scrutinizing this affecting scene of intense activity, and suddenly ... Suddenly, through the serried heads, I met full on, directed straight at me – I swear it! – Khrushchev's gaze. He had just finished joining in with Maiboroda: "Why am I not an eagle, why have I not wings ..."; had only that moment been smiling broadly, and his face, a trifle exhausted from the sun, was relaxed or, rather, reflected contentment. Only just now, a second ago, a fraction of a second! Now in between other people's heads, what I saw at a slight distance was an entirely different face – not mollified, not relaxed, but tense, taut and hostile. Though that face still seemed furrowed with exhaustion, the gaze he directed at me was one of distrust and suspicion, almost menace. The sort of gaze one visits on one's enemy.

He had never seen me before, had no way of recognizing me by my face, had no grounds for considering me an enemy. Yet none the less ...

I had no cause to be afraid. I was perfectly well aware that the solid wall of sycophants and the intervening ten paces formed a reliable defence. I did not lower my eyes but continued to stare with astonishment at Khrushchev's transformed face.

Our glances cannot have met for more than a second. Someone's bald patch interrupted my view of the Head of State and the next time I caught sight of him, Khrushchev was again beaming benevolently and talking to someone.

Well, well, well! . . . The smiles, the jokes, the musical impromptu, the appearance of someone relaxing – all my eye and Betty Martin: inwardly he is tense, on his guard, consumed with suspicion. And I involuntarily feel sorry for him. "You must have it tough, Nikita Sergeevich. It's no bed of roses when you have to turn it on like that."

Even my wife, who was standing elbow to elbow with me, failed to notice our exchange. True, I did tell her; she was momentarily interested . . . and immediately forgot about it. It wasn't all that significant an event to attach any particular importance to it.

But I was unable to forget it. We left the hub of activity and went for a stroll along the paths, exchanging greetings with people we knew, and again landed up in the vicinity of the Government scrum. Once more I paused for a moment and took a long look at good-hearted, genial Khrushchev, waiting to see whether our glances might cross, in the hope that there would be a replay which would confirm to me that I had not been dreaming.

But this time Khrushchev failed to spot me.

7

Everyone who today had been invited to the island of Communism – both those who had not ventured to draw near to the Government and those who by pushing and shoving had secured themselves a place nearby, like wasps round a jam jar – belonged to the intelligentsia, or that part of it most prominent in our country.

The intelligentsia . . . People professionally engaged in mental labour, or in other words directly related to what constitutes man's highest attribute – his intellect. One would think that this part of the human race would be publicly recognized as its most important, and would benefit from unfailing, universal respect. Alas! The attitude taken towards the intelligentsia has always been one of caution and, at times, outright dislike. For it has usually been the source of ideas and opinions which run counter to received stereotypes, and which confuse the man in the street and complicate the work of Government leaders.

Lenin did not like the liberal intelligentsia, did not trust it, considered it the appendage of the bourgeoisie. "The influence of the *intelligentsia*," he wrote in 1907, "which took no direct part in exploitation, which was brought up to conceptualize in general terms and notions, which peddles all kinds of 'good' injunctions, and which sometimes from sincere obtuseness sublimates its own inter-class position into the *axiom* of ultra-class parties and ultra-class policies – the influence of that bourgeois intelligentsia on the people is dangerous."

Once he had become head of government, he then openly challenged the intelligentsia: "We never had any doubt of your flabbiness. But we do not deny that we need you, because you are the only existing cultural element." In other words, just as the intelligentsia had been an appendage, that was what she was to remain. To the end of his life Lenin often spoke with bitterness of how he lacked genuine like-minded intellectuals.

Stalin moulded the principle of subservience into the basis of the existence of the new State: the junior in line compliantly, unquestioningly and automatically obeyed the orders of his superior, the latter those of his superior, and so on upwards, up to the final summit presided over by someone who obeyed no one's orders but subjected all to his – Stalin's. The most representative figure in society became a sort of governmental Janus whose face on the one side was that of a dictator and on the other that of a lackey.

Only those directly engaged in productive work escaped being invested with dictatorial powers of some sort. If you're ploughing a field, ploughing it yourself as distinct from giving orders for it to be ploughed, then there's no one for you to dictate to, to order around. If you're writing a book, composing a piece of music or solving a scientific problem, you can't become a dictator, however much you wish to. Only by reassigning to someone else the field about to come under the plough, the book, the musical composition, or the scientific discovery, can you acquire the option of converting yourself into a dictator. Creative activity excludes the possibility of dictatorship but it doesn't stop one being a lackey. You're not in a position to give orders to anyone but then – why not? – people can give orders to you. And if you then prove insufficiently submissive, display awkwardness, why shouldn't they use duress on you, up to the point of isolating you in strict regime camps, subjecting you to physical maltreatment, torture, and, finally, execution by firing squad.

Stalin converted the intelligentsia into a submissive appendage dutifully carrying out – mostly obtusely, though at times with flair and inventiveness – the Government's instructions, be it for the construction of new bombers or be it for the "philosophical" substantiation of the supreme scientific value of Stalin's works on linguistics.

And here we had this tight, almost sweaty scrummage of bodies – the persons who had been members of the intelligentsia in Stalin's time. And Khrushchev and his entourage, the focus of this vortex, had been Stalin's civil servants. Promoted by Stalin, reared and raised by Stalin, two-faced Januses who were both dictators and lackeys.

Khrushchev never visualized any system other than that prevailing under the late Stalin. Khrushchev genuinely considered that the world was split asunder by enmity and hatred, that the State must strengthen itself every hour of the day, every day of the week, observe the iron discipline of subordination, seek to preserve absolutist power . . . The Party's general line in the years of Stalinism was correct, though . . .

He had been nurtured by Stalin, brought up by Stalin, and was therefore in a better position than anyone else to know how painful and fraught such an upbringing was. Before his eyes State leaders had been seized and lined up against the wall . . . Up against the wall was a relatively happy outcome; otherwise it could be having one's nails torn out, or one's kidneys kicked out, a series of bestial brutalities, of ignominious humiliations, before being dispatched to the other world. Khrushchev himself for many years waited for his hour to strike, fell asleep at night not expecting to see the morning in, answered summonses to call upon Stalin without hope of returning alive. He lived in anticipation, existed in terror. Nurtured and brought up by, but feeling no gratitude towards his tutor.

"Yes, in Stalin's time the Party's general line was irreproachably correct, only Stalin himself was wrong – one was nauseated by his cruelty, dumbfounded by the amount of innocent blood being shed." Khrushchev was thus not proposing to change any part of the Stalinist legacy – it could all remain as it was! – but Stalin had to be condemned and removed from History. It is difficult to conceive of a more absurd decision. Given that the former leader was a full-fledged dictator and issued bad instructions which were carried out to the letter, how could it be that the Party and the country had to be correct in the way they lived and the way they acted? Either he was no dictator, his authority amounted to nothing, and there was nothing to condemn or expose, or else he was a dictator – in which case condemn him together with the path down which his iniquitous authority had led him. The two are closely connected . . .

If only Khrushchev had been able to relate the cause to the effect, the particular to the general! . . . Happily for him, he was as simple as a baby: what I want, I want – and that's all there is to it; logic is not my master! Simplicity is as capable of daring deeds as intellect. Khrushchev resolutely dethroned Stalin at the Twentieth Congress: get thee behind me, Satan! Yet another venturesome jump into the unknown . . .

Were it not for that act, we should be having it drummed into us: we are following Stalin's path! The Black Marias would still be scouring our city streets, the master torturers plying their trade in the dungeons, and we would doubtless still have a frenziedly aggressive foreign policy with no question of there being such a thing as peaceful coexistence. One might even have had thermonuclear explosions spawning their mushrooms above the planet and mankind dying off from radioactivity. Who knows how great the role of the chance factor in history may be – of "Bradbury's notorious 'butterfly'", which changes the shape of the future?

All power to the hand of chance indeed! All laud and honour to simplicity and its daring exponent, Nikita Sergeevich Khrushchev! The peoples of all the continents should remember his name with gratitude!

But if Khrushchev in his simplicity paid no attention to elementary logic, others were not able to permit themselves this liberty. Stalin's conduct has been condemned – that's splendid. However, as the saying goes: "in for a penny, in for a pound".

The genie had been released from the bottle; the seed of doubt had been sown. There were so many restive readers at the meeting in the Moscow Writers' Club to discuss Dudintsev's book that the mounted police had to be called out – an unprecedented occurrence! And in friendly Hungary a revolt had to be put down by armed force and led to an abrupt change of the government installed by Stalin.

At the last meeting Khrushchev had resorted to abusive bad language, but this time he knows he has the intellectuals as his guests and not only those who want nothing better than to kiss his hand. And there was that momentary glance from behind our hospitable host's mask.

I had had an unauthorized sight of our King Midas's long ears.

8

The sun overhead was starting to sink behind the treetops. With the painter Orest Vereisky and his wife, we explore further along the deserted side paths. Not only should there be a well-tended forest here, but somewhere there must surely be a Government weekend residence. For the time being we come across no sign of any buildings. I call our small group to one side. "Let's have a snoop around. There's nothing else to do, in any case."

Muffled voices in the far distance; modulated sound of holiday conviviality. But here a woodpecker taps away undisturbed. A hallowed silence, making one want to converse in whispers.

A passer-by emerges from a side track, heading towards us. And we fall silent, overcome by involuntary confusion: the man coming our way is well known to us, though he has not the least idea of who we are. How does one behave in such circumstances? Walk past, pretending you haven't recognized him, which is unnatural? But is it natural to greet him? May this not be taken for sycophancy? Shall we not receive in exchange a blank look and an offensively patronizing nod? Such is the eternal reflex of the Russian intellectual, torn apart by self-regarding contradictions on the slightest pretext. The stray walker comes up to us and is the first to exchange greetings. Not a trace of superiority. It is Leonid Ilyich Brezhnev.

From deep in the woods comes the sound of shots being fired. No, we do not start quivering or exchange puzzled glances. The maniacal thought – Is it an attempt on someone's life? – never enters our minds. It's obviously some sort of holiday entertainment. Taking our time, we go towards the firing, accompanied by the tick-tack of the undaunted woodpecker.

A clearing in the middle of the forest. Two knots of spectators. On the grass are several chairs and two tables, on one of which there are shotguns and on the other a whole pile of china bric-à-brac – prizes for the best shots. Around the tables are Khrushchev, Mzhavanadze and various other people quite unknown to me.

At a distance of a hundred paces are some barely noticeable bunkers overgrown with grass from which saucers fly into the air, one after another, at set intervals. They shatter into pieces at the shots of a tall, well-groomed, corpulent young man.

The young man finishes shooting, lays down his shotgun and moves away proudly and coolly. He must be close to Khrushchev to allow himself such a display of nonchalance, untinged by diffidence or obsequiousness. Mzhavanadze, however, is clearly not feeling at ease. He is trying to stay close to the boss but at the same time is afraid of offending him by excessive propinquity. He stays a variable one-and-a-half paces to the rear and guffaws jerkily. He bears a remarkable resemblance to an alcoholic who has fallen among teetotallers, is dying for a drink, and is not very sanguine of being brought a lifeline.

With a proprietorial gesture, Khrushchev motions Mzhavanadze towards the table.

"Have a go!"

And Mzhavanadze lifts the gun from the table with alacrity.

A saucer flies into the blue sky. Bang! Shatter! A new saucer . . . Bang! Shatter! And again, again and again . . . With a happy smile, Mzhavanadze, his entire body expressing the utmost deference, carefully restores the gun to its former place. The prize is already being held out for him to receive – a porcelain statuette heavily encrusted in gilt. He clutches it to his groin.

Khrushchev resolutely strips off his jacket.

From the group standing to one side of the tight throng of bystanders come openly mocking remarks. "Hold on there, you're going to get a shower of fragments down on your head!" I look more closely, with interest: who, pray, is permitting himself such liberties vis-à-vis the Head of State? I recognize among the spectators the heavy figure of his wife, Nina Petrovna, and realize that they are members of Khrushchev's family. They're allowed such licence.

In his embroidered "Jew-baiter", with his stubby legs set wide apart, and his pink ears sticking out alertly, Khrushchev steadies himself with the gun.

A saucer zooms up in the air. Bang – a miss! The saucer falls earthwards. A second shot – a miss! Bang! Bang! The saucers are untouched . . . Mzhavanadze, his golden prize still clutched to his groin, goes rigid.

Khrushchev scores a hit on only one of the ten saucers. He puts the gun back and sits down in a chair.

His podgy shoulders droop, his arms fall to his sides, his gleaming head drops, his innocently pink ears stick out laterally in pique and there is something of the inconsolable schoolboy in his entire pasty figure. Indeed, one feels like going up, patting him on his bald patch and saying: "Don't take it so hard, old son. It's no great deal; you'll have other occasions to prove your mettle."

And, to the side, more merciless taunts.

"He's got so many birds to his credit, how can we cope?"

And Mzhavanadze stands in front of a downcast Khrushchev, clutching his trophy to his groin, fidgeting and not knowing where to turn. Not someone to be envied . . .

And those cutting remarks from the boss's family.

Suddenly Khrushchev rises to his feet. His slumped body stiffens; his movements become economical; his face grows undeniably grim, and his pink ears now obtrude not in pique but threateningly.

The taunts from the wings carry on regardless, but Mzhavanadze emerges from his stupor, straightens his shoulders with relief and with canine fidelity and expectation watches Khrushchev lifting the gun.

The sleeves of his "Jew-baiter" are taut with the effort, his feet splayed apart, his heavy trunk thrust forward, his head lowered – a bull in the middle of the road, just try driving round that!

A saucer flies up . . . Fire! The fragments scatter down to the ground. Fire! More fragments. Fire! Fire! Fire . . . Good heavens! How is it possible! Only one saucer falls intact to the ground.

Khrushchev triumphantly replaces the gun.

I do not know whether some sort of underling's sleight of hand was involved. I do not know how the saucers are projected into the air. Can it be possible within the space of a few minutes to arrange for them to fragment in the air and if so, moreover, to coincide with the shots. But if it was a nimble underling's trick, Khrushchev believed in it with all his soul.

After putting down the gun, he strode to and fro beside the tables. His shoulders swung assertively; his chest and stomach, in mutual competition, thrust themselves forward; his gait had an upward lift to it like a dancer's on the point of joining the circle. At a distance one could sense that under the tight covering of fat every muscle, every vein was pulsating with energy. One would really have to be an actor of genius to give such an uninhibited, such a lifelike impersonation of triumph incarnate, with shoulders, stomach and feet, even ears, all joining in! But that was not the case; only someone genuinely possessed by his own sense of victory could behave like that . . . He wanted to keep it in check, but just couldn't: it simply burst out of him.

His relatives continued making fun of him, in no way surprised or impressed by his success, but I, for my part, was puzzled.

Even now this small episode is for me an insoluble riddle, almost a miracle. The only explanation I can put forward lies in Khrushchev's remarkable strength of character. One cannot deny him his irresistible push and his peasant's unyielding obstinacy. His struggle with Stalin was the proof of that. Even unmasked and from his grave, the Leader of the Whole People put up a desperate resistance. He was removed from the Mausoleum but he returned to reoccupy his bier inside it. They tried to erect a wall of silence around him, but he continued to serve notice of himself, by the thousands of bronze, marble and plaster models standing in every city and village, however remote; by the place names; by the subdued rumble from his admirers. However, Khrushchev did finally eject Stalin from the Mausoleum, did demolish the monuments to him all over the country, did obliterate his name from maps, and failed to be daunted by the million-strong rumble of his admirers. There's no denying the man his strength of character!

On this occasion he was exhibiting pure childish glee in winning: he had shot down the saucers and proved his dexterity, and how! Yeah, yeah, yeah!

People rushed up to hand him his china prize. He received it with dignity – even the gravitas becoming a figure of State – and . . . glanced across at Mzhavanadze's prize. Mzhavanadze was in seventh heaven, beaming with joy – thank God, it had all passed off all right! – and looking adoringly into Khrushchev's eyes . . .

The smile left Mzhavanadze's face; he intercepted the boss's glance and lowered his eyes to his own prize, which he was still awkwardly clutching with both hands to his private parts. Oh dear, oh dear, there had been a small blunder: Mzhavanadze's ornate little statuette clearly had the more gilt on it . . . Khrushchev scrutinized more closely the prize he had not been given.

And Mzhavanadze jumped to it and hastened to proffer it to him.

"Let's swap, Nikita Sergeevich."

No, I'm not inventing a single word for the sake of a story; it was all just as I'm telling you, please believe me. Yes, yes, Khrushchev did a swap: took Mzhavanadze's prize, which had more gilt on it. And both were clearly content with their exchange.

At that point there was an announcement over the loudspeakers, the words booming through the forest.

"Dear guests! Dinner is served! Dear guests! Please come to table! . . ."

And everyone made for the large striped marquee, erected among the pines. Under it long tables stood in serried ranks.

I was there, I partook . . .

So as not to be accused of making things up, I append a document I retain – the menu card.

DINNER

Caviar; fish patties
Stuffed carp
Danube herring
Turkey with fruit
Vegetable salad
Crayfish in beer

Cold meat soup with sour cream
Consommé with pasty

Trout in white wine
Shashlyk
Cauliflower in cream sauce and breadcrumbs

Melon
Coffee, pastries, petits fours, fruit

Semyonovskoe village, 17 July 1960

The drinks on offer were not mentioned, for the sake of delicacy. Connoisseurs affirm that the last time the fare was infinitely more abundant.

N. S. Khrushchev and I. V. Stalin. January 1936

Could he have foreseen?

March 1974   Publication and preparation of text by N. Asmolova

Translated by Michael Duncan

ANDREI BITOV

The Doctor

A SUNNY DAY recalls a funeral. Not every sunny day, of course, but the one we speak of as sunny – the first one, sudden, at long last. It is also clear. Perhaps the clear sky is what matters, and not the sun. At funerals, first and foremost, there is weather.

. . . My aunt by marriage, my uncle's wife, was dying.

She was "such an *alive* person" (Mama's words) that we found this hard to believe. Indeed she was alive, and indeed it was hard to believe, but the fact was that she had long been making preparations, even though secretly from herself.

First she tried her foot. Her foot suddenly became painful and swollen and would not fit into her shoe. But Auntie did not give up. She would tie a prewar slipper to the "elephant" (her word) and come out to the kitchen to wash dishes with us; then Alexander Nikolaevich, her chauffeur, would arrive, and she would drive to her Institute (disability evaluation), then to a board meeting of her Society (therapeutics), then to some sort of alumnae committee (she was a Bestuzhev graduate), then make a house call on some titled bandit, then swing by to see her Jewish relatives (who, by a tacit agreement of forty years' standing, did not visit our house), then return home for a moment, feed her husband, and have trouble deciding whether to go to the banquet celebrating the dissertation defence of Nektor Beritashvili, an assistant professor at the institute's Tbilisi branch: she was very tired (and this was more than true) and did not want to go (but this wasn't quite true). Secretly from herself, she wanted to go. (Having repeated this "secretly from herself", I begin to realize that the emotional capacity for such a thing can be maintained into old age only by people who are very . . . alive? pure? kind? . . . good? . . . I mutter this incomprehensible, now defunct word – secretly from my own self . . .) And she went, because she took all human gatherings at face value, she loved them, she had a passion for tokens of kindness, the whole brocade of honour and respect. To forestall possible mockery she had even taught our self-important family the Jewish word *koved*, which means a respect that does not necessarily come from the soul and heart – respect *pro forma*, according to status, as a display, respect as such. (Russians have no such concept, no such word, and here one might say, with the affectionate smile of a person who secretly from himself is an anti-Semite, that the Jews are a different nation. But although this insincere word does not exist in our language, it has become a fact of our life – and besides, why is everyone so convinced that rudeness is sincerity?) "You understand, Dima," she would say to her husband, "he's Vakhtang's son, do you remember Vakhtang?" She would sigh with distress, and go. Her desires still outweighed her fatigue. Nowadays we can't understand this – people used to be different.

At last she returned. She never stayed long, only for the ceremonial part, which she loved very poignantly, imbuing its every ostentation and hypocrisy with her own generous good sense and faith. (It is curious that they sincerely believed themselves to be materialists, these people. We will never be like them; to achieve such a paradox, one must possess exceptional . . . again, that incomprehensible word.) So she came home promptly, because in addition to her foot she suffered from diabetes and could allow herself nothing at the banquet, yet she came home high: the speeches of the ceremonial part affected her like champagne. Younger, pink-cheeked, she would buoyantly and happily tell her husband how nice everything had been, how warm . . . Gradually it would become clear that she herself had said it best of all. If you looked into her face then, you could hardly believe that she was about to turn eighty, that she had the foot. But she did: it was tied to the slipper, you had only to look down. And after she finished chattering, after she gave her husband his tea, after he went to bed, she would fill a basin with hot water, lower her foot into it, and sit for a long time, suddenly lifeless and shapeless, "all in a heap" (as she put it). She would sit there for a long time, all in a heap, staring at her already dead foot.

She was a great doctor.

Doctors like her *don't exist* nowadays. Easily I catch myself using this ready-made formula, which has struck me as absurd ever since I was a child. I tell myself (with a "sober" grin) that things have always been the same. Identical. No better. Easily I catch myself, and easily let myself off: from the altitude of today's experience, the formula "they don't exist nowadays" strikes me as both legitimate and accurate. Expressive. So they don't exist . . . It wasn't that Auntie cured every-one. Medicine was the subject on which she had the fewest delusions. She didn't feel that everyone *could* be helped, so much as that everyone *must* be. She well knew (not in words, not from science, but from . . .

again, that nameless quality) that she had *no* way to help, but then if she had even a *small* way to help, you could be sure she would do her *all*. This inability to do even the slightest bit less than her all, this need to do absolutely all she could – this imperative was the very essence of "the old-time doctors that don't exist nowadays", doctors like her, the last of them. And it was provocatively simple. If you had a cold, for example, she would inquire whether you were sleeping well. You would ask in surprise, "What does sleep have to do with it?" She would say, "He who sleeps poorly will feel the chill, and he who feels the chill will catch cold." She would give you a sleeping pill for your cold (allergy was still a fiction of the capitalist world), and suddenly this forgotten tempo of Russian speech and Russian words . . . "feel the chill" . . . made you so happy and affectionate that all was right, all in good order, all ahead of you . . . you glimpsed an unreal morning with grey sky and white snow, fever happiness, someone riding by under the window on a horse, smoke curling from the chimney . . . If you said, "My nerves are playing tricks, Auntie, could I have something for nerves," she would give you an icy look and say, "Get hold of yourself, there's nothing for nerves." But another time you wouldn't even ask for anything, and she'd thrust a medical-leave certificate into your hands: "I saw you smoking in the kitchen last night. You need rest."

If an observant intellectual had articulated it for her – even this way, in her own words – she would never have understood. She would have shrugged: What are you talking about? For she knew no mechanisms of experience. The way she entered the patient's room! No amount of self-control could have wrought such a change. She was simply transformed. Nothing but ease and steadiness – no eighty years, no handsome young husband, no thousands of snotty, sweaty, blue, pathetic patients breathing in her face – no experience, either professional or personal, no vestige of the residue of her own self and her own life, her eager life. How she let the patient complain! How affirmatively she asked, "It hurts a lot?" Precisely – *a lot*. There could be no "It's nothing" or "You'll get over it" from her. At this moment only two people in the whole world knew how it hurt: the patient and she. They were the elite of pain. After she left, the patient was all but proud of his initiation. Never in my life will I see again such a capacity for *sympathy*. One doesn't take an exam in sympathy in medical school. Auntie showed sympathy instantly, and at the same moment renounced forever her old age and pain. If you were truly sick she had only to turn and see your face, and with the speed of light you were bathed in her sympathy, that is, in a total absence of the sympathizer and a total awareness of how you felt, what it was like. This astounding capacity, devoid of everything except its own self, empathy in pure form, became, for me, the Essence of the Doctor. The Name of the Physician. And nothing false, nothing forced, no "old chaps" or "my dear fellows" in the Moscow Art Theatre style (although she believed religiously in the Moscow Art Theatre, and when it was on television she would settle down in her chair with a ready expression of satisfaction, "which nothing modern can bring, isn't that so, Dima dear . . . Ah, Kachalov! And Tarasova is the ideal of beauty . . ." At the word "Anna" she shapes her fluffy hairdo with trembling hand . . .).

From her hairdo, I begin to see her. To the end of her days she wore the same hairdo, which had once suited her best of all. As someone's compliment had stuck in the young woman's mind – "She has beautiful hair," he had said – so her certainty of this had lasted for half a century and a whole lifetime, and so the greying, medicinally tinted wave was fluffed up every morning and a tortoiseshell comb was jabbed – her hands trembled violently – was jabbed into it in three tries, back and forth, higher and lower, and at last exactly in the middle, always in the same place. Her unsteady hands were very skilful, and in my mind's eye I can also see her adjusting their tremor, like artillery fire: undershooting, overshooting (a narrow bracket) . . . – bull's-eye. That is, I can still see her hands, shaking but always hitting the mark, always doing something. (That's not my typewriter tapping, it's Auntie washing dishes, the characteristic clink of her cups against the faucet. If she broke a cup, which did happen, and her cups were expensive, then of course she felt very bad about it. But – with an indescribable femininity, also arrested in the era of her first hairdo – she immediately announced the event to all the kitchen witnesses, as one of her eternal charming blunders. "Again," she would say. Even her figure changed as she tossed the fragments into the garbage pail; even the curve of her waist (what waist? . . .) and the tilt of her head were once more maidenly . . . because the behaviour most forbidden to the witnesses in such an incident could only be pity. We must not notice her age.) Even now I long to kiss Auntie (which I never did, even though I loved her more than many I have kissed) . . . as the cups clink against the faucet.

She tossed fifty or a hundred roubles into the pail with the gesture of a very wealthy person, forestalling our false chorus of sympathy . . . but what came next was the most difficult for her, though she was resolute by nature and did not dawdle or procrastinate: for just an instant, with an assortment of cups in her hands, she stood frozen before her door . . . became still more willowy (even her round back straightened, it was hard not to believe the optical illusion) . . . and promptly threw open the door and fluttered in, almost with the summery chirp of a Serov morning early in the century – again, in her youth. Washed sunlight through washed leaves dappled the polished parquet, a bouquet of dawn lilacs stood motionless in droplets, there was all but a peignoir and a Scriabin étude . . . as though the reproduction on the wall were not a reproduction but a mirror. "Dima, such a pity! I've broken my favourite Chinese cup!"

Ah, yes! All our lives we remember how we were loved . . .

Dima, my dearly beloved uncle, remains beyond the door in these memories. I see him in shadow, his legs crossed, next to the bouquet, a kind of bouquet. He drums on the tablecloth with a surgeon's musical fingers, waits for his tea, smiles attentively and gently, a good man who has nothing to say.

So first I see her hairdo (or rather the comb), and then her hands. Right now she is stirring jam: an antique (pre-catastrophe) copper kettle, burnished like the sun; in it, a scarlet layer of very expensive select strawberries from the market; and on top, the coarse sharp slivers of old-time (loaf) sugar, shining faintly blue. All this is precious, a crown, sceptre, and orb all together (in our family we like to say that Auntie is as majestic as Catherine) . . . and over this empire rules the hand with the golden spoon – it catches itself trembling and pretends that it had planned to make exactly the motions that occurred (this is very picturesque: governance by chance as an artistic method).

I see the comb, the hairdo, the hands . . . and suddenly, vividly, all at once, my whole aunt: as though I have been laboriously rubbing a transfer picture, and finally I peel it back, holding my breath, tormenting my own hand with my smoothness and slowness – and it works! no rips in the film! here come the brilliant big flowers on her crimson Chinese jacket (silk, buttoned) . . . her round back, with a bouquet between the shoulder blades . . . and the foot with the bandaged-on slipper. The flowers on her back are splendid, lush, a Chinese variety of chrysanthemum, the kind she loves to receive for her eternal anniversary (every day a basket is brought to us from grateful people, and my aunt's room always looks like an actress's after a benefit performance; every day, in exchange, the next faded basket is set out on the stairway). The flowers on her back were the same as in her coffin.

In our extensive family, all living together, we had a number of standardized formulas for admiring Auntie. What I don't know is how

the questionnaire data – age, sex, marital status, and ethnic origin –
were factored into them. Naturally, our family was too well bred to
stoop to the level of a personnel department. Such things were never
spoken of. Yet a hundred-per cent silence always speaks for itself: the
silence said that one did not speak of these things, one knew them.
She was fifteen years older than Uncle, they had no children, and she
was a Jew. For me – as a child, a teenager, a youth – she had neither
sex, age, nor ethnic origin. Whereas all the other relatives did have
these things. Somehow I saw no contradiction here.

We all played this game – of unconditionally accepting all the
conditions she set – for our indulgence was too lavishly encouraged,
and our clumsy performance had a grateful spectator. God knows who
outplayed whom in nobility, but everyone overplayed. She could
nevertheless see it from a higher perspective, I think; we could not.
Weren't her pre-established conditions a lofty response to our own
unconditionality? Wasn't this why the only person she feared, and
cultivated beyond all measure, was Pavlovna, our cook? Pavlovna did
not need to play our game. She *knew*: both that Auntie was a Jew, and
that she was an old woman, and that her husband . . . , and that they
had no . . . – that death was near. She had a knack for revealing her
awareness of these simple but mercilessly precise facts with exaggerated
servility, stopping just short of verbal expression. In return for her
silence, with bustling gratitude, she helped herself to anything she
wanted, even those cups.

We really did love Auntie, but our love was also proclaimed. Auntie
was a "Fine Human Being"! This has a bitter ring to it. How often we
speak with a capital letter, specifically in order to hide the questionnaire
facts; our automatic membership in the human race is racist. Inordinate
delight in someone's virtues always smells. Of either toadyism or
apartheid. She was a *fine human being* . . . great, broad, passionate,
very alive, generous, and very *meritorious* ("Meritorious Scientist" –
that was another title she held). In sum, I now believe that throughout the forty years of her marriage she *worked* as an aunt in our household, with all her remarkable qualities, and came to be *like one of the
family*. (That was another reason why she and Pavlovna were able to
develop a special understanding; Pavlovna, too, was a "Fine Human
Being.")

We had every cause to extol and deify her: none of us did as much,
even for ourselves, as she did for everyone else. She saved me from
death, she saved my brother, and three times she saved my uncle (her
husband). The number of times she helped just for the sake of helping

(when there was no threat to life) cannot be counted. With the years the list grew and was canonized, item by item, down the list. Our custom, however, was to remind about these things but not remember them, so that the phrase I let slip a moment ago is correct: like one of the family . . . She was also – as I learned considerably later, after her death – *like a wife*. In all those forty years, it turned out, they had not been registered as married. This old news immediately acquired legendary chic: the independence of truly decent people from formal and meaningless formalities. The rest of the family, however, were registered.

Time drains away. A silted river bottom. The rustily protruding framework of a drama. This, it turns out, is not her life but its plot. It is lifeless from retelling: years later, in our family, information germinates in the form of a tombstone.

And I'm now constructing a pedestal from it . . .

She was a great doctor, and I've never been able to resolve my uncertainty: what did she herself know about her own illness? Sometimes I think that she *must* have known; sometimes, that she knew nothing.

She tried her foot, and then she tried a heart attack.

The heart attack nearly cured her foot. One way or another, she pulled herself through the heart attack. Knowing that she had squeaked by (as a physician, she could tell herself this with confidence, in this case), she felt so much happier and younger, and even fitted her foot back into her shoe, that we could not stop rejoicing. Again came the meetings, governing boards, dissertation defences, house calls on officials (cure the murderer! unquestionably, a sacred principle of the Physician . . . but isn't it wrong to treat them more vigorously and responsibly than their potential victims? . . . no, it's all right: the law is alive where its paradoxes are alive, as in England) . . . and I see her again in the kitchen, ruling over her gleaming sun-kettle.

But her sun had not risen for long.

Auntie was dying. This was no longer a secret from anyone except herself. Even she had lost so much strength that every day she wearied, forgot, and took a small, involuntary step toward death. But then she would catch herself, and again fail to die. Her foot turned quite black, and she resolutely insisted that she wanted it amputated, although everyone, except her, knew that the operation was already beyond her endurance. The foot, the heart attack, the foot . . . a stroke. And now she clutched at life with fresh strength, of which she alone, among us all, had so much.

A bed! She demanded a *different* bed. For some reason she was especially counting on my physical assistance. She summoned me to give instructions. I did not understand her thickened speech very well but agreed to everything, seeing no great difficulty in the task. "Repeat," she said, suddenly articulating clearly. And oh!! with what annoyance she turned away from my unparalysed stammer.

We brought in the bed. This was a special bed, from a hospital. It was complicated, in the clumsy way in which a thing can be made complicated only by people remote from technology. Naturally, none of the contrivances for changing the position of the body was operative. Many times recoated with a prison shade of oil paint, the bed was both nonadjustable and ugly. We carried this monster into Auntie's mirrored-crystalled-carpeted-polished coziness, and I did not recognize the room. All her things seemed to stampede away from the bed, hide in the corners, huddle up in presentiment of social change. Actually, it was just that a space had been hastily made for the bed. I remember an absurdly youthful sensation of muscles and strength, an exaggerated awareness, inappropriate to my task as a mover. My biceps were emphatically alive, on display for the paralysed, dying old person. Because of this a peculiar awkwardness pursued me: I kept bumping into corners, tripping, and banging my knuckles. The bed seemed to be forcing me to resemble it.

Auntie sat in the middle of the room and directed the move. That is how I remembered it – but she could not have sat in the middle, for she could not sit up, and the middle had been cleared for the bed. Her gaze burned with an ember light; she had never had such deep eyes. She passionately desired to move from her bed of forty years, she was already in the bed that we were just carrying in, and thus I remembered her in the middle. We must not damage the "apparatus", since we knew nothing about it; we must flatten it a little here and bend it a bit more there and set its permanently fixed planes higher-lower-higher, we were doing everything wrong, we couldn't possibly be this thick-headed, she herself would obviously have to . . . The impression also stayed with me that she herself finally rose, arranged everything right – see, nothing to it, just use your head – and after adjusting it lay back down into her paralysis, leaving to us the transfer of pillows, feather beds, and mattresses, a task more nearly accessible to our stage of maturity, although here, too, we made scandalous blunders. Good heavens, she hadn't changed in thirty years! When we sawed firewood together in that same kitchen, during the winter of the blockade, she (a woman of fifty) used to get just as cross with me (a child of five) as she was now. With our saw flexing and groaning as we rescued each other's fingers, she would be aggrieved to the point of tears in an argument over who should pull in which direction. "Olga!" she would cry to my mother at last. "Make your hooligan stop! He's tormenting me deliberately. He's sawing the wrong direction on purpose." I, too, was greatly aggrieved, not so much by her outcry as by the fact that they suspected me of "on purpose", when I had no ulterior motives at all, I would never have done anything for spite or on purpose . . . at the time I was a tolerably good little boy; quite good, it seems to me now. Sobbing, we would abandon the saw in the half-sawn log. Ten minutes later she would cheerfully come and make peace with me, bringing her "last", something mouse-sized: perhaps a little crust, or a crumb. Well, I alone had changed, it turned out. And she still could not accept the only change that lay ahead for her in life: she did not believe, of course, in the Next World. (No, I will never comprehend their generation! Confident that God did not exist, they carried Christian commandments higher than I do . . .).

After we moved her, she spent a long time arranging herself, with obvious satisfaction and not another glance at her deserted conjugal bed. Now I imagine I heard a great sigh of relief when we tore her from it. Of all the things that she still, despite her medical experience, did not understand, this she understood irreversibly: never again would she return to that bed . . . We did not understand. Like idiots, we understood nothing of what she knew perfectly well, better than anyone: what it meant to be sick, how the sick person felt, and what he really needed. Now she herself was in need, but no one could repay this debt to her. And then, when she had arranged herself, she told us "Thank you," with profound first meaning, as though we truly had done something for her, as though we understood . . . "Was it very heavy?" she asked me sympathetically. "Oh, no, not at all, Aunt! It was light." That was not how I should have answered.

Yet this bed did not suit her either: it was objectively uncomfortable. And then we brought in the last one, Grandmother's, in which all of us died . . . Once she was in it, Auntie put the pillow right for the last time, smoothed with her trembling hand the nice, even fold-back of the sheet on the blanket, half-closed her eyes, and sighed with relief: "At last I'm comfortable." The bed stood like a coffin in the centre of the room, and her face was at peace.

She passed away suddenly, that very day . . . the woman who had been the subject of the drama.

Auntie survived her. "At last I'm comfortable . . ."

The bed stood in the middle of the strangely deserted room, where her things were abandoning their owner a little more hastily – an instant sooner – than their owner abandoned them. They wore cheap expressions: these sides and surfaces, precious since childhood, turned out to be merely old things. They shunned the metal bed in the middle, they were mahogany, they were Karelian birch . . . Auntie was comfortable.

She would not be able to take them with her . . .

But she did.

In the middle of the burial mound stands a bed with nickel-plated knobs, some of them worn down to the brass. Reclining comfortably in it, with her eyelids half shut and her jaw bound up, Auntie wears her favourite Chinese jacket; on her lap is the sunny kettle filled with strawberry jam; in one hand she holds her stethoscope, in the other an American thermometer that suggests a timer for a bomb; a Riva-Rocci blood-pressure machine lies at her feet. Not forgotten are the surviving cups, the dissertation submitted for review, the yellow Venus de Milo with which (as the story goes) she arrived at our house . . . Uncle, with the chauffeur behind him, stands modestly at her side, already half covered by the earth falling from above . . . Driving soundlessly down upon them is a car with a gleaming deer on the hood (she regularly transferred the deer from one model to the next, ignoring the fact that it had gone out of style). So the deer is here, too . . . And our whole apartment is already here, under the loose, friable time that is showering down from above, bringing with it my entire past and slivers of blockade ice, everything for which I am indebted to anyone is sinking into the burial mound, time showers down with its living humaneness and Darwinian humanity, with principles and decency, with everything that the principled and decent could not endure, with everything that made of me the pathetic creature who is called by analogy a man, that is, with me . . . but I myself manage, shaggily, after throwing the last shovelful, to be transformed into the blackly glimmering warmth of honest bestiality . . .

Because, since they passed away – first my grandmother, who was still better, still purer than Auntie, and then Auntie, who took my grandmother's place as in a relay race, and now her place stands empty for . . . I will not forgive them this. Because, since these last people passed away, the world has grown no better, and I have grown worse.

Lord, after death there will be no memory of Thee! I have already looked into Thy face . . . If a man is sitting in a deep well, why shouldn't he think he's looking *out* from the world, rather than *into* the world! And supposing I extricate myself from the well, what if there's nothing there? all level, all empty, in all four directions? except for the hole of the well I've climbed out of? I hope the terrain in Thy country is slightly varied . . .

Why has Thy inept but diligent pupil been incarcerated at the bottom of this bottomless cell and forgotten? In order for me to spend my whole life observing one star? Granted, the star is farther than the eye can see without the aid of the well . . . But I have already learned it!

Lord! Uncle! Aunt! Mama! I weep . . .

Sun. The very sun I began with.

In your native city there are apt to be spots you have never visited. Especially in the neighbourhood of tourist attractions that overwhelm their surroundings. The Smolny Institute, and on its left the bell tower of the Smolny Convent – I had always known that they were here, that this was the place to bring a stranger, and I no longer felt anything more for them than for a postcard. But now one day I had to locate an address (there were also houses and streets here, people living here, it turned out), and off to the left of the bell tower, to the left of the Regional Komsomol Committee, to the left of the honeycomb of convent cells, I found a crooked street (a rarity in Leningrad), century-old trees, Auntie's institute (the former Invalid Home, which is why it was so handsome; not very many medical facilities are constructed – sooner or later you will come across an old building), and suddenly I was in such a good mood that even the blank fence looked beautiful to me. Everything seemed to have survived here, in the shadow of the tourist attraction . . . Well, there was a checkpoint instead of the watchman's booth, a board fence instead of the eliminated grill-work . . . but the main gate was still intact, and a handicapped old door-keeper was at his post by the entrance to the Invalid Home (one of their own, probably). Both halves of the flowery baroque gate stood open in expectation. On the plaque I finally read what Auntie's institute was properly called (Ministry of Public Health, Regional Executive Committee . . . a great many words had replaced the two, Invalid Home). I had to step aside for a black Volga with an epaulette flashing in its interior. The invalid, on his stump of a leg, jumped up and saluted. Low to the ground, with a surfeited swish, the general moved away down the brick lane in his fur coat of "black Volga". I followed along, on to the premises. "You're going to the funeral?" the invalid asked, not from severity, but from a sense of dedication. "Yes."

The red brick of the lane matched the maple leaves that were being raked aside by a diligent mongoloid. He looked like a homemade stuffed toy, of a poverty-stricken wartime pattern. Another man, a little brighter, proud of the tool entrusted to him, was spearing papers and cigarette butts. A cripple with a brick-red face, who stood confidently on a wooden leg with a black rubber suction disk on its tip, was crushing brick for the lane with a heavy instrument that resembled his own inverted wooden leg. Drab, laundered old ladies hovered here and there about the park like the autumn cobwebs – senile Ophelias with nosegays of sumptuous leaves . . . Outdoor work therapy, a nice sunny day. The air had grown empty, and the sunlight spread evenly, unobstructed, as if it were the air; the shade was gone, illumined from within by rays from the flaming leaves; a premature puff of smoke (don't let children play with matches!) had collected an intent, retarded group around it . . . The ancient smell of decaying leaves, the revivifying smell of burning ones. The fall clean-up. Things were all strewn about, but a forthcoming order was beginning to show through the chaos: space had been tidied up, the air had been changed, even the lane was freshly reddened. The morning's half-asleep retarded people, early-to-rise cripples, and autumnal old ladies were in great harmony with autumn. "Over that way," an extreme oligophrenic told me respectfully. Where was I going? . . . I was standing at the end of the lane, which had brought me to the hospital courtyard. I had to step back off the shoulder into a pile of leaves, which sank agreeably under my feet, and the oligophrenic wisely got off on the other side: more Volga sedans drove between us, two at once. Aha, over that way. That was where I was going. Auntie was already there.

At the morgue there had been a hitch. We hadn't recognized her: she was lacking her hairdo. None of us could lift a hand to fluff up the usual locks. Nor could she . . . Nektor Beritashvili was the one who proved to be her true friend. He arrived leading a hairdresser, practically in handcuffs. "No one needs the money!" he said indignantly. "How much?" we wondered. "Oh –" He brushed us aside. "A hundred." The answer was as crisp as a new banknote. Auntie had not stinted.

Now Auntie looked nice. Her face was properly calm, beautiful, and significant, but slightly on guard. She was plainly listening to what was being said and did not find it fully satisfactory. They were listlessly cataloguing her merits, piling up the corpses of epithets – not a single living word. "Her radiant aspect ... Never ... Eternally in our hearts ..." The general who had been first to speak (three Hero stars, a good general, stout, preoccupied, and lifeless) drove away: through the conference hall doors, open to the autumn, we could hear the disrespectfully hasty departing roar of his Volga. "Sleep in peace," he had said, bowing his head over the coffin, and already he was slamming the car door: "To the Smolny!" He would make it to his meeting. He had found time to dwell chiefly on her wartime services: "We will never forget!" They had forgotten already – both the war, the blockade, the living, and the dead. They no longer had time to remember Auntie: I realized that she had been written off long before she died. The changed historical circumstances allowed them to appear at the funeral service – that was something, at least. Times were different now, how could old men be expected to keep up. And if the general, panting for breath, could still make it to his next Hero star, it would be on just one condition – that he not leave the carpeted race track for an instant ... After the general, people were shy to speak, as though his white-haired ear and the golden gleam of his shoulder board had been left behind when he sped away. The next orator droned on exactly as he had, and so did the next ... they simply could not catch fire. The deceased's family, parted by the coffin like the streams parted by the prow of a boat, looked like poor relations of the orators. We were clustered on the left, the Jewish relatives on the right. I hadn't known there were so many of them. Not a single familiar face. One man, I thought, I had seen briefly in our foyer. He caught my glance and nodded. Grey eyes, attentively perplexed, as if nearsighted. But why had I never ... none of them ... I didn't realize it, but I had begun to feel awkward, ill at ease – in sum, ashamed. But I supposed I disliked the orators, not us, not myself. "Your merits were duly ... with a medal ..." Auntie was a fine human being ... her merits could never be ... Death is death: I was beginning to understand something after all, and the cultish flush left my cheeks ... Stalin was dying a second death, fifteen years later. Because in all that time I no longer had anything to remember except Auntie, a pure and honest representative, it nevertheless turned out, of the Stalin era.

Auntie was more and more strongly dissatisfied with the droning of the orators. At first she had thought rather well of them – they had come, after all, the academicians, the professors, and the generals – but then she utterly died of boredom. At one point I distinctly felt that she was ready to stand up and make a speech herself. *She* would have found the words! She knew how to speak from the heart ...

Her temptation to give a person joy was always strong, and she contrived to find heartfelt praise for people who did not deserve even one degree of her warmth. This is no exaggeration, no figure of speech: Auntie was more alive than anyone at her own funeral. But here, too – just as she had not been able to come to her own aid when dying, and no one else had come, though we were all clustered around her bed – so now, around the coffin . . . here, too, there was nothing left for her but to turn away in vexation. Auntie lay back down in the coffin, and we carried her out, along with her bed and her utter dissatisfaction, into the autumn sunshine of the hospital courtyard. Once more I lent my strong shoulder, of course, side by side with the attentive, grey-eyed man, who nodded to me again. "Not at all, Aunt! It was light . . ."

The courtyard could not be recognized. It was thick with people. Nearest the door were the nurses and aides, sobbing with unusual respect for the deceased's merits, as evidenced by the guests who had come. Sullen, hung-over orderlies mingled with the cripples to form the next rank, their shared navy blue shoulder forcing back a crowd of retarded people, who in turn forced back the old ladies humbly standing behind an invisible boundary. The steady light of a timid ecstasy illumined their faces. That light fell on us, too. We assumed a dignified air. At a funeral the relatives, too, have rank. The coffin tassels, the galloons, the lid, the little cushion with the medal, the sobbing head nurses . . . the general!! (it was another one, who had not been in such a hurry) . . . the cars with chauffeurs opening their doors . . . the autumn gold of the brass band, the breathless sun of the tuba and cymbals . . . oh, my! They stood humbly and solemnly, patched but clean, never breaking discipline, leaning on rakes and shovels, this antirebellious mob. The general got into his car and gleamed inside it as if the tuba were being carted away . . . they watched with a united gaze, unblinking. The coffin sailed like a ship, its prow parting the human wave into two humanities: the defectives on the right, the above-normal, successful, and distinguished on the left. The two streams, separated by the breakwater of orderlies, did not close up behind the coffin. "We're just like them!" – that was the pride I read on the shared, unformed face of the retarded. They gazed ecstatically at what they would have become, had they risked going out in society, like us. They were what we had all started from, so that now, at the end of our careers, we could flash our noble white hair and rattle our medals. They were part of us, we were part of them. They had not risked it for fear of the orderly; we had suborned and then subordinated him. Arduous and glorious our careers had been, as doctors and professors, academics and generals! Many of us possessed exceptional talent and vitality, and all this vitality and talent had gone for advancement – so that the door would obsequiously slam shut on the prestigious coffin-on-wheels . . .

If they were only half a man, so were we . . . They had not taken, and we had lost. But the half that we had lost was the very half that they still kept intact. We ought to sort ourselves into pairs as in kindergarten, hold hands, and pass ourselves off as a whole person . . . only thus can we come before Him without fear . . . Never, never should we forget what we would have been, had we not embarked on all this . . . Here we stand in a grey, respectful column, with large heads and tiny flowerlike heads, the micro- and macrocephalics, with the border-guard orderlies and the coffin of the last living person in between! . . . We trudge along, we who have given our all to become the objects of your merited ecstasy; we who are dead bury the living, we blind the living with our brilliance! . . . They're *alive*, the retarded! Like an autumn chill, the thought ran between my shoulder blades, my taut young muscles. Alive and sinless! For what sin do they have, other than in their fists, in their pockets . . . and their pockets are prudently sewn shut. But here we are, with the coffins of our achievements and experience on our shoulders . . . If you look first into the soul of an idiot, if you see in his eyes the near, blue, inmost depths of his soul, and then abruptly look into the soul of that general, or indeed of any of us – my God! better *not* look and see what we deserve. We deserve much, as much as we have paid for this. And we have paid our all. No, far be it from me to peer into the musty, treacherous blind alleys of our life, the inevitable peristalsis of a career. I fully believe that everyone in our procession is a hard-working, crystal-pure, talented, dedicated human being (even with a capital letter!). Only this soul do I propose to look into . . . our own, under no suspicion . . . and I turn away, frightened. That's why they don't cross over to us – they are rooted to the spot, not merely by ecstasy, but by horror! Not only the retarded, after all, but we, too, are hardly able to separate horror from ecstasy, ecstasy from horror. And we never will, never having understood. How could the retarded person . . . Wisely, he took fright at the very beginning. Even then, in the cradle, or even earlier, in the womb, he would not come here, to us . . . There he stands in the cradle, with his toy rake and shovel, and does not weep for his doctor: The doctor is alive, you are dead. Not one of us could truly look Death in the face, not because we feared to, but because *we already had*. The

souls of the unborn in Paradise, the souls of the dead in Hell; Auntie
flowed between us like the Styx.

We filed lifelessly along the blood-red lane of the park. It had been
thoroughly neatened up (when had they found time?). Kept back by
the orderlies, the retarded had stayed at the end of the lane, still in
formation, like a grey wall, and now they melted into the board fence,
vanished. My last glance saw only an utterly empty world: beyond the
cold, painted park rose the burial mound, whither the patients, one
by one, were departing to their doctor.

Which of the two of us is alive? I myself, or my conception of
myself?

She was a great doctor, yet even now, after all these pages, I still
haven't resolved my banal uncertainty: what did she know, as a
physician, about her own illness and death? That is, she knew all right,
to judge by the pages I have written . . . but how did she deal with
her feelings about her own knowledge? I never did answer my own
question, and I still wonder what methods a professional employs to
deal with his own knowledge, in an instance when he can apply it to
himself. How does the writer write letters to his beloved? How does
the gynaecologist go to bed with his wife? How does the prosecutor
take a bribe? How does the thief bar his door? How does the chef
feast? How does the builder live in his own house? How does the
voluptuary manage in solitude? . . . How does the Lord see the
crowning achievement of His Creation? . . . When I reflect on all this,
of course, I conclude that even great specialists are also human. For
in these critical instances, the narrow and secret manoeuvres by which
their consciousness bypasses their own skill, reason, and experience
are such a triumph of the human over man – always and in every
instance! – that we can only turn our long faces once again to Him,
who for our sake consists of blue, stars, and clouds, and ask: Lord,
how much faith hast Thou, if Thou foresaw even this!

Translated by Susan Brownsberger

VLADIMIR MAKANIN

Those Who Did not Get into
the Choir

"WELL, SON, DO you want to go to Pioneer camp? Out with it,
eh?"

Her son stayed silent.

"You can't imagine the difficulty I've had in fixing it up," she said
to the women of the village.

"Yes of course," the women nodded. They agreed with her.

"You can't imagine the effort I put into it. The wear and tear on
my nerves!"

"Yes, of course . . . It stands to reason!" And the womenfolk started
telling her what a stout lass she was and what a hard time she was
having with Kolya and how tough life was in general. They loved her
and, of course, were slightly scared of her. They were standing around
in a circle, chewing sunflower seeds after their sauna bath. They were
red-faced and limp from the hot steam. They clutched bundles of
varying sizes in their purpling female hands – in the bath they had not
only washed themselves but also done their washing; Kolya's mother
had done her washing and her soaping along with the rest of them
and now, depositing her bundle of washing on the bench, she again
enquired, gleefully and excitedly: "Well, son, do you want to go to
Pioneer camp?"

With complete self-possession, extinguishing a knowing and sardonic little smile, Mister replied quietly: "Fer crying out loud, just
pack me off where yer thinks best."

The women gave a collective start and turned round to stare at him:
a small, wise, elderly mannikin stood there looking, yet not looking at
them, spitting out sunflower seed husks. He always answered his
mother quietly, with one hundred per cent compliance, which was
itself inwardly insolent. Unable to grasp the nuance, his mother and,
following her example, the rest of the womenfolk turned away after a
brief pause, and resumed their conversations about their barrack hut
and the minute rooms in which they lodged. At that time Kolya's
mother had ideas of getting herself on to the Factory Committee (later

she did climb up that particular ladder) and of being in a position to allocate the sparse reserve of housing under construction in the village. In her sleep she pictured herself in the full plenitude of her righteousness, dividing up the individual rooms between applicants and, perhaps, granting them flats: flats were then an unheard-of luxury. She threatened: "Just wait. I'll get in there and show them what allocation means."

Kolya's father was a weak-willed man who had never recovered from the war, and lived under his wife's thumb, a quiet or, more exactly, subdued soul, yet with an inner, carefully concealed longing – to fulfil his life potential. Unbeknown to the others, Kolya's father held conversations with himself, on such lines as: "I already have my whole life behind me, and I've never had a moment's rest."

Or: "My life's over and I've not seen a thing . . ."

Or: "I've had my life and I've never really loved anyone properly . . ."

He was a teacher in a technical college. Now and then, in the course of lecturing his students about insulating materials, he would contemplate a platonic relationship with one or other young girl, spending much time trying to make up his mind and decide whether she was or was not worthy of his love and whether he should or should not devote to her what remained of his life. He scrutinized them, turned them over in his mind, picked on each one's weak points, and made timorous passes at them with his eyes. The girl students considered him a weirdo. They regarded him as a case of shell shock. He delivered his lectures in a slow, lugubrious voice. He treated his son as his latest setback in life. The father considered himself as deserving something better; he considered himself better than his son.

"Here, too, I was out of luck . . . You're the cross I bear," he suddenly ventured with a sigh. And sought quietly (and semi-warily) to place his hands on his son's head.

At times during the night the father would drop his legs over the side of the bed, go out to the corridor of the hut and have a smoke – to think over his arduous life. The years were passing and, as it seemed to him, he had learnt very little and seen very little.

"I never once," he began, in quiet self-reproach, "tried my hand at netting fish. Not once . . ."

Or: "I've never once been to Guryev."

And off he would go with someone to nearby Guryev. Or to some lake or other to fish. On his return he would gently defend his action, and quietly and submissively endure his wife's hysterics: he wanted no more than to live out his life on a quiet confessional note. This was all he thought of, and he was like someone who pointedly fails to understand why rain simply cannot be reassembled from individual drops.

There were two American families in the village: engineers. They lived in what were by the standards of those times handsome, purpose-built cottages, located at a discreet distance from our hutments. The wind often blew in our direction and we would catch the smell of dinner being prepared just as, as if air-borne, Americanisms took root in the village. And the most persistent one, the appellation Mister, attached itself to Kolya. Kolya was one of those young boys who behaved quietly and sedately. He owed his shape to an enlarged spleen which gave him the appearance of possessing a small but solid professional *embonpoint*. Otherwise he was thin and scrawny. He had a catheter sticking out from his left side through which he passed water. He had one year left to live: he was twelve years old and he died at the age of thirteen.

His sister – and she was three years older than Mister Kolya – was first and foremost an outstanding student. True, she was a profoundly decent person: she had not inherited the least trace of her mother's energetic, artistic busyness nor her father's hidden, quiet pretence. But for that very reason her inner being had drawn in on itself and become prim and proper. She was a little grey mouse at school. A little mouse in the street. A little mouse at home. A prize pupil, watching carefully over her marks, she kept herself to herself, awaiting the day and the hour when she would, at the earliest possible moment, obtain her gold medal and depart for one or another university – Sverdlovsk or Saratov – depart, leave, run away and, resurfacing somewhere else, start to live afresh and anew. Kolya's sister was unshakable on this point and was quite impervious, to say the least, to the reproaches of her girlfriends and schoolmates on the score of currying favour with the teachers: she was above all that. She went to see one or other teacher in the evening, sat with her, had a chat, drank tea and picked out the odd book to read. The teachers were not that fond of her but honoured the letter and the spirit of their calling by leaving their doors open and laying on a ready supply of tea.

"You'll bring shame on our family. Thief! Little thief!" thundered Kolya's mother when she caught Mister Kolya and me with the potatoes we had lifted to take into the hills. Without a word, her face dark with anger, his sister there and then bundled her school books

together and went off to see the teacher. His sister's name was Olya
– Olya, the Prize Student. She visited the teacher in order to get in
some practice with her logarithms. She would walk along the village
street, clutching her books, and repeat to herself (so as not to waste
precious time) the lines she had learnt by heart:

> "October's here already. The grove is casting off
> The last surviving leaves from its naked boughs."

Mother had, by special request, secured a day off work and come
back to give Mister a whipping for petty theft and to ensure that
sinfulness did not secure any foothold in him for the future. Mother
arrived not on her own but accompanied by one of her friends,
and here were two forty-year-old women getting down with grim
determination to the task in hand. A task that was, in general, a routine,
simple one. They did not lay a finger on me: my own people could
deal with me in their home. But neither did they let me go. "Let him
stay and watch it." They grabbed me when I tried to get out through
the window.

"No, you don't!" And they shut the window. I stood there, like a
wolf cub at bay, until I realized the complex nature of what they had
in mind. Mother started yelling at Kolya: she needed to work herself
up; she shouted that their family was and, so long as she was alive,
would be decent and honest. It was just then that her brigade had
again been singled out for commendation and Mother was, as it were,
on the up-and-up. Perhaps that was why she and the other woman
painter chanted in full awareness of the rectitude of their words: "One
learns honesty in childhood!" "Spare the rod and spoil the child! . . ."
They kept interrupting and egging each other on. Their object, the
small elderly mannikin, stood opposite them, calm and shrewd, and it
was only the immediate concrete threat that kept the sardonic little
smile from crossing his face.

Finally they seized him by the shoulders like a doll, but the doll, it
turned out, was on its guard and managed to find its voice – quietly,
as always.

"Hey, be careful. Don't snap my pee-pee."

They hesitated . . . For a moment they stayed their heavy hands,
whereupon Mister, now reassured that they would not lay into him
in hot blood, went across to the bed unaided. He lay down with his
head buried in the pillow. His face was half turned towards the wall.
The women started yelling again, calling on their inner reserves of
ineluctable retribution. "How can he want to be a little thief for life?

Surely he realizes that, for once and for all? . . ." The strap appeared and Mother beat Mister across his scraggy bottom – not all that hard or viciously but gradually getting into the swing and with gradually increasing fervour. Meanwhile the other woman painter kept yelling her head off as if to provide a pedagogical accompaniment to the blows. She bellowed for all she was worth. Then more softly. And more softly still. And then there appeared in her voice the first mini-notes of didacticism.

"Now he'll understand . . . Now he'll know better."

And, turning to me, she said: "You just take it in and think about it. It'll do you good."

Mister rose to his feet. He was white but not enraged. His lips trembled. But he sat on the bed quietly, looking maybe at me, maybe at some point in space, and seemed to be about to come out with one of his off-the-cuff sayings: Fer crying out loud, they had to have their pantomime, didn't they.

Mother burst out: "We want you to be a good, decent boy. I love you, you know. Who do you think I love most on earth?"

"Me," asserted Mister compliantly and quietly. He tucked his shirt back into his trousers. It had worked itself free.

"So there . . . You're my favourite, you know that yourself, my own sick little son. What do you think, why does a mother always love a sick child the most?"

"It's not necessary, Ma, not necessary," he said calmly, patiently and, as ever, quietly. He finished adjusting his shirt and shook himself as if the beating had left a coating of dust on him which he now needed to brush off. His lips no longer trembled but his hands kept making small fluttering movements.

He started early to save, and put money aside against a rainy day as people do in their old age: time, as everyone knows, is relative and Mister Kolya's life was running out, so that at the age of twelve he was already into his old age. His father, noticing the money he had put aside, took the opportunity to say reproachfully: "If you're that way inclined now, what are you going to be like when you grow up?" Kolya stayed silent and did not respond as to how he would be when grown up: he had already grown up. He had a job in an atelier and tramped around at night; he was a fully self-sufficient and non-dependent person, in other words a grown-up. For him life had to be fitted into an extremely tight schedule; eleven to twelve years for him was the equivalent of sixty for other mortals and once one has reached sixty it is the most natural thing in the world to put money by on the side. But it was the small things about him that struck me at the time. How he caught marmots. Or how he learnt to suck the goat let out to pasture in the area behind the village, towards the mountains: we would approach her armed with breadcrumbs, we crawled up to her cautiously, uttering various forms of reassurance, until she became compliant. Mister Kolya was as resourceful in pursuit of his quarry as in defence of himself. He was already looking ahead. On one occasion we sucked the completely docile goat dry and he sighed as only sagacious old men can do.

"You'll see, any moment now the owners will cut her throat."

Frightened out of my wits, I mumbled: "Let's suck her less often, and then they won't."

"To hell with her," Mister said. And added, with another sigh for good measure, like a little old man: "It's something else I'm afraid of."

"What?"

"Their trying to cure her."

Which was very much to the point. They wasted no time in stuffing the goat with some restorative, home-brewed concoction; her eyes clouded over and she stood as motionless as the post to which she was attached, but we found ourselves the victims of colic and acute diarrhoea. That first day we barely survived, we clutched at our stomachs and clambered up the slopes on all fours, while the goat stayed put among the brambles on the far side of the stream. At midday the post cast a short shadow. The goat stood two paces from the brambles and chewed the grass. For me it is still standing there, like a scene taken direct from life. My uncle came to visit us from the depths of the countryside, spotted the animal and said tersely: "That's no goat." We were out on a walk with him through our village and I was showing him over our "empire": the school, the wasteland, the hills. And I well remember him sizing up the scraggy, miserable creature and doggedly repeating: "That's no goat." Uncle was seventy, a hulking, unkempt, peasant figure, with a grey beard. The following day I went with Uncle to his village. Why I was packed off with him, I no longer remember, but I do remember our climbing down from the lorry and that on the way back Uncle turned aside to visit an old church on the outskirts of Novo-Pokrovka; he went in and spent an hour or so listening to the choir practice, while I stayed seated outside, picking my nose and growing ever more exhausted from the heat and the tedium.

Uncle finally emerged. He reappeared in the porch, followed by a cluster of depressed-looking youngsters.

Uncle told them severely: "There's no point in you're being here . . . Go home."

They were the rejects. They hesitated and then moved off down the road; and for some time I could still see their thin cotton shirts in the haze. They were about my age, even a bit younger, and all of them from different villages; at the crossroads they went their various ways and the dusty tracks and the white haze now swallowed them up, one by one. They were children who had not got into the choir.

When I got back home, I learnt that Kolya had been taken ill. He was lying in bed. I walked round the bedstead. His eyes were open, and I came into his field of vision. "Kolya," I called to him. "Mister . . ." I felt terrible. His face was puffed up: a black, bloated, charcoal biscuit. He made no reply except to move his lips in a bitter, hostile grimace.

The room was in semi-darkness. A heavy smell hung in the air: someone in the hut was cooking haricot beans. Kolya's father and mother were out at work. Olya – the Prize Pupil – was also not around.

"Has someone come?" In the cubicle the other side of the partition there was the sound of movement and shuffling steps. Kolya's grandmother put in an appearance. She was his mum's mother, a thin old lady, permanently undernourished, for the reason that they forgot to feed her and she, equally, forgot to feed herself. She made her appearance, took one look at my hands to see whether they perhaps held anything edible; they did not, so she moved off.

His mother was full of fire and fury; she kicked up a scene with the village doctor, who had given her to understand that Mister was doomed and one could start counting off the days. How could that be so? A doctor, if he was a proper doctor, had no right to say such things! Mother worked herself into a fit; she acted it out – the scene with the doctor and her own pain – in public, here, there, everywhere; at school even, under the hut windows, she shrieked and carried on without pause, so that the entire hutment and the whole settlement was quick to learn that Kolya was doomed. Mother's next job was to paint the fence, a five-foot high one, which had just been put up around the boilerhouse. Mother swiftly and rhythmically, with a professional ease of stroke, applied the brush from the top downwards. She was good at her job. She gritted her teeth. If the brigade fell behind, they wouldn't come down too hard on her: her little boy had died, her beloved sick child; everyone knew and everyone would understand. And so as to reduce the load of grief and pain she started thinking about the impending death from a different perspective: she would go and visit his little grave, sit for hours at her little son's side, bur without tears – her enemies would not catch her crying. All of a sudden the still unshed tears spurted forth; through the mesh of her everyday thoughts she caught sight of Kolya's face, no, not just his face – his sweet little face, at the moment when they had pressed him to her breast in the maternity home, rosy, featureless; a happy, chubby biscuit of a baby – her little boy.

"Get a move on girls!" she shouted. "It'll soon be dinnertime . . . Let's get it finished, eh? We've never let anyone down yet!" And energetically, authoritatively, with a dexterity and ease that won the others over, she whisked her brush across the horizontal face of the stone fence, and all the rest of the brigade jumped in to follow her example.

The doctor, terrified and browbeaten by Mother (and she was well up to browbeating anyone), suddenly fell prey to a fit of optimism. He went around wreathed in smiles, gesticulating expansively; he now announced that Kolya would not die; what is more, he would even make a breakthrough for the better, as he said to Mother.

Mother nodded.

"Yes . . . Kolya's a chip off the old block. He's a tough one . . . We've managed to get out of worse holes."

Forgetful of the fact that it was she who had put the selfsame words into the doctor's mouth, Mother enquired of him, as if even cajoling something out of him: "Seemingly, a breakthrough in his condition; maybe, a week more, eh?"

"Yes," the doctor assented, "about a week." The hut fell silent. It was some two years since any one of its inhabitants had died and the impending moment was a strain on their nerves and their hearts. Mister Kolya's spasmodic breathing could be heard through the windows of the hutment.

"Ssh . . . ssh . . . ssh . . . ssh." The whistling in his breathing could be heard from the street.

Grandmother made a big fuss, motioning towards the open window. "The whole house is wide open, and what's the use of that?"

"He needs air," Mother told her in a tone brooking no response.

Mother and Olya-the-Swot opened the windows at hourly intervals, only for them again to be shut tight on the quiet by the old lady. She grumbled: "Air – what air? They've just thought it up. The little lad is dying – he should be allowed to die in the warm."

"Shut up, Mama!" her daughter butted in.

The old lady screwed up her lips in offence. It was hot outside in the street. The sun had baked the grass black but the old lady was still afraid of catching cold. Her bones were frozen and aching. "My bones are turning to water, turning to water," she complained to passers-by in the street. Or she would all of a sudden open her jaws wide to reveal a terrifying toothless expanse, reminiscent of the interior of a deserted church.

"Have a look. Is there any swelling there?"

The answers she got were abrupt, hasty ones – no, there was no swelling. But she would again return to the charge.

"What d'ye think, my dear? Haven't I caught a chill on my chest?"

There were no lessons at school and Olya went off as early in the morning as she could to the small village library, where she stayed up to the time it closed. Apart from her, there was no one else inside. Olya could not put into words why she was unable to stand the secretive little world of her own family; and she was, in fact, concerned not with finding the words to do so but only with sitting working at the wobbly table opposite the semi-somnolent old lady librarian. Somewhere far away from her (far enough away) a new life awaited her and Olya knew it; she kept her heart well under lock and key, intent on not releasing it until she had got away from here to Sverdlovsk or Saratov.

Her father drank. He called on his wartime pals or simply on his neighbours. Afterwards, when he had been ushered out at some late hour, he would find a perch in the small, deserted, open-air market (a huddle of dirty stalls enclosed by a fence), sit himself down on one of the stalls, and have half an hour's shut-eye and half an hour communing with himself. He always talked to himself on the same lines: life was running out, had already run out, and where was happiness to be found? He had not properly lived. He had never visited the city of Kiev, the founding mother of all our cities. He had never been to a seaside spa. Even at the front he had seen very little. He had even chosen himself the wrong wife – a boisterous, pretentious woman. And to top it all, now his son was dying . . .

At night, to give Kolya more air, they all slept in the one small cubicle, on the other side of the partition. Mother and Olya. And the old woman. Father, who was the last to arrive home – by which time it was pitch dark – turned on the light, but he was most reluctant to join the others behind the partition and be given the night-time order of the boot by his wife. What worse fate was there? He was tottering on his feet. He peered at the floor and thought: "I'll just lie on the floor, next to my son . . ." After pulling off his boots, he discovered that his dying son's eyes were open. "Can't you sleep?" he enquired timidly. There was no answer from the mannikin. The sound of his laboured breathing was now on a lower note. That night he had already started rattling in his throat.

Without waiting for an answer, his father, in an uncertain, tipsy way, volunteered: "I'll sing you something, son . . . Right now, when I've put my shoes away." He tottered but stayed upright. He sat down beside the bed and began a quiet, long-drawn-out song, intoned to himself to compensate for what he had failed to say to himself during his lonely, late-night vigil in the deserted market.

Kolya, who had no desire to see him or listen to him, attempted to interrupt. The rattle became even louder and his shoulders jerked. He was physically incapable of uttering a word.

"I'll sing to you," his father ventured again uncertainly. "I'll do you a song . . . Son, it's a very nice song."

But then the dying boy rattled so hard that his father shut up instantly and murmured in fright: "OK, I won't, I won't, I understand . . . It's night-time, everyone's asleep. I understand." He lay down beside his son and curled himself up into a ball. He forgot to put out the light – a job that was done by Grandmother when she got up in the middle of the night. In doing so she gave his father's sleeping figure a kick. And carefully closed the windows.

Kolya grew thin overnight. The following morning his puffy face had dried out, his features had gone peaky, and his head resembled a small clenched fist. Mother sat beside him: there was the change in him and there was a change in her. As happens in the case of generously endowed spirits, his mother saw not the slightest contradiction between her saying "God does not exist. Only matter exists" and her now whispering about God to her dying son. "Don't cry, my little son," she sobbed piteously and quietly. "Don't cry, my angel. The Dear Lord is kind. He will be there to welcome you, my son."

There was a lump in her throat. She gulped for air. She whispered: "The Dear Lord is kind . . . The Lord is kind. Don't be afraid of Him."

The dying child wanted to say something but his stertorous gasps prevented him doing so.

His mother hurried on to say: "He understands – he understands everything – you're my little angel, my own pure little angel – He won't hold it against you that you misbehaved or that you stole – you are only a child and besides the times are so dreadfully hard."

Mister's eyes had sunk deep into their orbits and you could have put a small apple into each cavity. And, lo and behold, two meagre little tears surfaced unwillingly in the right-hand corners of his eye sockets (his head was tilted to one side). Kolya was moved neither by deep sorrow nor by compassion. He was sorry for his mother, but not that sorry: he looked at her with the look of an old man on the brink of death, knowing for good or for bad, life is over and one has to cross to the other shore.

The entire population of the hut now converged on his bedside, with restrained, mysteriously deliberate movements. All had been told and all knew that he was dying. They looked in on him, wiping their feet at the threshold, women and children alike.

"He's completely shrivelled up," the old ladies sighed.

"Not a person but a little shrunken lump . . ."

By the evening the same shrunken lump, in which not a spark of life seemed to remain, had started to yell in a penetrating human scream. He had lost consciousness but the pain was there – or maybe it wasn't the pain. His yells were inchoate, wordless, undifferentiated. It was a single, intense, uninterrupted wail which gradually and quite naturally switched into an animal's death howl. One had the impression of not only the hut but the entire settlement falling into silence. The shrunken lump had yelled for five hours at a stretch. His life or what had been called his life had now emerged from him and was dissipating in space. His father was on the wasteland, beyond the lean-tos – at the spot where they tethered the goat and disposed of outworn pails – amid the weeds, sitting on a couple of bricks laid on top of one another. He was drunk and maundering. Hiding away from the yells of his son and the eyes of his wife, he in turn invoked the Good Lord, in whom he did not believe for a single moment, and asked Him to accept the soul of his son kindly and lovingly. It was a sort of conjuration. "Whatever the bloody thing is called, matter or non-matter," muttered Father, "You follow me . . . by and large you do understand me, don't you, God?" Father spat into the weeds. "In short, just see to it and make him welcome. OK? Got it?" And Father tipsily waved his finger at someone among the weeds.

The person for whom he was interceding continued to cry out loud. His cries only broke off when night was far advanced – and from that moment Mister's body called off the struggle and only somewhere deep in its recesses was there a barely audible gurgle.

Two youths had been standing by the hut, shifting from foot to foot. The cries had come to a halt, and they made for the hills to poke around there in the dark and sit beside a campfire. They thought no more about Mister Kolya. The feeling of compassion exceeded the confines of their understanding, and the finite capacities of their juvenile souls were unable to yield or draw out any more than they had already done.

"It's a pretty sad business," said one.

"And how . . ."

And they left.

I too was intending to go up to the Yellow Hills that night but they wouldn't let me at home. "Why at night? Why do you have to go there at night?" "I need to. I need to, that's what," I kept on, shuffling my feet. I knew that the other two had already left . . . Then as luck would have it, some incident occurred among our hut population, between our neighbours; they had forgotten all about me, and at the height of their loud night-time altercation, I squeaked softly: "OK, Mum, I'm off," and hurtled out of doors. I ran to start with. Then I slowed down to a rapid lope. The path was a well-trodden one, a path we were all familiar with, and the lads would soon be lighting their fire, and either on the one hill or on the other I would, of course, be bound to spot it. And I had the idea that above my head, in the moon's beam, Mister Kolya's soul was flying in the air, maybe following the route I had taken. Before finally soaring into the heavens his soul had taken a course parallel to the earth, accompanying us to the Yellow Hills. Why not fly for a while over the earth, the lad had thought to himself. So I ran and ran, looking up at the moon's nimbus.

It was the dark of night, everyone was asleep; only the old grandmother (she was again starving) was wandering round the room, and it was she who heard his last raucous rattle.

"My little child." The old lady went nearer and saw in the shafts of moonlight how he was agonizing. She clasped him to her, embracing his cold, dessicated legs. "My little child . . ." And, as if realizing they were trying to hold him back, he uttered this final rattle, jerked his little body and crossed over. Burying her face in his legs, the old lady mumbled to herself that this was a small lump of her own flesh and blood and did her utmost neither to ignore it nor to relinquish it.

Translated by Michael Duncan

VASILY BELOV

A War like That

DARYA RUMYANTSEVA'S SON, Vanya, was killed at the front in
'42, but the bit of paper didn't arrive till the spring of '43. This bit of
paper, with its rubber stamp and highly suspicious, impossible-to-
make-out signature, had taken more than a year to reach her. And
because it had taken so long, but more because the signature – a hook
with a little loop – was impossible to make out, Darya decided it was
a fake, forged by some cruel person.

Whenever gypsies passed through the village, Darya went and had
Vanya's fortune told. And every time the indications were that the
piece of paper wasn't genuine. The cards were kind, Darya always
getting Sevens, and the King of Hearts being joined now by the Ace
of Diamonds, denoting an official house, and now by the Six of Clubs.
And the King with the Six could only be the way for Vanya to go –
now into the official house, now out of it. True, that black Antichrist,
the King of Spades with his sharp sword in his heathen hand, was
always hovering near. Which, you see, couldn't be helped – it wasn't
a picnic Vanya had gone to, but war. Against that, neither the Ten of
Spades denoting a bed of sickness, nor the Ace of Spades denoting a
fatal blow, ever came out together. Feeling more at peace, she made
a round of all the houses, simply to say: "He's alive, my Vanya, alive.
There's nothing to that piece of paper. It's wrong." And everyone,
the old women especially, sincerely and readily backed up this idea of
Darya's, and she, returning home, set the samovar boiling, and drank
hot water with dried turnip for sugar long and pleasurably. The
samovar sang away happily on the table, giving forth jolly ringing
sounds from within. Beneath the white pine floor a guileless mouse
set up a gentle rustling. The clock tip-tapped on the wall as it had
when Vanya was there. And Darya waited patiently for the war to
end.

In the evenings, winter and autumn, she slipped a broken padlock,
a contemporary of the samovar, into the gate fastening, rammed a
birch stick into the staple, and went to the stables to guard the horses.
Her little bunkroom in the stable was heated by a crackling stove,
and smelt of leather and sweaty felt collars. On wooden pegs hung

harnesses. Darya counted them aloud, lit the lantern and made a round of the stables.

The long, dry corridor with two rows of stalls was clean and comfortable. The horses were all munching hay, their munching merging into one rhythmical never-ending sound like that of the fine, warm gentle rain that brings the mushrooms. The sound of horses feeding was something that Darya loved to hear. Walking the long corridor, she was filled with a radiant feeling of peace and satisfaction, without knowing it for what it was – joy that horses, worn out during the day, should now be stilling their hunger. Here, there, not greedily but in unhurried peasant fashion, they took soft mouthfuls of fodder, following the light of the lantern with deep snorts. Darya walked the stables from end to end, and, well satisfied, dozed all night in her little room, and thought about her son. She would return home with the dawn, dragging some bit of dead wood, an abandoned stake or rotten plank. Firewood was a torment to her, especially in winter. In summer she only had a fire every other day, to save wood. She had the bright idea of boiling potatoes in the samovar. It was simple and convenient. If of the smaller size they boiled quickly, and the hot water was, as it were, a more interesting drink.

For the first two years of the war, Darya kept a goat. "Didn't have a goat and haven't got one now," she used to say, driving it out of other people's kitchen gardens. The goat was a prize wanderer. Now it was for ever getting on to the roof by some means, where it would dash to and fro, bleating, not knowing how to get down again, and the terrified Darya would have to summon old Misha to help. Another time it would get into the collective farm's corn, and then Darya, like other offenders, would be given five to ten days' work by way of a fine. And what's more, she couldn't drink its milk, which had a disgusting, wrong smell to it. For all of which reasons Darya nicknamed her "cow" now "Loony", now "Ninny", but always without any special malice, and in general felt sorry for the animal.

One day in early spring, to Darya's surprise, the goat went into kid, and, put out to graze, gave birth to two fluffy kids with big, prominent foreheads. The little she-kid she swapped with a neighbour for three pounds of sheep's wool to make boots out of. The he-kid grew unnoticed, becoming a lascivious, prominent-browed idiot, leaping at people, snorting, impudently curling back his lip and swishing his tail. His beard was a tangled lump of burdock burs, and his horns were perpetually bloody, urchins having trained him to butt. So when she lost her billy goat, Darya did not grieve specially, although she thought it a pity she'd not managed to get him credited as a meat delivery. If she had, and at the proper time, there would not now be these arrears to her name.

Being not yet over the age limit, Darya was assessed at the full rate for eggs, meat, wool and potatoes. All of which she delivered, buying some, bartering for others, and was in arrears only as regards meat. But there was still the whole of the monetary tax to pay, not to mention insurance, State loan, and the voluntary community payment. Under these headings she had not yet settled up for the previous year, '42, and in January Pashka Neustupov, known as Creepy, who was the same age as Vanya, but excused call-up on medical grounds, had brought her fresh liabilities. She'd put the green and pink pieces of paper carefully into an empty tea tin, and Pashka, after fastening his satchel of papers, had started telling her off. "So there we are, Comrade Rumyantseva! We won't bandy words. Obligations to the State have got to be met. Got to be."

"As we well know, Pashka," Darya said. "No two ways about it, dear man." And genuinely pleased at having company, she fetched out the samovar. Pashka and Vanya had been to parties together before the war, had even stayed in each other's houses, and Darya looked on him as one of the family. She wanted to offer him something, to have a talk, but Creepy set off to the next house, and Darya watched him go, remembering Vanya.

And so in winter, when the billy goat had grown, Darya was keen to have the animal credited as a meat delivery, but didn't manage it. What happened was that one day the farm manager arrived in the village and put his gelding in an empty stall. Darya wanted to take off its saddle and bridle, but was told by the drunken manager not to touch them, as he'd soon be riding back to his office. Darya went off home, having nothing to guard during the day, and the gelding being from a different stables. The gelding, still bridled, ate hay, biting its tongue and ruining its mouth, and had to be put down. And Darya was called to account by the collective farm board, together with the manager. The latter paid his fine in cash – sold something, and paid. But Darya had no money, which everyone knew, and in the record of the proceedings the board entered as its decision "That for negligent injury to a gelding of the Collective Farm, Watchwoman Rumyantseva be deprived of her personal billy goat."

Famine amongst the people began somehow imperceptibly and gradually. And very likely it was because of this that there was no wringing of hands when, on the collective farm, the first old woman died of exhaustion. Nor was there surprise at the near-impossibility of shutting doors on account of all the beggars.

Walking the roads were all manner of strange old men from afar, with knapsacks and sticks. Wretched old women and cripples wandered with baskets, teenagers came with their canvas school bags. From village to village, from house to house, went children of every sort, from those who had barely learnt to talk, to those who were a bit bigger. And women would ask: "Are you a boy or a girl?" – it being hard to tell from their clothing, and women having a constant need to know everything about everything.

The children begged, using phrases they had learnt, now it was because of a place that had been destroyed by fire, now because they were orphans. They would stand at the door, impassive, with downcast eyes. People gave, but if they had nothing to give, the children, still impassive, would turn and go. The old men were quicker about it, so as not to let the cold in. Looking towards the ikon corner, they would cross themselves and say: "Lord, send this house abundance and peace, preserve it from fire and loss of life, protect the master from sword, bullet and evil men. Give alms for the sake of Christ." The old women would whisper prayers, humbly, fervently.

The beggars found themselves somewhere to sleep while it was still light, so as not to be benighted, and it was a rare house that refused them shelter. The women would sit them at table, ask their names, what family they had, whether they had a home, what the news was from their parts. The beggars would warm themselves at the stoves, and those good at telling stories would find listeners. The hut would be lit by an almost smokeless birch torch; there would be the noise of the wind at the windows; and the magical autumn nights would be the shorter for tales, cheerful and terrible, of actual happenings.

"You've not heard, I suppose, what happened at Dikov this summer," a beggar woman would begin quietly, placidly, turning to the wife, and all would fall silent.

"No, grandmother, I've not. At where?"

The old lady in question would blow her nose neatly into some piece of rag she had, fold her hands, bloodless and waxen with age, and shake her head, as if in reproach. "Everyone, they say, knows what happened at Dikov."

The wife would sit nearer the fire, the children would elbow each other in the ribs to get closer.

"Well, my dear, living in Dikov was a family, husband and wife and two children. When the war came upon the land, the husband was, of course, called into the army. The wife saw him off, and was left alone with the little ones. The wife, a large, big-boned woman, was called Maryuta. Well, a year went by, and another, and suddenly, mistress, would you believe, folk heard something making noises in Maryuta's cellar at night, either a little dog or a piglet. Come nightfall, my dears, there'd be a squealing and a wailing."

"In the cellar?"

"In the cellar, mistress. And now it was that folk saw Maryuta's belly getting bigger, and wondered how this could be, with her husband at the war, and never a breath of sin about her." The storyteller made a number of quick token crosses upon her narrow breast. The wife, clasping her hands, said: "Oh, my goodness!" and the children listened in terror to the story of the devil. This Maryuta, they learnt, shut the devil up in her cellar by day, but at night he would squeal and beg to be set free, and let him out at night she did. And one day she gave birth to a baby. And when they were bathing the baby, it appears, one old woman could see it had a tiny tail no bigger than a thimble. And when folk gathered and fumigated the whole house with heather smoke, not a thing did they see, except that leading from the cellar, in the snow, there were hoof marks. The old woman, in her simplicity of soul, had failed to notice that, in the terms of her story, this must have occurred in summer, at hay-harvesting time, and the summer snow escaped the attention of her listeners, too.

In the morning, the beggars would rise early, at the same time as the wives, and set off God knew whither, and in their stead came others, wave upon wave of them, and to that twilight time of hunger no end could be seen.

Soon there was absolutely nothing to eat. Small stocks of corn accumulated before the war had been consumed long since, and the old women had swept the bins and boxes clean with grouse feathers. In houses where cows had been cut up for meat, there were potatoes to help survival. In addition to which, the women went to distant collective farms still producing grain, to barter goods. Fetching out of trunks festive things reminiscent of former days – shawls, kerchiefs, men's jackets, boots – they piled them on to sledges, and after a brief lament over it all, went purposefully to collect their bitter spoils. Ten pounds of grain for new calfskin boots, eighteen pounds of potatoes for a rich lace kerchief. The women kept back their tears, didn't haggle, and sledged home with their tiny amounts of grain, their counted-out potatoes. Their burdens being light, there was no creaking of sledges over the snow, and the roomy pre-war trunks very soon had even more room in them.

True, even here there were some laughs. One woman, in cheerful despair, bartered a bright-as-new and as yet unworn cashmere wedding veil for two earthenware pots of yoghurt, saying that at least she'd have a good blow-out for once. Another, after twenty kilometres in freezing weather, came home with a bottle of cabbage soup. Yet another, for a wad of crisp new State bonds, bought a lame hen. As the proverb has it: "Laughing or weeping, the same mouth does for both."

Darya had a good wool-mixture suit of Vanya's. He'd bought it three weeks before the war, and had hardly had any wear out of it before the dreaded express couriers came galloping, and the men were marching away, accordions playing, and the girls and women were howling at the edge of the village.

When things became unbearable and she was very sick at heart, she would bring this suit out of the hay loft and iron it, catching, though overlaid by the mustiness of the trunk, a faint whiff of her Vanya.

One day she noticed a button loose on the sleeve. Another time, turning out the pockets, she found a kopeck-piece and some tobacco dust. Smoking was something he'd taken to during his army training. And Darya sat long alone, much agitated, seeking relief in tears. She hid the tiny kopeck-piece in the sugar pot, and taking her time, so as to spin out the pleasure, sewed the button on the sleeve. She could not bring herself to go bartering with the other women, not even when her legs began to swell.

On the 1st of May, a neighbour, that grey-haired old gossip Misha, bought her goat from her. One half of the price Darya took from him in potatoes, the other half in cash. The cash, seventy-five roubles, Darya handed over to the financial agent, and the potatoes she also divided into two: one basket for eating, one for seed. So that she could, like all good folk, plant at least one little row. But to keep herself alive, she soon had to boil these in the samovar too, and when people started ploughing their kitchen gardens, she was desperate. She must plant at least one little row, at least one little half-row, and, mind finally made up, she went with the other women.

Vanya's suit she bartered for half a sack of potatoes, and taking a segment from each potato, planted one-and-a-half rows. On the basket of cut potatoes that remained, and cakes of weevil pupae, she fed herself until – incredible as it seems – the 8th of July.

*

The village had a warm, pleasing summer.

Each day Darya went off with the women mowing. In company, time passed more quickly, you were less hungry, and anguish, as it were, abated.

At breaks for rest, Darya would sit near the other women, warming her swollen legs in the sun, and feeling all the time like falling asleep. She seldom joined in the conversation, and at times she didn't notice the mosquito bites.

"You ought to go home, Darya dear, have a lie down," they would sometimes say, and she, rousing herself and ashamed of her weakness, would say softly, tenderly: "My head's spinning, girls, just spinning, spinning . . ."

Overhead the clouds filed by. Among the hot grasses, tirelessly, for all the world, grasshoppers chirped, and their chirping merged with the unrelenting ecstatically shrill din in her ears.

Again Darya was sleepily drooping her head, smiling at the caress of the breeze on her palsied brow, and with difficulty she got to her feet and took up her rake.

For the first minutes of work she thought she was going to fall. But again, gradually, to her own surprise, some sort of fresh strength came to her, and when she did set off home, it was with everyone else. On her way she, too, gathered the drying sorrel, and picked sweet, succulent stems of angelica from under bushes, peeling off the coarse outer skin in strips and eating the crisp flesh.

The sun, now large and red, was sinking towards the horizon. The cows were coming in from the pasture, and the corncrake was practising his call by the stream, as if there wasn't a war anywhere.

Once home, Darya began to feel better. She set the samovar to boil, putting in three or four of the cut potatoes. Her samovar came to the boil very quickly. She didn't bring it to the table, but left it on the hearth, and while eating her potatoes, looked at it and talked to it. "Just you give another gurgle, just you dare. There, now it's really off."

She'd chatted in just the same way to the goat and the little underfloor mouse. But the goat had long since been bought and slaughtered by neighbour Misha, and the little mouse didn't live under the floor now, and so she chatted to the samovar. "It won't do. You'll catch it in a minute! I'll come and close your chimney, then you'll stop."

The samovar composed itself, went over to producing a quiet, church-chant sort of sound, then something inside chirped softly, and after one final cheep, it fell silent.

Often, singly or in twos, the women would come and visit Darya, or the old, broken-in-half-looking hunchback Surganikha would drop in. The women would sometimes bring a pot of whey that hadn't been fed to the cattle, sometimes some leftover broth in a bowl, and Surganikha would treat her to a clover cake, taste and praise what Darya had baked, and drink a cup or two of hot water. They would sit long over the samovar, telling their dreams and complaining of their illnesses.

Two or three times that summer, grey, venerable old Misha came. Once he hafted an oven fork, and on another occasion he bound round a split scythe handle.

And always everyone asked whether there'd been a letter from Vanya, and learning that there hadn't, would cluck their tongues in sympathy and distress, and comfort Darya. "There will be one, Darya dear. Why should there not? There must be. Just think what war's like nowadays – all the men, ours and other people's, all mixed up. And the post; sometimes it doesn't get through."

"Yes, my dear, yes," Darya would cheerfully agree, dabbing her eyes with her apron.

"Then, again, take the bombings. Shouldn't wonder if they've lost count of the mail trains that don't arrive. And Vanya, maybe sometimes he's got nothing to write with, nothing to write on. It's not like home, you know, mother."

"No, my dear, it's not."

"If they've been taken into the thick of it, they've maybe no time to eat, those lads, let alone write a letter."

Darya herself did not go visiting other huts.

One day, when thundery rain had been threatening since early morning and hayricks had to be built, she was suddenly afraid that she'd left the samovar uncovered.

Lightning was already flashing directly above the village, a black cloud was bearing down on the white roofs, and with ebbing energy, Darya set off at a run for home, crossing herself at each clap of thunder, and cursing herself for not having covered the samovar with a tablecloth and closed the damper of the stove.

She had barely reached the hut when a deluge descended. The sky was one great peal of thunder; the corners of the darkened hut were lit by the smoky yellow light of the flashes. Weak with fear, Darya closed the damper, wrapped the samovar tightly in a linen tablecloth, and then came such a bang that, with no time to cross herself, she fell feebly to the floor and lost consciousness.

But the thunderstorm passed as quickly as it had come, creeping away beyond the forest ridge, and with gold drops still falling from the sky, the sun peeped out. Darya managed to drag herself just as far as the porch. Her head was spinning, her legs refusing to obey her. She gazed tenderly at the fresh, rain-washed grass, listened to the twittering of the white-breasted swallows, and cursed herself for forgetting to put a tub to catch water from the eaves. Weakness and a dull ache in her head did nothing to remove her sense of grievance against herself. And suddenly, softly, soundlessly, she started whispering something to herself, and had the strange feeling of being no longer Darya but someone else, and of being told off by this other Darya for not putting out the tub. It was a pleasant, easy, comforting sensation to be, as it were, watching and hearing herself, as if her body had become separate from her, and she now felt easy in her mind and happy.

The thunder died away in the distance completely. Bright, warm steam rose from the bright pure grass. The steep, bright rainbow was high, yet almost touchable. The broad band of unsullied iridescence described an enormous arc, descending in a green field, and osier beds in the shadow of the band shone pearly pink. Darya seemed to be trying to remember something and not succeeding. Her eyes lighted on an ancient pannier hanging on a wooden peg in the passage, and now, looking at it, slowly and with difficulty, she remembered.

Getting to her feet, and as if in a dream, she took the basket down, and slowly, supporting herself against the wall of the cowshed, she set off for the kitchen garden. She opened up the allotment, and went to her row. The potatoes were already showing plenty of greenery. It was good to see the fleshy, succulent little stalks, the rough broad leaves ready to be decked with pale-yellow flowers.

Kneeling, she dug trembling fingers into the earth, feeling and breaking from the roots the mother potato that had given life to those green stems. The tiny, fragile white roots had, she could see, no potato buds as yet.

She dug beneath another plant, then another, putting into the basket the black, limp segments of potato that she had planted. She counted eight, wiped them on grass, and returned, calm and contented, to her hut.

In the hearth stood the samovar, bright and cheerful as before a grand occasion.

She slowly brought a tub of water from the well, stripped half-a-dozen splinters off a log, but failed to kindle them.

In, noisily, walked Creepy. "Is the mistress at home?"

"She is, good man, she is. Come you in, Pashka. Sit yourself down."
She put a stool for him, but he didn't sit on it. He sat on the bench
at the table, opened his satchel and turned over papers, not looking
at Darya, who watched deferentially. Then, deftly, he sharpened a
pencil with a little knife. "Well, what about it, Comrade Rumyantseva?
Are we paying up, or aren't we? You are the only persistent defaulter
in the village. Measures will clearly have to be taken."

"It's a terrible thing, Pashka, but I've got no money at present. You
could wait just a bit, couldn't you?"

"I could not."

"You couldn't?"

"Not on any account."

Darya fell silent, sighed, and without knowing why, scratched the
tabletop with her finger, while Pashka looked the hut over in a
purposeful fashion and said: "I'll take an inventory."

"Yes, but you see, what . . . If . . . Well, it's up to you, good man."

Pashka spent a long time writing out some document, making a
carbon copy, and Darya waited patiently.

Afterwards they went around the hut together. Pashka himself
opened the storeroom, and while Darya stood in the door, raised the
lid of an aspenwood trunk, and looked under the bench. The storeroom
was dark, and he was constantly striking matches. "So, one trunk, one
old sieve. That won't do. Loom reeds . . . No good. Anything else?"

"There is, Pashka, yes. There's an empty kerosene bottle here, and
nine or so skeins of bark."

"That's not what I'm asking about." Pashka sneezed. "Any clothing,
any linen?"

"No. Only two-and-a-quarter pounds of wool I was going to make
into footwear for the winter."

"Where?"

"There." She handed him the wool, stuffed into an old cotton
pillowcase.

Nothing else in the storeroom, nor in the attic, nor in the dark
cellar smelling of mould, was of interest to Pashka. He went back into
the hut, opened the cupboard, inspected the sleeping bench and its
locker, and flung back the lid of the trap door by its ring, but there
was nothing more anywhere. "Here, Comrade Rumyantseva, your
signature to the document and the inventory."

"I've not got the schooling, Pashka."

Pashka had known anyway that Darya couldn't sign her name. He
tugged at the tags of each of his box-calf boots in turn, slipped his

papers into his satchel, and again not looking at Darya, said severely: "So, Comrade Rumyantseva."

Darya poured water into the samovar, and tried to light a shaving from a match of Pashka's, but he moved the match away, and having lit his cigarette, blew it out. Darya was at a loss. It was only when Pashka picked up the samovar and went to empty the water out that she burst into tears, and heading him off, pleaded: "Pashka, dear, how can I live with no samovar? Take the wool, but leave the samovar . . . I'll pray for you for ever."

But Pashka carried off both wool and samovar, and Darya sat down on the bench in tears. Her head was spinning again, splitting. With no samovar the hut was now completely unwelcoming and empty. Darya wept, but her tears, too, came to an end.

Outside the window, it stayed light for some time. Far beyond the forests the frightening thunder rumbled until late into the night. Gadflies flew in, and after buzzing about, flew out again. Others banged into the window, spent a long time beating their heads against the panes, and wearily fell silent.

Darya heard nothing of this. She devoured one of the potatoes that had exhausted itself in the ground, then another, and climbed on to her sleeping bench above the stove. There she lay, not knowing whether it was night, morning or evening outside, feeling her arms and legs growing weak.

She was still trying to separate reality from dream, but was quite unable to, and the distant thunder seemed like the din of a vast war. War, to Darya, took the form of two endless lines of soldiers with rifles. The soldiers, ours and the Germans', stood in lines facing one another, firing at each other in turn, and between theirs and ours lay level green grass. These lines of soldiers were lost to sight far away on the horizon, and Vanya, her son, was standing in full view on a little knoll, and for some reason was carrying no rifle. Darya was terrified, thinking he would be killed at any minute, standing there with no rifle, and tried in her torment to shout to him to grab his rifle, but no shout came. And in extreme alarm, she set off towards him at a run. She wanted to run faster, but her legs would not obey her, and something heavy, all-powerful, was stopping her from running to him. And slowly and inexorably the lines of soldiers moved farther and farther away.

Two or three days later, Surganikha, going to the shop to buy a whetstone for the scythes, saw Darya's samovar on the counter. Amazed, she went so far as to turn the tap. The samovar was, in truth, Darya's. "Oh dear, oh dear! They must have taken it," thought Surganikha. "That devil Creepy's taken the old woman's samovar!"

At haymaking, Surganikha told the other women about having seen Darya's samovar on the shop counter.

The other women groaned, out of sorrow for Darya. At which point it emerged that it was now more than two days since Darya had been to the fields, and their alarm grew.

"How much is it?"

"I say, you girls, do you think she's all right? Darya, I mean."

"Creepy by name, creepy by nature."

"Pig of a man."

"Oughtn't we to buy it for her?" someone asked, and frightened at the suggestion, the women fell silent. But then, one after the other, they again groaned, and got talking, and somehow it was decided that there was nothing for it: the whole village must club together and buy the samovar back.

The shop stayed open in the evenings at haymaking time. The women made their collection, bought back the samovar, and, well pleased, set off together to Darya's hut.

However, the gate had a padlock on it, the one that didn't lock, and a birch stick was protruding from the staple.

"She's gone, the poor dear thing, that's clear. Gone begging," said Surganikha.

They opened the gate, and went around the empty house. It was all swept, the cupboard was shut, the oven forks were standing tidily by the stove. Surganikha saw at once that the pannier wasn't in the house or in the little passage.

The women put the samovar in its usual place, sighed, and left, locking up with the same padlock.

"She's gone, gone into the wide world."

"Maybe Christian folk will not forsake her."

"One amongst others can never be poor, only one alone."

"True."

"Beggar's scrip, like prison bars, will be with men for ever, they say," Surganikha said, inserting the same birch stick in the staple. "God send that the war will end and life be as it was."

"And maybe dear old Darya will come back."

Haymaking took its course.

Hundreds of beggars passed through the village that summer, old men, children, old women. But not once was Darya seen, not by anyone. Her hut stood alone. The row of potatoes for that hut flowered and withered, a dozen or so rotten planks slipped from the yard roof. But Darya did not return to the village.

The women questioned beggars as to whether they'd seen or come across her somewhere, but nobody had.

One day, in winter, a rumour reached the village that, some ten kilometres off, in a hay loft on forest wasteland, they'd found an old woman dead. They'd gone for hay, and found her. From the fact that the scraps in her basket were completely dried out, and she was dressed for summer, the women, as one, decided that it must be their Darya – indeed, that it could not be anyone else. But old Misha merely mocked them. "Yes," he said, "you blow on a puddle, and you say, yes, that must, simply must, be our old Darya. But is Mother Russia really short of such old women? Try counting them, these old women, and there'll very likely not be numbers enough to number them. But all you can say is 'Darya, Darya!' These old women . . ."

The women, defending their firm and clear opinion, made despairing gestures, saying that he, Misha, should sit quiet and stop arguing. It *was* Darya in the hay loft, and nobody else. Misha was dismissive.

"Well, off to God in heaven with you, you chattering magpies; there's no getting the better of you."

And indeed, there was no point in one old man's arguing with them.

And who knows? Maybe they were right. They, women that is, almost always are, especially when there's a war like that going on.

Translated by George Bird

IRINA POVOLOTSKAYA

The Rosy-Fingered Dawn

There we both were: "I'm at the chemist's!"
"But I was looking for you at the pictures!"

Words to the tune of an old foxtrot

YOUR AUTHOR KNOWS nothing about agriculture. Once he spent
the whole summer tending a radish, but it bolted, reaching out
for the sunlight, its leaves in riot and its feeble straggly roots like
threadworms in the rain. In his garden three solitary flowers have
spent three winters unsheltered. They huddle in affront, muttering:
"The scoundrel, the scoundrel . . ."

But I'll take a chance all the same, and tell you a story that does have a
connection with agriculture, in a way. In the background to this agricultural narrative, or to be more exact, in its central field, a boat looms up: a
river steamer, nothing out of the ordinary, the usual sort, white-painted,
with a restaurant in the bows and another in the stern.

Over the fifty years during which the doomed love of my very
ordinary heroes runs from start to finish, the boats that ply the rivers
have changed far less than other machines, their blood brothers, and
the old swan simile still exactly fits the magnificent grace of their
motion.

Once the author's delight in such a boat nearly caused him to
swallow whole mouthfuls of sludgy Volkhov river water. A magically
white steamer first floated in view above the grass and flowers of the
bank, then, rounding the peninsular, struck up a tune, like a great
symphony orchestra, in the middle of the river. Cows lifted their
horned heads, and the cowherd made his ritual exclamation, proving
once more how true is the general belief that river boats have an
extraordinary effect on the Russian psyche. No doubt the roots of this
excitement can be traced back to the time when we, that is our
ancestors, idly grazed our cows and got our children in subconscious
expectation of the Varangians' arrival, which would put us on the path
to statehood and set everything – everything even yet unfinished –
in motion.

But the author is cowardly! How timidly he hesitates, how fearful he is to miss out what is most important. How easily he lets himself be distracted in the hope that he may not have to finish what he has begun. In fact he would never have written anything at all, had it not been for insomnia or the demon of some kind, roused by boredom, which climbs on to his windowsill of a moonlit night – a night like this one, in fact – had it not been for Memory, God rot her . . .

Take the soul-stirring word "pro-to-pla-sm" for example, which once uttered, will exist for ever. "Protoplasm" – that was exactly the word my grandmother's cousin Uncle Sasha used about me in my childhood, when my grandmother made me climb on a chair and recite one of Turgenev's glorious nature descriptions.

Or perhaps my third cousin twice removed was talking about Turgenev? It is by no means impossible, after all, that he disliked the great author, especially if a certain lady named Anechka did not . . . For Uncle Sasha had a difficult character, cross-grained, as they would have said in the old days.

Sometime long ago Uncle Sasha had been young. He was the eldest son in the large family of a landowner in Perm. His father was a widower, with masses of daughters and one other son, Sasha's younger brother Petka, a lively and feckless youth who dreamt of becoming the pilot of a flying machine, but vanished into oblivion along with the fragments of his absurd vehicle. Uncle Sasha had been studying abroad at the time. He got back to Russia just before war broke out, itching for great deeds, and found his elderly father in the clutches of a soubrette, his sisters still spinsters and bewailing Petka's fate, and the estate gone to rack and ruin. It was summer on the Kama, the air was full of nightingales . . . Soon he left home again. Agriculture was what Uncle Sasha had been studying during his time abroad, and so he quickly found work as the estate manager for a rich relative. But a month later he had a terrible quarrel with him, a real exchange of insults. Apparently his extraordinary pride had been stung by the relative's suspicion that Uncle Sasha was hoping for a little something in his will.

In truth there was no "apparently" and "suspicion" about it, for the relative had no children and no wife, and he was sinking fast. His disease was incurable: "consumption", they told the girls, but the men knew how things really stood.

Well, anyway, Uncle Sasha came back home, forgetting even to pack in his fury. His luggage came on after him soon enough, but that was later, when his sisters' friend Anechka quarrelled in her turn with Uncle Sasha and went rushing off to Kazan.

When she was little, he called her the "Tatar girl" because of her narrow dark-blue eyes set in her sallow high-cheekboned face. He thought she was ugly, but that was his mistake. She turned into a real beauty . . . They used to play croquet together in the garden. He knew the rules better than she did, of course, and took care to let her know it. She lost her temper, but he still would not let her alone. So she picked up the mallet in her pretty little hand and with startling force flung it – no, not at his head – into the lilac hedge which bordered the croquet lawn. She had wild blood in her, did Anechka; maybe the "Tatar" bit was right. Her parents were merchants in Kazan.

It was then, in those long-forgotten times, that they began to argue. Anechka had a stubborn belief in the need for social change and had no time at all for mysticism or fashionable decadence. Half-jokingly he contradicted her, and was privately delighted by the red spots of indignation which burnt on her enchanting cheeks. It was all a game: he would be as provocative as he knew how. Once, he said that he loathed Tolstoy, and she got breathless with fury. But at that point his sisters all joined in, and the daughters of the parish priest (who had poured scorn on their poor father since Tolstoy's excommunication) added their voices to the chorus. Anechka shut her mouth straightaway: she wanted to be a soloist or nothing. He tried to sting her into a response, but his efforts seem not to have been up to much. Such at least was the message in her eyes and contemptuously wrinkled nose. In vain did he expand on Dostoevsky and eschatology, on the Russian peasant and systems of land tenure and even – for reasons best known to himself – on the stallion at her cousin's stud farm, who (the stallion not the cousin) was somehow not properly thoroughbred about the rump. But even this last bit of idiocy was received in fastidious maidenly silence.

On other days, in other years, how he hated her for that mulishness, but now, in the spring of 1914, he could see only her glorious face and was certain she was silent for his sake, as before she had argued for his sake – yes, that was it!

Afterwards the young ladies drank their tea with dollops of cream and sang to an accompaniment banged out on the out-of-tune baby grand by the eldest daughter. In silence Anechka moved to the swing at the edge of the terrace, in silence she sat down and began to swing back and forth, one-two, her white flannel skirt beating time softly and catching on her white lacey stockings.

Uncle Sasha was the first to walk off. He had a glass of port in his father's study – it was empty, his father was off in Kazan with his soubrette. But when he'd finished his glass of rich ruby liquid, he went back to the young ladies. Nothing had changed: she was still sitting on the swing, face like a Scythian idol. Uncle Sasha froze in the door a moment, then leapt to the piano and ripped his sister's hands from the keys, planting a smacking kiss just above her wrist, and started to thump out the chorus of a stupid popular song which had just come into his head. "Annette, oh ho . . . not yes, not no . . . Annette, God bless, not no, not yes . . ." The young ladies were convulsed, but Anechka gave him not one look, the baggage, she just went on swinging with her Tatar stoicism.

When at length they all went off to their rooms, he went too, but he soon realized he would not be able to sleep, for he was desperately in love with Anechka. He dressed quickly and went into the garden. Anechka, too, could not sleep, it seemed. Light reflected from her room lay etched in a neat triangle on the damp grass of the lawn. He formed the word "Anechka" with his lips. At that moment the light went out. "She's gone to bed," he guessed, but for some reason he took one more turn round the house and stopped once more before her darkened window before going back to his room.

Suddenly there was a crunch of gravel on the path. Anechka was standing two paces away from him. He took her chilly hand and led her behind him, stumbling on the thick roots of the centenarian limes, led her down to the river, which opened out before them with each step they took, glittering and stretching to the pale May sky. The deep sound of a ship's hooter made them quicken their steps, and when at length they ran out on to the broad sandbank, they saw the ship right in front of them.

Brightly and festively its many lights glimmered as it sailed on the calm water, as solitary as a night-time walker on a road. The engine thumped dully and the sound of the water was fresh and musical as it slapped against the metal body. The ship seemed to quiver with tension and excitement . . . A sharp sense of fatefulness cut into Uncle Sasha and Anechka. There was no mistaking it: this was meant. Anechka groaned softly. Uncle Sasha pressed her to him gingerly, but she broke away from him and, fully dressed but for her light summer shoes – she had trouble finding them afterwards in the warm sand – ran headlong into the river towards the boat . . . Her gauzy skirts spread out like a bell on the water, flowing round her like a ballerina's tutu. Laughing with pleasure, she raced back to Uncle Sasha.

"Madwoman . . ." he said to her. "Darling . . . Madwoman . . . Mine . . . Mine . . ."

"Madwoman, darling, yours" – she seemed to agree, eyes flashing black in the darkness. And she shivered not only from cold, but from a mixture of shame and delight, as he covered her slim, quickstepping feet with kisses.

In the morning they went out into the meadows in a droshky. That was another thing people liked to do in those days.

The heat beat down mercilessly. Uncle Sasha was driving. Anechka had pulled her white hat down low over her brows, and beads of sweat glimmered on her upper lip. The hat tumbled into the road as he kissed her. The horses swished their tails lazily, and the gadflies hummed – summer had come.

"Let's go to the Crimea," Uncle Sasha said. "To Yurzuf."

"It's too hot there now," Anechka said. "Spring would be better."

"Autumn," he said and kissed her. "After the wedding, in the autumn."

"Whose wedding?" she said, screwing up her eyes, but he kissed her again. "I'm going to Switzerland."

"Why?"

"Why not?" she laughed. "Would you like to come too?"

"Where?"

"Switzerland!"

"I've been there – and anyway, Switzerland is boring."

The horses jerked forward, covering the hat with dust. But that wasn't the quarrel. The quarrel was later, on the terrace, when Anechka, dressed for dinner, sat down on that wretched swing again.

Now it was her turn to talk. After she got back from her travels – and, please note, Uncle Sasha was expected to wait for her – they would begin work together . . . Anechka had schemes of transporting fruit from the south to the north, she had socialist convictions about all kinds of things. Uncle Sasha was silent. She narrowed her eyes to slits . . .

At length he asked: "So you think the peasants will eat your fruit and like it?"

She flared up, but a demon seemed to have taken hold of Uncle Sasha: he liked making her angry. All the more so since listening to her idiotic speeches gave him a sense of possessing them and her, and he was delighted by this new sensation.

"'In the sweat of thy face shalt thou eat bread.' It's the scriptural curse," hissed Uncle Sasha, no longer taking good care what he said.

"And the most important thing in women is mystery, indefinability. It's difficult enough to preserve that in marriage anyway, but if you labour hand in hand . . ." He burst out laughing. "Let me out! I'd not stand it for more than a month!"

She said that there would be no need for him to stand it, she would leave straightaway herself, this minute.

She did not even stay for dinner, despite the sisters' pleas. He hid behind the portière and watched his restless lady-love go. How like a thoroughbred mare this Tatar girl was – and he adored horses. How proudly she shook her head at him, believing it was for the last time! How he shook with joy in his hiding place when she flashed her eyes in victory at him, consumed by pride and self-love!

How well he knew the gloomy Gothic hall of the best flower shop in Kazan, the stifling greenhouse smell behind the heavy wooden door with its brass hinges; and there, in the half-light, coloured by the fashionable spherical shades with their dangling ornaments, behind which that ugly new invention, the Edison lamp, was modestly concealed, there Uncle Sasha had seen a living magic goblet – a little bell of wondrous purity, two lady's hands fused at the wrist in the mystical eroticism of an oriental dance; the white petals of a unique flower with a golden dusting of stamens and a flaming pistil.

How vividly he imagined all this, sensed it, as he hid behind the portière . . . But he could not guess, could not, whether perhaps something quite different might happen or he might not recognize this mystery when it did happen. Might it not be like the fairy tale about the three wishes? The soldier and the devil strike a bargain, and the wishes come true; the devil tries no tricks, yet the soul is still lost . . .

So the owner of the flower shop, Uncle Sasha's friend Zakhar Abramovich, plump beyond his years and with the beautiful dark eyes of the convert Jew, chooses lilies for Uncle Sasha with his own hand . . . Lilies, for what other flowers could the infatuated Uncle Sasha possibly choose? Zakhar Abramovich chooses the flowers, seeing all, silently guessing the future, sealing his fate, and Anechka's, and Uncle Sasha's; the red-haired freckly assistant smiles ingratiatingly and wraps the flowers passed to him by his master's sapphire-ringed hand. And now our heroine herself, Anna Nikitichna, Anechka, is burying her golden head in the flowers in that absurd way women have, sniffing and raising her eyes to Uncle Sasha, her nose sprinkled with yellow pollen . . .

Why did they shoot the archduke? Why did they kill Zakhar Abramovich two years later? Why did the gingery assistant vanish to parts unknown – quite by chance, by some oversight on the part of Providence or that Emperor of Darkness, who had just appeared in Uncle's musings – whilst Uncle Sasha and Anechka survived, and, indeed, lived on and on?

Having survived the war, and then a year's prison sentence in Nizhny-Novgorod when the tsarist officers were purged, Uncle Sasha found himself free again by a happy chance; but, giving rein to the contrariness which had always marked his character, he chose not to go to Moscow, though his youngest sister was summoning him there – she had a job in Narkompros. But neither did he remain in Nizhny, where he could have lodged with his aunt on his mother's side and found himself a sinecure in a Soviet institution. Instead he went home, that is, to his father's estate. The house was still standing; clearly the local "revolutioniks" (so Uncle Sasha called everyone in the new regime from top to bottom without discrimination) were sober, sensible individuals. Incidentally, this neologism "revolutioniks" had been the occasion for one of Uncle Sasha's endless quarrels with Anechka. He had heatedly, though without regard for the rules of etymology, assured her that the word "revolutionary" was an absurdity. It was the suffix -ary which had provoked our hero's sardonic irritation, and all Anechka's angry, and well-founded, retorts on the score of "apothecary" or "luminary" were in vain.

All his life Uncle Sasha had been "gainfully employed in the service of his motherland" – so he would himself again and again assert. First he had worked as an accountant on the state farm; then, much later, as an agronomist there, and when the big house was turned from a school into a children's sanatorium, he married one of the lady doctors.

His sudden return, so soon after the Civil War, to what had been his father's estate, had surprised many people. But one can even cope with surprises, and over the years our Uncle Sasha became an indispensable fixture in local life. Besides, he was an outstandingly good agronomist – like the ones you can see on that television programme *An Hour on the Farm*. "Take a look at so-and-so," they say. "He's still quite young, but he knows a thing or two, reads poetry in his spare time, knows the soil, and he's not going to go rushing off to town the day after tomorrow, works every hour God sends and, more to the point, he's raised the crop yield." Funnily enough, when Uncle Sasha was running things the crop yields really were good: both during collectivization and later, after the war . . . (That was the phrase Uncle Sasha used to use: "when I was running things at home . . .".) All right, so his harvests didn't get his picture in the papers, but then again, who cares? For, long after he got back, if he met one of the old women on a forest path or in the standing corn, and there was no one around to see, she would give a low bow, or if she were a bit younger and bolder, even kiss his hand – "If it isn't the master, good day to ye, yer honour." There were people who thought that was his main reason for staying put so long – and foremost amongst them was Anechka, that damnable Lilith of our far from biblical narrative.

"Lilith", because the place of Eve was now taken by the lady doctor from the children's sanatorium.

Anechka was quite sure that Uncle Sasha's motivation for not leaving his home was low and despicable. Oh, and how she despised him for it! Later, that is – in 1921, when they finally did get in touch with each other (not without the aid of her allies, his sisters), and it turned out both were alive and, as it happened, living not so far apart as might have been imagined – for one might have expected him, at least, to be in Constantinople, if not in Paris. Before plunging into the dark hungry sleep which was all she, like most regional Young Communist League organizers, had a chance to enjoy, Anechka gave herself over to charming fantasies of his slim elegant figure dressed in white flannels, his little moustache above the mouth she herself had mocked as an "aristo's", and, as she finally sank into sleep, the tender despotism of his mouth allied to his schoolboyish clumsiness. Well, that is probably not all that she imagined after those six years which they had both somehow survived.

I expect that you think they had not met in all that time, for how otherwise had they not united two lives so constantly yearning for unity? But you would be wrong. They had met, and on two occasions. The first was in 1915, when he snatched one day's leave by a miracle, and they spent the whole time sitting in opposite corners of a hotel room, idiotically mute. The other was at the end of 1916, when he got a week's leave to collect his George Medal, and they made up for lost time. The war had sharpened Anechka's socialist convictions out of all recognition, whilst Uncle Sasha's patriotic monarchism had hardened in the trenches.

Anyway, in 1921 they had a ritual exchange of quite meaningless letters. Though one thing of substance *was* arranged: they were to meet in the autumn. He would come to Nizhny to visit his aunt; she had a friend living there too. Judging by their letters, it was these visits to the aunt and the friend which were the only purpose behind their meeting, now inexorably approaching.

Here again, asking Uncle Sasha why he had not gone to Kazan as soon as he knew she was there, what on earth had stopped him – or, God forbid, interrogating Anechka on the same subject – would be as much of a waste of time as cross-questioning Fate. We are not in the theatre. We have spent enough time discussing how and why as it is . . . What use is it examining other people's lives, when you can't even get to know your own, no matter how many questions you ask it?

. . . How he started towards her in that louse-ridden, lumpish throng when he caught sight of her standing on her own to one side, hands raised to her neck in agitation! How his poor heart pounded, as if in pain, when he saw her inexpressibly "Grecian" outline, the curve from hip to knee – an amphora, a Cretan goddess, God knew!

How magnificently she perched on her pedestal above the crowd, without a trace of self-consciousness, looking for him only; hoping not to miss him, fearing she would, hoping he would not miss her, fearful he would!

But though she had given her whole being to looking for him, she (as so often happens) did in fact overlook him, missed him in the crowd. He ran to her, jostling others as he ran, but she still did not see him, and only when he was close by, an arm's length, when he reached out and touched the hem of her skirt – she was standing high up – only then did she see him, let out a gasp, go still paler than before. Then she frowned and plunged towards him, dirty and unshaven from the journey as he was.

"Sasha!"

But in a flash, the impulse once past, her usual arrogance returned. She narrowed her bright eyes and asked off-handedly: "Going to your aunt's first?"

"Yes." He too was coming to grips with his agitation. "Of course."

Anechka said nothing about the splendid breakfast and coffee which it had cost her such time and effort to assemble in these times of food shortage, nor did she mention that her friend was out at the moment . . .

And when at length our hero, shaved and perfumed with the fragrant Houbigant his aunt had brought back from her last trip to Paris, reached the wretched room lit by one narrow internal window on the fourth floor of a hideous tenement block, Anechka was alone no longer.

Her friend Fira, a long-nosed girl in a red scarf, had got back from

work and was fiddling about meaningfully with the primus. She gave
Uncle Sasha an unfriendly stare, pursing the scarlet bow of her lips as
she sniffed suspiciously at his Parisian chic. She was boiling with
revolutionary contempt.

"The name's Esfir Zinovevna," Anechka's friend announced.

"There's no such name as Esfir," Uncle Sasha said immediately,
locking eyes with her. Exactly so does a well-trained dog seize a
stick even when not wanting to: out of habit. Reflexes, damn
them!

"Now *Esther* certainly exists – a wonderful biblical name," Uncle
Sasha continued. "The point is that in the course of its long travels
round the earth your race has simply forgotten its own language, and
now only has the corrupt German of the shtetls to call its own."

He finished this statement at a gabble, for behind his back he
suddenly heard Anechka give a low, agonized wail from her corner as
if she had violent toothache.

"My name is Esfir!" the "she-revolutionik" snapped. She had taken
an instant dislike to him. What on earth could her golden-haired friend
see in this dandified bourgeois down on his luck!

All three of them sat there till late. His hatred for himself and
Anechka mounting, he squabbled endlessly with this Fira who would
not call herself by her proper name. At last, voice hoarse, he went back
home to his aunt's. True, just before he left Fira ostentatiously went
out into the corridor of the communal flat to sleep on top of a trunk,
leaving them alone at last. Worn out and furious, head propped on
his long fingers which already had the dessicated look of an old man's,
he smoked his cheap tobacco with loathing. Anechka sat opposite him
on the bed – the only thing there was for her to sit on. Before that
dreadful young chit Fira had gone out, both girls had sat there
together, wrinkling their noses at the tobacco smoke, eyes dazed with
fatigue and watering with contempt.

Anechka was silent, and when Uncle Sasha got up from his stool
and kissed her soft ringless hand with its nails gnawed to the quick in
frustration, she snatched it away in embarrassment and hid it in the
pocket of her cardigan.

"So I'm off now, Anna Nikitichna," he said, phrasing it as a question.

"Of course." She screwed up her eyes and nodded.

"See you tomorrow."

For some reason she did not answer, simply shaking her head. For
so long he was to remember – indeed, he never forgot – how she sat
on the bed that night, head sunk on her shoulder as though her neck

were broken, as he gave her a farewell bow on the threshold and opened the door into the dark corridor.

And there in the corridor, of course, he tripped over Fira's trunk, bruising his knee on the sharp metal edge under its cover of cloth. There wasn't a whisper from that direction. He knew full well that she was awake, that she was watching him in the darkness with her round cat's eyes . . .

Then he had trouble with the outer door: he could not find the lock by feel, and kept dropping his soggy spluttering matches. But at last he mastered it, and went out on to the tiny landing where moonlight was streaming through the broken window – the only one in the building which light could come through, for the others in this hellhole had all been blocked up with plywood long since.

Stumbling a last time on the broken steps, he went out into the street and, despite himself, looked upwards – to where he thought her window must be. The movement brought back a vivid, bitter memory of that wonderful lilac-scented night and the crunch of her light tread on gravel. He even stopped for a moment and waited, although what was there to wait for?

When he reached his aunt's house at around dawn he heard the sound of a ship's hooter; for this was a river town too.

The following day he did visit her after all, but she said she had to leave. Whether it was the truth or a decision taken in anger was unclear, and it hardly mattered, but once more he pleaded with her, standing before her in that hateful room.

"No, stay!"

"Why?" She smiled coldly, appearing not to notice what lay behind his question: something evil had got into her today.

And again Uncle Sasha begged her ineptly: "Come back with me!"

"So I suppose you mean I should leave my work here and decamp to the . . . bosom of your family?"

Anechka looked incredibly beautiful despite her sleepless night – she had even managed to wave her fringe; heaven knows how she had made time. Her eyes sparkled. She was sickened inside by her show of coquetry, by her inability to curb it – and more, by her own helplessness before this new life which had so abruptly and irremediably put an end to the old. What was more she had no money. What was more that young idiot Fira obviously had no intention of removing herself to the trunk; there she was sitting on the windowsill next to the dried herring in newspaper bought to provision Anechka on her journey back.

But the author should not expend too much effort on describing the scene which was to follow, judging by the twitching at the corner of Uncle Sasha's mouth and the grim expression in Anechka's eyes after she had uttered the words "the bosom of your family", but before he had made his response "You – suffragette!"

The years had not softened their characters, only enhanced their vocabularies. In their letters to Sasha's sisters they would write things about each other, sometimes, that made those good ladies cry – since all their lives the sisters loved both Sasha and Anechka dearly; Sasha's wife, on the other hand, or "the lady doctor" as they called her, they most heartily disliked.

Incidentally, the lady doctor was a handsome woman; later, when the Civil War ended, the local executive committee chairman fell in love with her. He was a bachelor of oriental extraction, who could hardly tell the difference between wheat and rye. Or so Uncle Sasha asserted, face dark with rage; the lady doctor did not turn a hair. In general she had a talent for not noticing things it was better for her not to. And although she returned his sisters' cool feelings, she never said so. It is impossible to say for sure whether she knew about the correspondence between Uncle Sasha and Anechka, which lasted all their lives – and when they were not writing to each other they were writing to his sisters, though there were unexpected gaps from time to time, which according to the teaching of the Ancients must of course have been caused by cataclysmic events in the astral worlds, where planets keep crashing into each other and exploding – rather like people in the queue outside the wine shop by the Tishinsky market.

In the wake of one such cosmic event Uncle Sasha went and married the lady doctor who knew how to hold her tongue. She had little taste for conversation either – not a talker in any sense. All her husband's many and various relations were encapsulated for her in the skinny, ascetic person of the oldest sister Nadezhda, her pernickety genteel poverty, her tall one-eyed husband, a violinist from the Orenburg opera house. The lady doctor was infuriated by the persistent atmosphere of unhappiness rising from the pair of them and their children: the children were skinny and nervous, and the younger one even had a tic. The lady doctor – a paediatrician as it happens – thought health was the most important thing in life. She doted on babies above all, those "little bundles of fluff". She had produced four of her own by the time the Second War started, and if Uncle Sasha had not protested vigorously, and if it had not been for the war, she would no doubt have had a stab at getting a medal for her efforts in that line.

Sasha's sisters each wrote to their brother once a month, and Sasha would reply to every letter punctiliously. The lady doctor thought privately that her husband would have been better writing some kind of dissertation than wasting time on such fripperies. But she was wrong there, for Uncle Sasha had a hearty contempt for dissertation writing, if only because Anechka had been awarded a high degree.

After graduating from the Agricultural Academy in Moscow (a course on which she had embarked in order to rile her non-lover in her turn), Anechka had gone off to some institute in Poltava, where she had launched into a detailed study of grassland crop rotation. All in order to spite Uncle Sasha, who ground his teeth when he heard the name "Williams" – and Williams was not even the worst of them!

"'Bonnets in the air'!" Uncle Sasha would yell on receipt of the predictable missive from one of his sisters, full of gush about Anechka's dissertation and the fête which had followed it. "The empty-headed little patriot! Squatting on her branched wheat like a mermaid beached on a rock!"

It was nonsense about the branched wheat, of course: Anechka had written her dissertation on clover. But the lady doctor seemed oddly delighted by the vicious sallies Uncle Sasha launched into whenever he got a letter from one of his sisters. Naturally she had no idea what was getting him so het up (or then again, perhaps she did), but at any rate over all the years of their marriage she had only once asked him who Anechka was.

That was after the war, after Anechka's dissertation was finished – but here begins an independent story within our shaggy-dog story about Anechka and Uncle Sasha. A globe within a globe, like those ivory toys made by the Chinese as presents for the generalissimo, as the Friendship of Nations took its unpredictable course – a smaller one inside the larger, and so on *ad infinitum* – and just so my tale runs on, who knows where . . .

It was then – after the journey about which the reader and the lady doctor have heard nothing, after the journey arranged without warning, in secret – when Uncle Sasha had been about to set off to the Crimea as usual, but had changed his mind, repacked his suitcase at dead of night and sneaked off to Kazan, and then arrived back home three days later, again without warning – it was then that the lady doctor had asked, by the way as it were: "So who is Anechka?"

"Cousin of mine" – the lie was uttered defensively, but then he added with a clear conscience: "Gone mad on clover, the minx!" And when even this seemed putting it too mildly, "It's her time of life," he said.

"Sasha!" the lady doctor chided, pointing at her daughter, who was all ears (she was the youngest child, with bright brown eyes – "Just like her father," as the lady doctor would explain with a sigh to her lady friends).

It appears that Anechka had herself put forth the olive branch and encouraged this journey. It was she who had wished to kiss and make up; and, after a conference in Gorky which she had attended as the Poltava institute's representative, she had sent Uncle Sasha a note. True, if I am not mistaken, Uncle Sasha had just prior to that sent her congratulations on her birthday via his sister Nadya, but it is not at all clear whether the latter had passed them on. For she had enough to preoccupy her on her own account: fussing now about her one-eyed violinist husband losing his job in the orchestra, now about her son being called up . . .

When Anechka suggested a trip down the river (as a conference delegate she had the right to book tickets on the steamer), Uncle Sasha, surprisingly enough, responded immediately. He did not go on his usual autumn trip to Gurzuf, as he had every year in the last twenty-five (excluding the war, of course). Anechka loved the Crimea as much as he did, but *she* always went there in the spring. Perhaps we may suppose that they did think of one another despite everything when they scrambled out of the stifling heat of the charabanc on to the narrow Gurzuf square after hours of torment on the winding Crimean roads, perhaps we may suppose that each experienced a similar feeling of liberty as, six months apart, they walked down to the sea with its famous backdrop, on which the shadowy outline of the Ayu-Dag is sketched.

No doubt each wished the other would give way, give up his or her dreadful behaviour. That Uncle Sasha, head still shaved in the fashion of the 1930s, would suddenly appear when the almonds were in bloom and stay with one of the friends with whom he always stayed when he was in Gurzuf, the Tatar or the honourable old gent who had once been the president of a club for mountain guides. Or that, in autumn, Anechka would suddenly appear in the midst of the famous juniper thicket that edged the serpentine hillside path . . . But even then (my spiteful reader observes), even then they would never have met; or else things would have continued just as before. And in fact that was exactly what did happen on that boat trip which I have just mentioned: true to themselves, they had a terrible quarrel. He had a fit of jealousy over her feelings for Trofim Denisovich Lysenko. (Here I had better explain: that very same biologist and academician who was enjoying fame at the time for his work with branched wheat.) So there we are!

When Uncle Sasha and Anechka quarrelled it was always hard to tell who had started it: to an outside observer it looked as though a tide of black water had welled up from the depths of their tormented souls – a fatal, annihilating tide – and then subsided, leaving the river banks bare and battered.

But anyway . . . "Why, Anna Nikitichna, you haven't changed a bit!' said Uncle Sasha to Anechka on the quay when she turned up, late, in a grey Pobeda with chequerboard markings on the door, to find him waiting there with his Chinese mackintosh flung over his shoulder.

This was a comment made for effect, not meant to bear scrutiny – and, in fact, that very minute he noticed the fine web of wrinkles on her Tatar cheekbones and felt a stab of pity for the inroads made by the years on her, as on him. But immediately Anechka's eyes glittered vengefully, with the old dangerous light, and he said again, voice not quite steady this time: "You haven't changed a bit, Anna Nikitichna!" – and this time the statement had a greater flavour of sincerity.

His sisters informed him she was still unattached, *still*, they would say, dropping their voices, and always, but always, giving him meaning looks. And they would never forget to mention it in their letters, too. "Anechka is still unattached."

Anechka had a new hairstyle. Being single, she took good care of herself, and that was especially obvious now, in this crowd of provincials. He had always been struck by how she stood out in a crowd, and he was so now as she strode towards him with steps whose lightness the years had done nothing to decrease. Her hair was done in two plaits round her head and pinned at the temples. She still had the look of a finely bred horse . . . He was tormented by the riddle of why she should have stayed single and independent; sometimes he tried to imagine her life and would often fantasize about a bastard son. Yes, it had to be like that: the "unattached" his sisters insisted on did not convince him for a minute. And what was Anna Nikitichna thinking? Who could say what thoughts flashed every night through her head with its covering of now not so blonde locks? But at this moment she was thinking that she didn't look half bad in spite of everything.

What self-deception is possible as one looks in the mirror, glad that one looks more intelligent than when one was younger! Oh, one says to oneself, one's mouth was nondescript then, one had round shoulders – hunched to hide the embarrassing, unfamiliar bosom . . . But only those who remember otherwise can tell of the indescribable charm of those pouting lips on the sweet, bland young face.

Happily, Uncle Sasha did not remember the former Anechka as he looked at the new one. And this new Anechka was softened and charmed by the autumnal beauty of the river banks, and also by seeing Uncle Sasha face to face again. She sighed faintly.

Her square-toed Czech patent shoes (she'd just bought them, at the conference) set off her long slim legs a treat as she followed Uncle Sasha down the central carpet of the ship's restaurant, sniffing in pleasurable anticipation of supper. A tangy scent wafted from the plates of pickled herring and onion, nestling by carafes of chilled vodka veiled in droplets, which the waiters carried past on their silvery nickel trays . . .

Swishing her pleated skirt, Anechka sank gratefully into the heavy armchair which Uncle Sasha had gallantly pulled out for her, hitched her patent handbag to the back with affected negligence (what luck, it matched her shoes *exactly*) and sat smiling vaguely into space.

The champagne went to her head immediately, and this was when she decided for some reason (but then again, why shouldn't she have decided to share her happiness with an old friend?) – decided to tell Uncle Sasha about her dissertation. Knowing how conceited Anechka was, his sisters had kept quiet, in their letters to her, about Uncle Sasha's virulent tirades on that very subject. She poured out all the amusing details of the fête and, tipsy from lack of habit, threw caution to the winds as she switched to an excited analysis of the recent conference in Gorky and the talks given by all the most famous scientists in the country. Then she suddenly clapped her hands and with girlish gaucherie requested a bottle of that delicious cream soda.

Uncle Sasha called the waiter and ordered some cream soda as she had asked, but Anechka's behaviour, all her little airs, suddenly struck him as affected and overdone. She failed to notice his morose expression as he listened to all her "mad euphoria" and delirious chatter on the subject of corn and clover and soil types, and how harvest yields were getting better and better (when he knew damn well there had been a drought for the last two years). He was getting more and more angry. His hand shook with rage as he poured out the vodka and drank glass after glass – he had long stopped pouring her any or clinking glasses. Now she was nattering on about Trofim Denisovich's visit to the institute – yes, that was what she called him, "Trofim Denisovich".

It came into Uncle Sasha's head that she might be fifty years old, but she was still a damn fine woman, and everyone knew that the single ladies were a lot more mettlesome than the married ones, and if this was the way she was carrying on with Sasha, who was nothing out of the ordinary, God knew what she might have been up to with an academician . . . He started to beat a tattoo on the table with his fist.

Eventually even Anechka noticed the strange look in his eyes and stopped in her tracks.

"What is it, Sasha?" she asked anxiously.

Well, there you have it, that stupid forgetfulness of women's. If that is the right word! Try a simple test: stop a woman in the street, any woman, and ask her if she can tell her right from her left. If she doesn't get all huffy or fail to understand the question, she'll answer it – but she'll have to think for a minute first. And that's what they're all like, all the time! Anechka should have shut up long ago and let a man tell her about what *he* was doing, putting in an encouraging word or two and making goo-goo eyes at him. But instead she had to give him all this rubbish about Trofim Denisovich this, and Trofim Denisovich that, and if you knew what he was *really* like, Trofim Denisovich I mean! Well, he's just brilliant! And do you know they've sown two hectares of his branched wheat in the next sector! And I *must* tell you about my clover!

And, hoarse with jealousy, Uncle Sasha bawled: "Your academician's nothing but a cock!"

Shot him down in flames. But then he added in honeyed tones: "A worn-out old cock in a miserable Poltava henhouse."

"Alexander Vasilevich!" Anechka's eyes had narrowed, but Uncle Sasha was unstoppable.

"Cock-a-doodle-doo! Cock-a-doodle-doo! And the hens all go: cluck-cluck-cluck!" he cried, mimicking their expressions.

"You're not just stupid, you're common too!" Anechka said, sounding almost surprised at herself.

"Maybe I am!" There would be no end to it now.

"And a boor!" Anna Nikitichna's blood was up now.

"Yes, I'm a boor!" said Uncle Sasha triumphantly. "But *I've* got a head on my shoulders, though – not a prick, like your academician!"

Hearing him pronounce this coarse word with a sort of special flourish – or so it seemed to her – she went as white as a sheet and, scarcely knowing what she was doing, seized at the white tablecloth and hauled it towards her. The bowls of black and red caviar, the plate of sturgeon and salmon garnished with flirtatious twirls of celery leaf and rings of cooked carrot, the carafe of vodka and the two glasses into which Uncle Sasha had so recently, yes, really so recently, only half an hour before, poured the *Abra-Dursu* Moroccan champagne brought to him on the shiny metal tray – all this went crashing and tinkling over the table. And when Anechka's fork (which was first to reach the edge) went flying out on to the floor, Anechka frowned darkly, twisted the cloth round her muscular hand and flung the whole bundle, all the fruits of sea and shore the restaurant had harvested, to the floor in an explosion of anger.

The bottle of cream soda, Anechka's favourite, bounced under the next-door table without breaking and landed right by the top boots of a colonel still in early middle age, who was spending his leave in the company of the wife of a lieutenant in his regiment. The lieutenant's wife let out a squeal.

"Ah, the sufferings of our great nation!" said Uncle Sasha for reasons best known to himself. Who knows to whom he addressed this – hardly to the colonel and his lady-friend, and if it was to Anechka, then there was no point, for she had vanished in any case.

Choked with sobs, she was running to her cabin in the stern, to her tiny single cabin. Once there, fully dressed – not bothering to remove even her Czech patent leather shoes – she flung herself on the bunk, and lay there till at last her sobs abated.

That night she got out at the very first stop, so that she would never have to see him again. They both knew it. He watched her go. He sat the whole night in a deckchair, teeth chattering with cold, so that he was hidden from view and could watch her go down the ship's ladder, patent shoes flashing in the gloom.

It was a tiny, ancient landing stage, and the hour was past midnight. Apart from Anechka, the clucking hen, the she-idiot, no one got out there.

What the devil had got into her? This was more than slamming the door in his face – as she'd done fifteen years ago, slammed it and gone out God knows where, left the little dining room in his sister's flat in Moscow and gone into the bedroom next door . . . But now? Mind you, Anechka had behaved quite badly enough even that other time: she hadn't come out to eat for two days; in fact, she hadn't emerged at all so far as he could tell, she'd just stayed like a statue on his sister's bed with her feet up and her hair down, reading the *Short*

History of the Communist Party (it had been published not long before) and chewing a lock of hair she'd twisted round her finger – even at that age she still had the habits of a schoolgirl.

And when Uncle Sasha met her eyes at unexpected moments – for instance, when the door of the bedroom was open, and he appeared at the midpoint of the axis between her silly golden head and his sister's narrow hand on the latch – when his gaze met hers, she would immediately turn her back, but all the same he would glimpse the red spots of uncontrollable hatred on her high-cheekboned face.

And that last evening before he left for home, Anechka was still behind closed doors in the bedroom. At supper with his sister and her husband he asked loudly (for he'd had a glass or two of vodka): "So what does Anna Nikitichna do about going to the loo? Does she climb in and out through the window? Or does the lady have a po in there, like some merchant's wife?"

"Sasha!" his sister cried indignantly and rushed into the bedroom, but there she must also have heard something not to her taste, for she shot out again, and her husband, who was a mild-mannered man for all his military calling, lit himself a cigarette at table, which was unheard of: normally he would go out on the balcony to smoke, or in winter would smoke through the open window. For two days already a deathly hush had reigned behind the bedroom door, but now it became quieter still. Until at last the silence was broken by the bedroom door opening and there she stood, hair unbrushed, Tatar eyes narrowed – the Medusa, that was the only word for her – on the threshold in his sister's dressing gown, which was several inches too short for her.

His sister was weeping in the kitchen. "Why do you say such terrible, stupid things to each other!" His sister's husband made a sudden decision to smoke on the balcony after all.

That was dreadful. But, as he lay panting with hatred on the broken-backed camp bed, which creaked and heaved its coarsely darned canvas skin under him, as he lay all that long sleepless night, waiting for the morning trill of his alarm clock, signal to get up and start the journey home, begin his other life again, he knew that she was sleeping beside him. In the next room. And that no one but he could hurt her. He would kill anyone who tried.

He called that night to mind as he stood in the shadow of the bridge, numb with the damp cold rising from the river, and watched over her sad escape. And it seemed to him that all those long years before, during and after the war had never been; there were only those two nights on end, those nights when he had lost her for ever.

Ten years later his younger sister, her favourite, had died, but Sasha and Anechka still had not met. She had arrived a day late for the funeral, after he had gone. It had been in August and she had not been able to get a ticket.

Uncle Sasha had learnt of this from a long letter sent by his sister's husband. After the death of his beloved wife he had begun writing to Uncle Sasha in her stead. Uncle Sasha also heard that Anechka had been ill a lot the previous winter, that she was now in poor health and still unattached. This last fact now surprised him no more. The letter also contained a slip of paper with her address on it in her own hand. Uncle Sasha recognized her scrawl immediately: it was unforgettable. The corner of the paper was torn: she had obviously written in haste. He could not work out whether she had written it specially for him or had given it to his sister's husband when she left there. The husband did not explain, though he did say that Anechka was still working in the Poltava institute, where she now had a senior research fellowship. She had not yet retired and had no intention of retiring in the immediate future; indeed, why should she, when the directors of her institute thought so highly of her that she had just been allocated a new two-roomed flat?

Naturally Uncle Sasha had no intention of writing to her, but he put the paper away in case.

Another five years later another funeral – cousin Georgy's this time – finally did bring them together.

Remember Georgy? Do you mean to say I really haven't mentioned him in all this time? Have you forgotten that evening on the terrace long ago when Anechka was sitting on the swing, a week before the archduke's untimely death? When the priest's daughters were drinking tea with cream, and Uncle Sasha was making his jokes about how the horses at her cousin's stud farm would make good drays for Ukrainian breweries? Why "Ukrainian"? That's just Uncle Sasha's nasty sense of humour. But, to be fair, Anechka herself was hardly all sugar and spice.

This time they did both manage to get there, and on the same day. Both arrived in Kuybyshev, he from Kama and she from Poltava, in time to climb the steep surburban side street behind the coffin carrying her cousin Georgy, a humble retired physics teacher.

And perhaps it was the moment, drawn out by the mourners' slow footsteps, when the procession (if that is the right word for the huddle of the deceased's nearest and dearest, to boot his wife, also a retired schoolteacher, fussing beside the coffin in her black plush hat, and a few of his friends), when Anechka and Uncle Sasha (for let us so address them to the bitter end) turned the corner and glimpsed the great river with the ever-present shade of the steamer on it, perhaps it was then – or perhaps it was that moment at the station, whither he had been forced to accompany her and a woman friend of hers – they were both leaving on the same inconvenient night train – when the train moved off and her face appeared at the carriage window smoothed by the thick pane, and when she smiled the smile he had not seen for decades, and Uncle Sasha's legs turned to cotton wool as he remembered how wild she had been in the past and the stupid events in Nizhny, and he shook inwardly as he recognized in the wrinkled little old woman with tightly waved hair that Fira whom he had so hated long ago, and was astonished to realize that these women had been friends all these years, but the train was going, she was off again . . . In fact it doesn't really matter when, the point is that it was this meeting, sad though the attendant circumstances were, which made Uncle Sasha and Anechka understand that their relations, which seemed to have ended for all time, would continue against their will; that, besides, they had reached that strange stage when the physical presence of one adds nothing in the eyes of the other but, on the contrary, irritates by its inadequacy to convey the inexpressible, overwhelms by its lack of appropriateness.

How should we explain the essence, which is in any case a mystery, the Kantian "Ding an sich" as Uncle Sasha put it? And if that mysterious "Ding an sich" should take root in our soil . . . Oh! We can only cry Oh! That is all that is left to us.

In vain does the steamer stranded on a sandbank somewhere near the town that was once Samara call out in the fog, waking the solitary widow on her metal bedstead with its nickel knobs. The phials of heart medicine and tranquillizers lined up on the bentwood chair (the very one for which the stage managers of so many Chekhov productions have searched in vain!) – the phials rattle against each other as the bed's wire netting heaves under the weight of the widow's grieving soul, whose transient covering dries up with her every sigh – for only in old age does that covering seem to enchain the soul; in youth, by contrast, the soul seems to look out of every cell of the tender female body, which is, of course, the essence of satanic temptation, for the soul is the soul, it is all or nothing.

Let us leave the widow and Samara, now the industrial town of Kuybyshev, let us omit from our narrative all the idiocies and misunderstandings of the correspondence now resumed, let us forget about the absurd quarrel when he sent her a New Year's card with a snapshot of himself in his new suit and the bowler hat which he, ignoring the protests of his wife, had begun to wear in his old age, and Anechka responded by sending him a photograph of her cat on a cushion embroidered by her own hand . . . To the devil with all that!

Once again they had bought tickets on the same boat – by "they" I mean Uncle Sasha and Anechka, of course.

He saw her straightaway. She was standing with her suitcase at her feet, elbows on the plaster balustrade above the steps stretching down to the river, hair sleek and face alight. She was wearing a raincoat of good grey cloth – that was modern, but her two plaits were pinned up over her ears as they had been that earlier time, in 1950, the way she had started to wear her hair after the war, and the sight of her bare neck below the stupid hairstyle was like a blow to the solar plexus. His wife was better looking, younger, had kept her figure, but over the years he had stopped caring whether he ever saw or thought about her again. He had not given her a thought now; the lady doctor has only been mentioned because of the author's silly habit of going off the point – there is no reason at all to speak about her, or their grown children, even the youngest of whom, the little daughter, has long moved away from home, is married and working as a supervisor in a shop. Uncle Sasha himself eventually went up to Anechka with an air of self-importance – trying to favour the leg which had been a bit lame since his recent stroke – and she turned to face him, sensing his presence. He took off his bowler and held it in his hands.

And where on earth had he got the bowler, come to mention it? Surely it couldn't date from "an earlier era", as the euphemism has it? How could he have kept it?

And why hadn't Uncle Sasha's bowler turned to dust under the assault of wind, weather and war? All that is dim and mysterious, but that the bowler existed is confirmed by documentary evidence. For it was in that very bowler (of which the reader would gladly hear no more) that Uncle Sasha sat on the deck of the steamer *Ivan Nekrasov*. No, that is no misprint: the steamer which took Sasha and Anechka on their river trip really was called the *Ivan Nekrasov*, for it was named not after the poet, but after a ship's mechanic and hero of whom my snooty Moscow reader may not have heard. And it is just as well that his surname *was* Nekrasov and not Gogol; many people are not too sure of Nekrasov's first name; they might think it really was Ivan, but everyone knows Gogol's was Nikolay and that's that.

So Uncle Sasha sits in his deckchair, crossing his long thin feet in their shiny shoes, and Anechka stands over him in her severe hairstyle, leaning her elbow on the back of the chair. They are both staring at one and the same point, but the birdie we are always told to watch never does fly out, and it hasn't flown out for them either. It's a bad photograph: it's turning yellow and it was taken into the sun in the first place, so you can't see their eyes and their wrinkles stand out, but compositionally this ugly little piece shows its affinity with those pompous, respectable pictures of the turn of the century, decorated all over (even on the backs) with eagles and medals. And so it's not hard to work out who must have taken the photograph, especially since the *Ivan Nekrasov* was not a cruise ship, but an ordinary passenger steamer: there was no music booming on either of her decks, she stopped at every landing stage, and the passengers, like our two heroes, were all more than familiar with the journey.

Well now, the bowler hat and the photograph have helped me to cut from his tender glance at her greying elderly plaits, the unforgettable second when they looked into one another's eyes, to a later scene, when, having got their things unpacked in their respective cabins, they met up on deck again.

"Where shall we take our promenade, dear Anna Nikitichna?" Uncle Sasha asked with an ironic bow. "In the stern or the bows?"

Don't worry, dear reader, for . . .

"I don't mind, Sasha," said Anechka.

And here for the first time in their lives they were in a strange dilemma: neither of them cared, so one of them had to decide. They would have stood even longer, astonished at one another, had not the evening sunlight peeking behind the steep bank caught their eye. Anechka turned round and made a move to the right; Uncle Sasha sensed her movement and set off for the stern.

They were quieter this time, more earnest. Perhaps it was a premonition of parting, perhaps it was the deaths of certain Great Academicians in a symbolic sense as well as the everyday one – and above all the Chief and Premier Academician – or perhaps it was the purchase of grain overseas which had curbed their pride and put a stop to their quarrels. At any rate the words "grain", "soil" and "Russia" were not mentioned. True, at one point she did say that she enjoyed watching the gymnastics on television, and Uncle Sasha said drily as he sipped his mineral water that he didn't approve of sport for women.

"That Marx of yours, Anna Nikitichna, were he still living (God rest him), would think as I do!"

Uncle Sasha was, after all, not letting the past go unavenged here, as he touched on the great man's frivolous reply to a home questionnaire –

in his day such things were fashionable – asking: "What do you value in women?", to which he responded: "Weakness!"

But Anechka's heart could beat no faster in anger; for she was already suffering from tachycardia and stenocardia, the after-effects of her service on the Poltava front in the war for clover improvement.

After supper Uncle Sasha untied the black lacquer stick which he had lashed to the handle of his suitcase, and she took off her new brown sandals (sandalettes, as she called them), wrapped them in newspaper and pushed them under her bunk, and put on some comfortable checked slippers.

For a long time they circled the snow-white decks of the *Ivan Nekrasov* as it moved into the night; then, without a word, they walked to the stern. They were alone.

At first, to be sure, they shared the deck with a big man in a leather coat and a scarf up to his ears, but soon he started feeling chilly and left.

Silence . . . The steamer's heart thumped. The water slapped. Stars spoke of eternal life.

. . . As the early June sun came up, or to be more exact, as the light of dawn showed, tingeing the fluffy clouds with pink, Anechka said dreamily: "The rosy-fingered dawn." She was smiling.

"Don't talk like some blushing virgin," Uncle Sasha sneered.

"But I *am* a virgin," said Anechka.

"I know," said Uncle Sasha. And, dropping to his knees before her, he began to weep.

Anechka was choked by tears.

And the author is choked by tears, too, though he is neither young nor old, but has "grey hair here and there", neither one thing nor the other, and so lives on, a mixture of hopes and memories.

Translated by Catriona Kelly

YURY KAZAKOV

You Cried so Bitterly in Your Sleep

IT WAS A hot summer day.

I stood talking with some friends near our house. You wandered up to your shoulders amongst the grass and flowers, or squatted down to gaze at a pine cone or a blade of grass with a vague half-smile on your face which I tried in vain to fathom.

Our spaniel Chief bounded up every so often, exhausted from his exertions among the nut trees. Stopping at a slight angle to you, he would hunch his shoulders like a wolf, slowly crane his neck and fix his coffee-coloured eyes on you, imploring you for a kind look. But for some reason you were afraid of Chief and backed away, hugging my knee and throwing back your head to gaze into my face with blue eyes that reflected the sun. "Papa!" you murmured happily, as though returning from a long journey.

The touch of your little hands filled me with an almost painful joy. My friend also seemed moved by your casual embrace, as he suddenly fell silent, ruffled your downy hair and stared at you thoughtfully.

Never again will he look tenderly at you, for he is no longer alive. And you cannot remember him, of course, like so much you cannot remember . . .

He shot himself in the late autumn, just after the first snow. Did he ever see the snow? Did he look out of the verandah window at the suddenly lifeless countryside, or did he shoot himself at night? Was the ground covered with snow the previous evening, or was everything dark when he returned on the suburban train and walked home to his Golgotha?

The first snow is so soothing and melancholy, and plunges us into such languid, leisurely thoughts . . .

At what moment exactly did the idea enter his blood, insistent and terrible as poison? It must have been there for a long time. He frequently told me of the bouts of depression he suffered when alone at the dacha in early spring and late autumn, and of how he would feel like shooting himself there and then to put an end to his misery. Yet don't we all say these things in moments of depression?

He had had the most terrible nights, though, when he was unable to sleep and kept imagining that someone had slipped into the house, casting spells and filling it with cold. And this someone must have been death!

"For God's sake give me some cartridges!" he begged me once. "I've run out. I keep thinking that someone is creeping around the house at night, yet it's silent as the grave ... You will let me have some, won't you?"

I gave him six.

"Now you'll be able to shoot your way out!" I joked.

What a hard worker he was! I used to feel reproached by his energy and enthusiasm. Whenever I went to his house – during the summer months people would drop in on him from the verandah – I used to look up to the open attic window and call softly: "Mitya!"

"Hello there!" would come his reply, and his face would appear at the window. For a full minute he would gaze down with blank, cloudy eyes, then he would smile weakly, wave his thin arm and shout: "Coming!"

A moment later he would be downstairs on the verandah in his thick sweater. He always seemed to breathe more deeply after he had been working, and looking at him, one would feel the same envious pleasure one feels at the sight of a young horse straining at the bit and breaking into a trot.

"You're letting yourself go!" he would say, whenever I was ill or out of sorts. "You should follow my example. I swim in the Yasnushka till late autumn! Don't lie in bed or sit in a chair – get up and get some exercise!"

The last time I saw him was in the middle of October. He came to see me one glorious sunny day, well dressed as always, and wearing a woollen cap. He looked sad, but we had a cheerful conversation – about Buddhism, for some reason, about the fact that it was time to write great novels, and that working every day was the only happiness, but that one could only do so when writing something really big ...

When I went to see him out, he suddenly turned round and burst into tears.

"When I was the same age as your little Alyosha, the sky seemed so high," he said, when he was a bit calmer. "But is it just my age? Perhaps it's still like that? I'm terrified of Abramtsevo, you know, absolutely terrified! The longer I live in this place, the more I love it. But isn't it a sin to be totally committed to one place? Did you carry Alyosha on your shoulders? I used to carry mine too. Later on I took them for cycle rides in the forest, and talked to them about Abramtsevo, about the region of Radonezh. I so much wanted them to love it properly – this is their native land . . . ! Oh quick, look at that maple tree!"

Then he started talking about his winter plans – even though the sky was still blue, and the dense foliage of the maples gleamed like gold under the sun. We said goodbye with especial warmth and tenderness.

Three weeks later, when I was staying at the Black Sea resort of Gagry, the news came to me like a thunderbolt, as though the shot in the night had come winging its way across Russia to find me. I am writing now in that same place. Then as now, the waves in the darkness beat the shore and spewed up the pungent smell of the sea's depths, while far away to the right, a gleaming pearly necklace of lights encircled the bay like a curved bow.

You were just five years old then. I sat with you in the darkness, listening to the invisible roar of the surf, and the wet slap of the shingle as it rolled back after each retreating wave. I do not know what you were thinking about, for you said nothing, but I suddenly imagined myself going home to Abramtsevo from the station, and taking a different path from the one I usually took. I no longer saw the sea or the mountains of the night, scattered with the lights of a few cottages. Instead I was walking along a cobbled road dusted with the first snow, my dark tracks clearly visible behind me on the ashy-white ground.

I turn left, past the gleaming banks of a dark pond, into a dark clump of fir trees. I turn right . . . Looking straight ahead to the end of the path, I see his dacha, shaded with fir trees, lights blazing in all the windows . . .

When had it happened? Was it in the evening, or was it at night? For some reason I longed for the uncertain early November dawn, when one could sense the approaching day only from the gleam of the snow and the outline of the trees looming out of the prevailing darkness.

I go to his house, open the wicket gate, climb the steps of the verandah, and see . . .

"Listen," he once said to me. "Is small shot powerful? At close range, I mean?"

"I'll say it is!" I replied. "If you shoot from eighteen inches at a little aspen tree as wide as my hand, you'll slice it clean in two!"

I still torment myself wondering what I would have done if I had seen him sitting there on the veranda, his gun cocked and his shoe off.

Would I have wrenched the door open, smashed the glass and shouted for help? Or would I have looked the other way and held my breath in terror, hoping that if I didn't alarm him he might change his mind, put down the gun, carefully pull back his big toe, release the hammer and put on his shoe, sighing deeply as though awaking from a bad dream?

And if I had smashed the glass and shouted, what would he have done? Would he have thrust aside the gun and joyfully thrown himself at me? Or would he have looked at me with dead, hate-filled eyes, and hastily squeezed the trigger with his toe? In my thoughts I am constantly flying to him, to that house, that night, longing to become him, to follow his every movement, to divine his thoughts. But I cannot.

I know that he returned to his dacha in the late evening. What did he do in his last hours? First of all he changed his clothes as usual, neatly hanging up his city suit in the cupboard. Then he brought in firewood to light the stove, and ate some apple. I don't suppose the fatal resolve came over him at once – people don't usually eat apples and bring in firewood when contemplating suicide.

Then he decided not to light the stove after all, and went to bed instead. It was probably then that it came to him. Did he recall the past in his final moments? Or merely plan his next move?

He washed and changed his underwear.

The gun was hanging on the wall. He took it down, felt its cold weight and the chill of its steel barrels. The fore-stock lay obediently in his left hand. The tongue of the lock yielded stiffly to his right thumb. The gun broke at the lock, to reveal the cross section of the two, tunnel-like barrels. Into one of these barrels he smoothly slid the cartridge. *My* cartridge!

All the lights inside the house were on. He switched on the veranda light, sat down in a chair and took off his right shoe. With a resounding click in the deathly silence, he lifted up the safety catch and put the gun in his mouth, gripping it with his teeth and tasting the cold oily metal of the barrels . . .

Did he sit down and take off his shoe at once? Or did he stand there all night, pressing his forehead to the window, so that the glass streamed with his tears? Or did he wander through the garden bidding farewell to the trees, the sky, the Yasnushka and his beloved bathhouse? Did his toe grasp the loaded trigger at once? Or did he with his habitual clumsiness squeeze the wrong one, then spend the next few minutes sighing and wiping away the cold sweat before he summoned

up the strength to try once more? Did he screw up his eyes? Or did
he stare ahead as the final flash entered his brain?

No, this was not weakness. One needs immense courage and strength
to end one's life as he did.

But why did he do it? I keep searching for answers, yet I can
find none. Perhaps his cheerful, energetic life concealed some secret
suffering. Yet we all suffer. This was not what drove him to take up
his gun. It may be that he was marked from birth by some fatal sign;
perhaps each of us unknowingly bears a mark foretelling the course
of our life . . .

My soul is wandering in the darkness . . .

Then, however, we were all still alive, and the sun was at its height on
one of those long, long summer days which seem endless when recalled
in years to come.

After saying goodbye to me, Mitya again ruffled your hair and
brushed your forehead with his bearded lips, which tickled you and
sent you off into peals of happy laughter. Then he went home, and
you and I took a big apple and set off for a walk which we had been
looking forward to all day. When Chief saw us leave, he rushed out
to join us. Leaping up into the air and almost knocking you to the
ground, he bounded ahead and disappeared into the forest, his ears
flapping in the wind like butterfly wings.

Oh, what a journey lay ahead of us – almost half a mile! And what
variety! You had already been here before, of course, so it was partly
familiar to you. But each walk is totally unlike another, just as
one hour is unlike another. Sometimes it was cloudy and sometimes
it was warm, or the grass was wet with dew, or the sky was heavy
with clouds, or thunder rumbled, or it drizzled with rain, and
beads of moisture weighed down the lower branches of the fir trees,
and your little red boots gleamed, and the path grew dark and
slippery. Or the wind blew, making the aspens murmur and rustling
the tops of the birches and firs. Sometimes we went in the morning and sometimes at noon; sometimes it was cold, sometimes it
was sunny. Each day, each hour, each bush, each tree was unlike any
other.

The sky on that day was not the piercing blue which floods our eyes
in early spring, or grips the soul as it breaks through the low clouds
in late autumn, but a peaceful, cloudless pale blue. You were wearing
brown sandals, yellow socks, red shorts and a bright-yellow tee shirt.
Your knees were scratched, your legs, arms and shoulders were pale,

and your big grey pistachio-flecked eyes looked darker and bluer than usual.

We set off away from the main gates and towards the wicket gate, stepping over large fir roots and soft springy pine needles on a sun-dappled path. Suddenly you stopped still and looked around you. I knew at once that you wanted a stick, and would not go on until you had one. Breaking off a switch from a nut tree, I handed you your stick.

You lowered your head, overjoyed that I had sensed what you wanted. Then you took your stick and ran off, brushing it against the trunks of the trees which came down to the path, and the tall, shaded ferns, their damp tips like violin scrolls.

Looking down at your running legs, the silvery strands of hair on the nape of your neck, and the downy tuft on the crown of your head, I tried to remember myself when I was young. Memories instantly crowded in, yet for some reason I was unable to remember my early childhood, I was always older than you.

Then suddenly into the forest clearing from the left, across a gulley lapped by the Yasnushka, sprang the warm smell of sun-baked meadows.

"Al-yo-sha's feet," I said in a mechanical sing-song voice.

"Go down street," you responded, and I saw from your quivering transparent ears that you were smiling.

Yes, long, long ago I too ran like you, and it was summer, and the sun shone, and the fragrant smell of hay wafted over the meadow . . .

I saw a large field somewhere outside Moscow, which separated two groups of people assembled there. One group, standing on the edge of a thin row of birches, consisted only of children and women, many of whom were weeping and wiping their eyes on their red kerchiefs. On the other side of the field stood a line of men. Behind them rose an embankment, on which stood a long row of reddish-brown goods vans, with a chuffing steam engine far in front emitting a tall column of black smoke. Patrolling the line of men were soldiers in military uniforms.

My short-sighted mother was also weeping. Wiping away her tears and screwing up her eyes, she kept asking: "Where is Papa, dear? Which end is he at? Can you see him?"

"Yes I can!" I replied, and I did indeed see him, standing on the right of the line. He saw us too, and smiled and occasionally waved to us, and I could not understand why he didn't come to us, or we go to him.

Then a current seemed to pass through our line, and some boys and girls timidly darted out into the meadow with bundles in their hands. Hurriedly shoving a heavy bundle of underwear and tinned food into my hands, my mother pushed me out too, shouting: "Run to your father, son! Give him this and kiss him, and say we'll wait for him!"

Happy to escape from the exhausting heat and the long wait, I set off across the field with the others, our bare sunburnt knees flashing. My heart leapt at the thought that in a few moments my father would be hugging and kissing me and lifting me in his arms, and I would again hear his voice, and smell the lovely smell of his tobacco – it was so long since I had seen him that my short memory of him was covered in ashes and I felt pity only for myself, alone without his rough hands, his eyes, his voice. I ran on, looking first at the ground under my feet, then at my father. I could already see the birthmark on his temple. Then suddenly I realized that his face was unhappy, and the closer to him I ran, the more anxious grew the men in his line . . .

Emerging from the wicket gate into the forest, we turned right towards our neighbour's half-built rotunda, whose grey concrete dome and pillars, looming up starkly amidst the green firs and alders, always gave you endless delight.

To the left of us the Yasnushka spurted over the pebbles. It was still concealed from view by overgrown nut and raspberry bushes, but we knew that beneath the rotunda the path led down to a steep embankment, at the bottom of which stray leaves and pine needles circled slowly in a small dark pool.

The sun burst through the undergrowth in vertical columns of light, in which oozing resin gleamed like honey, wild strawberries flashed like drops of blood, and swarms of midges crowded weightless and invisible in the foliage. Birds called out to one another, a squirrel darted across a sunbeam and leapt from tree to tree, making the branches sway. Everything was filled with fragrance . . .

"See the squirrel, Alyosha! It's looking at you . . . !"

You looked up, saw the squirrel and dropped your stick. You always dropped your stick when something new caught your attention. You gazed after the squirrel until it disappeared, then you remembered your stick, picked it up and went on.

Bounding towards us on the path came Chief, leaping high in the air as though trying to fly. He stopped and looked at us for a moment with his deep, gazelle-like eyes, asking whether he should run ahead, or whether we were going to turn back or to one side. I silently showed him the path along which we had come, and he understood and dashed off again.

A moment later we heard frantic barking. The sound came from one place, which meant that he was not chasing something, but had found something he wanted us to come and see.

"Listen!" I said. "Our Chief is calling us!"

I picked you up so you wouldn't scratch yourself on the trees, and we followed the barking sounds to a clearing of lilac, yellow and sharp-green moss. Under a large and lovely birch tree, standing slightly to one side, we saw Chief, his barking interspersed with frenzied, gasping sobs and sighs.

He had found a hedgehog. The birch stood some thirty yards from the path, and I was amazed as always by his sense of smell. The moss around the hedgehog had been trampled down, and on seeing us, his barking grew even louder. I put you down, pulled him away by his collar, and we squatted down beside the hedgehog.

"That's a hedgehog," I said. "Say 'hedgehog'."

You repeated the word, and touched it with your stick.

The hedgehog snuffled and gave a little jump. You jerked the stick away, lost your balance and tumbled into the moss.

"Don't be frightened," I said. "But don't touch it. See how it's rolled itself up in a ball with its needles sticking out. When we go away it'll put out its nose and run off. It's taking a walk, just like us. It needs lots of walks, because it sleeps all winter. It gets covered in snow, and falls asleep. Do you remember the winter? Do you remember us taking you out in your sledge?"

You smiled enigmatically. I longed to know what made you smile like that when you were alone or listening to me! Was it some wisdom which transcended all my knowledge and experience?

I remembered the day when I fetched you home from the hospital, a heavy, tightly wrapped bundle, which the nurse for some reason handed to me. On the way to the car I realized that this bundle contained a warm, living creature, although your face was covered and I could not feel you breathing.

We unwrapped you as soon as we got home. I had heard that newborn babies were red and wrinkled, but you were not in the least bit red or wrinkled. You gleamed with whiteness, and stirred your tiny, amazingly delicate arms and legs, and gazed solemnly at us with your large greyish-blue eyes. You were a miracle of beauty, marred only by the plaster on your navel.

You were wrapped up again, fed and put to sleep, and we went into the kitchen. As we drank tea, the women discussed nappies, bathing, expressing milk and other blissfully important subjects, while I kept getting up to sit beside your cot and gaze into your sleeping face.

The third or fourth time I went to you, I saw your face tremble and smile. What did that smile mean? Were you dreaming? What could you be dreaming about? What did you know? Where did your thoughts wander? Did you have thoughts at all? You did not merely smile, either. Sometimes your face would acquire a look of lofty, prophetic wisdom, then clouds would pass across it . . . Your expression was constantly changing, yet it never lost its fundamental harmony. Never in your waking hours – laughing, or crying, or staring quietly at the coloured rattles over your cot – did I see the expression which so amazed me when you were asleep, when I would hold my breath and wonder what was happening within you. "When babies smile like that," my mother told me later, "the angels are playing with them . . ."

As we bent over the hedgehog on that day, and you replied to my question with your usual enigmatic smile, I had no idea whether you remembered your first winter or not. Yet that winter in Abramtsevo had been magical. The snow fell thickly at night, and by day the pink sun cast a rosy glow over the sky and the birch trees, shaggy with hoarfrost. You went out into the snow bundled up so thickly in your fur coat and felt boots that your mittened hands stuck out from your body. You sat down in the sledge, grasped your inevitable stick – sticks of various lengths were propped up by the porch, and you always chose a different one – and we pulled you through the gates. A wonderful journey began. Tracing patterns in the snow with your stick, you talked to yourself, to the sky, the forest, the squeak of the snow under our feet and the sledge runners. They all understood you, but we did not, for you had not yet learnt to speak, and all your trilling and warbling told us was that you were happy.

Then suddenly you fell silent, and looking back, we saw your stick lying far behind us in the road, and you fast asleep with your arms thrown out, your firm cheeks blazing with colour. We pulled you for another hour, then another, and you remained so fast asleep that you did not even wake when we finally took you into the house, undid your coat and scarf, removed your boots and clothes, and put you to bed . . .

*

Having stared our fill at the hedgehog, we returned to the path and soon reached the rotunda. You saw it before I did and stopped. "Big tower!" you said happily, as you always did.

You looked at it for a while from a distance, repeating in amazement, as if seeing it for the first time: "Pretty tower!" Then we went up to it, and you touched each of its pillars with your stick. Finally you dropped your eyes to the small transparent pool. I reached out to help you, and hand in hand, we cautiously scrambled down the embankment towards the water. A little lower downstream was a tiny waterfall. The water there was green, but the pool itself seemed motionless, and the movement of the current could be seen only by staring hard at a floating leaf which moved towards the waterfall as slowly as the minute hand of a clock. I sat down on the trunk of an uprooted fir tree and lit a cigarette, preparing myself to wait until you had exhausted all the delights of the pool.

Dropping your stick, you ran up to a convenient root by the bank of the stream, and lay face down on it to stare into the water. You were strangely uninterested in toys that summer, but you were fascinated by minute objects. You would endlessly move a grain of sand, a pine needle or a blade of grass over your hand, and a little chip of paint which you picked off the wall of our house afforded you hours of contemplative delight. The life of bees, flies, butterflies and midges interested you far more than that of dogs, kittens, cows, magpies, squirrels or birds. What an infinity of life you discovered in this pool, when you lay on the root, brought your face close to the water and gazed into its depths! How many grains of sand did you see, and pebbles of every imaginable shade, and boulders coated in velvety green weed, and transparent minnows, now frozen in immobility, now darting off to one side! How many microscopic objects were there, discernible to your eyes alone!

"Fishes swimming . . ." you said after a while.

"They're baby fish. They haven't swum off to the big river yet," I said, coming up and sitting beside you.

"Baby fish!" you repeated happily.

The water in the pool was so transparent that it was visible only from the blue of the sky and the tops of the trees reflected in it. Hanging over the root, you scooped handfuls of gravel from the bottom. A cloud of fine sand formed, then dispersed. You threw the gravel into the water, and the reflection of the trees wavered. Then you suddenly stood up, and I realized that you had remembered your favourite game. It was time for you to throw stones.

I sat down on the trunk again, and you picked up a pebble, inspected it lovingly from all sides, went to the water and threw it into the middle of the pool. There was a splash, surrounded by undulating currents of air, then rippling circles appeared in the water as the stone thudded to the bottom. You happily watched the splash, the bubbles, the ripples, and after waiting for everything to subside, you picked up another pebble, inspected it as you had the first, and threw again.

You threw again and again, admiring the splashes and the waves. All around you was silence and beauty. We were out of earshot of the suburban train, not one aeroplane flew overhead, nobody walked past, nobody saw us. Only Chief would appear every so often, his tongue lolling, and would splash into the brook, noisily lap some water, look at us enquiringly and run off again.

A mosquito settled on your shoulder. It was a while before you noticed it and drove it away. Then you came to me.

"Mosquito . . ." you said, frowning.

I rubbed your shoulder, patted it and blew on it.

"What do you want to do now? Throw more stones, or go on?"

"Go on," you decided.

I picked you up and waded across the Yasnushka. We cut across a damp gulley lined with a cascading mass of lungwort, whose foaming white tips seemed to float in the sun, and were filled with the happy buzzing of bees.

The path climbed up, through fir trees and nut bushes, then through oaks and birches, until it brought us out at a large meadow, framed on the right by a forest, and passing on the left into a rolling pasture. We climbed up and up until we reached the top, where we could see as far as the horizon, marked by the barely perceptible hyphens of aerials and a thin haze of smoke hovering over invisible Zagorsk. In the meadow the haymaking had only just begun and the grass had not yet been gathered, but a slight fading smell already wafted over the earth. We sat down in an unscythed patch of grass and flowers, which came up to my shoulders and your head, with nothing but the sky visible above us. Remembering the apple, I took it out of my pocket, rubbed it on the grass till it shone and gave it to you. You grasped it with both hands and took a bite, leaving little squirrel-like tooth marks.

All around us stretched one of the most ancient lands in Russia, the quiet Muscovite principality of Radonezh. Soaring high above the edge of the field in slow, swooping circles were two kites. Nothing of the past remained. The earth, the trees, the forests had all changed, and all but the memory of Radonezh had vanished. Yet those two kites still circled in the sky as they might have done a thousand years ago, and perhaps the Yasnushka too still flowed along the same course.

You had finished your apple, but I could see that your thoughts were far away. You had noticed the kites too, and you gazed up at them for a long time. Butterflies hovered around you. Attracted by your red shorts, they would try to land on them, then dart up again, and you stared at their magical flight. You spoke little, but I could see from your face and eyes that you were deep in thought. How I longed to be you for a moment, to know your thoughts! Why, you were a person already!

Beautiful and blessed was our world! Bombs did not fall, towns and villages did not burn, flies did not swarm over babies sprawled out in the roads. Children did not grow stiff with cold, or go about in lice-ridden rags, or live in caves and ruins like wild beasts. Children's tears flowed now, but for different reasons. Was this not blessedness, was this not joy!

As I looked around, I thought that this day – these clouds which perhaps no one else at this moment and in this place had seen; the forest stream below lined with pebbles which you had thrown, and the clear currents flowing around them, and the meadow air, and the white, well-trodden path through stooks of corn already touched by silvery hoarfrost, and the lovely little village in the distance, and the shimmering horizon beyond it – this day, one of the most beautiful of my life, would remain with me for ever. But would you remember it? Would you look back one day as though the intervening years had not been, and you were a child again, running up to your shoulders in the flowers and startling the butterflies? Would you remember us walking together in the sun, and you burning your shoulders, and all the smells and sounds of that impossibly long summer day?

Where does it all disappear to? By what strange law is the past cut off from us and buried in the mists of oblivion? What happens to those blindingly happy years of one's early life? It even made me wring my hands in despair that we cannot remember the greatest moment of all, that of birth itself.

Then I thought of you. You knew so much, you already had your own character and your own habits, you had learnt to talk, and more importantly to understand others, you had your own likes and dislikes. Yet ask anyone you like, and they will remember themselves only from the age of five or six. Why is this? Could it be that we do not forget everything, but that every so often some childhood event from the dawn of time will flash upon our consciousness? Has not everyone

been struck suddenly by some sound or smell, or the sight of something
as obscure and ordinary as a puddle of rain on an autumn road? I
know that, I have seen that before, we say to ourselves. Yet when and
where was it? Was it in this life, or another? And we try in vain to
grasp that moment from our past.

It was time for your afternoon nap, and we started home. Chief had
run back a long time ago, and had dug himself a little hole in the grass,
stretched himself out and gone to sleep, his paws twitching.

The house was quiet, and bright squares of sunlight lay on the
floors. While I was undressing you in your room and putting on your
pyjamas, you told me about everything you had seen that day. Then
you yawned twice, I tucked you up, and I think you were asleep before
I was through the door. I sat by the open window of my room,
smoking and thinking about you, and imagining your future life. I did
not want to think of you as an adult, shaving, smoking and chasing
girls. I wanted to think of you for as long as possible as a child – not
as you were then, but aged perhaps about ten. What journeys you and
I would make, what adventures we would have!

Then I returned to the present, and to the aching conviction that
you knew something that I had known but forgotten . . . That the
things on this earth were made for children's eyes alone. That the
kingdom of heaven belonged to you! These words were said over a
thousand years ago. Was it because people then sensed children's
mysterious superiority over us? And if so, why? Is it their innocence,
or some higher knowledge which we have lost with age?

More than an hour had passed, the sun had dipped and the shadows
lengthened when I heard you crying. I crushed my cigarette in the
ashtray and went into your room, thinking that you had woken and
wanted something.

But you were fast asleep, with your knees tucked up to your chin.
You were weeping so bitterly that your tears had soaked into the
pillow. You were sobbing with despair. When you were hurt or
naughty, you simply howled. Now it was as though you were weeping
for something irretrievably lost. You were choking with sobs – even
your voice sounded different.

Are dreams merely a chaotic reflection of reality? If so, what was
the reality of your dream then? What had you seen in your life but
loving eyes, smiles and toys, the sun, the moon and the stars? What
had you heard but the noise of water, the rustle of the forest, the
singing of the birds, soothing raindrops on the roof and your mother's

lullaby? Other than these calm joys, what could you have discovered that made you weep so bitterly in your sleep? You had not suffered, you had no regrets, you did not fear death. What had you dreamt? Can it be that we grieve even in infancy for the suffering that lies in store?

I woke you gently, patting your shoulder and stroking your hair.

"Wake up now, Alyosha!" I said, tugging at your arm. "Time to wake up!"

You woke, sat bolt upright and reached out to me. I took you in my arms, picked you up and said with deliberate cheerfulness: "Don't cry, little boy, it was just a bad dream! Up you get now! Look at the sun!"

I drew back the curtains and the room filled with sunlight. But you went on sobbing, burying your face in my shoulders, gasping for breath and digging your fingers painfully into my neck.

"We'll have supper . . . Look at that bird . . . Where's our fluffy pussycat? Don't cry, everything's all right now . . . Who's that coming? Is it Mama . . . ?"

I said the first thing that came into my mind, trying to distract you, and gradually your sobs subsided. Your mouth was still twisted with suffering, but a smile was breaking through. Then you caught sight of your beloved little glazed jug hanging by the window, and you beamed with joy. "Jug! Jug!" you said tenderly, delighting in the sound of the word.

You did not grab for it, as children usually grab for their favourite toy. You merely looked at it with tear-stained eyes, marvelling in its shape and its patterned glaze.

After I had washed your hands, tucked your napkin under your chin and sat you down at the table, I realized that something had indeed happened to you. You did not bang your foot against the table, or laugh, or shout: "More! More!" Instead, you stared at me seriously and unblinkingly, and I felt you were leaving me. As though your soul were no longer one with mine, but was moving away from me, and would go further away with every year that passed. I felt that you were no longer a mere continuation of me, that I would never catch up with you, and that soon you would leave me for ever. In your deep, adult gaze I saw your soul abandoning me, and your eyes were filled with compassion as you took your final leave of me.

I reached out, longing to draw you closer to me. But I knew it was too late, and that life would take me on my way, while you would from now on be travelling along a different path.

I felt overwhelmed with grief.

Then I heard the weak, hoarse voice of hope. Our souls might one day be reunited, it said, never to be parted again.

Yes, but where would this be, and when?

Now it was my turn to weep, my friend.

And that summer you were only one-and-a-half years old.

Translated by Catherine Porter

LEONID BORODIN

The Visit

A DOCUMENT CAME into my possession recently. Its author was reputedly a provincial priest who died only last year. The document is so extraordinary, I felt unable to pass it on to anybody else, but it was equally impossible to remain silent. I decided to be devious. I wrote a story. And by doing so relieved myself of all responsibility.

The service in the village church had finished an hour ago, but Father Venyamin had only just left for home. He'd been discussing an important matter with one of his parishioners – the rebuilding of the church fence. The existing one, which had been up for longer than anyone could remember and been patched and re-patched, was rotten beyond repair. The discussion had been about posts and palings, about paint, in other words which colour was fitting for God's house. Pale blue, of course. But the shops only stocked red and yellow. They would have to pay over the odds. Father Venyamin stroked his beard, the peasant scratched the back of his head. Finally, they struck the best possible bargain: the posts and such would come for nothing, while they'd have to allow a bit extra for the paint and the palings. It was a deal.

The bargaining over, Father Venyamin was still in no hurry to go home.

We all know how it is: you do something, then find more things to do, keep busy, knowing that once on your own you will be besieged by melancholy thoughts, thoughts that will nag you till cockcrow.

The priest, however, was in his seventies. He knew from experience that melancholy has to be properly identified if it was not to lurk as an ill-defined torment in the soul. Understanding melancholy meant finding its source, and the source was always a concrete instance of some kind and every such instance has its own little shelf where it can be tucked away forgotten.

As soon as he arrived home and studied the ikons, he recalled the source of his melancholy. It was the face of a young man who had come to the church today at the beginning of the service and stood by the door to the very end, without crossing himself once. Then left without crossing himself. What had he read in the young man's face? For Father Venyamin that face held a memory. Many years ago, in his younger days, he had known faces like that, Russian faces, with suffering in their eyes. Those faces then began to disappear from Russia. The ones which replaced them weren't necessarily beardless; beards were not the point, they were simply different faces and they spoke a different language, in which the words were either barbed or spoken through gritted teeth. And that was the end of the old Russia. It was like living under a foreign heel. There were good Christians who didn't abandon the faith, but the Russian radiance left their faces, too, and there was only fear, despair and the pain of the godforsaken written there.

Father Venyamin had passed through schism and prison and survived by a miracle. He had brought God's word to people, like the cross the priest holds up to the prisoner condemned to die.

The priest had grown used to the idea that Russia was finished. But now, fifty years on, after all that had happened, he suddenly began to recognize familiar faces here and there. He studied them with surprise and anxiety. At first he had always felt let down, for they gave the impression of being a mask, Russian faces rented for the day, ignorant of everything truly Russian.

One day he saw two young men in town. Chestnut beards, blue eyes, sensitive hands, standing aside from the crowd, talking heatedly. Father Venyamin tried to guess what it was they were discussing. The meaning of life? God? The ideal woman, perhaps? He came closer, and it was as if they had spat on all that was sacred! They were talking about hockey. They had the faces of Alyosha Karamazov and were discussing hockey!

And yet. And yet it was a sign. Perhaps the Russian faces would come first, to be followed by Russian souls.

Today one of these new young men had stood through the entire service at Father Venyamin's church. He had taken a good look at him. There was no sign of faith in the boy's eyes, but there wasn't that militant emptiness, either. Which meant there was something there. And that "something" was the cause of Father Venyamin's melancholy. Those eyes, he reflected, really belong to a man behind bars or the incurably sick or someone who has lost the thing he values most in life . . . He felt he ought to pray for those eyes, ask the Lord to deliver them from pain and sorrow, felt he ought to do something himself to help, to relieve, to alleviate. He knew he would spend the night in prayer and tears, and he had a conviction that his prayer would of a certainty be heard.

Father Venyamin prepared his supper mechanically, frying eggs and making a cup of tea, and when he was sitting at the table, about to say grace, he heard a knock at the door. He was surprised, he had not been expecting company. His surprise was the greater when, on opening the door, he saw the person who had been at the centre of his thoughts.

"May I? I haven't disturbed you?" The young man sounded uncertain, hesitated to cross the threshold.

"Certainly not," Father Venyamin replied. "I was about to eat on my own. The Lord has sent me a guest and I am very glad. Come in."

The young man stepped through the lobby into the room. He didn't ask a blessing or cross himself in front of the ikons. It was as if he knew he ought to, but deliberately chose not to do so in order to stress his attitude and avoid any ambiguity. His manner was unaffected. He sat gladly to table, and while he refused any eggs, he drank tea with pleasure, out of a saucer, holding it in both hands like his host, as though re-enacting an ancient custom.

They sat opposite each other, looking at each other and smiling, each perhaps at his own thoughts, but an intimacy of some kind was undoubtedly born. At the same time, though, a vague sense of alarm crept into the priest's heart.

"My name is Alexey," the visitor said at last. "I've known about you for a long time. My aunt told me a lot of good things about you. She lives in the next village and comes to your church."

Father Venyamin sat silent. He sipped his tea and looked at his visitor.

"I've come to you for help, Father . . . Though I'm almost certain it's not within your power to help me . . . All the same, I've come . . . I had to try, didn't I?"

"Of course," the priest agreed.

He could feel the young man was finding it hard to begin. It wasn't the words he was searching for, but the form of words, as if he wanted to say very little himself, yet obtain an answer to the most fundamental questions. Father Venyamin did not hurry him, nor did he encourage him to be frank. He knew that people open their hearts either out of need or out of faith. His guest was without faith. So it had to be need . . . He would open up.

"Probably I'll tell you everything," the visitor went on. "Probably. But not immediately. To begin with I'd like your answer to one question, one which is a very important one to me. And I beg you, don't hurry to answer. I have a training in philosophy and I am familiar with theology. The standard textbook answer won't do. I want to know what you think personally. You've been through a lot. I need an honest answer from a man who has seen life. Treat it as though my life depends on the sincerity of your reply."

Father Venyamin was much troubled. "You may be certain I won't lie to you, no matter what the question. And should you really let your life depend on the sincerity of any person, even a priest? It is so very hard, after all, for one person to understand another. And if I have understood you right, you want to ask me something it will not be easy to speak about?"

The young man was somewhat abashed. "Well, I was overdoing it, I suppose. Essentially, my question . . . I mean . . . I could ask any priest . . . but knowing you by reputation, I felt more like . . ."

He was suddenly tongue-tied.

"Well, when you do give me an answer, please bear in mind I'm not a believer and what I've already told you. It's very important to me."

He was silent, then fired his question: "What's a miracle, Father?"

The priest was taken aback.

"A miracle? But . . . You're placing me in an impossible situation. You ask what a miracle is and say you're not a believer. So how can I answer you? You see, to me a miracle is the manifestation of Our Lord's existence, a sign of His presence in the world . . . if we're talking about so-called supernatural phenomena . . . But to me, believe me, all God's creation is a miracle. You find that hard to understand, but look at the world through the eyes of a child or as an alien would, then every bug, all human life, it's all a miracle, and nothing can be explained without God . . ."

The priest watched the sparkle go out of the young man's eyes and stopped in full flow.

"No. That's not it. Not it at all," the visitor mumbled. Suddenly he jerked, his whole body convulsed in a kind of spasm. He saw the alarm on the priest's face and muttered, embarrassed: "It's nothing . . . I'll explain later . . . it happens every so often . . ."

Only then did Father Venyamin notice there was something unusual about the young man's appearance, about his manner, his posture, the way he sat. Hard to define precisely what. Was he ill, perhaps?

Now the young man was sitting sideways, gripping the back of the chair, and the tension both in his hands and his face was palpable.

"That's not what I wanted to hear from you," the visitor said, pulling a face.

"What did you want?" asked the priest, thinking what a thorough waste of time this was.

"You must at some time – you personally, I mean, you've seen a lot in your lifetime – you must have witnessed a miracle yourself, surely? A genuine miracle."

"No," the priest replied.

"And yet you believe in miracles?"

"I find it hard to answer you, young man. If I were to tell you that the resurrection of Our Lord Jesus Christ, His life, His death, that this was the supreme miracle, testified to by the apostles, you would not be convinced by my answer. Maybe after this sublime moment people were utterly unworthy of God's attention, since there was now so much to bear witness to. But that is merely my own opinion, sinner that I am. The Lord is infinitely merciful. And the miracles which happen to people are the manifestations of the goodness, the mercy, the fullness of love of God's heart. And may the one who rejects it find forgiveness . . ." Here he stopped and looked uncomprehendingly at the young man. "But . . . if you do not believe in God, even miracles do not exist. So why . . ."

"I believe in miracles, Father. Or at least I admit the existence of miracles."

"Impossible! Without God, what kind of a miracle could it be? If we are surrounded by matter, by matter and strict causality, where can a miracle spring from? If you recognize the existence of miracles, it presupposes the existence of at least some kind of power, some kind of origin for the miracle . . ."

"Meaning," the visitor interjected with a certain malice, "one must presuppose the miracle has a cause, yet what were you saying a moment ago about causality? Tell me."

"Don't try to trip me up. That's not good. You know what I mean, you understand my train of thought." Father Venyamin was not so much offended as disappointed.

"Of course I do. But the whole point is that certain phenomena are possible which violate causality. Is such a viewpoint tenable?"

"Certainly," the priest replied calmly. "But you will not find the answer to your question and you will not be satisfied. An answer of that sort does not solve the question, it raises endless new ones."

"But doesn't the hypothesis of God generate doubts and an endless number of questions?"

The priest was silent for a little while, and when he spoke again he chose his words carefully.

"To see God as a hypothesis is the lot of the stiff-necked and proud. It is not faith that gives birth to doubt, but our weakness, our sinfulness, our inability to follow the path of faith. But faith is tested by doubt. Tried and tested. The vanquishing of doubt is a great joy which the godless can never know . . ." Father Venyamin suddenly felt that he was growing tired, that his words were feeble and unconvincing. "Do you not think, Alyosha, that we are discussing a topic on which, as you said, your mind is made up. I cannot get to the heart of your question. I can only speak of miracles as a Divine Manifestation, and you do not believe in God. How can I help you? Try to find the answer in science . . ."

Alexey snorted sarcastically: "Unfortunately science is even less help!"

As he spoke, he jerked again. His face contorted. It was a grimace of annoyance, however, rather than pain . . . He stood up and staggered across to the window. He gripped the windowsill with his left hand and the window latch with his right, standing in profile to the priest.

"Nobody can help me," he whispered with a kind of melancholy despair.

"Are you ill?" Father Venyamin asked hesitantly.

"Ill? I wish I knew what was wrong with me myself."

"I don't understand . . ." the priest murmured. His attention was riveted by his visitor's face. He was obviously in despair, but he did not look sick in the usual sense. What then?

It was Alexey who broke the silence. "Where were we? Ah, yes . . . God as hypothesis . . . So, you believe miracles are in all cases a manifestation of God?"

"That's right," the priest answered reluctantly.

"If that is the case, there is meaning of a sort in every miracle? A kind of intimation?"

"Precisely. Why should God manifest Himself, unless to give a sign? However, God manifests Himself without imposing His presence, without imposing His will."

"I don't understand." Alexey spoke nervously, hastily.

"A person who is obstinate in his unbelief cannot be helped even by a miracle. That is what I believe."

"And what if he isn't obstinate? If he wants to believe?"

"He will believe," Father Venyamin answered with conviction.

Now the visitor was smiling. It was a smile partly of condescension, partly of regret.

"Well, Father, what if you saw a man walking on water? How would you react to that?"

"I would go down on my knees in joy and give thanks to the Lord God for His grace . . ."

He was cut short by laughter, rude, cynical laughter. But the priest did not even have time to take offence. His visitor suddenly lifted away from the window, just as he was, standing, upright, and slowly floated towards the ceiling. Now the laughter fell on the priest from above, words fell, interspersed with laughter. "Well now, Father, go down on your knees and give thanks!"

At this the visitor swivelled to a horizontal position, reached out his arms and with his fingers outspread floated at the priest, laughing wildly.

Father Venyamin came to on his bed in the corner, brought round by the touch of something cold on his forehead. Alexey was holding a wet towel to his head. He looked scared and there were tears, yes, tears in his eyes. They were the first thing the priest saw.

"You're alive! Thank God. Forgive me, please, if you can bring yourself to. It was a rotten thing to do. Forgive me, I beg you. Do you feel better now?"

"What was that?" The priest's question was barely audible. He was white.

"I'll explain. I should have told you everything. But it all came out stupid and wrong . . ."

"Are you a hypnotist? Have you come to make fun of me?"

"No. Word of honour, no. I'll explain. Now. Believe me, I didn't want it to happen like that. You had me frightened, you went so pale . . . Water?"

"Please . . ."

Father Venyamin closed his eyes, but immediately seized Alexey's arm.

"Was it a hallucination or were you really flying?"

"I'll fetch some water . . ."

The visitor still sounded rather scared and ashamed, but as he rushed out to fetch water, it seemed to the priest the young man's feet were not touching the floor. When Alexey came back with a dipper of water, Father Venyamin was on the verge of passing out again. He gulped down the water; his eyes closed. Then he groaned: "What was it you were going to tell me? Please. I'll lie here . . . Draw up a chair and sit next to me . . . And tell me . . ."

It wasn't that easy to begin, apparently, and the first sentences came rather haltingly, but only the first few. After that the confession began to flow.

"I graduated in philosophy ... I was about to carry on as a postgraduate ... Do you have any idea how tempting philosophy is, Father? The word itself is full of mystery. And the names of the great exponents have a magnificent ring – Hegel, Kant, Plato, Fichte. They don't mean anything now ... But there was a time the mere mention of those names made me go weak at the knees. And the excitement when you begin to get into the thinking of a great philosopher, as if you've had to go through the whole process with him! You feel so proud. But that's nothing. Now when you spot the first slip-up, the first tiny flaw in the logic of a great philosopher you've spent years trying to understand, that really does something for your ego. Later on, when you're able to form your own opinion of the greats, you don't even want to share it with anybody, you feel so pleased with yourself. A lot of people are perfectly satisfied with that and stop there. They go on to make a career at nit-picking commentators, but they never make philosophers. I didn't want to stop, only something else happened: I suddenly felt it was all a sham ... There are as many philosophies as there are people. Every one of them is right in so far as that is how the world appears to that individual ... You won't find truth in philosophy, only more or less talented insights, original constructs ... nothing more. And that's it! How to put it? ... just walls ... partitions ... labyrinths ... but no roof ... there's no actual building. In the sense of a truth ..." He broke off. "I'm rambling, I know. But I have to say it, believe me ..."

The priest seized his hand. "Speak. There's no need for explanations. Speak!"

"It was then I became interested in religion. It was fashionable to wear a crucifix, have ikons ... I read the Gospels and told myself I'd found what it was I'd been looking for. Here was a wisdom I could feel, even though it was beyond my powers to grasp intellectually. It was beyond my capabilities. I realized that for the rest of my life I could absorb this wisdom a bit at a time, more than enough for one lifetime. And if there is such a possibility – to comprehend the ultimate wisdom – does that leave room for anything else in your life? At that point I declared myself to be a believer."

"Declared?" Father Venyamin echoed in surprise. "Hadn't you actually found faith, since you had come to the understanding that there is no greater wisdom?"

Alexey smiled involuntarily.

"I declared I had found faith. I thought that to recognize Christianity's truthfulness and to believe in God amounted to the same thing."

"But isn't that the case?" asked the priest in astonishment.

"Certainly. Yet on the other hand, you might see Christianity as no more than a coded philosophy for preserving the human race we acquired, for example, from intellectually superior aliens from outer space."

"Yes," the priest concurred sadly, "people are prepared to believe anything except the plain, obvious truth."

"The obvious is a subjective category . . ." the young man began, and then fell silent. A moment later he continued: "So I became a believer. Grew a beard, stopped smoking, stopped fornicating . . . With my philosophical baggage I became something of a guru in my circle of friends. I started going to church, of course, and even began observing the fasts . . . Then a month ago . . ."

"Please could you fetch me some more water." The priest drank. His hands were shaking visibly and the palor seemed to have returned to his face. "Well . . . I'm listening. Carry on."

"You probably think it happened while I was praying or meditating or reading the Scriptures. Actually I was lying on the beach, my mind was a blank, no thoughts of any kind, sacred or profane . . . I went to stand up, pushed my hands into the sand and suddenly I felt I was suspended above it . . . four centimetres or so . . . I didn't dare breathe, just thought, and I lifted a bit more. I went dizzy, in other words roughly the same happened to me as happened to you half an hour ago. I passed out. Only for a second or two. And when I came round, I knew, I had this physical sense, that I could rise in the air without the slightest effort. And God didn't even enter my mind, remember that, Father. It was incredible . . . I resisted the temptation to try it again, pulled on my clothes, jumped on to a bus . . . It was full but not packed, and I pressed my legs together and hung between the other passengers . . . I got back to my room, locked the door and never even glanced at the ikons. I took a deep breath, plucked up courage and levitated to the ceiling. I floated up, came down again, turned somersaults, all the junk fell out of my pockets . . . It was like a dream . . .

"You say all miracles are God's work . . . But if that's true, I would have felt something in my soul. But I felt nothing! You understand, there was nothing, except maybe a feeling I was a bit outlandish, a

freak . . . It didn't feel like a miracle . . . Only a paradox of causality
. . . And then came the blinding insight. I had never been a believer
. . . More than that, I felt, well, how shall I put it? The emptiness of
the universe, the godlessness of the world; I felt I was quite alone in
the world . . ."

"How can this be?" exclaimed the priest. "You can fly! Fly! And yet
you speak of the emptiness of the universe, of your being alone . . .
Lord! What's wrong with people? They refuse to accept either reward
or retribution!"

He got up from the bed, walked over to the ikonostasis and fell to
his knees.

"Lord, be Thou not angry at the ignorance of Thy servants. Their
minds are clouded and their souls defiled. Great is Thy patience and
great Thy love, O Lord!"

Alexey stood aside. He looked vexed, or sad, or perhaps both at
once. When the priest had finished and went to bow, Alexey's voice
broke in harshly, jeeringly even. "I haven't told you everything yet,
Father!"

The priest went back to his bed and covered his face with his hands.
"Tell me. Tell me everything. Leave nothing hidden in your heart."

Alexey walked over to the ikonostasis. "Symbols! The symbols of
your God! And does God recognize these symbols as belonging to
Him? Blasphemy? Right?" He sat down next to the old man. "That
time in my room, after discovering I was a freak, right at the end, I
ripped an ikon from the wall. I flew about with it and mocked God.
Risky, wasn't it? But nothing happened, except the ikon shattered
when I dropped it from the ceiling. A pity! Now if I'd gone smash on
to the floor and broken my arms and legs . . ."

"You would have believed?"

". . . Not half," laughed Alexey.

"No, even then you would not have believed . . . But perhaps not,
no, I don't know."

Father Venyamin was embarrassed somehow, regretting having said
what he did.

Alexey ignored it.

"And so I began a new life. Living with a miracle. I even forgot to
think about God the first few days. Flying's quite something. Lord!
Can you imagine the pleasure, the sheer pleasure of flying. At night,
over the steppe or a lake. Spread your arms and cruise and dip and
soar. You don't need anything else in life. It's so easy . . ."

He stood up, put his hands on his head and, smiling drunkenly, floated about the room in a semi-vertical position. Apparently he suddenly thought better of it, because he dropped quickly to the floor, almost as if he'd jumped down, and glanced anxiously at the priest. Father Venyamin stood there, pale and solemn.

"A miracle. A miracle," he whispered. He sounded so full of joy, the young man looked frankly jealous. "Now I can go to my grave!"

Father Venyamin suddenly frowned. He looked worried.

"Why did God permit me to witness a miracle?" he asked, looking anxiously at Alexey. "Why? Am I not burdened with sin more than others? Surely . . ."

He blenched, as if he was about to faint, and swayed. Alexey hurried to help him, but was gently pushed aside and he retreated in surprise to a corner. The priest sank on to the bed and stared blankly past him.

"There was something else you wanted to tell me . . ."

"How are you feeling? Some water, perhaps? . . ."

"No," the priest replied. His tone was detached. "Speak. I know you still have something very important to tell me . . ."

Alexey shrugged.

"I've told you the most important things. Strange . . . First you were happy when you found out . . . Now you look the most miserable person in the world . . . I had my suspicions, but now I know. My miracle will bring misery to everybody in the end . . ."

"Everybody?" Father Venyamin hastened. "Was there somebody else . . . ?"

"We didn't get round to that," Alexey sniggered. "I'll start with me, though . . . What am I supposed to do with this miracle? Life has lost all meaning. I can't live amongst people any more because I can't control myself." He smiled. "Ah, if only you knew, Father, how many times I've had to resist temptation. More than Jesus, believe me! The number of times I've wanted to levitate in the middle of the street and enjoy watching the reactions of my fellow citizens, all of them permanently drunk on the determinism of the natural world. And don't you think I didn't want to liven things up a bit at your church today?"

"But you didn't," the priest said quietly.

"I didn't. But it wasn't out of a sense of decency. If I demonstrate it in public, they'll either turn me into a scientific guinea pig or I'll be exploited by the church. I have my vanity. I've no intention of becoming an object of study!"

"And until now nobody . . ."

"Regrettably . . ." Alexey interrupted. "But you need to be in the right frame of mind before I tell you."

He was trying to be ironic . . . But that was not how it sounded and so the priest answered in all seriousness. "I'm ready."

"I cannot live among ordinary people. It's too boring. It's not that I feel I'm a superman. I simply want to fly. I've turned into a bird of the night, Father. I can't fly by day . . . I came to the country, dropped my studies and everything as if they were so much waste paper . . . I never wanted to drink . . . haven't a clue about drugs . . . and yet it seems I'm suffering the same kind of addiction. I sleep during the day, and I keep flying in my sleep . . . I always wake up frightened: perhaps it was all a dream? If I'm alone, I have to try and see if I can still do it. I literally go shooting up into the air. When I'm certain again it's not a dream, that I really can fly, I weep with joy. If I go somewhere where it's impossible, I get this nagging doubt that the miracle's over, so I rush off to try it out and make sure . . . The worst thing, Father, is that the time I can do without gets less and less . . . People irritate me just by being there . . . I've become rude . . . cruel . . . All I want to do is fly.

"But the story I wanted to tell you is this . . . One day I went off away into the trees and began chasing birds. The uproar! . . . Birds, Father, are determinists as well. They hate to see the laws of nature violated . . .

"Anyway, I was completely carried away, and then I suddenly looked down and saw a man . . . He was standing there gawping with his mouth wide open . . . I should have got out of there, but instead I flew down towards him . . . He never uttered a sound. He just fell flat on his back. By the time I reached him, it was all over . . . I've killed a man. That's what I've done. And you very nearly gave up the ghost . . ."

The priest leapt from his bed. His eyes were wide and staring, his hands shaking . . . Alexey darted away from him.

"That's it," Father Venyamin shouted. "That's it. I, too. You, and the man, and me!" He clutched his head.

"This is all I need," muttered Alexey, backing towards the door.

"Stop," shouted the priest. "Forgive me!"

He suddenly fell on his knees before Alexey. "Forgive me! For the love of Christ, forgive me. I preached you a sermon about faith. Forgive me, I had no right to. I was myself deluded and so deluded you. And the Lord. And the Lord. You are honest . . . forthright . . . While all my life I . . ."

He fell to the ground, sobbing. Alexey was in despair.

"Damn this miracle," he yelled. He knelt beside the priest. Father Venyamin looked up, struggled back to his knees and embraced Alexey.

"No. You mustn't talk like that. You do not understand. We have all betrayed God. I am the first. By His miracle He has exposed my lie!"

The priest's voice sank to a whisper. "I was frightened, you see. Understand? I was frightened. Like that man who did not believe what he saw. And you are frightened, too, when confronted by a miracle because you are without faith. I am, too. Oh, Lord! Can I be forgiven? I have been a hypocrite and a Pharisee! Do you understand?"

Alexey extricated himself carefully, straightened up, and lifted the priest to his feet.

"I'm terribly sorry," he said, and his voice was hard, "but subtleties like that are obviously beyond me. I can't think straight when it comes to my own problems . . . I'd better go . . ."

"Wait! Wait! I beg you!"

Father Venyamin urged him to the chair and sat on the bed next to him, never letting go of Alexey's hand.

"We cannot, please understand, we cannot part like this. The Lord in His mercy has bound our lives together . . ."

"Mercy?" snorted Alexey. "What do I need His mercy for? I have recognized Him of my own free will. That was how it all happened. With this miracle He challenged the freedom of my faith and destroyed it."

"No, no, no," Father Venyamin objected hotly. "It was you who admitted there was no faith in your heart, was it not? Do not be stiff-necked! You want to be more free than God, but to be free of God means to be a slave. Understand?" He was so agitated he could only whisper. He gripped Alexey's hand hard, much harder than you would have thought possible for a man of his age. "You think of God. You thirst for faith. Overcome your arrogance, be like the infant who is just discovering the world, listen to the promptings of your own heart. That is where your truth lies."

Alexey made a dismissive gesture, but the priest did not give him time to speak.

"You do not want to accept a miracle. But think, you would have been one of those who rejected Christ. You would have crucified Him!"

Alexey looked at him attentively.

"There is a kind of logic in what you say . . . But has logic ever been a reason for anybody to have faith?"

"It's not because it's logical, it's because it's the truth. An age-old truth, which the whole world acknowledged at one time."

"The whole world acknowledged Ptolemy as the truth. So what?"

"Lord," Father Venyamin whispered, his eyes closed. There were tears on his cheeks. "Lord, give me reason. Give me words."

Alexey tried to shake himself free. He had not found comfort and the discussion had become burdensome.

"Listen," the priest said with passion. "Today, now, go home, fall on your knees and compel yourself with all the strength of your heart, compel yourself to be utterly sincere. And pray. If you feel nothing, pray harder. Pray for one hour, two, three if you have to, until you hear. You will hear, because you will be heard. My dear boy, your life is at stake, and not just this life, so fleeting and false, but life eternal, which is real, and for which the Lord, with His special mercy, is preparing you."

He embraced the young man, and continued: "I, too . . . will pray all night. And the Lord will hear the two of us if we ask for the same thing. My years are thrice yours. And I have to pray for forgiveness for all of them. Will I have the strength? I beg you. Go home and pray. Promise me."

Alexey finally freed himself. He stood up.

"I promise you, Father, that I will go home now . . ."

He stopped, his eyes glowing with a secret joy.

". . . It's dark now, right? So I can fly. I'll think over what you said while I'm doing it. I can't promise more than that."

Hastily he said goodbye to the priest. Father Venyamin, on the verge of tears, said nothing. He merely made the sign of the cross and whispered something.

By the time the garden gate banged shut behind Alexey, Father Venyamin was already on his knees.

The night was dark and warm. A man stood on a hill. Invisible to all except himself. Perhaps God saw him, too.

The night was still. All around men huddled asleep in their shelters, dreaming their sinful dreams. The past had seen it all. Abel murdered and Christ crucified, both murder and crucifixion forgotten by mankind, as a child's naughtiness is soon forgotten. And the man on the hill under the starry sky, the son of Adam, was only the image and the likeness of Adam – of Adam, not of God, because he knew nothing of God, and he would not believe the person who knew of Him by hearsay.

The night was dark and warm. Mankind yelped in its sleep, like a dog cheated of a bone. The man on the hill heard the yelping, but felt no sympathy. He no longer belonged among men, cut off from them as he was by the warmth and darkness of the night.

The man looked up into the depth of the stars and thought: "Suppose there is something that unites this infinity of matter and space, something which embodies a meaning for all the world's diversity. I might imagine it as some kind of immanent reason. I might call it God. But what contact can there be between me – dust created of dust - and what one might assume under the term God? How does this Something reduce and simplify itself in order to speak the same language as me with my puny concepts? It'd be easier for a human to make contact with an amoeba. At least there's the same general principle at work . . . cells, proteins and so forth. The very idea of God is absurd . . . and I can fly!

"That's enough. Why rack my brains any longer? That's for humanity at large. Tomorrow it will discover who I am. I'll spit in the eye of both science and religion at once. I'll show the creeps! I can fly. Fly!"

He moved back from the edge of the hill, took a run and lifted off, arms stretched forward. He was intoxicated by the sensation, his mind was drained of thoughts, cleared of problems and contradictions. He didn't feel his body, he was conscious only of himself, as if he was now what he ought always to have been since birth – an immortal free spirit, liberated from all the cares of the flesh. His life was flying, it had no other meaning.

He lost all sense of time. He flew and knew that he would never tire of it. He changed direction automatically, not thinking about where he was flying to, or how far.

Quite some time must have passed. Suddenly the stars vanished, covered by unseen clouds. He lost his bearings. He had lost his sense of horizon; his sense of spatial relationships had vanished. Earth and sky vanished. Climb and descent were indistinguishable. Yes, he was now upright, but where the ground was, above or below, to the right or left, there was no knowing. Fear, something he had not experienced before, gripped his heart. He hunted desperately from side to side, in all directions, but they were infinite, as many as there were facets to his imagination. He shouted, wildly, despairingly, but mankind, even if it was somewhere close at hand, slept on and did not hear his cry. He knew he had lost the earth. And without it, it seemed, life was impossible. God had given him wings and the earth had given up its gravitational force.

He screamed and hurled himself into headlong flight.

Father Venyamin spent the night in prayer. Towards morning he dozed, exhausted, on the floor in front of the ikonostasis. He was woken by the woman next door, who brought him his milk as usual at seven. Worried, she asked if he was feeling well. Then she told him about the accident in the village. A man had been killed during the night. The girls found him on their way to milking. A young man, good-looking, too . . .

"Where is he?" shouted the priest, giving his neighbour a bad scare.

"The militia came from town and took the body away."

The villagers stared curiously as the priest hurried down the village street, hair and beard flying.

The village nurse was taken by surprise when the priest burst into her office.

"Tell me, did you see him?"

"Who?"

"The young man . . . who was killed . . ."

"Yes," she replied, not understanding what was required of her.

"What happened?"

"I don't know, he looked like he'd fallen out of a plane . . . all smashed up . . ."

Father Venyamin ran back to his lodgings. He didn't stop to shut the door, he collapsed in prayer in front of the ikons and burst into tears.

Translated by Frank Williams

YURY DOMBROVSKY

An Arm, a Leg, a Gherkin too . . .

THAT STIFLING JUNE evening he was lolling on the sofa, half asleep or just in a state of uneasy oblivion, when through his feverish doze he imagined they were talking to him on the telephone again. The conversation was rough and menacing; they were threatening him: they promised to break his bones or worse – lie in wait for him somewhere in the entrance hall and smash his skull in with a hammer. That had actually happened not long before, except that the murderer had used a heavy bottle instead of a hammer. He had struck from behind, on the back of the head. The man had lain in hospital for a week and died without regaining consciousness. He hadn't even turned thirty, and had only just published his first book of verse.

These thoughts roused him into an awareness that the phone really was ringing.

He went over to it and glanced through the window. By now the light was fading; it must be after seven. I'll get back home after dark again, he thought, and picked up the receiver.

"Yes," he said.

The answering voice was youthful, resonant, with a hint of insolence.

"And who is speaking?"

It's somebody else now, he realized. Is there a whole gang of them over there, or what? He asked: "Well who do you want, then?"

"No, who is this speaking?"

"But who do you want?"

"Maybe I've got the wrong number. Who . . ."

"No, no, it's right, it's the right number. Four of you have rung me already today. So carry on."

"Ah, it's you, you filthy sonofabitch, bloody rotten writer. Just you remember: we're warning you for the last time, swine – if you don't put a stop to your foul . . ."

"Wait a minute. I'm getting a chair. Listen, do you all get given copies or something over there? Why do you all keep harping on the same old thing? I can't see any free creativity there, no flight of fancy. Let's have at least one word of your own; it's all uncle's as it is."

"All what uncle's?"

"Uncle Dick's. No, but seriously, have you got no minds of your own? Just 'filthy sonofabitch', just 'we'll smash your skull in', just 'vile activities'. Incidentally, one of you pricks pronounces it 'activities'. Activists! Give him my regards!"

"OK, stop trying to charm away the toothache. My teeth are sound."

"Ah, I'd enjoy smashing them in!"

"Why you!" For a second the receiver was positively stupefied. "I'll eat you alive."

"And are you far from here?"

"Wherever I am, we'll get you. So we're warning you – and for the last time . . ."

"Hold it! Somebody at the door. Just don't hang up."

He went over to the door, took a look through the eyehole and saw her standing there, the woman he'd been expecting for three days now, the one he'd had desperate need of that morning. The whole country knew and loved her and she was due to have played a part in his film. Her pictures – young, beautiful, smiling – hung in the foyer of practically every cinema; her photos adorned every newspaper kiosk. She was always recognized whenever she appeared in the street with him. He had waited and waited for her these three blasted days, and now she was simply no use to him.

"More trouble," he thought. "Why has everything started piling up on me all at once?"

He opened the door. She didn't just come in, she flew in and rushed at him. Not towards him, at him. She was in such a state and breathing so heavily, puffing and panting, that she couldn't get a word out for several seconds.

"Well, what's the matter?" he asked, somewhat roughly. "Get a hold of yourself, now! Look at you, just look at you!" He shook her lightly by the shoulder. "Now then!"

She moistened her dry lips.

"Oh, I'm so pleased to see you're all right. Your phone's engaged all the time."

"That's right. I was having a sleep and took it off the hook. All sorts of riff-raff kept calling up."

"They rang my brother too, asking for you; they were threatening to get you in the entrance hall. I'd just got back from the set and he told me. I rushed round here straightaway. You can see I didn't even get changed."

She was in her working clothes, slacks, blouse, big sunglasses.

"Well, sit down and catch your breath then. I'll just finish talking.

You still there, peasant?" he asked the receiver. "Good man. So have you got far to come?"

"What do you want to know that for?" The voice held a genuinely disconcerted note now. It sounded as if other voices were in the background. "You want to track me down, is that it, swine?"

"No, I want to make a practical suggestion. You've often been round here and know the lie of the land. So then, if you intend killing me, you know all you need to know. So this is it. Diagonally opposite here there's some waste ground. It used to be a derelict building and now it's been demolished. The drunks hit the bottle there till eleven. You know the place?"

"Well, so what are you leading up to, you old goat?"

"This is what I suggest. There's nobody there just now. The boozers are still at home. In fifteen minutes I'll walk out there and wait for you. You just come along. With a hammer or a bottle, on your own or the whole pack of you – I'll be waiting for you. Is it a deal?"

"What do you mean, you bastard . . . Why, I'll . . ."

"Wait, don't start swearing, thickhead! I'm fed up with all this!" He gently fended off the actress as she dashed over to him and gripped his fingers.

"For God's sake," she said, "it's . . ."

He waved her away.

"So that's it. You come along. We'll have a little chat. But come prepared, don't forget. If you make a mess of it – it's the ambulance for you, I can guarantee you that. I know how to do it. You know very well the places I've been and the things I've seen – and the kind of roast chicken I've had stuck up my backside."

"Don't try and frighten me, you swine. We'll be lying in wait for you on the waste ground as well. Just you wait!"

"No need for ambushes. I'm volunteering. I'm sick of you dumb-bells shooting your mouths off, you bastard, sick to death."

"One fine specimen of your sort's been shot already; that dauber. From a car . . ."

"There, you see the way they treat you, dummy. They haven't even told you who was killed, how it was done or what for. He wasn't a dauber or a doctor, he was an artist. And he was shot by accident; a cop did it. Lost his head and let him have it from the car. The one murdered in the entrance was a poet."

"There you are . . ."

"And it wasn't you who killed him, it was somebody a bit more serious than you lot. All you buggers are good for is two kopeck's worth of yap from a telephone box. Dickheads is all you are. When they want to kill people they don't ring them up. So that's it. You be there in fifteen minutes, on the dot. Got that?"

"Are you going to get the vigilantes in?"

"Don't do it in your pants before you have to. I'll be on my own. It's all open ground. That's all. I'm hanging up."

The actress was sitting on a cushion, regarding him. Her face wasn't even chalk white, it was the colour of cocaine; it had that same ghastly crystalline glow.

"What on earth was all that?" she asked softly.

"What do you mean? A most businesslike conversation."

"And you're going?"

"Certainly . . ."

He went over to the table, opened a drawer and rummaged among his papers till he found a Finnish knife. Some black-haired individual had jumped him on the stairs with it a year before. It had been on the eighth floor, about eleven at night and the bulbs had been unscrewed. He had broken the swarthy attacker's wrist and the knife had dropped out of his hand. As a parting gift he had smashed him another twice across his off-white, livid-crimson features, adding peaceably: "Off you go, deary." Say what you like, he'd been taught to handle himself properly in a fight when he'd been inside. The knife was handcrafted, a beautiful inlaid job, and he thought a great deal of it. He gripped it in his fist, brandished it and admired his belligerent arm for a moment. It looked fine at that. The knife glittered, blood-red coral.

"That's how it is, madame," he said.

The actress was on her feet, staring at him, her eyes almost crazed.

"I'm not going to let you go anywhere. It's plain suicide. Not while I'm here . . . No, no!" she cried.

He frowned and tossed the knife on to the table.

"Well, it's just like my stupid scenario! Listen to me, silly," he said affectionately. "They won't eat me. On my honour! On mine and yours! They're yobs, drunks, trash; they just talk big. They're the sort that used to steal our rations in the North, and we used to duck them in the latrines for it. Not kill them; just so they got a good taste of it. And I'll teach them a lesson today."

"There'll be a dozen there. They won't give you time to turn round. There's the bushes, remember."

"Well, I'm not blind either. I'll see them. The sort of gentry they are – punch one on the nose and knock another one down and they all run away. But see how they've terrified you. Now how can I not give the idiots a lesson after that?"

He spoke lightly, with confidence and conviction, and she gradually calmed down. He could always make her believe anything he said. She shot a glance at him at that moment – at ease, unhurried, collected – he wasn't like that in his private existence – and almost believed that nothing awful was going to happen. They'd just have a talk, man to man, and that would be it. He too realized that she had recovered herself, laughed and clapped her on the shoulder.

"There, there, be a good girl. Just sit and wait . . . Afterwards you can take me to the station. I'm off to the dacha. As it is, I've been hanging around here for three days, drinking with the riff-raff, and the work's not getting done. Get your bag, powder your nose and wipe your eyes. They're redder than a sea perch's – and your mascara's run. Just take a look in the mirror. Pretty Masha, eh?"

"And there's no getting out of this?" she asked, picking up her bag.

"No. You must realize that! They're getting brazen. Once they realize I'm scared, they really will finish me off round some corner or ambush me in the entrance, like that poor chap. Here it's all in the open!"

"Oy!" and she jumped up again.

"Sit still! I'll be back directly. You can look out of the kitchen window. You can see everything from there."

"Then you and I . . ."

"Thanks a lot. So we're going to put on a show for them, are we? Julian Semyonov in four parts? Just sit there, that's all."

And he again pressed her down on to the sofa.

However, less than five minutes had passed since the phone conversation. The waste ground was only a couple of steps away, a matter of crossing the street. So should he stand about in full view?

He sat down at the table again and brooded, head propped on hand. The phone started ringing. He picked it up reluctantly, listened, then brightened and said: "Yes, hello. Of course I recognized your voice." He listened for a moment and replied: "I'll be there all day. Not at all. No, it's not too early. I get up at six. I'll be waiting, then." He replaced the receiver and smirked. "This meeting on the waste ground's nothing! Tomorrow the editor's dropping in on me first thing . . ."

She realized at once who he was talking about, and offered condolences.

"You really dislike him so much?"

He scowled.

"No, no, it's not that I dislike him, it's just . . ."

She got up from the sofa, went over to the mirror, then got hold of a stool and sat down next to him.

". . . It's just that you don't like him." And suddenly she began painstakingly drawing with her finger on the green paper – something longish, rounded, twisted, with lots of bulges and hollows this way and that, inwards and outwards.

"What's that? A snake?"

"Nearly. A curve. A ruler that draws curved lines. That's him. And this is you!" And she swiftly – one, two, three! – turned out an oval, with two little lines at the bottom, two at the top, and a little circle above them, and on the circle lots and lots of little lines sticking out above, below and to the sides – a head, long hair, hands and feet.

He laughed.

"I was taught that when I was young as well. An arm, a leg, a gherkin too – and there's a little man for you . . ."

"There you are, there's your little man for you." She smiled into his eyes.

"Hmm! So that's what I am – an arm, a leg, and tufts of hair. Not too flattering, you know."

"Not very, of course, but the curve is far worse."

"Worse? And so elegant?"

"I hate it. It's cunning, twisting its way round everything, enfolding everything, creeping up on everything. There's nothing straight about it, it's all bends, turns and breaks."

"You know a lot of people like that?"

"Everybody's like that at our place. Me above all."

"Marvellous! But I'm like that . . ." He indicated the invisible drawing.

"Yes, you're like that." She had used the intimate "thou" for the first time.

He thought for a moment, then stood up.

"Well, time to go, it seems. I'm off. You sit tight. Shan't be long."

But he was a long time coming back. She sat placidly now because she could see that nobody came up to him or even set foot in the derelict plot. He just wasted half an hour sitting about on a Moroccan orange box.

"The rotten sods. All mouth," he said crisply. "Well, just let them tangle with me another time!" He banged his faceted tumbler – the boozer's saviour – down on the table. He had a cupboard stuffed with them; someone had told him they brought a house good luck. "Look, here's a dandelion chain I made while I was sitting out there. See, just like the sun. Have a smell. There're bees in there, bees; you can hear the buzzing. Have you got your car? Hands steady? Show me. Excellent. Can you drop me off at the station?"

"Oh, today I can take you all the way home."

"No, not home today. It's the holidays you know. Traffic cops everywhere. Quicker by train."

"Why not stay? Tomorrow would do."

"Can't. The wife thinks I've got lost. The cats are yowling. They're fond of me. Let's away!"

There was a good half-hour before the last suburban train, but there were few people about. By now it was becoming quite dark. The station lamps were on. After a sultry and oppressive day the air was still and somehow stagnant. The dusty poplars stood stupefied in the lilac glow of the lamps. A man came up and sat down next to him.

"You don't happen to know the time, do you?" he enquired of this neighbour.

"Oh, the train will be here in five minutes," came the response. "Don't you recognize me or what, old man?" The neighbour called him by his Christian names.

"Good lord!" he exclaimed. "What brings you here? Do you live on this line now?"

"No, no. I'm just staying with a friend. Actually you know him." He mentioned the name of a fairly well-known essayist. "I fixed him up with a dacha out there, so now and again at holiday time I go and spend a night with him. We take a walk in the morning, have a swim, drop of vodka. Very nice."

"I should think it is!" he replied, smiling as he surveyed his companion.

The latter had worked at one time for a regional newspaper and was now the chairman of the provincial bibliophile society. A couple of years previously he had phoned one day and asked him to speak at one of their meetings. Just to talk or read an extract. The evening had been a great success – lots of applause, a bouquet of gorgeous carnations cut on the spot and brought to him, a whole crowd to see him off, pressing requests to come again. Since then not so much a friendship as an agreeable acquaintance had grown up between him and the bibliophile, whose outward appearance had greatly taken his fancy. He was a husky individual, with a round face, hazel-flecked eyes and a droll turned-up nose. Every inch a tractor driver or team leader, you'd say. The bibliophile used to invite him all over the place, either to read a story, or give a lecture on somebody's anniversary, or just to chat about writers and writing in general. He was very courteous and unfussy and always paid well, something the writer also valued, since he was chronically short of cash. He rarely got into print and was never reissued. A year ago now he had finished his great novel and it was going the rounds. This was when all his troubles had started raining down, beginning with the telephone calls and ending with editorial rejections. Still, he had foreseen it all and was not disposed to repine too much.

"Where are you getting off?" he asked the bibliophile.

He mentioned a station, not exactly near but not all that far, about half an hour from where the writer was now living.

"Well then, we'll be able to talk our heads off. You know, I've missed you."

The train pulled in. The carriages were practically empty. The lights were on at half-power.

"Well, how is it with the novel? Any prospects?"

"Not on your life! It's the off season for me and no mistake!"

"You spent eleven years on it, I hear."

"And a bit."

"Yes," the bibliophile sighed again and even shook his head. "And now I hear you're having some sort of harassment? Some yobs threatening you . . ."

"Yobs is just what they are. It's all right, nothing serious. The usual filth."

"Don't be afraid. If anything happens, we'll stick up for you. Like this!" He showed a small but solid fist.

"Oh, I'm not afraid." The writer smiled. "But thanks all the same."

The bibliophile suddenly plucked at his sleeve.

"Look! Why don't you get off with me? We've got a half-litre of Young Man's Education left, what do you say?"

"You tempt me!" The writer smiled again. "Serpent! The green serpent of Eden, that's what you are!"

"No, but seriously? Tomorrow morning first thing you could go on to your place. Why drag on in the dark? Your wife will be fast asleep by now, don't worry. I could introduce you to one of your keenest readers. He lives there as well. A young chap. Writing a historical novel. He'd be thrilled. Shall we?"

"Very very tempting! Half-litre, you say? What's this novel the young man's writing?"

"Oh, I haven't read it, actually. I know it's historical though."

"Our history or some other country's?"

"Abroad."

"What country?"

"Denmark."

"Really now? He knows Danish history as well as that, does he? That's not something you often come across. What's his name?"

"Name! Blast! That's gone as well. I use his Christian name normally, you see. Hell knows what's happening to my memory."

"Yes, indeed, hell knows what's happening to the world," the writer thought. "Everybody going mad somehow. Everyone losing their memory."

"So, have you made your mind up to go with me?" the bibliophile spoke again. "It's ten minutes' walk from the station. It would be really nice."

"It's my wife, you see. I'm scared in case she runs off. What does she want with a husband like me? Drinks, disappears lord knows where to or who with. Otherwise it would be a real pleasure . . ."

"Splendid woman, your wife," said the bibliophile feelingly. "She doesn't have a very high opinion of me though."

"Whatever makes you think that?" The writer was greatly surprised, recalling that his wife had in fact seen the bibliophile only on one occasion and immediately taken against him. Or rather, something about him had put her on her guard.

"Oh, for some reason she thought I was, you know . . ."

He tapped his finger lightly against the seat.

The writer said nothing because that was true as well. They had discussed him together – where had he sprung from, such a good man, just at the time of their greatest anxieties? She had confided her doubts only to a single acquaintance, however. His had been the name mentioned by both the bibliophile and his female companion, indicating that they had mutual acquaintances. His wife had phoned up this mutual acquaintance, but had learnt nothing concrete. "No, that woman is perfectly all right," he had said. "It's just that she behaves rather indiscreetly at times. She has undesirable friends. She reads all kinds of literature and passes it on. Her tongue wags too much. They might have something more serious on her, perhaps, so it's possible he's keeping an eye on her. Although I doubt it; otherwise I'd have known."

That had been the sum total of the conversation. How had the bibliophile found out about it? The common acquaintance couldn't possibly have let it slip . . . Then all at once, it dawned on him! They had talked on the telephone, hadn't they? That meant . . .

The train began to slow. Station outbuildings and little brick chateaux began flickering past.

"Well, this is me!" said the bibliophile as he got to his feet. "So what's it to be, do we get off?"

"No, I'm going on to the wife!" snapped the writer. A chill entered the atmosphere.

"Well then, au revoir!" The bibliophile spread his arms.

"All the best, now." The writer nodded, thinking: "No, I'm definitely a sick man; all sorts of weird ideas getting into my skull. I should get to a psychiatrist, quick!"

He automatically followed the bibliophile with his eyes. He was proceeding along the platform when all at once he halted and waved to somebody outside the writer's field of vision. It was then he realized that this wasn't the station the bibliophile had mentioned at all; that one was several stops further on. He had barely time to think: "I'll be damned!" before the bibliophile rushed back in, hotfoot, and dropped heavily into his former seat.

"Wrong station!" he said. "Brain like a sieve! Incidentally, I've remembered that writer's name – it's Birmashov. And his book's set in Hamlet's time, the seventeenth century."

"You mean Shakespeare wrote his *Hamlet* in the seventeenth century, but Hamlet himself lived a lot earlier – in the eleventh! That's what Saxo Grammaticus says at any rate. There aren't any other sources, so maybe there never was a Hamlet at all!"

"Such a lot you know," said the bibliophile sweetly, taking out a notebook.

"So it's Barmashov?" asked the writer, deliberately getting the name wrong. The bibliophile nodded. "Got half a litre, you say?"

"Yes, maybe more. They made some moonshine over there for a wedding."

"Oh well, I'll go with him," the writer resolved swiftly. "It's the only way to cure myself; otherwise I'll simply go off my head. What have I got to be scared of anyway? The novel's written, and I'll be sixty-eight in a week's time! Enough's enough. He's a grand chap. It's me who's the dummy; hell knows what I'll dream up next. I'm just giving myself the willies . . ."

"All right," he said. "We'll go together."

"Now that really is splendid." The bibliophile was delighted, positively rubbing his hands.

The writer automatically put his hand in his pocket, but the Finnish knife wasn't there. "Well, to hell with it," he thought. "You can't get rid of fear by being frightened, the only cure is to be fearless . . ."

They got off two stops further on. It was a little forest halt, or rather not a halt, a platform. It was completely dark now. The cool blackness was barely illuminated by a solitary yellow lamp. There was probably a pond nearby, as there was a whiff of slime and stagnant water and there were frogs swarming everywhere. Large, warm, still pools were standing on the asphalt and in the surface hollows. Tiny brown froglets were hopping about in all directions. The writer stooped to brush his hand along the tall grass.

"It's been raining here," he said, breathing deeply in the resin-laden air.

As the bibliophile took the writer's arm, the latter felt the other's pocket against his hip. "Browning, light-calibre, Belgian probably," he decided.

"What have you got in there?" he asked.

"A Browning." The bibliophile smiled. "Watch this!" He instantly whipped the gun out and levelled it at the writer. "Now then," he said, placing it against his own temple. Something clicked. A transparent blue flame darted high into the air.

Both men laughed.

"I got it off a drunk for a fiver," said the bibliophile, stowing the lighter away. "German. Burnished steel. Comes in handy when you want to give somebody a fright. Like the people who keep phoning you, for example."

"Oh, blow them. Is it far?"

They had entered the forest and the scent of resin and pine needles had intensified. The bibliophile retained his hold on the writer's arm, gently pressing it against his side, allowing the other to feel his firm masculature, unmoving, as if cast in metal.

"Oh, nearly there. What's the matter, are you very tired?"

"I am," sighed the writer. "I'm very tired, dear comrade of mine. Lately times have been so hard."

"Writing for eleven years . . . Well, never mind, now you can rest from all your labours." The bibliophile seemed to find something to smirk about.

"Death grip," came the sudden poignant thought. "Pistons, not muscles. The ones that drive locomotives. No escape from them. The forest, and in the forest a hut on chicken's legs . . ."

The bibliophile halted suddenly and switched on his torch. Why on earth hadn't he used it earlier? It revealed a door. It was obviously a woodsman's hut. It stood by itself, and anyone living there would have to be extremely daring or well armed. The bibliophile touched the door and it sprang away from him as if automatically. They entered and the door closed behind them with a wolfish click of steel.

"This is the end," thought the writer, going cold, despite sensing a kind of relief. "And no one will ever know where my grave is. Just got on a train and never got off. Vanished into thin air. No one to accuse. No traces. Complete annihilation."

A second door opened. Two brawny toughs were sitting at a desk covered in oilcloth; the floor was also covered in oilcloth. White, slippery, terrifying. The light burned inside a green glass shade. "Father used to have one like that in his study," he thought. One fellow was plump and had a neatly shaven head; he was ruddy from the sun, like a winter apple. The other resembled a horse with a white mane. They gazed at him in silence. Ruddy-face smiled. White-mane said nothing. The bibliophile stood behind him. Nobody said anything. There was, after all, nothing really to say.

"So, it's on a box on waste ground is it?" asked White-mane. "And here's us inviting you to a little dacha, everything laid on." And he smiled, displaying flat teeth, also equine. He was absolutely still, but frighteningly, deathly tense, and this tension of his created in this room of white oilcloth an invisible but oppressive force field.

"Yes, that one will rip you to bits as soon as look at you," thought the writer.

"Now he'll have a little box with a lid on," smiled Ruddy-face. "That's what he's won for himself. The game's up; his little bit of sabotage is over, and his slander and his drinking our blood, the bastard."

The writer wanted to leap backwards but was unable to do so; although his legs were standing perfectly straight, they did not move; it was as if they were gripped in a force field. Something steely and implacable squeezed his neck and crushed his throat. His attempt to cry out was choked with blood. Clearly the bibliophile was a past master in his line of work. The haze of blinding, hot crimson light hovered in front of him for a few more split seconds, but now it was in his brain rather than his eyes; his body, however, which had over long years become hardened to anything, even death, was still alive and answering evil with evil. The bibliophile doubled up from a terrible kick in the groin. The pressure was released. "Now then," said his body, instantly springing away and pressing itself against the wall. It was horrible – covered in blood and some sort of vile sticky stuff, crimson, with eyes starting from their sockets. All this had taken place in a matter of seconds. Ruddy-face leapt to his feet, grabbing for his pocket, but at once sat down again. At this, Horse shouted: "You lying swine!" and rushed at this man by the wall, still grim and terrible and ready for mortal combat. He hurled a flat paperweight at him, striking him full on the temple. The body crumpled to its knees. But when Horse closed in to deliver another blow, it seized him by the leg and brought him down. They rolled around the floor, Horse at once finding himself underneath. At this point Ruddy-face came over and with a deft, well-calculated movement struck the upper figure with a lancet. The blow landed precisely in the hollow at the base of the skull. The hands relaxed. The struggling heap fell apart. Ruddy-face struck again in the same place. Horse picked himself up. He was dripping wet and racked with coughing. Ruddy-face, meanwhile, had bent down and checked the man's pulse in a professional manner – as he turned, his medical badge flashed crimson – and then glanced into the rapidly dimming eyes.

"All over," he pronounced.

"Well, thanks, boys," croaked the bibliophile, straightening up and recovering his breath. "Stand back though, just stand back! You can see the mess! Ah, hell! So much for lack of preparation. He could easily have killed somebody, the swine! The car will be here presently. It followed us along. I got out to signal it."

Horse was standing and staring. He had really caught it. He was breathing with a sort of whistling, sobbing sound.

"Whew!" said the bibliophile, savagely lashing his boot into the corpse's temple. "Whew, the swine!" He lashed out again and again, but the head merely lolled softly on the oilcloth.

Horse was standing with his mouth half open, teeth gleaming.

"He's tough all right!" he said. "You know I never thought he'd go with you. 'Come along, peasant!'" It would be hard to convey the peculiar inflection in his voice at these words. But it was certainly there. It made the bibliophile glance at him.

"Sit down now, just sit down; you're all of a tremble," he said. "Where did he catch you? Ech, it's a pity you can't shoot anybody here."

"He talked to me on the phone, swore at me, called me a peasant.

That woman went running to him, tried to make him change his mind, cried over him. I heard it all – but no, he went out. He picked flowers for her, dandelions. You can't persuade people like that, can you?"

"What's the matter? Sorry for him are you?" The bibliophile said, angered. "Didn't hit you hard enough, is that it? Get yourself a drink."

The white-haired man shook, his face streaming, and not because he was on the point of vomiting.

"Go on, give him a hug!" jeered the bibliophile. "Fine sort of baby I've been landed with. If you're going to cry over every swine . . ."

A siren sounded.

"Coming, coming," said the bibliophile and went out.

"He's the one I'd like to get," said White-hair. "No messing, I'd . . ."

"But what's he got to do with it?" The ruddy-faced one with the medical badge was astonished. "He had his orders and we had our orders from him. That's all there is to it."

White-hair seated himself at the table, opened a drawer and took out a bottle. He bit off the metal top, poured out a full glass and tossed it down in one gulp. He sat for a moment, gritting his teeth, then suddenly lashed out with his foot at the side of the desk. The desk groaned and rattled. It was made of plywood; everything here was artificial – plywood, oilcloth – everything apart from the bolts on the door: those at any rate were steel and automatic.

"I'd take him apart, no messing," said Horse. "I heard that order. When I told him on the radio that this one here was coming out to meet me, he said: 'Oh no, that won't do. You go and wait in the duty post. If he's not afraid, warnings are out; the job has to be done.'"

"Well, what of it? It's right enough," said Ruddy-face. "That's what we've done."

"Then after a bit he gets through to me, says: 'Go to the forest guardhouse. You're not required. He's gone to his dacha.'"

"He sent three others to the dacha in the car. He'd had it either way," said Red-face, "so don't fret about it."

"And that doll couldn't hold him. Even brought him herself. Brainless bird."

"Quiet! They're coming. Cut the speeches."

"So it's Barmashov?" asked the writer, deliberately getting the name wrong. "Got half a litre, you say?"

"Even more, probably. They've made some moonshine. Let's go, shall we?"

"No, no," smiled the writer. "It looks like I'm headed for home, the old shack." But all of a sudden, when the bibliophile was already on the step, he shouted: "Just a second! A counter-suggestion. Why not come on to my place? What if they *are* asleep? We'll sit out in the hall. I've got something special tucked away. For heaven's sake don't say no! As it is, I've started going crazy. Here I am sitting with you and imagining things in broad daylight."

At this the bibliophile obediently returned and lowered himself into his seat.

"I'll go with you wherever you like."

And the other, an old man, engineer of human souls, as someone once put it, reflected despondently, in profound self-disgust: "What cowardly creatures we are, when all's said and done. Another couple of phone calls like that and we'd run away from everybody. Those swine know just what they're doing. Here am I plucking up courage, going out to meet them, coming back proud of myself – I'm not afraid, oh no! And after that I'm scared witless the whole time." He felt so wretched, he didn't know what to say or do. After all, a simple, ordinary chap was sitting opposite him now, someone who was really fond of him, and here he was starting to see even affection as a fake and a pretence. So had he ever been worthy of real affection? He thought about this while they journeyed on, and later, while they were walking, and in consequence kept up a steady stream of trivial nonsense, just so as to stifle the sense of shame he felt. No, no, by now it was more than shame: he positively ached and burnt like an open inflamed wound. All mouth! The pipsqueaks! Twopenny jam, as they used to say in the North. Nothing straightforward, everything devious. Nothing in their hands but plenty in their hearts! Wriggling like adders in a swamp, at each others' throats like curs in a dog catcher's cage. An arm, a leg, a gherkin too . . . If it had only been that, but it was nothing like that, was it?

"Curve," he suddenly said aloud, then paused. "Damned curve."

"Now why be like that?" The bibliophile was pained. "I used to be a draughtsman myself. You can't manage without a curve there."

"That's right, but I'm not a draughtsman, am I!" he cried out despairingly. "Whatever you say, I'm a man, I'm an arm, a leg and a gherkin too! I'm not a curve."

Somebody laughed in the darkness, and a woman's voice explained: "That's the only sort you get on these electrics coming back from Moscow. They get sozzled up there . . ."

They walked another half-block and the bibliophile said: "Well, we seem to have arrived. There's the 'Writer's Lodge' sign. Au revoir. I

. . . I'm sorry . . ." He set off at a run. "Otherwise I'll miss the train. And I absolutely have to be there. Today."

"So you're not coming?" the writer called after him, disappointed.

"I'm sorry. I can't! Another time! I was just seeing you to the door. I can see you're not quite yourself. I haven't a minute. So long!"

"What about the half-litre, then?"

"But I'm a teetotaller." The bibliophile laughed. "You hadn't forgotten that, had you?"

Yes, yes, he had forgotten everything. Everything.

Translated by Alan Myers

LARISA VANEEVA

Lame Pigeons

I'VE NEVER LIKED singing in the choir. And I can't bear PE either.
I'm always trying to get out of those sorts of things. But thanks to
Schneidermann, our singing teacher, our school always comes top at
the local festivals and so everyone gets driven into the gym for choir
practice. Us fourth formers get separated by height and voice on to
the benches we usually have to sit freezing on all the way through PE,
just for the sake of jumping over the horse three times. Midgets on
the floor, normal-sized ones above them, then us at the top. And I
stick out like a water tower even amongst the beanpoles.

It's real torture! Open your mouths children . . . Ah-ah-aaah . . .
You do it, now you, now YOU . . . In front of all the Bs! What
torture! In front of Egor Novikov and Garry Mikhailovsky from the
Bs . . . In front of all the other forms! The foghorns are honking. It's
a piece of cake for them. They can honk right from the bottom of
their stomachs. The teacher pulls a painful face, like an old monkey in
a zoo. But I'm frightened of just moving my lips, let alone singing.
And if I do start singing, it's ghastly. It's just *so* out of tune! Good
old Lenochka is in front of me, so close I could even blow on her
golden hair. She's little Miss Perfect, and she's got a silvery kind
of voice which just comes tripping out. A silvery voice, she loves
singing, and as if that was not enough, she's pretty too. She gets
called out of the ranks and now she's singing solos with the teacher.
Solveig.

You can get complexes here from a very early age.

Our singing teacher wears a bohemian scarf, carries a cane, and is
driven by a manic desire to enamour us of singing. That's exactly what
he says. "I vant to enamour you of singing. I vant to enamour you of
singing – school home break street . . ." "Lesson!" prompts the choir.
Titters and giggles . . . The old fellow shakes his noble ape-like head
and, all of a sudden, produces with a great flourish a dark pointer from
goodness knows where. He stands up on tiptoes, as if trying to reach
something high up with it. Then having finally reached whatever it
was up there to the accompaniment of our sniggers, he pauses for a
moment, then begins to bring it down quietly, then even more quietly,

bending down after it, straining his ear. There isn't any music at all and everyone is still larking about, but he keeps on bringing it down more and more quietly, listening to some sort of music on his own and, believe it or not, the racket dies down. The entire choir falls silent and submits to his mute power. After bringing the silent note to the very bottom, the old fellow gives himself a shake and then gets on with the lessons.

"Children, I vanted to repeat today . . ." He chews over his words with endearing little mistakes, because he is German, our singing teacher, like many of the pupils from school number 47 in the Siberian town of N, offspring of the Volga Germans who were exiled there in the war.

"Children! Schumann; 'The Evening Star' . . . *Kinder*! 'The Trout' by Schubert . . ."

The trout splashes in the living water, glinting like silver . . .

To this day I still don't know what sort of voice I've got. So I don't sing. But I could if I wanted to. I've got perfect pitch after all. I might have sung, if what happened had not happened. I was a mute fish before and I've remained one. A splashing trout . . . Once, though, the only time in my life, when I was in the eighth form, I started singing after school one day in a low contralto or a mezzo-soprano (God knows what the difference is), like Maria Callas or rather Leonarda Daine. Everyone was so amazed that they almost fell over, and I almost fell over too. I slid off the desk which I had been sitting astride and scampered home on my shaking extremities. Since then absolutely nothing has happened. It's a shame really. I open my mouth dumbly, but the thought of actually singing . . .

"Young lady, yes, yes, you, young lady, come to me after school today. Tell your mother that I am going to work with you. You have got a good ear but you're too embarrassed to sing. That's bad. It can't be a good thing to be embarrassed about singing, my child. We will stretch your voice. It's crucial to stretch the voice. Then you will be able to start singing like . . . a nightingagaga . . ."

He got stuck on the last syllable.

Jumping up and down in excitement on my spindly legs, forgetting my superstition that stepping on the cracks in the pavement was forbidden lest my mother and father should start ignoring each other again (I never knew coming home from school whether they would still be talking to each other or had ceased all communications for a month), I skipped past a pigeon on a manhole cover.

I turned back.

The feathers on its neck were all ruffled up like a jabot. It looked at me out of the corner of its eye, shivering . . .

Aaaghh! I tore home with a wild, choked howl, my satchel full of pencils bashing against my shoulderblades, the pigeon on my outstretched hands. I was holding it alternately against my chest and on my outstretched hands . . . I was yelling my head off, bounding up the steps in our huge entrance hall, where there are such huge gaps in the mesh between the banisters, and for the umpteenth time, I wanted to fall out of my life.

I do not want to live, folks. It's abnormal, but it's true. All of us here are condemned to life, folks.

My sensitive forebears who had endowed me with an acute sensitivity perhaps felt guilty about it and so they would never protest if I or my sister brought into the flat various of God's creatures with broken limbs. As someone once said, all you can do is not torture animals. That was the idea. My mother would rub iodine into the creature in front of me, bandage it, give it some medicine and force something down the bird's throat with her fingers. And then she would send me to bed. Also with force. Never mind what time of day it was. With a tranquillizer or some valerian. Traumatized, I would recover with the aid of sleep. Homework later. The kid is asleep. Everyone would go round on tiptoes. Otherwise my eyes would become bloodshot, or my nose would start bleeding, or I would get a headache . . . The sensitive child had to learn to treat its sensitivity with sensitivity, putting on brakes when going past an object which had caused pain before, or (this came later) sensitively giving all sharp and jagged objects a wide berth.

The problem was not the pigeon, but me. And so I rushed home in great excitement, wanting to throw the pigeon into the faces of those who had given me life, because someone had broken its leg, but it was *I* who felt the pain. Someone had broken its leg, but I was feeling the pain and I wanted to fall down and writhe in a fit. But there was no one at home.

Only my little sister Sonya was at home.

"Quick, a box! Cotton wool and iodine!"

I stopped in front of the mirror that had been fixed into the door of the wardrobe and displayed the pigeon to myself in the mirror – the pigeon together with me . . . Then I stuck out my tongue at myself. And I grew even paler.

"I don't know where any boxes are," lisped my little sister Sonya, waddling in.

"I don't know where any boxes are either, but I'll kill you if you don't find one, so there! Go to the shop and ask for one."

At last she found an abandoned shoebox somewhere, although it was too small for the pigeon.

We decided we ought to tie it by its good leg to the balcony, so that it would not fly away or fall from where we lived on the seventh floor.

"Bring some cereal!"

From the balcony, which ran round the whole seventh floor of the building (the seventh and last floor) with its little cupids above the arches of the windows, one could see far and wide, including the domed roof of the opera house amongst the froth of young foliage.

"Bring some water."

The fat plaster railings were covered all over with a disgusting layer of bird droppings. The birds would scuttle up and down on the balcony all day cooing to each other, until someone came out and scared the whole flock off. Plaster and bird droppings had become so mixed up you couldn't tell which was which. Sonya's eyes were round with fear.

"Don't you dare howl!"

I moistened the cotton wool with iodine and applied it to the pigeon's broken leg. As it tried to break free, the pigeon began to quiver, beating its wings painfully.

"Bandage! Gauze!" I shouted.

Sonya rushed into the flat.

"I'm going to tell your parents what you are doing here, you shameless little girls." I hadn't noticed that Valera had come out of his room on to the balcony we all shared. "Why are you bringing muck into the building, eh? Why did you have to go and break its leg, eh? It's so small too. You shouldn't have done that . . ."

Behind him, a disgusting muslin-like cloud of faded greyish-brown smoke arose out of his smelly room. He stubbed his cigarette out in a tin can that had been tied to the railings with a bit of wire. Then suddenly he dropped to his knees and started to shuffle towards us. We stared at him in horror whilst his wobbly brown eyes remained fixed on us . . .

"Why do you girls paint your lips? Such red little lips you've got . . . You're too young to paint your lips. I'll have to tell your mother. Come on, I'll wipe it off for you . . ."

He held out his hand. Sonya clung to me as we stood rooted to the spot, scared to death.

"Come on, girls . . ." He had come up quite close to us.

He was so near now that I could see his rough dry lips, which he was licking with his fat tongue. Amongst the pine needles of rusty-grey unshavenness.

"Little girl," he croaked.

And then he shaped his lips – like this. Amazing charm. *Charmant* . . .

"Did Teofil Petrovich do some work with you today?" I looked round. Behind us in a wheelchair, its tyres moving as silently as a snake on sand, blonde-haired Linda was smiling at us.

There was this portrait. Of an extraordinary face. I have never seen anyone since with such a beautiful face. Countenance. Athenian maiden. Wet locks streaming down her cheeks, catching on the outer shell of her sensual lips, parched with suffering. Torment, unimaginable levity and bliss. Beautiful, wax-like purity. Like a burning candle, her whole being stretches upwards, her eyes wide open. Looking towards the observer. And all this in the shower, against the backdrop of wet tiles . . . Half of her chest is cut away by the camera frame. It is clear she was photographed naked.

It was her husband Perepletchikov, when he was still around, who photographed her. Leaning over without worrying about whether he would get his fashionable haircut wet, he kissed the groove at the back of her neck, the hollow of her collarbone, where drops of water had collected. To be more precise, he drank the water from her, putting his Zenith behind his back, as if hiding his hands so as not to touch, in a semblance of pious devotion. His profile reminded one of "The Kiss of Judas" by one of the minor Dutch masters. And Linda, stretching out like a candle in the wind, flickering, her eyes shut, thought that she would gladly give up her life for such a moment. Then she fell, banging her back sharply on the cold tiles.

What a funny habit, risking everything for the one moment. But oh, that moment! How many such moments have there been and how many will there be in the future . . . But no, life will not teach her anything. Yet again she leaps into the flames: "Let me feel bad later, let me feel really bad later, just as long as now . . . now . . . No, give me the sort of love I can throw myself into . . . A broken heart . . . Who cares?"

She had been more cautious before. Sharp angles of bones, the interlacing of collarbones, the heavy – rather heavier than others – but gaunt, mortal body, tightly wrapped in parchment, yet another cumbersome corset of flesh, just like the other one clattering with metal bits, straps that squeaked and clamps that dug into her skin, which they put her into for many years after she had fallen from the seventh floor as a girl. Her fragile little body had wafted through the air like a feather after bouncing off the branches of the poplar tree, and she thought then that she had not fallen by chance, but deliberately in fact, because of her fear of life, her desire to get it over and done with as early as possible, so as not to suffer. To skive off lessons. There are those who get As and those who get Bs and those who skive off . . . Stupid lessons. And they make me sing as well. Not just learn their lessons, but ring and sing the whole day through.

But things turned out in a strange sort of way. The whole idea of falling, it seemed, was in order not to have to suffer any longer, not to see them any more, not to hear, not to know. But it was that which brought the real, sweat-laden torment, the cross and Calvary, and now there was no one to help, to carry you or lend a hand. From now on there would be injections, clinics, operations, wheelchairs, from now on and for ever more. It was as if a premonition of the pain had provoked the pain itself, and the desire to avoid it brought it closer . . . And so she had fallen right into the hands of her tormentors, straight into their strong, animal embrace . . . And they took him away, not in a Black Maria, but in an ordinary van with hard seats, bars on the windows and a smell of vomit, into which the police patrol in the evenings would bundle the various labourers strewn along the roadside, although – and this is funny, of course! – he had dreamt, yes, actually dreamt, however funny it may seem, that he would be invited into a black Volga, with a gentleman at each side. The click of handcuffs, skyscrapers, Europe, cross-eyed passers-by gaping, too slow to shut their mouths . . . He would pity them with a weary but triumphant smile . . . The car would lurch into motion and a flock of pigeons on the chequered square would brush against the bodywork, while one sweaty, down-covered wing would pierce the air like a sharp trajectory before his very nose, and he would then sink back limply on to the supple, stitched seat, which with its leather comfort and stability he had suspected in himself all his life and carried within him like a true German. He would also think though that he was a bit Russian too, already a bit Russian. The Russian never talks of liberty but demands freedom . . . Freedom equals space to breathe equals room to swing one's arm . . . Anathema! But wasn't it actually freedom that

he wanted, he would think, in order in the end to . . . oh, very soon
. . . and at this point he looked with lively curiosity at the stone profiles
of those accompanying him . . . in order in the end to gain liberty?

"Well then . . . what did he say about your voice?" Linda smiled at us
serenely. Serene bitch. Valera brushed the dust off from his knees.

"Like a nightingggg · · · gg · · · gg."

"Quite right. You've got a very nice teacher, girls. But I don't advise
you to talk to this particular gentleman, however."

Linda's eyes shone a destructive light on to Valera like the beam of
pale headlights.

"This is a shared balcony, and the bird will make a mess. They
brought it here. A bird should fly, not jump. It'll die anyhow in the
winter. Should be given to the cat. A new by-law is coming out soon
– they are working on it now – which will order all pigeons to be
destroyed, because they are damaging monuments," Valera droned,
averting his eyes. "They leave their mess on the heads of statues who
can't clean it off by themselves. I can clean myself, but they can't. But
perhaps I don't want to clean myself, maybe I don't give a damn either
when it's on me!" Valera gave a wink and fastened his eyes on Linda.

"But who would behave like that . . . to you, dear Valera?" Linda
asked playfully, but with a tinge of unease.

"I . . . it's . . . I just know who."

"But who?"

"Someone,' Valera said triumphantly. And darkly.

"Are you sure you're not mistaken?" Linda asked again playfully,
but already feeling threatened.

"Sappers only ever make one mistake in their life!"

"Well, maybe." Linda pursed her lips ironically. But they became
dry again instantly. "Do you want to see the portrait?"

"No, I don't!"

"How come you don't want to any more?" Linda's smile was
strained.

"I'll look at it when I feel like it!"

"Don't listen to him, girls; you are still young," Linda interrupted
anxiously as she started pulling at her wheelchair. "Let's go and look
at the portrait, Valera. Come on! Let's go . . . Take me."

That's how I remember Linda. From her portrait. Along the whole
wall above her couch, just like photographic wallpaper composed of
different sections . . . Her portrait quite frankly told the amazed
observer, who could not but be struck by its nakedness, that she had

also been loved once and it even led one on to think that there was still a possibility of love yet. Her neighbour Valera certainly wanted to know her in that way . . . And wasn't it really thanks to the portrait, which was not all *that* distressing or frightening to look at? One could project into it all one's desire for a strange woman, who was ugly too, and so aroused even more carnal interest, aroused life, to set against the angry flapping of the wheels of her invalid's chair with its eternal rattle and, through the chink in the door, her cross shouts of irritation at her mother, mumbling away quietly to herself. I can remember her so clearly, it is as if I can see her face in my mirror, still waiting, still waiting for her Perepletchikov, painting her face and then pushing away the cold glass . . . We can't quite remember Valera visually (and I say "we" because there were two of us in front of him, as he shuffled towards us on his knees, me and my sister Sonya, like two mushrooms growing in a field, one a bit bigger, the other a bit smaller, but grown from the same spore), but even if we can't remember him, we would be able to recognize him in a crowd with our eyes shut because of the mystical horror and attraction he inspired in us. Valera was set in a particular mould for us: the Valera who wandered the streets.

Oh, how my frightened little heart beat as I even joined in my sister's wailing, whilst I scraped at the plaster-covered wall with all its cracks that made up the profiles and designs I knew by heart, the pictures on that bare wall I loved so much. I picked off thin and semi-transparent pieces of paintwork, then great chunks of old plaster, which dropped on to the skirting board by the bed, while you Valera, having drunk your fill of Linda's portrait behind the wall, and yielded to her, were beating up your wife Nina. Whilst she let out her peculiar euphoric cries, you tied her up with a towel, and having twisted it as much as you could, like they tighten skating boots, you reduced her to shreds with your kicks. You didn't strike each blow at your full strength, though. You left a certain incompleteness, a certain imposs- ible aching sweetness, in which was contained the prolongation of Nina's life. She was screaming: "Beat me, beat me, you sadist . . . Kill me! Go on, hit me! Hit me!" She began to shout this as soon as you turned up drunk in the yard. As she heard your dull, hard, stone footsteps on the stairs, heavy with the lead of anger, resounding with a concrete echo like in a torture chamber, she rushed around the flat, grabbing the children, asking to be hidden, at one point even squashing herself into the cupboard on our corridor. But then she went and threw herself at your feet, screaming: "Well, Nina, my dear, you asked for this . . . Hit me, hit me, sadist! Go on, kill me!" Grinning stupidly, you neatly arranged the bags of sweets for the children on the table, then turned round slowly and thumped her on the ear . . . The first blow.

"Imagine insulting a person like that! When is this all going to stop? It's insulting to all of us! I can't let this go on, I really can't!"

"Don't you dare go in there! They can sort it out themselves. I forbid you to go in there!" My father blocked my mother's way, like a shadow running across the beam of a passing car.

"You don't care, you're just despicable!" mother said. And like a soft, gentle blue cloud of silk, she slid along the moonlit squares of the night-filled room away from him. She hovered beneath the ceiling.

"OK, so I'm selfish." My father fell silent and a black hole formed in the middle of the room. "But why did they give us a flat and not other people?"

"Because I went round knocking at everyone's doors . . ."

"Other people do too," father snapped. "Other people also wait for decades, *and* they go round knocking at everyone's doors, even more than we have, and they still get damn all for it . . . but my wife goes to some Fedotov or other and abracadabra, we get a separate flat . . . And quite right and proper too. The concern of the State for the population is really *touching*!"

The little cloud began to tremble.

"What are you trying to say?"

There was a luminous wail, like a smoking rocket, trailing a fiery white ribbon behind the wall.

"The idea of living in a flat obtained by those sorts of means . . ."

"What means?! Obtained by what means? What are you implying?"

"You're the one who knows what methods . . ."

"Go on, say it!"

"I get it. The family, the children hear these shocking things every day on the other side of the wall . . . You women have a thousand justifications for everything. But I'm sorry, I really can't go on living with you any more after this . . ."

"You . . . you . . . just how can you say that . . . how could you think . . . ?" The little cloud wrung her hands in desperation and tore up and down the room like a caged bird. "Agh, the pain . . . How come I didn't see all this earlier . . . I'm an idiot, an idiot . . . Well, you had better get out, you've wanted to for ages, so why don't you just get lost! We'll be even better off without you! Do you think I won't be able to cope?"

"You'll cope all right, I've no doubt about that. But there's our daughters."

"What do you mean, our daughters?"

"Legally I could take them with me. A depraved and frivolous woman does not have any right to bring them up. But bearing in mind your attachment to them, I'll just take one of them. And she and I will stay here."

"Here?"

"Right here. And you can move to a new flat. With your Egorov."

"What Egorov are you talking about? Ha, ha . . . you bastard . . . ha, ha . . . You thought this up. You have no intention of moving out. You think I don't know, you think I can't guess . . . that you spend the whole time round her portrait . . . What bastards!"

"And you were happy enough! Didn't you throw yourself round my neck, shrieking: 'They've given us a flat!'? So there was Fedotov, then . . . who else . . . the president of the executive committee . . . Zakharov, Egorov . . . You did the rounds of all of them." Father groaned through his clenched teeth as he tensed.

"Aieee . . ." A rabbit-like squeal broke out from behind the wall followed by a thump. Silence.

"I'm staying with Mama! I'm staying with Mama too!" Sonya and I howled.

Was he caught or taken unawares? Behind the bars of the gym windows (of course not . . .), as Mr X was laying out scores by German composers on the scruffy piano, it was no coincidence that he caught sight of the approaching van.

In the honeycomb of classrooms the second shift was humming. Lesson time. The corridors were empty. They had picked the right time. But he didn't think it would happen at school. Any minute now, the children from the first shift would arrive, having had their lunch. Lenochka from 4A, Svetik from 4B, Annchen . . . and a tallish girl, painfully shy, also from the fourth form. Linda had put in a word for her . . . Adorable little kids . . .

Yes, I was supposed to come in order to have my voice stretched and coordinated with my ear. I've got perfect pitch, you see. I was sitting at the kitchen table, choking on soup and tears.

"Don't talk rubbish! And don't dangle your legs!" my mother shouted, her eyes swollen from her night-time and morning crying.

"But what if . . . what if he wins the case and takes me away?"

"He won't!" mother said angrily.

"What about Sonya?"

"He won't get Sonya either."

"Well then, tell me . . . tell me that you love me more than her!" Linda was sitting in her wheelchair on the open kitchen balcony. She had let her hair, which was looking transparent in the sun, right down to the ground, and was crumbling bread for our sick birds and smiling enigmatically. She was warming a little sparrow on her chest. When she blew on to its little beak it closed its eyes and when she blew on its neck it made a little crater of down. The sparrow was the favourite bird of the goddess of love. Every Roman girl used to keep a sparrow, or perhaps a parrot or a canary. Catullus wrote a poem "On the Death of a Sparrow", and invented the lyric in doing so.

The four men got out of the van, stretching their legs and adjusting invisible shoulder belts, leaving inside the shadow of the driver, who pulled down his cap on to the bridge of his nose and slid down into his seat to have a snooze.

The four walked idly up to the school porch, unhurriedly, as if cracking whips. They stopped on the warm concrete porch and looked around, exactly as though they were calculating something in the windows . . .

Teofil Petrovich Schneidermann leapt away from the bars of the gymnasium windows when their gaze reached him (he wasn't after all behind bars yet; indeed, at the moment he was still in front of them). His short shadow darted across the horses and the mats, and jumped over the thick shafts of dusty sunlight . . . Mr X threw back the lid of the piano and sat down. He was just about to lower his fingers on to the keys, mimicking the teacher, when Schneidermann pulled them away, as if singed by the sound. He scooped up all the scattered scores and jumped to his feet. Again his shadow bounced like a little ball over the benches and the dust. The music flew everywhere but as he bent down to pick it up, he realized he had to start running – he really had to run!

Like a monkey, light-footed and wiry, he ran up the worn steps, his scarf trailing behind him and his cane tapping out of step. His grey mane was like the floss of a halo. Here came the tunnel; the cleaning lady had been mopping the floor of the corridor and it was drying in patches. He slipped and slid like a gallant dancer, the dancing teacher one-two-three, the singing teacher, the ill-fated *Konzertmeister*, and here was what he most feared – the schoolboy pioneer returning from the toilet with a lascivious filth in his red eyes. "He went that way, sirs! I'll geddim for you if you want, sirs, I'll geddim right away!"

He had just enough strength to get to the staff room on the second floor . . . As if he was just a teacher and nothing more. A teacher, and behind the teacher's mask, nothing and nobody. But anyway, what else could he be? There was no one and nothing, no sweat, no blood, no desires, no functions. Dried up already. Old.

The headmistress was busy writing a report in the airy room. Puffing and panting as he slowed his delicate step, his cane catching on the tables, he went up to her and . . . and . . . "I can't say . . . anything . . ." He gripped the polished edge of the table with the sweaty palms of his hands.

The headmistress raised her long, horse-like face and then uncontrollably began to flush a bright tomato red.

"It's a misunderstanding . . . Please . . . you must explain . . . to them," the old man began to babble, urgently, his head on one side like a bird. His eyes remained fixed on the headmistress, as if he were trying to disappear into her, hide in her, become her . . . and then he realized that she already knew . . . They had rung her already . . . they had warned the school in advance that they were coming . . . Maybe she had even rung herself. Forty-five minutes, that's the length of the gap in the schedule between the two shifts; "Do try to be finished by then, dear comrades . . ." His eye fell on the telephone and seeing his eye fall on it, she blushed from her neck upwards, leaving a red triangle exposed on her crimplene breast.

They had already left the empty gym . . .

Well, they obviously could not arrest him at home. Unwanted publicity. At home there were neighbours on all sides. And they were Germans too. What could you do? He was the only intellectual in this small ethnic group of Russianized kolkhoz farmers from the Volga, exiled in the war. They still just about managed to mumble in their native language while they ate their borsch, sat on the benches outside their front doors or queued in shops, but their grandchildren could now barely scrape Bs in German and so he *had* to save his culture. What did those fat hens have to offer though, that could be taught to their children and grandchildren?

Nothing. Precisely nothing.

So Schneidermann taught. He taught them to sing. In German too. He taught everyone to sing.

So that is how it came about that a German taught us to sing and that's an indisputable fact.

He urged the headmistress towards the door, almost lovingly, tickling her inflamed flabby breast with his whiskers, murmuring

affectionately and earnestly, hurriedly nudging her foot by foot towards
the open door in his frenzied state, cajoling her, impelling her, pushing
her and finally throwing her out into the cool corridor. He then leant
across, viciously yanked the door shut in front of her forlorn blue nose
and turned the key.

He wedged the leg of a chair and his cane into the bracket of the
door handle. Crisscross. Sword and rapier. Let them try now!

Immediately the door began to shake.

"Teofil Petrovich, have you gone mad? Open up! Teofil Petrovich
. . . Comrade Schneidermann! This is outrageous!"

He rubbed his now dry hands and chortled.

The main thing now was to wait for the bell. The children would
get in the way. A horde of children would come pouring out. They
would protect their favourite teacher. They would not dare to arrest
him then. He would be saved.

But had children ever stopped them before? Had they been stopped
by the son of his Communist friend Heinrich, when they came for
him at night, way back in 1937? The ten-year-old boy in his pyjamas
had leapt like a squirrel at the person standing in the doorway and bit
his finger. Then the person emptied his pistol on him. They took his
father away whilst his son remained for ever slumped on the floor, his
face buried in the shoes beneath the coat rack, lying by the wheel of
his mud-splattered bike.

Those times are long since past, you will say, and all that remains is
a certain instinctive feeling of persecution felt by the older generation,
the generation of our fathers and mothers, on whom we concentrate
our poison-tongued fearlessness, who drive us mad, whom we despise
for reminding us about the distant past, about such trivial things, such
crap. Is it all worth remembering?

"He's locked himself in," the headmistress said in a muffled voice.
She knocked.

"Mr Schneidermann, my dear *Freund*, what do you mean by this?
I need to mark my class books . . ."

The empty gym was deserted. The music scores were wandering
about the floor in the breeze. The quadrangles of sunlight made bars
on the floor and climbed up the walls. I stood in the middle of the
resounding emptiness while the headmistress thrust her wet, blue nose
down my neck, into my lace collar, and gurgled into my ear.

"Your beloved Teofil Petrovich, children, has turned out to be a
wicked man, children, and from today that old German goat won't be
taking choir with you any more, because he is . . . hee, hee . . . a

debauchee who has debauched all the prettiest girls in the school under the pretext of wanting to teach them to sing, whilst in fact he has photographed them in their sports kit, and also without their sports kit. Photographed them in their pants and vests or even without their vests and combinations. Photographed them just in their pants, or even without any knickers on at all, children. He made them open their legs under the pretext of teaching them to sing and wanting to turn them into famous singers; that's the sort of person that our naughty, bad Mr Schneidermann has turned out to be . . ."

So Lenochka, in that case . . . Lenochka whom I had envied so much, in that case, Lenochka had opened her legs . . . and he had asked me to come too . . . And now everyone will think that I had already gone to be photographed in my sports kit, which I look so horrible in, or even without it . . . Everyone is bound to think that, since he asked me in front of everyone to come and see him after lunch. And Lenochka, Svetik and Annchen . . . How are Lenochka, Svetik and Annchen going to live now . . . after such a disgrace and such an exposure? They often used to stay behind after lunch and now they are in his collection . . . pornography, that's what it's called, and now their parents will really thrash them . . . photographs, like the one Linda has on her wall . . . so he must have photographed Linda too! Well, it figures of course; they all came to see her. They locked themselves in and talked as quietly as if no one was there. They put on music while in actual fact they were being photographed! It wasn't for nothing that old Valera eavesdropped and looked through the keyhole . . . So does that mean I am pretty too? No, it's embarrassing, too embarrassing to think about . . . How can I look people in the eye now . . . after such a disgrace and such an exposure? No, I would rather hang myself, poison myself . . . with matches . . . I would rather eat a whole box of matches, gnaw off their tips . . . When is this lesson going to end? The setting sun throws squares through the giant windows, the curtains are rippling like muscles, the board is black and I have to look at green trees and the sky in order to get my mind off all that, feel better, so my head won't spin . . . Suddenly a disgusting, drivelling old man creeps out of the blackboard. All the surfaces of the classroom home in on him strangely, as if saliva was being extracted from the desks and walls. The headmistress is striding up and down behind him, rapping the old man on the skull with the pointer. And in his spiderwebs and dirt, he calls me into his lair. He calls me, calls me, winking with his red eye, snorting shamelessly and wiggling his fingers, wiggling his fingers lewdly. As if I weren't myself, as if hypnotized, I go towards him. Slowly and steadily I go to him, as if I were bewitched. The icy, curled fingers are already running all over my body and running in there . . . and it's so unbearable, so awful and so . . . Darkness.

The door was coming away from its hinges from all the shaking. The mad old man was cracking his finger joints, either running up to the door to reposition the chair that was slipping out of the bracket or running off behind the cupboard at the other end of the room, to the mirror and soap dishes around which the young teachers usually hovered during break. What could he do? The chair had become loose and was now coming adrift. "What am I doing? None of this will make any difference anyway . . ." The lock snapped like a piece of string . . . His cane was now showing exposed wooden flesh . . . He risked coming nearer. He picked up the chair, in order to drive the leg in once more, but then sat down overcome by weakness.

"Why did I have to put up with all of this? Why? *Mein Gott*, what a *Dummkopf*, what a stupid old blockhead I am . . . A country cottage, a fishing rod, the riches of nature and the tranquil and serene days of old age . . . But instead of that, all that prittle-prattle at table, all that tea drinking, their snotty kids, who did not know about . . . Useless leadership! The Redikops, the Webers and the Fruschenbachs had . . . *mein Gott, mein Gott* . . ." It was as clear as day that it would all lead to nothing and he knew that beforehand . . . Did he want to be different then? Show off? "*Mein Gott*, let me survive this ordeal . . . Linda, my child – I wanted to show off in front of that poor thing, in front of that hunchback, that devilish freak, *Donnerwetter, noch einmal!*"

And suddenly Mr X-Schneidermann, his eyes fixed on the dancing floor, which was noiselessly opening wider and wider as it was shaken, suddenly withdrew into himself. He straightened up, inhaled the air, then began sniffing around like a dog. He blushed like a young maiden and threw up his hands in comic horror. Unable to bear the disgrace in his panic – the door was already open – he leapt through an open window into the spring air, landing straight on to the silvery grass that was blowing in the wind, on to his bent leg, which immediately gave a sharp crack, like the cane in the door.

So tell us, Teofil Petrovich, are you really Schneidermann . . . or is it going to transpire, if one thinks hard on it, that you are not Schneidermann at all, but a Mr X without kith or kin, brought to our land of coal mines to spy and carry out subversive activities, to get our mines and pits blown up and make yourself happy, shaking your beard like a wicked old lecher? . . .

"You just wait! That's nothing to what I'll make him say!" In his rage, Valera was yelling and thrusting himself forward like a cockerel. Everything was red and concrete like, the beam of the lamp was merciless, and red too. Everything was red . . .

And you would be glad, wouldn't you? Come on now, don't turn away, my dear fellow, this is our shared fate now. The light too bright, you say, the pulsation, you can't think. But who wants you to think? You should have thought about that before, it's too late now . . . We will leave you your braces now. Sorry, my dear friend, I overlooked, I forgot, I confess, I am sorry, I'm leaving you your braces . . .

"May I?" Valera the model pupil jumped forward and had to be pushed back again and shoved into the corner.

Oh, you're not a fascist, you are a *Communist*. You were a Communist when I was still a toddler . . . I agree. But racial or nationalist narrow-mindedness is alien to us too though, don't forget. In fact, foreignness inspires warm feelings in us. The nationality clause – that small physical imperfection – inspires pity in us . . . We harbour a great affection for Negroes, for example, so that they can to keep their spirits up, so they don't feel so unfortunate . . . Ah, how kind we are! We want happiness for everyone, we want to help everyone, support them by the elbows on both sides . . . Yes, every coloured inch on earth concerns us, we wish to pour out peace and happiness from the great cup of plenty to everyone, in great ladlefuls. How can you, grey and primitive, compare with us? Calm down, Valera, we will need you later . . . The singing teacher, with a false idea of himself as an upholder of national traditions, sadistically forcing our children to break their tongues on some mumbo jumbo . . .

"No, I can't stand any more," wheezed Valera and tore at the sailor's shirt on his chest. A fist like a hammer. The skull would crack under his sledgehammer . . . The delightful stab of pain in the crotch! His skull would smash to pieces!

You can help the gentleman with his braces, but alas, he still has something to sign so that I'll just get off with a reprimand for lack of caution . . . I've had plenty of reprimands before now . . . But for that we need to investigate who is who amongst our friends and enemies, whose beer it is that I'm drinking, who their friends are, who their enemies are . . . And who am I, you want to know? Why, haven't you worked that one out yet, Mr Teacher? I am eternal; not a Jew of course – you're the Jew, my dear fellow, although you killed plenty of them in your war, not enough mind you . . . Well I'm your eternal loving friend, my dear teacher, and you and I will mate together, just you wait, in our eternal vicious circle, executioner and victim, hating, loving . . . Take a look for example at your good neighbour Valera . . .

Doesn't he beat his wife? He beats her really badly. He beats up his beloved Nina like anything, and soon he will beat her to death. And why? Because that is what he is used to and he can't do anything else. He can't get it up otherwise, you naive old crank. But what about you? When you were secretly putting together your German choir, when you were waving your baton, didn't you realize you were starting to emit the smell of a female insect? I will come flying to you, I will sense you a thousand miles away and will fly to your call. I will always be ready to mate with you, because you've thrown down the challenge . . . although all the while you could have been sitting quietly and not exuding any smells. Couldn't you? Country cottage, river, fishing rod – wasn't it something like that? Did I know? Well if I didn't know, I guessed . . . So you see, eh? I feel sure that you and I are going to find a common language. You want to sign, do you? You want to sign as quickly as possible? You'll sign anything? Well, hold on, hang on a minute, what's all the hurry? I'm not ready for that yet.

Let's settle one thing before we can ask our friend Valera to assist with the braces. Let's settle this once and for all with all the right artistic detail, so that no one will be able to find a single flaw. Those girls, you old devil, you didn't just want to stretch their voices, did you? Well, own up, don't blush, monkey face. How old are you and you still haven't grown out of blushing like a child . . . Hadn't you better tell me what it was all about, hmm? Here is where we will find our weakness, our little human touch. We'll hunt out the weakness and indulge in it. Good idea? So you didn't expect things to turn out the way they did, eh? Brilliant! You expected anything but that. You photographed the daughters of your best friends, your respected Germans. We won't go into who they were. They can sort it out themselves and cover up their family disgrace, whispering in corners and pointing fingers at each other . . . No, no, we won't overdo it, my drooling, impotent old man, but you did photograph those adolescent girls, didn't you?

"Aagh, you filthy reptile! I won't choke him by his braces, but with his scarf instead," screamed Valera.

Unease had settled in our flat. Linda was not talking to anyone, nor was she letting anyone into her room to look at her portrait. She played Bach to herself all day. Sonya and I collected another dozen pigeons on the street with broken wings. Someone was catching them, breaking their wings and then letting them go. Valera was sitting at the oilcloth kitchen table and confessing to our father. Father had a habit of periodically "going to the people". He would bring home some old drunk, a vagrant alcoholic with a long history, and would order mother to dish up some meat and put a bottle on the table. None of this could be questioned. Just from the way our father sat, you could see he had a powerful intellect. The drunks were frightened of him and they would spill out their whole story to him; it was seldom that anyone tried to pit their strength against him.

He had a drinking session like this with Valera a couple of times. And Valera cried. Father's blue gaze at first registered an embarrassed look of surprise with a light tinge of disgust. Then his eyes grew cold and all the pain and melancholy showed through. He sucked through his teeth as he filled Valera's glass and then sucked through his teeth again. Valera was slumping lower and lower before him, as if he was sitting on a park bench. He was feeling more and more nauseated with himself and was starting to hallucinate. He hallucinated that the person who had inspired cold terror in him, that legendary man, was once again striding up and down in front of the line of young cadets, one of whom was Valera. That man looked straight into their souls. Hardly alive, their stomachs stuck to their spines, their eyes glassy, streams of sweat pouring down their vertebrae, they looked loyally straight ahead into the void without blinking. They looked straight ahead while he kept pacing up and down, peering into their eyes as into keyholes, his searing gaze burning its way through them. What could he see there? Their country manure-filled childhood, cows in the meadow, the river with its whirlpool, a windmill, a single cloud in the deep-blue sky, mother carrying a bucket of milk . . . and the stink of raw vodka, stolen from granny's cellar and drunk on the quiet under the haystack . . . On the next day half the year was missing. Every second person was shot.

And every first person from then on . . . Crying, Valera shook his inebriated head and clenched his teeth so as not to blab. Nina spent her time groaning in bed, or like a quiet shadow with her huge bruises, washing nappies and hanging them out silently in the bathroom or on the balcony in a contented sort of way, almost happy even. It was as if the thunderstorm had passed and everything was now clean, shining from within, the broken fragments turned towards the rays of the life-giving sun, absorbing its warmth. The dome of the opera house threw off a sharp, metallic light.

Towards evening, Valera hanged himself in the lavatory. Without finding anything suitable, without having washed himself or prepared himself the way a person should. Valera just hanged himself on his own imitation leather belt. He suffered for a long time, writhing in agony to make the noose tighten. It wouldn't for a long time but then finally it did. Valera shuffled his holey socks along the tiles; he had tied his hands, in order not to prop himself up on the narrow walls. He was just about to stand on his toes and put off the whole business until a better time when he gave a wheeze and died . . . The belt, stretching like a sinew of a colourless, transparent plastic texture, eventually snapped and Valera's corpse landed smoothly on the lavatory seat. When his eldest son looked in from the bathroom through the little window, he shouted out to Nina, his mother, that father had got drunk again and had gone to sleep on the lavatory.

Hour after hour passed. They knocked on the door but in vain. It was time to go to bed, and my sister and I were embarrassed at having to pee in the bath. Valera would not wake up and open the door. My parents were sitting in their room gloomily, from long habit not interfering. The nervous Nina ran off to fetch the superintendent, threatening arrest.

The superintendent turned up with some plumbers who kicked the door with their boots.

"Come on, you bastard, are you ever going to wake up? Open up!" One of them took a run up and threw himself at the door. The latch inside snapped off and the door swung open. While the plumber extracted the splinters from himself, the unfortunate and ashamed Nina, with one boy in her arms and the other at her skirt, waited patiently to take Valera out of the lavatory. It wasn't the first time Valera had gone to sleep on the lavatory and not the first time they had to break down the door. Once he had set himself alight in there while he was on the lavatory, and the lino had produced clouds of poisonous smoke . . . "Mama . . . his willy is sticking out," said the elder child and hid himself in embarrassment in the folds of Nina's skirt.

Valera was slumped on the lavatory seat, his trousers down without the belt to hold them up, and the blood had drained from his body and gathered in the pillar of flesh between his pale, hairy thighs, which had swollen in a most disgusting manner and turned the colour of the headmistress's nose, its size exceeding all known norms. Valera's cap had fallen off his drooping head on to it, so that one could not make out at first which was his head and which was his cap.

I lay in a plaster cast by the wall and picked off the plaster, immobile after my flight now, like a chrysalis, when I so wanted to become a butterfly. I thought that when they peeled this coat of armour off me I would immediately become like Lenochka. I would dance and sing and smile, always be dancing, singing and laughing, for my own pleasure and for the pleasure of everyone else. "Look at that girl! What fun she is, and always laughing – you couldn't get bored with her. How nice to be so light-hearted. You are lucky to have someone so easy-going. My old hag is a real witch, and a bitch too. It's written all over her face."

"Come to me, my little girl!"

Translated by Rosamund Bartlett

DMITRY BAKIN

Lagopthalmos

I HATED THAT bloke. As bad luck would have it, I served with him.

. . . Every day I would see his ungainly, skinny body, hidden beneath a uniform which was too big for him, and which he would slip off without undoing the buttons: his heavy boots were worn out by crooked feet, their heels, without segs, eaten way; narrow shoulders like oar blades; a face as ugly as a hardened clot of magma – I should like to see the woman who gave birth to him and find out in which month this calamity occurred – but Bragin told me that only very gifted people tended to be so ugly and unhealthily weak. And then: "Just look! His neck doesn't support his head! Look! Look! It's fallen on one side, like a two-month-old baby's." But, Monashka, who once cleaned cages in the zoo, said: "A pack of wolves always destroys the weak wolf because ultimately his life costs the strong and healthy ones too much."

I hated this bloke, even before I knew that he was an ex-pianist and that his surname was Vensky. Vensky had been sent to us from the radio operators' training sub-unit. He came to the company on one of the most boring evenings, an hour before evening roll call; he stood silently in the gap between the bunks, having put his kit bag and rolled-up greatcoat down on the floor, looking around with a lost gaze, as if he had fallen into a hole and did not know how to get out. He scanned each of us with an anxious and frightened look until he finally came to me. For a few seconds, we stared into each other's eyes. My muscles tensed against my will. I froze as if preparing to dodge a knife. He smiled and calmed down.

Vensky acted like a man about to ask for a loan.

An unconscious desire arose in me to keep my distance. I did not know why on earth he was sticking to me – in the army that kind of thing is just not done. Maybe he felt something, maybe he saw something in me, and his attempts to get next to me were like those of a blind man searching for a firm path.

He would wander forlornly amongst the soldiers, air squishing in his boots; he would twist his face and wrinkle his brow under the pressure of a dull hypochondriac pain – a requiem for one of us weighed on him – a mixture of pain and music.

His face gave me no peace. Much later I understood that I used to turn to this face at night when I did not want to live.

He was always at my side, smiling guiltily and trying to strike up a conversation.

I would say to him: "Listen, get your mug away from me!" He would stand there smiling guiltily, just like a child, before taking it away.

I could not keep looking at a man the very sight of whom made me feel like running away.

I used to say to him: "Get your ugly mug away from me."

But it was all useless. His choice had been made.

I changed drastically. I was afraid, as people are afraid of the dark and of open graves. The charge of rage which had built up in me would have been enough to blow up bridges. I became dangerous. I developed a fear of man like a dumb animal. Ever watchful, I saw danger in everything. I was blind in the face of the enemy, and the longer that lasted, the more clearly I understood that my enemy would live as long as I lived and would only die within me, together with me, but not outside me.

I was inclined to see in the actions of this skinny, weak runt the indestructible, obstinate accuracy of a magnetic compass – life directed by the unfailing sense which guides one's feet to step where the ground will never give way, makes the body avoid thousands of deaths and drunken lives, closes one's eyes where one will be blinded, takes one away from a place where anyone else would be crushed by a tree – the exact infallible calculation of an ancient instinct confirming a man's vague, unhealthy belief in the incomparable meaning of his own life and in the gift of creating greatness. Raised in purity and innocence, he was afraid of blood, threw up at the sight of other people's vomit, did not like stray dogs, but felt boundless love for his mother, who had protected and tutored him – a wise female.

In spring, Vensky was taken into the medical unit.

The medical block overlooked the barrack square. Whenever I walked past, Vensky's head could always be seen behind the cross in the windowframe. He looked at me, clutching the windowsill, twisted his yellow face and smiled anxiously. He looked in a really bad way. I felt like breaking into a dance.

Moved by malicious curiosity, I went into the medical block and tried to look at Vensky's medical record, but, apart from the fact that he was ill, I could not understand anything – if an ape were taught to write holding the pen between its feet it would write far more neatly and legibly than doctors do.

Vensky was discharged after a fortnight.

He came into the canteen and sat down at my table. I was slowly eating my barley porridge, looking at my filthy hands. Vensky had somehow managed to get his hands on half a length of smoked sausage and was handing out slices to those sitting at our table.

"Damn you! You're back again," I growled. "Damn you! Swine!"

I reached for the bread. Vensky quickly leant across the table and placed a piece of bread with sliced sausage by my plate. For a few seconds, I looked at the bread basket, feeling my brain become suffused with the thick juices of rage, and then I thumped my fist on the table and sent both his stinking sausage and my plate crashing on to the floor.

Everyone fell silent. There were no officers in the canteen. I got up and left.

Golden grains of sunlight streamed in from the sky.

I wanted to be alone.

I wanted to be alone like five years ago when I lay on the seashore. It had started raining, everyone had gathered their belongings and left. I had stayed on the wet pebbles and watched the wind lift small, salty splashes above the sea, shape a waterspout into a strange female figure and smoothly lead it over the waves as if waltzing.

But no one would leave this place, even if bones started pouring from the sky.

That night, I could not fall asleep for a long time. I was delirious. Ghostly white blurs of human faces slowly moved past, and gradually the number of faces increased and moved more quickly – millions of human faces, immortalized by historians – those impartial pedlars of lies – in heroic deeds and shame, in depravity and wars. The owners of these faces suffered cold, hunger, malaria, poverty, impecunity, inferiority, drunkenness, but they offered thanks to God, they tried not to stick their necks out, not to put themselves in danger, not to fight, not to die; they – the sick, the healthy, the illegitimate, the madmen – wanted quietly and without being noticed to slip by under the sun, quietly and without being noticed to have children – a noiseless crowd, millions strong. From time to time one of them would break away and shout: "Stop! Not like that" – and be killed, squashed by a slab of envy, poisoned by a horse's dose of brucine, riddled with bullets, or disappear in a wood where he had gone to pay his respects to fate.

Everything comes to an end just when one is ready to begin. I woke up – fell asleep – the huge wall of faces crumbled.

At 5 am, I awoke fully, lay motionless, listening to noisy breathing, snoring and squeaking, rusty bedsprings under slumbering bodies. Then I got up, put on my boots, picked up my cigarettes and went to the washroom. I had a smoke, inhaling deeply, and looked out of the window. The place smelt of strong Lysol solution and dirty linen.

Someone entered the washroom. I turned round and saw Vensky. He was wearing baggy, black shorts and a vest which was torn, as often happens with sets of clean linen coming back from the divisional laundry. He smiled guiltily, his whole appearance a picture of sympathy.

The whites of his eyes were yellow, like unclean teeth.

He took a few steps towards me.

I laid my cigarette on the windowsill.

He twisted his face, preparing to say something. But I didn't give a damn about anything he might have to say. I had the opportunity to do the very least which could be done. I waited for him to come closer, and, without pulling back my arm, hit him sharply. His head reeled to one side, his legs gave way and he fell. Screwing up my eyes, I watched him get to his feet. I waited to hear what he would say, feeling that each of my blows would bring him relief, and that afterwards, fate would free us from each other. He understood that sooner or later I would beat him up, but he still sought one-to-one encounters, which meant that this was what he wanted. Besides, he wanted to explain something.

He got up and said: "That's no use."

It seemed he knew very well that he had to be with me come what may and would have to put up with my vicious outbursts.

I felt like running away, but I hit him once more. He fell and couldn't get up for a long time.

Blood streamed from his mouth.

He said: "Look, that's really no use."

The next day I was given seven days' detention.

Vensky went to the captain and said that he had started the fight himself and if anyone was to be put in detention, we both should be, but the captain knew me inside out and would not listen to him; so then Vensky insulted the sergeant and got three days. He knew very well that he had to be with me everywhere. But, before detention, everyone had to have a medical. The medical unit would not allow Vensky to be held.

Two days later, I was taken to the glasshouse.

The guards confiscated my money, documents and all sharp objects; they searched my pockets for cigarettes, pushed their fingers under my Sam Browne, shook out my boots, removing the insoles, and felt along the seams of my clothes. They then drew up a list of everything which had been confiscated, gave it to me to sign, led me to a cell, took the lock off a collapsible wooden bed and told me I could sleep until tomorrow, because today did not count as part of my sentence, and that there would be no grub today.

It was a four-man cell, with an iron-clad door which was painted green, with a little surveillance window at eye level. It had grey concrete walls. On the wall opposite the door was a rough-hewn air hole into the yard; in one corner a forty-litre tank of drinking water and a mug. Nothing else.

I threw myself on to the wooden bed and fell asleep. I was woken by the heavy stomp of boots in the corridor. It was late. The detainees were coming back from work. After lights-out it became clear that there would be two others in the cell with me. A swarthy marine and a tall, fat Uzbek. They entered the cell, gloomily cast a sidelong look at me and threw themselves on to their wooden beds. The guards closed the door from outside, and inside the cell, above the surveillance window, the security light – a bleak twenty-watt bulb – lit up like a cat's eye.

The marine muttered under his breath that he hadn't managed to relieve himself and would have to suffer until morning as no one was allowed out of the cells at night. The Uzbek kept silent, pretending not to understand Russian.

Both had been given ten days for having gone AWOL. The marine said that he had gone to see a woman, but where the Uzbek had been, nobody knew. So far, the marine had served two days, the Uzbek, three.

At night it was cold and damp in the cell.

In the glasshouse, reveille was at 5 am.

We lined up in the corridor and gloomily waited for detail.

We were split into groups of ten to fifteen people, taken outside, given shovels, crowbars, barrows, and allotted places to work. Our group was herded to a deserted wasteland a long way off to dig ditches – either for rubbish or for slops. We were watched over by two guards with machine guns. One of them, a lanky, melancholy fellow, sat apart on an upside-down rusty bucket with the machine gun on his knees and the barrel pointing at us, and leisurely making toys from scraps of rubber.

I hadn't run so much in a long time and I'd never run so much with a wheelbarrow and a crowbar.

By lunchtime the Uzbek was half dead. After lunch and until dinner he wafted his shovel listlessly around the freshly dug hole.

We were as filthy as twigs pulled out of a swamp.

At night I got cramp in my legs.

The marine snored so loudly that it sounded as if a three-metre-wide wardrobe were being dragged across concrete.

Soon, I got used to the routine and did everything automatically, almost without tiring. But the Uzbek could not get used to it and cried every day.

Stretched out on his bunk after lights-out on the sixth day, the marine said: "Tomorrow you'll be out. I've got one more day to go." Looking at the Uzbek, he grinned – "Not bad here, eh?" – and laughed.

The Uzbek shook with rage.

The marine said: "What counts is that time flies in here and they feed you well."

In the morning, the Uzbek was sent back to his unit. The rest of us were lined up for detail.

That day they gave me another five days for a fag end found under my bed. I didn't know whether the Uzbek had thrown it there or whether the guards had simply been smoking in the cell.

The next day the marine was released.

I was left alone. During the day, I worked until I dropped. At night, I thought about Vensky.

Then my time was done.

I was driven back to my unit.

I wanted to sleep more than I wanted to live.

The weather was marvellous. A golden net of sunlight hung above the rooftops, trapping all the birds over the town. Out there, the streets were full of people who would never meet Vensky.

Nobody from my company was in. They had been taken to the firing range to cut turf for camouflaging pillboxes.

I sat on my bed and tried to remove my boots, but they wouldn't budge. I got a bayonet from the sentry, unstitched my boot uppers almost down to the soles, tossed the boots under my bunk, put on someone's frayed slippers and shuffled in to see the sergeant-major. I bought two packets of cigarettes from him, took some magazines, grabbed a stool and went into the washroom. I sat by the window, smoking and reading. I read a story about a little village girl and a huge sow, then I read some poems above which there was a photograph of a beautiful young woman. The poems were bad, but the woman was so beautiful that not to publish her poems you would have to be impotent. Then I glanced through the cartoons.

Someone touched my shoulder. I looked up and saw Vensky.

He gave a pained smile and said: "I haven't told anyone about the fight."

I said: "Drop dead!"

He went as red as a dog's tongue and said: "I haven't told anyone about the fight," turned and left. He seemed to be crying. I provoked some kind of feeling in him, I'll be damned; I always aroused a feeling of guilt in him.

On Thursday, the captain lined up the company and told us that in seven days' time we would be going on a hundred-kilometre route march in the mountains. For the driver mechanics, this meant seven days without surfacing from beneath their armoured personnel carriers. He read out the crew lists. My radio man was Monashka. Vensky was radio operator with the crew of 204, which, according to numerical order, would go in front of my 205 in convoy. The driver mechanic of 204 was Bragin.

We were led to the motor pool.

Any other time I wouldn't have lifted a finger. I would have hung around the repair shop or slept in the boxroom. But I felt a growing sense of foreboding.

I changed the oil in the engine, put in a new fuel pump, replaced the starter, checked the generator and relay regulator, and changed the fuel filters (and that was at a time when many people drove without one at all). Passers-by seemed to think I'd flipped. I adjusted the clutch, checked the steering and the entire brake system thoroughly. Then I remembered that during the last exercise the hub on the offside front wheel had overheated. I removed the wheel and the hub, changed the bearings and greased them thickly with Solidol. I was just putting the wheel back, using the heavy jack, when something made me look round. I turned and saw Vensky, who was standing twenty paces away, near a big black canister of Nigrol, never once taking his eyes off me.

I understood: whatever I did was useless. I squatted, looking inanely at my filthy hands and at the wrenches under the wheel. I felt as a man does at the end of a war, when he has no strength left to live by hatred, nor the will not to live by anguish.

On Saturday Monashka got a twenty-four-hour pass. He got some obliging brunette's address from Bragin, brushed his teeth, pressed his uniform, got dressed and set off into town.

He came back on Sunday night, radiant as a rakish comet, just about managed to get through evening roll call, undressed, straightened his back latticed with scratch marks, and went unhurriedly to the washroom, leaning his head to one side so that everyone could see the oblong, lilac lovebite under his left ear.

For the next two days and nights he chattered nonstop. On the third day, someone saw him come out of the toilet with a leaden step, go to his bedside table without a word, take out a clean sheet of paper, an envelope and boot polish. He removed one boot, smeared the sole with polish, placed the clean paper on the floor, put the boot back on and trod on the sheet with the whole of his foot. Then he folded the sheet with the footprint, placed it in the envelope, wrote the brunette's address on it and tossed the letter into the company postbox.

After lunch he came up to me, his mournful blue eyes gazing into the distance, raised his head, as though expecting rain, and said: "It looks as if I'm really in it this time."

I lit a cigarette, looked at Vensky, who was hovering nearby, wearing his vile and guilty smile, and grunted: "I got myself in it too – by being born."

Monashka said: "I've got to go into hospital."

I asked: "What for?"

He said: "For tests." He fell silent for a short time, then continued: "I went to the captain and said: 'I'm sick, I need to go into hospital.' I told him: 'You'll find a replacement for the exercise.'"

I asked: "And what'd he say?"

Monashka said: "And he says: 'OK, Vensky'll take your place.'"

I waited a moment and said: "You'll be going into hospital straight after the exercise."

He stared at me and asked: "Why?"

I said: "Because you're my sparks. And that's that."

Then I went to the medical centre. The first-aid instructor and I rifled through all the drawers and medicine cabinets, where we found *Vibramycin, Diazemuls* and *Nystatin*. I took the pills to Monashka.

On the 24th of April our company was raised by an alarm.

The convoy of armoured personnel carriers left the camp, skirted the town, crossed the plateau and rolled on into the foothills.

The road was narrow and winding.

Up, then down, up, then down we went.

I drove my APC, listening to the hum of the engine.

I spat over my shoulder.

And then, on one of the rises, the APC stalled. I switched off the ignition, switched it on again and tried to get the engine going with the starter, but it would not catch.

Monashka said: "Something's burnt out."

I told him to belt up. Then I got out on to the armour plating.

The two APCs behind us stopped, the rest drifted on. Bragin's APC in front of us also stopped. The front four disappeared around the bend.

From 208 the captain shouted through a megaphone: "Hey, what's going on there?"

I saw that they could not get past – the road was too narrow.

The roar of the engines pressed on the eardrums like water at a depth of ten metres.

"Tow him!" shouted the captain through the megaphone. "Bragin! Take him in tow!" he screamed at Bragin, and at me: "Untie the rope!"

I jumped to the ground and untied the towrope. Bragin inched backwards. I hooked up the rope and climbed into the APC. Bragin jerked forward. I saw blue exhaust fumes through the triplex windscreen and heard the rope snap, and Bragin's APC drove on up the mountain. Vensky, who sat on the body of 204, leant over the hatch and cried to Bragin that the rope had broken. Bragin braked and started slowly to edge back. Cursing everything under the sun, I climbed out again, but Vensky beat me to it. His boots were covered in white dust. In his hands he held another rope.

He said: "It's all right, I'll fasten it."

I stood aside and watched his agile, dexterous, pianist's hands clumsily attach the rope to the hook, and I wanted to laugh maliciously. Finally, he had fastened the rope to Bragin's APC, turned his back on it and started to tie the other end to my hook. And only by the shadow creeping over Vensky's boots did I realize, and then see, that Bragin's APC was rolling backwards – this often happens when you're sitting at the wheel, thinking of God knows what, unaware of anything around you.

Vensky stood with his back to Bragin's APC trying to fasten the rope.

I saw the shadow on Vensky's back and knew that in a couple of seconds he would be squashed between the armoured personnel carriers.

Everything resolves itself, and the more you talk about it, the longer it remains unresolved.

I did not want to think and did not want to yell, because, when the grim reaper comes calling, to think or to yell is risible.

I jumped at the very moment when Vensky lifted his head and when the rear end of Bragin's vehicle was a few centimetres from his back. And I put my whole life, everything which had been and everything which would have been to come, into a punch. And before my bones crunched between the steel plates, I caught sight of Vensky's skinny body, thrown into the air by my blow, spin like an unbreakable doll, then drop two metres from the armoured personnel carrier.

They laid me on the roadside in warm, soft dust. Somebody removed my helmet and stroked my head. Probably Vensky.

Look, stop messing around.

I'm telling you, don't carry me anywhere. Movement has meaning for you. Meaning for me lies in motionlessness.

But you don't hear me.

I don't open my eyes because I know what I'll see – the whole convoy halted, except the front four armoured personnel carriers which disappeared around the bend.

I don't know if I'll be able to open my eyes at all. I don't feel anything inside. Your voices are one with the rumble of falling rocks and the rumble of the artillery range. Everything alive is one with the dead.

Don't carry me anywhere.

. . . For a long time, she's been coming to me down grey roads, with a light noiseless step, like ashes settling.

Don't touch me.

I want to see this.

Translated by Sylva Rubashova and Milena Michalski

OLEG ERMAKOV

Safe Return

A GIANT OF a general, smirking, was saying that now Orshev was in the regiment for good; Orshev tried to slip away, but the general overtook him everywhere he went, so Orshev decided to kill the general, and he slithered up to him in serpent's form, then in the shape of an old man, a child, a woman, a tank, but the giant recognized him each time and hid behind an iron door: *Orshev was delirious in the soggy bed sheets.* He hunted a general, banqueted with black, swollen, stinking corpses on a white summit, grew light, like a wood chip, and was afraid of the wind, then suddenly became heavy, like a granite monument, and was swallowed by the earth up to his knees; sometimes he saw his own lungs, transparent sacks stuffed thick with worms; he ran into his own house and threw a grenade into a cake on the festive table, darted back out of the door and threw all his weight against it, while friends, parents and children screamed and pounded on the door, but he didn't let them out, and the grenade exploded; then, naked, he chased a frisky old woman around a garden; somebody was helping him catch her, and then everyone together, snarling and biting, fell upon the old woman . . .

Orshev was raving in the suffocating, overcrowded hospital ward at the same time as his recently demobilized comrades were flying back to Kabul. Those soldiers, with whom he had lived side by side these two years, had flown out of here for ever. They had wanted to return to the Union together. For two years the return had been their favourite topic: they imagined it aloud in contented tones while on night watch, after a battle, or in the evening around a fire behind the bathhouse, where they usually baked potatoes, drank tea and smoked anasha. They spent a lot of time imagining how, medals clinking, they'd finally come down the aircraft steps in Tashkent, buy up all the cognac, get seats on a train, and start to drink, laugh and reminisce, while frightened civilians would cower in the corner with gaping mouths, listening and watching as the suntanned soldiers, sinewy and fearless, would drink, laugh, and remember the war.

But this was how it had turned out instead.

During the last operation – for three weeks his battalion together with Government forces had laid siege to the Urganskoe gorge – the soldiers had gone for a swim after a routine patrol into the mountains. The river was swift, clear and cold; filthy and sweaty, the soldiers waded into the current and submerged themselves, allowing it to carry them downstream. Then they jumped out of the river and stretched out on the hot white sand; their frozen bodies quickly heated up, whereupon they dived back into the stream again. Orshev stayed in the water longer than anyone else – a stupid idea: to chill himself to the bone so as to stave off the heat and thirst at least until evening. He searched out a boulder under the water in the middle of the river, grasped it and let his body float full length. He was rocked up and down and swayed from side to side. In the sky stood the sun, small and hot; upstream arched the mountain ranges, with occasional patches of cedars. Along the left bank of the river stretched a strip of fine-grained white sand, and on it lay dark, muscled bodies; the soldiers talked, joked back and forth, smoked, and didn't think about having to return to the mountains next morning. Things were fine. But towards evening Orshev became violently ill. It was pneumonia, and his temperature climbed to forty-two degrees.

Orshev's comrades were already long since home by the time he was released from the hospital ward. Gaunt and yellowed, Orshev arrived at the regiment. The cots of his friends and even his own cot, located on the prestigious bottom level, were now occupied by the new "granddads", the senior troops who called the shots in the regiment. Orshev set out for the officers' quarters, and found the company commander. The commander spoke easily with him, allowing him to smoke in his office, and poured him some tea, served up with white bread and sugar. The commander told him the helicopters would be sure to bring in some new troops any day now, and Orshev would be able to leave for Kabul. But what exactly was the meaning of "any day now"? That could be tomorrow or the day after, in a week or two. Now then, tomorrow morning there's a column setting out for supplies in Kabul. "Of course, travelling by truck to Kabul's a risky business, you know that yourself, Orshev. But there it is: tomorrow afternoon, carved in stone. That means you're in Kabul by evening, and the next day, if you're lucky, in the Union. I'm not advising you one way or

the other; make up your own mind." Orshev agreed to leave. With a
smile the commander handed over his orders. "Well, congratulations,
soldier, your hitch is up."

Orshev wandered around the tent city, which was flooded with the
steely light of the sun, and stood for a while at the boundary of the
regimental area, smoking a cigarette and peering into the steppe,
empty, mute and endless. He'd have to go to the bathhouse. But it
was hot, and besides, the illness had softened his solid frame. Orshev
felt lazy, weak and listless. But he'd have to go to the bathhouse.
Orshev gathered his strength and left for the baths used by his battalion.

The rotund attendant sat with a book on the porch of the clay-walled
bathhouse. Orshev greeted him and asked if there was any water.
"Hey, for you we'll find some," answered the attendant. Orshev
wearily sat down next to him and saw that this bath somehow wasn't
going to be pleasant. "Your eyes are bloodshot; obviously they've let
you out too early," said the attendant, closing his book with a thud.
"When d'you fly?" Orshev replied that he was leaving tomorrow with
the column. The attendant's face wrinkled in displeasure: "I wouldn't
go. Better to wait a month for a chopper. Why not stay here, spend
the night at my place. Tomorrow I'll scrape up some good shit, we'll
roll a few joints and fire up, what say?" Orshev shook his head:
everything made him sick, he was even sick of anasha, sick to death
of everything.

He washed in tepid water, dried himself, and before he dressed,
attentively inspected the seams of his new tee shirt and shorts – new
things from the supply depot were often already lice ridden. While
Orshev busied himself in the bathhouse, the attendant heated a mess
tin of water on the little fire behind the building and brewed the tea.

They sat on the porch, sipped tea, nibbled hard tack and sugar and
peered out at the little regimental city. The tents, the wooden-planked
sentry boxes like so many mushrooms, the toilets, rubbish bins, mess
tents, the headquarters and the commissary store, the officers' quarters,
the parade ground and supply dumps – all were grey from the dust
and the sun.

Orshev stayed at the attendant's until evening, and was left alone
there – the attendant slept in the dressing room of the bathhouse –
but he felt like spending his last night in the tent; after all, for two
years it had been his home . . .

In the twilight Orshev returned to his tent and lay down on his cot
without undressing or making up the bed. The security detail made
the evening rounds of the company area, and in the tent all was quiet.

Orshev peered up at the mattress springs of the top bunk and warily took inventory of himself. Something wasn't right, maybe he really was still sick. Or was it the usual lethargy after an illness? Orshev drifted into a light slumber.

A touch on the shoulder woke him. He opened his eyes and saw an unfamiliar young soldier. The soldier smiled, embarrassed. Orshev interrogated him with his eyebrows and a slight nod: well? "I was sent by 'Grandfather' of the Soviet Army Khmyzin," muttered the youngster. Orshev remained silent. "He asked me," the soldier cautiously continued, "to pass along a message that this is his place." Orshev raised himself up on an elbow, glanced around: there were no granddads, no Khmyzin in the tent, only the newer troops, the finches and the scoops. "Well, why didn't he come himself to tell me, if he's got so brave?" asked Orshev mockingly. "Is that an answer?" asked the young soldier. "Go on, get out," Orshev gently rebuffed him. The youngster quickly left. But soon he returned and said that Granddad Khmyzin had warned him: by the time they finished smoking, the place had better be vacated. Orshev didn't reply. "They're finishing their cigarettes; that means they're all together, the jackals," thought Orshev. The youngster waited for an answer but lacked the courage to prompt him again.

Orshev lay with eyes closed. Finally the granddads walked into the tent. Khmyzin, a stumpy, squat, broad-chested fellow, looked around at his comrades and marched over to Orshev's cot, proclaiming loudly: "Orshev! Get out." Orshev opened his eyes and glared at Khmyzin. Khmyzin glanced at his comrades and kicked the iron bedrail. "Orshev!" Orshev rose up sharply, pushed aside the frightened young soldier and stepped towards his adversary. Khmyzin's comrades came to life. "Back off, you bastards," yelled Orshev, raising his arm in a threatening gesture. The granddads stopped dead. "Khmyzin," said Orshev, "you feel like a scrap. Fine with me. But are you man enough for it? Then take care of your own business. I always take care of mine." "That's only fair," one of the granddads finally said. "But he called us bastards," muttered another in an uncertain tone. No one answered him. Despite the insults they'd suffered under their former granddads – Orshev and his comrades – they were reluctant to join the fight against Orshev. In the first place, the worst of the former crowd, those who really deserved a lesson, were already long since home, and why should Orshev have to answer for all of them? In the second place, there was nothing unnatural about holding grudges against former granddads – no, that's the way it was, and always would be: yesterday they were dumped on, today they did the dumping. In the third place, beating up a "demob", that is, a veteran, a soldier who'd been to hell and back, could spoil the junior soldiers who now submitted to the senior troops as if they were gods – wise, powerful and fearless. Besides, Orshev wasn't a bastard, far from it – true, he gave it to you right in the teeth, and he forced you to do all the work, but he wasn't greedy or vengeful, and had never devised any exquisitely refined humiliations for the finches and scoops. So now they forgave him calling them bastards, and agreed that it was only fair: one on one. The granddads chased everybody out of the tent, cleared away the stools, fanned out in a wide circle and peered avidly at Khmyzin and Orshev. Orshev wasn't wearing a belt, so somebody told Khmyzin to take his off, and he did. It became quiet. And awkward. "Hey, Khmyzin, let him have it!" somebody shouted out, and Khmyzin stepped towards Orshev, clenched his fists and ducked his head.

They went into a clinch. Khmyzin dipped his left shoulder, distracting Orshev's attention, and struck with his right from the side, slamming a fist to his temple. Orshev staggered and grew pale. Khmyzin launched a stomach punch, but Orshev covered himself just in time. Khmyzin again jabbed with his right, grunting from the gut – Orshev deflected that blow as well. All this time Orshev defended himself, trying to come back after the blow to his head. Flushed with newfound courage, Khmyzin attacked, no trace remaining of any indecisiveness – after all, how could he fight with a former granddad, someone he hadn't had the courage to look straight in the eye! Seeing that Orshev was only defending himself, Khmyzin flew into a rage and, grunting furiously, began to rain down blows on his opponent. His rage turning to a white heat, he became reckless, and was amazed, as was everyone else, when suddenly he found himself on the floor. Khmyzin jumped up, spraying golden droplets as he shook his head, but Orshev quickly slashed an elbow across his cheekbone from the left, while planting his fist on the right side of his jaw. Khmyzin began to groan, closed his arms over his lowered head and started to retreat. Orshev pressed hard, landing solid and accurate punches to the head, to the back, and to the kidney. Everyone watched silently. Suddenly Khmyzin stopped, uttered a roar, rose up and threw himself on his enemy, trying to turn the fist fight into a wrestling match, but Orshev adroitly recoiled and struck Khmyzin on the nose. Panic-stricken, blood now flowing from a lacerated lip and both nostrils, Khmyzin again rushed his adversary and this time was able to break through his fists, grasp Orshev in a bear hug and throw him to the floor. Khmyzin ended up on top, grabbed Orshev's hair and began to beat the back of his head against the floor, until Orshev, tears flowing from the pain, tore himself from under Khmyzin, hammering him in the sides with his fists. The onlookers were silent. Finally Orshev, soiled with Khmyzin's blood, managed to cinch a throat lock, but a wheezing Khmyzin bit into his hand. Orshev grabbed Khmyzin's ear with his free hand and began to tear it away from the skull. Khmyzin screamed and let go of his opponent's hair, but Orshev continued to twist his ear, and Khmyzin had to crawl away from him. Puffing and panting, Orshev got up on all fours. Khmyzin also. They slowly got to their feet, not taking their eyes from one another. "You . . . had enough?" asked Orshev, supporting himself against the bedrail of the cot. "No . . . that's . . . for you . . . that's enough for you," answered Khmyzin, spitting blood and wiping his nose with his sleeve. Orshev pushed away from the bedrail and with the edge of his hand gave a chop to Khmyzin's neck. Khmyzin's head buckled from the blow. Orshev stood and waited. Khmyzin looked to be just about finished. "That's all," said Orshev, but suddenly Khmyzin sprang up and butted Orshev's face with his forehead. Clutching at his gurgling nose, Orshev was thrown back on to the cot railing. Now they both had bloody noses. Staunching the blood with his hand, Orshev stood there leaning on the cot, following Khmyzin with foggy eyes, and held his right hand at the ready. One more blow and he was going to collapse. But Khmyzin had no strength left to attack either. He was bathed in sweat, wiping away the blood, his breath coming in short dry rasps as he staggered on shaking legs.

"Looks like it's all over," someone said in a loud voice. Orshev and Khmyzin kept silent. "Go clean up," voices suggested to them both. Everyone filed out of the tent, and outside the younger soldiers poured water for them from their mess tins.

Orshev was the first to return to the tent; he tore off his ripped and bloody clothes and collapsed over the cot on top of the blanket.

Khmyzin walked into the tent. He approached the disputed cot and said in a hoarse voice: "Orshev, give it up." Silence in the tent. "But it's my cot," answered Orshev after a short pause. Khmyzin stubbornly insisted: "Get into the top bunk, there's a free cot up there. I won't be up on top ever again. I've had enough. A year and a half. That's enough." "Go to hell," said Orshev. Khmyzin spoke slowly in a strained voice. "You're nobody. Get up on the second floor." Orshev sat up. "Get going," repeated Khmyzin. Orshev stood up and hit Khmyzin, but the blow was weak and landed on his chest. Khmyzin took two steps back, stumbled over a stool and seized it by the leg. "Khmyzin!"

everyone screamed. Khmyzin didn't turn around at the outcry. He stood half turned towards Orshev, poised to strike, but Orshev didn't wait: suspending himself with bent arms from the edge of the top bunk, he lashed out at Khmyzin with his feet. Khmyzin flew away with a crash, collapsed among the cots, and was quiet. Orshev dropped down on to the conquered bed. "Wow, you killed him," voices were saying.

The orderly woke Orshev at five o'clock; the column was setting out at six. "What's with that one?" asked Orshev, yawning. "Sleeping," replied the orderly. Orshev, grunting and screwing his face into a grimace, got up and went outside in his shorts and tee shirt.

It was warm. Birds whistled. The sun, standing red in relief against the sky, lay at the edge of the steppe.

The orderly scooped up a mess tin full of water from the barrel and poured it out for Orshev. Orshev gingerly washed his beaten face, nodded to the orderly and, cautiously dabbing at his face with a towel, returned to the tent. On the railing hung his dress uniform – before waking him, the orderly had brought it over from personal storage. Orshev dressed, picked up his satchel and dress cap, walked to the middle of the tent and looked around. He saw Khmyzin. He was sleeping, arms akimbo and mouth wide open; bruises were beginning to show on his face, blood had caked around his nose, and a jagged black weal cut across his lower lip. A faint, satisfied smile crossed Orshev's lips; with a flourish of his hat he waved at the sleeping Khmyzin and walked out of the tent.

The commander of the column, glancing at Orshev's swollen face, smirked: "Well, look at the piss artist, had a good drink?" Orshev replied that he wasn't a drunk, far from it, he had simply slept a lot in the hospital. "Yeah, sure . . ." exclaimed the captain. "No doubt our young stud blew through a bottle or two, right? Well, where do you want to ride? In a truck? In a BTR? . . . In a truck? Well, take your pick."

Orshev passed along the column and stopped alongside a truck. "Lift?" "Grab a seat," exclaimed the driver. Once in the cabin Orshev immediately took off his dress coat, hung it on the hook, asked for some water, drank his fill from an aluminium canteen, leant back against the seat and lit a cigarette.

Ten minutes later the column set out. At the head, tail and middle went BTRs – armoured transports with infantry – for defence. The column slowly made its way past the perimeter checkpoint. As

Orshev's truck drew level with the little stone house, Orshev whispered to himself: "Amen!"

Gaining speed, the column bounced along the steppe road, kicking up dust, shaking and roaring. The sun shone from an angle, needles of light penetrating the dust cloud that blanketed the vehicles. The dust filtered into the cabin and caked on eyes and lips, tickled nostrils, settled into the scalp. The driver unhurriedly smoked a cigarette in the dust. The moist end of the butt was already dirty. Orshev rocked back and forth on the springy cushion seat and peered out at the blurred outline of the canvas tarp stretched over the truck travelling ahead. The driver, thank God, was not a talkative type; he'd only been interested to know why Orshev had been delayed back at the regiment, and commented that in six months he too would be heading home, and that was all. Orshev was grateful. After two years he was tired of these army conversations: going home, women, medals and decorations and good grub. Not only that, but after the fight his head was killing him, as if he'd been drinking home-made brew or smoking anasha straight through the night.

Sometimes the truck's wheels sank into a pothole, and the two passengers flew around on the seats. From the regimental camp to the paved highway was twenty kilometres; on this section the rebels loved to plant mines, and the road looked like the face of the moon. Of course, even on the highway trucks were blown up. But at least there wouldn't be any dust. "The sooner we get to the highway, the better," thought Orshev.

For half an hour the column travelled in clouds of dust along the steppe road, then took to the highway and headed off along a straight grey ribbon to the north. Orshev took out a handkerchief and wiped his face, reached for the canteen, washed out his mouth and took a huge swig. The driver lit up a cigarette and said happily: "No sweat, in six months I'm out of here." Orshev thought a bit: "Six months — that is, twenty-four weeks, let's see, one hundred and eighty days" — and his jaw ached from the sheer tedium.

All around lay the steppe with little inclines the colour of lead, and tiny ridges along the horizon. In the lifeless desert an occasional village was outlined in green. Sometimes these settlements came to the very edge of the highway. They were cheerless gatherings of mudbrick dwellings surrounded by high walls; the houses, the walls and the wooden gates were all grey and lacklustre. The people — men in turbans, cloaks and wide trousers, women in dark loose overalls — occasionally brought timid life to the sun-drenched alleys and cramped squares. But beyond the courtyard walls overflowed lush gardens – fresh, verdant, gentle gardens . . .

The column moved forward at a good pace. The mountains advanced, seeming weighty, set against the sky in rust; the valley was tapering. And soon the column was travelling between mountains coloured copper and ginger. The road started to wind around in loops. The ascent into the mountain pass had begun.

Orshev threw his cigarette butt out of the window and lit another smoke; he glanced warily at the cliffs, grown huge on either side. The driver, knitting his brows and moving slightly forward on the seat, kept turning the steering wheel and in barely audible tones began to whistle a monotonous snatch of melody. Orshev squinted at the sky and asked for the automatic rifle. The driver shook his head. "Sorry, no can do." Orshev smiled crookedly and muttered, justifying himself, that being without an automatic was like being without arms or legs; he never went anywhere without an automatic any more. Sturdily grasping the wheel with one hand, the driver managed to free an ammo pouch with a couple of grenades, and pushed it towards Orshev. Bouncing up and down, the driver transferred yet another pouch. Now Orshev had four grenades, and breathed easier.

The column climbed along the stone road, torn by craters. Cliffs loomed over the trucks. The foot of the cliffs was black from soot; to the right yawned a shallow gulch with burned-out vehicles, wheels, scraps of iron and shreds of rubber at the bottom. The lead trucks had already crawled through the saddle of the mountain pass. The engines roared, and a black haze hung over the road, with blue sky pressing the grey cliffs. Orshev held the ammo pouches in his lap and smoked, while the driver whistled his primitive little ditty more and more insistently. But suddenly the trucks in front began to stop, one after the other, and Orshev's truck slowly came to a halt as well. "One of the old goats broke down," suggested the driver and once again took up whistling. Orshev took a swig from the canteen – the water was already warm. The driver whistled and drummed with his fingers on the steering wheel.

A minute passed. The column stood, engines at a low rumble. The driver whistled and drummed his fingers. Orshev glanced down at the charred wreckage and debris. It was hot, breathing was difficult, brown drops rolled down their faces. What the hell was going on up there? No doubt an armoured transport had overheated – typical for noon on a summer day. Or a truck engine had died.

"Hey, chief, change the record," requested Orshev. The driver stopped whistling and drumming, narrowed his eyes, leant back against the seat and began to breathe evenly and deeply, imitating sleep. Orshev let out a laugh. "I should've waited for a chopper," he thought. "What the devil ever possessed me to paddle up this creek . . . Right now I could be . . . yeah, at home . . . fresh sheets . . ."

The engines roared to life, and Orshev's driver opened his eyes and began to whistle again. The column set out. "Well, if nothing's happened so far, then nothing's going to happen," thought Orshev, and then corrected himself: "– at least in this mountain pass."

The column gained the pass and began the descending crawl. The mountains retreated a little from the road. The sun stood at its zenith; the stone faces of the mountains mirrored the light, and the sky scalded the eyes. The driver donned a pair of teardrop reflective sunglasses and took on the enigmatic appearance of a Sicilian mafioso. The stone heights and the boulders alongside the road shimmered, and the hood of the truck burnt. Orshev squinted, eyes closing, and drifted off to sleep.

"They really caught it," voices said loudly, and Orshev gave a start and looked at the driver. The driver caught his glance and directed it with a nod to the left. The column was skirting several military vehicles with Afghan insignia on the doors, and a red and white passenger bus lying on its side in a ditch with its chassis, blown away, facing the road. Gathered around the bus was a crowd of civilians and soldiers. There were no wounded or killed to be seen; they had probably already been loaded into vehicles. A wizened, moustachioed soldier who looked like Don Quixote was pouring water from a canteen on to his comrade's red hands. The turbans and cloaks of the civilians were torn and stained with oil and blood. At some distance from the others, bending his face to his knees and rocking back and forth, sat a bony old man. There was also a knot of women in chadoris standing and sobbing. Two barefoot urchins, having eyed the column and lost interest, began to investigate the bottom of the bus. Together they stuck their heads through the opening, until a grey-haired officer yelled at them. The Afghans stared at the column.

The transport truck in which Orshev was riding worked its way down into the ditch, proceeded parallel to the road for a bit and then returned to the hard surface. The driver took up his tune. Orshev glanced at his watch and asked: "Listen, do you guys stop for lunch or eat on the move?" "We stop. There'll be a river soon, that's where we usually chow down." "Hmm. The thing is, I haven't eaten since yesterday." "Then have at it, what's the problem? Or didn't you bring

anything?" "I've got something. But I don't feel like eating alone."
"Forget it, chow down." "No, not alone, I'll wait."

Again Orshev was jolted and awoke when the column stopped
before a bridge. Two sappers with a sniffer dog were already wandering
over the bridge, while the remaining soldiers smoked, strolled around
the vehicles, or tossed aside their sweaty, stiff jackets on their way
towards the river to wash off. Orshev and his driver walked down to
the river too. Refreshed, they returned to the truck, left the doors
wide open, and laid out the meal: black bread, sugar, two tins of
smoked mutton and two tins of cheese. They ate in silence. First they
devoured all the mutton with the sour bread, and then the sugar and
cheese. They gulped down some water and then lit up cigarettes. While
they were smoking they spotted a caravan far off in the steppe – a tiny
chain of camels, miniature walking figures of humans, and white herds
of sheep. "Ah, Pushtuns," drawled the driver, and yawned. "They
couldn't give a damn, war is war, but they roam by themselves."
"Gypsies," responded Orshev. "We once had a Gypsy with us," said
the driver, suddenly becoming animated. "Nobody to speak of, a
Gypsy like any other: dark skin, huge eyes, a real operator. One time
we were headed down to Kabul, but in the mountain pass we had a
surprise party thrown for us. And afterwards the Gypsy took sick. Off
with him to the hospital, then to Kabul, and from there to the Union;
we didn't see any more of him." "What was his problem?" "Something
like liver trouble. Or his stomach. They say he always swallowed his
tobacco. What an idea – sending a Gypsy into the army." "What, not
the type, was he?" "Of course not. A Gypsy even in Africa's still a
Gypsy; give him a whip, a horse and the wind. But all he got was the
whip. I love them." "Who?" Orshev didn't understand. "Why, the
Gypsies. They'd spit on anything. A horse, a whip and the wind. And
we're just mules." The driver peered gloomily into the steppe where,
at the foot of the bare mountains, the tiny camels and the finely etched
silhouettes of the humans moved along, and the wool of the sheep
showed softly white.

Kabul was illuminated by an evening sun which was viscous, hot,
bloated, and darkening as it set on the snowy peaks. The city lay in a
valley between the mountains, a vast city of clay, stone, glass and
concrete. Everywhere there were gardens like fluffy down, with poplars
sticking up like pyramids and, among the gardens, gleaming windows
and whitewashed walls, while the cupolas of the mosques shone sky
blue and yellow minarets soared.

The column halted at the edge of the city in an enclosed marshalling area. Orshev put on his dress coat and cap, picked up his satchel and turned towards the driver. The driver, hanging his heavy palms on the steering wheel, gazed at Orshev. "Well," said Orshev and hesitated. "Until we meet in the Union?" He stretched out his hand to the driver. The other shook it limply and replied that there was hardly a chance of meeting, the Union being a big country. "Half a year – no sweat," said Orshev and slipped down from the cabin.

He searched out the captain and asked to be driven to the transfer station. "Hey, listen, that poor cattle hauler's been overworked; why not get an early start outa here tomorrow?" the captain said merrily. "What's your hurry? The jets aren't flying any more today; nothing but lice at the transfer station. Spend the night at our place. We can shoot the bull all night long. What, don't want to?" The captain laughed heartily. Orshev looked at him gloomily and remained silent, and at that instant a jet roared in the sky over Kabul. The captain, the infantrymen and Orshev looked up. In the sky, gaining altitude, soared a white aircraft with scarlet stripe from nose to tail. "Uh-oh! See there, your jet – bye-bye!" exclaimed the captain, laughing. "That's not ours," objected one of the infantrymen. "Ours are white and blue." "But a new regulation just came out for ours to have a red stripe; what, haven't you heard? Listen, you guys, life has left you behind," said the captain. The infantrymen were astounded: was this really true? "It's a fact. Listen: is our flag red? A Pioneer's scarf? How about a passport or military ID? So why should the jets be white and blue? After all, they fly abroad, but there's absolutely no ideological cargo, there's no ideological cargo in that colour scheme, see. So how come? It's either an oversight . . . or a provocation." The captain looked at Orshev. "Uh-oh! The vet's gonna tear me to pieces, ha-ha-ha!" "Comrade Captain," said Orshev, and then grew silent. "Hey, admit it, if I weren't wearing shoulder boards – epaulettes, that is – wouldn't you give it to me right in the face? Ha-ha-ha! Be honest now. Wouldn't you?" asked the captain. The infantrymen and the driver of the armoured transport grumbled: "Comrade Captain, what are you doing? Good God, just get the fellow on his way." "You sure would, oh, how you'd love to," said the captain. "I can see it in your eyes. No doubt you've finished off quite a few spooks, young stud? But hold on, hold on, I'm joking. Take it easy, we're leaving. We'll get you there in one piece. Get the warrant officer over here!"

Orshev, four of the infantrymen and a warrant officer sat down on top of an armoured transport and drove off towards the road. Orshev's

eyes searched out the taciturn truck driver, and then he waved to him
– the driver was still sitting in the cabin, smoking. "You'd better get
inside," the warrant officer advised Orshev. "Don't tempt fate –
snipers!" Orshev shook his head – no. "OK, up to you," said the
warrant officer, tossing a good-natured glance at the solid figure.

The green armoured transport, gently rocking back and forth, sailed
along the broad main road bordered on either side by poplars and
cedars. Along the way they passed automobiles, buses, trucks and
bicycles. Ragamuffins crowded the verges pulling two-wheeled
wooden carts weighted down with sacks, bales and firewood – transport taxis for the poor. People walked along the pavements: old men,
thick white beards against black European coats, officers and soldiers
with automatic weapons, curly-haired teenaged boys in brightly
coloured shirts, jeans or white trousers, grubby barefoot children,
women in chadoris, and young girls with fair faces and dark hair
wearing short denim skirts and light blouses. Everywhere the taverns
were doing a lively trade, shop windows and restaurant signs gleamed.
In the streets people roasted spits of lamb, while homeless dogs
howled, children chirruped, engines roared and brakes squealed; the
evening breeze shifted the leaves of the poplars and plantains, and
high above the city glowed the mountain tops, just now hiding the
sun.

The transfer point, a tent camp surrounded by barbed wire, was
located on the opposite edge of the city, not far from the airport. The
evening was still translucent as the armoured transport rolled to a stop
in front of the camp gates. Orshev bid farewell to the infantrymen and
the warrant officer, and jumped to the ground. A sentry appeared near
the gates.

Orshev didn't sleep. He lay on a bare cot with his satchel tucked under
his head, smoking and peering at the ceiling. New conscripts – the
camp was crammed full of them – puffed and snored in unison. Orshev
felt loathsome: his head ached, his hand hurt where Khmyzin had
bitten him, and it seemed his temperature was rising. Orshev thought:
"I'm still sick." He smoked, now and again glancing at the luminescent
face of his watch. Time was crawling.

At one in the morning a sudden bang disturbed the quiet, then a
wail and an explosion were heard. An instant later another burst, now
closer, as shrapnel whistled over the tents. The camp security forces
opened fire with their automatic weapons and a heavy machine gun.
The new recruits jumped up and yelled to one another: "Hey! What?

Alert! What is it?" They leant out of the tent and saw the black mountains and red tracer bursts. "Shelling! They're shelling us!" they exclaimed noisily, when a third round suddenly exploded right next to them, somewhere just beyond the barbed wire. Orshev lay in his cot smoking his cigarette and thought: "That's the way it has to be," and he had a premonition: "That's exactly the way it will end: the final curtain! . . ."

"Are they mortars?" they asked him. Orshev replied: "Mortars." The raw recruits pressed up to the door, stared out of the windows. Orshev suddenly and distinctly saw it all: there they are camouflaged in black, now one man stuffs a scrap of pig iron with metal tail fins down a tube, then skips away as the mortar throws out the shell. Whistling a tender and bewitching refrain, it sails off into the night and soars down through the top of the tent. Orshev heard and saw the recruits being killed, thrown about, screams piercing the air, gasping, they whimper and squeal, not believing that such a thing could happen on their very first day in the country, and Orshev saw himself pressing the damp, hot, oozing tear in his own stomach – and now . . .

But the mortar didn't strike again. The perimeter defence forces poured bursts of tracer fire over the mountains, and after half an hour everything quietened down. The camp stirred, talked, lit up cigarettes; no screams were heard, which meant that all the shells had missed their mark. Orshev finished another cigarette and, lulled by the conversation of the new troops, fell asleep. In a dream he thought: "Please let there be good weather, and let there be a jet, just good weather and a jet, weather and a jet . . ."

The weather was good, and there was a jet. It was the transport from Bagram with coffins and their escorts, taking on more cargo in Kabul. Orshev found out the first stop would be in Orenburg, then to Minsk and Moscow. That was a bit of luck. Usually the demobilized vets were shipped to Tashkent, and from there they were on their own getting home, which in winter wasn't a problem, but during the summer season when the train station and airport were overcrowded, there was no choice but to kill time in Tashkent for a few days. Orshev had to go to Moscow and further west. He was extremely lucky.

Orshev settled into a folding seat in the tail of the aircraft. It was suffocating. He removed his coat, tore off his tie, and unbuttoned his shirt.

Sunburnt soldiers in pressed and laundered field uniforms with snow-white undercollars looked sullenly at him – before them lay the task of escorting the coffins out to all the homes and saying something over the graves and at the funeral dinners. Among the escorts were two officers, which meant that officers were also among the slain. Oblong mat-finished metal coffins, crudely soldered down the middle, were stacked on board the aeroplane in pairs. The officers were discussing something. The soldiers were silent.

Finally the pilots passed through the cabin in their sky-blue flight suits. The rear exit hatches were tightly secured, it became twilight inside, and the overhead cabin lights began to glow dully. The jet engines roared to life, the plane began to roll, taxied out on to the straight runway, gained speed and lifted off. Those with seats at the few windows glued themselves to the thick panes. Orshev felt like looking at Kabul one last time, but he wasn't near a window, and to approach somebody and ask to peer over his shoulder for a minute – no, it wasn't worth it to walk up and ask. Orshev looked at the soldiers, at the metal boxes, at the overhead lights, at his own two feet . . . He gently closed his eyes.

The aeroplane laboriously gained altitude. It was hot. Sweat poured off everyone's faces. Orshev felt like having a cigarette. He hadn't smoked for a long while – he had sat for an hour in the shade underneath a wing while the plane was being loaded, but smoking wasn't allowed on the flight line. His body felt weak. He took a deep breath and felt a sharp pain in his back opposite the left lung. Or was it his heart? No, his heart was healthy, it had been silent these two years, that is, it had worked perfectly, even though in the mountains they ran like horses. No, it was his lungs. He simply hadn't fully recovered yet, that was all. Although maybe Khmyzin had landed a good punch right there, and that's why it hurt. But this damned feeling of weakness . . .

"How long until the border – half an hour, an hour?" thought Orshev. "Until we cross the border, it's too early to cheer. But we've gained good altitude, now they won't knock us down, they can't reach us. So why not – Hip, hip . . . Hurrah!"

Translated by Howard Swartz

IZRAEL METTER

Ryabov and Kozhin

EMERGING FROM HIS suburban train, Ryabov flipped through his address book once again. Kozhin's address, which he had had such difficulty in obtaining, was not down under the appropriate letter of the alphabet but had a page to itself – so that he could later rip it out and forget it for good, if that were to prove possible.

A number of buses stood in an untidy huddle on the dusty square in front of the station. Their destinations were indicated on tin markers fastened to posts. The buses stood by them like horses tethered to a rail. Ryabov looked them over until he found ZVONAREVKA and took his place at the back of the queue of people who had jumped off the train before him.

Mushroomers, anglers, anguished weekend cottagers – the loads they carried on their backs or in their arms immediately gave them away. The only person to have a thin briefcase projecting from under his arm was Ryabov.

The bus, crammed with passengers, lurched through the village streets. For a short while it rattled along the edge of the fields, and was then swallowed up in the forest. Here there was no more dust, the mildly astringent aroma of pine needles was sucked in through the open windows, and the passengers' faces gradually shed their look of urban frenzy.

A lake suddenly loomed up on one of their sharper turns, almost as if the bus were about to drive full tilt into it, but the gravel track swung to the left and followed the shore for quite a while.

This was where Zvonarevka began. The lake sprawled on the edge of the village and the single main street climbed the rise beyond it.

From the bus stop Ryabov walked back towards the edge of the lake. He did not know where Kozhin's house was, but the address stipulated Lake Street, so it had to be there somewhere.

Looked at from the rise, the lake was broad and unconfined: it basked in the clear expanse of sunlit sky and faithfully reflected its image. Though when Ryabov made his way down the rise and came close to the lake, it suddenly disappeared from sight: the entire shore was occupied by individual building plots, and bushes, houses and trees obscured the water from view.

Here the garden areas were generous in size and luxuriantly green. After finding the right number on one of the fences, Ryabov refrained from opening the gate but went on further and to one side. There in the sand stood a veteran pine, already half dead; its roots jutted out like bones from a coffin.

Ryabov sat down for a moment on one of the petrified roots, and surveyed Kozhin's house, visible through the greenery bordering the fence. Constructed from logs and painted a uniform brick red, the house squatted solidly on high cement foundations. Swallows flew in under the edge of the slate roof.

He heard children's voices coming from the garden and beyond them the sound of someone splitting logs. These sounds, and all that his eyes were now taking in, had nothing to do with what he had come here for.

He went in by the lych gate and, skirting past some bedraggled clumps of lilac, emerged beside the verandah. The door to the house was open. There were babies' nappies drying on the balcony.

Ryabov enquired loudly from the verandah steps: "Is anyone at home? May I come in?"

No one answered.

Through the open door of the verandah he could see a table laden with apples picked from the trees, and dishes heaped with redcurrants and gooseberries. In one corner there was a heap of discarded Wellingtons and various remnants of clothing.

"Hi there, is the Master in!" Ryabov shouted once more.

And again no one answered him.

He made his way down the track towards the shore of the lake – the children's voices had come from that direction.

Two little boys were hunting crayfish off the wooden jetty. They were diving down under the steep bank and resurfacing, snorting out the water from their nostrils. They swam to the side of the jetty and, with triumphant cries, chucked their booty into a pail.

Ryabov waited until one of them, feeling the cold, climbed out of the lake. Hopping about on one foot, his head tilted to one side, he was getting the water out of his ear. Only then did the young boy notice Ryabov.

"Is it Grandfather you want?" he asked.

"I want Kozhin, Sergey Mikhailovich," said Ryabov.

"That's right. That's Granddad. Wait a moment, if you please, and I'll just get my trousers on."

"Heavens!" thought Ryabov. "And the bastard has such a polite grandchild!"

He followed the little boy to the furthest end of the garden. There, beside a wooden shed, a shortish, effeminately corpulent man, in frayed pyjamas that were much too long for him, was splitting logs. Ryabov had already noticed while some way off that he was performing his task in a most odd manner, giving the block of wood a couple of taps with the hatchet and then looking to one side in the direction of the bushes. Then he would give it another tap and take another sideways peek. Under the bushes, in the shade, was a pram with a one-year-old baby sitting in it. Its gaze was fixed on the man: the moment the man stopped, the baby's face twisted into a tearful grimace, while after each blow, it bounced up and down and clapped its hands in ecstasy.

"Grandpapa," said the young boy accompanying Ryabov, "this uncle is asking for you."

Turning towards them, his puffy face damp with sweat, and using his sleeve to mop his bald pate with its damp, silvery wisps, the man grumbled: "Found something to amuse him, the little bugger!" He motioned towards the child in the pram.

"You see, he likes my chopping up logs . . . And only last year I had a stroke . . ."

Burying the hatchet in the log, he gave orders to his elder grandson to "keep an eye on little Oleg", and walked tiredly towards the house. Ryabov followed. Behind them, in the bushes, the child immediately started yelling.

"What have you come about?" Kozhin asked without turning round.

"I don't even know how best to explain it to you," Ryabov said.

They went inside. After removing two bowls full of berries from the table on the verandah to clear a space, Kozhin flopped panting on to a battered sofa, jerking one foot out at the toys scattered over the floor.

Ryabov sat himself down on a chair, opened his briefcase and extracted a bottle of vodka and some sausage wrapped in a piece of paper.

"I have come about my father," he said. "It will be a painful conversation. Let's have a drink. Do you have glasses."

"We'll find some," said Kozhin.

Without getting up from the settee, he stretched out a hand to a small cupboard, rummaged among its contents, and brought out two opaque tumblers.

"As a rule, I never drink during the day. The doctors say not . . . What can we use to soak it up with? Apple? It's been a bloody awful harvest this year – the aphids really hit them, no matter what I tried."

"I've brought some sausage," Ryabov said.

"You must have got it in town? We scarcely see anything made of sausage in our village. We mostly get by on what we grow ourselves . . . Where might you be from, yourself?"

"My surname is Ryabov," said Ryabov. "Does that say nothing to you?"

Kozhin thought for a moment.

"As a matter of fact, no . . . There was one lad at our Workers' High School – we studied together – with a name something like that . . . No, that wasn't it. His name was Mikhail Ryabchik, a red-haired skinny-looking chap – where he went after that, I've forgotten."

Ryabov poured two tumblers of vodka and knocked his back. He moved the other across to the edge of the table, towards the sofa. Kozhin drank half of his, cut himself a chunk of the sausage, topped it with a slice of apple, ate it, and downed the other half.

"To help with my memory," he said, "I use sea cabbage – something I read about in the papers. I must have chewed my way through almost a hundredweight of it . . ."

"Very well," said Ryabov. "May I now remind you? My father, Nikolay Semyonovich Ryabov, passed through your hands in connection with the Komintern Factory case."

"What year was that?" Kozhin asked.

"In '39. You handled the case. I read the records of the interrogation: I was shown the entire contents of the file after my father's posthumous rehabilitation. I didn't then try to trace you, in the immediate aftermath. I was in no state to do so. I didn't have the strength . . ."

"Well, well," sighed Kozhin.

Ryabov paused to see whether Kozhin had anything further to add. But the latter said nothing.

"I have come here from a desire to look into the eyes of the person who forced my father . . ."

"Grandfather!" came a yell from the garden. "Oleg has done something in his pants . . ."

The pram came rattling up to the verandah; the young boy had wheeled his brother towards them. Kozhin moved happily into action, stomped down from the porch, plucked the baby from its pram, placed it on the sofa and set about changing its nappy.

"Blasted parasite," he mumbled affectionately. "What a little rascal . . . How can I hope to have enough nappies to keep up with you . . ."

In his stooping posture, he had his back turned to Ryabov, and his large bottom stuck out aggressively. Kozhin bundled together his grandson's soiled garments and thrust them at the young boy.

"Go off and rinse them in the lake."

"Grandda, it'll frighten the crayfish away."

"No it won't. They like faeces."

Ryabov waited patiently. To him, time now seemed divided into two unequal segments: a protracted one, out of which he had come here; and this one – a fleeting, nonsensical one.

After putting a fresh nappy on the child and covering him, now asleep, with a quilted jacket, Kozhin, who was already perspiring from his ministrations, turned to his guest.

"As you see, I'm run off my feet from morning to night, from dawn to dusk . . . And d'you suppose my daughter sympathizes? Up she turns on her day off and even has a chuckle at my expense: 'After all, Papa dear, you've been awarded a personal pension for the special purpose of bringing up a successor . . .'"

Ryabov enquired: "Listen – unless I'm mistaken you actually were a senior police investigator in '39?"

"I served . . ." Kozhin replied. "I joined the 'organs' in 1932 by direct recruitment from the Komsomol."

"And therefore you are bound to remember all that happened to my father!"

"My dear chap . . ." Kozhin was about to continue and even gave Ryabov a friendly smile, as he sought to clarify the point.

But Ryabov persisted relentlessly: "From the records it is evident that for the first few days Father kept rejecting all the accusations you brought against him. And then all of a sudden put his signature to everything . . . You don't need to be afraid: I haven't come to settle accounts with you, or seek revenge. The thought of vengeance never crossed my mind . . . In fact, I'm not at all certain just why I needed to come and see you . . ."

Ryabov measured out the vodka into the glasses. His hand started to shake, but, after he drank, it stopped. Kozhin then swallowed his. He was growing tipsy but this escaped Ryabov's attention. At that moment alcohol had no effect on Ryabov except to underline his apartness, to make him feel isolated.

In this state of isolation, he found himself thinking aloud, oblivious to the sound of his own voice.

"At five years of age I was sent to a juvenile detention centre. Mother was banished and died there. I don't now have a single photo of them. If I were to meet my parents in the street, I would not recognize them. They crop up in my dreams, but maybe it is not them. It's strange, but I am now more of an orphan than I was in my childhood. It used to seem to me that grief grows less acute with the passage of time. In all probability, it does do so when the reason for it is clear and explicable: where the people concerned died from old age or illness or perished at the front. When the reason is non-explicable – when you can't come to terms with it – then the passing of the years causes havoc: I live in the past not the present. I now live a second time round, powerless to alter or correct any part of it. Even had I then known, in advance, that that was what had to happen, I would have been unable to prevent it happening, I would have been unable to save them. And no one was able to . . ."

By now Ryabov was no longer sitting in his chair but roaming aimlessly over the verandah.

He did not look at Kozhin. He was incapable of looking at Kozhin. Whatever Ryabov looked at, it failed to register: the berries and apples in their bowls, the multicoloured glass panes of the verandah, the children's toys scattered over the floor – it was all snapped by his eyes' shutters but immediately exposed to the light before it could be recorded in his mind.

He asked: "You interrogated my father. Why did he confess? What did you do to him?"

"I must have put questions to him. There was material evidence."

"There could not have been any material evidence. And there was none. Do you remember what he was accused of?"

"How can one hope to remember all the cases? Judge for yourself – how many years have gone by since then . . . And then maybe it was not I who conducted the interrogation."

"You conducted it. Your signature is on the records."

"If it's my signature, then it was me," Kozhin agreed.

From the vodka and the sun burning into his neck and his back he was feeling quite queasy. He had a lot on his plate today: he had to gather the windfalls, to hoe the currant bushes, to glue his old garden shoes again – they'd never really wear out – and little Oleg had not had a bath since Friday, the day Varya shoved off to town to rejoin her stud; he needed to get some lime into the greenhouse – the soil had turned quite sour – and he could, of course, simply kick this fellow out, but it seemed a pity, the chap was not to blame – he was only a kid when his father had been arrested, and it was no picnic to grow up without parents, and now people were stuffing his head with stories about violations of socialist legality and he, in his innocence, thinks there never were any enemies, that the people were just told a pack of fairy tales, and now they themselves don't know which way to turn; and the blackcurrants also needed picking, those damned thrushes are after them . . .

Looking down from his height Ryabov was unable to see Kozhin's increasingly soporific face. All he could make out from above was the other's bald cranium, mottled by the sun's rays, and his body's bulbous outline.

He addressed the shapeless lump.

"May I now remind you? You brought the charge against him of intending to blow up the railway bridge."

The word "bridge" served to unblock something in Kozhin's memory. He had had to deal with a dozen or so cases relating to this bridge. Various persons and various groups had wanted to blow it up. And they had, in fact, all come clean about it . . .

After that Kozhin's sequence of thought started to trail off. He had been desperately busy all morning, hadn't had a bite to eat, and the vodka had hit him on an empty stomach. Ryabov's voice came to him from a distance in waves, as if a long goods train were on the move – individual words rattling over the points. Occasionally the odd phrase emerged intact and then the whole thing continued its even rumble into the distance.

"I don't understand how you can live with it," said Ryabov. "How can you manage to live with it?"

"There he goes brandishing his rights," Kozhin just had time to think from out of the haze which was sweetly engulfing him.

Ryabov paused beside the table, poured what remained of the vodka into his glass and said: "I want nothing of you. Absolutely nothing. I merely want to understand how it's possible to bear such a burden. It sticks in my gut and, as for you, how you manage . . ."

Then he noticed Kozhin was sitting quite motionless, his head bowed down on his chest. In that first moment, Ryabov decided the old man had been taken ill. Bending over him, he peered at his face.

Kozhin was asleep.

Taking one pace back and, without looking, feeling for the glass on the table with his hand, Ryabov hurled its contents as hard as he could into Kozhin's face.

He covered the distance back to the station in no time at all. It was only after taking his seat in the train that he came to his senses.

It was noisy inside the compartment, a transistor radio was playing, and a game of dominoes was in progress next to him.

And all of them were people ignorant of why he had come to Zvonarevka.

As he himself remained quite ignorant.

Translated by Michael Duncan

VIKTOR EROFEEV

Sludge-gulper

SPRING IN THE Moscow countryside is incredibly beautiful. Everything stirs, rustles and flows. Autumn too is terribly beautiful. The woods are ablaze. And the silence! Your ears are filled with it! The only sounds are of builders hammering, buzzing saws scattering fragrant sawdust, and the warbling of autumn birds. Just beyond the forest is the Moscow river, as full and wayward here as a mountain stream. At midday in July it entices in scrawny men with white vest marks on their shoulders, nervous women with deep-set, socket eyes, and rowdy young pioneers and schoolchildren. Thanks to the river's tricks, some of these end up drowned, and their spiritless bodies are dragged as far as Zvenigorod, where they surface like submarines opposite the malodorous monastery, as a warning to sinners. The young Herzen once lived in those parts. A spider's web clung like a veil to the delicate face of the young bastard.

Here in Kubinka there is an aerodrome. The silver carcases of red-starred fighter planes soar up into the sky. The hammering stops, and the builders throw back their heads in their bright holiday caps. They're ours! They breathe heavily. It was planes like these that shot down that Korean passenger jet! Mushroom soup bubbles in a bucket. Their eyes become bloodshot. "Serve it sodding right!"

It will soon be lunchtime. The youngest has been sent off to the shop. He sets off along the forest path, his frog-like mouth grinning from ear to ear. He has large worker's hands. Suddenly he tenses, steps off the path, squats down under a little fir tree, grunts, rummages through some rotting leaves and pulls out a large firm white mushroom. He turns it around in his hands, croaks appreciatively, and slips it inside his jerkin.

During lunch it starts to rain. The builders sit in their dacha. Let it pour! They don't care so long as they've got a roof over their heads! They drink beer and soup, and eat. The most educated of them is Viktor. He spent a year at aviation school. After he left, he served in the German Democratic Republic, then Prague during the upheavals of 1968. Now he always wears his tank helmet in memory of his service in the armoured corps. The most skilled amongst them of course is

Evgeny Ivanovich, and he gives the orders, because although Pavel is the actual foreman, Pavel's talents lie elsewhere, and he usually spends the evenings at the local rest-home – although he's getting a bit lazy now and specializes in taking things easy, so he'll consider anything in a skirt aged forty, fifty or upwards. Sometimes a scented, painted beauty, with sweet tooth and thinning hair, will sail into the building site to pass the time, watch him bang in some nails, or invite friends over. But Evgeny Ivanovich doesn't like having the girls around; he's through with that sort of thing and prefers work, even though the dacha job keeps them on their toes and is designed in the most outlandish fashion, with a steeply pitched roof like a Swiss chalet, so that the rafters on one side touch the ground, while the window on the other looks up into the sky.

Viktor says it's great, he's seen houses like that in Germany – and the women there don't give you any trouble either, he tells Pavel. At which Evgeny Ivanovich angrily tells him to cut it out and concentrate on the house instead. But his eyes are glassy, and he's drinking more and more these days – old age is a curse, and the boss is an idiot. Why does he want a dacha in a style no one can understand? He ordered that staircase on the first floor to be done all over again, just because he didn't like the curve. Who does the bastard think he is? Evgeny Ivanovich feels like putting a match to the whole bloody thing. As he dozes bad-temperedly, the others finish off a second bottle and cheer on the rain, which means they don't have to work. Zhenya says he's not going out again in this weather, at which point the rain really lets loose, lashing the earth as though fighter planes were tearing the sky apart, and persuading the youthful Boris to join them on his motorbike. Boris is the most up to date of them. He dresses fashionably, his work is competent, though not especially modern, and he plays the accordion at a House of Culture in some village on the other side of Moscow. He recently got married, and somehow it shows. Viktor too has just had a few days off because of family problems, and you'd never guess that his father had just died: our boys hide their emotions deep within their souls!

The owner of the dacha comes every Sunday to check up on them. They prepare for this, but not too hard. On the first floor, in what is to be the master's study, Zhenya scrapes up a pile of his vomit which has been congealing on the floor for the last three days. Evgeny Ivanovich puts on his glasses and starts resetting the staircase, cursing and checking it against the boss's design, while Boris drives off on his motorbike into the rain for a third bottle. Then they all fall asleep on the floor in their clothes, Viktor still with his tank helmet on, and they get up in the night only to drink water and piss out of the window.

Next morning Pavel comes back, soaked to the skin and terrified. He gets them up. They all stumble downstairs, fall out of the front door and stare.

While they were asleep, torrents of muddy water have flooded the cellar of the house. They light cigarettes. It's clear that if the sandy foundations are washed away and the reinforced concrete piles sink, the whole pile of Swiss shit will topple to the ground. It's clear too that it's all their fault. When they dug out the cellar they completely forgot that it would get filled with rainwater. The new iron roof sparkles ominously. The house howls softly in the wind.

The owner of the house was still lounging in his bed on Gorky Street when he was roused by an early Sunday morning telephone call. He arrived half an hour later in his cherry-coloured Volga motorcar, and Pavel spun him a long tale about a dam bursting its banks. The boss's unhealthy face, exhausted after a long week in the office, was yellow and unpleasant.

"Well, don't just stand there!" he snapped. "Bale it out with buckets!"

"It'd take us three days with buckets," said Pavel. "What we need is a sludge-gulper."

"What may that be?" enquired the boss, frowning with distaste at this ugly, alien word. They explained to him what it was.

"And where might one find such a thing?" he asked.

"Old Kolya the night watchman will know," they told him.

"Well, find him then," he said curtly, and told Pavel to come with him.

But since the gang had just put the roof on, the boss was expected to treat them all to drinks, so they knocked up a table near the house and put benches around it. They discussed the Korean jet. "Do you think it had an atom bomb on board?" Zhenya asked.

"I've told you a hundred times that it couldn't have had a bomb on board!" shouted Viktor, who knew everything about planes, although Zhenya was still not convinced. The boss liked these lads. They loved their country, and they only drank so much because they were depressed by the shortages.

"I think I ought to warn you," murmured Viktor, bending his helmeted head towards the boss, "Pavel has been flogging off building materials on the side. That's why we're short."

It grew dark. They lit a bonfire, and Zhenya told them how he had once been arrested in Mytishchi. In the courtroom he had led them a merry dance, and stripped off to his underpants. The police rushed at him, and the trial had to be adjourned. Then Evgeny Ivanovich cockily asked the boss why he wanted a dacha in a foreign style, and the boss told him, but next morning Evgeny Ivanovich had completely forgotten what he said. Then Viktor whispered to the boss that it was all a load of rubbish about the dam, there was no dam. But next morning the boss took Pavel with him anyway.

Old Kolya had been drunk since breakfast. He welcomed his guests noisily, banged his fist on the table and broke into a song. Then he told them that in his youth he had been an engineer, but that immediately before the war he had been unjustly arrested. The boss suspected that old Kolya might be filching stuff from him. Maybe he and Pavel were in it together, but where was he going to find anyone else? Kolya told them that his leg had been broken in the camp, and now he walked like a pair of compasses which was why people had nicknamed him "Shufflefoot". In queues, old Shufflefoot always passed himself off as a war invalid.

"Sludge-gulper, sludge-gulper . . ." the invalid mused. Then he yelled triumphantly. "I've got it! Let's go!"

He explained that they would have to go to the village to find a certain stove repairer, who was a friend of his, a relative you might say. Old Shufflefoot settled himself in the front seat of the car, and Pavel sat in the back, his hands crossed on his knees. With his blue eyes, and fair, pleasantly thinning hair, he looked rather like a diligent student. If the hero of Gogol's *Dead Souls* had sinned with a servant girl, the fruit of their union would surely have been the spitting image of Pavel.

After they had driven for several kilometres through the autumn forest, a green fence flashed by.

"Here we have a special sanatorium," announced old Kolya, solemnly smacking his lips. "It's guarded by a special patrol."

The boss appeared not to hear.

"There's a fridge in every room, and Arabian cabinets filled with cut glass," Kolya went on, turning round to face Pavel. "Every morning the fridges are loaded up with bottles of vodka, brandy and even sherry."

A sour smile passed over the boss's stale face.

"You get caviar there three times a day, any kind you want, even the pressed stuff," Kolya continued.

"It's too salty if there's a lot of it," Pavel demurred.

"Not there it isn't," Kolya said sternly. "It's a special kind."

"That's not bad!" Pavel livened up. The boss still said nothing.

"The guards have machine guns." Old Kolya licked his lips. "And even a cannon! They make a real racket!"

"Come now," the boss said quietly.

"I've seen it with my own eyes!" exclaimed Kolya. "They're in the bushes by the entrance."

Just then a huge red combine harvester came straight at them from around the bend.

"Stop him! Stop him!" yelled Kolya.

The boss flashed his lights. The harvester stopped, Kolya dragged his leg out of the car, and circled around the harvester.

"See here, my friend," he said at last, approaching the young man at the wheel. "Tell me where we can find a sludge-gulper around here. Do you think the fire brigade would lend us one?"

"No, I don't," said the young man.

"You're right," agreed Kolya. "So where can we get one, Mikhail?"

"I don't know," said Mikhail. "Try Vovka."

"Which Vovka?"

"Vovka at Hero Worker Farm."

After being demobilized four years earlier, Komsomol member Vovka Sorokin had returned to his village and got down to some hard work on the farm, so that his livestock breeding was now the envy of the district.

"Where would we find him?"

"Where do you think?" asked Mikhail in amazement. "With his piglets, of course!"

"Goodbye then, Mikhail," Kolya said severely, shaking Mikhail's hand.

"Why don't you ever come and see us, Uncle Vasya?" said the man with the harvester.

"Too much work on," replied Kolya. "Besides, I'm not Uncle Vasya, I'm Uncle Kolya."

"Of course you are!" The boy smiled broadly, showing a row of fine, sugar-white teeth. "And I'm not Mikhail, I'm Alexander Bodunov!"

"Bodunov?" Old Kolya peered at him. "Well I'll be damned! So you are!"

After chatting for several more minutes about various other important matters, the two men went their separate ways.

"To Hero Worker Farm!" commanded Uncle Kolya. "I'll bet he's got a brand-new sludge-gulper, shining like a mirror!"

Hopeful but still grim faced, the boss stepped on the gas.

"Tell me more about that sanatorium, Uncle Kolya," Pavel begged earnestly.

"The sanatorium?" pondered Kolya. "Well all right," he finally agreed. "There's two specialists, a nurse and several auxiliaries for each patient. And the drugs are all American . . ."

"What are the nurses like?" Pavel interrupted.

"Absolutely gorgeous," Kolya assured him.

"Where do they live, then?" asked Pavel ingratiatingly.

"Stop that, lad!" Kolya interrupted him. "They live behind the fence. They're out of bounds!"

"Like nuns . . ." Pavel murmured to himself.

"Never mind about the nurses!" said Kolya impatiently. "What they have there is a special department."

"So what's that?" asked Pavel timidly.

"It's like this," the invalid explained in a leisurely tone. "They have special underground vaults, where corpses lie in glass bullet-proof coffins."

The boss cast an anxious glance at Kolya.

"It's true." Kolya returned his look. "You think the top brass are buried in the earth like everyone else when they die? Fat chance! They have plaster dummies of themselves buried, and their real bodies are frozen and put here. They're all there: all the marshals, including Comrade Zhukov, and our great strategist Zhdanov, and the Big Chief Himself, and Malenkov, Molotov and Suslov. And at the door of the main office the fiery fighter Klim Voroshilov lies like a frozen statue, ready for anything. When they're needed they'll all be defrosted," Shufflefoot concluded solemnly. "So they can lead the country again!"

"What, in case there's a war?" gulped Pavel, clapping his hand to his mouth.

"Anything may happen, my boy!" Kolya said tendentiously. "That's why they've got machine guns and a cannon there."

"Look here," the boss snapped. "Will you please stop talking this dangerous rubbish in my car!"

"What do you mean?" Kolya protested in an injured tone. "They're all there, with their uniforms and medals on . . . Even Beria! At his trial, he said: 'Don't shoot me, I'm a talented organizer, I can still be useful to you!' And Khrushchev thought and thought, and he finally granted his bloody enemy's request."

"But hold on!" said Pavel, flustered. "How can they fight a war, what with all the new technology now?"

"I suppose they give them lessons down there!"

"How can you give lessons to a corpse?" demanded the boss, white with rage.

"Search me!" shrugged Kolya, lighting an evil-smelling cigarette. "Look, why should I make up stories?" he said angrily. "When they unfreeze Stalin I'll be the first person he throws into prison!"

"Why?" asked Pavel stupidly.

"Because everyone he put in prison then will be put straight back there!"

"What if they're all rotten by now?" Pavel asked anxiously.

"No chance of that." Kolya shook his head. "Every coffin is attended by a military doctor of the rank of colonel. And sometimes one of them is quickly defrosted and turned over, so they won't get bedsores."

The bedsores were the final straw for the boss.

"Shut up!" he bellowed at Kolya. "I've had enough! There's nothing there! No machine guns, no coffins, do you understand? I stayed in that bloody sanatorium last summer, so I should know!"

Old Kolya gazed thoughtfully at the road ahead and dragged on his cigarette. The forest was a flaming yellow. He frowned. "So it isn't true then about the Arabian cabinets filled with cut glass in every room?"

Translated by Catherine Porter

EVGENY POPOV

The Situation

The Electronic Accordion

"IT'S GONNA BE really nice back home now! Katya will be stirring the borsch with her ladle. And the borsch will be as red as a banner. And what's the little darling going to prepare for the second course? If it's a bit of chicken . . . or mutton she's stewed . . . with fresh cabbage . . . a few potatoes in it, and tomatoes – that'll be great! But even if she's only fried up some eggs and salami, that'll be nice too. Jesus! How come a simple man like me can have such happiness? Little Vitya will grab me round the knees, shouting: 'Dad! Dad! Let's get the building bricks and make a moon buggy to go to the moon!' He's growing up, the clever little devil, but he won't get spoilt for all that he's got. When we were his age we didn't live like him at all, no way. Never enough grub . . . just a bit of bread and salt to eat . . . Jesus! How come I've got all this happiness? All this just for me, just for a simple man like me!"

Such, roughly speaking, were the thoughts of one Pyotr Matveevich Palchikov, an honest man, a good, middle-ranking specialist, thirty-seven years old and, as you see, a family man, as he wended his way home after a stressful day at work.

And his home, like those of dozens of other manual and blue-collar workers, was situated deep in the foothills of the Sayansky mountains, on the right bank of the river E, a fair way from the centre of town and, as it turned out, from Pyotr Matveevich's place of work, whence he now betook himself by tram and bus.

The only inconvenience was the means of transport. Apart from this, in accordance with all the demands of present-day town planning and construction, there was to be found in their district absolutely everything that the modern man required to lead a full-blooded and interesting life, replete in every respect.

Judge for yourself: in addition to the bathtubs in the houses, a large, splendid public baths was always steaming in the winter frost, complete with laundry and a dry-cleaning collection point; and don't even mention the knitware, baker's, grocer's and fishmonger's shops – there they were, right under your nose. And not far away was the smart collective farm market with its reasonable prices, and for get-togethers and entertainment there was the club run by the rubber technical products factory, and there was even a pub in the district, while at the service of those who were keen on such things there was a real music school. Yes, you could live a thousand years in a district like this and never want to die!

Well, naturally enough, Pyotr Matveevich did not go to the pub. It was dirty and smokey in there, and people were shouting. Drunks would pester you for twenty kopecks. And anyway, Pyotr Matveevich was not a great one for beer, though he had heard more than enough about its magical properties. They said it did this, and it did that . . . Bucked you up, got you going. Yet beer always made him want to doze off, when, in fact, Pyotr Matveevich always wanted to live, not sleep. So he'd picked up a quarter-litre of vodka in the shop. He walked through the darkening streets, the ice crunching underfoot, and yellow lights were already lit in the houses, and the blue mountains were already darkening and merging with the sky above.

He was taking his usual path, but it had been badly churned up by people's feet, and the mud, despite the ice, was still slippery in places. Pyotr Matveevich stepped in it once, then a second time, then he swore and decided to encroach on the territory of the music school. An asphalt path ran right from the palings there to the palings on the other side. All he had to do was hop over the fence, and then he'd be home – there was his house within spitting distance.

Pyotr Matveevich himself did not in general encourage such trespassing on the school's territory. He enjoined his son Vitya in this respect and warned off Vitya's pals. "It's not nice, chaps," he urged them. "After all, you're grown-ups now, aren't you? The caretaker has put a lot of work in there. Go and play somewhere else, learn to respect other people's work, lads . . ."

He did not encourage it. But at the moment he was most anxious not to get his new brown half-length boots all covered in mud. "Over the boards and over the bricks," whispered Pyotr Matveevich. "You'll get home somehow," he hummed.

And though he was utterly absorbed in his cares about preserving his personal cleanliness, as well as in thoughts concerning his imminent family happiness, he suddenly saw that the school windows were illuminated in a way that was rather unnatural for that time of the evening: every single one of them was lit up, and brightly too. Usually at that time, well, there might be a light on here, or a couple there, where someone was scraping away on a fiddle, or thumping the piano, or opening their mouth wide, though you couldn't hear through the glass what sort of a song was pouring out of it.

In his curiosity Pyotr Matveevich pulled on his spectacles and discovered by the door the following handwritten text on a piece of white paper:

The electronic accordion
played by Kudzhepov
Works of the classics and by Soviet composers
tickets on sale

"Tickets on sale!" said Pyotr Matveevich slowly. And he spat angrily. "What a God-awful thing to think up – an electronic accordion! They've gone completely nuts!"

He condemned it, but he did not budge from the spot.

Because he had seen a lot of accordions in his life, and he had known an extraordinary number of concertinas, but an electronic accordion, now that was something that he just could not picture, no matter how he tried. And his swearing only inflamed his curiosity, so he decided to go in, so that, should the need for it arise, he would have an opinion on this subject too. As they say, it's better to see something once than to hear about it a hundred times. And in addition to that, he could describe this interesting phenomenon to his family afterwards, and discourse to his workmates on the practical use of it or its harmful effects. So Pyotr Matveevich decided to go in anyway, and sparing no expense, he made ready with a rouble note.

However, on entering the foyer, in the first place he saw that there were no tickets on sale at all, indeed no box office at all. And in the second place he heard the sounds of organized human speech emanating from behind a white door.

Pyotr Matveevich put his cap in his pocket, cautiously opened the door a crack, and then found himself in the back row of a small auditorium.

People looked at him absent-mindedly. No one asked to see his ticket, they just whispered: "Quiet" when he scraped his chair. Everyone was listening to the man standing on the stage.

"Thus, dear friends, the electronic accordion is a very interesting innovation in music. And we all hope that soon our industry will start mass production of these remarkable instruments, which at present we are purchasing from abroad, and unfortunately, comrades, only for

hard currency." The speaker shook his mane. "So, comrades, the day
is not so far off when a huge number of our listeners, our lovers of
music, will delight in the deep sounds of this instrument, which, as I
have already said, is, in its richness of tone, close to the organ and the
clavichord, yet combines all this with compactness and requires no
special performance skills."

This was, apparently, Kudzhepov himself. From a distance Pyotr
Matveevich could not make out his face in detail. However, he could
see that he was evidently a man not in the first flush of youth, had a
receding hairline, his mane notwithstanding, and was wearing a black
suit, rather dapper in appearance – well, that's how people like that
are supposed to look.

And the accordion didn't look anything special. You couldn't see
anything electronic about it either. Were there really wires running
off into the wings? It was just an accordion like any other.

"Common trickster," grunted Pyotr Matveevich. "What a God-
awful thing to think up!"

But while he was grumbling he missed what was being said. Because
Kudzhepov said something else and then deftly extended the accordion's bellows.

Suddenly it got him! Took hold of him, sent him spinning, carried
him away; his heart was in his mouth, he was caught, shivers ran down
his spine, it warmed him up – sweet weariness, giddiness. The tune,
and the sweet pain, and youth and old age, all together!

"What's this?" whispered Pyotr Matveevich. "Wha-at is this?"

"Something you need to know, young man," said his neighbour
with dignity, a shrivelled old woman, wearing glasses tied up with
thread.

"I'm not talking about that, what's happening to me?" whispered
Pyotr Matveevich.

"Stop bothering me while I'm listening!" said the old woman,
losing her temper.

"I didn't mean anything," said Pyotr Matveevich in confusion.

And suddenly the tears started to stream silently down his cheeks,
and he was ashamed of them, but still wept, in utter silence, while
continuing to look straight in front. The little auditorium, the black-
clad musician and his magical musical instrument all swam before his
eyes. And the music swam and swam too.

Pyotr Matveevich felt for his handkerchief and suddenly found the
quarter-bottle of vodka. Such a sudden anger seized him that, to the
profound amazement of his neighbour, he leapt up from his seat,

stamped his feet, waved his hand absurdly, shouted out something, and shot out on to the street like a bullet.

There was the same night outside, a streetlamp creaking in the wind, a steady light burning in the windows of the houses, everything around exuding night, quiet and tranquillity.

In his agitated state Pyotr Matveevich was on the point of smashing his bottle on the asphalt, but then he changed his mind, his face grew darker, he pulled his cap determinedly over his eyes, and set off home, without picking and choosing his route.

"Jesus! Look at the state you're in, just like a pig! Your trousers all covered in mud," gasped his wife. "Where the hell have you been?"

Pyotr Matveevich took off his things without a word, but seething with rage.

"Have you been drinking with someone, or something?" said his wife, examining him.

At which point Pyotr Matveevich cracked.

"'Drinking'! 'Drinking'!" he yelled. "I'll give you 'drink'! All you can think of is drinking and stuffing yourself! You haven't got a thought in your head! You live like a carp under the ice! Are you going to drag me into the grave with you? Don't you know how other people live? What is there on the television for you today? Stierlitz? Or who?"

"It's 'The Thibaut Family'. France," said his wife, her voice trailing away. "We can eat now and watch it all afterwards."

"You fool!" shouted Pyotr Matveevich, filled his lungs with air and then repeated: "You fool! You fool!"

His wife gasped, while Vitya abandoned his moon buggy construction kit and retreated into a corner, sobbing: "Daddy! Daddy! What are you doing? Why are you telling mummy off?"

"Clear off!" said father, stamping his foot at him.

By now the son was crying fit to burst. Then Pyotr Matveevich more or less came to his senses, more or less returned to his old self. He looked slowly around. The house was still a house. The flat still a flat. The furniture still furniture. The people were still people.

"Well, actually . . . I . . . it was . . ." He rubbed his temple with his finger. "Katya, don't be angry with me. You get all wound up at that bloody job of mine, pulled every which way . . . We had it again today: they've allocated us funds for sheet aluminium, and when I get over to the stores, they tell me there isn't any. Real struggle to get it . . . they've been on at me all day, and you get yourself all worked up. And then I was going along past the music school – do you know what a God-awful thing they've thought up? A real circus turn this one – an electronic accordion, can you imagine that?!"

"Oh, you gave me such a fright, such a fright, you really are a performer yourself," said his wife, laughing with relief. "I thought to myself: 'He's drunk or something. Or he's gone round the twist, just like that Misha who worked as an assistant in our factory . . .'"

Pyotr Matveevich laughed as well. They both laughed and slapped each other on their fleshy backs.

And only their little son Vitya looked on like a wolf cub. The tears on his cheeks had dried, but his lips were pressed tightly together.

The Reservoir

And yet to start with Bublik seemed to us to be a respectable man. He outbid others and paid a good price for a small two-storeyed house and some tilled land which he bought from the grass widow of Vasil-Vasilek, who was in prison for embezzling the nation's wealth, selling on the side iron roofing, Metlakh tiles and central heating radiators. Whenever he offered us something "out of neighbourliness" though, we just listened politely to him but did not get involved, preferring to take the path of honesty. Because we were all original inhabitants of Siberia. As if I couldn't get hold of some rubbish from Metlakh in my home town off my own bat! That would be a joke, and anyway it would, to a certain extent, run counter to the policy of improving our life and the principles of mastering the outlying regions of our huge homeland. We're not some kind of kulaks, but these days everyone lives like this, and a sight better than those halfwit kulaks of former days, who overdid things when the time wasn't right and pushed themselves up front without taking anybody else with them. For which they were most severely, but justly, punished.

But – Jesus! Jesus! God Almighty! What for? There was just so much work to do! On Saturdays the gas cylinders had to be delivered. Kozorezov was a smart operator here. He took care of things, thanks very much, detailed a lorry, and a man . . . And if you wanted raspberries, there they were by the bushful, and if you wanted straw-berries, there were beds of them . . . Fine beautiful sight like that went straight to the head, softened the eye and soothed the soul . . . Fine beautiful sight like that went straight to the head . . .

And the main thing was the reservoir. Jesus! The reservoir! This reservoir was constantly being replenished with crystal-clear underground waters, and it was a sheer delight for us on those muggy summer nights. A jolly flock of wayward lads frolicked in its loving waters. And their girlfriends and fiancées like Youth itself, the little kittens, lay on the crisp quartz sand. Preparing for exams or merely succumbing to the usual maidenly dreaming – their future working life, the family, marriage, bringing up the children, the proper relationship between the sexes.

And all around were we, the parents. The women knitting something out of mohair, or talking about who was on holiday and where in the south, or who had bought something – some new acquisition for the family. Colonel Zhestakanov and Professor Burvich playing draughts in the rose willow bushes. Mitya the termite arguing with Lysukhin the physicist about the correlation between the number of degrees of Czech beer and its alcohol content. Someone solving a crossword, another questions of production. And me . . . I look back at it all, and on my word of honour, my heart is overjoyed and bursting. The hungry years of the war come to mind when I was recruited for defence duties, and afterwards – standing, No. 261, in a queue for flour, with my wife, on a stormy black morning in an archway by the "Red Front" cinema. My foot turned hard as bast, I just couldn't feel it inside my thin felt boot: we massaged it afterwards, smeared it with goose fat. As I remember all this, so, on my word of honour, I would personally strangle with my own hands all those chatter-boxes and whingers, stuffing themselves on kebabs and guzzling pepsi-cola! I'd have all those skunks standing in my place in that queue in 1947! Then I'd see what sort of tune they'd be singing, the snotty noses!

And as for that pair of young people, the ones that looked like actors, well to start with we even liked them as well, I won't conceal our gullibility, I won't try and justify us . . .

Bublik the director brought them, together with his pretty-looking singer wife. The only good thing about this nasty piece of work was that as a director, when he came, he made our day by arranging for various celebrities to visit Stuffen Nonsense (that was the name of our housing estate). One minute you'd look and see the singer M. walking by with a towel over his arm and roaring: "Glory be, glory be" and the next it would be the conjuror T. delighting everyone by making Zhestakanov's pocket watch disappear and turn up in Mitya the termite's shoe, or else there would be our famous portrait artist Spozhnikov sitting up on high and drawing a picture of the reservoir against a background of its surroundings. It was strange that these clever people were unable to detect Bublik's rotten inside before we did, really strange!

Yet at first sight this pair were the most straightforward of long-haired lads. But then again, it's not for nothing that common folk say a certain kind of straightforwardness is worse than theft, even though modesty makes man beautiful. One of them was on the tall side, a sporty type with blue eyes. The other one was more puny, a bit swarthy, and more lively. Our girls, our fiancées, almost turned somersaults when they saw all the skill those young men displayed at table tennis. And they weren't the type of lads to pass some tasteless remark or make a tasteless gesture to them, challenging them to a game. No! Look, they just carried on hitting the little white ball, modestly and with dignity, the rats. Until it happened.

And when it did happen, then everyone immediately started shouting that we had realized right from the word go. But precisely what we had realized we had no idea, until there ensued a good old-fashioned bust-up of the worst sort, the consequences of which are indelible, irreversible, sorrowful and shaming. Now the windows and doors of the dachas are being boarded up, small-time purchasers are swarming all over the place, autumn leaves are rustling, fruit trees are being dug up and removed, and there's no cheer on anyone's face, nothing but weary gloominess, disappointment and fear.

Though if you had a bit of nous, you could have guessed right away. After all, they *went around arm in arm*, not to mention the fact that they patently, patently showed no interest in our girls.

And the latter, the delinquents, were happy to snigger. They gave the little one plaits, just like an Uzbek girl. They made him up with brightly coloured lipstick, and then – oh, that seventeen-year-old Nastya Zhestakanov! – then, using a bit of force, they went and put on his chest, which was rather plump and out of proportion to the rest of his build, a loose-fitting bra they had to spare.

What a laugh that was! And at the time we all thought, mistakenly, that it was fun, and we were laughing away, reckoning the somewhat tasteless prank to be a relatively successful joke. We were just having fun and laughing away, until it happened.

Jesus! I'll never forget it as long as I live. So, the distribution of forces was as follows. There was the reservoir. The pair of them were on a raft near the bank, the girls were nearby, we were sitting in the bushes, but the director Bublik with his pretty-looking singer wife was actually nowhere around.

No sooner had the girls fastened their innocent female adornment on to the younger one's chest, than the elder one jumped up, turned pale, his blue eyes darkened, and he gave Nastya a sharp boxer's jab straight in the solar plexus, which caused the child to fall silently on to the sand, without even a yelp.

We all froze, our mouths wide open. Without a second's delay, he shoved off sharply from the bank, and in the twinkling of an eye the couple were out in the middle of the reservoir, where they set about indulging in some foul, filthy language. The tall one ranted and raged, while the small one only snivelled in answer, but also used swearwords. He even stuck his tongue out at the tall one, at which the latter twitched strangely and howled: "Oh, you tart!" and gave the little one a slap. The latter then fell on his knees and started to kiss his comrade's bare dirty feet, which were half covered by the lapping waves.

Jesus! Jesus! God Almighty! The latter kicked him as hard as he could, and the first young man gave a piercing scream and found himself in the water. However, this upset the equilibrium of the raft, which lurched and threw the second young man in the water too. Without even gurgling, they began to vanish into the deep. Then they came to the surface again, apparently not knowing how to swim, after which, once again without even gurgling, they went right to the bottom.

And a terrible silence descended.

We all stood there thunderstruck. Like a pack of frightened animals our girls all crowded round Nastya, who was now recovering, women and cleaning women woke up, babes in arms started crying and dogs started barking.

Colonel Zhestakanov was the first to come to his senses. With a cry of "I'll rescue those poofters so they'll answer to a court of law!" the excellent swimmer, who had won various championships more than once in his youth, threw himself into the water and disappeared for a long time. When he came up, he lay on his back resting for a long time, and then, wasting no words, dived down again.

However, neither this second, nor the subsequent dives by Colonel Zhestakanov beneath the surface of the reservoir, produced any positive results. The colonel mumbled: "How could it happen?" but the fact was they had disappeared.

We hit on the idea of rushing off to see Bublik, the party responsible, so to speak, for the "festivities". But he had vanished together with his pretty-looking singer wife. A pine-scented wind wandered around their empty dacha, ruffling the lace curtains, an upturned cup of coffee lay on the carpet, its contents spilt over a copy of a glossy magazine, clearly not one published in our country, bright orange, orphaned flowers wilted in beautiful ceramic vases, but Bublik and his pretty-looking singer wife were nowhere to be seen.

When we sent a delegation of our people to him to the musical comedy theatre a few days later, the management told us, looking at the floor, that Bublik had resigned from there completely, and cleared off; his whereabouts were unknown. And it was only later that we understood the reason for the embarrassed demeanour of these honest people, when it was finally ascertained that the whereabouts of the director Bublik were the United States of America, whither he had brazenly emigrated together with his pretty-looking singer wife practically in full view of everyone. Which fact isn't after all so surprising, since in the USA it would apparently be easier for them to pursue that debauchery which in our country has such a strict embargo placed on it. It's not surprising.

But there was something else that was surprising. It was surprising that when the police and the frogmen arrived at the reservoir they could not find anyone at all either. We pleaded with the frogmen, and they tried very hard to cover every centimetre of the bottom, but all in vain. The couple had disappeared.

You know, we talked about it afterwards: damn it, if we had had enough money – they'd had to go to some real expense anyway – we ought to have drained the lake to figure out what had happened and get to the bottom of things, so that the business would not smack of devilry and religious superstition, and leave us with this sense of weary despondency, disappointment and fear. But the opportunity was missed, and now we are paying severely for our misguided credulity and giddy carelessness.

Because literally the day after everything allegedly settled down again, the housing estate was ringing with the terrible howls of a man being murdered, a man who turned out to be that lover of night-time bathing, Comrade Zhestakanov. The poor man was close to suffocation, his eyes popping out of his head, and all he could do was point to a trace of moonlight on the water and keep repeating: "It's them! It's them! There! There!"

Fortified with a glass of vodka, he came to his senses, but kept insisting that at twelve o'clock, all by itself, the raft had floated out to the middle of the water and suddenly two sorrowful skeletons embracing each other had appeared on it, softly singing a song: "Don't be sad, you have all your life ahead of you." So there you are!

Although Zhestakanov was soon being treated by the psychiatrist

Tsarkov-Kolomensky, this was no help to anyone. Prof. Burvich, Comrade Kozorezov, Mitya the termite and his mother-in-law, Eprev the metal worker and his colleague Shenopin, Angelina Stepanovna, Eduard Ivanovich, Yury Alexandrovich, Emma Nikolaevna, Fetisov, myself, and even the physicist Lysukhin, who, as a man of science was so shaken by the spectacle that he took to drink dangerously, we all saw and heard skeletons.

We tried to scare them away, shouted at them, and fired double-barrelled shotguns at them – but nothing worked. True, the skeletons were not always visible, but the raft really did float around by itself, and howls, singing, laments, hoarsely whispered vows, smacking kisses and entreaties rang out at night *constantly*!

I'm no Zhestakanov, I wasn't even at the front, nor am I a physicist like Lysukhin, I haven't got a higher education, I'm just an ordinary man, I don't even drink an inordinate amount of vodka, and *I personally swear to you that I heard all this with my own ears!* "My darling! My darling!" – and then a rattling noise enough to make your hair stand on end.

When we had tried everything – guns, stones, and even insecticide – then the end came: the end for us, the end for the estate, the end for the reservoir. So the windows and doors of the dachas are being boarded up, small-time purchasers are swarming all over the place, autumn leaves are rustling, the fruit trees are being dug up and removed, and there's no cheer on anyone's face, nothing but weary gloominess, disappointment and fear.

Well, what would you expect of us? We're not mystics or priests, but we're not fools either, to go on living in a place putrescent with debauchery, with skeletal lust gleaming in the moonlight beckoning, drawing, frightening and leading people straight into psychiatric hospitals, depriving women of their courage, men of their reason, and children of a happy childhood and a clear vision of life's and labour's prospects for the good of our huge homeland.

Jesus! Jesus! God Almighty . . .

The Drummer and his Wife

Once upon a time there lived in the wide world a quiet woman who was disabled, and there also lived in the wide world together with her a lively drummer in a funeral orchestra.

At one time this woman had lived with her husband in the city of

Karaganda in the Kazakh SSR and once she was travelling on a long-distance bus to work. Suddenly the engine in the bus conked out on a level crossing, and a train was too close.

The train hit the bus and produced a real mess and a lot of scrap iron. And the drummer's wife went flying out of the bus.

During the flight an iron-capped boot smashed her head open, and the bones stuck out, after which she started forever mumbling something, mumbling and mumbling, and also reading the same book over and over again. To be precise, it was Rasul Gamzatov's *The Mountain Woman*, in which he describes the new relationships between people in the Republic of Daghestan and their struggle for women's equality.

She had brought this book in the hospital kiosk immediately after she had sustained her injuries. And she had never parted with it since.

After her accident a good many people turned their backs on the woman, and the first to do so was her own husband.

But the drummer played the drum all his life. He beat the drum in the war at the front, and after the war too he beat the drum. He drank heavily. He drank and drank and drank, until he started playing in a funeral orchestra, making music as they followed the coffins.

And then a good many people turned their backs on him too.

And then he and the woman met, and they started to live together in Zasukhina Street in temporarily built quarters.

Their home was draughty in winter, but the stove burnt brightly. And in the summer the bird cherry trees blossomed in their little garden, and they could get by all right. True, the drummer still drank and drank, and the woman still mumbled.

And the woman was beautiful – black haired and slender.

And the drummer, apart from playing the drum, studied issues involving the durability of the things around him. He grieved deeply over the fact that there were no durable things on earth. And that if there was a more or less durable object, then there was most certainly a more durable object which could destroy it.

"You know, if it wasn't like that, then your head wouldn't have been smashed by a metal-capped boot," he used to tell his wife.

And she would agree with him.

Always mindful of his unsuccessful search for the meaning of durability, the drummer drank more and more. Then one day, in utter despair, he turned on the holiest of holies: he climbed on to his drum and started to jump up and down on it. Testing it.

The woman was sitting on the bed.

She was sitting quietly on the bed and reading her favourite book. The wall clock was ticking quietly. The wooden walls of the temporary building were nicely whitewashed. There was a washbasin and a rubbish bin in the corner. There was a mat on the floor.

And the drummer kept jumping up and down, though he was small and plumpish. He kept jumping and jumping and eventually burst the drum, his bread and butter, his drink.

Then he got really upset, and began behaving badly. He started accusing his woman of ruining his life.

"If it wasn't for you, you fool, I'd be playing in the Bolshoi Theatre now. I could give you a good hiding."

The quiet woman was very frightened. Because they had lived together for a long time and he had never spoken to her like that before. She took her book and ran out into the street.

But it was night-time, and the streetlamps weren't very bright so you would run off only if you were in really desperate straits.

The drummer understood this, and he started to feel very ashamed. Then he went over to the standpipe. He was hairy. He stripped off, doused himself in cold water, went back home and cut open the duvet.

He rolled around in the feathers, and then set off to look for his woman.

He found her by the mound of earth that ran along the walls of the house. She was trembling with fear and peering in all directions into the darkness.

"Well, what are you afraid of, you fool!" said the befeathered drummer. "Don't be afraid."

The drummer's woman said nothing.

"Don't be afraid, love," said the drummer, who was a lively individual. "I haven't smeared myself with tar, or with honey. I poured water over myself, and you'll have no trouble washing me down. Do you want to?"

"Yes," answered the woman. She climbed out from under the mound, and started mumbling: "Yes, yes, yes."

And they went back into the house. The drummer put his arms round his wife. She heated up some water in a large clothes boiler. She poured the water into a butt and started to wash him.

And he sat in the butt and blew soap bubbles, to stop his wife from crying, and to make her laugh.

Translated by Robert Porter

Broadbrow

ONE WARM SUMMER day a buffalo known as Broadbrow lay in the cool of a pond with several other buffaloes, male and female. A crow perched on his head, looked around from time to time and pecked at his head with its strong beak.

A couple of terrapins crept, one after the other, cautiously on to his back, to the high point sticking out of the water, shook themselves off and then settled down to bask in the sun.

Broadbrow liked having the crow peck out the ticks from his coat. He even enjoyed having the terrapins scratching his back and clambering over him to warm themselves in the sun. He understood why the terrapins preferred to do their sunbathing lying on his back rather than at the side of the pond. On the dry ground anything could happen, whereas on the mighty back of a buffalo, of course, nobody would dare to touch them. And Broadbrow liked it that way.

But he liked both the crow pecking ticks off him and the terrapins lying on his back mainly because they signified peace, tranquillity and rest. And with the whole of his powerful body sunk in the cool waters of the pond he was enjoying that peace and tranquillity, the blue sky high above and the hot sun whose very warmth enabled him to appreciate the pleasure of lying in the cool water.

Broadbrow was chewing the cud and, as always when he was in a good mood, was amusing himself by thinking about the tractor. The tractor had made its appearance in upper Chegem a couple of years previously, and since then Broadbrow and the other buffaloes had ceased to be used for ploughing, although they were still used for hauling logs from the forest and occasionally for drawing bullock carts.

Broadbrow had seen a motorcar many times and he knew that it was not a living creature. But it seemed to him that the tractor, ugly though it was, was alive because it was used for ploughing. Broadbrow was quite sure that only living creatures were used for ploughing. Buffaloes, oxen and horses were all used to pull a plough. And this strange being was also used for ploughing, which meant that it was alive. Only living things pulled a plough. He had observed this all his life, had learnt about it from his parents, and was sure that that was the way it was and would be for centuries to come.

What was so strange about the tractor was mainly the fact that it was not able, or did not want, to do anything on its own. Alone, so long as no one touched it, it slept the whole time, and it would wake up only when someone mounted it. If no one got up on to it it simply slept. Broadbrow once noticed that the tractor slept for twenty days alongside the farm. It just slept and slept.

Broadbrow admitted that it was very powerful, because he had often seen the sort of logs it hauled out of the forest. He usually called it the Sleepy Giant. But when he got cross with it he called it the Stupid Giant.

It was certainly very powerful, but strength wasn't always everything. Broadbrow had himself seen the Sleepy Giant disgrace himself on more than one occasion. Broadbrow saw it happen for the first time when, along with another buffalo, he was driven up a steep slope where the Sleepy Giant was grunting and groaning at the top of his voice but was quite incapable of moving a huge log that had got stuck on the slope. The Sleepy Giant had made such an effort that smoke came out behind him, but still he couldn't shift the log.

The foreman had signalled to the man sitting on the Giant, and he jumped down at once and the Giant fell silent, exhausted. They untied him from the log and harnessed the buffaloes in his place.

Then they tried to shift the log – how they tried! It was a very heavy log and, as usual on steep slopes, Broadbrow and the other buffaloes tensed their powerful muscles, going down on their front legs to increase the leverage, and finally got the log moving and dragged it to the top of the slope. Then they brought up the Sleepy Giant and harnessed him again to the log. It was then that the people of Chegem realized what buffaloes could do and that they couldn't manage without them.

Later there was another quite amusing incident. This time it was the Sleepy Giant himself, without any log being involved, who got bogged down in a stream and had to be dragged out of it by a buffalo. They were amused by and at the same time sorry for the Stupid Giant.

A few crows, perched on the buffaloes' heads, rose lazily into the air and, with a tired movement of their wings, flew off to settle on a half-bare alder that had dried out on the river bank.

Bardusha the stockman came across to the pond and started driving the buffaloes out of the water. Slowly they rose up from their familiar places and the terrapins slid off their backs and flopped into the water.

The buffaloes came up on to the river bank, flicking themselves with their tails, their dark wet bodies shining in the sun.

For some reason Bardusha separated Broadbrow from the others and drove him in the direction of the collective farm office. There was a truck standing there with some of the locals hanging around smoking. There were about half-a-dozen of them and Broadbrow was vaguely aware that they were local people.

Only one of them did he know really well. He was the man in charge of the cattle yard. Way back, a long time ago, Broadbrow had been in love with a she-buffalo, and the man in charge of her had subjected him to a frightful humiliation that Broadbrow remembered for four years until the time came for him to forgive the man's mean behaviour. But it had all been so long ago, and the man in charge of his beloved girl friend had only recently been put in charge of the farm animals.

The back of the truck was open and some planks had been laid up to it. Bardusha drove Broadbrow towards it and then tried to make him go up the planks into the truck. Broadbrow didn't like this very much, but he was accustomed to obeying humans because they were an intelligent force – that was the way the world was arranged, and so he obeyed. He was especially ready to do so since he had known Bardusha for a long time and was very fond of him.

Very carefully, because he was afraid the planks might break under his weight, Broadbrow walked up them and plumped himself down in the truck. He realized that the truck would soon move off somewhere. He thought they were going to take him to some village where there were no Sleepy Giants, and he resigned himself to his fate. But why were they taking only him? Probably because he was the strongest.

The stockman came up into the truck behind Broadbrow, took some rope and tied his legs together. First his forelegs and then his back legs.

"Why did you decide to hand over Broadbrow?" asked one of the men from Chegem.

"We get rid of one bull," the cattleman explained rather too eagerly – "He'll give a ton . . . And that way we'll fulfill the meat delivery plan for the year."

"Actually, the buffaloes' days are over," one of the men from Chegem said. "They eat too much and they're very stubborn."

"Does he eat off your table, then?" Someone else joined in the conversation. "It's because they eat a lot that they have such strength. You can cut buffalo yogurt with a knife."

Tongues gradually became loosened and various ideas about buffaloes were canvassed,

"It's interesting that the buffalo has the thickest skin but at the same time it tolerates the heat and the cold worse than any other animal."

"On the other hand it can swim in the sea like a boat. it can swim from Kengursk to Batum. In the water it blows itself up and consequently can never sink."

"All the same it eats too much . . . It's no good."

"What are you talking about – 'eats'! Do you always watch your guests so carefully when they're at your table?"

"What have guests got to do with it?"

"There aren't any more buffaloes with the sort of fighting spirit that Broadbrow has. Bardusha here will tell you I'm not lying. Five years back, in the spring, there was still snow on the ground, the buffaloes were grazing on the Top Meadow when a pack of starving wolves set on them. The buffaloes formed a defensive circle and kept the young buffaloes in the centre. We could hear the she-buffaloes howling and Bardusha and I grabbed our guns and lanterns and went to see what was going on. There were no fewer than ten wolves. Once they saw us they ran away. Broadbrow killed three of them himself . . ."

"How did you know that he killed them?"

"Bardusha here will confirm what I say. He was the only one with blood on his horns. I swear to you on my children he hurled one wolf twenty paces. I paced the distance out myself."

"You'll not find a prouder animal in the whole world. I once had a very fine she-buffalo. On one occasion I beat her up – gave her a real beating! She deserved it. And to the end of her days she never forgave me. If my wife sat down to milk her all was well. But if I went to milk her she wouldn't give a drop. If my mother milked her it was OK. But if I tried she would hold on to her milk. It went on like that for eight years until I slaughtered her."

"Like the mullah, the buffalo likes justice."

"Did you ever get much justice from a mullah?"

"Never mind me . . . That's what the people say."

Bardusha got down from the truck and took the planks away. The driver shut the back firmly. Then the men climbed into the front and the driver started up the engine. The truck moved off.

For the first time in his life Broadbrow wasn't hauling a load but was himself being hauled by an outside force. He suddenly felt terribly uncomfortable. He was even frightened. It was a law of life he had learnt in childhood that what you stood on had to be quite firm. And suddenly it was not his legs that were moving about but what he was standing on.

The truck had hardly driven out of the village Soviet's yard when Broadbrow tensed his muscles and the ropes snapped first from his forelegs and a second later from his rear legs and he leapt off the truck. He hit the ground with a force that shook his whole mighty frame, but he felt no pain and was on his feet at once.

People standing near the office all shouted out in chorus. The truck eventually came to a halt. The driver and Bardusha had not even noticed that Broadbrow had jumped out. Bardusha got down from the truck and drove the buffalo back towards the office. The truck reversed after him.

"The poor thing senses where he's being taken," said someone.

But Broadbrow had sensed nothing; he had simply taken fright at the unexpected experience of feeling what he stood on move about.

They dropped the back of the truck again, fixed the planks, and Bardusha urged the buffalo on to the truck again. Broadbrow didn't like going up the shaky planks, but there was nothing he could do, because he was accustomed to obeying humans as intelligent beings, and so he was in the truck again.

This time they decided that, to be quite sure, they would lay the buffalo down and tie his legs so that he couldn't jump out. The farmworkers clambered into the truck and, with a great deal of shouting and arguing, tried to pull his legs from under him. For a long time he didn't grasp what they wanted from him, but when he did he lay down himself, though the men believed that it was their doing.

The stockman Bardusha again tied his legs together, but Broadbrow no longer had any intention of jumping out of the truck. He realized that they wouldn't leave him alone until they had taken him where they wanted him. He was still convinced that he was being taken to another village where they had no Sleepy Giants.

This time the driver of the truck drove more carefully, but in any case Broadbrow had now decided to accept his fate. As the truck drove down the country road he tried to get accustomed to his new situation in which he didn't haul a load but was himself hauled. He even tried chewing the cud, but the shaking about destroyed any pleasure in that. He couldn't adjust the movement of his jaw to the uneven jolting of the truck, so he swallowed what he had and lost himself in his thoughts.

When the truck came out on to the main road his nostrils caught the sharp, strong smell of the asphalt, and along with the smell came agreeable memories of his childhood.

He had been only a buffalo calf still but already big enough not to be drinking his mother's milk, and he had been driven off along with his mother and other buffaloes to graze with the herd. On that amazing day, along with his mother, father and other buffaloes he had been eating grass in the Sabida valley.

It had been a terribly hot day, and his father recalled something from his past and decided to lead the buffaloes off somewhere. They walked and walked and walked, always downhill, until they came to a road that had that same strong, sharp smell and was black and soft. They crossed it and carried on until they came to a vast expanse of water. It was the sea, and the sea meant freedom and the happiness that it brought.

His father had entered the water followed by all the buffaloes, and they had begun to swim. It was so beautiful – on such a hot day the welcoming water smelling of freedom, his mother and his father beside him, and all the other buffaloes nearby – and they swam and swam and then lay still in the water in a state of bliss, noisily sucking in the air and puffing themselves out.

Towards evening Bardusha the stockman swam up to them with his son. At that time Broadbrow was still a real innocent. He thought that Bardusha had brought his son along just as Broadbrow's father had brought the herd of buffaloes and that they had met purely by chance in the water. Bardusha clambered up on to his father's back and his son got on to Broadbrow and with much laughter they drove the herd to the shore. Broadbrow could still remember how pleasant it had been to have the boy holding on to his ears with his little hands so as to stay on his back and to point the way he had to swim.

After reaching the shore they set off in the direction of Chegem. It was a long march, and from time to time the boy rode on the back of Broadbrow's father and then, tired of that, he rode on his own father's shoulders and there he went to sleep. It was late at night when they arrived back in Chegem.

So many years had passed since then, but Broadbrow always remembered that day with pleasure, and the vast welcoming water that smelt of freedom; and he would dream of once again experiencing that pleasure. Now he would himself have liked to lead a herd to the big water, to enjoy the sea and enjoy seeing others who had never seen the sea before enjoying themselves. But something prevented him. Probably the fact that there simply weren't such hot summer days any more.

How much time had passed since then? He didn't know exactly. Maybe since then snow had fallen ten times, maybe more, and maybe he had climbed up to the mountain meadows, always so fresh and tasty, ten times or possibly more. And his mother and father had disappeared somewhere. First his father. Then his mother.

Broadbrow had always considered life to be a wonderful experience. But there was one thing in that wonderful life that he found frightening and incomprehensible: everybody whom he had loved, absolutely everybody, sooner or later disappeared. Where did they go? He had no idea. First his father disappeared. Then, two years later, his mother. Then there came into his life an amazingly beautiful brown she-buffalo, his first love. But she also disappeared. And some of the buffaloes he had got to know in the herd also vanished. He supposed that cows and bulls also disappeared from time to time. Goats and sheep also disappeared somewhere, but they were so insignificant that you just couldn't keep track of them.

Other buffaloes, cows and bulls grew up to take the place of those that had disappeared, but, looking back over his life, Broadbrow could not fail to notice that the village herd was slowly but steadily shrinking. At times this caused him to feel a vague unease, a vague feeling of pain. His instinct told him that a law of life itself was being violated. The herd ought to have been fertile and growing in numbers, but it was slowly getting smaller, and if things went on like that, somewhere in the future, when Broadbrow was no longer among the living, the herd would die out altogether, and this distant but slowly approaching end caused him real pain.

According to a story his mother had told him he had learnt that there was in the world a terrible place, a sort of hell, known as the Place Where Horses Weep. His mother had told him that animals that fetched up there perished. They were killed by angry humans.

Only once did a buffalo return from that place. He was of an earlier generation than his mother, who had only heard stories about him. The buffalo had refused to do the angry humans' bidding and had run away from the Place Where Horses Weep and had made his way through many forests back to Chegem.

The people of Chegem were amazed to see the buffalo again and respected him for having escaped from the place from which no one returned. As a mark of their respect they did not make him pull a plough, haul logs or pull a cart. And from the fact that the people of Chegem were so fond of that buffalo because of his courage and stubbornness Broadbrow was quite sure that it was not they but some quite different people who picked on animals and dispatched them to the Place Where Horses Weep.

But if Broadbrow had been sure that all animals that disappeared fetched up Where Horses Weep it would have been impossible for him to go on living. No – he was an intelligent and observant buffalo and had noted on many occasions that buffaloes, cows, bulls and horses that had not grown up in Chegem would turn up there from time to time, having been born and brought up in a different place. He realized that people sometimes exchanged animals or simply made presents of them to each other. If a horse turned up in Chegem that had never been seen there as a foal it meant that many animals that had vanished from Chegem could have turned up in other villages. He found that a great consolation. But there was no way of knowing where a particular buffalo had gone, to another village or to the Place Where Horses Weep.

Once when the Chegem herd was grazing in the mountain meadows a man approached and separated Broadbrow from it. Accustomed to submitting to the intelligent will of a human being, Broadbrow went off in the direction the man drove him. He thought the man must be someone from Chegem whom he only vaguely recognized. Apart from the stockmen and the people he met at work Broadbrow had difficulty in distinguishing the features of one man of Chegem from another. Unlike animals, human beings were very like one another and the fact that they had only two legs made them almost indistinguishable.

So Broadbrow went where the fellow drove him. But then, without knowing exactly why, he suddenly suspected that the man was one of those wicked ones who drove animals off to the Place Where Horses Weep. Broadbrow stopped, turned, took a good look at the man and, realizing that he was not from Chegem, began to breathe with such fury that the man shouted: "What's up then, what's up?" and ran off. On that occasion Broadbrow did not chase after him because he hadn't yet made up his mind about killing such people. But later, when he had come to a decision, he regretted not having pursued him.

The man had in fact been a cattle thief. Broadbrow knew a lot about people, but he didn't know that humans were a tribe given to thieving. Unaware of this, he nevertheless suspected there was something wrong about the man by the urgency and haste with which he had separated him from the herd. A lifetime's experience had taught Broadbrow that people who led him out to work did so in a more measured and controlled way. Having correctly understood that he was not being led out to work, he mistakenly believed that he was being led to the Place Where Horses Weep.

On another occasion Broadbrow was grazing in the Sabida valley along with other buffaloes. Again some fellow approached the herd and after separating Broadbrow from the other buffaloes he drove him off into the depths of the forest. The fellow was no amateur but a professional cattle thief who drove Broadbrow at a quiet businesslike pace which misled Broadbrow for some time. They had already been walking for about two hours and had passed all the places where trees were being felled and everything around was strange. At this point Broadbrow began to suspect something, so he stopped, studied the man's features and realized that he was not from Chegem. That meant he was a murderer, leading him to the Place Where Horses Weep. As his rage mounted steadily within him Broadbrow started breathing heavily and audibly from his nostrils.

The man took fright and ran away from Broadbrow. But even a horse could not get away from a buffalo moving at speed, and Broadbrow, of course, knew that. Now he would avenge them all! But then something unexpected happened. The man jumped as he ran, grasped the branch of a young beech tree and scrambled on to it. In his fury Broadbrow began striking the tree with his horns. It was autumn and the beechnuts were ripe and came raining down from the branches. But for some reason the man was not to be shaken off. People were tenacious beings! Broadbrow got himself into a state of unbelievable fury and shook the tree with his horns. The nuts came tumbling down but the man didn't fall. Although the tree was young it was strong enough to withstand the blows.

Broadbrow was angry with himself as well. Again he had taken someone to be from Chegem. But people were so like each other. Leaving aside buffaloes, he could always distinguish two cows even if they were of the same colour. The same with horses. Goats and sheep could of course be confused – but they were just little things.

As for pigs, there was nothing to be said. The people of Chegem were sufficiently good Muslims not to eat pork, but not so good that they were above rearing pigs for the market. Broadbrow had long ago noticed that the Chegem people, when they were rounding up pigs or driving them into their sties, could not conceal a mixture of disgust and contempt in their voices. It stood to reason that pigs did not deserve better treatment.

A really loathsome and mean trick on the part of the pigs consisted in the fact that in the heat of summer they would find for themselves a pond and, thinking that this was the way to make themselves like buffaloes, would crawl into it.

It was one thing for a powerful buffalo, quietly chewing over a tasty cud, to lie peacefully in a pond with a crow on his head and terrapins on his back. It was quite another matter for a snorting pig to crawl into a muddy pond. That was not why Allah had created the pig – so that everything living should see this model of impiety. Broadbrow scorned the pig with all his being and in that respect, without knowing it, he was a real Muslim.

Tired of attacking the tree, Broadbrow tried another trick. He pretended to go away and return to the herd, but in fact he hid in the undergrowth and watched the man. Broadbrow waited a long time, but the man didn't get down from the tree. Broadbrow didn't realize that his back could easily be seen from up in the tree.

Then Broadbrow decided to attack from the rear and strike the tree unexpectedly. Perhaps the man would be taken by surprise and fall out. But from whichever side he approached he always came face to face with the man. Then he realized that the man was watching him closely all the time from up in the tree.

Broadbrow decided not to go anywhere so long as the man did not fall out of the tree. A man wasn't a bird who could live for ever in a tree. Having taken this decision, he quietened down and moved over to the beech tree. It was only then that he saw that there were lots of beechnuts lying round the tree. Broadbrow was very fond of beechnuts and he started gathering up with his lips the ones that had fallen out of their prickly shells. He spent a long time eating the nuts and listening to the curses coming from the tree. Broadbrow decided that the man was hungry and envied him. He knew that every living thing has to eat and that the man, weak from hunger, would eventually fall down.

Then Broadbrow decided not to leave the man in the tree any beechnuts so that there would be nothing for him to eat and so gather strength. He started attacking the tree again with his horns, but he didn't have to do it for long because he had already shaken practically all the nuts down. Broadbrow ate up everything that he had shaken off and then lay down beneath the tree. His decision to punish the murderer was unalterable. He would stay under the tree as long as was necessary.

As he dozed lightly beneath the tree that night he again several times heard the man's curses. Broadbrow quietly bided his time. On two occasions in the night some liquid poured out of the tree and Broadbrow guessed correctly that the man had relieved himself. "Never mind," Broadbrow thought, "it's easy to piss out of a tree but much more difficult to get something to eat up there."

Next morning the stockman Bardusha set out to track Broadbrow down and soon arrived at the tree that the buffalo was lying under. Bardusha had brought an axe with him.

When he saw Bardusha with the axe Broadbrow was delighted. Just like a lot of human beings today, Broadbrow had an exaggerated idea of the possibility of thought transference over long distances. He decided that his passionate desire to catch the murderer had been communicated to Bardusha, who had therefore come with his axe to chop down the young beech tree.

When he saw the man up in the tree and Broadbrow beneath it Bardusha suspected the man of being a cattle thief, and he started to shout at him. From the gestures the man in the tree was making Broadbrow guessed he was trying to prove his innocence, claiming that the buffalo had chased after him and forced him to climb up the tree. But it was clear from the gestures Bardusha was making, pointing all the time in the direction of the Sabida valley, that he didn't believe the man. A buffalo couldn't drive a person so far: he would have caught up with him long ago.

Why spend so long arguing with each other, thought Broadbrow – just chop down the tree and it would be clear what to do with the murderer who led animals off to the Place Where Horses Weep. But unfortunately it appeared that Bardusha believed what the man said and, still swearing at him, started to drive Broadbrow back home. Broadbrow felt terribly offended, but, accustomed as he was to obeying the good sense of humans, he set off reluctantly and dejected for the Sabida valley.

The main road the truck was driving down was approaching the sea. Broadbrow picked up that exciting, slightly salty smell of freedom mixed up, unfortunately, with the evil smells reaching him from the road. Raising his head he took a deep breath and tried to filter out of the air the smell of the sea and to take in less of the road smell. Dozing off, he again started chewing the cud, but the shaking of the truck and the smell of the asphalt spoilt the pleasure. He swallowed down a mouthful and began to reflect on life.

He recalled his first love. In the whole of his life Broadbrow had been in love three times. But now he recalled his very first love.

It was rather strange how it came about. He couldn't understand exactly how it had happened. The young she-buffalo usually grazed along with all the buffaloes either in the Sabida valley or in other meadows and pastures. She was practically indistinguishable from the other she-buffaloes, except that the others were rather darker while she was browner. She was fatter and her horns looked less like weapons and more like an embellishment.

At first he couldn't understand why he found it pleasanter to graze next to her. He decided that she had a sort of special nose for grass and that she always discovered the most tasty corners of the pasture. It was a pleasant surprise for him, every time he came close to her, to discover that the grass nearby was much tastier than usual. What a clever girl she was to find it!

Later he noticed that if the farmer was a little late in letting her into the herd the grass became quite unpleasant to the taste, and Broadbrow would raise his head and wait for her, still under the impression that she was making up to him with her ability to find the tastiest grass. It was only later that he realized that it was love that made the grass so sweet.

In the evening, when she went back home or the farmer would lead her off, Broadbrow would miss her and think about the next morning when she would reappear. Every morning her return to the herd was a cause for real celebration.

He revealed to her a little but quite agreeable secret he had. All the buffaloes already knew, of course, that the best place to scratch your side against was a walnut tree. It had the roughest bark and it gave the buffalo's coat a good combing.

But the Sacred Nut Tree differed from the other trees in that it had long and strong ridges in it. Because it grew on a steep hillside the other buffaloes mistakenly believed that it was difficult to get close to it for scratching. In fact it was very simple.

From the very first time that she rubbed herself against the Sacred Nut Tree the she-buffalo immediately took to it and, however far away from it they grazed, when she wanted to scratch her sides she would pass up all the other trees and accompany Broadbrow to this particular tree and rub herself against it, gazing gratefully at him.

There was one place in the pond where it was a lot softer to lie than elsewhere. There were practically no stones there. But she didn't know about it. The first time they went to the pond together he had to edge the silly girl towards that place. Later she would always settle down there herself, while he would lie next to her. Sometimes they would arrive at the pond to find her place occupied. Then there was nothing for it but to chase away the buffalo who had settled himself down in a place where it was not allowed. Broadbrow was young, but all the buffaloes and a lot of people already knew how strong he was.

That summer of his first love had been the most wonderful in his whole life, a time when he was still young enough not to know a anything about she-buffaloes being on heat in the autumn. He still thought that the sum total of love consisted in munching the most tasty grass alongside your beloved she-buffalo, waiting for her in the morning, longing for her in the evening, lying blissfully at her side in the pond or going with her to scratch your hide against the sacred bark of the Sacred Nut Tree.

Suddenly, one day in the autumn, she disappeared. She didn't turn up in the herd in the morning. Broadbrow waited and waited until he could wait no more and, somewhat ashamed, he went to her part of the farm and looked into the cattle pen. It was empty, quite empty. Overcome by a great grief, he came to the conclusion that she had disappeared as his father had disappeared in his day and as so many other buffaloes and animals had disappeared. The thought that his gentle, dappled she-buffalo could have finished up in the Place Where Horses Weep drove him out of his mind.

For two days he ate nothing at all. Sometimes he wandered aimlessly in the Sabida valley, at others he would go deliberately into the most prickly undergrowth so that the thorns that scraped painfully along his hide deadened the pain he felt inside. At times he just stood silently in the shade of the trees.

This period of great grief coincided with the mating season: perhaps it even brought it on. He would stand under the trees in the shade and listen to the way the love juices coursed within him; his legs became numb and his head swam. He had only to close his eyes slightly and she would appear before him, quiet, obedient, with her heavy-lidded eyes. He could see her standing there, dappled and plump, and, driven wild with love, he just could not understand one thing: how it had ever been possible for him to graze quietly alongside her, how he could lie peacefully next to her in the pond, or calmly rub himself against the Sacred Nut Tree along with her. If he were to lie down next to her in the pond now the whole pond would boil up with his passion. And if he were now rubbing his hide against it the Sacred Nut Tree would have gone up in smoke from his passion, just as it had done once from heavenly fire.

Then, on the third day, as he was standing there in the rain at the edge of the forest he caught the smell of his she-buffalo, and he drew in that sweet smell with such force that his sides nearly burst as his ribs expanded. And from behind the trees a cart appeared with his girlfriend harnessed to it. The cart was loaded with wood and the farmer was sitting at the front with a stick in his hand. So that was where she had been for those two days.

His joy at finding her drove everything out of his head, and Broadbrow rushed towards his loved one. There was a great clap of thunder, and then the rain turned into a downpour. When he saw the buffalo hurtling towards the cart the farmer tried to out-shout the storm and threatened him with his stick, but Broadbrow could neither see nor hear anything but his buffalo bride.

He descended on the cart, a veritable hurricane of adoration. The farmer went in one direction, the cart overturned in the other, and the straps that harnessed the buffalo into the cart simply snapped. But every time he tried to mount his bride and she out of modesty retreated from him, moving a few paces ahead, the cart was dragged along behind them. It seemed that some strap was still holding. Broadbrow was still so young and so excited by the proximity of his bride that he decided that the cart had also been smitten with an unlawful passion for his buffalo. He picked up the cart on his horns and threw it aside with such fury that as it landed it disintegrated into a pile of wood, while one wheel rolled towards the farmer.

Then, to the pitiful mutterings of the farmer, he possessed his beloved buffalo. The downpour from the heavens was matched by the outpouring of love, and then the mighty passion was assuaged, and the two of them, drenched by both downpours, turned to grazing quietly nearby, munching the grass, also freshened by the downpour.

Three days later the stupid farmer, having decided that Broadbrow would always follow his loved one and would in so doing cause him incalculable expenses, sold her to the next village. And now she disappeared for ever and Broadbrow had no idea where she had gone to. His grief was so great that, as a mark of sympathy for him, for a whole six months the sun shone hazily in the sky. Broadbrow had never known a worse period.

The truck sped down the main road in the direction of Mukhus. The August sun blazed down. The roadway continued to give off a disagreeable smell, and it was only the welcome wafts of sea air drifting into his nostrils from time to time that calmed him down. Traffic going the other way produced another evil smell.

Because of the heat Broadbrow stopped thinking of female buffaloes and began remembering all the watering places he had managed to visit and enjoy in his lifetime. Of course, his happiest memory was of the sea, but all watering places are welcome on a summer's day.

What was so good about the waters in the marshy lands below Chegem? There were plenty of terrapins! No sooner had you settled down there than a dozen terrapins would crawl up on to you and start wriggling about and scratching your coat. And the bottom of the pond was so beautifully soft. The mud was as deep as a buffalo's leg. But it was probably too warm, too comfortable. It was very pleasant, but afterwards you felt too relaxed, too pampered.

Then there was the pond at Chegem. It was a good one. The water was neither too warm nor too cold. It was just right. There were, of course, far fewer terrapins, but on the other hand, if there were no people about, the crows with their well-trained beaks would dig a lot of harmful insects out of your head and back. But what was wrong with it? It had to be said in all honesty that the Chegem pond was fine in every way except that its bottom was too stony. You didn't get the sort of soft mud that there was lower down. There was nothing you could do about it. There was no point in praising something simply because it was one's own.

Then there were the little mountain lakes. Very nice to look at – there was no disputing that. But the water was too cold. Those lakes were one of nature's most puzzling problems. They were, after all, much nearer the sun than other places on the earth, yet for some reason the water never managed to warm up. So you couldn't lie around in it for very long.

But on the other hand what was good about that invigorating water? It gave you an unbelievable appetite! As you came out of the lake into the meadow you immediately started to eat the grass. And you could go on eating to your heart's content. There was no tastier grass in the whole world; it was so tasty in fact that even later when you were chewing the cud you could tell by its aroma that it was mountain grass you were chewing.

Sometimes at night, especially in the first few days after the herd had been driven up into the mountains, you would forget where you were and think you were still in Chegem. But as soon as you tasted the cud in your mouth you knew you were in the mountain pastures.

On several occasions, along with the other buffaloes, Broadbrow went down to the swiftly flowing waters of the Kodor to cool off. That was quite a treat! The strong current of water washed you down and dragged at you, but you stood firm on your legs, because you were a buffalo and nothing and nobody could shift you by force. And curiously enough not a single fly would come near you when you were in the Kodor. Cowardly creatures!

Then there were the children! With floats hollowed out of a special kind of pumpkin tied to their waists to keep them from drowning they would swim up to you, climb on to your back, shouting and screaming and splashing and laughing. It was wonderful! Nothing like the flies. Meanwhile the strong current would try to knock you over and drag you along with it, but you stood firm and felt your own strength. It was very pleasant to overpower the fast-flowing river.

Recalling time spent in the water so cheered Broadbrow that, in spite of the smell from the road, he switched his thoughts again to his favourite she-buffaloes.

He had been in love with his next girlfriend for about two years. And he had thought it was to be for ever, for the rest of his life. But no one knows what the future will bring. With that partner he had an offspring, and they were so in love with each other that the people of Chegem often made fun of them. Why do people, when they notice that animals love each other, start making fun of them? Out of envy, probably.

Broadbrow always grazed alongside her and always lay next to her in the pond, having first, of course, taught her where the softest place was. In fact, to tell the truth, she didn't even need any teaching. Knowing that she enjoyed his protection, she just flopped down there of her own accord. And if, when she came to the pond with Broadbrow, that place was occupied, she would wait a little and then glance round for him to bring order into the place.

Broadbrow found it amusing to watch some lazybones of a buffalo who was occupying his beloved's place and pretending not to see what was going on around him, just lying there dozing and chewing the cud. Broadbrow would wait, knowing that even the laziest buffalo would sooner or later feel pricks of conscience. And, of course, in the end his conscience *would* awake. The lazybones would suddenly look round and see them standing on the bank and pretend to be surprised that they were standing on the dry land and not entering the water, but then, as though it had suddenly occurred to him that he had absent-mindedly occupied the place belonging to Broadbrow's queen, he would slowly stand up, move away a few paces and settle down in another spot.

Although Broadbrow was much in love with his new girlfriend he still did not reveal to her that the pleasantest thing to do in Chegem was to rub against the Sacred Nut Tree. Let that tree remain the rubbing post of his first love. Even now he went to it sometimes to give his coat a good scratch and abandon himself to sweet and sad memories.

Broadbrow always accompanied his present girlfriend home, stood next to her in the cattle yard while she was being milked, and then returned to the herd.

The people of Chegem used sometimes to come to look at Broadbrow as he came to the cattle yard where his loved one was kept. They explained to outsiders that they were looking at a buffalo known as Broadbrow who didn't belong to that farmer but to the collective farm, and that he came to the yard every morning just to visit his girlfriend. People were amazed that a buffalo could be so attached to a female not only when she was on heat but all the year round.

But the whole affair finished up in a very silly, very unhappy manner.

One day the farmer had been milking the buffalo as usual, and had driven off the calf with a stick. The calf hung around impatiently waiting until the farmer finished milking and it could suck out what was left of the milk.

Broadbrow was standing alongside his girlfriend when suddenly she made a move to rest her head on his neck and did it so awkwardly that she kicked over the pail full of milk with her hind leg.

Broadbrow would never have believed that the farmer was so mean. He grabbed a stick and started to beat Broadbrow with all his strength and drove him out of the yard. And that was very hurtful for Broadbrow, because he had felt that he had been accepted in that farmyard as a member of the family. He was at a loss to know what to do, not because of the beating but because of the farmer's shameful performance.

Broadbrow left the cattle yard at a fast pace. But the farmer kept up with him and kept on hitting him and shouting bad words at him. Broadbrow could of course have broken into a run, but to run would have been shameful, and because he didn't run the performance lasted much longer. His loved one saw all this, of course, and her poor little calf fell silent and nuzzled up to its mother. The cows also saw it, and the stupid goats looked on in amazement, and even the two pigs, for whom the farmer's wife had just filled their trough with swill, took the trouble to raise their heads, still munching away, to look at him. Only the horse, that noble creature, when he saw what was happening, sadly turned his head in the opposite direction.

Never in his whole life had Broadbrow suffered such humiliation.

Why on earth had he not picked that miserable scoundrel up on his horns and tossed him over his back? He had apparently lost his head. For a moment he had thought that his loved one was, of course, to blame. He was even ready for the farmer to take out his anger on him, Broadbrow. The man could have given him a couple of good whacks with his stick, but he ought not to have mocked him like that.

The cattle yard was about a hundred yards long and as he was going down it the farmer kept hitting him and shouting angry words at him. Finally it seemed to Broadbrow that even the stick broke in half out of shame. It could well have snapped sooner.

That night Broadbrow didn't sleep a wink. It hurt him to recall that he had previously felt himself quite at home in that cattle yard. Now he must have his revenge! The bad-tempered fool of a man who had humiliated him simply because of a pail of milk was not even able to understand that if the she-buffalo had not become pregnant because of Broadbrow there would have been no milk anyway. Broadbrow now knew that sooner or later he would pick that man up on his horns.

What he did not understand was how he should now treat his loved one. He would of course never escort her back to the cattle yard again. But how should he now approach her? It was not at all clear.

Next day they were grazing in the same herd, but he did not approach her. She raised her head several times and looked in his direction but he pretended not to notice. Finally she found herself near him and she raised her head and looked across at him and he saw quite clearly in her look the question: will you really not forgive us? His whole body stiffened with indignation. He would never be able to forgive her for that shameful "us". It meant that she took the farmer's part. All right. And he set about thinking up another way of getting his own back.

Now he not only kept right away from her, but when she was on heat in the autumn and a young and rather stupid buffalo tried to mount her Broadbrow drove him off with blows from his horns and then chased after him. He made him run twice round the Sabida valley until the young buffalo jumped the river and disappeared into the forest.

The she-buffalo remained barren for two years and, because he didn't understand what was wrong (that pail of milk was costing him dear), the farmer sold her to someone in the next village. Broadbrow never forgot, however, that the farmer who had owned his girlfriend had yet to be dealt with. But as luck would have it he never seemed to run into him.

Finally, another couple of years later, they met up. That day Broadbrow was grazing alongside the upper Chegem road when he caught sight of his former girlfriend's owner coming by on horseback. He might never get another chance like that.

Broadbrow rushed after the horseman. Whether it was because the horse heard him approaching or whether, as Broadbrow believed, his fierce determination to have his revenge transmitted itself to the man who had so humiliated him, the horse broke into a gallop. But Broadbrow was already going at top speed and was inevitably catching up with the horse. The rider let out a scream and, looking round all the time, urged his horse on. But he was already doomed. Broadbrow finally cornered him next to the garden of the Big House.

He picked the horse up on his horns and was about to toss it along with its rider over his back. But the rider somehow slid off, was thrown along with the horse over the fence and landed in the soft earth of a cornfield. The man jumped up and, with a shout of "Murder! Murder!" that could easily be heard in the Big House, he hid himself among the corn. The horse flailed about with its legs for a while, then rolled over on its back and remained still. The saddle had slipped off, one of its girths was torn off, and the horse looked very sorry for itself.

The cowardly way the farmer had run off, first along the upper Chegem road and then into the cornfield, was quite sufficient to assuage Broadbrow's desire for vengeance. The owner of the she-buffalo was of course a coward. Broadbrow had always suspected that cruelty was the bravery of cowards.

But now he felt ashamed of himself on account of the horse lying helplessly in the corner. He remembered that, of all the animals present on that cursed evening, only the horse did not want to watch him being humiliated. Then suddenly the horse rolled over on to its belly, stood up, and started to eat the corncobs, munching noisily. "Eat up the sweet-tasting corn," Broadbrow thought to himself. "You have earned it." But the horse did not go on eating the corn stalks for long. Soon they heard the voice of a man walking across the field, and Broadbrow went back to the herd.

It turned out that, when he fell, the horseman had put his arm out of joint. That same day he complained to the chairman of the collective farm that Broadbrow had gone mad and was now dangerous for people to handle. The farm management was about to hand over

Broadbrow for slaughter when the foreman Kyazym came into the chairman's office.

"What's up with you? Did Broadbrow toss you as well?" asked the chairman, surprised at Kyazym's appearance. The chairman already knew that there had been an accident near Kyazym's house.

"The horse brought him." Kyazym nodded, smiling sarcastically. "He abandoned it in my cornfield and came running over here."

"That cursed buffalo," the victim replied. "I forgot about him in the heat of the moment."

It appeared that Kyazym had returned home just after Broadbrow's enemy had left. When he learnt from the servants what had happened he led the horse into the yard, put another saddle on it, and rode it to the farm office.

"What's this you say about his going mad?" Kyazym asked when he learnt what the victim was after. "You said yourself that you broke a stick on his back."

"That was ages ago," replied the farmer. "Good God, it's four years since then."

"A buffalo never forgets an insult all his life," Kyazym said. "Did you really not know that? You've kept buffaloes after all."

"So what am I supposed to do now? Let the farm go to pieces and get out of Chegem?" The farmer pointed to his helpless arm.

"No," said Kyazym. "He will remember an insult until he can avenge himself. You can reckon that you've got away with it lightly."

So it was decided that if Broadbrow attacked another human being he would be sent for slaughter to help them reach the meat quota. It was the first time Kyazym saved his life, though Broadbrow did not, of course, know it.

Being surprised from time to time not so much at the smell of the main road as at how long it continued, Broadbrow lay there in the back of the truck as it raced down the road. In Chegem and many other places Broadbrow had often come across strong smells, but never one that lasted so long. Whenever the Sleepy Giant woke up and started to move it also gave off a pretty strong smell. But not for long. It soon went away. There was a strong smell in the barn where the tobacco leaves were dried. Well, and the pigs, of course. A pig was a little walking stink. But it also soon went away. But for a smell to last so long when you were driving along with it and it seemed never to end, he had never come across that before. "No," he thought, "we shall arrive in a village and everything there will be as it used to be:

the earth will smell of earth, and the grass of grass." But the Sleepy Giants must have increased greatly in numbers if it took so long to reach the village where there still weren't any of them.

Suddenly Broadbrow stopped short in anticipation of unbelievable happiness. Supposing his first love, his dappled lady, was alive and living in this very village? Of course, she would no longer be the two-year-old he had known, but then he too was quite a bit older. And he now knew so much more about life, about people and about buffaloes. He would take such good care of her. He now knew better than anyone what it meant to have a loyal spirit, a real friend. And they could have calves together – after all, they still weren't very old. Oh, if only he found her there! But better not to tempt fate; better not to think about it.

As his thoughts turned to the new village where he was going to pull a plough once again Broadbrow realized just how much he missed doing that work. When the Sleepy Giant had started rumbling across the Chegem fields Broadbrow had said to himself: "All right, if you think I shall pass away because of you, you are making a big mistake." And, of course, he did not pass away. But he liked pulling a plough. Of the three jobs he performed for humans – ploughing, hauling logs, and transporting loads on a cart – the only one he really liked was ploughing.

Sometimes he enjoyed hauling logs out of the forest and sometimes he didn't. He liked hauling the logs when it was really hard work – when the logs were difficult to get out of the ground or when the place was so steep that he had to get down on his knees and drag the logs to a flat place. He liked that work when there was an element of excitement about it and when he was himself amazed at how strong he was and could tell by the exclamations of the workers that they were amazed too. But he had never enjoyed dragging a cart. That was a stupid, monotonous occupation.

But ploughing – that was another story! To be turning the rich earth over evenly and smoothly – it made him feel so good, because he, a buffalo, was put in the position of a ploughman. It seemed that the man who walked behind the plough always felt he was taking part in good work, the most important task in life. He would turn over a layer of earth, like turning back a blanket, to place the tiny seed grain in the ground. Broadbrow had the feeling that, as he turned over the earth layer by layer, the ploughman was continually caressing it with the blade of the plough and preparing it to receive the seed and was himself involved in the great secret of its future fertility. And, no

matter how he shouted when they came to the turn and no matter
how tired Broadbrow was at the end of the day, he carried that great
secret with him when he left the field. But since they had started using
the Sleepy Giant to pull the plough Broadbrow had noticed that the
ploughman wasn't affected the same way. He would jump down from
the tractor bad-tempered and exhausted. Broadbrow believed that the
laws of nature itself decreed that it was sinful to make the earth more
fertile without actually being in contact with it. A good Chegem
peasant always ploughed barefoot.

Broadbrow then recalled the first time in his life that he had ploughed
a field of maize. Until then the people of Chegem had always hoed
the earth around the maize stalks in the same way as they treated
tobacco plants and everything that grew in the garden. Kyazym the
foreman was the first in Chegem to realize that they could use the
plough in a maize field so long as the maize was sown in rows. The
others didn't believe him and simply laughed at the idea that you could
make a buffalo or a bull walk between rows of ripe corn without
touching it.

When Kyazym harnessed Broadbrow to the plough and led him out
into the field a group of local people, joking and jeering, gathered
along the fence to see what would happen. Broadbrow himself thought
it was rather funny. How could one walk past ripe, tender and tasty
corn without biting off a cob or two? And what happened? Kyazym
was right.

It turned out that it wasn't all that easy to plough a cornfield and
at the same time sample what you were ploughing. What happened
was that you would pass down the rows of green stalks and some of
them would rub against your body so temptingly, but you had to carry
on, just ploughing the earth they grew in. Because it was very awkward.
In order to snap off a cob of corn you had to stop at least for a
moment, but you couldn't stop because you were pulling a plough
and there was a man beside you.

Broadbrow had noticed that since those days the people of Chegem
no longer hoed their cornfields or scattered the seeds at random.
Instead they sowed the seeds in rows and used buffaloes or bulls to
plough them. It was true that the stupider bulls did not always
appreciate the complexity of their difficult situation and tried occasionally to snatch the corncobs on the move. So they had their mouths
tied shut with rope, which was rather humiliating when you come to
think of it.

There is no point in hiding the fact that, in his younger days,

Broadbrow had enjoyed breaking the rules in the cornfields. With strength like his, of course, no barrier was sufficient to keep him out. And it was so pleasant to munch the sweet corncobs that he quite forgot about the punishment he was inviting. The trouble was that the other animals – donkeys, cows and goats – rushed after him through the gap he had made and started to eat the corn. He couldn't very well chase them out again because it was he who had broken into the field. In the end they attached a piece of wood to his horns so that he could see nothing but the grass under his feet. His world grew dark. Now he could no longer see, not just the cornfield, but the sky, the meadows, the trees and the pond. Broadbrow stuck it for three days. Then he lost his temper and started banging his head against the ground until he had smashed the piece of wood to bits. Once again he could see the vast, beautiful, multicoloured world. Never again did he break through a fence, and never again did they fix that horrible piece of wood to his forehead, that prison for his eyes.

The truck came to a halt outside a bar, and Bardusha and the driver went in to have a drink. When the truck stopped the smell seemed to go on ahead, but a moment later it returned and settled down alongside the truck like a faithful pig. Broadbrow continued to try to filter out from the air the smell of the sea. It was somewhere not far off, and penetrated through the stench.

As he lay in the truck Broadbrow recalled the story of his third love. A new she-buffalo had turned up unexpectedly in the Chegem herd. Broadbrow immediately took a liking to her, and so did another buffalo whom Broadbrow respected for his strength and courage.

One night in the springtime a pack of wolves, emboldened by hunger, attacked a young calf. All the buffaloes formed a cirle to protect their young ones, and the buffalo Broadbrow respected fought alongside him. He withstood the wolves' attack bravely, although he didn't manage to kill any of them. He simply had not mastered the art of cutting their legs from under them. He would attack a wolf head-on and try to get his horns into him, but the wolf would always manage to jump back. The way to do it was to attack his legs and throw him over, ripping his guts open in the act.

Anyway, Broadbrow respected that buffalo for his strength and courage and at times he felt he would like to take him on just to see who was the stronger. But there were no grounds for quarrelling. As the strongest of all they respected each other.

Then this new she-buffalo came on the scene. Broadbrow noticed that the other buffalo had also taken a liking to her. But when Broadbrow went up to her and rested his head on her neck and then started grazing alongside her, the other buffalo recognized them as a pair and made no further approaches to her. This state of affairs continued for three weeks, and Broadbrow thought the matter was decided.

One day he was sent into the forest to haul logs and then, having worked till midday, he went to the pasture and, finding no buffaloes there, he guessed, of course, that they were resting in the pond. So he went down to the pond and came across a remarkable scene.

His rival buffalo was lying next to his latest love, casually chewing the cud and glancing unconcernedly at the bank where Broadbrow was standing. They were lying so close together that the buffalo's tail would from time to time rise out of the water and splash water on his back and incidentally, as though by chance, touch the back of the she-buffalo. That was not very agreeable to watch, but still bearable. Then suddenly a terrapin which had been sitting on the she-buffalo's back slid off her and crawled on to the buffalo's back. In a burst of jealousy, encouraged by his belief that thoughts could be transmitted over a distance, Broadbrow decided that his latest love had made a present of the terrapin to the buffalo. Saying pitifully to himself: "Nobody ever gave me a terrapin!" and with a determined snort he dashed into the pond and drove all the buffaloes out into the meadow. The other buffalo realized that there was going to be a fight, and he was ready for it. And Broadbrow knew it too. His opponent had a certain advantage over him. After all Broadbrow had been working since the morning while his opponent had been cooling off in the pond alongside Broadbrow's girlfriend. They stood back from each other and then attacked head-on. There was a crack like a shot from a gun as the two sets of horns crashed into each other and there was a smell of burning bone. Locked together by their horns, they stood there rocking and circling round in search of better leverage, but neither could make any headway. Their horns had met with such force that their heads were hot at the base of their horns.

Having failed to throw each other at the first clash, they again retreated. Broadbrow was already standing still, preparing to rush at his opponent, but the latter continued to retreat and lengthen the distance between them. So then Broadbrow decided that that was not fair and he also lengthened his run. This time his opponent came to a halt before Broadbrow and when he saw Broadbrow increasing his run, he retreated still further. By now they were about fifty metres apart, staring straight at each other, taking aim and waiting. Broadbrow took off at high speed and his opponent shook himself and hastened to meet him, fearing that Broadbrow would cover a greater distance and thus gather greater speed.

Again they crashed into each other. Locked together, they pressed with such incredible force that both Broadbrow's and his opponent's forelegs sank deep into the grassy ground. The two buffaloes remained locked in that position, scarcely moving their horns, and again there was the smell of burning bone and their heads were hot at the base of their horns.

The task confronting each buffalo was, by means of the sheer force behind his horns, to twist the neck of his opponent so that the pain would force him to roll over and straighten his neck. All that would remain then would be to chase the defeated opponent from the field of battle. But this time again nothing came of the contest. Again they stood off a fair distance apart and, breathing heavily, eyed each other from afar, trying not to be caught off guard when the opponent decided to make a dash for it.

At this point it occurred to Broadbrow to adopt another trick. He would wait, letting his opponent be the first to attack, and then, very slightly, scarcely visibly, changing direction, he would concentrate the whole force of the blow, not on both his opponent's horns, but only on the left one. Then, perhaps, his neck wouldn't stand it and his huge body would be thrown over.

The other buffalo began his run. Broadbrow waited a little and then, mentally aiming the base of his right horn at the middle of his opponent's left horn and in his sad fury recalling that "Nobody ever gave me a terrapin!", hurled himself into battle.

Once again they collided. But this time there was not just the sound of contact being made but the sound of something cracking. The other buffalo's left horn had broken off and fallen to the ground! It was so unexpected that the buffalo lost his head and ran away. Feeling that something awful, wrong and irreparable had taken place, Broadbrow nevertheless chased after him in his rage and butted him several times on the run until the defeated buffalo broke off into the prickly undergrowth.

Broadbrow had, of course, wanted to be victorious and to use his victory to shame his opponent. But he hadn't wanted to go so far. He didn't even know that a buffalo's horn could break off. He had often come across cows and sometimes bulls with only one horn, but he had never seen a one-horned buffalo. It was really awful. He had not wanted to humiliate his opponent to such an extent. How could he now live with just one horn? It was like making a man from Chegem cut off half his moustache. Broadbrow had long noticed that, if a man from Chegem had a moustache, it always grew on both sides, like horns.

To complete the tale of misfortune a shepherd entered the pasture with his dog and some goats. The dog found the horn and proceeded to treat it without any respect, as if it were a dead crow. He seized the broken-off horn in his teeth and then for some reason dragged it along, although it was quite obvious that no dog, and not even a bear, could crack a buffalo horn. Broadbrow could, of course, have chased after the dog and taken the horn off it, but the dog was such a small creature it would have been humiliating to pursue it. A terrible situation!

Meanwhile his beloved buffalo raised her head and looked at Broadbrow, expecting him to join her. But she miscalculated. He did not join her. She went on grazing, raising her head from time to time with a puzzled look, as if to say: "Why don't you join me? Didn't you win the battle?" Her stupidity annoyed Broadbrow, and he did not approach her that day or even the next day, although she frequently raised her head and looked in his direction. The foolish girl just couldn't understand that he was sorry for his defeated opponent who was now grazing mournfully on the edge of the herd, an ugly stump sticking out of his head.

That was the end of Broadbrow's love affair. Never again did he approach that buffalo or lie with her in the pond.

The driver and Bardusha came out of the bar. Bardusha climbed up to the back of the truck where he could reach Broadbrow and stroke his neck.

"So what about it, Broadbrow?" he said.

Broadbrow could tell by his breath that he had been drinking and by the tone of his voice he gathered that Bardusha was sorry for him.

"Come on, come on," the driver urged him.

And as he sat down next to the driver and banged the door shut, Bardusha said: "I shall never see another buffalo like that in my lifetime."

The truck carried on down the road. The smell, taken by surprise, had briefly fallen behind. But it soon caught up with them and spread around in the atmosphere. The sea was somewhere not far away, and the smell of freedom occasionally reached Broadbrow's nostrils.

Now he turned to thinking about a day in the distant past spent on the mountain pastures. The herd of buffaloes and cows had arrived at a wonderful sloping meadow with a mixture of rich succulent grasses. They had set about eating that grass, moving gradually up the hill, and the grass became better and better. A she-buffalo grazed next to him. She had a grown calf with her.

At that time Broadbrow had not been in love with any of the buffaloes in the Chegem herd, and when the time came for them to be on heat he, like all the other buffaloes, performed the service laid down by nature and immediately forgot all about whichever she-buffalo chance had thrown in his way.

Ever since he ceased to be in love all she-buffaloes seemed to be just like each other, as human beings did. When he had been in love he had distinguished not only buffaloes but all other animals too, even if they were of the same colour. Love made him see clearly. But now, as he eyed the buffalo and the calf that did not leave her side, he just couldn't remember whether he had actually been with that buffalo in the autumn or with another one. In any case two years had passed since then. Strange.

And, as though he had heard Broadbrow's thoughts, a bear came out from behind the hill and started to amble slowly in the direction of the calf, as though sure that Broadbrow would not try to defend it when he had such doubts in his head. Broadbrow reacted with a truly noble fury. Letting out his usual mournful roar – "Nobody ever gave me a terrapin!" – he hurled himself at the bear and pinned him against the hillside.

The bear let out a howl of pain; clouds of evil-smelling breath left his mouth, and he drew his rake-like claws down Broadbrow's hide. But his paws were so weakened by the pressure Broadbrow brought into play that, despite his attempts, he was unable to get his claws deep into Broadbrow's neck.

The bear groaned. He frothed at the mouth but for some reason did not expire. Broadbrow did not gore him, but simply pressed him into the hillside with great force. He held him like that for a long time, and the bear's groans became weaker but the smell did not go away. Finally Broadbrow decided to put an end to the business, to get his horns into the bear and toss him over his back. But no sooner had he moved away than the bear collapsed and his lifeless body rolled off down the hillside, bumping on the rocks.

Broadbrow watched the bear roll down the hill, surprised that he had died so quickly. But then when it reached the very bottom of the hill the dead body of the bear stopped rolling, came to life most dishonestly, shook itself off and, as though nothing had happened, staggered off into the undergrowth. He had outsmarted Broadbrow!

Broadbrow was so upset by what had happened that he stood there for an hour breathing fiercely and noisily. Then suddenly Bardusha reappeared with a load of firewood on his back. He threw down his load and went towards Broadbrow, but the buffalo was still so furious that he didn't want even Bardusha to approach him. Why had Bardusha forgotten about the herd? What would have happened to the calf if Broadbrow had not been nearby?

Later he did, of course, let Bardusha approach him and inspect carefully the wounds on his neck. Broadbrow was fond of Bardusha. He always treated the herd to salt and encouraged them with his shouts. Broadbrow was, of course, afraid of nothing, but some of the she-buffaloes and all the cows were such shy creatures that it pleased them as they ate the mountain grass to hear a human voice. Moreover, no beast would approach if it heard a human being speak.

On one occasion Broadbrow fell sick on the mountain pastures. He had eaten some poisonous grass. For several days he lay at the shepherd's hut. Every day Bardusha brought him some little branches bearing fresh and very tasty leaves that he ate lying down because he hadn't the strength to stand up. Every morning and evening Bardusha brought a huge bowl of healing tea from his hut. Broadbrow drank it lying down. Life was wonderful on the mountain pastures. Nowhere else in the world was there such an appetizing mixture of rich grasses. There was only one thing wrong with it: after a heavy hailstorm the grasses and bushes became so cold that your tongue ceased to be able to detect the poisonous qualities of certain plants and leaves which animals normally detect very well. Even if they chanced to take such poisons into their mouths they spat them out at once. But after a heavy hailstorm the plants froze and your tongue could be mistaken. That is what happened to Broadbrow, but he had a strong constitution and Bardusha saved his life. Broadbrow didn't know that the senior shepherd had already suggested slaughtering him. But Bardusha had taken it upon himself to cure him and finally succeeded with his health-giving tea. Broadbrow had never forgotten how far Bardusha had to go to obtain the bunches of twigs with their fresh tasty leaves that he ate lying down.

The truck braked to a halt at the entrance to the slaughterhouse. The gates opened and the truck turned slowly and drove into the yard.

There it turned again and backed up to the scales on which the animals were weighed on arrival.

As soon as the truck entered the slaughterhouse yard Broadbrow could tell that the smell of the road had disappeared; instead there was the smell of blood. Apparently a long-lasting smell ends in blood, he thought. There was no mistaking the smell of blood. Broadbrow knew it well, because he had seen the blood of animals torn apart by predators and he had seen the blood of predators destroyed by his own horns. But along with the smell of blood there was an increasingly strong smell of the sea, because the slaughterhouse was situated near the sea. With a strange sense of alarm Broadbrow picked up two salty smells: the smell of blood and the smell of the sea and of freedom.

But he was still unable to make out what was going on. Ahead of him could be heard the continual unpleasant sound of heavy blows being struck and from time to time came the even less pleasant sound of bones being broken.

It was quite clear to Broadbrow that they had not yet arrived at the village. Because between the village and the smelly road there had to be a road that did not smell. That was the way it had been when they left Chegem. So they were not yet at the village. But where were they?

At this point Bardusha climbed into the back of the truck and started undoing the ropes that bound Broadbrow's legs. The buffalo was now rather confused because, if the ropes were being taken off, it meant that they had arrived somewhere and he would have to get down from the truck. Bardusha threw the ropes aside and patted Broadbrow lightly on the neck. That made Broadbrow feel much better immediately.

He was worried by that smell of blood and the strange clatter of machines, from which there came from time to time the sound of broken bones, painfully recalling something familiar. It was all very frightening, but Bardusha was beside him and that meant that he was protected by the good sense of a human being and Broadbrow had only to obey him. Bardusha then gave Broadbrow a more demanding pat on the neck signifying that he had to stand up, which he did with difficulty on his numb legs. Bardusha dropped the back of the truck, a slaughterhouse employee fixed some planks to it, and Broadbrow, encouraged by kindly pats from Bardusha, came down from the truck.

The rumble of machinery and the sound of bones breaking. The rumble and the crash.

"Over here," said the man in charge of the weighing machine, and Bardusha drove Broadbrow towards him.

To facilitate the business of weighing, the platform on which the animals stood was level with the ground and had already been tramped over by so many animals that it looked no different from the ground around it. Broadbrow thought that it was just like the rest of the ground, but when he stood on the platform he felt it concealed in itself an unpleasant instability. But he decided to be patient since that was what Bardusha wanted.

"Not bad!" said the man in charge of the weighing machine. "Nine hundred and fifty-five kilos!"

"There isn't another buffalo like this one in the whole world," Bardusha said, and then everything that he had ever thought about Broadbrow got mixed up in his head: his mighty memory, his touching attachment to she-buffaloes, his strength, his courage and his sense of his own dignity. "He broke off the horn of another buffalo in a fight – actually broke his horn!"

He felt his words did not sound very convincing. Perhaps the man at the scales didn't even know that nature had created nothing stronger than buffaloes' horns. But the man sensed that this fellow up from the country was putting too much weight into his words and decided in any case not to give him a way out.

"Listen, I don't need any lectures from you just now," he interrupted Bardusha sternly. "Meat is meat! Hold the receipt! Get on in!"

"Oh dear, Broadbrow, Broadbrow," said Bardusha and, stepping on to the weighing platform, patted the buffalo on his back for the last time. Then he turned on his heels and without looking back walked to the truck, climbed into the cabin and slammed the door. Meanwhile another truck drove into the entrance to the slaughterhouse with a load of cows. The two trucks drove off, and the Chegem truck turned right at the main road, gathered speed and went off in the direction of Chegem.

Still standing on the weighing platform and feeling its surface moving under his mighty weight, Broadbrow came to the conclusion that it was a bridge. Bridges always gave him that feeling. But where was the river and where did the bridge lead?

The slaughterhouse employee opened the gate into a narrow, board-lined passageway and drove Broadbrow into it. Ahead of him Broadbrow saw a couple of dozen cows standing, tightly packed in, continually shaking and nodding their heads. When he saw the expression in their eyes he recalled seeing the same expression in the eyes of animals in the forest when they sensed the proximity of a predator or believed a predator was near.

A strong smell of blood attacked his nostrils, but the smell of the sea reached him with the same force as before. From this he gathered that, by going into the narrow passageway, he was getting closer to the blood he could not see but was not moving further away from the sea.

Once again, through the clatter of the machines, Broadbrow could make out that unpleasant sound of bones breaking, now much more clearly distinguishable from the noise of the machines. The noise of the machines meant nothing because they were not living things. But the sound of bones being struck meant something because it concerned something alive and painful. Broadbrow now remembered where and when he had heard that sound before. One winter the whole herd had been crossing a bridge covered with ice and one of the she-buffaloes had slipped and fallen down on the bridge with that same sound of bones breaking. And at that point a frightening picture formed in his mind: first they fell down for some reason and then there was blood.

Despite the horror and alarm that the noise of the bones aroused in him, Broadbrow was firmly convinced that Bardusha would come to fetch him. He would lead him out of this place. Broadbrow looked around several times, but there was no sign of Bardusha. Nevertheless, he remained quite convinced that the stockman would come for the good reason that it was so unpleasant here and Bardusha would never keep him for long in such an unpleasant place.

But then Broadbrow suddenly saw something he had often seen in his thoughts and in his sleep. He saw a horse! Whether it was because he had been studying the cows next to him too closely, or because the horse was standing with head hung down, it was only now that he noticed the horse. It seemed to him that the awesome master of that place had been hiding the horse from him until now, so that he had not noticed it. The horse, stretching out its neck and sniffing at the wooden barrier, could detect the smell of the sea. Then Broadbrow saw the horse's big, sad eye and tears trickling down its face.

So that's where he was! The Place Where Horses Weep! He and Bardusha had been tricked! And that was the end of the alarming, confused and lonely period of waiting for Bardusha. Broadbrow realized that he was left in this world with just two salty smells – the smell of blood and death and the smell of the sea and freedom. He now understood that he was alone and that he had only himself to rely on. He immediately felt the might of his own body and his own inner calm. He knew what he had to do.

Meanwhile the gates had opened and another load of cows were

driven into the passageway. They began to crowd him in from behind.
But nobody could push him around now.

With a side blow with his horns he quickly knocked out two boards
and poked his head through the gap. The smell of the sea became
stronger. Hearing the splitting of the boards, the cattle man who had
let the cows into the passageway ran up and grabbed Broadbrow by
the horns and tried to push his head back. It would have been easier
to stop a falling oak tree.

Having got his head into the gap to freedom, Broadbrow dragged
his body after it. The gap was rather narrow, but his desire for freedom
was so great that Broadbrow clambered out, ripping the boards from
the posts.

The smell of freedom grew stronger. But he was now in a big cattle
yard that was intended to hold a large number of cattle that could not
be dealt with at once. About twenty metres ahead he could see a fence
made of oak boards and he realized that he would have to break
through it. Standing still in the middle of the yard he sniffed the air
to determine from which direction the sea smelt strongest and where
he should break through the fence.

When he had broken through the side of the passageway the cows
had rushed out after him and, wild with joy, they started rushing to
and fro, mooing pointlessly. The horse came to life and started galloping round the yard. The noise brought the slaughterhouse employees
to the yard. They leant against the fence and waited to see what would
happen.

The man in charge of the weighing machine had quite lost his head,
but now took charge of himself. He decided that if he could get the
buffalo back into the passageway first it would be easy to restore order.
Having worked in the slaughterhouse for a long time and being
accustomed to handling confused and obedient animals, he was not
in the least afraid of the buffalo. He ran up to Broadbrow just at the
moment when the buffalo was taking aim at the place in the fence
nearest to the sea. The man grabbed him angrily by the tail and tried
to turn him in the direction of the passageway. With unusual agility
the buffalo spun round on the spot, dug his right horn into the man's
left side and tossed him casually over his back. The spectators on the
other side of the fence gasped in unison. The man had fallen to the
ground but managed in the heat of the moment to stagger to his feet
again. Broadbrow was surprised to see him move, turned his head in
the man's direction and was going to finish him off when he suddenly
recalled with the tip of his right horn the unpleasant flabbiness of

the man's flesh. He turned away and immediately forgot about his existence.

Having once more identified the place in the fence closest to the sea he trotted across to it, broke through it with one blow and found himself in the slaughterhouse yard. The upper crossbeam of the part of the fence he had broken through had got caught up in some way between his horns. Annoyed by this, he shook his head, but the piece of wood became more firmly fixed in his horns. So then he shook his head with such fury that the piece of wood broke free and landed some ten metres or so behind him.

When he came out into the cattle yard Broadbrow saw that people backed away from him and even ran off. Saying to himself as he went past them: "They're just small stuff!", he started sniffing in the smell of the sea. A stone wall and metal gates separated the slaughterhouse from the sea. He realized he would have to attack the gates: there was no other way. It was no more than twenty metres to the gates, and he would have to gather top speed as quickly as possible. The black ton-weight hurricane thundered into the gate and bent it back. Broadbrow ran back, took aim again, and, with muscles tensed, made a second run. This time the blow was so powerful that Broadbrow lost consciousness for a moment. The gate was ripped off its hinges, clattered and bumped down the pebbles on the shore and, somersaulting into the sea, lay still.

The sea was spread out in front of Broadbrow. Scattering the pebbles with his feet, he trotted quietly down to it and took a drink of it. Then, having slaked his thirst, he went right into it and swam away.

Twenty minutes later an ambulance drove into the slaughterhouse yard. The man at the weighing machine, his thigh pierced right through, was laid on a stretcher and driven away like a heroic matador.

The cows and the lone horse were again driven into the narrow passageway that had now been repaired. But the slaughterhouse workers took some time to calm down. Many of them stood there at the ruined metal gates and watched the buffalo swimming ever further and further into the distance.

The elderly worker Mesrop kept telling everybody that forty years previously there had been a similar affair. Only on that occasion the buffalo hadn't gone into the sea but had broken his way through some wooden gates leading to the town. After racing round all the streets it had run off into the mountains and hidden in the forest.

Meanwhile Broadbrow kept swimming in the open sea.

The chief engineer at the slaughterhouse then came to an agreement with the chairman of the nearby fishing collective that he would send a motorboat after the buffalo with people who would shoot the animal and tow it back to the slaughterhouse.

In view of the fact that the duties of a chairman of a fishing fleet did not include the capture and shooting of buffaloes swimming in the sea, the man demanded two bullock haunches from the chief engineer in recompense. The chief engineer agreed and the high contracting parties came to terms.

The chairman of the fishing collective now had a task, you might say, of treble difficulty. Finding fishermen not currently at sea was relatively simple. But that they should at the same time be in possession of clear heads was a condition which immediately posed an additional difficulty. And finally one of them had to know how to shoot, and that was something that simply had to be left to chance.

Three hours later everything was in order and the motorboat cast off from the quay and headed for the open sea. The man with the gun sat at the front of the boat and, as he watched the distant dark spot that was the buffalo's head, he was already feeling apprehensive. He knew what the buffalo had done to the man in the slaughterhouse.

Freedom was when, on a hot day, there was a lot of water around. And Broadbrow just went on swimming. He was in a very good mood. In the three hours he had spent in the sea all the passion he had felt in the slaughterhouse had cooled off, and he was now thinking of his beloved Chegem and of how surprised the people and the buffaloes would be when they learnt where he had returned from. It was a good thing that Great Buffalo had existed – the one who had been the first to escape from the Place Where Horses Weep. And it was a good thing that buffaloes preserved his memory. Who could tell whether Broadbrow would have dared to do what he had done if he had not known that there had already been another rebellious and brave buffalo before him?

Having swum about three kilometres in the open sea, Broadbrow began to feel drawn by instinct towards his home and he started gradually turning to the left so that, if he now swam in a straight line, he would cross the sea and finish up near the Chegem hills.

He felt he would have to swim for a long time. For the rest of the day and throughout the night. But there was a great feeling of joy inside him. He knew that he would reach the shore at the place where, long, long ago, as a clumsy buffalo calf, he had first experienced the sea along with his mother and father.

Freedom was when there was a lot of water on a hot day. And all around him, right to the horizon, there was freedom, vast, cool and caressing, and he found that good, very good. At that point he remembered the Sleepy Giant. Broadbrow smiled to himself when he tried to imagine what would have happened to the Sleepy Giant in the sea, if he got stuck in a little Chegem stream. In that part of the sea where the Sleepy Giant drowned even ten buffaloes would probably not be enough to haul him out on to the beach.

A seagull saw Broadbrow's head and horns from a distance and took them for a big branch of a tree. It decided that it was a good place to take a rest, dived down and settled between his horns. "That's fine," Broadbrow thought. "Now we'll see whether the white crows of the sea are any good at pecking ticks out of my head." And by the way, were there terrapins in the sea or not?

When he heard the noise of an approaching motorboat and when he caught sight of the people sitting in it Broadbrow was not worried. The freedom of the sea was so vast that even if the people were bringing the opposite of freedom, they looked so small in their little boat compared with the sea. With such a ridiculous balance of force there was nothing to be worried about. The sound of the motor grew louder.

As the sun was going down pink- and lilac-tinted patches of light spread over the sea. Here and there a fish would jump out of the water and, flashing momentarily in the air, would splash down again into its natural element.

The white houses of the town, the softly wooded slopes above them, the line of smoky mountains that reached up to the limitless sky, and the distant, though to an admirer quite distinguishable, patches of bare cliffs above Chegem – everything was drowned in the light of the setting sun.

ALEXANDER LAVRIN

The Death of Egor Ilich

IT ALL STARTED when Egor Ilich began to squeak. Oh yes, I do beg your pardon, I should make it clear that Egor Ilich is not a person, but a kind of bookcase. An antique bookcase. At one time my wife's late grandfather had bestowed a human name upon it. He had this strange habit of giving objects names. He called the escritoire Femistocles Makedonovich, a decadent, shell-shaped sofa Snandulia Kuzminichna, a solid sideboard made of ebony and stained glass Pyotr Mitrofanovich. Egot Ilich served us, as they say, loyally and faithfully; he withstood everything we packed into him – the tomes of encyclopedias adding up to poods in weight, the collected works of classic authors, which looked like the extended bellows of an accordion, annual subscriptions of thick magazines, and plush albums of family photographs.

But one day the bookcase began to squeal. His age, of course, was considerable, yet not terminal. Judging by the style – something halfway between mock Empire and early modern – he was born at the end of the last century, which means he was ninety, give or take five years. At his time of life, Voroshilov was still able to raise a spoon to his mouth without assistance; not to mention Vernadsky. But, then, Russians are like that: they can never fully accept what nature has given them. A German would, out of sheer pedantry, be prepared to live to a hundred. The same goes for a Frenchman: he races to one hundred like an express train, and does not even notice – perhaps he will suddenly realize in the grave . . .

Let me add that Egor Ilich was made mainly of oak: the veneer, the pilasters, the beading, and the mighty cornice – all this was made of unadulterated oak.

In addition to this, even the beams of Egor Ilich's frame were out of the ordinary, made not from worthless, soft pine, but from strong Russian birch. We might not have paid attention to Egor Ilich's squeaking for a long time, had it not been for our neighbour, the retired Colonel Matvey Petrovich Nechitaylo, who lived on the same landing. He was the first to notice something amiss. On the whole, this is understandable. Even thirty years after his retirement, Matvey

Petrovich religiously kept his professional qualities, chief amongst which was his nose for something out of place.

It was for that nose that the colonel had been valued in his department, which dealt with the supervision of surveillance. The name of this department had changed so many times in the years of Matvey Petrovich's service that as he approached old age he started to confuse the endless abbreviations. "When I served in the EFGHI . . . no, when I served in the PQRST . . . no, then we called it the XYZ of the ABC . . ." Anyway, the devil himself would split his head trying to get his tongue around them.

Let us return, however, to Egor Ilich. After the colonel's remark we started to keep an eye on the bookcase. At first, the squeaks were rather small – not squeaks so much as mouse squeals. But then everything went hurtling ahead like an avalanche, where you cannot only not stop, you cannot even look back. The squeaks grew louder and louder – especially at night. Hearing them, I used to wake up in irritation, but, understanding that it is foolish to get angry with an old man, I would temper my discontent to the size of a thimble, would get up from the divan and would stroke Egor Ilich's rough side covered in maroon bruises of peeling polish. This helped a little and I would go to sleep, only to jump up from the divan again in an hour because of the unbearable sound.

Finally, I thought of ringing Yakov Mironovich Shvartsenbakh, or simply Mironych, as we called our family doctor, who used to treat my late mama, and her father before her.

Mironych belonged to the good old school of Baumgarten and Koshko-Jordansky, who considered that three tablespoons of Cahors wine on an empty stomach and a glass of cognac after lunch would put you back on your feet better than a dozen newfangled drugs with semi-pronounceable names. And in truth, Mironych alone had cured many more sick people than any mandarins' hospital with doormen like bulldogs, carpeted corridors and palm trees on every floor, with electric bells above the beds for calling the staff, and scalpels made from Solingen steel. In the last few years, Mironych had given up his practice and only allowed the families of his oldest patients to consult him; us, in any case, he never refused. I suspected that in his youth he had secretly been in love with my mama. This opinion was strongly reinforced when I noticed how tense the doctor's expression became when he looked at her photograph in the brass frame, her curls like fading lilies in the hair of beauties, as painted in decadent magazines, not guessing that I could see each line of his face reflected in the angled cheval glass, in the antique mirror with glass as thick as a finger, coated with real silver amalgam and not the cheap aluminium powder of today.

To my good fortune Mironych was in Moscow, and, no sooner had he heard the essence of the problem, than he started to get ready to come to our house, as if he had been specially waiting for my call. He arrived in an hour and turned out to be just as round, jovial and good-natured as I remembered him twenty, thirty years back. Mironych's fullness was not a thickened or flattened fullness, like cotton wool which has been stored for a long time, the fullness by which one can immediately spot a bureaucrat in any crowd, but alive and unmoving like quicksilver.

Without wasting time on lengthy greetings, Mironych immediately proceeded to the study and gave Egor Ilich the most detailed examination. First he walked around him, grunted, tapped his finger on the pilasters and sidebeams, then took a plane with a well-sharpened blade out of his scuffed Gladstone bag and here and there carefully scraped the veneer. Having opened the little doors, he put his phonendoscope against their inner side, listened and felt the shelves. We did not take the books out, but then he did not ask us to.

I tried, by the expression on Mironych's face, to guess the final diagnosis, with the same growing anxiety with which a student, having sat his university entrance exams, waits for the decision of the Examiners' Board. But the expression on the doctor's face could have indicated sternness just as much as simple concern. At last he finished the examination and sat down to write out the prescription. I stood beside him, not daring to disturb him with questions.

"Here," he said, replacing the lid of his Chinese pen and handing me the prescription.

"Turpentine and kerosene. Mix them in equal parts and inject all the affected areas three times a day. Have you got a syringe? No? Really, old chap . . . It's an absolute must. Needles should preferably be sterilized."

I took courage and asked: "Doctor, tell me the truth, will he live?"

"There is some hope, but it all depends on the course the illness takes. You see, Vadim, dear boy, it's far gone, and the situation, I won't hide it from you, is dire. For one, the top beams are badly warped, the tenons will hardly stay in their mortises, and to perform an operation at such an age is very, very dangerous. Secondly, and most importantly, Egor Ilich's timber is badly damaged by deathwatch beetle."

Mironych got up from the table and pointed to the bottom of the bookcase. "See how many holes there are? The deathwatch beetle has made the bookcase frame too fragile and now another bout has begun. Complete eradication of deathwatch beetle, unfortunately, is impossible in domestic conditions. To do this, the bookcase has to be placed in a sealed chamber and fumigated with special gases. That kind of chamber is available only in the Fourth Department. About ten years ago, I would have been able to arrange it for you, but me then and me now are two big differences or four small ones, as they say in Odessa . . ."

Mironych raised his head and peered at me over his glasses with tearful, cow-like eyes. "From now on, my son, it's entirely in your hands. If you inject the medicine properly into all the affected areas, perhaps your Egor Ilich will last till doomsday; he may even outlive us, me in any case . . ."

Then we had tea, talked about this and that, remembered old times when things and people were somehow more resilient, more reliable – and if they did die, they did not do it bit by bit, but in direct combat, with open visor, so to speak.

"Oh, if only your bookcase were a big younger." The doctor sighed and his eyes lit up. "I would have prescribed polishing with light-yellow shellac in strong turpentine spirit . . . But now it's too late, his veneer is fragile – it would be burnt through in a minute."

As we were parting – I am ashamed at the thought of it – I started to slip Mironych a twenty-five-rouble note, at which he suddenly took great offence, in spite of the fact that in previous years this had been customary. I assumed that the sum was too small, but this made the doctor even more furious.

"I'm not practising any more!" Puffing heavily, he grabbed his raincoat from my hands. "I didn't come for money. If you had had a sick child, I wouldn't have lifted a finger – that's how it is. But this is quite a different matter. If you want to know –" Here he puffed even harder. "Once upon a time, Egor Ilich saved my life."

I nodded tactfully in no particular direction, suspecting that the old man's mind had, on the contrary, moved in a specific direction – towards the golden age of childhood.

"Your parents probably told you . . ."

"No . . ." I said, with mounting surprise.

"Yes, and how! In '53, some . . . people were looking for me, I couldn't show my face at home. I am, you see, a doctor and a Jew in one. And that's something like being an NCO's widow. Your folks sheltered me. I lived at your place for two months while you, Vadim, were packed off to your aunt's in Leningrad, just in case . . ."

Goodness gracious, it suddenly came back to me how out of the blue one night, without explanation, or anyway, one that made sense to me, I was made to get out of bed and quickly gather my things; a taxi was already waiting in the street and father and I rushed to Leningrad railway station. The winter vacation had only just ended, I had finally signed up for the ice hockey option and had suddenly fallen in love with the redhead Mayka Arkhipova from the next block . . .

I also remembered how during that night I had wanted to go into my father's study to fetch my favourite little bronze cannon, which if you loaded it with powder and pellets could really fire; my mother had seen me at the last moment, and with a stifled scream had grabbed me by the hand. "You can't go in there," she said with such an expression on her face that I didn't even dare ask why.

"I had been living at your place for two weeks," continued Mironych, "but then someone must have informed the authorities that there were strangers in the flat. The district policeman came, accompanied by someone in plain clothes. While Andrey Nikolaevich talked to them through the door, your mama – wise soul – had'an idea: she took the bottom shelf out of the bookcase and pushed me in. As you can see, the lower part of the doors is solid. You can't see in at all. And the upper two thirds are glass, and that's where the psychological effect comes in: if the little doors are made of glass, and behind the glass are books, and what books – nothing but Lenin and Stalin – it wouldn't even cross your mind that there might be a person in there . . ."

I eyed Mironych's figure doubtfully. He noticed and chortled with satisfaction.

"It's the truth! I'm telling the truth . . . In spite of my having been rather plump at that time, though less so than nowadays, I was as supple as a bow. Before the war I even did acrobatics. At one of our AviaChem Organization celebrations I imitated a bowstring: it was a little scene from 'William Tell and Mussolini', you know. And I was bending, would you believe it, I really was. So then, you understand, dear boy, you are to inject the mixture into every opening. And don't forget: use only pure turpentine, no substitutes. I bid you farewell."

Later, that same evening, our neighbour dropped in. He was even more agitated than usual, waving a newspaper, jabbing it with his finger and repeating the words "It should've happened a long time ago! Thank God we've lived to see it." Engrossed in thoughts of Egor

Ilich, I let all that the colonel said go in one ear and out the other. Noticing my distraction and not getting an answer to his questions, Matvey Petrovich snorted like a cat, pulled out his handkerchief, whose coarse embossed thickness and tattered fringe made you suspect that it had been cut from an old tablecloth, and began blowing his nose with a masterfully sustained, heart-rending sound. That was a sign of the greatest indignation.

And here, like novelists of old, we must digress and say a few words about our relations with the neighbour. After we had first moved in, we received Matvey Petrovich quite often; there were weeks when he turned up at our place daily – firstly as an old resident of these parts, who taught us all kinds of little tricks to do with using the shops, the laundry, the dry cleaner's and so on; and secondly, I admit it, in the words of the poet, I felt "somehow both joyful and fearful", as beside me stood a man above whom invisibly soared the shade of Azrael. For there was a time when on his will depended . . . Ah, but why spell it out, there's no need. The colonel's face resembled an over-cooked potato from Tula, when it has only just been taken out of the pot but not yet mashed; he wore a baggy coat of thick cloth, the sleeves threadbare from playing dominoes, but I fancied I saw firm, sculpted cheekbones and a tight-fitting, black leather coat, shiny as if from rain. Against this the wooden holster of a Mauser, with a cover which sprang open on a steel spring, gleamed yellow, like ivory.

Months passed, and the chill in my chest settled and thawed, our evening sittings started to irritate us, as did our neighbour's constant reminiscences about three episodes from his professional life. The first and second were like Siamese twins: in the former, he told us how they had captured a gang of robbers in Marina Roshcha; the latter also involved robbers being captured, only this time in Second Meshch-anskaya Street. The third case was striking: at the time when Matvey Petrovich's department had evolved a crystal-clear, geometically in-spired structure, work began on the crystallization of all the other departments and the colonel (that is, then he still had quite a way to go to being a colonel, but we will call him that for the sake of convenience, as I do not know his rank at that time) devoted himself to his work, night and day, with the passion of a neophyte, although he had already established years of professional service. So then, at that very same time he had someone brought before him for interrogation (Matvey Petrovich put it more delicately: for conversation) who was his exact namesake! Not to the second degree, but to the third.

That means a man whose forename, surname and patronymic fully coincided with his own.

It goes without saying that this was something extraordinary, one of fate's little games, and comrades in the service immediately came up with all sorts of jokes about it. On entering his office, they would deliberately confuse the conversationist (which means the one leading the conversation) with the conversationee (that is, the one who keeps up the conversation according to the demands of the conversationist) and would conclude by pronouncing the surname "Nechitaylo" in a Jewish or Causasian way (since Matvey Petrovich's conversationee had an unmistakably Eastern appearance). A joke is a joke, but the fateful coincidence could reach the ears of top bosses and then who knew what turn events might take? Or again, the restless minds of comrades in the service could embark on a path that went further than just little jokes and quips, and they might venture on to the wide road of innuendo. So, the crystallization of innuendo into certainty was taking place faster than ink dries on an official form – and no one knew that better than Matvey Petrovich.

Something had to be done!

To transfer the conversationee to another conversationist? Dangerous: unnecessary attention. And what motive could one give? All right, let us say a reason could be found, but what good would it do? – the bosses are all one. To believe in the crystal clarity of the namesake conversationee and to hell with him? But that would be putting one's head straight on the block. They would immediately suspect something improper, they would check, and instead of crystal clarity, there would be nothing but wooliness . . . And so on, and so on, and so on . . . Or what about changing one's own surname? Just like that, without a reason? Suspicious. Divorce, in order to remarry and take the wife's surname? Too long, devilishly long, and here every minute counts . . . And at that moment, Matvey Petrovich recounted, wind instruments began to play in his breast – it came to him!

In a second, he was ready and went to see his old mother, who was living out her days in a little village called Metkino near Moscow. He spent the whole day with her and, coaxing cautiously, so as not to overdo it (this is where experience came in handy), little by little, talked the old woman into writing a formal statement to the effect that Matvey, her own son, was fathered not by her lawful husband, Ivan, but by the neighbour, Pyotr, who perished later during the Imperialist War, and that meant that in fairness he should have a different patronymic – not Ivanovich, but Petrovich. And that was precisely what Matvey Petrovich's idea consisted of. Changing his patronymic would be such a delicate matter, hardly noticeable, and at the same time this change would significantly distance him from his namesake-conversationee. True, at first, his mother could not for the life of her understand why he needed this. She became frightened and lamented: "Motya, my darling, really, how can you, how can one renounce one's father's name? He will turn in his grave when he finds out . . ."

"One can, Mother," he retorted harshly, like a whiplash. "Nowadays, everything which is to the good is possible. Until now people lived in superstition; they were afraid of themselves."

"My boy, and how is one supposed to know what is to the good and what is a mere whim?"

"There are special people for this, mother, and they can tell . . . and as for a name, that is a relic from olden days. If necessary, I would renounce my father himself – let alone his name!"

"And me too, Motya?"

"What's it to do with you? I'm speaking figuratively . . ."

And he really did get himself out of the mess! He amended his documents properly with his new patronymic, brought the case of his conversationee to full crystal clarity and lived happily ever after. At first, his new patronymic sounded discordant to his ears, but soon he got used to it. He even began to like the fact that the sound of his patronymic was not soft, like a divan cushion, but hard and booming. And they say that the name Pyotr means "stone". And stone is the same as crystals – the nucleus of society, so to speak.

"So, you see," the neighbour concluded his story, "I am really Ivanovich, but judging by the life I've actually led, I am Petrovich. I sometimes even think that maybe my father *was* Pyotr, the devil knows! Besides, who cares? The main thing is, I was saved – and by my own wits."

And now let us return to that memorable evening when Matvey Petrovich became incensed at my lack of attention. I tried to justify my distraction by the doctor's visit and the discovery of Egor Ilich's illness. What a to-do! The colonel's eyes . . . No, these were not eyes, these were olives – overripe and ready to burst! My neighbour's face turned the colour of over-used carbon paper, his hands began to shake, he contorted himself like the roots of a tree growing over a precipice. For one or two minutes, he said nothing, puffing out his cheeks like a trumpeter in a silent film, but then the floodgates burst.

"Your! Bookcase! Malingerer!" screamed the colonel in telegrammatic style. "Healthy! As! Bull! You could! Plough! With it . . . See! See!"

The colonel jumped over to the bookcase like a cockerel and, with all his might, thumped its wooden side with his fist. I gasped. Poor Egor Ilich wobbled, every fibre creaked, but he managed to withstand it.

"Aha! You see!" Matvey Petrovich waved his iron fist triumphantly in the air. "So much for your invalid! I ask you! A malingerer, that's all he is!"

"But the doctor came today, examined him and said . . ."

"Doctor?" My neighbour's face twisted so much that it seemed to be about to disintegrate. "They're all . . ." Here he added words with which a Russian ear is familiar since childhood, but which do not bear repeating in literature just to pander to the crowd's bad taste.

In short, that evening, the colonel and I parted as virtual blood enemies. The neighbour left and I sat on the divan and thought my sad thoughts. The night was drawing in and the last rays of the sun darted through my study. I lifted my head and there stood Egor Ilich mournfully, as if reading my thoughts, and I felt that his suffering was greater than mine. "Look," he seemed to be saying, "how much trouble I give you. A different owner would have taken me apart or put me in a home for the aged long ago, but you show concern for me, you suffer, you protect me . . ."

"No-o-o, you aren't just a bookcase for me, Egor Ilich, you are a living memory. A memory of those who brought you to life, carved and polished your sides, who put the treasures of wisdom – books – into you, who were reflected in your glass. You're my hope that I won't be forgotten when my time comes . . ."

Here it seemed to me that the glass on Egor Ilich's doors shone in a special way, as if tears were running down them. I wanted to get up and touch him with my hand, but for some reason I did not have the strength. And I, myself, blinked once or twice. And even to this day, I do not know: was good old Egor Ilich really crying or was it all a trick of the evening light? God knows!

Within a week, I managed to get hold of turpentine and kerosene, and also of a syringe, risking a reputation as a drug addict. I started to give injections painstakingly: everything as Mironych instructed. Alas! Egor Ilich got worse and worse. His frame evidently could not withstand the load, the squeaking at night was terrible; any minute now, you felt, he would collapse on to the parquet – a shapeless heap of debris.

To ease, to abate Egor Ilich's suffering, I removed the collected works of Stalin, but this did not help. I had to take Lenin out too. Then came *The History of the Russian State* and, a bit later, slimmer volumes had to go, like *Memoirs of a Reformed Robber*, Emin-Agi Borchalinsky, a brochure by L. Shkolnik, *The Odessa Monte-Carlo, The Life of Collective Farmer Vasyunkina – In Her Own Words, The Correspondence of Nicholas the Second and the Great Princes* and many, many others – at first glance, an ill-matched collection put together by chance not, in reality, full of that mysterious meaning by which all occurrences in life are bound.

Meanwhile, the illness became more acute. One night, Egor Ilich felt so bad that I had to call an ambulance. Oh! Our so-called "free medicine"! First of all, the ambulance took a full forty minutes to arrive; secondly, the doctor happened to be some kind of novice, almost a student doing his training. He did not even have a hammer or a pair of nail pincers! Thank God that the nurse's bag happened to contain some spare casein powder. She dissolved it quickly in cold water and, after adding sawdust, rubbed it into the most visible cracks on Egor Ilich's body. But they could not reduce the squeaking. They blamed this on the fact that nowadays they were given three times less PVA glue because of the increase in glue-sniffing. The doctor even told me that because of the PVA shortage, an ebony bureau, which could almost have been the work of Mazhorel himself, died before their very eyes and they had been unable to do anything about it. "Absolutely nothing!" added the nurse with a sob.

After the ambulance had left, I stood on the balcony for a long time and smoked . . .

Ah, Russia, my Russia, unforgettable bird-troika! You have taken flight like a seagull, and nobody can bridle you, you race on, your hooves thundering, sleigh bells ringing, the coachman shouting like crazy, and you cannot hear my quiet voice over the noise. I do not ask you to give me bread made with poppy seeds, or sugar cake, nor Central Committee rations, nor mansions in Moscow. I ask only one thing: listen to your little children who have fallen out of the cart on a sharp bend, who have been left to lie there like newborn kittens whose eyes have not yet opened. Slow down, turn your face to them, for they are also the flesh of your flesh, have suckled your milk, have gurgled up at you from their cradles. Do not turn them away from your kingdom, give them bread and medicine. I know, I know that in your rushing forward, in your eternal striving, there is no place for anything earthly, temporal; you even change your coachman on the way! But still, try to remember your poor fledglings, the children of the Arbat in their white clothes, punks and heavy-metal fans, milkmaids and tractor drivers, poets and drug addicts, Afghanistan veterans and even Egor Ilich himself – remember them!

The bouts of illness became more frequent. The bookcase trembled, the glass-covered doors shook as if a heavy goods train were passing by. The ambulance became a regular guest at our house; there were nights when we called it three or four times.

At night, I kept guard in the study by Egor Ilich's side; by day, I slept it out. I had to take unpaid leave to do this. My wife, a good enough person, could not bear it in the end.

"Why are you fussing around this bookcase like a mother hen?" she used to say. "If you can't bring yourself to throw him out, let's give him to Tolik and Alka. Tolik has golden hands, he'll dismantle Egor Ilich and make some shelves out of him. Don't you remember how deftly he fixed the top section of the sideboard above the toilet?"

"But the bookcase would die!" I retorted.

"So what? None of us is immortal," my wife replied calmly. "Let the dead bury their dead, we must think of the living. Do you think at your age, and with your weak heart, these all-night vigils are good for you? God forbid, if anything were to happen to you, how would your son and I live? Did you think about that? OK then, if you don't want to give him to Tolik and Alka, put him into a home for the aged."

"That would be certain death!"

"That's none of our business. Signed away – and off your back . . ."

"My God, I didn't know you were so cynical!"

"You'd be cynical in my place! The flat's been turned into a madhouse and you still aren't satisfied!"

I looked at the bookcase. A silent plea was reflected in Egor Ilich's glass. It even seemed to me that the little curtains behind the doors were fluttering with timidity and humiliation: "Forgive me, I myself understand that I've outlived my time, but for the love of God, don't turn an old man out of his home . . ."

"No," I cruelly cut her short. "No Toliks, no homes for the aged. Remember what Gogol said: an example is more effective than a rule. Today we drive Egor Ilich out, tomorrow our children throw us out."

"Well, then I'll leave," rejoined my wife with feeling. "I'll live at my mother's until your bookcase gives up the ghost."

With all these problems, there were a couple of occasions on which I did not greet my neighbour in passing. This was taken by him to be a sign of the highest degree of contempt on my part. Umbrage became the colonel's driving force. He started to churn out letters to everyone full of accusations directed at me – accusations so absurd that I do not know where he could have got them from, unless he copied them from Kafka. Time and again I was visited at home by officials – either it was the local policeman, or a delegation from the House Committee with the house manager, or an official from the district Social Security office. It goes without saying that they all understood the absurdity of my neighbour's claims. But paper is paper and you have to reply. And besides, in our fatherland, there is no smoke, however sweet and pleasant, without fire, as we all know. So, all those visitors who came on plausible pretexts – "Don't you have leaks in your flat?"; "Isn't there someone living here illegally?"; or "Maybe someone old and lonely needs help?" – all of them without fail endeavoured to enter my study to get at least a brief glimpse of Egor Ilich.

These comings and goings lasted about a month. But then, on one such night, I think Saturday/Sunday, I suddenly woke up in a cold sweat. It was stuffy in the flat, but I felt as if I were wrapped in an icy sheet. With a pounding heart, I got up from the divan, feeling such pressure in my temples it was as if my head were submerged in the depths of the ocean in some kind of sea bed hollow. I could sense, without even looking at Egor Ilich, that something was wrong. And so it was: just as I turned my head, there was an indescribable crash and a scraping noise. Before my very eyes the veneer, the veneer which had been torn apart, curled up like a snake; the carved panels flew off with the crack of a pistol shot; the intarsias popped out; the pilasters slanted and the glass doors exploded . . . A horrific internal rumbling came from the gut of the bookcase; withered beams sprang out from their brackets; everything started to fall apart.

Frozen with horror, I watched the agony. It seemed that nature herself was taking part. Complete darkness yawned from behind the windows. The trees rustled. The wind beat against the glass with sabre-like thrusts. Somewhere above us, one floor above, an unsecured little window flapped; on the fifth or sixth bang, the glass broke. I gave a start. Jumping up from the divan, I ran to Egor Ilich. I tried to hold him up, to prop him up with my shoulder at least, but it was too late. The walls of the bookcase came completely apart and fell down with a crash. One of the little doors bounced sideways and hit me very painfully on the knee. Trying to catch it, I misjudged my movement and managed only to cut my hand on the splinters of glass. In the heat of the moment, I did not notice, but when I turned on the light, I saw that the remnants of the bookcase were spattered with blood. Still in a frenzy, I hurriedly bandaged up my hand and, suffocating with the stifling heat, ran to the window. I wrenched it open and at that very moment, as if it had been waiting for this, there was a flash of lightning and a roar of thunder. After this, there was a torrential downpour . . .

Gusts of wind threw handfuls of spray into my face, but I was afraid to move away from the window or turn my back to it, because I did not want to meet the glassy gaze of the dead Egor Ilich . . .

In the morning, while I was bustling around preparing all sorts of things – trying to get hold of some nails and some polish to make Egor Ilich look decent, phoning my wife, friends, the funeral parlour, and so on and so forth – the neighbours from the flat opposite came round with the news that during that very same night the colonel had also died! I took this news calmly, although with slight surprise: I had always thought that such people did not die, or that they went into the forest to die, like dogs do. Matvey Petrovich's death was discovered by chance: the previous evening, he had forgotten to bolt the door of his flat, and at night the door had blown open in the draught. In the morning, one of the neighbours had noticed the open door and called the colonel, but had got no reply. Sensing something was wrong, the neighbour had entered the flat and discovered Matvey Petrovich lying on the kitchen floor, face down with a piece of paper clenched in his mouth and a wildly twisted hand.

In some sense one could say that Matvey Petrovich had been lucky. Had he bolted the door, he would have been lying there till the end of the century, because he had lived a solitary life and there were practically no people willing to visit him. The colonel's only relative, his nephew Nikita, lived in the back of beyond, either in Chertanovo, or Biryulevo, and he used to turn up at his uncle's barely once a year.

The colonel's death completely reconciled me to him. I even began to help Nikita, who had quickly been found and had come, with advice on the organization of the funeral, for it became clear that he did not have the slightest idea how to go about it.

In those hours, I also valued good advice. It became clear that one could not get a place in a single cemetery in Moscow to bury Egor Ilich. The only thing suggested was cremation – and even that, God knows where, at some Nikolo-Arkhangelsk crematorium behind the ring road: this did not suit me at all. Firstly, I did not want Egor Ilich to be burnt according to a pagan custom, against the tradition of his forebears; secondly, three times a year – on the day of the bookcase's

death, at Easter and on Parents' Remembrance Day – I would have
to make a great deal of effort to get to that Nikolo-Arkhangelsk.

For old times' sake, I went to the Vostryakovsk Cemetery, where
about ten years ago I had buried a comrade, but the old director had
been imprisoned, and the new one was a miserable jobsworth; hardly
had I managed to open my mouth when I was showed out of the yard.
It is true that as I was leaving, one of the workmen caught up with
me and gave me to understand that, in principle, he could help me in
my misfortune, but he quoted such an unbelievable sum to grease his
palm that I was lost for words.

Returning home, I found Nikita in financial distress. Contrary to
rumours, the nephew had not managed to find in his uncle's flat either
the hidden money box, or a stocking full of gold sovereigns, or a
savings book with fifteen thousand in fixed investments – not anything
at all, in fact.

In general, Nikita, who had been counting a great deal on that
money box, had to fork out the money for the funeral himself. He
returned from the funeral parlour totally defeated. It transpired
that they only had two-and-a-half-metre long coffins in stock with
some kind of special silk brocade – little silver snakes on a golden
background – costing one hundred and twenty-one roubles, thirty-
seven kopecks. These thirty-seven kopecks particularly outraged
Nikita.

"Judases! Blasphemers!" Nikita poured his indignation out to the
whole entrance. "They fleece the dead of such amounts. Shame on
them!"

I tactfully pointed out that it was not actually the dead who were
being fleeced, but the living, because it is not the dead themselves who
pay, but their still living relatives.

"What's the difference!" said Nikita, waving his hand dismissively.
"Nowadays you can't tell who's alive and who's dead. It's easier to die
oneself, anyway, than to bury someone else . . . What an idiotic life!
And I still have to order the funeral repast and pay for the bus, the
grave diggers, the orchestra . . ."

I expressed surprise at this.

"For goodness' sake," I said, "if your expenses matter so much to
you, why be so extravagant as to hire an orchestra?"

"Well, you see, I was told that my uncle must be buried at the
Novodevichy Cemetery as befits his rank, and it would be embarrassing
not to have an orchestra there."

My wife took me aside. "Listen," she whispered, "I've thought of something. We can easily come to some agreement with this milksop. Suggest that he bury his uncle in our bookcase."

"My God! What are you saying?" I was shocked.

"Be quiet!" hissed my wife. "I've kept my head, but you seem to have lost yours. You seriously hope to get a place at a cemetery? Who the hell are you – *nomenklatura*, a merchant, a speculator? You see, there you are. And besides, work it out: for two, the expenses are halved."

"Why not?" I suddenly thought. "Perhaps there is something in what my wife says."

All this fuss confused me so much that I clutched at my wife's idea as at a straw. I took Nikita by the elbow and led him aside, away from inquisitive ears.

"Listen, my friend," I said stealthily, ashamed of my sugary voice, "I understand you are not well off."

"Indeed not," admitted the nephew quickly.

"So what if I suggest the following to you: we bury your uncle in our bookcase. Don't rush your answer, just think what advantages there'd be . . . You won't have to pay anything for the coffin and secondly . . . secondly, I'd be paying half the funeral expenses."

Nikita, open-mouthed, painfully tried to work out if there were not some dirty trick behind it, but one could tell that my suggestion seemed highly tempting to him.

"Yes . . . But, how can you have . . ." he muttered hesitantly at last. "Two in one grave, who'll allow such a thing? And a bookcase instead of a coffin is somehow odd . . ."

"But they won't lie separately. They'll be one inside the other," I explained to Nikita, "and we won't need permission. I'm telling you that as a former lawyer. You are the owner of a corpse and you have the right to bury it inside any object you please. And as for the bookcase, don't think twice – it has the shape of a typical coffin! Even marshals aren't buried in such coffins. Oh, why talk about it . . . Come, I'll show you . . ."

No, Egor Ilich did not shame us, even after his death. Even his remains, tacked together by me, looked so imposing that Nikita was impressed. He was particularly taken by the pilasters with their mother-of-pearl intarsias – which is further proof that tinsel and trinkets have more power over man than the actual object they adorn.

The matter was settled.

But, as they used to say in the olden days, no sooner do you make a plan that you have to make a hundred modifications.

On the very day that Nikita went to the XYZ Department to correct some essential paperwork, it suddenly transpired that the colonel's papers had either been lost, or placed for safe keeping in some archive from which it was impossible to retrieve them – the lion will lie down with the lamb and be led by a child first.

There and then, Nikita's mood of euphoria changed into one of melancholy, and you can hardly imagine the depth of my own sadness. In my thoughts I was already feasting my eyes upon the noble, ichorous walls of the Novodevichy Cemetery with white flower ornaments and a guard at the entrance, the austere rows of graves with their majestic pyramids of marble, granite and labradorite in the new grounds and the picturesque little chapels, crypts and tombs in the old part of the cemetery, which is closer to the monastery . . . The fact that Egor Ilich would be lying in the cemetery where the remains of Gogol and Bulgakov had been laid to rest made me tremble with a sense of awe . . .

The blow which destroyed my hopes was so strong that I remember all the rest only vaguely, as if in a dream. But, even had I retained a crystal-clear memory, how could one describe, even using the Russian language, the abundant, blessed Russian language, all the chaos which came afterwards instead of music?

What Marquez could describe how, after prolonged ordeals and humiliations, we at last found a cemetery rat at Vagankovo who sold us a plot on the sly, one which was being kept for sale under a false label reading "Major Petrov"; how, ten minutes before the body was supposed to be carried out, the funeral parlour rang and informed us that the bus we had ordered had broken down and there were no other cars available, because some buses were out on the job, and, as for the remaining ones, the staff at the car park had gone off to the collective farm to dig potatoes, and "generally, the whole of this month we've been in such a sweat, such a sweat, just imagine, out of six promised accumulators, they sent us only two, we haven't got any sleeve couplings, we haven't got any stuffing boxes, we've forgotten what an axle looks like and Ivan Gavrilovich couldn't care less – he has half a year till his pension, that's why he muddles through any old how, but we'll send you a bus, don't worry, not now, but a bit later, in about three hours, when number 48-74 returns, it just left for Mitino, so you'll have to wait"; how, after sending the undertakers to the place where they take their clients, Nikita and I dashed out into the street and, for half an hour, tried to stop a vehicle in the rain; how, at last, we got a furniture van from the Mostrans agency and arranged, for an enormous sum, with the driver and haulers for the transportation of the bookcase; how, after getting into a taxi, we told the lorry carrying the bookcase to follow us; how the driver, drunk as a lord, took off at the Nizhnaya Maslovka, driving away from us, off towards the Bolshaya Akademicheskaya, having decided that the bookcase had to be delivered to the second-hand furniture shop; how, after arriving at the shop, they unloaded the bookcase and took it on to the sales floor; how, at that very moment, the bookcase doors opened and out fell the unfortunate colonel in his army cap and barely worn full dress coat; how the senior goods manageress, an elderly woman, mother of three, fainted on seeing him and an ambulance had to be called; how, in the meantime, we went round the whole of Moscow in search of the lost lorry; how we were cursed and scolded by the grave diggers and the musicians who had also arrived at the cemetery and also by the staff in the canteen where the funeral repast was booked . . . No, one cannot describe all that . . . In defeat I throw away my fountain pen . . .

I will say only that we located the bookcase and took it to the cemetery, with the colonel inside, just before midnight. Of course, everyone was long gone, and only Nikita and I, plus two workers who had stayed on for a big inducement, stood at the graveside.

I came to my senses only as the bookcase with the colonel inside was being lowered into the grave pit on ropes, and clods of clay started to thud on to Egor Ilich's wooden body. Nikita shone the torch down into the grave, at the risk of falling into it. I was watching with indifference . . . when suddenly something inside me turned over. Heat, as if from a bonfire, hit me in the face. For an instant, I felt the earth yawning at my feet, breathing at me the horror of a frightful abyss, the bottom of which no voice could reach. Everything around me became unsteady, shaky like the ocean bed; my gaze blurred, as if a rubber glove had been pulled over my face . . .

God Almighty!

I suddenly understood that it was not Egor Ilich, but I, who was lying at the bottom of the grave – yes, exactly, I. Look: the same nose, cheeks, eyes, and even the lenses in my glasses are cracked in the same way! And the colonel, in his severe full dress coat, with a stony face, the colour of ivory, rested inside my belly . . . And now they would cover me with earth, load a thousand-pood burden on to my chest, and the colonel would toss around in my belly, trying to find a comfortable position for the eternal sleep. His knees would lean against my insides, so bony, so sharp that the pain from them would be stronger and more unbearable than the pressure from above. And nowhere could I escape from that pain, for until the transformation of my last atom into the eternal substance of the earth, until that time, I would not be able to be rid of the colonel inside me.

"Stop! Stop!" I shouted, returning to my senses. I rushed to the diggers, grabbed the shovel from one of them and pushed the other out of the way. "Get the bookcase out! Immediately!" My voice faltered.

"Some schizo!" The grave diggers grimaced in puzzlement and looked questioningly at Nikita, who was settling the account with them.

"I'll pay! Twice, three times – whatever you want," I kept shouting. "Just leave the bookcase in peace!"

The way I looked – an expensive suit and tie, totally covered in clay, my eyes bulging, the shovel raised – was probably so absurd and frightening that they did not dare contradict me. Perplexed, Nikita said nothing. The grave diggers, at whom I immediately thrust twenty-five roubles each, promptly arranged the ropes, lifted the bookcase out and removed the colonel . . .

God knows what would have happened next, but fortunately, it became clear that one of the workmen had a good pine coffin stored away, hidden in the granite workshop, there at the cemetery, and if that was how things were, he was prepared to part with it for a goodly sum. "I was keeping it for myself," he added. "But, what can you do? . . . Use it." However, he took more than a fair price; but thanks to this, Matvey Petrovich, at last, attained peace.

I do not know if it is worth continuing . . . However, my duty as a storyteller obliges me to say a few words more.

A week later, I also buried Egor Ilich – at an old cemetery in Zvonnitsa, a suburb of Moscow where my decrepit aunt lives. There are many little suburban houses there, which have grown waist deep into the earth, like heroes from epic folklore; the air is filled with a marvellous pine freshness. It is quiet and peaceful in the streets, as it can be in a small provincial town where the iron heel of MinAgFish or the Coal and Oil Extraction Ministry has not yet reached. True, the roads are covered with asphalt, but cars seldom pass through; you are more likely to see a nanny goat chewing up a club poster in front of the sunken, leaning, two-storey, bourgeois, Empire-style town hall, or five geese strutting along to the general store situated in the derelict little church with those lancet windows in the very top of the apse,

due to which the light falls on to the counters as straight as a carpenter's
plumb line.

Several times a year, early in the morning, I set off for the Paveletsk
railway station. At that time of day, there are few people on the train,
and I manage to sit right by the window. The whistle blows. The train
jerks and gathers speed quickly. Depots, warehouses, grey houses,
more depots . . . I do not mind. I am patient. A little further and I
will be able to see the winter field, and beyond it the thin black edge
of the forest. I lean back against the seat. In my hands I hold a little
bunch of dry heather. If you put it to your ear and squeeze it gently
in your hand, you can hear a light rustling – as if a butterfly is beating
its wings against the windowpane.

Translated by Sylva Rubashova and Milena Michalski

VALERY POPOV

Dreams on an Upper Berth

WHAT A TRAIN! Where've they got it from? Given it a three-day roll
in mud, from the look of it. Funny thing is, though, where would
they have got the mud? It's been snow all round for ages. Kept some
back from summer, clearly. Still, this is no time for pondering finer
points: everyone's started edging down the platform, the numbering
of the coaches being unexpectedly back to front! My *Coach 1* is last.
There's not enough platform, so I have to climb down, run along and
haul myself up by the handrails. The attendant, ominously unshaven
and wearing a kind of old woman's cardigan, stands impassive in the
rear vestibule of the coach. I didn't exactly expect him to be in a
snow-white tunic, but still . . .

"This a sleeping car?" I asked hesitantly, surveying the gloomy
vestibule, with its little door leading to the heating boiler and a tangle
of rusty pipes.

The attendant looks at me long and hard, grins darkly, offers no
reply. Strange! I enter. Good sort of coach to travel to prison in – life
ahead wouldn't seem so bad. The shabby berths, the musty smell, call
to mind the grimmest moments of my life – not so much those past,
as those to come.

On top of which, although they're supposed to be two-berth compartments, a two-berth being what I've paid for, calmly and without
so much as a batted eyelid, I'm put instead into what is clearly a
four-berth one. What's the game? I head smartly for the attendant,
but halfway, stop dead. It's not worth it. He'll take another look at
my ticket, and that, as they say, could be a bit fraught. The fact is, it's
marked *Complimentary*. It was got for me by a little old man with a
stick, to save me queueing. (The queue had been enormous, and no
tickets were to be had.) And it wasn't until he'd taken my money and
hopped it that I noticed what it said, and woke up. But the little old
man was no more. He, as a bona fide railwayman, was entitled to a
complimentary ticket, but I was not. So better not to widen the field
of enquiry. We're none of us so beyond reproach that we can go
asserting our rights, which is why they do what they like with us. One
minus point after another. But one small, if dusty, plus is the window.

I try to wipe it, but the grime's chiefly on the outside. The main thing is to have a bit of warmth. The heating apparatus in the vestibule looks terribly complicated and antediluvian. I blow on my fingers. Our attendant's thick cardigan inspires increasing apprehensions, as does also his failure to shave. I slide the creaking door and go out into the vestibule. Immediately behind me, also determined on action, comes the passenger from the next compartment.

"Will there be any tea?" he enquires of the attendant in friendly fashion.

"No," says the attendant hoarsely, without turning his head on its fat neck, and you could print the word on the cloud of steam that issues with it.

"What do you mean, *no*?"

"Just no. Can't heat without coal, can you?"

"So there's no coal."

"Just imagine," he grins.

"No coal on a railway!" I exclaim. "Well, go along to the engine."

"Bit late. Steam locomotives have been out for donkey's years."

"And this coach is from the days of steam," I venture to suggest.

The attendant turns and looks at me, as if these are the first words of sense he's heard. "It is."

"So why use these coaches?"

"Got any others?" grins the attendant, again taking up his position in the door giving on to the empty vestibule.

"But in this snow," says my neighbour, nodding towards the window, "we'll freeze."

"That's your worry," says the attendant, who couldn't care less.

"Outrageous!" I cry, unable to contain myself. "Which coach is the train commander in? Not this one, I take it."

With a sudden squeal the door of the service compartment slides back, and out looks a red-faced little sailor in naval striped vest. I wonder if he's a fare dodger.

"Hi," he says. "What the hell's the matter with you? We'll get there somehow. We're men, not mice!"

Shamed, I and my neighbour return to our freezing compartments. Probably not worth tackling the train commander: the question of my dubious ticket might arise. At last, the train eases creakingly forward. Patches of light become elongated and vanish, a process which speeds up until the light comes to an end, and all is plunged into darkness.

"Is there," I wonder, "such a thing as electricity in this compartment?" At which a ceiling bulb glows faintly, revealing tatty empty bunks and the steam from my mouth. I sit for a while, arms clasped about my chest, rocking gently. But with my blood congealing and a constant pricking of the skin, which may for all I know be the precursor of frostbite, I can't stay sitting for long. No! Stupid to wait patiently for the end! I leap up.

Not all the coaches will be so cold. Some may even be heated. There'll be a stove in the dining car, if nowhere else; after all, that's where they do the cooking, isn't it? Just so. I recall seeing the words *Dining Car* slap in the middle of the train. I open the door, and crouching, negotiate the swinging, clanking crossover between coaches. The next coach is even colder. People wrapped in blankets sit motionless in dark compartments, not wanting, for some reason, to turn on the light, which I can also appreciate. The only signs of life are little puffs of exhaled steam. The next coach is exactly the same. What *is* this? What year are we in?

I go on, looking neither to left nor right, just automatically opening, for the umpteenth time, doors for my chilling crossing, standing in the freezing cold, warily crouched until, managing to get the next door open, I end up in the next coach, which is equally dark and chilly. And suddenly, on the crossover from one coach to the next, I get stuck. I tug at a door, but it doesn't give. Clearly it's locked. The iron plates forming the crossover clank, one sliding under the other, and then sharply away, sideways, beneath my feet. Panic, from the feet up. I tug and tug. The door doesn't open. I turn my head. Even more terrifying to have to go back. I hammer on the door. Finally a face appears behind the glass, stares out into the darkness, and wags from side to side to indicate nothing doing. Again I hammer.

"What d'you want?" the face shouts at last, opening a tiny chink.

"This the dining car?"

"It is. What d'you want?"

"What do I want?" I tug the door. "Can't you see?"

"It's out of the question!" The face is that of a female. "We're being inspected!"

She tugs the door. I get a hand around it – let them crush it if they want.

"How can you be, with no customers?" I yell.

She stares, interested. Clearly that line of thought has never occurred to her.

"All right, come in." She edges open the door just a tiny bit.

I burst in. Never have I had such difficulty, or been exposed to such risk, in getting into an eating place. It's no warmer than my coach, but warmer than the space between coaches.

To my surprise, a man in black tail coat, starched dicky and velvet bow tie, hair sleeked into a side parting, rises from a little table apart, and comes to meet me. "Welcome," he says, indicating the row of empty tables with a smooth gesture of the arm.

Lost in wonderment, I take a seat. Was it really me who, a minute ago, was darting between coaches? And now dignity, peace . . .

"In just a moment you will be brought the menu. We are under inspection for quality of service. Any observations, however trivial, should kindly be made to me immediately."

"Of course," I reply in the same cordial tone.

With dignity and a dead straight back the head waiter retires to his little table. Twenty minutes later an unshaven waiter approaches.

"Goulash," he says, as if confusing which of us should do the ordering.

"Will that be all?" I ask, making the rejoinder usually made by the waiter.

"Cold goulash," he says in amplification.

"Why cold?" I ask stupidly.

"Stove's not working," says the waiter with a shrug.

I look in the direction of the head waiter. He, as before, sits towering above his little table, face set but radiant, but not looking my way.

"All right, then," I say, surrendering.

The dining car's gloomy and cold. The dark window shows nothing but reflections.

At length the waiter appears and plonks a plate in front of me. A scatter of vermicelli creates a crater-like rim. The crater itself is void. For a while I sit numbed, then charge over to the head waiter, whose face is now set in a smile.

"Call this goulash?" I exclaim. "Where's the meat?"

Inclining his irreproachable parting, the head waiter proceeds to the kitchen regions, where there's an immediate rumpus in which can be distinguished the voices of waiter and head waiter. The latter then appears wearing the same smile. He removes the plate from my table. "I'm sorry. You shall be brought another immediately. The waiter tells me that he was attacked by someone in the dark corridor by the kitchen, and that this someone snatched the meat from the goulash."

"Where does that get me?" I mutter, freezing once more into immobility before the totally dark window. At last, forty minutes later, I get the urge to stir. "Well, where's my waiter?" I enquire of the immobile head waiter.

Again he politely inclines the perfect parting and disappears into the kitchen regions.

"Been arrested," he announces, returning with a cheerful smile.

"What do you mean 'arrested'?"

"And rightly so," says the head waiter severely, as if I too was involved. "It emerges that it was he who snatched and ate the meat from the goulash."

"So that's all right, then," I say. "But what now?"

"Now," he declares with dignity, "you shall be sent another waiter immediately."

"Thank you," I say.

After the second waiter takes my order, I wait for over an hour. He, of course, may well be straight, but *where is he*?

"Arrested," the head waiter informs me without waiting to be asked.

"Him too?" My legs are being literally cut from under me.

"Needless to say," he continues, "they've all turned out to be members of the same gang. We only needed to make sure, and we have."

"Well, of course, that's wonderful," I mutter, "but what about my goulash?"

He regards me with scorn. All this going on, and me talking nonsense.

"I will endeavour to find out," he says coldly and not particularly reassuringly, and disappears into the kitchen regions.

An hour later, losing patience, I poke my head in. "Head waiter about anywhere?" I enquire of a man in a severe-looking suit wearing an armband.

"Arrested," he says with a weary but contented sigh. "Turned out to be the head of the criminal gang that bossed it here."

"Wonderful!" I say. "But any chance of getting something to eat?"

"Everything's under seal," says the inspector severely. "But if you want to be a witness, come in."

"Thank you."

I sit in the kitchen regions. The waiters are led in in chains, and taken off somewhere, then, elegant as ever, the head waiter. I'm so hungry, but that's clearly something it's not appropriate to be.

I plod back through the coaches.

"Something else I could do with at the moment . . . How about here?" I wonder, desperately tugging at the toilet door.

"Locked," says my neighbour, appearing like a ghost behind me.

"What? Permanently?" I ask, enraged. "And how about that one?" I nod towards the far end.

"Also locked."

"But why?"

"The sleeping car attendants keep chickens there."

"In the toilet?"

"Where else can they?"

"But what for?"

"Apparently they were going to deliver them to the dining car, a few at a time, but the dining car's undergoing inspection, they say. So that's out."

"What's to be done, then?"

"Nothing."

"How do you know it's chickens?"

"By the sound," is the melancholy reply.

Despondent, I sit in my compartment for a bit. But that's a quick way of turning into a snowman. I must move, do something. I set off again for the attendant's compartment. As I approach, the door squeals open and out comes the little sailor, red as a beetroot, bare, powerful arms protruding from a sleeveless vest. With a jaunty wink, he turns to the dark, snow-streaked corridor window, and in a thick falsetto sings:

> "Farewell, farewell, r-r-rocky mountains,
> The sea summons us to great deeds!"

I attentively hear it out, then slide back the attendant's door regardless.

"Whadya want?" he snaps, looking up from his table.

Their compartment, if not warm, is at least fuggy. The table's heaped with the remnants of a banquet. The walls are insulated with blankets, the window's blocked with one.

"Where's the train commander?" I ask, through lips glued together by frost.

"I'm train commander," says the little sailor brightly, entering the compartment. "What's your problem?"

"No problem."

I go back to my compartment, climb on to my upper berth – which at least has less cold window by it – muffle myself in my blanket, which has no warmth to it, and freeze. Luxuriant scenes of the south float past. Those who say that freezing is quite a pleasant form of death are right. And only one troublesome and, as it turns out, salutary thought prevents my sinking into that blissful state. I've left the dining car without paying! For bread which I'd smeared with mustard! Those very kopecks are maybe playing some part in the investigation. Who can tell? Of course, the question arises whether there is any need for honesty towards sharks, but I, purely selfishly, still think there is.

Creaking like a snowman, I climb down from my bunk, and again make my way from coach to coach over the clashing, blizzard-bound crossovers. In the vestibule I encounter an inspector of inspectors of inspectors, as can be seen from his three armbands.

I enter the dining car. They're all sitting at tables singing: inspectors as trebles, inspectors of inspectors as baritones, and inspectors of inspectors of inspectors as basses, all fairly harmoniously. And here, timidly joining in, sit the waiters in chains and the head waiter, there having so far been no stop.

"Whadya want?" asks an inspector of inspectors of inspectors quickly, intimating the pause between lines of the song to be a brief one, and the desirability of conforming to the fact.

"Here." I pull out ten kopecks. "I had bread and mustard. I want to pay."

"People like him," says the head waiter with feeling, clearly trying to ingratiate himself, "should have monuments raised to them in their lifetime." He looks at the inspectors, clearly offering to engage in that noble task here and now.

"Fine. I'm agreeable to a monument, so long as it's not here, in the diner," I mutter, and set off back.

At which point I notice that the train is braking. The coaches are juddering, banging against each other. Getting from one to another is becoming even more complicated.

In our vestibule, I encounter the attendant in grubby, tattered attire, with a sack on his back. He leaps from the steps and disappears, clearly setting off in search of feed for his chickens.

This no longer troubles me. I have done my duty towards humanity. I can take my rest in my sarcophagus. I climb up and roll myself into a ball. The train remains stationary for a very long time. Not a sound. Liberated, my consciousness takes wing. Really, why should I attempt to bring order to the railway, which I come into contact with once a year, when my own life is complete chaos, when I can't even establish the least vestige of order in my own house! Three years ago I suddenly realized that on the other side of my wall there was a vast empty area, and boldly tried to get permission to make it my own, to create a sitting room there, a study. Then I worked out how much it would cost me, and tried to get my application turned down. Anyone observing me would have been entitled to cry: "What an idiot!" I put in any number of formal letters saying: "Beg that my request be rejected . . ." I scrippled a heap of anonymous letters to myself. What if they were to take away what I had!

I subside into slumber. Suddenly I see myself in some courtyard, with dark figures all round, closing in . . . Any minute they'll be thumping me. "Let them try!" flashes the triumphant thought. "They don't know, the fools, that it's all just a dream." The courtyard vanishes. I'm in the dining car. For some reason it's full of flowers. Floating past the windows is the torrid south. My friend the head waiter appears in a dazzlingly white tail coat.

"Your food," he announces in triumph, "is not served!"

A minute later he emerges in an orange tail coat.

"Your food," he announces, "is again not served!"

"Maybe there's something I *could* have," I beg.

"Two janitor coffees!" he commands, flinging open the door to the gleaming kitchen.

Suddenly I have the sensation of flying in a state of complete bliss, stretched at full length on my berth, having thrown off the heavy blanket with my feet. Warm? I'll say!

So the attendant, when we stopped, was going not for chicken feed, but for coal. Wonderful. Better, in that case, not to wake. Now for pleasant dreams.

In my next dream I'm in a beautiful toyshop, and in the shape of a young frog, being inflated by way of a tube, harder and harder.

All is plain. Irresistibly so. Got to get up.

The attendant is sitting in the vestibule on an upturned bucket, eyes blissfully screwed up in contemplation of the orange flame in the furnace. At my approach, he turns, barely able to focus after staring into the flame. "All well?"

"Wonderful," I cry. "OK to pop into the toilet?"

"Go right ahead," he says, softening in the warmth. "Only don't upset the chickens." He proffers the key.

"Why should I do that?" I exclaimed in all sincerity.

I burst into the toilet. The chickens, taking fright at first, calm down, and resume their resting places, regarding me out of beady little eyes in cocked heads. "Who," I wonder, "do I seem to be, to these representatives of what is, in essence, a different civilization? Do I worthily represent humanity? Will they," I wonder, "be upset by what I'm going to do here?" No, they're not.

Completely happy, I return to my berth, stretch out. What will my next dream be? The sun is rising over the sea. I draw nearer, flying on a chicken. Close to, it turns out to be an enormous stove. Beside it sits the attendant.

"Shows a lack of respect for the galaxy, bad heating," he says severely, plying his poker.

Translated by George Bird

VIKTOR ASTAFIEV

The Blind Fisherman

THE TEAM OF municipal gas workers, headed by a large man, resilient to wine and cold weather, Kir Kirych, had at its disposal a powerful, covered truck, to which swamps, ice and mud presented no problems, because its driver came from a category undesignated anywhere in any documents. He was able to drive cross-country or over places where the roads had been built during Peter the Great's reign and had not been repaired since then.

The driver, who was called Grisha, was a somewhat puny man; skinny and white haired, he never raised his voice, but was well aware of his own strength and of his secret mastery of the technical side of his work, and was quietly proud of this, and, when those in the work association who dealt with him spoke approvingly of him, he received their restrained praise with equanimity, or even resentment, but in his heart he rejoiced, and felt proud of himself: he needed such praise "for the sake of his independence". His wife, Galka, a woman of well-rounded mind and body, had been able to achieve only one thing in her life – she had given birth to a child weighing five-and-a-half kilos – and this had given her an inflated idea of herself, and so she despised her husband as a person, but respected him as a technician, for he knew how to do everything about the house, and to her surprise, almost amazement, was highly esteemed in his work collective, which was seized by one common passion – fishing, especially winter fishing.

Grisha did not like fishing, and did not even have his own rod. While the valiant work association was plying its trade, he always busied himself with household matters – he fitted out his truck, and how! The first time I got into the "saloon" of his truck, I was struck by its amenities: the plywood seats along both sides were trimmed with tin and had raisable tops, in which the anglers' stools were stowed, and the fishermen's clothing and footware, and there was a separate compartment for axes and other ice-breaking tools, and yet another compartment for saucepans, plates, and spoons, and another one, felt lined, for bottles. There were little boxes fitted in wherever possible for herbs and salt. A gas ring was installed at the head of the bed, the cylinder tucked away under the seat. And there were folding bunks as well – though Grisha had never been in prison, he had profited from seeing how someone, probably a gas worker with one of the mobile work teams, had made a trestle bed. There were draughts, chess, dominoes, a few books and journals long past the return date to their respective libraries, mainly on technical subjects. But when the ceiling was taken down, turned upside down, folding legs were opened out and it became a table, everyone gave me a meaningful look. Even Uncle Yasha, the fifth man there, the sixth counting me, an eternal pensioner and indomitable fisherman, admitted to the family circle of gas repair men on the basis of his angling talent, smiled triumphantly and asked me with his eyes: "Not bad, eh?" I rocked the table and said: "Yes!"

As far as the gas workers were concerned, there were no barriers on earth to them, so they went off fishing to deserted reservoirs and made it to such remote districts that the occasional inhabitants, seeing out their remaining years, whom they did encounter there, came out to stare at them as if they were dentists or visiting officials at the time of elections to the Soviets.

The gas workers had held their own election this time, and decided to try the Voronovka river system, where there was timber felling. In the depths of the now silent woods and the depopulated villages someone unseen, most probably a recruited worker, had felled and cut the timber, but it had taken a long time to think of a way of moving it. Help came from some specialists in land reclamation: they pointed out on the map a chain of lakes into which the river Voronovka poured its waters in spring when it woke up and linked them into one great reservoir more than a hundred versts long. All you had to do was clear certain bottlenecks here and there, fell the old trees, hack away the undergrowth, deepen the river course where there were any blockages, and keep your eyes open during the floods.

In the summer the Voronovka lakes filled out, went quiet, the waters stopped flowing, and lilies bloomed on them, a huge rash of water lilies bursting out on the water's surface; masses of small fry, roach, ide, ruff, all fed off water-logged timber, and having stuffed themselves all spring on this free caviar, beat a drunken path to anyone and anywhere, biting lazily, but irresponsibly, at anything they came across. Rotting debris in the lakes led to the extinction of dace and grayling, and crab disappeared, but on the other hand pike and perch were given complete scope for their vandalism and pillage.

When the gas workers had cut a path through to the Voronovka lakes, they kept quiet about it and for a long time did not divulge to anyone the whereabouts of their propitious spot, except to Uncle Yasha, who knew how to keep his mouth shut. They stopped overnight in a village with the gloomy name of Muryzhikha. It stood on top of a hill surrounding a silent, many-spired church. There were still a few families living in Muryzhikha but for the most part there were only single old women, those unchanging custodians of the now silenced Russian village and her overgrown fields. The other little villages around were empty, ramshackle, strewn with rubbish, and those deep in the woods had been converted into logging "bases" and lumberjacking sectors.

Hard by a bend which connected two neighbouring lakes there stood a big peasant hut, black with age, with some outbuildings which had collapsed, a wide dormer window in the roof, the glass of it broken and one frame flapping in the wind, banging in the night, but not falling off, for it had been made to last. The outbuildings were being sawn up for firewood, and where they had once stood, there was now a wall of giant burdock, wormwood, bristle-stem hemp nettles, and common nettles, and long since untended brambles with their coarse time-honoured foliage running riot over it, producing no berries. The osier which had been pushed aside by the lumberjacks, the spurge, alder trees, bird-cherry trees and elders had all retreated from the banks on to the once fertile fields and vegetable gardens, and had got into the gardens and choked them, were threatening the huts, surrounding them, devouring them. Half of Muryzhikha, if not more, was already captive to the freebooting wild forest, and only in the centre of the village could you find well-trodden paths, dogs barking and cats fighting. Here, still alive and opening once a week, was a miserable little shop, with some foresight renamed, according to the sign, a storehouse for everyday goods, and thus, as it were, utterly alienated from people. But the people, especially village folk, were used to signs being changed, they knew from their children and grandchildren, who all came back to visit in the summer, that no matter what happened elsewhere, in the Russian village no amount of renaming or permutation of the unit parts had any influence on the end result, or rather it did, but only in one direction – downhill. No goods of any kind – neither everyday necessities nor consumer durables – were to be found in the newly named trading centre; all that remained from the erstwhile shop were moth-eaten felt boots, some horse collars and bridles for animals now deceased, a child's iron toboggan, though there had been no children here for ages, some iron sheets with naked mermaids etched on them, some bug-eyed plastic dolls, a few scythes, rakes and iron stoves, which no one had bought. There was no one to do any scything, digging or raking: the people who lived in the lakeside area were living out their days, and gradually forgetting the land, the trades, rituals and toil; once again, just as in the year dot, the Slavs were washing themselves by their Russian stoves, poking about in their vegetable patches at meagre, enfeebled potatoes that were turning black in the middle, the odd carrot or radish growing here and there, while to get cabbage, onions and garlic, or apples, they travelled in to the nearest little town on the lumberjacks' tractor. The women had forgotten what to cook and how to cook it, they'd lost the art of rustling up something to eat, or of weaving, doing needlework or saying prayers, but everyone swore like troopers, gossiped and found the "wherewithal" for booze, earning a kopeck by handing over some cranberries, mushrooms or herbal medicines to the shopping association, "renting out" to drinking lumberjacks, or in summer to random tourists and holiday-makers, who, under the pretext of a fishing trip, snooped around in empty huts in search of ikons, spinning wheels, doormats, kerosene lamps, samovars, old-fashioned flasks and other antiques.

In the spring a tractor, caked with mud up to its cab roof, brought dirty sacks to Muryzhikha containing grey bread, which when it was heated fell to pieces, and when it was cooled down became as hard as concrete, nasty little cakes the mice had got at, yellow, damp granulated sugar, a tub of vegetable oil, three or four boxes of Bulgarian pepper, which none of the villagers bought – they did not know if you were supposed to eat it or not. Squat, bulging pots of what was called "tourist's breakfast" containing rotten sprats, which had poisoned people more than once in the past, death-like bluish sweets stuck together, and above all one trump card, a delightful commodity – "grunter" home-brew – and the enticing ornamental bottles almost full to the brim with "gleaming child's tears" and bearing labels not written in Russian: "Russian Vodka".

From out of the woods, from beyond the hills and the lakes and the swamps, the folk, who led their own separate lives throughout the villages and hamlets, rose up, as if going to an ancient *veche*, and made their way into Muryzhikha, and if it happened that someone from some village or other failed to show up on hearing the roar of the tractor, then it meant that for yet another Russian the allotted span on earth was at an end: he had drunk the cup of life to the full and no longer needed either the affordable "grunter" or the expensive "gleaming child's tears" they drank on public holidays; he needed

nothing – neither favours, nor pensions, nor rewards. He lay in bed
without God watching over him, in an empty village, in a half-rotting
peasant hut on a cold stove, lay there unconscious, belonging to no
one, needed by no one; and he would lie there until he was torn to
pieces and dragged off bit by bit to dark garrets by wild cats, and the
mice finished nibbling him, until his remains were crushed by the
rotting roof of his own hut – his last refuge, his own home now
transformed into a tomb.

"God rest his soul!" his or her fellow countrymen would say, crossing
themselves by the shop, and them promptly forget about the deceased,
for there are more important things to attend to: keeping an eye on
your place in the shop queue, listening to news brought from afar,
and getting nearer to the grunter, which drowns out the memory, and
attacks the kidneys, liver and spleen – "let God be the judge of these
people whom we have forsaken."

The gate of one house which stood on the river bend girded with
cornel and dogwood was still intact, and there were rusty little stars
on the timber gatepost, hung up there as it were. Five of them.
The top one, the biggest, was for the owner, the head of the household, the other four were a bit smaller; no one had come back from
the war to this house, there were no father and no sons to tend this
yard.

The woman of the house had boarded up the summer half of the
property, which was difficult to heat. But the winter half, which
consisted of a kitchen and a "hall", was spacious: the hut had been
built for a large family. The woman may have been toothless, but she
still had her wits about her, and she was well disposed to the gas
workers. To start with she charged each of the fisherman twenty
kopecks for a night's lodging, but when Grisha mended her roof,
patched up the floor in the kitchen and on the porch, used the power
saw to cut up firewood for the winter, and more besides, she, with
sinking heart, refused to take any rent. And how could she help but
refuse: when the fishermen went away, they left behind piles of empty
bottles that she could get the money back on, as well as bread, salt
and occasionally rolls, cakes, and "tinned meat", and sugar lumps, and
they'd give her a little tipple of something for nothing, and chatted
to her and cheered her up.

It was more fun with fishermen in the house. God give them strength
and a bite for their bait!

I noted with interest that the woman of the house never gave her
patronymic, but the fishermen-cum-gas workers teased her over this:

"Go and ask old patronymic there!' they'd say, and this would have them all laughing. And in reply the woman would say: "I couldn't care less about a patronymic! I'm no Lady Muck to be putting on airs and graces." Uncle Yasha informed us on the quiet: "She's called Adolfovna. As if the priest was taking the mickey out of her, as if the long-haired rascal knew that Adolf Hitler would gobble up all her family . . ."

Oh, Russian land! Where is the end to your majesty and suffering! . . .

A spring sun shone over the Voronovka lakes. Black specks of larks traced blue circles in the well-washed, fathomless sky. The starling houses in the villages had all fallen down, but the starlings still came and trilled and whistled, setting up home in the hollows of old trees; rooks cawed in the fields, breaking twigs with their beaks and dragging them off into their rotting nests, to carry out repairs; snow was still lying around the woods and swamps, but it had been eaten up on the lakes and along the Voronovka river; the ice on the banks had been sucked in, and the winter land underneath was just about ready to be raised and dried out, but for the time being there was water pouring into the lakes and river from all directions, pouring in with helter-skelter panache, bringing rubbish, fir needles, old foliage, branches broken off by the wind and the heavy winter snow. The dirty water on top gushed through the gullies towards the fishing holes, and swirled around in them in eddies, devouring the ice. Though freezing cold in the morning, by midday the fishermen were throwing off their capes and short fur coats and Kir Kirych stripped to the waist – to get a tan. Grisha, having nothing better to do, had knocked up two starling houses and climbed up on to the gate to fix them to the posts: he was shouting out cheerfully from afar, while the others waved their arms at him, approving his actions, and pointing to a great big fish, a large pike which had got at the live bait during the night; they kept on pointing to it and from different positions, Grisha thought they had caught three bags full of pike.

The perch bit condescendingly, only by the banks and then only going for grubs or the yellow-coloured weighted hook: they had eaten too well, sod them, and thought too much of themselves, so they fed off the weed and roots, whereas the roach and ruff did not even give the line a chance to get under the ice. Uncle Yasha had stuck to the fishing hole on the river bend since morning and had not straightened his back, just tugging the line now and then, and deftly pulling it out of the hole with its booty. Fish of all shapes and sizes were writhing on the ice all around him, like a silvery halo.

A warm wind from off the fields, which unevenly abutted the lakes, was wafting a now green haze over the little passes between the hills, drying the slopes, and hastening the yellow, murky rivulets on their way, augmenting their girth and passage, encouraging the fleshy marsh marigolds along the banks, and breaking the ground with just a pinch of dove-blue lungwort shoots. There were gentle, white anemones all over the wet alder groves, and above in festive heaps were the yellow pussy willows, the osier, while the catkins in the aspen and alder groves showered everything with a brown dandruff.

Peace and springtime reigned over the sleeping Voronovka region, and spring strove to warm it up, and wake it up from its tedious slumber, populate it with cattle, fowl, and all living creatures, with flowers, grass and seeds. But there was no reciprocal joy to be heard, none of the springtime, festive hustle and bustle to be felt; no cocks crowed in the villages, no cows lowed, no sleepy, moulting horse neighed in the empty field, and there was no ploughman kneading in his hand the drying earth, or sniffing the new grass, or cracking the seed in his teeth to sense in it its yearning to be planted; and then the fertile earth itself, devalued, empty, squeezed on all sides by undergrowth and weeds, cringing orphan-like in the wind, giving admittance to the impure, uneven waters of the thaw, dried out into wrinkles, crumbled and cracked, turning into ravines, and then mysteriously disappearing somewhere.

At midday, when it had got really warm and the air was clear, by an isolated hut which stood on the other side of the lake opposite Muryzhikha – the only surviving hut of what was once a riverside farm – there appeared a man, carefully making his way down the slope over the wet grass. He shook hands with Uncle Yasha, stood next to him, had a word with him about something, and turning his cheek to the wind, took mincing steps sideways along the lake edge, stopping by each fisherman and not failing to offer him his hand. In this way he eventually reached me, tested the fishing hole with the heel of his rubber boot, threw into it a lure which gleamed in the sunlight, and jerked at the fishing rod. After a couple of jerks, he looked over my head and asked: "You're new to the lake here, aren't you?"

Suddenly it dawned on me – he was a blind fisherman! In my surprise I could not say a word.

"Go on, carry on with your fishing," said the fisherman reassuringly.

"Don't pay any attention to me. I've been blind since the war. My name's Zhora. A piece of shrapnel hit me in the head. I was laid up in a field hospital. It was all right, I could still see a bit. When I got home I managed to get married. I should have gone into the town and let the doctors have a look at me, but there was work here. The collective farm was still in one piece. Crippling taxes. Then my sight really started to fail, from strain, I suppose. And I got shocking headaches. Then I went completely blind. When that happened, my head got better. I could remember our lakes from my childhood. I was really miserable with nothing to do. So I went out one day and tried with someone else's rod. It was all right. Easy. Sometimes I caught a ruff, sometimes a roach, sometimes a perch; more often than not I'd catch my own sleeve or my trousers. Once I caught my lip. Look 'ere – they cut it out." He poked his finger into his upper lip, where there was a little red scar like a bird's wing. "They were biting so good that I asked the other fishermen to cut it out with a knife, so that I wouldn't waste time going to hospital."

The garrulous fisherman told his story to every new person he met, in an ordinary voice, using ordinary words, and explaining that he most often went out to the lakes when there was a wind – it was easier in the wind: he would turn his cheek to it and sense where and which way to go; he knew all the winds by their sound, smell, force and other features. If it was an easterly it was damp and nasty – a "piddler" they called it in these parts – and then the fish in the Voronovka lakes hardly bit at all, and then only ruff; the north wind was cutting, often cold, inhospitable, that's the northerly for you – the fish hardly biting in that too, maybe a starving hungry pike, if you stuck a lure right under its nose, will take a snap at it like a dog, and tear the lure off out of sheer disappointment, just stand there chewing the fatherland's metal. Then the Moscow wind, the westerly, and also the southerly, the south wind – they're a blessing, they're a treat, the fish bite, and the old sun warms you up, even in winter, and it really brings the folk out from all over the place, and he, Zhora, loved people, and he came out not so much to do a bit of fishing as to have a chat, learn what's new and make a bit on the side out of fishing tackle: they didn't sell anything in Muryzhikha, no hooks, no lines; well, there was no one to do any fishing there – all the "fishing" was done in the shop.

That very day the lumberjacks' shop, rigged up on a tractor sledge, arrived in Muryzhikha. Things started to liven up throughout the lakeland region: the shop had wine labelled "Volga", and vodka labelled "Special" and "Pepper" – specially for those who got cold and wet. The gas workers had a whip-round, even though they had vodka back in the house, but Grisha was adamant – he would not let them have a drop before they'd finished fishing, before evening, that is, before they had had the fish soup, for "it wouldn't tear their trousers or beg their bread off them" to save it for a while. Even I put a green three-rouble note into Kir Kirych's horny hand – how can you escape the collective, especially one as fine as ours? And Zhora put his hand in his shirt front, and felt around in there for a long time, muttering: "Where is it, that torn one I had? . . ." The other fishermen gave me a warning wink, as I was about to pay the invalid's share out of the three roubles I'd put in. At last Zhora fished a rouble out of his old, patched coat; it barely resembled present-day money, it was such a crumpled, worn-out, tatty little rouble note. "There you are, lads, order me a drop," he said, proffering it to the fishermen with the advice: "Don't get 'Volga', it's not very strong, better and nicer to spend a bit more and get vodka. That'll do the job! And cheer you up. And it won't give you a bad head afterwards."

Of course the fishermen refused to take Zhora's rouble, and he stood there, with hand outstretched in the direction of the one who was sent to do the buying. "What's going on? I'm not used to sponging off others. Take it, lads . . ." And the wind actually stirred that tattered one-rouble note, blackened at the corners, which, as it turned out, had been known for many years among the fishermen as "Zhora's non-negotiable", and had helped its owner "preserve his good name" and sense of equality with other people.

Ah, what a fine, soft-hearted man he was, but not humiliated by grief – in aspect and manners so like his own native northern land. I used to see all sorts of people when I was out fishing. I even met people with no arms. Among these Major Kuporosov sticks in my mind best of all. He had been the commander of a separate battalion of sappers and was used to giving orders and wielding power. He bore his misfortune not so much with pride as with bad temper, shunning people, refusing their help and assistance. At home, among his own kith and kin, he probably accepted some sort of help, but when he was in the company of others, especially when he was fishing, he ranted and roared at anyone who offered to lend him a hand. The bones in one of his arms were splayed out, and the major moved them about like sticks. The bare flesh had grown over them unevenly and was itself covered with red skin, and tufts of hair, black here and there, but gradually thickening, so that on the healthy part of his body it covered not only his chest, but his shoulders and back as well, just like an animal's coat.

Major Kuporosov kept his bifurcated stump tucked away in his chest, under a short fur coat: the poor bones used to get freezing cold, and he wore a woollen cap on the left one. If he got a bite, he would pull out his claw and clamp it on his rod, and lifting it up, he would catch the line in his teeth and step back from the hole, pulling the fish out on to the ice. Then he would put a worm on his knee – he couldn't cope with grubs or weighted hooks – and spend ages fixing it on to the hook or lure.

Major Kuporosov always did his fishing on Holy Lake, travelling there in an invalid carriage that creaked and belched smoke, and he always set a lure under the ice together with the rod. His lures made you envy their efficiency, being made in various shapes and of rare metals. Before Holy Lake became polluted with fertilizers and effluent from the pig-breeding complex, zander and pike often took the bait here, and just as often the stubborn, bad-tempered major found that he could not cope with the huge fish, and banged it against the ice and dragged it along . . . And then the retired major would sit on his box, staring motionlessly into the distance over the lake and the heads of the other anglers, his eyes filled with deep suffering, his face turned to stone, the bones prominently outlined, each one separately, and the thick grey stubble becoming more noticeable on his grey cheeks and under his blue lips, lacerated by the line.

But if Major Kuporosov did succeed in pulling a large fish out on to the ice, he would crow loudly and triumphantly, roar, look at everyone, and even offer people a drink with him in honour of such a victory. But no one ever responded to his invitation, and he drank alone. Everyone who knew Major Kuporosov thought how hard it must have been for those who were near and dear to this man, embittered by his invalidity and his own vanity.

Grisha set up the starling houses, which had been made out of some old offcut boards, on long poles and they towered proudly over the last hut in the village. In no time two pairs of starlings had trodden down the "saucers" in the houses and were flitting in and out of the hole, and soon fighting with those who hadn't got anywhere to live. The people still milling around the lumberjacks' shop looked at the starling houses, listened kindly to the mockingbirds, and kept saying: "Look at it! Look at it! . . . Husband-to-be has cleared off! And the bride has spread her wings! Look at her wagging her tail, wagging her tail, just like Akula from Khomutovka playing up to that soldier!

Do you remember, in '43 the woods were swarming with soldiers . . ."

As he went down to the lakeside, Grisha kept stopping and looking back at the starling houses, feeling as pleased as Punch with himself. There were masses of ruff all over the lake, it was just a question of sorting the wheat from the chaff. The crows stood with their legs apart, like men, and swivelled their heads in a businesslike fashion as they walked, gobbling them up, jerking their necks and tails, and then standing still for some time, listening carefully to their own bodies, as the coarse food gave them a peculiar sensation. Grisha collected the ruff up in a basket, and the crows, flocking away from him over the lake, cawed out their oaths: the ruff had been caught for them, and you shouldn't rob poor little birds!

Grisha boiled up the roe-bearing ruff, poured them out into a tub, and concocted a whole bucketful of fish soup out of the water they had boiled in and the striped, hunchbacked, pot-bellied Voronovka perch. You could smell the aroma of the soup as far away as the lake! The gas workers reeled in their rods, took Zhora along with them, and set about celebrating Easter. When they had found out from their landlady that the Easter festivities began on that very day, the respectful work brigade had decided to celebrate the holy day: the brigade revered, and enjoyed revering, public holidays, the old ones as well as the new.

The ikons were covered with clean towels. Beneath the Virgin Mother of God and Fertility, which was positioned in the middle of the ikonostasis – even though no seed had been sown in these parts for many years and there was nowhere to pray to God – they praised the Virgin, and an ikon lamp burnt below the ikon, which was crumbling away at the corners. As there had been no holy oil in the house for many years, it was sunflower oil, brought in by the lumberjacks in a barrel, that was giving off fumes and crackling in the ikon lamp. In the centre of the broad, round tabletop with its chipped, crenellated, carved edge, in a patterned, rustic dish, stood some resplendent, beautiful small eggs which the gas workers had brought; the eggs were from incubator hens, coloured with the water from boiled onion skins. There were no chickens in Muryzhikha, nor sheep, nor cows. Though there was half a dozen cats in every house. When people left, they abandoned their houses and their cats. The latter did not want to die: in summer they survived all right in the woods, but when winter came on, they crept in to the old women in the houses – nothing could get rid of them! The cats had litters three times a year, hiding the kittens in empty houses away from people until they had their eyesight and were playful. So how could you throw them out then, and where to?

As the atmosphere among the friendly company became even livelier, the gas workers broke the fast with the eggs, each man recalling something from the past, and expressing the view that there was no finer colouring for an Easter egg than that produced by onion skin, mainly because you got three colours from it: the first gave you an egg with a nut-brown, thick, ancient colour; the second colour was thinner, but gave the egg little circular stripes and little blotches at the top and bottom; and the third colour was very watery, all the strength boiled out of it, and that gave you yellowish eggs – they came out like dandelions – and there was no difference, all of them were nice, all of them were pretty!

Before tapping it on the tabletop and shelling the egg, I held it in my palm. Screwing up my eyes, I could see a little village street with close-cut grass and smartly dressed little children rolling painted eggs down it. If someone broke his egg, then he lost. This was a game of skill: you had to acquire the knack, and know which hen to take your egg from. If a hen's comb burned red after winter, she would lay larger eggs with brighter yokes, and tougher shells. My grandmother had known which hen's eggs to give me. I was always lucky at this game. I used to clean the lads out: I'd stuff my pockets full of eggs – brown, pink, violet, yellow and blue – and I'd be cock of the walk, while all around me there would be tears and grief. But what a holiday! It was spring, it was warm, there was the holy spirit of a public holiday, nature and the soul were both infused with it and appealed for your mercy and sympathy, so that having tyrannized my "victims", I would give them back their broken eggs. And then the merriment, the boys' jumping for joy, and my soul softening, having performed a deed of mercy, and the desire to keep performing them over and over again, to bring myself and others nothing but joy, to swell with happiness and a feeling of goodness . . .

What had happened to us? By whom and for what have we been flung into an abyss of evil and troubles? Who has extinguished the light of goodness in our souls? Who has blown out the ikon lamp of our consciousness, tipped it into a dark, eternal pit, and left us groping around in it, seeking the bottom, seeking some support and some guiding light for the future. Why do we have it, that light leading into fiery Gehenna? We used to live with light in our souls, a light acquired long before us by the performers of a feat; it was lit for us so that we would not lose our way in the dark, so that we would not bump into trees in the taiga, or into each other in the world, and not scratch each other's eyes out, nor break our neighbours' bones. Why was all that stolen from us and nothing given in return, engendering faithlessness, all-embracing faithlessness? Whom was there to pray to? Whom could we ask for forgiveness? After all, we used to know how – and we still haven't forgotten how – to forgive, even forgive our enemies . . .

The work team raised their glasses – just before the fish soup. The landlady brought in a little old vodka cup of tarnished silver from the "hall".

"It used to belong to my grandmother, God rest her soul! Christ is risen, men!" And those of us round the table who still remembered how to respond sang out individually: "Risen indeed!" – and for some reason felt a childlike embarrassment. Smacking her lips, the landlady took a sip of wine from the vodka glass and then addressed herself to the cup of fish soup, repeating: "May God grant you health, men! God grant you health! Look what a celebration you've put on . . . and for an old woman like me too! . . ."

Grisha was wearing the landlady's apron, and was serving out the fish soup on the plates and dishes. "Well, what's it like then?" he kept asking, and on receiving approval, beamed brighter than the Holy Saviour, Who had been placed next to the Mother of God and Fertility and looked as if He were supporting her under the arm with His secret affection, and with a suggestion of eternal bliss and salvation.

Then they got on to the singing. With a resonant voice forged in frost and wind, the veins standing out on his throat, Zhora shouted with all his might:

"Oh my rifle, hit the mark,
And ruthless strike the foe!
With my sabre sharp,
To your aid I'll go-o-o . . ."

The gas workers, not knowing these old war songs, willingly joined in with the "go-o-o . . ." But Zhora knew some city songs as well, which he had learnt off the radio, and he lent the team a hand when they roared: "Unfortunately, your birthday comes only o-o-once a ye-e-ar."

Having soaked up the sunshine, fresh air and fish soup, the fishermen had soon had enough, and crawled off in various directions – into the "hall", up on to the sleeping ledge, on to the stove, on to the floor, or beneath the ikons. The hut was filled with resolute snoring. As she helped Grisha to clear the table, the landlady was shaking her head, and saying with a laugh: "You should have seen the size of the cockroaches. They could have run off into the forest. The smaller ones died . . ."

For some reason Zhora was in no hurry to get home, and no one was pushing him. He started to look sluggish, and tried to tell stories about the war. I realized that he had seen very little of the war, and maybe hadn't been in it at all; maybe on his way to the front their train had been bombed. Zhora had listened to the radio too much and now made up stories about the war, which the kids in the kindergartens, children in the lower forms and pensioners who had lost their memory liked listening to and believed.

I offered to see Zhora home, but at this the landlady said: "He'll get there by himself. It's all the same to him whether it's day or night . . ."

In the yard outside we stopped and listened to the rustling of the weeds' pointed shoots, shedding their old seeds and thorns, and to the spring torrents babbling in the night . . . It was a warm night. The air, heavy with humidity, filled everything around with the slightly bitter freshness of buds, of waking grass, and of herbs peeping out from under the grass. And in a thin layer, sweet and tender, the willow exuded its honeyed fragrance. The chill of the expiring snows, washed away, blew in from the forests in a feeble gust, carrying with it the breath of clinging mould, filling the soul with faint regrets over the transcience of life, its short duration, and the inevitability of renewal.

A kerosene lamp was burning in the little porchway of Zhora's house, but there was no light in the house proper. Zhora took his shoes off carefully, and did not so much walk as creep stealthily into the hut, pressing his finger to his lips so that I would keep quiet. But as soon as the door opened a crack, a figure in white in the bed stirred, and a hand groped around for matches.

"Ah-ah, you blind-eyed drunk! You've come home at last, have you, you hopeless alcoholic!" said a clumsy, large-mouthed woman wearing a shift of Chinese silk, who, striking and breaking matches, jumped off the bed and lit the lamp. Without mincing her words she gave vent to her anger, which had accumulated in the dark, shaking her fists in Zhora's face. "Up to your old tricks again! Again! Why don't yer peg out? Why don't yer choke? I picked you up out of the gutter . . . Washed yer, clothed yer, fed yer, and you . . ."

"Nyusha! Nyusha!" prattled Zhora, trying blindly to grab his wife's hands. "Don't hit me. I'm a sick man. I'm going to die soon. Calm

down ... I understand ... I understand everything. I was with
friends, people from the town ... It's Easter today ... It was for the
religious festival. Don't ruin yourself, don't tear my soul apart. I would
go away to the invalids' home, but it's too far. I'm going to die soon,
I didn't drink my own money away. Look, here it is. They were friends
with good consciences, Soviet people, they didn't take it ... Look,
my friend here will tell you ..."

"Ah-ah, a friend! Another alcoholic! Another tramp from out of the
gutter! ..."

I sat Zhora on the stove and went out of the hut to the accompaniment of the housewife's shouting, which gradually turned into a
lament: "A poor wretch like me, who have I linked my life with! I've
ruined my life! What a miserable fate I've landed. I'd as soon kick the
bucket, or run off into the dark woods ... My mother, God rest her
soul, used to tell me, warn me ..."

I did not like the women in these parts. They had low backsides,
and their buttocks banged against their heels when they walked along;
they were colourless, flat-chested, common, they had been possessed
since birth, quarrelled among themselves, and nagged the menfolk,
young and old, to death. For every thousand or two like these, you
might get one white-haired beauty in the world with sky-blue eyes,
sweet-natured, and fertile, as if to prove that this earth, forgotten by
God and man, can still produce miracles, only that it lacks something,
or perhaps that the will is not there – after all, giving birth to something
bad and evil is simpler and easier, it doesn't require any intelligence,
effort, or love.

For a long time I sat on the porch of the hut, from which came the
low rumbling of the gas workers' snores, like the distant peals of a
gathering storm, and listened to the spring night, attending to the
sounds of the earth, filled with soft breathing and the distant, unceasing
hum of awakening. I thought of nothing, wanted nothing. My soul
heeded trustingly this springtime, night-time, restive quiet, which
filled it with bright hopes and the expectation of changes to come.
You could believe that no man could help but heed this age-old
tranquillity of the earth, and her humble, efficient readiness to love,
give birth, multiply. I also wanted humbly to trust all that was taking
place in the night, in the expanses under the stars – hark, oh, you man,
the assured progression of spring, unite with it; you must not work
at cross-purposes to nature, you must not fight against yourself,
otherwise everything around will be laid waste, and become over-

grown with weeds, and man will degenerate within himself, will turn mangy, and be deprived of his finest reason.

In the morning the distant woods fell silent, the waters went quiet, and a faint rustling through the dry cocklebur grass surviving from the previous year and over the timbers of the old roof reached my ears. A whispering arose in the willows and the alder trees. I felt the tender kiss on my lips of the first spring rain, in which there was more willow pollen than moisture.

I moved off to the shelter of the awning, pressed my back against the cracked boards of the old hut, and fell into a deep sleep to the gathering sounds of the teeming rain, after which people still sow wheat, barley or oats in places, and the newly washed winter crops shine green out in the fields. Once they have stirred from their sleep, the grass and flowers grow apace; people plough and harrow the rich earth, showered with heavenly abundance. Spring gathers pace, the woods fill with foliage, and the birds' nests with eggs; spring does not pass by in hustle, bustle, worry or work, but all the same, the long-awaited spring still flies by.

At night the ice on the lakes was covered with a thin layer of meltwater brought from the taiga by the Voronovka. We went out to fish on the raft, hacking away with icebreakers at the loose edges of the porous ice floe, where it had begun to get thin and had bulged out with grey surf.

Zhora, who still looked half asleep, came down to the bank. "Well, how are things?" we asked him. "Oh, it's no problem, I'm used to it," he said with a wave of his hand and . . . then he ordered us to get off the ice floe so that there wouldn't be an accident, saying that he'd heard the Voronovka pouring its upper waters into the lakes.

The water in the holes had indeed begun to stir and froth up; debris began to well up in the sluices and the ice strips on the banks, and suddenly the water burst out in a gush from the ice holes, as if from a fire hose; everything was in a whirl, there was a roaring noise, and everything was awash; reeling over and floundering around, everybody started gasping, oo-ing and ah-ing, snatching up the fish and rods as they ran for it, dashing like mad to get off the ice. Two of the gas workers got water in their boots on the lakeside ice strip and collapsed on the ground, lifting their feet up in the air to pour the cold water out.

From the opposite bank, now receding because of the headlong torrent of water, in full view of the widening lake, whose ice was now washed and cleansed of debris and had been smoothed out, flights of ducks soared skywards. The torrent of meltwater was covering the hump of the ice more thickly. All you could see was the glitter of the winter armour as it submerged into oblivion, disappearing under that deluge of reckless water. It made you think of a new eternal flood, of everything that was yet alive in the stilled heart disappearing. Birds, especially the crows, jackdaws and rooks, cawing with excitement, added to the disharmony and anxiety in the heart.

From the area on the other side of the lake, from the mouth of the Voronovka, now thrown wide open into the lake, the figure of a solitary fisherman, cut off by the flood, kept waving his hat at us. When we left Muryzhikha a herd of young cattle, about two hundred head, forced our truck off the road, just on the edge of the village. The lads on horseback were beating their dumb beasts with savage ruthlessness and making them bleed, just as foreign invaders, slant-eyed warriors, used to whip their Russian captives when they swept down into the forests from the dusty steppelands. The calves and bull calves, which had grown up indoors, unused to the herd life and the free range, ran into the bushes and the mire, trying to escape the knout, bunching together, piling on top of one another, and the drovers shouted at the senseless cattle, whipped them, and rode their horses into the dirty mass of that plodding, panting, wheezing herd. One man, with a billowing clown-like jacket on his back and a smart knitted hat with a foreign caption on its red brim, evidently the leader of the drovers, was especially vicious. He had a little steel nut tied on to the end of his knout, and he had already used it to knock out the eye of one meek white calf, which was caked from its horns to its tail in mud, so that it looked motley coloured rather than white.

The lads stopped for a smoke and explained willingly that they were driving the young herd off to be fattened, taking them out to abandoned pastures, fallow fields and meadowland, and if their first experience of fattening the herd turned out successful and brought down the cost of producing a kilo of meat, then they would repair the roads, and the living quarters, and perhaps even build a complex for a thousand head, open a permanent shop, and even a club, start ploughing again, sowing rye and oats and barley, so as not to have to bring fodder to the cattle.

By the pen, which had fallen down, just as in the good old days, the herd was met by the meagre population of Muryzhikha. Our landlady, Adolfovna, immediately fed the calf with the blinded eye a bit of bread and scolded the loudmouthed drover. "You ought to have a taste of the whip yourself," she said. "How would you like it? . . ."

"Well you kiss the calf better, go on, you old woman," said the kid of school age, with his pimply face and his greasy hair down to his shoulders, badgering the old woman. A little gadget with flashing lights was bouncing about on his belly, and playing some foreign song.

Our landlady, quickly putting on the huge, much-repaired boots that Kir Kirych had left behind at the end of last season, not even bothering to put on socks, wiped away her tears of pity with one hand and tried to get the mud off the calf and somehow clean it up with the other.

"I will kiss him better! I will!" she shouted in a trembling voice. "What are you grinning for? You've never sat in an empty hut, listening to the wind in the chimney, and wept over those killed in the war . . ."

The long-haired youth was going to taunt Adolfovna further, but the leader, the one with the fancy hat, came over, brandishing the knout with the steel nut in it.

"Pack it in! Aye, women, who's gonna put us up?"

"Put up you devils? You robbers!" said Adolfovna, throwing up her hands in horror, and trying to stamp her foot; however, the boot slipped off, and while she was pulling it back on properly with her twisted, rheumatic fingers, and hopping around on her other foot, another old woman, tall, hollow-cheeked, wearing a man's hat with earflaps and with a cigarette in her nicotine-stained fingers, told the lads to come to her place.

Sensing that the lodgers were being snatched from under her nose and that the profit, the living profit, would slip from her grasp, Adolfovna shouted: "Don't you go to her! She smokes! Her hut's cold . . . My place is – just you ask the men here . . ."

"Oh, fuck you!" said the long-haired one with the transistor, rounding on her with his filthy language. "You shouldn't make trouble, so we're not going to see your place!"

"Oy, you, whippersnapper!" shouted Kir Kirych, looking straight at him from the open door of our "saloon". "You use that filthy language again, and I'll knock your teeth out! Right now! Got it?"

"Ooh, look what a hard man we've got here!" was what the long-haired one was about to say. But when Kir Kirych appeared in the doorway of the truck, filling it with his bulk, the lad realized that it would take more than a horse to trample him underfoot, so he just lashed out with the whip at a calf or two, thrust his finger into his belly, and the transistor blared out all over the Voronovka region: "Forrrgive me, my countreeee, forrrgive me foreffer, a ma-han has offffended you . . ."

"There you are then, woman!" said the long-haired youth in a conciliatory tone, poking himself as if unintentionally below the belt. "That's a time machine singing, woman. Our time. Your time's finished."

"You call that singing? You call that singing?" she retorted, putting her arms round the calf, still cleaning it up and getting the mud off, feeling its head with the protruding little horns, and with her age-old peasant experience, assessing from the bumps on its head, its lips and its tongue, how many young it would have, what its milk yield would be and even what its quirks as a future cow would be. "Shouting and bawling, as if he's been castrated this autumn . . ."

"Castrated?! Ha-ha-ha! Ho-ho-ho! Now come on, you old cow, shift yourself! Get cracking! Otherwise the shop will be closed. The la-a-ast parrra-ade is co-o-ming . . . Goodbye, you peasants!" And he pressed another button. Someone with a voice like a ram started yelling even more barbarously (in English), and the long-haired youth joined in skilfully: "Goodbye, girls, boys, granny and aunts! Till new meetings and parts! Adios! Partings!"

"What language is that?" asked Adolfovna in a timid whisper.

"Heathen language! What language! Don't you criticize others! Don't! . . ."

Adolfovna pretended not to hear or see anyone; she just stroked the calf, kept talking to it, and perhaps she really did not hear or see anyone.

"Look how he's beaten you, the monster! Beaten you. They've taught them no different from what they know themselves! They've taken the last crumbs away . . . He grew up in the town, in the town, and he's got a brick there instead of a heart, and a cast-iron stove where his head should be . . . I'll give it to you!" she said, shaking her fist at the prancing horseman. "There was a time when we didn't give a damn either, didn't graze cattle, didn't look after anything. So take a good look at our farms now. We spoilt it all, wasted it, frittered it away . . ."

"So what yer gonna do now then? You can't turn the clock back." The old woman smoking the cigarette sighed, then suddenly she yelled out desperately in ringing tones: "You used to run about carrying a lighted torch, you did!" She spat the cigarette out into the mud, and went on, louder and more determined: "Down with the church, the opium of the people! Let's have a club! God don't exist and we don't need a tsar, we'll live our lives up on a hummock! And we've stayed on a hummock ever since."

"Forrrrgive me, my countreeeee!" sang Adolfovna, mimicking to a T the transistor. Apparently at one time she had been a great actress in Muryzhikha. "Is there anyone to give forgiveness, eh? And who's to be forgiven? Us? You, you wretches?" she said, glaring at the drovers . . ."O-oh, you devils! I won't have any swearing in my house in front of the ikons, or any smoking. Don't burn the lamp for too long – the kerosene has to be delivered."

Grisha pressed the starter, and the truck immediately roared lustily into life and set off at a brisk pace. When we bounded up the hillside and began to run into the roads that were turning to slush at the sides and the fields ragged with weeds, we saw through the open door of the "saloon" a great piece of ice, glistening like silver in the sunlight, rise like a white moon in the middle of the swollen lake, which pushed its surplus water over the edge and down the ravines, ruts, gullies, gorges, round corners, and through cracks. A sunlit haze danced hesitantly above it, and bright rays of light shattered against the edges of the ice. Seagulls hovered above the lake in sweet, drowsy sleep. Then suddenly something appeared on the ice, flashed by and was lost, breaking the ice to pieces as if in a silent film. "An elk! An elk!" the cries rang out. Kir Kirych pulled out his binoculars from under the seat, held them to his eyes, then muttered gloomily: "It's a calf. They've run it to bay out there, the rats! Turn round, Grigory."

The engine roared as we turned around in the mud. Women carrying poles and planks were running from Muryzhikha to the lake edge. The drovers were using their horses to force the stricken herd, which was ready to fling itself into the water after the first calf, on to the ice. On the other side of the lake, from the direction of the former farmstead, a man, his shirt ruffled by the wind, and a woman, also wearing white, were rolling an old boat over logs towards the water, to help the people save the cattle and generally to find out what was going on in the lakeland region, in Muryzhikha, and the reason for all the noise and for all those people, what it was that had almost brought back to life this long-silenced little corner of abandoned land.

Oh, Russian land! Where is the end to your majesty and suffering!

Translated by Robert Porter

SERAFIM CHETVERUKHIN

Tsarevich Dmitry

THE WINTER AND early spring of '37 I spent in Leningrad transit custody. At the beginning of May I was called for staged transit. What staged transit was, and what a camp was, I had already experienced briefly and terrifyingly. Still . . .

Firstly, nothing is worse than anticipation. Secondly, being in a cell for – to judge from the number of bunks screwed to the floor – twenty-five, in the company of two hundred, taking turns to sleep on the floor, worn out by uproar and commotion by day, and listening to ramblings and snoring by night, was, as our prison doctor used reasonably to inform us, of course, no health cure. Thirdly, there was the torment of weekly reunions with my wife. Across two barriers and a little window – for two young people in love . . . Better to go. Where didn't matter. Besides, they didn't ask. Just summoned us. North.

And to my surprise and joy, it was a happier start than last year. While we were still in the cellar, the escorts did a weed-out, sorting "clean" from "criminal" scum.

In the sealed goods wagon, it was pleasant to drowse to the hammering of the wheels. Places by the tiny, half-boarded windows were occupied by the fortunate, and in our semi-darkness it wasn't possible to do anything. No one felt like talking. People mused, remembered, prayed.

The railway terminated at a small town. Mighty poplars with countless nests overshadowed the station square. A piercing cawing could be heard from afar. Our huts stood above a deep ravine a short way from the town. Below flowed a well-known northern river. The opposite bank had been flooded by the spring high water, and the villages looked like islands. Boats darted about between the houses. It was a panorama that breathed wide-openness, repose, except for the chilly breeze ruffling the water, and the cloud shadows gliding over water and land. But for us, all this was cancelled out by the barbed wire. From here it was that we began our staged transit.

Now and then, during the first three days, we came upon old villages on the banks of rivers, and temporary forestry settlements. And then, nothing. On both sides of the road, forest, nothing but forest. Dense, difficult to penetrate. Encumbered by trunks of fallen trees and enormous discs of torn-up roots. Choked with thick undergrowth. Sometimes, for many kilometres, ravaged by fire. Yellow trunks with charred tops standing like snuffed candles on the grey ground. However high we climbed – and the road crossed ridge after ridge – all that could be seen was a single tousled green and reddish-brown sea, with rare gaps in the form of coffee-coloured lakes. The gravelled road, the ditches and telegraph poles beside it, or interminable stretches of brushwood and logs which gave wearisomely beneath our feet, were the only signs of man. About twice a day halts were organized. After five or six days' march there would be a day's rest, when blistered feet were attended to, clothing darned, boots repaired by ourselves unaided, and we could lie about all day. It was at one of these "stations" that I chanced to hear a story which I'm still unable to fathom.

There was a man with us whose name was Sergey Alexeevich Zolotaryov. But to his face and behind his back, everyone called him the Professor, and more as a respectful nickname than as a title. The Professor was an old man of seventy, tall, sturdy, prominent-featured, loud-voiced, keen-eyed. Like everyone's, his grey head was close-cropped, and his little grey-green beard and his moustache had a prickly look. The Professor was invariably courteous, but not on close terms with anybody. He sometimes joked that the judge had paid him a compliment in sending him to the camps for ten years.

My friend Seryozha, who at halts would sing songs by Vertinsky, said that he had studied under the Professor at a German-language school, where the latter taught Russian language and literature. In transit custody the Professor had been in the next cell, and had given absorbing and daring lectures on, for example, Mayakovsky. Enterprising fellow cell mates contrived to attend them, but I, lacking the courage, remained merely envious. There were also rumours to the effect that, in his youth, the Professor had been a socialist revolutionary, and that this was not his first taste of prison. On our marches, I very much wanted to get to know the Professor, who greatly reminded me of an uncle, also a teacher, but I was afraid of seeming obtrusive.

One day, at the end of the march, we came to our "station", which this time proved to be a log cabin, the sight of which prompted thoughts as to how a hundred of us were going to fit in. We were let in one by one, and by the time I got in, the bunks, both upper and lower, were crammed full. Looking round, I saw the Professor go down on all fours, and crawl under the bunks, dragging his sack behind him. I followed. Just in time! Those who came after spent the whole night huddled together on the floor. But beneath the bunks, once we'd spread a coat out, it was almost comfortable. Except for a rain of garbage.

After stretching legs and easing muscles, we spent a long time in silence. But having eaten our "swill", we fell into conversation. The Professor said with satisfaction that beneath the bunks was the most restful place to be, and that he preferred it to any other. We discussed the events of the day. Our route had led us not only away from general habitation, but also, as it were, into the depths of time. Tiny towns, ancient-looking buildings, absence of human life, dense forest, swamps – it was all like the Rus of old. And we discussed history. It was a subject that had always fascinated me, its murky pages particularly. I liked reading about the Time of Troubles, and I was under the spell of Platonov's work. I told the Professor.

"Yes," he replied, "an interesting time. But are you aware, young man, that the main character of the drama survived it all?"

"Who was that?"

"Tsarevich Dmitry."

"Which – the Uglich Dmitry or the Pretender Otrepiev?"

"Neither. The *real* Dmitry, son of Ivan IV!" And the Professor related as follows. "I am, as you may know, by occupation a teacher. For forty years I've taught literature. While still a student, I became interested in the part played in a writer's work by his parentage. Take Pushkin: his *Genealogy of the Pushkins and the Hannibals*, his *Negro of Peter the Great*. Lermontov has his Scottish motifs and his Duke Lerma. Tolstoy, in *War and Peace*, portrays a whole gallery of relatives, from his grandfather to his sister-in-law, and so on. I started collecting anything that might put life into the dead family trees of our writers, found out about the talents, tastes and ways of those they might have inherited their gifts from, and of those they might have passed them on to. This information was entered on cards whose number became enormous. There was no time to process this material. And now they've been confiscated, and probably lost. They contained so much of interest, those cards! Ties of kinship, family secrets, unexpected, sometimes scandalous explanations! Everyone knows how much Pushkin inherited from his mother's side. And to the present day, the Hannibals have been very original. While the Pushkins, even after becoming related to the Gogols, have been ordinary. Sofya Perovskaya, assassin of Alexander II, was a near relative of A. K. Tolstoy and of the Zhemchuzhnikov brothers, and all were descendants of Hetman Razumovsky. It's possible that the adventuress Princess Tarakanova was of the same family, but there are no proofs one way or the other. The writers with the name Tolstoy were not interrelated, and two, to be honest, weren't Tolstoys at all. But Lev Nikolaevich was a nephew four times removed of A. S. Pushkin, while A. N. Tolstoy was possibly his great-grandson.

"Depending on circumstances, the very same qualities of character, passing from generation to generation, have seemed at one time estimable, at another ridiculous. In a nutshell, each discovery has presented something unusual. My friends laughed, but thought it their duty to pass on anything that might, in their view, be of interest to me. Amongst those who favoured me, student though I was, were two elderly spinster sisters, baronesses" – the Professor gave a short Baltic German name. "These ladies travelled a great deal, were acquainted with the famous, and knew some surprising things. And one day they told me how, in the middle of the last century, a French lady of mature years had presented herself at the Russian embassy in Paris, and requested a meeting with the ambassador. Her forebears, she told him, had owned a château, but lost the title deeds in the Revolution, and neighbours had started a lawsuit. This lawsuit, which had been long and ruinous, was still not concluded. She had no relatives, and were she to lose, would be left a pauper. She had searched the whole château and found a box of old papers which might be the ones that were needed. But as they were written in strange letters, she was unable to read them. Someone had suggested them to be Greek or Russian. Would the ambassador kindly take a look at them? The ambassador did take a look at them, and suggested that they be left with him. The Frenchwoman" – another unintelligible name – "agreed. The papers were examined. They were written in Old Russian in Cyrillic script. Their content was repetitious: lists of 'victuals' dispatched from Muscovy to a person resident in France. But the addressee was styled 'His Highness the Tsarevich and Grand Prince Dmitry Ivanovich'! From the dates, the documents had clearly been written over a period of thirty to forty years, that is, from the reign of Fyodor Ivanovich to that of Mikhail Fyodorovich Romanov.

"The embassy officials sought to discover from the papers how the Tsarevich had happened to be in France, when and by whom he had been taken from Russia, for what reason, whether to protect or dispose of him, who had had the care of him in that foreign land, and who, at home in Russia, had been remembering him. But the papers gave no answers. Apart from the name of the addressee they contained no other. Still, the duration and the value of these consignments were evidence of the fact that the Moscovy Tsars must have been in the know. What could be gleaned, however, was that the Tsarevich had married in France, had children, been buried there. But as no one was corresponding any more with the children and grandchildren, it had to be assumed that they had become so Gallicized as to have forgotten not only their Tsarist but also their Russian descent. Meanwhile, Mademoiselle, the last Tsarevna of the House of Ivan the Terrible, had not even an inkling of the commotion that she and her old papers had caused in the embassy.

"What was to be done with them? How to avoid publicity? How to deal with a suppliant possibly possessing as good a right to the Moscow throne as His Majesty the Tsar? The ambassador decided to extract from his staff a solemn promise to keep the secret. He decided also to offer some pretext for not returning the documents to their owner, and to forward them to St Petersburg. And that's what happened. The French lady was assured that the documents had nothing to do with her lawsuit, but that they were of value to Russians as historical relics, and she was offered a generous price. Mademoiselle was distressed, but she agreed to the sale. Subsequently, it seems, and at some personal trouble, the ambassador obtained a small pension from the Russian Court for her. Beyond that, nothing further is known. My old ladies' father, as a junior official at the embassy, had actually handled those documents."

"Where are they now?"

"No one knows. They may have been destroyed at the command of the All-Highest, or got mislaid in the archives."

"Didn't you tell people about them? Try to locate them?"

"I did. The historians shrugged. When, after the Revolution, secret archives began to be published, I hoped they would come to light. But they didn't. To go burrowing in archives myself wasn't possible. I was a teacher of literature, not a historian. I wouldn't have had the time. And who would have authorized me?"

"Isn't the whole thing a fabrication?"

"The old ladies said their father had told them this story when on the point of death, and not disposed to talk lightly. He entrusted his secret to them alone, and they related it only to me."

"May not the documents have been false?"

"Who knows? Except that a bad forgery would have been instantly exposed, and a good one costs too much. Nothing in all this remotely resembled blackmail. Besides, what had the French lady to blackmail with? A journalistic sensation, no more. There'd have been talk, spiteful things said, and that would have been that."

"So you don't believe this story, Professor."

"I believe the worthy old ladies. As for Dmitry, there's so much contradictory evidence about his fate that the present version is no more dubious than the others. Of course, as regards the discovery and analysis of the documents, there's nothing firm to go on, beyond the plausibility of this version, and the fact that one can, by means of it, satisfactorily explain things that have hitherto remained obscure. For instance, the marks of royal disfavour incurred first by Bogdan Belsky, whom Ivan the Terrible had appointed guardian of his son, and then by the Romanovs. The official accusations were so foolish as not to be believed even at the time. And the concealing of the Tsarevich, of which rumours had filtered through to the people early on, and were, of course, known to Godunov, may have been precisely the reason. Of Otrepiev's past, very little is known, but there's no doubt that he was close to the Romanovs, and particularly to Alexander Nikitich, who was chief accused in the Romanov case, and who perished. As a bold conjecture, might not Otrepiev have penetrated the secret, or had it entrusted to him, and even have been sent abroad to the Tsarevich? And hearing, on the way, of the death of him who had sent him, might he not have decided to exploit the situation for his own purposes? Hence the jewelled cross, the gift of godfather Mstislavsky to his godson Dmitry, by which Otrepiev, as the False Dmitry, proved his royal descent. Also his unwillingness to relate the circumstances of his 'deliverance', and his generosity towards the surviving Romanovs. One can also better understand the behaviour of Ivan the Terrible's widow, Tsarina Mariya Nagaya, who took the veil, becoming Sister Marfa. Sister Marfa was constantly making contrary claims about her son's fate, now holding him to be alive, now dead, and both recognizing the Pretender, and rejecting him.

"A certain Dutchman living in Moscow at that time wrote an account in which Gudonov, not knowing how to halt the Pretender's army, has Dmitry's mother fetched from her convent. She's taken to the palace at the dead of night, and brought face to face with Boris and his consort, 'Tiny' Skuratov's daughter. 'Where is your son?' asks the Tsar. 'I don't know,' answers Marfa. 'Creature! How dare you say you don't when you do!' cries the new Tsarina, poking a burning candle at the old woman's eyes. Godunov only just manages to deflect her arm. Then Sister Marfa announces: 'They told me that my son was carried off to foreign parts without my knowledge. But those who told me are dead. Whether he is alive or not, I do not know . . .' The unfortunate woman is returned to her banishment. Not remembering her son by sight, and not knowing Otrepiev, she could have confirmed the Pretender's identity and acknowledged him affectionately. Or by detecting the deception, she could have disowned him, at his fateful hour. Although saving Otrepiev's life would have meant her being, as before, the Dowager Tsarina, by disowning him, she went back to being a disgraced and, moreover, mendacious old woman. After the death of the first Pretender and of the second, the name Dmitry was so disgraced that another attempt to resurrect it would have been rash. And the real Dmitry Ivanovich was forced – or preferred – to stay abroad in the country he grew up in, till the end of his days.

"If you think it strange that a Russian Tsarevich should become the progenitor of French noblemen, don't be surprised. The mathematician Sofya Kovalevskaya, née Korvin-Krukovskaya, had as an ancestor the Hungarian King Matvey Korvin. The landowning Durasovs were descended from the Sicilian Kings of the Anjou Dynasty, and had the right to the title of Dukes of Durazzo, and also to address any Bourbon as 'cousin'. Amongst the Russian nobility were descendants of Kings of Castile, Ireland, Scotland, and even of the Knights Hospitallers. Besides, all noble houses owe their origins to alien princes and khans. Clearly the process has been a mutual one, and fugitive Russian princes and boyars have filled the aristocratic *Who's Who*s of Europe with their progeny."

And lying beneath the bunks the Professor gave me a brilliant lecture on the labyrinths of that forgotten science, genealogy, and on the seventeenth century. On and on he went, and the surrounding darkness receded before the pictures he painted, and the people he summoned out of non-existence ousted the unwilling companions lying beside me. I fell to thinking. No longer listening, no longer hearing. The wall I had erected around my own experiences, thinking them so exceptional, was broken down by a torrent of unusual thoughts. Vague analogies suggested themselves. I could feel the threads linking people over decades and centuries and binding them into one human family. It seemed very important to find out, to understand for myself, what the abandoned Tsarevich had felt, being deprived not only of his native land, but also of his name. Did he, I wondered, writhe in impotent rage? Weep vain tears? Did he, finally, know that in his not properly understood native land a great many people were raising, in triumph and disaster, the one cry "Dmitry", but think that it had nothing whatsoever to do with him, the real Dmitry? Or had all that been pushed into the background by simple worldly pleasure? And what was a native land? And what was a name? And what was history? And what was truth?

I felt somehow sorry for my old textbook with pictures, where it was all elucidated so assiduously and categorically. I felt sorry for Pushkin, Mussorgsky, Nesterov. For their heroes, magnificent in suffering, dignified even in crime. It was distressing to play with the idea that it had, in fact, all happened completely differently, in a more commonplace way, in uglier, worse fashion. I felt upset, as if at losing something, as if I'd come from my cosy chimney corner out to a cheerless crossroads. My beloved history! What if the absurdity which has been our lot should endure in your pages also? And I shuddered.

"No need to get so agitated, young man," the Professor said, sensing my confusion and guessing my thoughts. "Everything remains as it was, you know. One tiny brick's been replaced by another. No one's even noticed. We've had murder at Uglich, we've had the death of the Godunovs, we've had Pretenders, we've had Poles . . . And if, in the final analysis, the bones reposing in honour in the Cathedral of St Michael the Archangel are those not of a Tsarevich but of a priest's son, what does it matter? Does it make any difference *whose* child has been murdered? What matters is that *a* child has been murdered. To whom is the actual fate, the essential man, of interest? To those close to him. Not to history. History deals with appearances, forever changing its heroes' attire from bright to dark and back again. You and I have become 'objects of history' too. What do, what will, people know about us, so ordinary, so different, suffering and thinking in our own ways? All that we have understood will sink into oblivion with us. And all that's left will be a label . . . Annoying, of course. Still, colleague, time for sleep!" And rolling on to his side, the Professor slept.

I could not sleep. My thoughts were buzzing in agitation. And suddenly, keenly, cravenly, I felt I wanted not to be "an object of history", not to wear a villain- or martyr-label, but just to sleep at home, in an ordinary bed, and not on an earth floor beneath bunks, far, far, far away from all that I loved.

The wind raged with increasing fury above our holed roof. The trees creaked, heralding bad weather. No day's rest to look forward to beyond the darkness, and tomorrow we'd have to march. I had to sleep. I did sleep.

But even in sleep I was not free of anxiety. My dreams were of lights, cries, pursuits. And of the tearful face of my little girl in the headdress of the Tsarina Mariya. Then, absurdly, of piles of bricks, hurled down by someone yelling: "What have bricks got to do with it? Feeling sorry for them or something? Enough lying around!"

"Enough lying around!" the guard was shouting, banging a stick against the bunks.

Frantic haste ensued.

The weather really had turned bad. Snow was giving way to rain. The wind was shaking the grey clouds, tatters of which were clinging to the pine-tops. The road was a mire.

Muffling ourselves up as best we could, we set off. Not feeling like talking or thinking.

Halfway through our march we came across lorries with guards. We were halted. The old men and the weak were weeded out, and whisked off ahead.

No time for farewells. They took the Professor, too.

Those who had been driven off were neither at the next "station", nor at the end of the march.

But for me the road of life was still a long one.

Translated by George Bird

YURY TRIFONOV

Archetypal Themes

ON ONE OCCASION a long time ago I took a number of short
stories to the editorial board of a famous journal. They were, in fact,
short short stories, of no more than five pages each, some thirty pages
in all, a pitiful offering, the more wretched for my having been unable
for a number of years to get anything worthwhile down on paper.
People had written me off. This batch of short stories was my first
output after a long interruption. It meant a lot to me, an incalculable
amount: no one would have known, glancing at the slender pile of
sheets, just how much it did mean to me. I could never have explained
it – can you ever explain such things? – and, besides, you never
recognize your fate at the time when it is being settled; the knowledge
comes later. I merely sensed that the moment was a decisive one for
me, and had a vague feeling of disquiet, a sort of icy tremor, part fear
and part impatience – and here I was coming to get my answer from
an ill-lit building on one of Moscow's oldest streets. I slowly climbed
the stone staircase, trying to calm my pounding heart. I paused when
I reached the top landing and stood there for perhaps a minute. I
wanted to look like someone quite other than the person I in fact was.

Finally I felt that I was ready to fling open the outer door, proceed
the length of the corridor and knock casually at the appropriate office.
Fate turned an unprepossessing face to me: a blotchy yellow one, with
sunken cheeks, a greying crew cut and a look that was at once sad and
pitiless. Sitting half turned towards me, wreathed in the smoke of a
cigarette protruding from a wooden holder, the man behind the desk
said: "They're all on the same archetypal themes."

I tensed my muscles, waiting for the blow. But none came. It was
already clear enough. The stories would not be published in the famous
journal because they were about archetypal themes. I should have left
but I continued standing there beside the desk and then sat down on
a small sofa, pulled out a cigarette and started to smoke. All my actions
were pointless but I could not stop myself: I settled back into a more
comfortable position, crossed my legs and asked what were archetypal
themes? The man behind the desk curled his lips a fraction.

"Come off it. You know perfectly well what I'm talking about."

"No, I don't," I said. "Do please explain."

"Don't be so silly! There's nothing to explain."

"But I genuinely don't understand."

"What's there to understand?" The man shrugged his shoulders. He gave me a bored, contemptuous look. "Archetypal themes are archetypal themes. Well, if you want . . . Let's say . . ."

Twenty-two years went by. At the Hotel Phoenix in Rome I was handed a note by Reception – and the reception in that hotel was located in a spacious, glass-enclosed corridor connecting the two buildings, like a conservatory; through the glass you could see the courtyard with its neatly cropped, lush green, all-the-year-round grass, its palm trees, a brick wall and a brilliant blue segment of sky above it. The note said that so-and-so was in Rome and would like to see me. I was astonished: during the intervening twenty-two years, ever since we had had our discussion about archetypal themes, we had not exchanged a word. Not because of any hostility ensuing between us, but because nothing had ensued between us: we had remained strangers. We exchanged salutes whenever we met and then immediately forgot one another. He came somewhere among my three hundred nearest acquaintances and I among his nearest five hundred. But there was one thing we had in common – the famous journal, for which we had once worked and in which I had once published my pieces. Yet the connection was so formal and distant that it seemed odd for him to look me up in Rome. What on earth did he want of me? But then it suddenly transpired that my wife also knew him. She enquired with alarm: "He's the very small chap? With a dark face? And a short haircut? I used to live in the same house as he did. He scares me."

"Why?"

"He brought bad luck. Whenever I met him in the yard or in the street, something unpleasant always happened."

"What, for example?"

"On one occasion when I met him, Vixen ran under a car. Another time, they tore my scenario to shreds. And the same sort of thing happened on other occasions, several times. Once I came face to face with him in the lift, and an hour later I got the telegram about Valery's death. There's no need to phone him. You're in no way obliged to meet him."

We were sitting in a chilly room – they only put on the heating in the evening – and were at a loss as to what to do. The note with the telephone number lay on the bed. There was a knock and in came a fat chambermaid, who asked something in Italian, smiling and showing us a large yellow tin. Not knowing what it was all about I said: "Prego" and waved my hand. The chambermaid started scattering the powder on the floor. The powder had no smell, and that seemed suspicious to me: how could powder that did not smell be capable of dealing with ants? There was a vast number of small ants and at nights they swarmed into the bed. As she sprinkled the powder the chambermaid said something ironic, perhaps rude, glancing saucily at us. My wife said that in Italy people who bring misfortune are called "portanero". And one must never use the word aloud. One may resort to any device to indicate who is meant, short of actually using the term. Because they dislike being named aloud. She had read all this stuff somewhere and fixed it in her mind. She used to read a great deal more than I did.

"Do you know him?" I asked.

"Only casually. We used to say 'good day' to one another, and that's all there was to it. Then I started avoiding him."

"He probably spoilt some little rendezvous of yours," I said. "You were running to get there on time and he crossed your path in the yard and you never made it."

"You were the one who did the running," said my wife. "You were always so afraid of being late. And took it all so much to heart, you poor old thing."

"You did more running than I did."

"I never ran, I went by car."

We fell silent. I thought about my wife's last words. When the chambermaid left, I said: "I'll give him a ring. I wonder what he wants me for."

"I beg you: don't ring. Everything has been going so well for us . . ."

"No, I'll call him. Nothing terrible will happen. And what if he needs help?"

"Did he help you at the time?"

"Well, that was when . . ."

"In that case I'm going out," my wife said. "I don't want to see him. I'll go for a stroll and you meet him by yourself. I'll go to the Pincio."

It seemed unfair: she would go off to the Pincio, maybe look in at the Villa Borghese, and I had to sit there in the dreary hotel and wait for a half-forgotten, arrogant, and now unwelcome gentleman.

Over an hour went by. The gentleman had a long way to come. Then I realized he must be coming from Trastevere on foot, as I had once walked everywhere, economizing on lira. His face was the same blotchy, flabby, contemptuous one I remembered, but something important was missing. It was a somehow forlorn face, with the look of desolation that an old square can acquire at twilight. We had seen just such an old square in Lucca, in the evening: it was circular, quiet, dusty, empty of people and cars, everything around it was torpid, as if tired of living; only the washing on the clothes lines against the grey walls spoke of life the eye did not see. Alongside its uninhabited stone meadow ran the hurly-burly of the high street. But the latter had nothing to hold one's interest, just goods for sale. Nothing apart from goods. The crowd surged past the buildings in a thick torrent. A single omnivorous millipede. The old square in Lucca with its quiet and its age – that was what my visitor's face put me in mind of.

He extended his arms wide and said, as if in apology: "You see what it's come to . . ."

His first wife had died of blood poisoning fifteen years before. His second wife had suffered the same misfortune. He was now married for a third time. His present wife loved the children from her first marriage intensely and could not imagine living without them; that was the cause of his present predicament. There was no other way out. Her daughter and son-in-law had gone to America three years ago – they had a little girl who had succumbed to a severe nervous disorder and his wife could not bear the thought of their being over there on their own. She loved them to the point of madness. With a somewhat unnatural love. Everything had become unbelievably complicated. The fact was that his wife's ex-husband, the father of the young woman now living in Atlanta, was the person responsible for my guest's anguish. He himself was therefore being made to suffer and refashion his life because of his grandchildren. He had left his own father in Leningrad when the old man was ninety-one. It was all such a mess. Had I ever been to see the Colosseum at night? I simply had to go and see it at night! I asked him why he was telling me all this? After all, we knew one another hardly at all.

"Why 'hardly at all'?" he retorted. "We know one another. I remember we were on holiday together in Yalta. Then we met on one occasion at the Gradovs'. I know your wife's ex-husband. By the way, do give her my warm greetings."

"I will pass them on," I said. "You are right, everything has got into such a mess."

We sat in the basement restaurant until 10 pm. There was no sign of my wife. We heard the sound of shooting. The waiter came up and said that there was an ambush in progress on the Gorizia; they had found a hidden ammunition cache, evidently belonging to the neo-Fascists; someone had been arrested, and the whole area round the Nomentana had been cordoned off and no one was being allowed through. There was nobody left at the tables in the restaurant apart from the two of us. The waiters and the chef were sitting in front of the television, watching a bicycle race. I began getting nervous. My guest was in no hurry. He had eaten two helpings of spaghetti Bolognese; then we had melon and cups of tea and smoked. The longer we remained seated, the more there appeared on his face his old expression – that of the sad executioner.

He enquired: "Aren't you fed up?"

"With what?"

"With keeping on writing. Are you still hoping to astound the world? Do you imagine that the world will start clucking when it reads your opus? Forgive me my venom. I am bitter because I am taking my leave. Yes, of Europe too. That's why I'm saying to you: one must visit the Colosseum at night. Because neither you nor I will ever have a chance to do so again. Apropos, that goes only for myself . . ."

He hid his face in his hands and sat there. I got up, went out into the street and stood there for a while by the hotel entrance. Two *carabinieri* were strolling up and down, and the electric light from one of the windows of our residence lit up their faces, still fresh from a country upbringing, frozen into immobility. At the corner where our side street came out on to the Nomentana a throng had formed and a car screeched to a half. The pavement had been dug up, someone was jumping the gap. The *carabinieri* turned round and started jogging in that direction. I had the impression that it was my wife shouting: "Let go of me!" I ran towards the spot and caught sight of men in civilian clothes pushing a woman inside a van. She was resisting. Another woman in the crowd started shouting. The Nomentana was ill lit and I elbowed my way nearer to make sure. There was no sign of my wife. When I returned to the restaurant, my guest was still sitting there, his face in his hands.

The next day my wife and I left Rome for Milan. The train came to a halt in a tunnel. The light flickered on and off. When it finally came back on, I pretended to be reading a journal. An acrid smell of burning began to creep into our coach. We closed the windows. There were just the two of us in the compartment. My wife's face suddenly looked crumpled, ashen with fear. She whispered: "I did say to you that there would at once be trouble. You should not have agreed to meet him."

I said: "It's he who's in real trouble."

Then I added: "Now I know everything about him. He knew your ex-husband."

She gave me an intense, puzzled look as if trying to work out whether I really did know everything about her. I gave her a hug. Far away to the north was our house; it would now be in the grip of frost, the roads would be obscured beneath the snowdrifts. In the morning one would have to call out the bulldozer and the warmth would emerge through the roof in a cloud of white smoke.

Translated by Michael Duncan

ELENA RZHEVSKAYA

On the Tarmac

GIVE ME BACK that man in the shoe cleaner's booth, the glass-fronted booth on the corner of Bolshaya Gruzinskaya and Gorky Street, next to the Anchor restaurant. That man with the black beard and the beret, that Aisor from the shoe cleaners' tribe, a tribe which is now nearly extinct, for over the last quarter-century they have prospered in mysterious ways and their children have blended into the background of modern urban life. But the tribal elders still cling fast to their roots, those tribal booths, newer and smarter now, hung with laces and insoles and stacked with boxes of soles and heels and boot tacks – all the wares of a cheap-jack, undemanding trade.

No, it is not the copper or two for shoe cleaning that keeps them going – that is not the half of it, there are wheels within wheels here. But that is not what concerns me now – God forbid! Suppose there *are* wheels within wheels – who cares? I have something else in mind. Every day you might walk past a million minor miracles in this frenzied, driven, deafened city of ours and never notice. It was only once, on that baking 9th July, when I was wending my way home, wrenched from everyday life by a visit to the cemetery, that a miracle of this kind was revealed to me. It was all to do with that man I mentioned a moment ago.

He was sitting on a stool by his booth reading. I had all but gone past when I stopped to have a second look – could that really be Hebrew he was reading? In fact his Bible was a parallel-text edition, with each page split down the middle. As he read he was making pencil marks on the Russian side.

Now in the West, there would be no mystery in that. Every hotel guest there is supplied with a crisp new Bible as well as a telephone directory. But here things are different. We don't publish the Bible. Somehow, by a combination of immense effort and sheer good luck, people "acquire" a copy. Invariably it looks as battered as the world God made, as old as the very Old Testament. Its print has faded to nothing, but a divine presence hovers over the pages, whose surface has been rubbed off by hands at prayer or in thirst for knowledge.

In short, for us Bibles are fabulous beasts.

And to see someone in the middle of Moscow, and on the main street, what's more – and not just someone, but a shoe cleaner, in the middle of his working day – with the Bible on his knees in full view – well! You could live a whole lifetime without that happening.

His beard brushing its surface, he was making his pencil marks on the pages in a businesslike fashion, almost as if he had a seminar to prepare for. All the more unexpected, then, that he should suddenly seize my arm and launch into a stupefying Old Testament homily. And what a homily it was. Poetically seductive, yet with a flavour of charlatanism; a challenge, yet tinged with hypocrisy. It took my breath away.

Giving up his stool to me, he dashed to the booth and preached at me from inside its open doors, squatting, as he did for work, on a low shelf only two foot off the ground. No one could possibly sit lower than that, closer to the tarmac – and so he would sit all day, down at the level of other people's filthy boots.

And from this lowest point of street existence he poured out a diatribe on his view of the truth, on his own talents and his superiority to the heathen rabble. But how to summon up or reproduce the torrential romanticism, the depravity of his sermonizing? Odd fragments only have stayed in my mind.

"The enemy has sent you, for today they distribute meatballs. That in their vanity folk may forget the Holy Ghost."

Leaning out of the booth, he surveyed the vain bustle of the street with a prophet's fiery gaze and said something about how that was where his mission lay.

"But the heathen will remain. There will be smoke and the pit of fire."

Gagarin is a sorcerer. God has called the heavens together. Yea, verily, Satan is but five miles away. God is beyond.

The traffic roared by and the stream of people flowed past and past. When people came up to make a purchase or have their shoes cleaned he would refuse, making it clear by gestures they were not wanted. I expressed my anxiety that he should not lose a day's earnings on my account. But he waved my worries aside, saying that his time was not being spent in vain.

"There is something spiritual in you, deep though it lies. You are no daughter of anger, or I should not have spoken to you, but a daughter of light." And he urged me: "Get yourself baptized. Then the flames of your soul will be lit." For if he converts me, God will grant him a pillar of gold.

But just then, at the bottom of the street, something stirred, started to creep towards us, moving close to the tarmac. Something which goes unnoticed by me and you, who are separated from the tarmac by our great height, who merely trample such things underfoot. Something mouse-coloured, hangdog, belonging to the evening hours, bustling along with its bag of the *Moscow Evening News*, hurrying to carry its cargo wherever it was needed in that sea of tarmac.

My interlocutor pulled out his cash box, flung two kopecks into the palm of the petty trader with his *Evening News*. But hardly had the latter moved off before he tore the paper to shreds.

"What are those lies to me? Fruit of machines! Pulp! I made the purchase out of charity. For my Book is eternal."

"Did your father give it to you?"

"I have only one Father – God. And Christ is my Teacher."

He muttered something about the ordeal by fire which awaited him and about those who hounded him – here there was something about that chief hellhound, his wife, who also worked shifts in this booth.

"Where will you go?"

"Where God shall command."

In the months that followed I rode past in a trolley bus several times and would always look out for the man with the black beard in his booth. I would see him cleaning someone's boots and in full homiletic flight. One winter evening I even met him as I walked past. But he was padlocking the booth and making haste to be gone.

"I must make an effort to go and see him," I told myself; but the dark quotidian fog swallowed me up.

It is too late now. No longer can he be seen in the shoe cleaner's booth at the corner of Gruzinskaya and Gorky Street. Now his wife, the hellhound, is there all the time – a woman with a tight rubbery face and a wreath of synthetic-looking black hair. He is not there and he will not return, it seems. The ordeal by fire which he called down on himself has hounded him away.

Translated by Catriona Kelly

VYACHESLAV PIETSUKH

Anamnesis and Epicrisis

IN OUR SECTION there lived two independent minded tom cats nicknamed Anamnesis and Epicrisis. We – that is Ward 12 – had no idea that these were indeed independent self-sufficient animals who had long since lived on the territory of the Gamaleya Hospital for infectious diseases, so that's why we had bought the tom cats for a fiver from the plumber Konstantin. This Konstantin, who was evidently light-fingered, used to sell everything for five roubles for some reason – from a tablet of Nembutal to concoctions produced in Yugoslavia; it is possible that this was his special eccentricity, like claustrophobia or blind faith in the power of the number thirteen. Our ward bought the cats to pass the time, in so far as at that point we had not yet had time to get to know one another properly and we had nothing to talk about, apart from our common illness, which was incidentally as ridiculous as it was dangerous, and thus not something one felt much like talking about. For those who are interested I shall merely hint that with this illness alcohol is contraindicated on pain of losing one's life; I shall also hint that from it the Blessed Emperor Alexander I passed away in Taganrog.

Anamnesis and Epicrisis turned out to be marvellous tom cats: they were friendly like brothers, melancholy like shop assistants, amusing like talking dolls and as sharp as royal poodles. The person in charge of our section, Vera Sergeevna Osipchuk, used to chase away our cats, but they used either to hide from her in the autoclaves where the nurses in charge of medical procedures sterilized the medical instruments, or else they vanished and returned to the section in the evening, approximately five minutes before the nurses on duty closed the door.

But now I can't even figure out why it is I am going on about these tom cats. For the point at issue has nothing to do with them, but with the fact that there were six of us in the ward, six different-minded blokes, so to speak; at first we lived comparatively peacefully, but then divided into two warring camps and finished off with an abominable incident. Strictly speaking, there was nothing surprising about the fact that we ended up by causing an abominable incident, because a Soviet hospital is truly a democratic institution, with the exception of

special clinics for big-wigs, for their personal assistants and body-
guards and the rest of the politically active powers-that-be, and it is
not strange that in our ward had ended up all sorts and sizes of
everything that creepeth upon the earth, and moreover creatures with
the most diverse moral orientations. In concrete terms: on the left side
as you entered the ward lay the policeman Afanasy Zolkin, beyond
him a furniture warehouseman Sergey Chegodaev, and next to the
window some unimportant trade union official whose surname was
Ottomanchik; on the right side as you entered the ward, lay, as they
say, your humble servant, beyond me a metalworker-adjuster from
the "Manometer" works, Vanya Saburov, and by the window the
professional thief Eduard Masko. As I have already mentioned, all of
these people were unlike each other in the highest degree, each with
his own quirks and weaknesses, his nasty and pleasant sides. About
each of them separately one may say the following . . . The policeman
Zolkin was a fine chap with a light forelock and with eyes that seemed
to be seeking something, although he looked a bit of an imbecile; in
contrast to the rest of us he read nothing, but simply lolled about,
for hours staring at the ceiling, or else went shooting sparrows, arming
himself with a fistful of bullets from a Makarov pistol and a catapult.
The warehouseman Chegodaev was not at all like a warehouseman for
he possessed a most ordinary complexion, read books about the theory
of small numbers, and ate delicately, just as if he were some sort of
attaché. The trade union official whose surname was Ottomanchik was
a middle-aged, unprepossessing, bald man with a well-formed paunch;
he read papers and was also such a secretive person that we didn't even
know his first name; and we had only found out his surname from
some medical paper or other that had by chance been left lying around
on the ward sister's desk. Vanya Saburov read promiscuously, was also
getting on in years, but, as they say, had lasted well and was young
looking, and stood out by virtue of that stamp of Slavic physiognomy
which inspires unqualified affection, and his features were arranged in
such a way as to give the impression that he was all the time remembering the happiest moments of his life: Ivan had come to us direct from
the Botkin hospital, where they had first cut out two thirds of his
stomach, and then had infected him with our disease by means of a
disposable syringe. The thief Masko, who, incidentally, was not at all
ashamed of his profession, although he didn't especially boast about
it either, was an unattractive little chap about thirty-five years old
with an expression of disgust on his face and protruding ears; he wore
a silk dressing gown with a Chinese hieroglyph on the back and read

only detective novels, of which he had a whole mobile library, but he spoke in such confused and deformed language that it was as if he'd suffered a stroke. Naturally, I shall pass over myself in silence.

To our company one must add the quiet madman Viktor Semyonovich Pertsinsky from ward 4, who always came to us to play chess and cards.

We spent our time in the following way: in the morning – treatment, to each his own, then walks along the corridor, smoking in the toilet, calls home using the lone public telephone, which hung on the wall by the exit from our section, playing with the cats, finally breakfast, for which we were always given semolina; after breakfast reading, playful conversations with the duty nurse Nina, the only nurse who would enter into playful conversations with us, walks along the corridor, smoking in the toilet, unauthorized strolls in groups around the building, playing with the cats and then finally lunch, for which we were given water with cabbage, a meatball with pearl barley kasha and the Venerable compote made from . . . well you couldn't even say from what exactly, but incidentally, Masko the thief assured us that we were fed a great deal better than people under investigation and far better again than prisoners; the second half of the day was spent in a more productive and interesting way: in the so-called quiet hour we would each take to our own beds and pick up our books, but almost immediately we would put them aside, because lively conversations always started up of their own accord.

"It's interesting," I, for example, would begin, "why have you, Afanasy, got such a fossilized name – Afanasy?"

Our policeman will answer me:

"Because my grandfather was one of the Old Believers from the Rogozh ancient Russian Orthodox grouping. I'm still more or less normal, my brother has the name Yanuariy – isn't that something!"

"In general these relatives cause nothing but problems," – Ivan Saburov, let us say, will join in. "My grandfather, just imagine, was run over in 1936, then during the war my father was also run over, then my elder brother Nikolay was also run over, and what's more by an ambulance, because they go like madmen. And now I am lying here and am amazed that I have a stomach ulcer, from which in all likelihood I'll die. Why am I amazed? because being run over is a sort of hereditary disease in our family."

Then it would be the turn of the trade union official Ottomanchik, who would always tell different fantastic stories, for example:

"But in 1974 I had an absurd, mysterious illness, I didn't even go to the polyclinic with it – that's the type of illness it was! I was walking, you know, along a street somehow and for some reason I suddenly became desperately thirsty – this took place in summer, in stupendously hot weather. You know, I drank my fill from a tap in some toilet, because everywhere there were absurd queues for fizzy mineral water, and I just go on, and on and on, and suddenly – what the hell is this – something inside me suddenly started speaking! Just like that it started speaking in a clear voice in the vicinity of my stomach, as if a radio had set up there inside me. Well, you know, it says bluntly: 'But if only the engineer in charge of the safety equipment, Comrade Lomeiko, had conscientiously fulfilled his immediate duties and had checked that the wires were insulated . . .' 'Wait a sec!' you know, I say to this foreign voice. 'Who are you, exactly, and why are you talking about safety equipment from inside of me?' The voice correspondingly answers me: 'I,' it says, 'am the shift foreman from the "Elektrolit" works, Grigory Arkadievich Ivanov, and just who are you?' I answer: 'That's none of your business! What sort of a puffed-up peacock do we have here, who has smuggled himself into a man and what's more is asking all sorts of questions?!'"

"Hey, the dirty dogs!" Masko will occasionally howl at the most exciting place.

In such an event someone will ask him: "Why are you getting so het up, Eduard?"

"Well you see this one – what d'you call him . . ." and he turns the cover of the book towards him – "this Boileaunarcejac, those Western cops . . . they went and caught one expert crook out in the open, with nowhere to hide – by the balls. The fool should have, you know, hidden for a while, but he, the idiot, kicked against the pricks! So they nabbed him for his troubles! Well, everywhere the cops are raging, whether you're the age of stagnation or whether you're that . . . capitalism!"

The policeman Zolkin will without fail react to this by saying: "We don't crush vermin like you half as much as we should! If I had my way I'd leave all your gang to rot in the uranium mines!"

And Masko will reply: "No chance, you filthy cop!"

"Hold on, for goodness' sake – honestly!" Chegodaev, let us suppose, will stop the quarrel. "Let's hear the end of the story about the mysterious illness . . ."

"Well then, you know, I say to him," continues Ottomanchik with animation in his voice: "'What sort of a puffed-up peacock do we have here, who has smuggled himself into a man and what's more is asking all sorts of questions!' He answers me, but already without arrogance, as if answering in a conciliatory way: 'Suppose that I crept into you not of my own free will, but by virtue of the natural water cycle. And then, a mass of questions have accumulated in me concerning the socialist method of production. Why is safety equipment in such a run-down state? Why is a working man paid a pittance? Why is our lathe park on a par with science fiction accounts written in the eighteenth century?' I then say to him: 'In as much as I am a trade union official, I refuse to answer such malevolent questions. And in general in my work I am responsible only for the special protective clothing. But in as much as we haven't got any protective clothing, then you may say that in concrete terms I am not responsible for anything.' 'That's the whole point!' says this noxious voice, 'that you answer for nothing, you troublemakers, and therefore have brought a once great state to a dead end. You all really deserve to be dispersed to vegetable storehouses to sort potatoes before you reduce the USSR to the international position of some Ethiopia or other.' 'I – I say – 'refuse to listen to such arrant anti-Soviet propaganda, especially when it issues directly from inside me! This is scandalous,' – I say – 'I'm a party member, selflessly devoted to the cause of socialist construction, and you're making some sort of dissident out of me! I' – I say – 'shall now go to the police, you anti-Soviet bastard! . . .' The voice answers: 'It's precisely you who are the cause of all our national woe, all you who are devoted to socialist construction, because you yourselves don't know what type of a vegetable it is or where you want people to put it. And if you go to the police, then before the duty officer I'll say such things that the relevant State organizations will take an interest in you. You see, they'll put you away, you fool, in Lefortovo!'"

At this time, that is somewhere in the middle of the quiet hour, the madman Pertsinsky usually comes into our ward, sits down in silence at a table and starts to set out the chesspieces.

"Naturally, of course, I didn't go to the police, in as much as that would have been an absurd step: well how would I have proved to the relevant organizations that it was not me spreading undoubted slander about our social systems, but that pest which had ensconced himself inside me! But he keeps on nagging, do you see, nagging away with his narrow-minded opinions . . . There's nothing to be done, I think, I'll have to go to our local polyclinic, let the doctors work out what's going on, after all they do have their oath of confidentiality, and, perhaps, this mess won't get as far as Lefortovo. And at this point I suddenly needed to relieve myself. Well, I couldn't hang on, what with the nearest public convenience being, as you yourselves will understand, a minimum of four trolleybus stops away. There was nothing to be done: I urinated in the first courtyard entrance that came my way. And suddenly a miracle: no sooner had I urinated than the foreign voice inside me fell silent! So what was all this? Personally to this day I can't understand what type of absurd, mysterious illness seized me . . ."

I am able to offer the following suggestion: "Perhaps you suffered from a temporary fit of madness, similar to the temporary paralysis people have, but only, so to say, a transient one, like a second-long fainting fit on your feet."

"No," Pertsinsky will object, "this was something else. In the psychiatric literature there are no such incidents described. I state this with full confidence, because I've read everything about psychiatry. And then, Comrade Ottomanchik, you do not resemble a madman one little bit. They are all sort of weak and at the same time hostilely pensive, just as if they are working out a plan for a political assassination."

"And how do you know?" Masko will without fail wind him up.

"How can I not know when I myself was a madman! I, comrades – forgive me for the openness – have passed through all the psychiatric hospitals and even after this have remained alive. In Kuibishev, for example, the conditions are excellent, they'd never even heard of cockroaches there. But in Matrosskaya Tishina a male nurse walks around the wards with a whip as big as this – if he hits you once you'll soon forget what's wrong with you! And many of the diagnoses of what was wrong with the lads were odd, because their crimes were pretty odd too: in the Gannushkin clinic one even spoke the whole time in Prakrit! – he most likely thought himself Buddha."

"What a nice male orderly," Vanya Saburov will say thoughtfully. "That's a real disorderly for you, not an orderly at all."

"By the way, about Buddha", Chegodaev will keep up the conversation. "Most likely of all is that by chance the spirit of some dead man took up residence inside you, Ottomanchik. You see for Buddhists the human soul is continuously transmigrating into different objects and organisms, let us say, from a man into a tree, from a tree into a fish, from a fish into water . . ."

"Hang on a minute, this is already mysticism!" said Ottomanchik, refusing to accept Chegodaev's hypothesis.

"But why?" said Chegodaev, not agreeing with him. "It was with good reason that the very same fellow who by mistake ensconced himself in you mentioned the circulation of water in nature. I dare say he really was Grigory Arkadevich Ivanov, a shift foreman from the 'Elektrolit' works, and then he was electrocuted owing to the oversight of the engineer Lomeiko who was responsible for the safety equipment, and then Ivanov was buried and his soul, in accordance with Buddhist teaching, went into the subsoil waters, and then you Ottomanchik drank, as it were, the shift foreman, and he started to make these criticisms. And eventually you freed yourself of him by pissing in the first yard you came to. In my opinion, this forms a totally logical picture . . ."

Ottomanchik probably will wonder for a certain time how to overturn this fantastic theory and simultaneously revenge himself against the joker, but nothing will come to mind and he will merely turn away from us towards the wall, pretending that drowsiness has overcome him.

After the quiet hour and right up until supper we played chess and cards for stakes of two kopecks, sometimes organizing short breaks, because it was usually at this time that our players were visited by, as it were, strangers from real life – acquaintances and relatives. I was the only one, poor fellow, not to be visited by any swine, but, incidentally, I myself had most strongly forbidden them to trudge out to the hospital to see me, for I was embarrassed about showing myself to people who respected me in that mocking jester's uniform in which they robe patients in our country; I am referring to the undershirt cut to a military model, the sort which, most probably, General Suvorov's great heroic warriors used to wear, wide baggy monsters of trousers made of flannelette of a pale and gloomy shade and a most comic top with sleeves made to measure for an adolescent, which befitted perhaps only a beggar at a railway station. In order to dispel my quiet longing for a visitor who had disobeyed my command, I started to amuse myself with the cats and immediately forget everything. This is no wonder: Anamnesis, by what seemed to be mere random shuffling of his paws, was able to construct various geometric shapes out of matches, while Epicrisis would meanly destroy them; or I would sit the cats on the bed and would retell them *Alice's Adventures in Wonderland*, and they would listen attentively and, it seems to me, would act out the story with their eyes; or I would teach them to stand on their heads, something which, to tell the truth, they couldn't stand, but which they nevertheless endured out of respect for man.

The most exhausting and sad time was the period from supper to midnight, when the section gradually went to sleep and step by step a silence, precisely a hospital silence, a sick silence, would spread everywhere. We would wander about alone, spending too much time thumbing in our heads our own unhappy thoughts, continually smoking in the washroom and for long periods at a stretch gazing at the black windows, some foreseeing insomnia, others nightmares. Before sleep we always had time for a collective safari after mosquitoes, which were unbelievably abundant in our section, and killed them down to the last creature due to the justifiable fear that they would spread infection from the fourth floor, where our AIDS patients were fading away. Nearer to midnight Masko the thief would start to receive exotic phonecalls, and he would depart for the duty desk for one or another of his mysterious conversations – and this even though the patients were strictly forbidden to use the staff telephone – and then Ivan would go to visit Nurse Nina and they would lock themselves away in a room marked "Laboratory", and then a female doctor from the administration block would appear and give Chegodaev a mysterious injection – Chegodaev would craftily claim that they were injecting him with a certain somnambuline – with the result that his face would soon acquire uncharacteristic features and would start depicting such profound contentment that it was as if he was lying there with a voice from above whispering pleasant prophecies to him. Round about midnight all of my fellow patients in the ward would doze off, and gradually all of our wide section would become pacified too, in general all noises of life would fall silent, and only the quiet madman Pertsinsky would for a long time yet still wander back and forth along the corridor, talking to himself. At night nearly everyone was delirious: I do not know whether I was delirious or not, but whenever I happened to wake up in the middle of the night a wild and incoherent chorus of voices, one may say, could be heard in the ward:

"Hands on head, spread your legs . . ." let us say, would be the command of the policeman Zolkin.

"Fool!" Vanya would splutter angrily in his sleep. "Here the thread is 0.2, but you went and took a 0.4 screw thread die . . ."

"Inquorate, inquorate! . . ." is Ottomanchik's unpleasant howl.

Masko would dream of the camp and he would yell: "Fifth detachment, prepare to be frisked! . . ."

In the mornings we would wake up because the sister on duty would have stuck a thermometer into us, and the day would start in accordance with the established pattern.

And then we divided into two warring camps and we gradually fought more and more until the thing ended with an abominable incident. Spring was already winding up, it was the middle of May, and I clearly remember that the previous day it had got colder, and then suddenly the protective greenery of the oak had appeared. On that memorable day the whole ward deliberately went to look at this whim of our native land's nature, that is even before breakfast we set off for the two young oaklings which had sprung up by the entrance to the morgue, and moreover Eduard Masko even stroked the new-born leaves a few times with his iniquitous hands; and why this sensitivity towards botany had taken us over I don't understand; but, possibly, it possessed us because our ward sort of symbolized a life which was, if not perhaps guttering, was then at least uncertain, and this life which was practically healthy and young stirred us, though the excitement was not free of an undesirable tinge of envy.

On returning to the ward we took to our beds, and no sooner had Vanya Saburov said, not addressing anyone in particular: "And why don't they bring us our medicine today?" – when duty nurse Nina came into our ward and announced that the medicinal treatment had been temporarily postponed owing to the fact that the medicines hadn't been delivered. Masko indistinctly howled something in response to this announcement, since in general he reacted fearfully to any restrictions of his rights, but we calmed him down by saying things like "it hasn't been delivered, and who cares, and we don't sodding mind that they haven't delivered it." However Afanasy Zolkin enquired all the same: "It would be interesting to know, incidentally, exactly why the medicine hasn't been delivered today?"

Nina said to him: "I can't answer that question. That's a question for the head physician, who's building a summer home in Ilinskoye."

"This, lads, is an entire Slavic mystery!" I noted with sad delight. "Just imagine, who in the West would be able to understand such causation: patients are ill in hospital in part because the head physicians are building themselves summer residences . . . For the West this is truly a conundrum, it's just as if one were to prove that the reason why the moon revolves around the earth is because there is no washing powder in the shops . . ."

"It's just that there each person has only two teaspoonfuls worth of brains," was Ottomanchik's reaction to my observation. "Therefore they understand nothing, whereas for us – thanks to our Russian native wit – everything is as clear as noonday."

Also after breakfast Konstantin the plumber looked in to see us, and suggested that we buy from him for a fiver a whole file of blank hospital forms, which Eduard Masko acquired; moreover he enquired of Konstantin why all his goods had the one fixed price, but the plumber kept an enigmatic silence.

After breakfast the medics did their rounds: Vera Sergeevna Osip-chuk appeared, accompanied by a long-legged female duty doctor, whose name and patronymic we didn't know, and they started to inspect each of us in turn. When it was the turn of the thief Masko, and when Vera Sergeevna had as usual asked him: "How's business?" – he answered in his incoherent language:

"Chebrikov is in charge of all the business. Us . . . we have . . . this is – just trivial business."

When it was the turn of the policeman Zolkin, he made his complaint: "Well, what a system you have here, Vera Sergeevna," he said. "Are you aware that the medicine hasn't been delivered to our section today?"

"It doesn't matter," said Vera Sergeevna. "You won't die. Our vegetable shop hasn't had any deliveries of vegetables for two weeks now, and everything's OK, somehow we manage to survive. All the more so because the medicines are given to you as a mere formality, as it were, because your illness can't be cured by using medicines anyway, but it just passes of its own accord. For you the only real medicine is rest and sleep."

To this I replied: "Soviet medicine has fallen on its feet very nicely!"

"And what are you particularly dissatisfied with?" The long-legged doctor turned to me and evilly raised her eyebrows.

"Oh no, I am, strictly speaking, satisfied with everything, and I'm even happy: I have my sight and my hearing, my heart sends the blood round – that is, I'll survive here under your care, and for that one should be grateful. The only thing is I wonder at Soviet medicine, which only knows how to supervise nature's activities. Or is this Soviet medicine's special strategic direction? Or has it also come to a dead end here?"

"It's all the result of our poverty," said Ivan somewhat ruefully. "The doctors would perhaps be all too glad to swamp us with every possible type of medicine, but where can you get hold of them in the midst of such ruin? . . ."

The long-legged doctor advised: "In your position, comrade patients, you should lie quietly and think about pleasant things, and not start criticizing."

"And indeed you shouldn't worry at all," added Osipchuk.

And they left, having forgotten unintentionally to examine Cheg-odaev and me.

At half past nine we had breakfast, then went to phone home, smoked in the washroom, started up playful conversations with Nina, wandered along the corridor and, lying on our separate beds read our various books. After my eyes became seriously dazzled owing to the fact that my volume of Kleist had been published before the orthography reform I pulled Anamnesis and Epicrisis on to my bed; my intention was to continue telling them *Alice's Adventures in Wonderland*, but for some reason the cats listened to me inattentively; so then I fell silent and came over all pensive about the fact that to be a tom cat was by no means the worst fate that could befall one, not the worst if only for the reason that a normal cat can diagnose its own illness infallibly, will unerringly go out and find the necessary medicinal plant and, consequently, has no need whatsoever of head physicians who build summer residences; and a few minutes before lunch my train of thought got stuck on the idea that, perhaps, the Creator made a mistake in choosing the monkey as the half-prepared raw material to use in creating man.

After lunch, during the quiet hour, an argument occurred in our ward, which led us to split into two warring camps, a fact to which I have already referred.

"The main point is that there's really no one to complain to," Ottomanchik suddenly started saying. "Those on high would see our complaints and suggestions in the grave. I'm saying this from bitter experience. I've written to every institution in my time, right up to the main office of UNESCO, and even they sent me a bureaucrat's formal non-reply from abroad, saying, as it were, all things considered, they didn't have the right to interfere in our internal affairs, even though in our country they were as white as soot, as everyone knew . . ."

Chegodaev interrupted him.

"Commander, I didn't expect such renegade opinions from you, and, moreover, I didn't expect you to correspond with the enemy."

"So what did I complain about?" Ottomanchik started to try to get out of it. "You see I wasn't complaining about Soviet power, but I was uncovering individual outrages which distort the face of developed socialism! The thing is, the following incident somehow occurred with us . . ."

"Did someone once more set up shop inside you?" Ivan asked him and made a comical face.

"Hey, let the man finish!" said Zolkin in annoyance. "Let him have his say, and then you can even tie him in knots if he spins too unrealistic a tale."

"You . . . and everything . . ." said Masko, "you know, answer for your words, you. You're not in the duty room now."

Ottomanchik continued his story:

"So then in, when was it, 1980, the post of manager fell vacant. Our former boss got caught on a large bribe, that is, he bribed the wrong person, and he was quietly retired with a personal pension with all the fringe benefits the elite enjoy. Therefore the manager's job was open. Well, we were all of course in a trance, because we didn't know what type of crocodile they'd hang around our necks. For the old boss had been a dear; he would confer favours upon you, and would be kind to you, would not betray you, and would reward you – and all this, you know, in a way somehow like a family favour, as if he were not your boss but your brother-in-law on your wife's side.

"Usually such appointments drag on for three months at a minimum, but here literally on the third day there appeared an absurd little man about thirty-five years old, well-groomed, tidy, who directly took over the boss's office. We were all of course in a trance, because he was a painfully absurd type, unreliable, I would say, a fraught character, and, the main thing, as unlike a member of the Party elite as . . ."

And Ottomanchik showed the little nail on his little finger.

"Well, OK: the first day goes all right, the second day all right, but on the third day Babel starts! It transpires that this goblin has thought up some crazy way of organizing labour, in which you don't get the chance to exchange even the odd word with your workmates. That means, instead of the normal production process, we are all rushing round in small circles like rats in a treadmill, have to think until we sweat like pigs, have to construct some sort of graph, in short – the ancient Egyptian exploitation of human labour starts up. And if, let us say, they find you knitting or you've sidled off for an hour or two, then immediately it's would you be so good as to write out your own resignation . . .

"We endured and endured, and then we started to write complaints. I even sent a statement to the UNESCO headquarters, because our organizations were not reacting at all to the actions of this enemy of the people, but the capitalists just sent me a bureaucrat's non-reply, saying that we don't have the right to interfere in your internal affairs, even though they are as white as soot, everyone knows that. We also experimented with such a tried and tested weapon of the proletariat as actively ignoring our production requirements, but even this didn't help: our new goblin just went and threw out on to the streets about a dozen fathers, heads of households, condomn . . . condomn . . . , well, how do you say it, condomning young children to hungry vegetation. It would seem as if he'd fully unmasked himself as an enemy hireling, but our organizations didn't say a word.

"And then about six months later, when we had already produced such an economic effect that a commission was sent by the ministry to check up on us, it suddenly became clear that our Judas is in fact a False Dmitry and a Pretender. One chap from the personnel department somehow or other went hunting with one influential inspector and being one over the eight asked him: 'What did you' – let us say, Ivan Ivanovich – 'Ivan Ivanovich, mean by sending such an imbecile who makes the people groan in agony and flee in all directions?' And the inspector, also one over the eight, answered him: 'We haven't sent you anyone, the candidacies for the post of manager are still only just being worked out on high.' 'What do you mean you haven't sent anyone,' the man from personnel enquires, 'when we received an official phone call from the Soviet of Ministries, when' – let us say, Pyotr Petrovich – 'Pyotr Petrovich himself recommended this bandit to us? . . .' Then it is the turn of the inspector to take an interest: 'And who exactly might this Pyotr Petrovich be?' And at this point it transpires, that hell only knows who this very Pyotr Petrovich might be!

"In a word, the bastard had been unmasked! It turns out that he was a simple someone with a doctorate who had thought up an ancient Egyptian system of exploiting human labour and had even directly faked his identity to put this system into action. Of course, they pinned some other indirect crime on him, the scoundrel, forging the bonds of a State loan, I think, and slapped a long sentence on him. If I'm not mistaken, about seven years with especially harsh conditions."

"That is . . ." Masko reacted to the story he'd heard, "with specially harsh conditions also, what's it called . . . is nothing. You know, if you're a real criminal, it's no shit enduring such a régime."

Zolkin said: "Soon we'll be permitted to fire on criminals without shouting a warning. And then you'll dance like a louse in a frying pan!"

"O Lord!" I said. "How interesting it is to live!"

"What do you mean by that?" Chegodaev asked me, guardedly for some reason.

I held back a little with my answer, because at that moment the quiet madman Pertsinsky entered our ward and started to set up the chess pieces.

"I'm talking about the fact," I said after my pause, "that here the times of disorder have set in once again, and in such epochs it is always interesting to live. You see it's been like that with us since time immemorial: fifty years of vegetation, then – life, fifty years of vegetation, then – life. The Christians against the pagans, Suzdal against Novgorod, the oprichniks against the boyars, the peasants against the nobles, the Reds against the Whites, all sorts of scum against normal people – isn't all this interesting?!"

"Scum, to whom are you referring?" Ottomanchik asked me.

"To no one" I said evasively.

"No, you are truly the spineless intelligentsia," announced Ivan, turning to me. "I don't place any hopes on you, I place my hopes on the All-Soviet proletariat, which will sooner or later take power from the political mandarins!"

"You've already taken power once", said Chegodaev to him venomously. "And you took it in such a cunning way, that even to this day no one knows where this power is and to whom it belongs in actual fact."

"To be honest, such a thought also came to me," admitted Ottomanchik with a crestfallen air. "You see, one army general told me – and, by the way, we have only five such generals for the whole of the country – that he was planning to holiday on the Crimean coast, but, as they say, nothing of the sort. He sends his special messenger beforehand to get the railway ticket, but the messenger returns and reports that, he says, there are no tickets right up until the 4th of November. The general put his special messenger under arrest for several days and personally phoned his army ticket office and demanded a ticket in the direction of the Crimea. But they answer him, you understand, that there are no tickets and none is expected right up until the 4th of November. He went hither and thither, even got the Central Committee of the Party involved – after all he is a general in the army, and not any old mongrel – and, you know, in the end he got what he wanted: they gave him a ticket for some sort of absurd, highly secret train which has some special purpose. He got ready, travelled to the Kursk station, found his closed train, entered the carriage, and there, just imagine, everywhere without exception were dark-skinned lads from the Central Market, who had sold all the gifts of nature and were travelling to rest from their upright labours. One has to ask: who is really in charge of the parade here? I just can't work it out – for you see one has somehow to come to some sort of living arrangement with reality, with those who are really in charge of the ball . . ."

"There's no denying all of that," said Ivan. "No sooner were the people given a whiff of freedom than everything turned upside down; that is, some sort of foggy life has set in."

"And this . . . the cops have let themselves go . . . how is this?!" joined in Masko. "Earlier, just give a cop a hundred roubles and everything and all your problems were solved. But now, the dirty dogs, they don't even want to talk things over! . . . Their wage has been increased, perhaps . . ."

"Chance would be a fine thing!" said Zolkin angrily. "We risk your bandit bullets for, one may say, a mere pittance. And in general it's an unanswered question who's rooting out whom nowadays – that is, the police the criminal element, or the criminal element the police!"

Precisely as these words were being spoken the duty nurse Nina looked into our ward and told our policeman that his fiancée had come to visit him. Zolkin cheered up, that is, he momentarily lost his pained expression, examined himself with interest in the mirror, smoothed his hair, plucked out a few little hairs from his nose, borrowed some decent slippers from Chegodaev and set off for his rendezvous, mumbling something or other to himself.

"If it wasn't for my old mother," said Pertsinsky suddenly, still setting up the chesspieces, "I wouldn't stay in this life a minute longer than necessary. I'd open up the Kingston valves and go to the bottom."

"You're a real human steamship," said Chegodaev to him. "Your surname isn't by any chance steamship *Nette*?"

"Pertsinsky, get rid of these suicidal tendencies," I said. "They don't befit a decent man. The first obligation a decent man has is to live. His second obligation is to live well. Here you have all the commandments of a decent man."

"Well, a right Sermon on the Mount!" Chegodaev once again spoke maliciously. "Your surname isn't Christ by any chance?"

"Why are you always stirring people up?" Vanya intervened on my behalf. "Why are you always winding people up? Or do you find it very jolly lying here? I'll quickly spoil your little mood for you. Do you think I don't understand that you're no furniture warehouseman, but a pure-bred scoundrel, an enemy of the working people and a parasite? Hey, why are you looking at me like a horse looking at a bike? When I clout you on the head with this chair now you'll soon come to your senses!"

"You . . . and this . . . stop this, mate!" said Masko. "You'd better shut it . . . you know, stop throwing your weight around, or I'll give you a bloody nose."

"And you shut your gob too, you thieving parasite!" Ivan stood firm. "If I have to I'll sort your mob out without any help from the police!"

At this moment, to speak of the devil, a pensive and sad Zolkin returned to the ward.

"What's this, Afonya? Why are you so sad?" Ottomanchik asked him.

"Oh, to hell with her, the fool!" answered Zolkin and in a sort of aloof way waved his hand. "Let me, I say to her, at least cop a few feels – but she won't! . . . She says: 'You're infected, a girl could pick something up from you.'"

"But you should have said to her," advised Ottomanchik, "that, firstly, we haven't been infectious for a long time now, and secondly, that no infection can be caught by feeling. See, you could say, like, the AIDers from the fourth floor, you should give *them* a wide berth."

"But I explained everything to her in simple terms! Still she wouldn't give it to me – well, such a stupid cow, what can you expect!"

"Why did you choose such a woman then?"

"Well, I didn't choose her. I rescued her, when about fifteen young louts had ganged up to rape her. Then later she came to our hostel herself and said: 'Let us be friends, hero.'"

"Hey, the bastards, look what they're doing!" Ivan said with feeling. "Women can't go out any more, even if you take them on a short lead! . . ."

"The swine have really let themselves go, that's certain," I confirmed. "It's time, oh it's time to take these guys in hand."

"Well, let us say, all your progress is in vain," Chegodaev said to me as if he were doing me a service. "Strong men are ineradicable, I'm telling you this as neighbours, speaking with total candour. For as long as this mess of ours exists – and it has always existed and will exist for ever – the lord of life will always be the strong, the enterprising man. Therefore, don't fret needlessly; as they say in Odessa, don't break your heart."

Zolkin asked Chegodaev, with undisguised hatred written on his face: "Ever heard of the RT-70?"

"And what's that when it's at home?" Chegodaev took a lively interest and even sat up a bit in his bed.

"What it is is a new weapon against you lot: a rubber truncheon seventy centimetres long!"

"That's like trying to scare a hedgehog with your bare bum!" said Ivan, smirking sorrowfully. "Really, Afonya, have you gone mad or something? They are armed with light artillery most likely, and there you are planning to beat them off with sticks!"

"This country of ours is a bit of a wild one," I said, also sorrowfully. "And our police are the poverty-stricken detachment of an indigent population."

"Well, never mind," announced Ivan. "Cobblestones are also a weapon of the proletariat. If every worker takes a cobblestone each, then even heavy artillery won't save these criminal bastards."

"You'll be washing blood off your face, Mr Shock-Worker," said Masko calmly.

For a certain time everyone fell silent, and then Pertsinsky made an interesting observation.

"How unfriendly we Russians are to one another! For example, Hungarians or Germans are all bosom friends with their fellow countrymen, and an Egyptian will stand up solid as a rock for another Egyptian, but there is no love lost between Russians, not because there's any underlying class reasons for this, but simply there's no love lost between them and that's all."

"We have our reasons," said Ivan darkly.

"Hey, why are you always quarrelling, lads!" Ottomanchik suddenly pleaded. "Here, look at our tom cats: they too are Russian, but they're quite happy just to sit there on the windowsill . . ."

And in actual fact Anamnesis and Epicrisis were amicably stretched out on the windowsill, united in one ball of fur, and were warming themselves in the May sun.

"Oh yeah!" said Chegodaev. "You just let a she near them, and then we'll see what sort of relations develop."

Zolkin was very much intrigued by this experiment, and he ran out to look for a she for the experiment. By chance he very quickly found one in the hospital courtyard, and I had not even had time to receive an answer to my question – "I'm curious, why do you steal, Eduard? Especially seeing as there's nothing to buy now anyway . . ." – when Zolkin appeared with his kidnapped cat, which he lugged fastidiously by the scruff of her neck, and planted on the windowsill next to our young lads. Anamnesis and Epicrisis definitely livened up; however things didn't go any further than so-called sloppy sentimentality with this trinity: the toms simply licked the unexpected girlfriend, and even then somewhat coolly, as if taking preventative measures, or according to some feline rule, or else with the implied message that we should leave them in peace.

Out of disappointment my companions turned to chess and their beloved cards. But I got myself comfortable and woke up as a result of the scandal that had ignited by that time at the table.

"You . . . and everything . . ." said Masko to the poor Pertsinsky with a sort of tenderly dangerous note in his voice, "you may be a madman, but this . . . like a healthy-minded person, you're capable of understanding your own best interest. At the end of the day why did you throw down the King of Spades instead of the Seven of Clubs? Or was it you know . . . you think that I'm kidding? Here's a real devil for you, and everything, pretends he's a loony, but he can cheat like a real criminal."

"Just what do you think you're doing?" exclaimed Pertsinksy, and his voice welled up with psychopathic weeping. "Of course I am a mentally ill person, but I've never cheated in my life, because I am also a decent man."

Chegodaev said: "Leave him, Edik. If this passenger is proud of the fact that he's a decent man, it means that he is definitely mentally disturbed."

"Oh no, brother," disagreed Vanya with feeling, "I would ask you not to twist the facts! Mentally disturbed people – that's you, various cheats and thieves, whereas Pertsinsky is comparatively normal, because he wouldn't hurt even a fly."

"You, devil, that is . . . you've gone too far this time," said Masko threateningly. "If you don't, basically speaking, control yourself, I'll knock your block off!"

At this point I intervened in the exchange of fire.

"Listen, Eduard: you too should also keep yourself under control."

"We haven't given the rotten intelligentsia the right to speak at all," Chegodaev rebuffed me.

"Frankly speaking, there are already quite clearly two criminal offences here," announced Afanasy Zolkin and threw down his cards. "The threat to use violence and slander. Perhaps you want, you sons of bitches, to be taken right away from the hospital in handcuffs?"

"You . . . that thing . . ." Masko had wanted to say something, but Chegodaev interrupted him.

"Cool down, Edik," he advised, "or else this loony really will call out a detail and they'll lock us up in solitary the day before they start handing out the chocolates."

Masko unwillingly and grudgingly obeyed, but Zolkin, judging by everything, had got seriously carried away with his idea.

"No, I ask you: do you want, you sons of bitches, to be taken right away from the hospital in handcuffs?"

It is hard to say how this scandal might have ended if at the moment this threat was made Konstantin the plumber had not appeared and offered ten odd volumes of the Brockhaus and Efron encyclopedia for a fiver. I acquired these books and at the same time enquired: "And will you sell me a second-hand car for the same price?"

Konstantin made a sign with his eyes that seemed to indicate that he would even find a five-rouble car and that he was taking my crazy demand into consideration.

This episode had a pacifying effect on us: the ward suddenly calmed down, and everyone returned to his book, with the exception of Afanasy Zolkin, who took his catapult out of his bedside cupboard and went off to shoot sparrows in the yard, and also excepting poor Pertsinsky, who sat for a little while longer with us, his moist gaze fixed on some interesting point or other on the ceiling, and then with his heavy and unhealthy gait dragged himself back to his ward: everything clearly indicated that he remained seriously offended by the accusation of cheating.

About two hours later we were already having supper, gazing severely at our plates, and then the most tormenting period of the day set in, that time when there was nothing to do, well, nothing constructive to do, especially since that evening we didn't go on safari after the mosquitoes because of the words there had been between us. Just after ten Vanya Saburov went to visit the duty nurse Nina. At around eleven Nina herself looked in and said to Masko: "Masko, there's an international call for you from Monte Carlo . . ." and there was nothing else of note apart from this. However something unpleasant was hovering in the odorous hospital air, something foreboding, insidious, perhaps because the atmospheric pressure had changed, or else because I simply felt unwell. Nearer to midnight our ward was already asleep, and only I was tormented in my bed. I had already begun to get slightly drowsy when Anamnesis and Epicrisis suddenly started up some unusual and frightening game: some of the time they would leap up unbelievably high and let out a far from cat-like howl, then they would hurl themselves at the walls, scratching them with their claws, then they would crawl – the leopard crawl, I suppose you could say – on their bellies, giving out a snakelike hiss as they did so. I became obsessed with them and, putting on my slippers, went into the corridor, hoping to get sleepy by walking. There was some sort of commotion taking place next to Ward 4: the sisters were rushing to and fro, bringing and taking away weird medical apparatus, doctors unfamiliar to me appeared and disappeared. I set off for where the action was taking place, eaten up as I was with curiosity, and when I glanced into Ward 4 the first thing I saw was that Pertsinsky's bed was empty, and all the bed linen had been removed, and even the striped mattress had been rolled up.

"But where then is Pertsinsky?" I asked a cardiologist who just happened to turn up at that moment, trundling before him apparatus that was obviously cardiological.

"Your Pertsinsky's turned up his toes," the doctor answered, hesitating somewhat. "He's just been sent to the morgue."

Having said this the cardiologist with a nimble movement knocked his jaw, which had unexpectedly become dislocated, back into position.

"I feel sorry for the chap," I said, and there ran through me that sensation which always runs through a man when he is suddenly confronted with the demise of someone who was just recently wandering around, speaking, playing cards, an offended creature made in his own likeness; that is, the feeling in his soul is at once sort of horrid and simultaneously frivolous; moreover some part of me, let us say one sixth, put to shame the other five sixths, for the reason that they weren't all that shaken by the death of a creature just like myself. "But what did the poor chap die of?"

"The devil only knows," said the cardiologist. "In such cases we write 'severe coronary insufficiency'. But that is exactly the same as saying that suffocation is the reason why a suicide dies."

And he once more put his dislocated jaw back into place. It was only at this point that I noticed that the cardiologist was so drunk that he was, as they say, insensible, and, in all likelihood, had fallen over somewhere or had his jaw smashed in a fight; incidentally, he was drunk in the proper medical manner: if it hadn't been for the dislocated jaw, the strange pallor of his face and the delayed reaction to questions, you would never have said that he was drunk.

Finally I asked him, for no apparent reason: "You don't happen to know why the plumber here sells things for five roubles? Why is this – didn't he learn to count beyond five?"

"No, no," came the answer, "it's just that in our shop on the corner the port costs four roubles and fifty-two kopecks."

I said: "That is, there's absolutely no logic to it."

"No logic at all!" said the cardiologist, agreeing with my position and showing some exasperation.

Pertsinsky's death oppressed me, naturally, but when I had returned to the ward and settled down in my bed I continued to wonder at myself for a long time, surprised that I was nevertheless a thick-skinned unfeeling man, that a comrade had died but I was interested in the logic of dodgers as if nothing had happened. After a certain time I dropped off and I had such an awful dream that I woke up in a sticky sweat from fright: I dreamt that the head of our section, Vera Sergeevna Osipchuk, had for some reason decided to cut my nails and, armed with huge tailor's scissors, had set about cutting off the phalanxes of my fingers. On waking up, I wiped myself with a towel and once more went into the corridor. It was unpleasantly quiet and gloomy there as before, like in a cave lit up by a distant pitch torch, in as much as at night in our corridor the only light was a lamp above the office in the duty area, which gave out an illumination which was truly medieval. I walked around a bit, back and forth, and then I sat down near an open wooden window and lit up; I sat there and smoked, looked into the dark hospital yard, which was giving off the aroma of May, and offhandedly, in a slipshod fashion so to say, I reflected that in case of special emergency there was always death as a way out of the sticky Russian situation. Then a Georgian from Ward 3 approached me and asked for a light. I gave him a cigarette; then nurse Nina came up and asked for a light. I gave her a cigarette; and then Pertsinsky approached and also asked for a light. I gave him a cigarette too, but as I did so I asked him a question.

"But I thought you were a non-smoker, yes?"

"Being here's enough to make you start," said Pertsinsky bad-temperedly and rapidly vanished into thin air.

"Wait a minute! . . ." I uttered after him, realizing that I'd just been speaking with a ghost, but it was too late, and my cry hung stupidly in the air, like a sail in windless weather; the most curious thing was that Pertsinsky's appearance hadn't stunned me at all – it hadn't stunned me, and that was that.

Next morning my sleep ended when the duty nurse stuck a thermometer into me and in this way woke me up. I sat up in bed and told my fellow sufferers: "Lads, last night I saw a real ghost! Moreover, even in the other world we have total chaos: just imagine, a ghost came here to scrounge a cigarette – this means that even there there's poverty and shortages."

"And why are you amazed that you met a ghost?" Chegodaev, not without spiteful innuendo, dampened my enthusiasm. "If we can buy a second-hand car for five roubles here, then ghosts are just as unsurprising as poverty and shortages."

Vanya said to me: "You probably haven't woken up yet, lad."

"Me?" I stuttered. "That is, yes, of course, I wanted to say that Pertsinsky passed away last night."

"I'm sorry?" Zolkin said, sounding somehow as if he was in charge.

"I said that Pertsinsky died last night from severe coronary insufficiency, don't you understand Russian?"

Some time passed in silence, and then Vanya Saburov exclaimed, pointing in Masko's direction with the cast-iron gesture of the statue of Yury Dolgoruky: "It was you, scum, who brought him to his death! You're a cheap thief yourself, and you called a good man a cardsharp! 'Cos Pertsinsky undoubtedly died from stress, that is, as a result of you, you dog, calling him a cardsharp!"

"OK . . . and this . . . that's it!" said Masko threateningly. "My patience has burst and everything! Now I'm going to fill you in . . ."

I warned: "Just you try to lay a finger on Ivan!"

"And you just keep quiet a bit, passenger," Chegodaev threatened me and rummaged under his pillow — perhaps even looking for a pistol; happily it turned out that he simply kept his sweets there.

"Don't hit them, lads!" said a much cheered-up Afanasy Zolkin to Ivan and me. "*Now* I'll tame his mafia."

Quite naturally, at this point a bloody battle started up. At first the fighting was hand-to-hand, but then chairs were brought into action, glucose bottles, various small pieces of hospital furniture and even the chessboard. In the heat of battle Zolkin asked Ottomanchik: "And why are you shirking, not fighting for the interests of the workers? A fine name this — trade union! . . ."

"No," Ottomanchik tried to excuse himself, "I'll wait a while. I'll just see which way the wind is blowing."

Afonya Zolkin, one must assume, didn't take me into consideration to begin with, as I was a representative of the spineless intelligentsia, incapable of battling physically for justice; and he was right in not taking me into consideration to begin with.

Meanwhile Anamnesis and Epicrisis were so terrified by our fight that in their panic they huddled together beneath my cupboard and merely looked out from under it, revealing on their faces a mixture of horror and childlike wonder. From time to time I glanced under the cupboard and thought about the fact that tom cats were probably the most fortunate of creatures; not only had they been endowed with certain supernatural characteristics from the point of view of man, for example, the ability to dematerialize immediately after death, but they were also comparatively kind-hearted, peaceful creatures . . .

In general I suffer from the bad habit of being carried away with an idea, as if on purpose, in the most inopportune situations. All around the battle was raging, broken glass was ringing, the furniture creaked as it broke, savage cries disturbed the section, but I lay in my bed and in thought examined the following idea closely: obviously, the principal way in which the Russian people differs from all other peoples is that Russians – how to put this as carefully as possibly? – don't worship each other. The Dutch, for example, will stand up for each other like a solid rock, and the Pope is more likely to renounce Catholicism than a Dutchman is to disavow a fellow Dutchman. Even a raven won't peck out another raven's eye, but a Russian won't miss a single opportunity to punish a fellow Russian.

I think that such unfriendliness has its own underlying historical cause: on account of certain peculiar features of our past we have gone too far too fast in our development, we have so much overdeveloped in the past two hundred years that among us dozens of subspecies of Russians have hatched out, some of which are undoubtedly Russians, whereas others are also Russians, but different Russians. Let us say, in the West there occur just two subspecies of *homo sapiens* – workers and shareholders – between whom personal dissatisfactions are possible, but with us you can't go a single step without bumping into someone who's alien to you. From this come, of course, the deliberate acts of wrecking of various degrees of seriousness, shameless robbery in broad daylight, the warlike expressions on our faces and, the main thing, a slipshod attitude towards everything. Moreover, the number of contradictions which have grown up between the different subspecies of Russians is so deep and has so many different meanings that the contradictions between labour and capital are child's play in comparison.

So then what measure would it be good to take to pacify the Russian-speaking population? One needs some type of all-uniting idea. But, of course, not in the spirit of Nikolay Fyodorov with his idea of collectively resurrecting the dead and, of course, not "Rob back that which was stolen in the first place", but something not so delirious and criminal, something delicate, generally accessible and, above all, easily fulfillable, like one's morning toilet. This can be a political idea: for example, let's stop developing, comrades, in a destructive direction;

let us, while preserving our feeling of human dignity, even move ten steps back, to the aristocracy, to whom power can be entrusted, to the concept of "unhappy man", which was the way in which the people used to look upon the criminal elements, to those authorities which are created by genius and murderous labour and not by the media of mass information, to fantastic rates of pay for intellectual work . . . well, and so on right back to the First Philosophical Letter, to examine closely where respected Pyotr Yakovlevich really laid it on thick, and where he hit the nail right on the head. Or it could be a simple economic idea, that is to say, in as much as being still determines consciousness all the same, there should not be a word, not even half a word out of the Red Banner collection of spells, not a single sigh with an underlying ideological meaning, until decent trousers can be seen on every citizen and it won't be necessary to struggle for the elementary benefits of civilization: we'll get clothed and shod, then, and only then, will we talk our heads off about the advantages of the socialist method of production. Incidentally, there is the worry that in a clothed, shod and well-fed manifestation we will no longer be so keen to have heart-to-heart talks. But, strictly speaking, in what ways didn't the present moment suit us? . . . Well, the Russians don't love one another, well, the national consensus is breaking up, well, there's poverty, the syndrome by which the nation's fathers are removed, mass melancholy – well, so what? This was always so, as they say, this is what we stand for, and our literature is a witness to all this, but on the other hand, my God, how interesting it is to live! Probably the thing is that we are too human for our time, in as much as we develop without thinking and always either aim to teach our grandfathers to suck eggs or else try to race God to the gates of paradise, and therefore in the Russian environment there ripen contradictions of such gigantic force that it is terribly tempting just to live. On the other side of the Elbe the only amusement consists in spending money, but with us . . . well it's exactly as if we had prematurely completed the appointed gyre of development and had tumbled into a vigorous ancient life just under another sign: now we have this, now that, now something else, now something else again; every moment the ancients are threatening to behave eccentrically, and, above all, with a sinking heart one is always awaiting something – either some great festival or else the trumpet call of the Archangel Gabriel.

And thus, perhaps, this is precisely our advantage and our fate – that we live in such a style, sharp and trembling with the pulse of life? If so, then we don't need any all-unifying ideas apart from the native

Russian language, which despite all our blind efforts will itself decide everything and put everything in its proper place. Just as Anamnesis and Epicrisis there unreasoningly follow their ancient instinct, so too we ought to trust the Russian language unquestioningly . . .

At precisely this point I was accidentally hit on the head with a bottle of Narzan mineral water, and I lost consciousness. Afterwards I was told that the skirmish lasted for fifteen minutes, until the doctors and nurses separated our warriors. The results of the battle made an impression. I was discovered to have concussion. Ivan Saburov had multiple wounds on his head. Masko's pelvis had been dislocated away from his spine. Chegodaev turned out to have had a haemorrhage in his abdominal cavity and his forearm was fractured. Ottomanchik, who in the heat of the moment had been struck by the stand which held up the dripper, had received an injury in the genital region; and Zolkin, as a professional, had escaped with only bruises.

By evening we had all been moved to the Sklifosovsky clinic, and this is the most interesting part: they put us all together again in the one ward . . .

Translated by Andrew Reynolds

LYUDMILA PETRUSHEVSKAYA

A Modern Family Robinson

(An End-of-the-Twentieth-Century Chronicle)

FATHER AND MOTHER decided to be more cunning than the rest, and at the beginning of everything withdrew with me and a load of assembled provisions to a remote and desolate village somewhere beyond the River Mora. We had bought our house very cheaply, and there it stood, and there was where we would go once a year for the latter part of June, to pick wild strawberries for my health's sake. And then we would come in August, when from neglected gardens you could gather apples, sloes and tiny run-wild blackcurrants, and in the woods there'd be raspberries and mushrooms. The house had been bought as if for demolition, but we lived in it and made use of it without repairing a thing until, one fine day, Father came to an arrangement with the driver, and in the spring, as soon as the roads were dry, we set out for the village like the Robinson Family, with a load of provisions, all sorts of garden implements, a gun, and Beauty, the borzoi who, the conviction was, would be able to catch hares in the autumn.

Father commenced feverish activity, digging the kitchen garden, after first annexing a neighbouring plot by repositioning posts and moving the non-existent neighbours' fence. The kitchen garden was dug, three sacks of potatoes were sown, the soil beneath the apple trees turned, and Father went and cut peat in the forest. A two-wheeled barrow made its appearance, and Father extended his activity in general to the neighbouring boarded-up houses, stocking up with whatever came to hand: nails, old planks, tarred roofing felt, tin, buckets, benches, door handles, window glass, assorted good-quality junk like tubs, spinning wheels, grandfather clocks; and assorted useless junk like cast-iron items: stove doors, dampers, cooking rings and similar.

In the whole village there were three old women: Anisya, utterly unsociable little old Marfa, and red-haired Tanya, the only one with any family, and who received occasional visits from her children in their own transport, either bringing or taking away something – canned things from the city, cheese, butter, gingerbread being what

was brought; cabbages, potatoes and salted cucumbers being what
was taken away. Tanya had a well-stocked cellar, a good covered yard,
and living with her, a tormented grandson, little Valery, who was
perpetually suffering, now with his ears, now with scabies. Tanya was
a nurse by training, which training she had received in a camp on the
Kolyma, which she had been sent to at the age of seventeen for stealing
a piglet from the collective farm. The popular path to her door never
got overgrown, she kept her stove burning, and Vera, the shepherdess,
would come from the nearest inhabited village, Tarutino, and while
still some way off, I observed, cry: "Tanya, what about a cuppa?"
Granny Anisya, the only proper person in the village (little old Marfa
being of no account, and Tanya being not a person but a criminal),
told us that Tanya, in her day, had been in charge of the medical
station here, in Mora, and practically the key figure. Great things were
done: she took over a whole half-block for her medical station, money
flowed. Anisya had worked with Tanya for five years, and as a result
had been left minus a pension, not having served the prescribed
twenty-five years on the collective farm, her five years' sweeping in
a medical station not counting towards a worker's pension award.
Mother went with Anisya to the Social Security department at Pri-
zerskoe, but the Social Security department was shut, had been for
ages, with no hope of its opening and everything wound up, and
Mother swiftly plodded the twenty-five kilometres back to Mora with
the intimidated Anisya, and Anisya, with renewed zeal, set about
digging, felling trees in the forest, and dragging home tree trunks and
branches, so delivering herself from the prospect of death by starvation,
which fate would have been hers, had she been idle. A living example
of idleness was little old Marfa, eighty-five, with never a fire in her
hut, and the potatoes, which somehow she dragged home in the
autumn, freezing during the winter and now lying in a wet and rotting
heap. Still, Marfa had eaten something through the winter, and refused
to be parted from her rotten potatoes, the only goods she possessed,
even though Mother sent me round with a spade to scrape them out.
But seeing through the rag-stuffed window that I was coming with a
spade, little old Marfa wouldn't open the door. Whether she sometimes
ate potatoes raw, despite not having a tooth in her head, or whether
she sometimes lit a fire when nobody was looking, nobody knew.
She'd no firewood and no logs. In spring she would turn up at Anisya's
warm house wrapped in any number of greasy shawls, rags and
blankets, and sit there like a mummy, saying nothing. Anisya didn't
attempt to offer her anything either, and little old Marfa just sat. Once

I looked at her face, or rather that portion of it that was visible amongst the rags, and saw that it was small and dark, and that her eyes were like little moist holes. Little old Marfa had lived through yet another winter, but no longer went out to her kitchen garden, and was evidently going to starve to death. Anisya said artlessly that last year little old Marfa had still been fine, but today was quite the reverse, toes curled up, pointing towards heaven. Mother took me along and we planted about a bucket and a half of potatoes for little old Marfa, while she watched from the back of her little house, obviously fretting lest we were annexing her little kitchen garden, but not daring to come painfully out to us, and Mother went and gave her half a bucket of potatoes. Little old Marfa evidently took it that that was the price of her kitchen garden, and wouldn't accept them. That evening, Mother, Father and I went to Anisya's for goat's milk, and little old Marfa was sitting there. Anisya said that she had seen us in Marfa's kitchen garden. Mother replied that we had decided to help Granny Marfa. Anisya objected that little old Marfa was determined to enter the next world, there was no helping her, she would find a way.

It must be said that we paid Anisya not in money but in tins, and packets of soup. This could not continue for long. The goat had milk and was increasing its supply daily, whereas we were simply living on our tins. A more stable equivalent was needed, and following conversation with Anisya, Mother said there and then that our tins were running out, we'd nothing to eat ourselves, so wouldn't be buying milk. Anisya, like the keen-witted person she was, replied that she'd bring us a jar of milk next day, and we'd talk it over. She was evidently put out at our expending potatoes on little old Marfa, instead of on milk, for not knowing how many potatoes we'd used on the garden in the hungry springtime – "Month of May, month of dismay" – she'd got her imagination going like an engine. She had, it seems, been working out variations of little old Marfa's imminent demise, and reckoning on harvesting the crop for her, hence the anger in advance with us, the owners of the planted potatoes. Everything gets complicated when, in times like ours, it's a question of survival – survival of an old, feeble person, as looked at by a young, vigorous family (Mother and Father were both forty-two, and I was eighteen).

That evening we were visited first by Tanya, wearing a town coat and yellow gumboots, and carrying a new household bag. She'd brought us, wrapped in a clean cloth, a sucking pig that had been crushed by the sow. She was curious to know if we were duly registered for residence in Mora. She said that a good many of the houses had owners who, if written to, would be anxious to come, for the houses were not abandoned, nor were the items of property, and every nail had had to be bought and hammered. In conclusion, she reminded us of the moved fence, and of the fact that little old Marfa was still alive. She proposed that the sucking pig should be bought from her for money, for paper roubles, and that very night Father cut up and salted the dead sucking pig, which, lying in its cloth, looked very like a child. Little eyes with eyelashes, and so on.

When she'd gone, Anisya came with a jar of goat's milk, and over a cup of tea we quickly agreed a new price for milk – one tin for three days' supply. With hatred in her voice she asked about Tanya, why she had come, and approved of our decision to help little old Marfa, of whom she said, with a laugh, that she smelt.

The goat's milk and the crushed sucking pig were to keep us from scurvy, besides which Anisya had a she-kid fattening which we'd decided to buy, only a bit later, when it was a little bigger, as Anisya was better versed in the rearing of kids. We had not, however, discussed it with Anisya, and she, maddened by jealousy towards her former chief Tanya, came, triumphant, with the slaughtered she-kid in a clean cloth. Two tins of fish were our response to this outrageous behaviour, and Mother wept. We made an effort, we boiled the meat, but somehow found it impossible to eat, and Father again did some salting.

Nevertheless, Mother and I did buy a live she-kid, after walking to another village beyond Tarutino, ten kilometres there and ten kilometres back, walking as tourists, as if for pleasure, as if times were still as they used to be. We carried rucksacks, sang, enquired by the village well where we could get a drink of goat's milk, bought a jar of it for a small flat loaf, and admired the young kids. I started whispering to Mother, as if begging to have a dear little kid. Scenting a deal, the woman who owned them livened up, but Mother whispered into my ear a firm no, whereupon the woman praised me unctuously, saying she loved the kids as if they were her own children, and that was why she would give me both of them. But I said no, one she-kid was what I wanted. A bargain was soon struck. The good lady clearly did not know the modern state of money, and took little, even throwing in a small lump of rock salt. She, clearly, was convinced that she had done a profitable deal, and indeed, the she-kid soon became sickly, having suffered much on the road. The situation was saved by Anisya's taking over the kid, after first smearing it with dirt from her yard. The nanny goat accepted it as her own and did not kill it. Anisya was positively radiant.

We now had the basics, but my lame, undefatigable father took to going off deeper and deeper into the forest each day. He would go with an axe, with nails, with the barrow, leaving at dawn and returning late at night. Mother and I pottered about in the kitchen garden, proceeded with Father's task of collecting windowframes, doors and window glass, while still cooking, tidying, carrying water for laundering, and sewing. Out of old sheep- and hareskin coats found lying around in houses, we made warm boots and gauntlets for the winter and fur bedding for the beds. Father, discovering this bedding one night, instantly rolled up all three lots, and in the morning took them off on the barrow. He seemed to be getting another lair ready, in the forest, which subsequently proved to be very much to the point. Although subsequently it also proved that no amount of labour and foresight will of themselves save one from the common fate, and that nothing can, short of success.

Meanwhile we lived through June – "the direst month" – when supplies in the village usually run out. We munched dandelion salad, made "cabbage soup" out of stinging nettles, but basically ate grass, which we were for ever transporting in rucksacks and bags. We'd no idea how to mow, and anyway the grass wasn't very tall. In the end – for ten rucksacks of grass, which was a lot! – Anisya gave us a scythe, and Mother and I took turns at scything.

We lived, I repeat, remote from the world. I missed my friends of both sexes greatly, but nothing in the way of news any longer reached our house. Father listened to the radio, it's true, but rarely. He was saving the batteries. Everything broadcast over the radio was very deceitful and intolerable, but we went on scything and scything, our she-kid Raya grew, and needing to find her a mate, we set off again for that same village where dwelt the possessor of another kid, the one she'd thrust at us at a time when we'd not known its true worth. The kid's owner received us coolly, everyone knowing everything about us by now, but not that we had a she-kid, our little Raya, who was being fostered by Anisya. So she received us coolly: she'd sold to us, but we'd failed to take proper care, which was our affair. She wasn't going to sell, since we no longer had any flour or little flat loaves, and her kid was a good weight, and at this hungry time, three kilos of fresh meat cost any amount. We agreed finally only on the basis of our giving her a kilo of salt and ten bars of soap. But for us, this was the price of future milk, and we set off home to fetch salt and soap, warning the woman that what we wanted was a live kid. "So I'm to go on soiling my hands for you," was her reply.

By evening we'd got the kid home, and the grim days of summer began: haymaking, weeding the kitchen garden, clamping potatoes, all the time keeping up with Anisya. By agreement we took from her one half of the goat droppings, and enriched the soil as best we might, but we got poor, thin crops. Free from haymaking, Granny Anisya would tether the nanny goat and the whole goat kindergarten within sight of us, then dash off for mushrooms and berries, then come and take some of our work. The dill, which we'd sown too deep, had to be re-sown. We needed it for pickling cucumbers. Our potatoes came into leaf. Mother and I read *The Complete Gardener*, and Father at long last finished operations in the forest, and we went and had a look at the new dwelling. It turned out to be someone's old hut which Father had renovated, at any rate to the extent of caulking, putting in windowframes, window glass, doors, and covering the roof with tarred felt. Inside it was empty. In the nights that followed, we transported tables, benches, chests, tubs, stoves and our remaining stores to it, and hid them all. Father was now excavating a cellar, and something approaching a dugout with a stove, the third of our houses. He already had a flourishing little kitchen garden.

That summer Mother and I became simple peasants, with fat fingers and hands and coarse, fat, earth-ingrained nails with − and this was the most interesting thing − something in the nature of beads, bulges or nodes at the base of them. I noticed the same thing with Anisya, and with idle little old Marfa; and with our *grande dame* and medic, Tanya, the picture was the same. And by the way, Tanya's constant visitor, Vera, the shepherdess, hanged herself in the forest. She was no longer a shepherdess, since everyone had eaten her flock, and Anisya really did the dirty on Tanya by telling us her secret, which was that what Tanya had been giving Vera was not tea but *medicine*, and Vera couldn't live without it, and that was why she hanged herself, having nothing to pay with. Incidentally to which, Vera had left a little fatherless daughter. Anisya, who kept in touch with Tarutino, told us that this little girl lived with a granny. Then, from this same triumphant account by Anisya, it further emerged that this granny was a beauty after the style of our little old Marfa, only an alcoholic as well.

The three-year-old baby was delivered to our house in an old pram, completely unconscious. Mother always got more on her plate than she should. Father turned nasty. The little girl wet her bed, didn't talk, licked what she snotted, didn't understand what was said to her, and cried all night. This soon made life impossible, and father went to live in the forest. There was nothing to be done, and everything pointed towards handing the little girl back to her worthless grandmother, when suddenly there she was, Granny Faina, swaying on her feet and trying to wheedle money out of us for the little girl and the pram. Without a word, Mother brought out Lena, clean, with her hair cut, barefoot but wearing a little dress. Suddenly, without uttering a sound, Lena prostrated herself before my mother like a grown-up, and rolled into a little ball, clasping her bare feet. The grandmother burst into tears and went, without Lena and without the pram, evidently to die. She swayed as she walked, wiping away her tears with her fists, and her swaying was not from drink, but, as I later guessed, from utter exhaustion. She'd long been without anything in the house, and more recently, of course, Vera had not been earning. We ourselves were increasingly eating stewed grass in various guises, the chief being "mushroom soup". The kids had long been living with Father out of harm's way, and the track to him had grown over completely, the more so as, with an eye to the future, he usually took the barrow by different routes. Lena stayed. We set aside milk for her, fed her berries and our mushroom "cabbage soups". By the time we started thinking about winter, things were getting considerably worse. There was no bread, no flour, no grain either. Nothing had been sown in our region, petrol and spares having long been unobtainable; and the horses having been slaughtered even before that, there was nothing to plough with.

Father took walks and picked up the odd ears of corn that had got left behind in former fields, but others had been over the ground before him, and very often his haul was no more than a tiny bag of grains. His idea was to attempt a winter sowing in a clearing not far from the hut. He asked Anisya about dates, and she promised to tell him when and how to sow, and how to plough. A spade was of no use, she said, but there wasn't a plough anywhere. Father asked her to draw one, and, just like Robinson, started knocking some contraption together. Anisya herself had a poor memory for the details, even though she'd had, in distant days, to walk behind the cow with the plough. But Father, fired with the engineering principle, sat down to reinvent the wheel. He was happy with his new lot, and never reminisced about the city, where he'd left many enemies, including his parents, my grandmother and grandfather, whom I'd seen only in every early childhood, but then – to hell with them both! – it had been nothing but rows on account of my mother and their old-world flat with its *the General's ceilings, the General's privy, the General's kitchen*. We'd never lived there, and by now my grandmother and grandfather were very likely corpses. We told no one anything when we were departing from the city, even though Father had long been preparing for this departure, hence the whole lorryload of sacks and boxes accumulated at our house. These were all things that were inexpensive and, in their time, not in short supply. My father, a former sportsman, mountaineer and geologist, with an injured leg and hip, had been dying to get away for a long time, and now circumstance and his ever-growing passion for escape had coincided, and we'd escaped when there'd not been a cloud in the sky. "Over Spain the skies are cloud free," Father used to joke, literally every fine morning.

It was a beautiful summer, with everything filling out and ripening. Our Lena started talking, and would come running into the forest after us. She would gather no mushrooms, but stuck to Mother as if her life depended on it. It was no good my teaching her to find mushrooms and berries, a child placed as she was was incapable of going her own quiet way, free of grown-ups. Following Mother everywhere, running after her on her little legs, with her distended little tummy, she was trying to save her own skin. Lena called Mother "Nanny", having picked up the word somewhere, although we never used it. And me she called "Nanny" too, wittily and to the point.

One night, hearing a noise like a kitten mewing, we discovered a baby wrapped in an old, greasy padded jacket. Father, who had got used to Lena, and would even come to us during the day to do some job about the house, groaned. Mother's mood was grim, and she decided to ask Anisya who could have left it. So with the baby, and accompanied by a silent Lena, we set off in the night for Anisya's. She wasn't asleep, having also heard the baby and been much alarmed. She told us that the first refugees had arrived in Tarutino, so that we should look out for more visitors. The baby yelled piercingly nonstop, his tummy was hard and swollen. Tanya, invited next morning to look the child over, said, without even touching him, that he was not long for this world, that he'd got "infantile". The child was in pain, roaring, and we hadn't even a teat to feed him through. Mother dripped water into his parched mouth, and he choked. He looked about four months old.

Mother marched off to Tarutino, bartered a teat out of the natives for a heap of precious salt, and came racing back, happy. The baby took a little water from a bottle. Mother gave him an enema and a dose of camomile, and all of us, Father included, rushed about heating water to give him a hot-water bottle. It was clear to all that we'd have to abandon the house, the kitchen garden, and our well-ordered economy, or else we'd soon be swamped. To abandon the kitchen garden was to die of starvation. At our family council, Father said that we should move to the forest, and that he would take up residence in the kitchen garden shed with Beauty and his gun.

That night we moved off with the first batch of things. The boy, whom we named Foundling, travelled on bundles in the barrow. To the amazement of all, he had, after the enema, passed a motion, then taken some diluted goat's milk, and now here he was, strapped in a sheepskin to the barrow. Lena walked, holding on to the bundles.

We arrived at our new house towards dawn. Father immediately did a second run, then a third. He was like a cat bringing in all its new kittens in its teeth, only what *he* was bringing were all the inventions won by the sweat of his brow. The little hut was crammed full. Next day, when all of us slept, worn out, Father set off on duty. That night he came with the wheelbarrow full of young vegetables – potatoes, carrots and beetroots, little turnips and tiny onions. These we stored away in the cellar. Late as it was, he set off again, and when he came back, it was almost at a run, and with the wheelbarrow empty. Limping, downcast, he said: "That's it." A jar of milk for the boy was all he'd brought. Our house had turned out to be occupied by an admin. detachment. The kitchen garden had a guard on it. Anisya's nanny goat had been seized and taken to our former home. Anisya had been lying in wait on Father's supply route with this jar of yesterday's milk since the small hours. Father, although he grieved, was nevertheless glad at having again managed to escape, and with his whole family.

All hope was now in Father's little kitchen garden and in mushrooms. Lena stayed in the hut with the boy. We did not take her into the forest, but locked her in, so that she should not interfere with the rhythm of work. Strange as it may seem, in the company of the boy she would just sit, and not hammer on the door. Foundling would drink potato broth with a will, while Mother and I scoured the forest with little bags and rucksacks. We no longer salted mushrooms, but just dried them, as we had hardly any salt. Father was digging a well, the stream being a fair way off.

On the fifth day after our move, Granny Anisya came to visit us. She came empty-handed, without a thing, except for the cat on her shoulder. Her eyes had a strange look. She sat for a while in the porch, holding the frightened cat in her skirts, then leapt up and went into the forest. The cat hid under the porch. Anisya came back shortly with a pinafore full of mushrooms, some of which were fly agaric. She stayed sitting in our porch, and did not go into the house. We brought her out some of our unspiced, unflavoured soup in her empty milk jar. That evening, Father took Anisya to the dugout, our third emergency house. Anisya had a rest and cheerfully set about scouring the forest. I took her mushrooms off her, so that she shouldn't poison herself. Some we dried, some we threw away. One afternoon, returning from the forest, we found our foster children all together in the porch. Anisya was rocking Foundling, and generally behaving like a normal person. Something seemed to have been released inside her, for she was telling Lena: "They turned everything upside down, carried everything off . . . Never even poked their noses into little old Marfa's, but took everything from me, took my nanny goat away on a rope."

Anisya made herself useful for some time, tending our goats, sitting with Foundling and Lena, right up until the cold weather came. And then she climbed up on to the stove with the children, and came down only to go outside. Winter obliterated all paths to us with snow. We had our mushrooms, our berries, dried and stewed, potatoes from Father's kitchen garden, a loft full of hay, macerated apples from the deserted houses in the forest, and even kegs of salted cucumbers and tomatoes. In a plot concealed by snow, winter grain was growing. We had the goats. We had a boy and a girl for the continuance of the human race. We had a cat which brought us forest mice. We had the dog Beauty, who had no desire to devour these mice, but who Father was hoping soon to hunt hares with. Father was afraid to go hunting with his gun, or even to axe wood, lest the noise give us away. He did his axeing whenever it was snowing heavily. We had a granny who was a mine of popular wisdom and knowledge. All around stretched chilly wastes.

One day, Father switched on the radio, and spent a long time searching the air. The air was silent. Either the batteries were flat, or we really were alone in the world. Father's eyes shone. He'd again managed to escape!

If we are not alone in the world, people will come. That much is clear to us all. But firstly, Father has a gun, we have skis, and we have a keen-nosed dog. And secondly, *when* will they come? We live, we wait, knowing that someone is there, living and waiting while we grow our grain, and while our corn and our potatoes and our new lot of kids are growing. Then is when they'll come. And take everything, me included. Meanwhile, they are being fed by our kitchen garden, by Anisya's kitchen garden, and by Tanya's setup. Tanya, I believe, has long since gone, but little old Marfa is still there. When we are like little old Marfa, *we* will not be touched.

But till then, we've got to live on and on. And again, we've not exactly been dozing, either. Father and I are getting a new refuge organized.

Translated by George Bird

PAVEL PETROV

A Bit of Winter

WHEN WINTER CAME, old Mother Palanya took the cattle shed door, a bucket with lime in it and a pair of rubber boots down to the stream. They were soon all covered with snow which then set into thick ice.

In the spring, the Iskona overflowed its banks to such a degree that the door had to meander about for a long time between tree trunks and bits of flotsam and sodden rubbish. Meanwhile, the boot with the hole in it filled with water, tipped over, crawled awkwardly off the door, swallowed more water and drowned. But the door was not a door yet, because it was still moving along with the ice and there was still a lot of ice around.

Going past Sergovo, the bucket, which was a quarter full of lime, decided it was going to make its own way. It shrugged off its mantle of ice and started to swim along all by itself, hugging the bank.

Once past Ruza, though, everything started to go more smoothly, so that by the Krymsky Bridge there was only a tiny bit of ice left . . . just the smallest little bit. In fact, when there was only a week's journey to the Oka left, you could really have said it was just a door swimming to the great river.

At Sormov, a little tug, the colour of an orange that had lain awhile in a puddle, came up suspiciously close. The skipper had a go at picking up the door with his boathook, but carried out this manoeuvre so lethargically and ineptly that he only just missed ending up in the water himself. Once he had calmed down, however, and had taken some more air into his broad chest, he shouted out to the departing door: "Go on then, sail away, sail away, you bit of old iron! . . ."

The wind carried away the end of his words. Despite the fact that the door had not even the remotest hint of metal on it, it still carried on swimming further downstream. And only at Kuybyshev, when it was going through the locks, or, rather, attaching itself to the tails of ships, as it had been doing all along, did it hear from the deck: "Hey, just look at that!" one person was saying to another. "There's what looks like a door over there with a boot on it . . . What do you reckon? Do you think that door could get as far as Togliatti?"

"Togliatti? Well, that would be difficult to say now, wouldn't it?"

"Well, how about Kazan then?"

"Oh no, it couldn't get to Kazan. Kazan is further away, See, and higher. And not even a door like that could travel upstream."

The banks of the Volga were widening. They were getting smaller as they ran further away . . . "Might it not be the sea already?" thought the door, but the sea was still a long way off.

A motorboat chugged up to the door past the mouth of the Akhtuba. A man in a sleeveless anorak picked up the boot with two fingers.

"Hmm – it's a boot of some sort!" he said with great thoughtfulness. And then he even took off his cap. "So it's swimming somewhere then . . . but where to?"

Anyway, having held the boot in midair for goodness knows how long and thought about it, he put it neatly back on its side, hooked up the door with the boot on top of it and started to tow it along. He might have taken it off God knows where if he hadn't encountered another motor launch, which also had an anorak on board. They ended up arguing.

Apparently, the anorak with sleeves was trying to explain to the anorak without sleeves the full meaning and significance of the floating boot and door; that it was not right to meddle with things that did not concern him, and that if the boot was swimming somewhere, then he should just let it carry on swimming.

It should be added that more and more questions and answers along these lines were beginning to be heard, for all kinds of little vessels were coming up to the door. They all expressed their opinions on the matter and examined the boot and, what is more, not just once. They couldn't stop picking it up and putting it down again. And so it stood up, lay down and turned in all the directions under the sun. But what happened in the end, though, was that the door set off for the Caspian Sea with the boot standing upright on it.

A strong south-westerly began to blow at this point, and so the door started to turn back on itself away from the sea, until it wandered up one of the sleeves of the delta. And there it got stuck in a mass of gigantic reeds, rustling in the wind.

Old Nikitich and his grandson Dima happened to stumble across it.

"Well then, Dima my lad, let's see what's in this old boot, then . . ." said the old man, thrusting his hand into it.

He pulled out a rolled-up bit of old newspaper, a piece of tow and also some cellophane, held together with sellotape.

"Well I never . . . there's some writing in here. Let's have a little look at it, then, let's have a look . . ."

The old man jabbed a knife into the packet and drew out a yellowing photograph of old Mother Palanya. The old lady was sitting on a bench, her careworn hands folded on her knees. There was a basin by her feet and there were numerous chickens round the basin. One chicken, with its head on one side, was looking at the camera as if to ask: "What's in there, eh?"

There was a letter attached to the photograph.

"So there we are, Tikhonovna, I've decided to write you a letter. The photo you are looking at was taken in the summer. There're only a few of them chickens still around, perhaps just Khlusha, Porusha and Kocha the cockerel . . . It's winter here, and it just won't stop snowing. Snowdrifts right up to the window. There're bullfinches and jackstraws in the trees . . ."

The letter continued with everyday village news. The old man clutched the letter in his hands and squinted at the sky.

"Grandpa, what's the matter?"

"Oh, nothing . . . Do you see how everything is all . . ."

"Everything is all what?"

"Well, you know . . . We've got lotuses flowering down here, and flamingoes wandering about, but up *there* you know . . ."

"What about up there?"

"It's winter still."

"Come on, Grandpa, what do you mean? Winter will be over there too!"

"Yes, you're right, it'll be over there too . . . We've got geese and herons and flamingoes down here, but up there, you know . . . there's still a bit of winter left. Bullfinches and jackstraws in the trees . . ."

Translated by Rosamund Bartlett

NOTES ON THE STORIES
(prepared by the translators)

The Chip

p. 1 *Cheka*: an acronym from the Russian for "Extraordinary Commission (for Combating Counter-Revolution, Sabotage and Speculation)", which was the name of the Soviet Secret Police between 1917 and 1922.

p. 10 *Moscow does not believe in tears*: an old Russian proverb.

p. 11 *Kolchak*: one of the most important White Army commanders during the Russian Civil War.

p. 34 *RKP*: a shortened form of RKP(b), an acronym for "Rossiiskaya kommunisticheskaya partiya (bolshevikov)", which was the official name of the Russian Communist Party between 1918 and 1925.

p. 37 *Tavrichesky Palace*: built in Leningrad, between 1783 and 1789, originally for Prince Potemkin. Between 1906 and 1917, the Palace housed the State Duma, and from March to July 1917 it served as the headquarters of the Provisional Government. The democratically elected Constituent Assembly sat here in January 1918, until it was unceremoniously disbanded by the Bolsheviks.

p. 37 *The Winter Palace*: the former official winter residence of the Romanovs in Petersburg, and the building which housed the Provisional Government between July and October 1917. Its storming, on, the night of 25–26 October (7–8 November, new style calendar), signalled the start of the Bolshevik Revolution. Since 1918 the Winter Palace has been the site of the State Hermitage Museum.

p. 38 *Emile Vandervelde* (1866–1938): a Belgian right-wing socialist, one of the founders of the 2nd Communist International. In 1922 he travelled to Moscow to defend Socialist Revolutionaries (socialists to the right of the Bolsheviks) in political trials.

p. 38 *Alexander Fyodorovich Kerensky* (1881–1970): a Russian liberal revolutionary leader, Prime Minister of the Provisional Government (July –October, 1917), until overthrown by the Bolsheviks.

p. 39 *Egor Sergeevich Sozonov* (1879–1910): Russian revolutionary, expelled from Moscow University in 1901 for participation in an illegal student movement. He became a Socialist Revolutionary in 1902, but was arrested a year later and sent to internal exile in Siberia. After escaping he assassinated the Russian Interior Minister, V. K. Pleve, seriously wounding himself in the process. He later committed suicide, rather than face life imprisonment in a labour camp.

p. 39 *Ivan Platonovich Kalyaev* (1877–1905): a Socialist Revolutionary who assassinated Prince Sergey Alexandrovich in 1905, an act for which he was executed.

p. 39 *Stepan Valerianovich Balmashev* (1882–1902): a Socialist Revolutionary who, in 1902, assassinated the Russian Interior Minister, D. S. Sipyagin, and was subsequently hanged.

p. 39 *Black Hundred*: the name given to various armed anti-Semitic and anti-revolutionary groups in Russia, active between 1905 and 1907.

p. 39 *Malyuta Skuratov*: literally Tiny Skuratov, one of Ivan the Terrible's most bloodthirsty henchmen, employed by the tsar to crush the nobles.

p. 44 *Smerdyakov*: a character from Dostoevsky's novel *The Brothers Karamazov*, who is responsible for the murder at the centre of the novel's plot.

p. 55 *NACHOSO*: a post-revolutionary acronym derived from *Nachalnik Osobogo Revtribunala*, meaning Head of the Special Revolutionary Tribunal, set up in 1919 under the Cheka.

p. 69 *Peter's City*: literally "Peter", a colloquial and deliberately anachronistic term for Leningrad.

On the Blessed Island of Communism

p. 84 *Konstantin Paustovsky* (1892–1963): novelist, playwright, memoirist and editor of *Literary Moscow*, who played a prominent role in the liberal movement among writers in the post-Stalin years.

p. 84 *Alexey Surkov* (1899–1983): editor of *Literaturnaya Gazeta* (1944–46); Secretary General of the Union of Soviet Writers (1954–59). A promising poet who became a literary manipulator; nicknamed the "Candied Hyena".

p. 85 *Leonid Leonov* (1988–   ): a leading novelist and playwright. A complex figure who successfully adapted to the twists and turns of Party policy, while struggling to retain some integrity as a writer. His play *The Golden Carriage*, written in 1946, appeared only after Stalin's death.

p. 85 *Valentin Kataev* (1897–1986): beginning as a journalist in Rostov on Don and, later, Odessa, he was one of the leading "Fellow Travellers" in the 1920s. After Stalin's death, as editor of the literary magazine *Yunost* (Youth) he encouraged new talent. In later years he turned to works of autobiographical fiction and reminiscence. At times experimentalist in his writings, he tended towards othodoxy in his public activity.

p. 85 *Nikolay Dorizo* (1923–   ): a lyric poet and composer of popular songs.

p. 85 *Komsomol Pravda*: the national daily newspaper of the Communist Youth League. Founded 1925; circulation 10 million.

p. 85 *Alexey Adzhubey* (1924–   ): Khrushchev's son-in-law. In Khrushchev's heyday he became an important figure in the cultural world, rising to be editor of *Izvestiya*. He weaved and tacked in and out of successive de-Stalinization/re-Stalinization moves of the 1960s.

p. 85 *Ilya Ehrenburg* (1891–1967): a novelist and journalist of prolific output, who was originally hostile to the Bolshevik regime, but for a time became a fervent propagandist; after Stalin's death he played an important part in the liberal movement, first with his novel *The Thaw* (1954), and later with his memoirs, *People, Years, Life* (1960–65), which, despite censorship cuts, gave a fuller picture of the fate of the intelligentsia under Stalin than had before appeared in print.

p. 85 *Anatoly Sofronov* (1911–   ): best known for his numerous works, mainly plays, about the happy experiences of Soviet collective farmers.

p. 85 *Nikolay Gribachev* (1910–   ): a poet of little talent but undoubted malevolence towards all who did not share his brand of loyal jingoism.

p. 85 *Vsevolod Kochetov* (1912–73): a writer and publicist; one of those who sought to stem the tide of de-Stalinization. Two of his novels, *The Brothers Ezhov* (1957) and *What Do You Want?* (1969) are lampoons on the liberal intelligentsia. In 1955 he became the editor of the leading literary journal, *Literaturnaya Gazeta*.

p. 86 *Marietta Shaginyan* (1888–1982): a veteran Soviet novelist. Returning to Russia after her studies at Heidelberg were interrupted by the First World War, she became a minor poet on the fringes of Symbolism, welcoming the October Revolution as a mystic-Christian event. She wrote about Armenia, England and America, but her attempt to write thrillers and detective fiction in a Western style in the 1920s was decried at the time as "Red Pinkertonism". She was an indefatigable polemicist.

p. 86 *Literary Moscow*: a two-volume literary anthology published in 1955 after the historic Twentieth Party Congress. Edited by Konstantin Paustovsky and others, it was something in the nature of a collective gesture on the part of a whole group of Soviet writers. Its publication marked the highlight of the first phase of the post-Stalin liberalization – and was a contributing factor to its abrupt suspension.

p. 86 *Margarita Aliger* (1915–   ): a writer of talented verse, but of wholly orthodox views (despite her brief involvement in the publication of *Literary Moscow*).

p. 87 *Leonid Sobolev* (1898–1971): a writer whose modest literary output was dwarfed by his administrative activity in both the USSR and RSFSR Writers Unions.

p. 87 *Anastas Mikoyan* (1895–1978): of Armenian origin. One of the Old Bolsheviks; a Vicar of Bray-like character, who occupied senior Government and Party posts under both Stalin and his successors.

p. 88 *Samuel Marshak* (1887–1964): the celebrated translator of Shakespeare, Heine and Burns into Russian. In the 1920s and 1930s he had been a father figure among innovative writers specializing in children's literature. Though known for his political adaptability, he showed liberal tendencies after Stalin's death.

p. 88 *Valentin Ovechkin* (1904–1968): a shoemaker, teacher, then writer, of much talent and originality. Expelled from, then readmitted to the Communist Party, he was best known for a book published in 1952 in which, even at that early stage, he dared criticize official policy towards the peasants.

p. 91 *Jew-baiter*: an embroidered shirt: the national dress of the Ukraine, an area which had the reputation of being the location of some of the worst pogroms.

p. 91 *Kliment Voroshilov* (1881–1969): a prominent political and military figure; a Marshal (1935), and a member of the Politburo or equivalent (1926–60). In fact, distinguished for his military incompetence, political kowtowing and reluctance to intercede during the purges even for his associates.

p. 92 *Vyacheslav Molotov* (1890–1986): an Old Bolshevik who had a long-standing involvement in the Ministry of Foreign Affairs (on and off from 1939–56) until he was rusticated by Khrushchev, as a member of the anti-Party Group, to Ulan Bator in 1957. A man of impeccable orthodoxy, and total loyalty to Stalin, (even when Molotov's own wife, was condemned to a forced labour camp).

p. 92 *Lazar Kaganovich* (1893–   ): today, the only surviving full member of the Politburo from the Stalin period; currently writing his memoirs.

p. 92 *Dmitry Shepilov* (1905–   ): a senior Party functionary in Agitprop who became editor of *Pravda* in Stalin's lifetime. His very first spell as Minister of Foreign Affairs (1956) was cut short as a result of his participation in an unsuccessful anti-Khrushchev coup. He was rusticated to Kirgizia; now retired.

p. 92 *Sergey Mikhalkov* (1913–   ): a writer of children's stories and fables, and political lampoons (to order). A much decorated and much travelled senior writer, he currently heads the RSFSR Writers Union.

p. 97 *Bradbury's notorious butterfly*: the chain of association extrapolated by the science fiction writer Ray Bradbury, whereby a butterfly flapping its wings in New York could affect the climate in China.

p. 97 *Vladimir Dudintsev* (1918–   ): novelist whose *Not by Bread Alone* provoked fierce controversy in 1956 because of its outspoken portrait of a Stalinist bureaucrat. It was passionately defended by Paustovsky at a closed meeting of the Union of Soviet Writers but, after the Hungarian uprising in November 1956, its opponents prevailed; it was, however, never banned, and in later years came to be accepted (by Khrushchev himself among others) as a legitimate critique of bureaucratic high-handedness under Stalin.

p. 98 *Vasily Mzhavanadze* (1902–   ): a political figure who rose from political work in the army to be First Secretary of the Georgian Communist Party (1953–72) and thereby a Candidate Member of the Politburo or its equivalent (1957–72). He retired on a pension in 1972.

The Doctor

p. 107 *Valentin Serov* (1865–1911): a well-known Russian painter. The finest portraitist of his time, he enriched technical realism with the Impressionists' lyrical use of light.

Those Who Did not Get into the Choir

p. 119 *Pioneer camp*: summer camp for deserving young (pre-Komsomol) seven- to fifteen-year-old members of what was the 25-million strong Pioneer movement.

p. 122 *"October's here already . . .*": lines from one of Pushkin's elegiac poems.

p. 125 *The children who had not got into the choir*: the outstanding feature of Russian Orthodox choral singing is its togetherness, even though much of it is antiphonal. Thus it is not the strength or purity or beauty of individual voices that matters, but the ability to maintain over all balance.

A War like That

p. 133 *Age limit*: the age, probably 55, which, combined with the requisite number of years of work, would exempt Darya from Agricultural Tax liability in kind and in cash. The tax base being the amount of land used by a household, Darya incurs the same liabilities as when her husband and her son were alive.

p. 133 *Monetary tax*: collective farm workers receive no wage, but derive income from what they rear or produce on personal plots, in what time remains after the hours they are required to work on the collective farm. The collective farm demands, and makes token payment for, a quota of what is grown or reared on such plots, also levying a monetary tax on profits therefrom.

p. 133 *Insurance*: probably a contribution to the farm's insurance with the Central State Insurance Department in respect of buildings, machinery, livestock and crops.

p. 133 *State loan*: credit granted probably for the building or acquisition of the house.

p. 133 *Voluntary community payment*: towards public services and utilities, and cultural provision.

p. 133 *Green and pink pieces of paper*: probably statements of due and overdue liabilities.

The Rosy-Fingered Dawn

p. 144 *The Rosy-Fingered Dawn*: Eos, goddess of dawn in Greek mythology.

p. 150 *Narkompros*: People's Commissariat of Education, responsible for education and culture in the first years of the Soviet regime.

p. 156 *Vasily Robertovich Williams* (1863–1939): a Soviet botanist and author of many works on grassland crop rotation as a means to increase production and soil fertility.

p. 156 *Bonnets in the air*: a line from Griboedev's famous comedy *The Misfortunes of Being Too Clever*: the hero, Chatsky, is satirizing female enthusiasm for officers returning from victory in the Napoleonic Wars.

p. 158 *Trofim Denisovich Lysenko* (1898–1976): a biologist and member of the Soviet Academy of Sciences. With the support of Stalin, he tried to destroy all his opponents among the Soviet geneticists. He is now discredited.

p. 158 *A grey Pobeda (Viktory) with chequerboard markings*: the Russian equivalent of the Volkswagen, first built in the late 1940s. Soviet taxis have black and white checks on their doors.

An Arm, a Leg, a Gherkin too. . .

p. 203 *Julian Semyonov*: popular and prolific detective and thriller writer, best known in Britain and the USA for his novel *Tass Is Authorized to Announce*, a cold-war thriller seen from the Russian side.

p. 207 *He tapped his finger lightly against the seat*: a "knocker" is Russian slang for an informer.

Lagopthalmos

p. 235 *Lagopthalmos*: a condition in which the eye cannot be completely closed.

p. 241 *Solidol*: grease.

p. 241 *Nigrol*: lubricating oil.

Safe Return

p. 245 *Anasha*: a hemp-based narcotic native to Central Asia which was commonly used by Soviet troops serving in Afghanistan.

p. 246 *Grandfather of the Soviet Army (Granddad)*: during most of the Soviet intervention in Afghanistan a normal tour of duty was two years. Every six months soldiers rose in the unofficial Company pecking order: 0–6 months, "sons"; 7–12 months, "finches"; 13–18 months, "scoops"; 19–24 months "granddads". After receiving orders to return home, soldiers were known as "demobs", demobilized veterans.

p. 256 *Pioneers*: see note to p. 119.

Ryabov and Kozhin

p. 264 *The "organs"*: the Secret Police; successively the Cheka/OGPU/MGB/KGB.

p. 264 *Komsomol*: the Communist Youth League; in its full title, the All-Union Leninist Union of Communist Youth, membership of which is available to the politically deserving between the ages of 14 and 28.

Sludge-gulper

p. 273 *Georgy Zhukov* (1896–1974): the Soviet Marshal whose defence of Moscow in 1941 saved the city and proved that the German Army was not invincible.

p. 273 *Andrey Zhdanov* (1896–1948): a close associate of Stalin and a member of the Politburo from 1939 who implemented a tough ideological line in the postwar period, beginning with the expulsion of Anna Akhmatova and Mikhail Zoschenko from the Writers Union in 1946.

p. 273 *The Big Chief himself*: Stalin.

p. 273 *Georgy Malenkov* (1902–1984): Soviet leader who was disgraced and exiled by Khrushchev in 1957.

p. 273 *Vyacheslav Molotov*: see note to p. 92.

p. 273 *Mikhail Suslov* (1902–1982): the leading Party ideologist whose indictment of Khrushchev in 1964 led to the latter's downfall.

p. 273 *Kliment Voroshilov*: see note to p. 91.

p. 273 *Lavrenty Beria* (1899–1953): Head of the Soviet Secret Police from 1938. After Stalin's death he was accused inter alia of being a British spy and executed.

The Situation

p. 279 *Stierlitz* . . . *"The Tibault Family"*: popular imported television serials.
p. 280 *Kulak*: a rich peasant. The Kulaks were liquidated by Stalin in the 1930s
– hence the subsequent reference to "halfwit Kulaks of former days".
p. 286 *Rasul Gamzatov* (1923–   ): a staunchly conformist Daghestani poet
whose long narrative poem, *The Mountain Woman*, appeared in
1958.

The Death of Egor Ilich

p. 336 *Bus*: the English reader might expect "hearse" rather than "bus" here,
but hearses do not exist to speak of in the Soviet Union, and it is
therefore common practice to hire a vehicle such as a bus or a truck to
carry out the function of the hearse.

The Blind Fisherman

p. 352 *Verst*: an archaic measurement (3500 feet). The use of the term here,
and similar archaisms elsewhere in the story, is quite deliberate. Astafiev
is an admirer of the traditional Russian way of life.
p. 353 *Muryzhikha*: the Russian word "Mura" means nonsense or something
boring.
p. 354 *Veche*: a public meeting or council meeting in ancient and medieval
Russia.
p. 369 *Goodbye, girls* . . .: the original here is deliberately garbled, indicating
the cultural imperialism that Astafiev, and some of his characters,
think Russia is falling victim to.

Tsarevich Dmitry

p. 371 *Tsarevich Dmitry*: son of Ivan IV and his seventh wife, Mariya
Nagaya, died suddenly in 1591, aged 9, at Uglich. Official
inquiry ascribed his death to natural causes, but some claimed,
and some believe still, that he was murdered on the orders of
Boris Godunov. Whatever the truth of this, the legitimacy of his
claim to the throne was contestable, his father having exceeded
the canonical allowance of three wives. A False Dmitry, claiming to
have been miraculously saved from assassination, appeared in
1603. Godunov denounced him as an imposter, declaring him to be
Grigory Otrepiev, a truant monk, but failed in attempts to secure
his arrest. On the death of Godunov and the deposing of Godunov's
son, Dmitry succeeded to the throne in 1605, but was murdered
within a year. In 1607 False Dmitry II appeared, attempted,
unsuccessfully, to seize Moscow, and fled to Kaluga, where he was
murdered.
p. 373 *Rus*: from the 9th to the 13th Century, a rough synonym for Eastern
Slavs speaking a language identifiable as Old Russian, and also for
their lands and cities.

p. 373 *The Time of Troubles*: extended from the extinction of the House of
Ryurikids (1598) to the establishment of the House of Romanov
(1613). It saw popular unrest, invasions by Sweden and Poland, four
Tsars of doubtful legitimacy – of whom Godunov was one – and two
Pretenders, Dmitry I and Dmitry II.

p. 373 *Platonov, Sergey Fyodorovich* (1860–1933): distinguished historian
whose works include *Studies in the History of the Time of Troubles in
the State of Muscovy*.

p. 373 *The Uglich Dmitry or the Pretender Otrepiev*: see note on *Tsarevich Dmitry*
above.

p. 373 *The real Dmitry*: son of Ivan IV and Mariya Nagaya.

On the Tarmac

p. 386 *Aisor*: an alternative name for Assyrian, an ethnic minority of the USSR
and the Middle East; of Christian religion.

Anamnesis and Epicrisis

p. 389 *Anamnesis*: the ability to recall: specifically, the case history of a patient.

p. 389 *Epicrisis*: a critical evaluation, especially of a literary work.

p. 389 *Tsar Alexander I*: it is not really clear what was the cause of Alexander
I's death, indeed it is shrouded in mystery. It was certainly unexpected
– probably some stomach disorder – and gave rise to the legend that
he had not died but had fled to Siberia to escape the burdens of
office, and lived there as a "holy man", Elder Fyodor Kuzmich.

p. 393 *Lefortovo*: a notorious prison in Moscow.

p. 394 *Prakrit*: the colloquial language of the ancient Aryans.

p. 401 *False Dmitry and a Pretender*. See notes to pp. 371 and 373.

p. 402 *Central Market*: the biggest and best market in Moscow. People from
the south of the USSR, especially from the Caucasian republics, earn
large sums of money selling items such as fruit and vegetables which
are in very short supply in Moscow. The mixture of racism and
justified annoyance conveyed in the rest of the sentence is always present
in talk on this subject.

p. 403 *Theodor Nette*: a Bolshevik Diplomatic Courier killed in 1926, and the
Black Sea steamship named after him, are the subjects of Mayakovsky's
poem "To Comrade Nette, Man and Steamship".

p. 412 *Pyotr Yakovlevich Chaadaev* (1794–1856): Russian philosopher whose
"First Philosophical Letter" (published in 1836) was deeply critical
of the Russia of his time, in particular of its (spiritual) isolation from
the West. Publication of the letter resulted in Chaadaev being declared
insane and being placed under house arrest for a year.

p. 413 *Sklifosovsky Clinic*: the main casualty hospital in Moscow.

NOTES ON THE AUTHORS

VIKTOR ASTAFIEV (1924–   ) was born in the village of Ovsyanka, Krasnoyarsk region. He lost his parents in early childhood and was brought up in an orphanage. He was called up at the very beginning of the Second World War, was in the army for the duration, and sustained a war wound. Later he studied on the State Higher Literature Courses in Moscow, before moving to Vologda, and then back to Krasnoyarsk. His best-known works are the novels *The King-Fish* (1972–75) and *The Sad Detective* (1986), the novellas *The Shepherd and the Shepherdess* (1971) and *The Last Bow* (1976–88), and the short story cycle *Blazes* (1985).

"The Blind Fisherman" was first published in *Nash sovremennik*, 1986, no. 5.

DMITRY BAKIN (1964–   ) is the pseudonym of Dmitry Bocharov. After leaving school, Bakin did military service, and now lives in Moscow, where he works as a lorry-driver. In 1989 he published two stories in issues 12 and 26 of *Ogonyok*.

"Lagophthalmos" is the author's first story.

VASILY BELOV (1932–   ) was born in Timonikha, a village in the Vologda Province, and graduated from the Gorky Institute of World Literature in 1964. His first publications were of lyric verse (the collection *My Forest Village* came out in 1961), but it was with the publication of a prose text (*An Ordinary Affair* in 1967) that he achieved recognition. His later publications include *A Carpenter's Stories* (1968), the documentary novel *Our Yesterdays* (1972–81: the third part was published only in 1987, in *Novy mir*, no. 8; the continuation, *The Year of Crisis* also appeared there in 1989, no. 3). In 1987 Belov published the controversial *All is Yet to Come*, an account of some corrupt Muscovite intellectuals and their harridan female partners. Besides fiction, Belov is the author of *Harmony* (1981), a volume of essays on ethnographical subjects. He now lives in Vologda town; he is a Deputy in the Supreme Soviet.

"A War like That" first appeared in *Yunost*, 1985, no. 11.

ANDREY BITOV (1937–   ), an architect's son, was born in Leningrad, and studied at the Institute of Mining there; an expulsion forced him to spend some time in compulsory military service, but he graduated in 1962. He had published his first story in 1959, and immediately upon graduating he signed a contract for his first book, a collection of short stories under the title *The Big Balloon* (1963), which gained him wide recognition, both amongst literary critics and amongst the reading public in general. His fifteen collections include *A Country Place* (1967), *Apothecary Island* (1968), *The Days of Man* (1976), and *Seven Journeys* (1976). A selection of his stories has appeared in English translation (*Life in Windy Weather*, Ardis, Ann Arbor, 1986). His novel *Pushkin House* was finished in 1971; failing to find a publisher in the USSR, it was brought out in Russian in the USA by Ardis in 1978. In the 1970s and early 1980s his work came under official criticism ostensibly for its "excessive subjectivity", but in reality partly because of the publication of *Pushkin House* in the West and partly because of his involvement in the *Metropol* affair, at attempt to found an uncensored literary almanac. *Pushkin House* appeared in the Soviet Union only in 1987 (*Novy mir*, nos. 10–12), though it had in fact been well known there since its original American publication. He lives in Moscow.

"The Doctor" was first published in *Metropol* (1979).

LEONID BORODIN (1938–) was born in Irkutsk, and studied at the University there, but was expelled half-way through his course on account of his membership of the *Free Speech* group. He graduated from the External Studies department of the teachers' training college in Ulan-Ude in 1962, and then worked as the headmaster of a school near Leningrad. In 1967 he was sentenced to six years' imprisonment for his membership of the All-Soviet Social-Christian Union for the Liberation of the People. In prison he wrote verse, but on his release turned to prose, which was published in the Russian émigré journal *Grani*. His first collection of prose, *The Story of a Strange Time* (which includes "The Visit"), was published in 1978 in Frankfurt am Main: then followed three novellas. *The Year of Miracle and Sadness* (1981), *The Third Truth* (1981), and *Gologor* (1982). Borodin was a co-author of the samizdat journal *Veche* and the almanac *Moskovskii sbornik*. In 1983 he was again arrested, tried and given a sentence of ten years in a hard regime labour camp, followed by five years of exile. In June 1987 he was freed. In the last two years Borodin's work has been widely published in many Soviet literary journals on both the right and the left (*Nash sovremennik* and *Yunost*).

"The Visit" was first published in the USSR in *Yunost*, 1989, no. 11.

SERAFIM CHETVERUKHIN (1911–1983) was born in what is now Zagorsk, and grew up in Moscow, but moved to Leningrad in 1930 to study at the University. He was arrested in 1936 and sent to a camp in the Vorkuta region. After the War he stayed on nearby in exile. In 1960, after 25 years in the Arctic Circle, he moved back to Leningrad, where he remained until his death, working as a book binder and restorer for the Saltykov-Shchedrin Library. Chetverukhin wrote stories about camp life and other topics; none was published during his lifetime. He also painted ikons and watercolours.

"Tsarevich Dmitry" was first published in the USSR in *Novy mir*, 1990, no. 16.

YURY DOMBROVSKY (1909–1978) was born and brought up in Moscow; he was educated at the Higher State Literature Courses from 1926, graduating in 1932. He then worked in a museum in Alma-Ata. His earliest publications were of poetry, but in 1939 he brought out a novel, *Derzhavin*.

Immediately on its appearance he was arrested; he then spent fifteen years in prisons, labour camps and in exile. During this period he wrote a second novel, *The Monkey Collects its Skull* (1948–58, published 1959). On being rehabilitated he returned to Moscow. In 1964 (the year of Khrushchev's downfall) he published a further novel. *The Keeper of Antiquities*, in *Novy mir*; in the year of his death its continuation, *The Faculty of Useless Objects*, was published in the West. These two books together form his major work; it has just been published in the Soviet Union (*Novy mir*, 1988). Besides novels and poems, Dombrovsky was the author of a volume of stories (*The Dark Lady: Three Tales about Shakespeare*, 1969); he was also active as a translator of Kazakh poetry.

"An Arm, a Leg, a Gherkin too. . ." was first published in *Novy mir*, 1990, no. 1.

OLEG ERMAKOV (1961–   ), a veteran of the Afghanistan conflict, lives in Smolensk. His first stories, devoted to the subject of the War, were published in *Znamya*, 1989, no. 3.

"Safe Return" was first published in *Novy mir*, 1989, no. 8.

VIKTOR EROFEEV (1947–   ) was born in Moscow. The son of diplomats who spent some years abroad. Erofeev graduated from the Department of Languages and Literature of Moscow University in 1970 and went on to do postgraduate studies at the Gorky Institute of World Literature, completing his dissertation on Dostoevsky and French existentialism in 1975. A book reviewer and literary critic since 1968, he was briefly accepted into the Union of Writers before being expelled over the "Metropol" affair (see under BITOV). Despite subsequent reinstatement, his prose met with official resistance. However, as a result of glasnost, since 1988 he has been able to travel in the USA and several of his stories have appeared in Soviet magazines. Most notably, a bowdlerized version of his story "The Parakeet" was published in *Ogonyok*. "Anna's Body" has appeared in *Panorama* and two stories, "A Letter to Mother" and "Galoshes", have appeared in *Yunost*.

"Sludge-gulper" was first published in his collection *Anna's Body, or the End of the Russian Avante-Garde* (1989).

FAZIL ISKANDER (1929–   ) was born in Sukhumi, Abkhazia and graduated from the Gorky Institute of World Literature in 1953. He then worked as a journalist; later he was employed in the State Publishing House, Abkhazia. His first publications were of poetry (*Mountain Paths*, Moscow and Sukhumi, 1957, followed by *Green Rain*). He then moved to Moscow, where he began to write prose, and to publish in the central literary journals, beginning with a story in *Yunost* in 1962. These early stories were collected as *Forbidden Fruit* in 1966. With the publication of his novella *The Goatibex Constellation* in 1966, Iskander attained a wide reputation. His cycle of interlinked novellas, *Sandro from Chegem*, began to appear in *Novy mir* during 1973; publication continued in a variety of journals. The first Soviet edition of this work in collected form (1977), had censorship cuts of more than fifty per cent: a more complete text was published by Ardis, Ann

Arbor, in 1979–81. His other works include a cycle of short stories for children, *Chik's Day*, and the "African" fable *Rabbits and serpents* (Ann Arbor, 1982), as well as other collections of poetry and short stories. Today Iskander is one of the most popular Soviet writers. He still lives in Moscow, and is a People's Deputy.

"Broadbrow" appeared in *Yunost*, 1984, no. 1.

YURY KAZAKOV (1927–1982) lived all his life in Moscow. He studied first at the Conservatoire, from which he graduated in 1951. For several years he taught music in various Moscow orchestras and – when he took up jazz – in jazz groups as well. Later he studied until 1958, at the Gorky Institute of World Literature. His first work was published in 1952; he is best known as a master of the short story and his stories were collected in more than fifteen volumes, including *Arcturus the Hunting Hound* (1958), *At the Whistle-Stop* (1959), *Northern Diary* (1961), *Blue and Green* (1963), *Two in December* (1966), *Autumn in the Oak Woods* (1969). He was also active as a translator. After 1973 Kazakov almost stopped writing original work.

"You Cried so Bitterly in Your Sleep", one of his last stories, was first published in *Nash sovremennik*, 1977, no. 7.

ALEXANDER LAVRIN (1958–) was born in the town of Sovetskaya Gavan (Soviet Harbour), Khabarovsk Region, Northern Russia. He studied at the Moscow State Institute of Culture, and has been publishing since 1983, but first attracted attention with the narrative poem *Meetings at Night* (published *Novy mir*, 1988, no. 1). He is also the author of the novella *The Chase*, published in *Yunost*, 1990, no. 11. He is active as a literary critic, and was the editor of the *Mirrors* almanac (1989), in which many "new wave" poets and prose writers were represented [see also POVOLOTSKAYA and PETROV].

"The Death of Egor Ilich" was first published in *Mirrors*.

VLADIMIR MAKANIN (1937–) was born and brought up in Orsk. He graduated from the Mathematics Faculty of Moscow University in 1960, and then taught for nearly ten years at a college of further education, whilst also studying part-time on the Higher State Courses for Film-Script Writers. His first novel, *Straight Line*, was published in the journal *Moskva* in 1965, but he became well known only later, after the publication of several stories and novellas, including *Klyuchkarev and Akimushkin* (1979), *The Precursor* (1983), *Where Sky and Hills Meet* (1984), *The Loss* (1989). He lives in Moscow.

"Those Who Did Not Get into the Choir" is one section of the novella *Voices* (1982).

IZRAEL METTER (1909–) was born in Kharkov, Ukraine, of Jewish parentage and educated at the Institute of Economics there (1926–29). In 1929 he moved to Leningrad, where he taught mathematics in a number of different educational establishments. When war started, he at first remained in Leningrad, writing radio scripts. (After the war he became a scriptwriter for the famous Soviet satirist, Akardy Raikin.) He survived a year of the Blockade, but was then evacuated. He published short stories from 1928; his first novella, *The End of Childhood*, came out in 1936. He is the author of many other stories and novellas, among them *The Insult* (1960), *Mukhtar* (1960), *Meetings and Partings* (1984), *The Fifth Corner of the Room* (published in *Neva*, 1989, no. 1). Metter still lives in Leningrad.

"Ryabov and Kozhin", written in 1976, was published in *Lest we Forget* (1989).

PAVEL PETROV (1941–) was born in Moscow, and still lives there now. He is an animation artist by profession, and works in television. His first literary work was published in 1989.

"A Bit of Winter" was published in the almanac *Mirrors* (1989).

LYUDMILA PETRUSHEVSKAYA (1939–) was born in Moscow, and trained as a journalist at the University there, graduating in 1961, before getting a job in Moscow Television. In 1979, Yury Norstein's full-length animated film of her scenario *Fairy Tale of Fairy Tales*, was acclaimed in the USSR and awarded the Grand Prix in Zagreb, the Grand Prix in Lille, first prize in Ottawa and, in 1984, was named by an international jury of film critics as the best film in the archives of animation. She began writing short stories in the 1960s (her first publication was of two stories in *Avrora*, 1972), but it was her plays (*Cinzano, Music Lessons, Columbina's Apartment*) which first brought her real recognition. Widely performed in factory and amateur drama clubs during the early 1980s, since glasnost they have also been staged in various Moscow theatres. Recently, while continuing to publish plays (cf. the collection *Three Girls in Blue*, 1989), Petrushevskaya has been more and more active as a writer of fiction. A recent collection of monologues and short stories is *Immortal Love* (1988). She still lives in Moscow.

"A Modern Family Robinson" was first published in *Novy mir*, 1989, no. 8.

VYACHESLAV PIETSUKH (1946–) was born in Moscow, where he still lives. He trained as a history teacher; later he worked in several different schools in Moscow, and then had a job at Moscow Radio. He is literary adviser to the journal *Village Youth*. His first publication was in the *Istoki* (*Sources*) almanac in 1978; his first book, *Alphabet*, came out in 1983. It was followed by *Happy Times* (1988), *The New Moscow Philosophy* (1989), *Me and so on* (1990).

"Anamnesis and Epicrisis" came out in *Novy mir*, 1990, no. 4.

EVGENY POPOV (1946–) was born in Krasnoyarsk Region, Siberia. Popov graduated from Moscow Geological Institute in 1962. His first short story was published in 1976 in *Novy mir*. He was a co-editor of the *Metropol* almanac (see under BITOV), published in 1979, and some of his work was also published in the volume. This was a collection of avant-garde or politically critical prose and poetry, whose *samizdat* publication, followed by its appearance as an Ardis volume, excited much official disfavour in the last two years of the Brezhnev era. Popov's books include *Merry-making in Old Russia* (1981), *The Beauty of Life* (1989), *I Await an Unperfidious Love* (1989). His novella *The Soul of a Patriot, or Various Missiles to Ferfichkin* was written in 1982, but published only in 1989 (see *Volga*, no. 2). He lives in Moscow.

These three stories from the cycle *The Situation* were first published in *Novy mir*, 1976, no. 4, ibid., 1987, no. 10, and ibid., 1989, no. 10.

VALERY POPOV (1939–   ) was born in Kazan, and educated at the Leningrad Electro-Technical Institute, and at the All-Soviet Institute of Cinematography, from which he graduated in 1963 and 1970 respectively. He has been publishing from 1965, and has brought out five books for "grown-ups" and five for children, appeared frequently in *Yunost* and *Avrora*. These include *Normal Speed* (1976), *Life was a Mess* (1981), *Two Trips to Moscow* (1985). He also writes film-scripts. Popov lives in Leningrad where he is head of the prose section of the Leningrad Writers Union.

"Dreams on an Upper Berth", appeared in Popov's collection *The New Sheherazade* (1988).

IRINA POVOLOTSKAYA (1937–   ) was born in Moscow, where she still lives. She trained as a film director at the All-Soviet Institute of Cinematography, from which she graduated in 1962; she went on to direct several feature films. She also worked as a script-writer and journalist. Her first story was published in 1986; her work is also represented in *Mirrors*, an almanac published in 1989.

"The Rosy-Fingered Dawn" was first published (as "Uncle Sasha and Anechka") in *Oktyabr*, 1986, no. 12.

ELENA RZHEVSKAYA (1919–   ) was born in Gomel, Belorussia, but brought up in Moscow, where she still lives. On the outbreak of war she left the Institute of History, Philosophy and Literature, where she was studying at the time, and went straight to the front line. Working as a military interpreter, she stayed with the Soviet Army through the whole course of the Second World War, from Moscow to Berlin. She began publishing in 1951. Much later, she produced a volume of memoirs about the last days of the war, Hitler's suicide and the secrets of the Reichskanzlei; the volume, *Berlin, May 1945* (1965), ran into ten editions. She worked on the editorial board of *Novy Mir* whilst Alexander Tvardovsky was editor. Amongst her most recent books are *Close Moves* (1985), *February – the Crooked Paths* (1985), and *The Far-Off Roar* (1988).

"On the Tarmac" was published in *Punctuation Marks* (1989).

ARSENY TARKOVSKY (1907–1989), the father of the famous film-director Andrey Tarkovsky, was born in Elizavetograd (now Kirovograd) in the

Ukraine, and died in Moscow. He began studying on the Higher State Literature Courses in 1925, and graduated from there in 1929. During the Second World War he saw active service, and was disabled as a result of his injuries. Tarkovsky is best known for his poetry. He published his first collection, *Before the Snow*, only in 1962, at the age of fifty-five; it was followed by four other collections. Like many other Soviet writers who had had difficulty publishing original works, he was very active as a translator.

"Frostbitten Hands" was first published in *Novy mir*, 1987, no. 5.

VLADIMIR TENDRYAKOV (1923–1984) was born in the village of Makarovskaya, Vologda province, Northern Russia. Tendryakov saw active service in the Second World War, was wounded, and later worked as a teacher and Komsomol activist. From 1946 until 1951, after a year studying film-making, he studied at the Gorky Institute of World Literature. He began publishing in 1947; his first story was "Affairs of My Platoon". At this stage most of his work appeared in the journal *Ogonyok*. But it was only with the Khrushchev Thaw, and the publication of such prose collections as *The Fall of Ivan Chuprov* (1954), *Tight Knot* (1956), *The Wonder-Working Ikon* (1958), *Three, Seven, Ace* (1960), *The Trial* (1961) and *Not Suitable* (1965), that he began to achieve recognition as a writer. He was generally considered one of the most talented postwar Soviet writers, an early exponent of the so-called "village prose" school. In later years, until his death aged sixty-one in Krasnaya Pakhra, a writers' village near Moscow, Tendryakov wrote many works "for the desk drawer" [i.e. without hope of publication]. Since glasnost, thanks largely to the efforts of his widow, Natalya Tendryakova-Asmolova, there have been many posthumous publications of these works, amongst them short stories, novels and novellas, including *The Pure Waters of Kitezh* (1986) and *Attack on Mirages* (*Novy mir*, 1987).

"On the Blessed Island of Communism" was first published in *Novy mir*, 1988, no. 9.

YURY TRIFONOV (1925–81) was one of the best-known and most highly-regarded postwar Soviet writers, was born in Moscow, into the family of a highly-placed party official, who perished during the purges of 1937. Trifonov's mother was also exiled at this time. After working for a while at a Moscow aviation factory, he studied from 1944–49 at the Gorky Institute of World Literature, where one of his literary mentors was Konstantin Paustovsky. He began publishing in 1947, and speedily attained official recognition: his novella *The Students* was awarded the Stalin Prize in 1950. But genuine literary standing took longer to arrive: only at the end of the 1960s, during the last year when Alexander Tvardovsky, responsible for the publication of such other path-breaking texts as Solzhenitsyn's *One Day in the Life*, was editor of *Novy mir*, were the first two of Trifonov's famous series of "Moscow"narratives published. These were *The Exchange* (1969) and *Taking Stock* (1970). These two novellas were followed by two others, *The Long Goodbye* (1973), *Another Life* (1975), and then by the novels *The House on the Embankment* (1976), *The Old Man* (1978) and *Time and Place* (1981) – which last title appeared after Trifonov's death. *The Exchange*, for many years one of the most successful plays in the repertoire of Yury Lyubimov's Taganka Theatre, has been staged in the U.K. in a version by Michael Frayn.

"Archetypal Themes" is taken from the cycle *The Topsy-Turvy House*, which was published posthumously, in *Novy mir*, 1981, no. 7.

LARISA VANEEVA (1952–   ) was born in Novosibirsk and is a graduate of the Gorky Institute of World Literature. She has worked as a journalist and a night watchman. She began publishing in 1989. Her story "Venetian Mirror" appeared in an anthology of Soviet Women's Writing published in 1990. She is the editor of a collection of recent women's fiction, *The Woman who Recalls no Evil*, and the author of a collection of stories, *Out of the Cube* (1990).

"Lame Pigeons" is taken from *Out of the Cube*.

VLADIMIR ZAZUBRIN (1895–1938) was the pseudonym of Vladimir Zubtsov, who was born in Penza in Southeast Central Russia. Educated at a technical school, he was involved in the revolutionary movement from an early age. During the Civil War he was called up into the White Army and packed off to Irkutsk Military Academy. In the autumn of 1919 he joined a group of Red Partisans. He joined the Communist Party in 1921, but was subsequently expelled. From 1923–28 he lived in Novosibirsk and was employed as the secretary-in-chief on the literary journal *Sibirskie ogni* (Siberian Fires). The main moving force behind the Siberian section of the Union of Writers, he was forced to move to Moscow after a campaign of vilification in the 1930s, and began working in the State Publishing House (Gosizdat). His works include the novel *Two Worlds*, a pro-Bolshevik novel about the Civil War (published by an Armenian military printing house in 1925, republished 1959), *The Hostel* (1923), a much shorter prose piece in which he openly criticized the New Economic Policy, and a second novel *Mountains* (1933), the last major work to be published before his death. His novella "The Chip" was completed in 1923, but rejected by the editorial board of *Sibirskie ogni*; a later re-working of this story as a novel also remained unpublished, and the manuscript has been lost. Zazubrin was arrested at the height of the purges and shot on 6 December 1938. He was officially rehabilitated in 1956.

"The Chip" was published for the first time in 1989 by two journals simultaneously: *Enisey*, 1989, no. 1, and *Sibirskie ogni*, 1989, no. 2.

NOTES ON THE TRANSLATORS

ROSAMUND BARTLETT studied Russian at Durham and St Antony's College, Oxford, where she completed her doctoral thesis on Wagner's influence on Russian culture. She spent a year attached to Moscow University on a British Council scholarship (1987–88) and has travelled widely throughout the Soviet Union. As a translator she has worked in a variety of fields, including music and television. Amongst current projects, she is collaborating with the Théâtre de Complicité as translator for a dramatization of the writings of Daniil Kharms. She was recently a Frances Yates Research Fellow at the Warburg Institute, University of London.

GEORGE BIRD read Russian and German at Emmanuel College, Cambridge. He served in the British Army (1946–49), in Government service (1951–55) and was in charge of Russian Interpreter Training, Joint Services School for Linguists (1955–62). He was Assistant German and Russian master, then Head of Modern Languages at Bedales School (1962–88). His translations include *The Double* by Fyodor Dostoevsky (Harvill, London, 1957, revised 1988) and *The Diary of Richard Wagner* (Gollancz, London, 1980). Under the pen name John Lear he is the author of two novels, *Death in Leningrad* (Pluto Press, London, 1986) and *A War in Peace* (in Danish translation, KLIM, Copenhagen, 1989).

SUSAN BROWNSBERGER holds degrees from Radcliffe and from Boston College. In addition to Andrey Bitov's novel *Pushkin House* (Farrar, Straus & Giroux, New York, 1987, and Weidenfeld & Nicolson, London, 1988, and with the author's commentary in paperback from Ardis, Ann Arbor, 1990, and Harvill Paperbacks, London, 1990) she has translated *The Fur Hat* by Vladimir Voinovich; *The Hand* by Yuz Aleshovsky; and *Sandro of Chegem* by Fazil Iskander. She is currently working on a translation of Bitov's travel memoir, *A Captive of the Caucasus* (forthcoming from Farrar, Straus and Giroux, New York, and Weidenfeld & Nicolson, London).

MICHAEL DUNCAN studied Russian at the Ecole Nationale des Langues Orientales and on postings to H.M. Embassy Moscow between 1949 and 1983, and is still doing so. He has translated (or co-translated) *The Story of a Life* by Konstantin Paustovsky (Harvill, 1964), *The Trotsky Papers: (1917–1922* (2 vols., Mouton, 1971), *Within the Whirlwind* by Eugenia Ginzburg (pseud., Harvill, 1981) and *Boris Pasternak: The Tragic Years 1930–60* (Harvill, 1990). He has recently completed translations of two novels for Harvill, *The Fifth Corner of the Room* by Izrael Metter and *The Late Lamented's Birthday* by Gennady Golovin, both to be published in 1991.

DAVID FLOYD acquired his knowledge of Russian mainly in Russia, where he lived for four years during and after the Second World War, first in the British Military Mission and then in the Embassy. Later, in Prague and

Belgrade, he added Czech and Serbo-Croat to his knowledge of Slavonic languages. His many translations include *Front-Line Stalingrad* by Viktor Nekrasov (Harvill, 1962), *For the Good of the Cause* by Alexander Solzhenitsyn (Praeger, 1964), and most recently *Sofya Petrovna* by Lydia Chukovskaya (Harvill, 1990). He is also the author of several books including *Russia in Revolt* (Macdonald, 1969); he is currently working on an authoritative study of the Yugoslav leader, Marshal Tito.

CATRIONA KELLY is a Junior Research Fellow in Russian at Christ Church, University of Oxford. She is the author of various works on Russian modernist poetry and on popular culture, including *Petrushka: The Russian Carnival Puppet Theatre* (Cambridge University Press, 1990). Her translations include *The Third Truth* by Leonid Borodin (Harvill 1989) and *The Humble Cemetery* (with "Gleb Bogdyshev Goes Moonlighting", Harvill 1990) by Sergey Kaledin. She has also translated work by the Leningrad poet Elena Shvarts for the American journal *Nimrod*. She is currently working on a history of Russian women's writing, 1830–1990.

MILENA MICHALSKI graduated in 1987 from the School of Slavonic and East European Studies, University of London, where she then took an MA in Russian, specializing in the narrative technique of Alexey Remizov. She has taught Russian at the Working Men's Institute in London, and is now employed in East-West trade, where her work includes commercial and technical translation and interpreting using Serbo-Croat and Russian. She has research interests in early twentieth-century Russian literature and in cinema, on which she has recently published "Slobodan Pešić's Film *Slučaj Harms* and Kharms's *Sluchai*", in Neil Cornwell, ed., *Daniil Kharms and the Poetics of the Absurd* (Macmillan, London, 1991).

ALAN MYERS has translated a wide variety of contemporary Russian prose and verse texts, including *You Live and Love* by Valentin Rasputin (Granada, 1985, and Vanguard, 1986) and *Sign of Misfortune* by Vasil Bykov (Allerton Press, 1990). His translations of Joseph Brodsky include poetry and prose collected in *A Part of Speech* and *Less than One* (Farrar, Straus and Giroux, 1987, and Penguin Books, 1988), as well as his plays, *Marble* and *Democracy* (*Granta* 30, "New Europe!", 1990). In 1989 he published *An Age Ago* (Farrar, Straus and Giroux, 1988, and Penguin Books, 1989), an anthology from the golden age of Russian nineteenth-century poetry, preserving the metre and rhyme scheme of the originals. He has recently completed translations of *The Idiot* by Fyodor Dostoevsky for Oxford University Press and *Behind the Lines* by Lydia Ginzburg for Harvill. He is currently working on a translation of *The Faculty of Useless Objects* by Yury Dombrovsky, also for Harvill.

CATHERINE PORTER is the author of a number of books including *Alexandra Kollontai, a biography* (Virago, London, 1980), *Women in Revolutionary Russia* (Cambridge University Press, 1987) and *Larissa Reisner, a Biography* (Virago, London, 1988). Her translations from the Russian include *The Diaries of Sofya Tolstoy* (Cape, London, 1985), *A Ship of Widows* by I. Grekova (Virago, London, 1985), and *The Best of Ogonyok: The New Journalism of Glasnost* (Heinemann, London, 1990).

ROBERT PORTER is Senior Lecturer in Russian Studies at Bristol University. He studied Russian and Czech at Leeds University. He taught in the University of Wales, Aberystwyth for three years, before taking up his present post in 1974. His books include *Understanding Soviet Politics through Literature*, with Martin Crouch (1984) and *Four Contemporary Russian Writers* (Berg, 1989). He has published translations from Russian, Czech and Danish, and has recently completed a translation of Evgeny Popov's novel, *The Soul of a Patriot*, for Harvill.

ANDREW REYNOLDS graduated from Merton College, Oxford in 1986 with a Congratulatory First in Russian. From 1988 to 1990 he was a Senior Scholar at Merton College. He is at present working on the poetry of Osip Mandelstam and teaching Russian language and literature at Oxford University. He has written an article on Mandelstam's poetry for a collection of articles due to be published in Moscow in 1991, on O'Connor's *Boris Pasternak* for the *Slavonic and East European Review*, and his translation of Ya. S. Lurye's "Bulgakov and Tolstoy" is due to be published in *Oxford Slavonic Papers* in the autumn of 1991.

GRAHAM ROBERTS was born in Liverpool in 1964 and graduated from Manchester University with a degree in French and Russian. He has worked as an interpreter in both France and the Soviet Union, and has wide experience as a translator. He has also taught Russian at secondary level. He is currently a member of New College, Oxford, where he is researching the works of Daniil Kharms, Alexander Vvedensky and Konstantin Vaginov.

SYLVA RUBASHOVA was born in Riga, Latvia. After coming to the West in 1965 she worked first for the Russian section of the Israel Broadcasting Authority (Kol Israel) and then for Russian Service of the BBC in London. Since retiring in 1987, she has continued to work on programmes for the Russian Service, as well as contributing to Russian language newspapers. Her autobiography, *A Sparrow in the Snow*, written as Sylva Darel, has been translated into twelve languages, including English, an edition of which (translated by Barbara Newman) was published by Penguin in 1977.

HOWARD SWARTZ was born in 1952 in Pasadena, California, and earned his undergraduate degree in English Literature from Pomona College. After joining the US Air Force, he studied Russian at the Defence Language Institute, and received his MA in Slavic Studies from Indiana University in 1984. An instructor at the US Air Force Academy, he is currently studying the literature of the Soviet-Afghan War at Oxford University.

FRANK WILLIAMS used to work for the Russian Service of the BBC World Service (Russian Service) in London and now works for Radio Free Europe in Munich. He is the translator of Leonid Borodin's story collection, *The Story of a Strange Time* (Harvill, London, 1990), which won the *Independent*'s Foreign Fiction Award in its month of publication and from which "The Visit" is taken.